# The Lighthouse of Bhagavad-Gita

# The Lighthouse of Bhagavad-Gita

Transcend the ocean of worldly life

*Commentary by:*

**Dr. Shrikrishna D. Deshmukh**

*Translation by:*

Mrs. Mukta P. Walvekar

MLBD PUBLICATIONS

The Lighthouse of Bhagavad-Gita/ Dr. Shrikrishna D. Deshmukh

**First Edition : Delhi, 2020**

ISBN : 9788194243847


*Published by:*
MOTILAL BANARSIDASS PUBLICATIONS
93, Shyam Lal Marg, Darya Ganj, New Delhi - 110002
mlbd@mlbd.com

**MLBD Cataloguing-in-Publication Data**
The Lighthouse of Bhagavad-Gita
by Dr. Shrikrishna D. Deshmukh
ISBN : 9788194243847
I. Preface II. Acknowledgment III. Foreword IV. Introduction

॥ ॐ नमो भगवते वासुदेवाय ॥

शान्ताकारं भुजगशयनं पद्मनाभं सुरेशं
विश्वाधारं गगनसदृशं मेघवर्णं शुभाङ्गम् ।
लक्ष्मीकान्तं कमलनयनं योगिभिर्ध्यानगम्यं
वन्दे विष्णुं भवभयहरं सर्वलोकैकनाथम् ॥

*Śāntākāram bhujagaśayanaṃ padmanābhaṃ sureśaṃ*
*Viśvādhāraṃ gaganasadṛśaṃ meghavarṇaṃ śubhāngaṃ* ।
*Lakṣmīkāntaṃ kamalanayanaṃ yogibhirdhyānagamyaṃ*
*Vande viṣṇum bhavabhayaharaṃ sarvalokaikanātham* ॥

॥ ॐ ॥

# ACKNOWLEDGEMENT

The Bhagavad-Gita is widely regarded as an eminent spiritual treatise. But for many-a-like, the Gita is "A Way of Life." People from across the world have found unmatched solace in the teachings of the Gita. I feel blessed for being given the opportunity to translate this one-of-a-kind commentary on the Gita which distinctly shows how to perform spiritual practices amid all difficulties in worldly life and live a peaceful and blissful life irrespective of the condition of the surroundings. It gave me a chance to immerse myself in the exquisite teachings of Lord Krishna and assimilate them in mind. More than translation, this truly has been a journey of profound inner transformation.

Many people helped me earnestly and selflessly in this process. Dr. Jyotsna Patankar and Mrs. Irina Derwall worked day and night for proofreading the translation and took enormous efforts for improving the accuracy and readability of the text. Dr. Rucha Sane and Vassily Aliseyko gave valuable inputs to enhance the overall quality of this translation. Mr. Mahesh Gadre from Shrikrupa Prakashan graciously made the cover-photo of the original book available for us. Mrs. Sonali Phadke created the insightful cover-page effortlessly and promptly. Mrs. Manju Arya from MLBD publication helped me with all the nuances of the publishing process. My husband, Pramod Walvekar, did the intricate job of formatting the book with utmost care and meticulousness. My family has given me unconditional support throughout the period of the translation of this book. I am sincerely grateful to all of them.

Despite all the efforts that went into this translation, I am humbly aware that it is far from being perfect, and I certainly welcome any comments or feedback from our discering readers.

My revered Sadguru **Dr. Shrikrishna Deshmukh** has initiated and led me on the most beautiful journey of life in the light of the brilliant teachings of the Gita. He not only kept me anchored through the most demanding phases of this translation but also nourished me with precious life-lessons in the course. I am deeply indebted to him for everything in life. This translation is only a result of his heartfelt blessings, unswerving support, silent inspiration, priceless guidance, and supreme grace!

**Mrs. Mukta Walvekar**

(Translator)

Email: mwalvekar@gmail.com

|| ॐ ||

# PREFACE

The Bhagavad-Gita is the epitome of the ultimate knowledge Hindu scriptures have to offer. It truly imparts the lessons on how to deal with life for one and all. Everyone desires to live life happily; however, the Gita teaches us to attain Bliss, live life in that blissful state, and at the end, leave this body and world happily. There are many commentaries available by various masters on the Bhagavad-Gita. The text has been translated into many other languages as well.

It is gratifying to see the English translation of my Marathi book with the same name. It is heartening to note that this translation captures the spirit of the original text very well. I hope English knowing seekers will find this effort valuable.

**Dr. Shrikrishna Deshmukh**
Murgud, Kolhapur
17 Feb, 2020

|| ॐ ||

# FOREWORD

The Glory of the Bhagavad-Gita states –

**एकं शास्त्रं देवकीपुत्रगीतम् ।** (*Ekaṃ śāstraṃ devakīputragītaṃ*)

There is only one song in the entire universe which is meant for the supreme welfare of all beings. It is this scripture known as the **Bhagavad-Gita** which is expounded by Lord Śrīkṛṣṇa to Arjuna. Many philosophers have sung different kinds of Gita. E.g. Haṅsagitā, Gurugitā, Aṣṭavakragitā, etc. However, the Gita which is a dialogue between Kṛṣṇa and Arjuna has received the honor of being meritorious in all aspects of life. That same dialogue is called the Śrimad Bhagavad-Gita. Today, it is so widely recognized in the world that the 'Gita' connotes the 'Bhagavad-Gita' alone. This is analogous to the case that the devotional poetic text 'Haripāṭha' composed by St. Jñāneśwara is alone equated to Haripāṭha, even though other saints have authored their own Haripāṭha as well.

Countless scholars have sanctified their brilliance by writing commentaries, expositions, poetries, dissertations, etc. on the Gita. Intellectuals from the non-dual and the dual schools of thought, thinkers from all religions and sects, and philosophers from western and eastern regions – all have written commentaries in various languages on the Bhagavad-Gita. No other treatise has received such enormous recognition by people from all over the world.

For Indians, the Bhagavad-Gita is a matter of profound faith and genuine affection. This treatise is worshipped, recited, propounded, listened, held close to the heart and considered valuable by many people. The Gita is the literary incarnation of Lord Śrīkṛṣṇa.

Respected author Dr. Shrikrishna. D. Deshmukh, a.k.a Dr. Kaka, has authored many spiritual texts. He has written commentaries in Marathi on Brahmasūtras and Upaniṣads which are part of the Prasthānatrayi – the three renowned canonical texts of the Vedānta. His work on the Gita took a relative backseat in this course. It is true that remarkable text is authored by remarkable people. But the converse is certainly not true. One does not become remarkable by writing remarkable texts. Thus, it is certainly not the case that 'remarkable' Dr. Kaka will become any more noteworthy by writing a commentary on the Bhagavad-Gita. It is also not the case that the 'remarkable' Bhagavad-Gita will become more magnificent due to him writing a commentary on it. Dr. Kaka, who is well aware of this fact, did not seem too eager to commence this work. However, his disciples were always anxious that "Our Sadguru should present his thoughts on the Gita." I have heard that they lovingly persuaded their Sadguru to do so. It is only appropriate that they are insistent in this regard. I feel proud of such persuasive and insistent disciples. I am not aware that respected Dr. Kaka was insistent that he did not want to write a commentary on this treatise. It is his eminence that Dr. Kaka, who is content in every sense, does not become anxious about anything – I am certainly aware of this fact. In this course of strong insistence, selflessly compassionate Dr. Kaka – befitting his role of the Sadguru – granted victory to his disciples. Thereafter, in a short period, he built and erected this **Lighthouse of Bhagavad-Gita** in the ocean of worldly life. This Lighthouse is itself Self-effulgent. For many seekers, their path of happiness is being illumined by the radiance of this Lighthouse. Today, it is being published or revealed in its own light. Indeed, this concurrence touches the heart. The Līlā of God is truly inconceivable! What else can we say?

The instrument that saves other things from sinking in water is itself unsinkable, e.g. wood. Self-Knowledge is the instrument to cross the ocean of mundane worldly life. Knowledge itself has the ability to float. It is not hefty like Karma. The Bhagavad-Gita is the origin of this savior Knowledge of Ātman, the true Self. For an ordinary seeker, the Path of Knowledge is too arduous to tread on it, but there is no other option to it. St. Jñāneśwara says, "In case you choose to pursue things other than the Knowledge of Ātman, then be aware that those things will not eradicate ignorance, rather you will be drawn deeper into worldly life by pursuing worldly matters." The compassion of enlightened saints engulfs the seekers who have weak intellect. These saints see to it that the core principles of philosophy are directly realized by ordinary seekers. They avoid mere theoretical discussions and teach the seekers to see the philosophy through appropriate examples. This is precisely the task that Dr. Kaka has deftly accomplished in the lighthouse of the Bhagavad-Gita.

I have browsed through this commentary and here are some points which specifically stand out in the text –

1) This treatise begins with a conventional rendering of Gitāmahātmya, which is in accordance with the method of studying the Gita in a traditional Sāmpradāya. As a result, the traditional Sāmpradāyic community will approve of the stature of this treatise, even though it is of modern format, and new people will find it appealing. It is immensely important that the innate faith of faithful people is nurtured properly. Also, it is necessary for skeptics and discerners to develop faith in the path of spirituality. Both these aspects are addressed here. Modern intellectuals disregard the traditional faiths while emphatically pampering spiritual skeptics. On the other hand, faithful people expect the intellectuals to approve of their faiths. The Lighthouse of

Bhagavad-Gita has stricken a golden balance in this delicate exercise. The entire treatise is an excellent example of this fact.

2) Naïve seekers feel assured while reading this commentary since they start comprehending the meaning as they read the text. Their self-confidence increases, and they feel motivated for the study.

3) The enlightened saints pledge that they will only speak what is taught by the Vedas. There is also a guideline that one should follow the path laid down by saints. Dr. Kaka, being a true saint at heart, has followed this pledge and guideline in his entire exposition. This is a matter of great satisfaction.

4) The author has raised some fundamental questions:
   - Is the Gita meant for one and all?
   - Is the Gita meant for Arjuna?
   - Is the Gita meant for people like Arjuna?

   The beauty of the rendering in this commentary is that every reader feels, this treatise is meant for me! This itself sheds light on the answers to the questions above which are not answered explicitly in the text. The success of this treatise lies in this fact.

5) Ordinary people cannot think about what lies in their best interest due to the lack of *Viveka* (spiritual discrimination). Such people should faithfully embrace the guidance of enlightened saints like Sri Śaṅkarācārya, Jñāneśwara, Tukārāma, Ekanātha, Nāmadeva, etc. This elemental, precious, and valuable guidance is found in the Lighthouse of Bhagavad-Gita.

6) There is a verse in Gitāmahātmya that begins with the words 'Bhīṣmadroṇataṭā jayadrathajalā....' It describes the nature of the ocean of worldly life. This ocean is filled with vortices that cause drowning, rocks that cause wreckage, and crocodiles that devour the people. The Lighthouse of Bhagavad-Gita truly illumines the path to get past these

obstacles in worldly ocean and reach the shores of Pure Bliss. In other words, it deciphers and shows how to perform spiritual practices amid all difficulties in worldly life with the help of the teachings of the Gita.

7) A road needs light so that it can be seen and followed properly. Akin to this, the mind, too, should be filled with the light of alertness and discrimination. Tamoguṇa causes 'load-shedding' in the mind. Of what use is even the external light to such a person? The chapters in this commentary talk about the three Guṇas, the characteristics of a person who has transcended the three Guṇas, the characteristics of a sage having steady wisdom, the characteristics of a devotee, the indicators of Self-Knowledge, service to the Guru, and descriptions of Yajñas, etc. The seeker can cleanse and purify his mind by studying these topics, and as a result, the inner light in his mind will be more luminous. This commentary also sheds light on the code of conduct for external behavior in day-to-day life by giving the exposition on Karma, describing the Glories of God, and explaining the Cosmic Form of the Lord. In short, the commentary removes indiscriminate thinking, lethargy, disbelief, and skepticism. It delicately leads the seekers from being complacent and passive to become dynamic and active, from attachment to non-attachment, and from bondage to liberation.

8) The overall text rendition is impressive, the text structure is lucid and uncomplicated, and the language is instinctive and seamless as it is inspired from within – these aspects appeal to the mind.

9) The preface gives a concise abstract of each chapter to aid further study. It introduces the readers with the subject-matter of each chapter. As a result, they get a fair idea of which things to focus on while studying each chapter.

10) The preface mentions the three verses in the Gita which explain the nature of the three kinds of consciousness: Jiva-Caitanya – Jiva's action-filled life, Īśvara-Caitanya – Īśvara's governance of sentient and insentient entities in the universe, and Brahma-Caitanya – all-pervasive Brahman which is not attached to or encaged by anything. Indeed, this is a very captivating point.
11) The author has fearlessly given a perfect, clear, and imperative message, obviously with the support of the Gita itself. He says, "One who is wise should not create discord in the minds of ignorant people who are attached to action. He should not tell them stories of monastic life and discuss the Knowledge of Brahman with them." It is in the best interest of all that they adhere to this message.
12) 'Worship,' 'worshipper,' 'worship should be performed,' etc. – Respected Dr. Kaka has mentioned these words with great regard, warmth, and close affinity for their intended meaning. This is indeed satisfying, though astonishing at the same time. Since he has mentioned these practices with due respect, it will certainly help reaffirm the faith of those seekers who are eligible for these practices alone.
13) "Why should one study the Bhagavad-Gita?" this question has been wonderfully answered here. See for yourself: "The reasons for worldly fears and suffering are removed by the Gita and thereby struggle and conflict in life come to an end."
14) By taking cognizance of the present times and taking the support of the compositions of St. Rāmadāsa Swāmi, the text gives a crucial warning, "One should be cautious not to fall prey to pretentious or hypocrite Gurus."
15) There is a section in the preface that renders the following explanation, "The teachings of the Gita are on four levels: worldly (transactional), ethical, religious, and spiritual." The

beauty and efficacy of this message and the verses chosen to elaborate the message capture the mind.

16) 'The Lighthouse of Bhagavad-Gita' is a simple, straightforward, lucid, panoptic, inspired, and affectionately authored commentary on the Gita, which is replete with useful instructions for seekers. The possibility of any other treatise of this nature and stature being available cannot be assumed. The Gita was taught by that 'Shrikrishna' and its commentary was authored by this 'Shrikrishna.' Both the teacher and the author are One in essence. I heartily bow down to both and bring this foreword to an end.

**Ms. Mandakini Gandhe**
Amravati, Maharashtra

# CONTENTS

॥ ॐ ॥

# The Glory of Gita

॥ अथ श्रीगीतामाहात्म्यप्रारम्भः ॥

*॥ Atha Śrīgītāmāhātmyaprārambhaḥ ॥*

धरोवाच ।
भगवन्परमेशान भक्तिरव्यभिचारिणी ।
प्रारब्धं भुज्यमानस्य कथं भवति हे प्रभो ॥ १ ॥

*Dharovāca ।*
*Bhagavānparemeśāna bhaktiravyabhicāriṇī ।*
*Prārabdhaṃ bhujyamānasya kathaṃ bhavati he prabho ॥ 1 ॥*

**Meaning:** (The Earth said) O Bhagavān, the Supreme Lord! How can unswerving devotion awaken in him who is bound by worldly life (Prārabdha Karma)? Please tell me.

श्री विष्णुरुवाच ।
प्रारब्धं भुज्यमानो हि गीताभ्यासरतः सदा ।
स मुक्तः स सुखी लोके कर्मणा नोपलिप्यते ॥ २ ॥

*Śrī Viṣṇuruvāca ।*
*Prārabdhaṃ bhujyamāno hi gītābhyāsarataḥ sadā ।*
*Sa muktaḥ sa sukhī loke karmaṇā nopalipyate ॥ 2 ॥*

**Meaning:** (Lord Viṣṇu said) One who consistently studies the Gita – though immersed in his worldly duties – becomes free. He is not bound by Karmas, and undoubtedly, he is a happy man in this world.

महापापादिपापानि गीताध्यानं करोति चेत् ।
क्वचित्स्पर्शं न कुर्वन्ति नलिनीदलमम्बुवत् ॥ ३ ॥

*Mahāpāpādipāpāni gītādhyānaṃ karoti cet ।*
*Kvacitsparśaṃ na kurvanti nalinīdalamambuvat ॥ 3 ॥*

**Meaning:** Even the most severe sins cannot touch, taint or bind a person who contemplates on the philosophy of the Gita, just as water cannot touch the lotus leaf.

**गीतायाः पुस्तकं यत्र यत्र पाठः प्रवर्तते ।**
**तत्र सर्वाणि तीर्थानि प्रयागादीनि तत्र वै ॥ ४ ॥**

*Gītāyāḥ pustakaṃ yatra yatra pāṭhaḥ pravartate* ।
*Tatra sarvāṇi tīrthāṇi prayāgādīni tatra vai* ॥ *4* ॥

**Meaning:** Prayāga and other such sacred places of pilgrimage dwell in that place where the Gita is read and recited regularly.

**सर्वे देवाश्च ऋषयो योगिनः पन्नगाश्च ये ।**
**गोपाला गोपिका वापि नारदोद्धवपार्षदैः ।**
**सहायो जायते शीघ्रं यत्र गीता प्रवर्तते ॥ ५ ॥**

*Sarve devāśca ṛṣayo yoginaḥ pannagāśca ye* ।
*Gopālā gopikā vāpi nāradoddhavapārṣadaiḥ* ॥
*Sahāyo jāyate śīghraṃ yatra gītā pravartate* ॥ *5* ॥

**Meaning:** All gods, Ṛṣis, practitioners of Yoga, divine serpents, childhood friends, attendants, and devotees of Lord Kṛṣṇa (Gopas and Gopis), sage Nārada, Uddhava, and others go to help quickly to those places where there is a strong desire to study the Gita meticulously.

**यत्र गीताविचारश्च पठनं पाठनं श्रुतम् ।**
**तत्राहं निश्चितं पृथ्वि निवसामि सदैव हि ॥ ६ ॥**

*Yatra gītāvicāraśca paṭhanaṃ pāṭhanaṃ śṛtam* ।
*Tatrāhaṃ niścitaṃ pṛthvi nivasāmi sadaiva hi* ॥ *6* ॥

**Meaning:** O Earth! I Myself constantly and certainly reside where the Gita is read, heard, taught, and contemplated upon.

**गीताश्रयेऽहं तिष्ठामि गीता मे चोत्तमं गृहम् ।**
**गीताज्ञानमुपाश्रित्य त्रींल्लोकान्पालयाम्यहम् ॥ ७ ॥**

*Gītāśraye'haṃ tiṣṭhāmi gītā me cottamaṃ gṛham* ।
*Gītājñānamupāśrītya trīṃlokānpālayāmyaham* ॥ *7* ॥

**Meaning:** The Gita is my best abode, and I take refuge in the shelter of the Gita. I nourish and protect the three worlds which take refuge in the knowledge of the Gita.

गीता मे परमा विद्या ब्रह्मरूपा न संशयः ।
अर्धमात्राक्षरा नित्या स्वानिर्वाच्यपदात्मिका ॥ ८ ॥

*Gītā me paramā vidyā brahmarūpā na saṃśayaḥ* ।
*Ardhamātrākṣarā nityā svānirvācyapadātmikā* ॥ *8* ॥

**Meaning:** Undoubtedly, the Gita is My highest knowledge. It is, without doubt, of the form of Brahman and the half syllable (Ardhamātra) of the Om. It is the eternal, indestructible Self that is ineffable or inexpressible in words.

चिदानन्देन कृष्णेन प्रोक्ता स्वमुखतोऽर्जुनम् ।
वेदत्रयी परानन्दा तत्त्वार्थज्ञानसंयुता ॥ ९ ॥

*Cidānandena kṛṣṇena proktā svamukhato'rjunam* ।
*Vedatrayī parānandā tattvārthajñānasaṅyutā* ॥ *9* ॥

**Meaning:** Lord Kṛṣṇa, who is Pure Knowledge and Bliss, has Himself told this Gita to Arjuna through His own mouth. It contains the essence of all the Vedas, and it is full of Supreme Bliss.

योऽष्टादशं जपे नित्यं नरो निश्चलमानसः ।
ज्ञानसिद्धिं स लभते ततो याति परं पदम् ॥ १० ॥

*Yo'ṣṭādaśajape nityaṃ naro niścalamānasaḥ* ।
*Jñānasiddhiṃ sa labhate tato yāti paraṃ padam* ॥ *10* ॥

**Meaning:** One who regularly recites the eighteen chapters of the Gita with a steady, unwavering mind is enlightened with Self-Knowledge. He attains the highest goal, state or place.

पाठेऽसमर्थः सम्पूर्णे ततोऽर्धं पाठमाचरेत् ।
तदा गोदानजं पुण्यं लभते नात्र संशयः ॥ ११ ॥

*Pāṭhe'samarthaḥ sampūrṇe tato'rdhaṃ pāṭhamācaret* ।
*Tadā godānajaṃ puṇyaṃ labhate nātra saṃśayaḥ* ॥ *11* ॥

**Meaning:** One should recite at least half the Gita if the complete recitation is not possible. Even by that half recitation, he undoubtedly gets the same fruits as that of donating a cow.

**त्रिभागं पठमानस्तु गङ्गास्नानफलं लभेत् ।**
**षडंशं जपमानस्तु सोमयागफलं लभेत् ॥ १२ ॥**

*Tribhāgaṃ paṭhamānastu gaṅgāsnānaphalaṃ labhet* ।
*Ṣaḍaṃśaṃ japamānastu somayāgaphalaṃ labhet* ॥ *12* ॥

**Meaning:** He who recites one-third of the Gita attains the fruit which is the same as that of bathing in the sacred Ganges River. He who recites one-sixth of the Gita attains the fruit which is the same as that of performing Soma-Yāga, which is a fire-oblation Vedic ritual.

**एकाध्यायं तु यो नित्यं पठते भक्तिसंयुतः ।**
**रुद्रलोकमवाप्नोति गणो भूत्वा वसेच्चिरम् ॥ १३ ॥**

*Ekādhyāyaṃ tu yo nityaṃ paṭhate bhaktisaṅyutaḥ* ।
*Rudralokamavāpnoti gaṇo bhūtvā vasecciram* ॥ *13* ॥

**Meaning:** A person who regularly reads one chapter of the Gita with intent devotion attains the plane of Rudra. By becoming a Gaṇa, an attendant of Lord Shiva, he lives there for a very long time.

**अध्यायं श्लोकपादं वा नित्यं यः पठते नरः ।**
**स याति नरतां यावन्मन्वन्तरं वसुन्धरे ॥ १४ ॥**

*Adhyāyaṃ ślokapādaṃ vā nityaṃ yaḥ paṭhate naraḥ* ।
*Sa yāti naratāṃ yāvanmanvantaraṃ vasundhare* ॥ *14* ॥

**Meaning:** O Earth! If one reads a chapter of the Gita or even a part of its verse daily, he is reborn forever as a human being (instead of getting an inferior body like an animal, bird or tree) till the end of the Manvantara. [Manvantara is a very long period equivalent to the age of Manu – the progenitor of life on earth. Manu is also the creator of the treatise Manusmṛiti.]

**गीतायाः श्लोकदशकं सप्त पञ्च चतुष्टयम् ।**
**द्वौ त्रीनेकं तदर्धं वा श्लोकानां यः पठेन्नरः ॥ १५ ॥**

*Gītāyāḥ ślokadaśakaṃ sapta pañca catuṣṭayam ।*
*Dvau trīnekaṃ tadardhaṃ vā ślokānāṃ yaḥ paṭhennaraḥ ॥ 15 ॥*

**चन्द्रलोकमवाप्नोति वर्षाणामयुतं ध्रुवम् ।**
**गीतापाठसमायुक्तो मृतो मानुषतां व्रजेत् ॥ १६ ॥**

*Candralokamavāpnoti varṣāṇāmayutaṃ dhruvam ।*
*Gītāpāṭhasamāyukto mṛto mānuṣatāṃ vrajet ॥ 16 ॥*

**Meaning:** A person who reads ten, seven, five, four, three, two verses, or even one or half the verse of the Gita attains the plane of the moon. He lives there for 10,000 years. A dying man who is habituated to the daily study of the Gita is reborn as a human being.

**गीताभ्यासं पुनः कृत्वा लभते मुक्तिमुत्तमाम् ।**
**गीतेत्युच्चारसंयुक्तो म्रियमाणो गतिं लभेत् ॥ १७ ॥**

*Gītābhyāsaṃ punaḥ kṛtvā labhate muktimuttamām ।*
*Gītetyuccārasaṅyukto mriyamāṇo gatiṃ labhet ॥ 17 ॥*

**Meaning:** And there, he again studies the Gita and attains liberation. A person who utters the word 'Gita' at the time of his death accomplishes the desired or highest goal.

**गीतार्थश्रवणासक्तो महापापयुतोऽपि वा ।**
**वैकुण्ठं समवाप्नोति विष्णुना सह मोदते ॥ १८ ॥**

*Gītārthaśravaṇāsakto mahāpāpayuto'pi vā ।*
*Vaikuṇṭhaṃ samavāpnoti viṣṇunā saha modate ॥ 18 ॥*

**Meaning:** A person – though very sinful – who is attached to hearing the meaning of the philosophy of the Gita attains the plane of Viṣṇu, Vaikuṇṭha, and revels in great joy with Him.

**गीतार्थं ध्यायते नित्यं कृत्वा कर्माणि भूरिशः ।**
**जीवन्मुक्तः स विज्ञेयो देहान्ते परमं पदम् ॥ १९ ॥**

*Gītārthaṃ dhyāyate nityaṃ kṛtvā karmāṇi bhūriśaḥ ।*
*Jīvanmuktaḥ sa vijñeyo dehānte paramaṃ padam ॥ 19 ॥*

**Meaning:** A seeker who has performed many noble actions and regularly reflects on the meaning of the Gita attains the Supreme Goal after his death. He is known as 'Jivanmukta' i.e. one who is liberated while living.

**गीतामाश्रित्य बहवो भूभुजो जनकादयः ।**
**निर्धूतकल्मषा लोके गीतायाताः परं पदम् ॥ २० ॥**

*GītāmāŚrītya bahavo bhūbhujo janakādayaḥ* ।
*Nirdhūtakalmaṣā loke gītāyātāḥ paraṃ padam* ॥ *20* ॥

**Meaning:** Janaka and other such kings – purified of all sins – have attained the highest state in this world by taking refuge in the shelter of the Gita.

**गीतायाः पठनं कृत्वा माहात्म्यं नैव यः पठेत् ।**
**वृथा पाठो भवेत्तस्य श्रम एव ह्युदाहृतः ॥ २१ ॥**

*Gītāyāḥ paṭhanaṃ kṛtvā māhātmyaṃ naiva yaḥ paṭhet* ।
*Vṛthā pāṭho bhavettasya śrama eva hyudāhṛtaḥ* ॥ *21* ॥

**Meaning:** If a person who does not read or recite this Glory of the Gita after reading or studying the Gita, his reading becomes futile, and his effort remains fruitless. He is not benefitted from his study.

**एतन्माहात्म्यसंयुक्तं गीताभ्यासं करोति यः ।**
**स तत्फलमवाप्नोति दुर्लभां गतिमाप्नुयात् ॥ २२॥**

*Etanmāhātmyasaṅyuktaṃ gītābhyāsaṃ karoti yaḥ* ।
*Sa tatphalamavāpnoti durlabhāṃ gatimāpnuyāt* ॥ *22* ॥

**Meaning:** A person who reads the Gita and also this 'Glory of the Gita' achieves the aforementioned fruits. He attains a state which is otherwise difficult to attain.

**सूत उवाच ।**
**माहात्म्यमेतद्गीताया मया प्रोक्तं सनातनम्**
**गीतांते च पठेद्यस्तु यदुक्तं तत्फलं लभेत् ॥ २३ ॥**

*Sūta uvāca* ।
*Māhātmyametadgītāyā mayā prokta satātanam* ।
*Gītānte ca paṭhedyastu yaduktaṃ tatphalaṃ labhet* ॥ *23* ॥

**Meaning:** (Sūta said –) This eternal Glory of the Gita as proclaimed by Me should be read (recited) at the end of studying the Bhagavad-Gita. Thereby, one shall attain the fruits mentioned so far.

इति श्रीवाराहपुराणे श्रीगीतामाहात्म्यं संपूर्णम् ।

*॥ Iti Śrīvārāhapurāṇe Śrīgītāmāhātmyaṃ sampūrṇam ॥*

॥ अथ द्वितीयमाहात्म्यम् ॥

*॥ Atha dvitiyamāhātmyaṃ ॥*

गीताशास्त्रमिदं पुण्यं यः पठेत् प्रयतः पुमान् ।
विष्णोः पदमवाप्नोति भयशोकादिवर्जितः ॥ १ ॥

*Gītāśāstram idaṁ puṇyaṁ yaḥ paṭhet prayataḥ pumān ।*
*Viṣṇoḥ padamavāpnoti bhayaśokādivarjitaḥ ॥ 1 ॥*

**Meaning:** If a person recites this pious scripture of the Gita, with a pure mind and loving devotion, he becomes free of fear, grief, and other such traits and attains the holy plane of Viṣṇu.

गीताध्ययनशीलस्य प्राणायामपरस्य च ।
नैव सन्ति हि पापानि पूर्वजन्मकृतानि च ॥ २ ॥

*Gītādhyayanaśīlasya prāṇāyāmaparasya ca ।*
*Naiva santi hi pāpāni pūrvajanmakṛtāni ca ॥ 2 ॥*

**Meaning:** For a person who regularly recites the Gita and promptly practices breath-control (Prāṇāyāma), all his sins from current and past births are eradicated, there is no doubt about this.

**मलनिर्मोचनं पुंसां जलस्नानं दिने दिने ।**
**सकृद्गीताम्भसि स्नानं संसारमलनाशनम् ॥ ३ ॥**

*Malanirmocanaṁ puṁsāṁ jalasnānaṁ dine dine* ।
*Sakṛdgītāmbhasi snānaṁ saṁsāramalanāśanam* ॥ *3* ॥

**Meaning:** A daily bath in water removes only the impurities of a person's body. But bathing for even one time in the holy philosophy of the Gita can remove the impurities in worldly life of a person.

**गीता सुगीता कर्तव्या किमन्यैः शास्त्रविस्तरैः ।**
**या स्वयं पद्मनाभस्य मुखपद्माद्विनिःसृता ॥ ४ ॥**

*Gītā sugītākartavyā kimanyaiḥ śāstravistaraiḥ* ।
*Yā svayaṁ padmanābhasya mukhapadmādviniḥsṛtā* ॥ *4* ॥

**Meaning:** The beneficial text of the Gita was revealed by Lord Viṣṇu Himself through His beautiful lotus-like mouth. One needs to only sing and study, read, or hear this Gita sincerely. What is the use of reading any other scripture?

**भारतामृतसर्वस्वं विष्णोर्वक्त्राद्विनिःसृतम् ।**
**गीतागङ्गोदकं पीत्वा पुनर्जन्म न विद्यते ॥ ५ ॥**

*Bhāratāmṛtasarvasvaṁ viṣṇorvaktrādviniḥsṛtam* ।
*Gītāgaṅgodakaṁ pītvā punarjanma na vidyate* ॥ *5* ॥

**Meaning:** The Bhagavad-Gita is the nectar of Mahābhārata, and it is revealed by Lord Kṛṣṇa, who is the incarnation of Lord Viṣṇu Himself. By drinking the holy water of the Ganges of the Gita, a person is not reborn in this worldly life.

**सर्वोपनिषदो गावो दोग्धा गोपालनन्दनः ।**
**पार्थो वत्सः सुधीर्भोक्ता दुग्धं गीतामृतं महत् ॥ ६ ॥**

*Sarvopaniṣado gāvo dogdhā gopālanandanaḥ* ।
*Pārtho vatsaḥ sudhīrbhoktā dugdhaṁ gītāmṛtaṁ mahat* ॥ *6* ॥

**Meaning:** All the Upaniṣads are cows which are milked by Gopala, the son of Nanda. Arjuna, a man of wise intellect, is the calf who enjoys the milk i.e. the supreme, eternal nectar of the Gita. [The word Gopala used in this verse is a name of Kṛṣṇa.

The Sanskrit word 'Go' means organs, which include both sense organs and action organs. The term 'Gopala' means the one who has conquered his organs. Metaphorically, this verse implies that Lord Kṛṣṇa milks the Upaniṣad cows and teaches many ways to conquer organs to the readers through the nectarian milk of the Gita.]

एकं शास्त्रं देवकीपुत्रगीतम् एको देवो देवकीपुत्र एव ।
एको मन्त्रस्तस्य नामानि यानि कर्माप्येकं तस्य देवस्य सेवा ॥ ७ ॥

*Ekaṁ śāstraṁ devakīputragītam eko devo devakīputra eva* ।
*Eko mantrastasya nāmāni yāni karmāpyekaṁ tasya devasya sevā*

**Meaning:** The philosophy of the Gita revealed by Lord Kṛṣṇa, the son of Devaki, is the only scripture worth studying. Lord Kṛṣṇa is the only Supreme Lord. His Name is the only Mantra worth chanting. Serving to such Lord is the only worthwhile duty on this earth.

## Meditation on the Gita

॥ अथ ध्यानम् ॥

॥ *Atha dhyānam* ॥

ॐ पार्थाय प्रतिबोधितां भगवता नारायणेन स्वयं
व्यासेन ग्रथितां पुराणमुनिना मध्येमहाभारतम् ।
अद्वैतामृतवर्षिणीं भगवतीमष्टादशाध्यायिनीं
अम्ब त्वामनुसन्दधामि भगवद्गीते भवद्वेषिणीम् ॥ १ ॥

*Om Pārthāya pratibodhitāṁ bhagavatā nārāyaṇena svayaṁ*
*Vyāsena grathitāṁ purāṇa-muninā madhye mahābhāratam* ।
*Advaitāmṛta-varṣiṇīṁ bhagavatīm aṣṭādaśādhyāyinīṁ*

*Amba tvām anusandadhāmi bhagavad-gīte bhava-dveṣiṇīm* ॥ *1* ॥

**Meaning:** Om. The teachings of the Bhagavad-Gita were imparted to Arjuna by Lord Nārāyaṇa Himself. The Gita was compiled by ancient sage Vyāsa as a part of the great epic Mahābhārata. It consists of eighteen chapters, and it showers the nectar of non-duality. I contemplate on thee O Bhagavad-Gita, the Divine Mother, the destroyer of attachment to worldly life!

**नमोऽस्तु ते व्यास विशालबुद्धे फुल्लारविन्दायतपत्रनेत्र ।**
**येन त्वया भारततैलपूर्णः प्रज्वालितो ज्ञानमयः प्रदीपः ॥ २ ॥**

*Namo'stu te vyāsa viśālabuddhe phullāravindāyatapatranetra* ।
*Yena tvayā bhāratatailapūrṇaḥ prajvālito jñānamayaḥ pradīpaḥ*

**Meaning:** I offer my salutations to you, O Vyāsa! You are known for having a great intellect and eyes like the fully blossomed lotus petal. You have lighted the lamp of knowledge by filling it with the oil of Mahābhārata.

**प्रपन्नपारिजाताय तोत्रवेत्रैकपाणये ।**
**ज्ञानमुद्राय कृष्णाय गीतामृतदुहे नमः ॥ ३ ॥**

*Prapannapārijātāya totravetraikapāṇaye* ।
*Jñānamudrāya kṛṣṇāya gītāmṛtaduhe namaḥ* ॥ *3* ॥

**Meaning:** I salute Lord Kṛṣṇa who is Pārijata, the wish-fulfilling tree. He fulfills all desires of those who take refuge in Him. He is the wielder of the whip in one hand and the holder of the Jñānamudrā in the other hand. [The whip indicates action, while the Jñānamudrā indicates knowledge. This verse implies that Lord Kṛṣṇa is actively engaged in actions, and at the same time, He revels in knowledge.] He has milked the nectar of the Gita.

**वसुदेवसुतं देवं कंसचाणूरमर्दनम् ।**
**देवकीपरमानन्दं कृष्णं वन्दे जगद्गुरुम् ॥ ४ ॥**

*Vasudevasutaṃ devaṃ kaṃsacāṇūramardanam* ।
*Devakīparamānandaṃ Kṛṣṇaṃ vande jagadgurum* ॥ *4* ॥

**Meaning:** Lord Kṛṣṇa is the son of Vasudeva, the destroyer of Kaṅsa and Cāṇūra, and the supreme joy of Mother Devaki! I offer my salutations to Lord Kṛṣṇa, the world-teacher!

**भीष्मद्रोणतटा जयद्रथजला गान्धारनीलोत्पला**
**शल्यग्राहवती कृपेण वहनी कर्णेन वेलाकुला ।**
**अश्वत्थामविकर्णघोरमकरा दुर्योधनावर्तिनी**
**सोत्तीर्णा खलु पाण्डवै रणनदी कैवर्तकः केशवः ॥ ५ ॥**

*Bhīṣmadroṇataṭā jayadrathajalā gāndhāranīlotpalā*
*Śalyagrāhavatī kṛpeṇa vahanī karṇena velākulā* ।
*Aśvatthāmavikarṇaghoramakarā duryodhanāvartinī*
*Sottīrṇā khalu pāṇḍavai raṇanadī kaivartakaḥ keśavaḥ* ॥ 5 ॥

**Meaning:** Bhīṣma and Droṇa are the two banks of the war-river of Mahābhārata. King Jayadratha is its water, Śakuni is a massive stone, Śalya is a crocodile, Kṛpa is a tide, and Karṇa is a powerful wave. Aśvatthāma and Vikarṇa are the dangerous alligators, and Duryodhana is a whirlpool. Pāṇḍavas crossed this perilous river indeed because Lord Kṛṣṇa was their helmsman.

**पाराशर्यवचःसरोजममलं गीतार्थगन्धोत्कटं**
**नानाख्यानककेसरं हरिकथासम्बोधनाबोधितम् ।**
**लोके सज्जनषट्पदैरहरहः पेपीयमानं मुदा**
**भूयाद्भारतपङ्कजं कलिमलप्रध्वंसि नः श्रेयसे ॥ ६ ॥**

*Pārāśaryavacaḥsarojamamalaṃ gitārthagandhotkaṭaṃ*
*Nānākhyānakakesaraṃ harikathāsambodhanābodhitam* ।
*Loke sajjana śaṭpadairaharahah pepīyamānaṃ mudā*
*Bhūyādbhāratapaṅkajaṃ kalimalapradhvaṃsi naḥ śreyase* ॥ 6 ॥

**Meaning:** This epic Mahābhārata composed by sage Vyāsa – the son of sage Parāśara – is a lotus without any blemishes. It has an intense sweet fragrance of the teachings of the Gita. Many stories are the filaments or stamens of this lotus. The lotus has fully opened and become vibrant due to the story of Hari and His teachings. Its nectar is drunk ardently with love, day and night, by the sages who are like bees that gather around the lotus for its nectar. May this lotus of the Gita destroy our sins, which arise from the Kaliyuga tendencies, and lead us to our highest benefit i.e. Mokṣa.

**मूकं करोति वाचालं पङ्गुं लङ्घयते गिरिम् ।**
**यत्कृपा तमहं वन्दे परमानन्दमाधवम् ॥ ७ ॥**

*Mūkaṃ karoti vācālaṃ paṅguṃ laṅghayate girim ।*
*Yatkṛpā tamahaṃ vande paramānandamādhavam ॥ 7 ॥*

**Meaning:** I bow down to that Mādhava who himself is the source of Supreme Bliss. By his grace, even the dumb are able to speak i.e. they become brilliant, and the crippled or lame people can cross mountains.

**यं ब्रह्मा वरुणेन्द्ररुद्रमरुतः स्तुन्वन्ति दिव्यैः स्तवैः**
**वेदैः साङ्गपदक्रमोपनिषदैर्गायन्ति यं सामगाः ।**
**ध्यानावस्थिततद्गतेन मनसा पश्यन्ति यं योगिनो**
**यस्यान्तं न विदुः सुरासुरगणा देवाय तस्मै नमः ॥ ८ ॥**

*Yaṃ brahmā varuṇendrarudramarutaḥ stunvanti divyaiḥ stavaiḥ*
*Vedaiḥ sāṅgapadakramopaniṣadairgāyanti yaṃ sāmagāḥ ।*
*Dhyānāvasthitatadgatena manasā paśyanti yaṃ yogino*
*Yasyāntaṃ na viduḥ surāsuragaṇā devāya tasmai namaḥ ॥ 8 ॥*

**Meaning:** I salute that God whom Brahma, Indra, Varuṇa, Rudra, and the Maruts praise with divine hymns. He is praised by the singers of Sāmaveda who sing the Vedas and Upaniṣads by duly following the word-sequences. The Yogis who immerse their minds in Him can see Him [understand His true nature] through meditation. Even Devas and Asuras do not know His bounds or limits.

|| ॐ ||

# Introduction

The Bhagavad-Gita has constantly enchanted those who wish to find happiness and satisfaction in this life full of struggle and conflicts. Intellectuals are drawn towards it out of sheer philosophical inquisitiveness, while pragmatists prefer to actually use this philosophy to improve the quality of their worldly lives. Their perspectives of studying the Gita are inherently different from each other, and rightfully so. There are many peripheral aspects of studying the Bhagavad-Gita such as giving scholarly discourses, finding new interpretations of its verses with incisive intellect, making academic comparisons with other philosophical treatises, analyzing the Gita from a literary or poetic perspective, and discovering newer social, political, and psychological references in its text. The essence and spirit of the Bhagavad-Gita may get lost amid these scholarly exercises.

## The backdrop of the Bhagavad-Gita

The Bhagavad-Gita is a part of Mahābhārata, one of the most renowned epics of ancient India. Mahābhārata is the story of the classic war of good versus evil between the paternal first cousins – Kauravas and Pāṇḍavas – of the Kuru dynasty. Kauravas were hundred sons of Dhṛtarāṣṭra, the blind ruler of kingdom Hastinapura. Pāṇḍavas were five sons of Pāṇḍu, the younger brother of King Dhṛtarāṣṭra. The two eldest amongst Kauravas were named Duryodhana and Duḥśāsana. Pāṇḍavas were named Yudhiṣṭhīra, Bhīma, Arjuna, Nakula, and Sahadeva. Mahābhārata is the acclaimed story of the giant war between

Pāṇḍavas and Kauravas that took place with the sole aim of deciding the rightful heir of their kingdom. Before the war commenced, Arjuna was overwhelmed with deep compassion and stricken with grief due to the mere idea of fighting against his kinsmen and the possible destruction of his clan. He was ready to abandon the war due to his delusion. Arjuna's charioteer was Lord Kṛṣṇa – the incarnation of Īśvara. To get Arjuna ready for doing his duty of fighting the war, Lord Kṛṣṇa imparted priceless spiritual teachings to him on the battlefield of Kurukṣetra. This eminent dialogue between Lord Kṛṣṇa and Arjuna, which took place amid two giant armies, is called the Bhagavad-Gita!

**The beneficiary of the Bhagavad-Gita**

Arjuna is the sole direct audience to whom Lord Kṛṣṇa imparts these teachings. Sanjaya and Dhṛtarāṣṭra are the two indirect listeners. Sanjaya was Dhṛtarāṣṭra's courtier and also his charioteer. He was bestowed with special divine powers by sage Vyāsa through which he was able to remotely see and hear the events on the battlefield and narrate them to his blind King Dhṛtarāṣṭra. Both Sanjaya and Dhṛtarāṣṭra were situated distantly in the palace in Hastinapura at the time.

Apart from these three listeners, who else is this spiritual treatise meant for? It is certainly true that Lord Kṛṣṇa imparted the teachings of the Bhagavad-Gita to each one of us and the entire mankind through Arjuna as a medium. However, would it be right to say that the Gita was told for the sake of the aforementioned peripheral aspects? It is believed that Lord Kṛṣṇa instructed Arjuna only the very gist of the spiritual philosophy, and Sage Vyāsa later elaborated His succinct teaching into the current form of the poetic the Gita which has 18 chapters. But can we say that the purpose of this exercise was to promote the scholarly activities mentioned above?

To determine the real beneficiary among those who study the Gita, it is necessary to evaluate the effect of the Bhagavad-Gita on its three direct and indirect listeners: Arjuna, Sanjaya, and Dhṛtarāṣṭra. Only then can we rightfully decide who can benefit by studying this treatise.

Arjuna says after listening to the Gita –

**नष्टो मोहः स्मृतिर्लब्धा त्वत्प्रसादान्मयाच्युत ।**
**स्थितोऽस्मि गतसन्देहः करिष्ये वचनं तव ॥ १८.७३ ॥**

*Naṣṭo mohaḥ smṛtir labdhā tvatprasādān mayācyuta* ।
*Sthito'smi gatasaṃdehaḥ kariṣye vacanaṃ tava* ॥ *18.73* ॥

"O Acyuta! My delusion is removed by Your grace. I have regained the memory of my true Self, and now I remember my duties. All my doubts are resolved, and I shall obey Your command."

Sanjaya says to Dhṛtarāṣṭra at the end after listening to the Gita –

**राजन्संस्मृत्य संस्मृत्य संवादमिममद्भुतम् ।**
**केशवार्जुनयोः पुण्यं हृष्यामि च मुहुर्मुहुः ॥ १८.७६ ॥**

*Rājan saṃsmṛtya saṃsmṛtya saṃvādam imam adbhūtam* ।
*Keśavārjunayoḥ puṇyaṃ hṛṣyāmi ca muhur muhuḥ* ॥ *18.76* ॥

"O King! I rejoice again and again by repeatedly reminiscing this extraordinary and valuable dialogue between Lord Kṛṣṇa and Arjuna." [Sanjaya was also reminiscing the most wonderful and remarkable Cosmic Form of Lord Kṛṣṇa, over and over again. *18.77*]

There is no verse in the Bhagavad-Gita that depicts the mindset of Dhṛtarāṣṭra after listening to its teachings. However, we can infer Dhṛtarāṣṭra's reaction when we study the very last verse of the Gita. In *18.76* and *18.77*, Sanjaya addressed Dhṛtarāṣṭra respectfully as "O King." However, after expressing his own mesmerized state in these two verses, Sanjaya came to normalcy and observed that Dhṛtarāṣṭra was completely blank and untouched even after listening to this remarkable philosophy. Sanjaya probably said the very last verse of the Bhagavad-Gita after seeing the uninfluenced, unaffected face of Dhṛtarāṣṭra –

**यत्र योगेश्वरः कृष्णो यत्र पार्थो धनुर्धरः ।**
**तत्र श्रीर्विजयो भूतिर्ध्रुवा नीतिर्मतिर्मम ॥ १८.७८ ॥**

*Yatra yogeśvaraḥ Kṛṣṇo yatra Pārtho dhanurdharaḥ* ।
*Tatra Śrīrvijayo bhūtirdhruvā nītirmatirmama* ॥ *18.78* ॥

"Wherever is Lord Kṛṣṇa, the Master of Yoga and Arjuna, the expert archer, there is prosperity, victory, wealth, and firm ethical policy. This is my conviction." Sanjaya's expression underscores the fact that the divine, magnificent dialogue between Śrīkṛṣṇa and Arjuna had no effect whatsoever on Dhṛtarāṣṭra. The king was rather immersed in his thoughts about the impending war, its result, and potential loss or victory of his side. It was not feasible for Sanjaya to explicitly state to his master that Kauravas would lose the war. It would have been a mark of insolence and antipathy to answer a question which was not asked in the first place. However, the impact of the dialogue on Sanjaya was very deep. He was spellbound when he saw the magnificent Cosmic Form of Lord Kṛṣṇa and understood who Kṛṣṇa really was. As an instinctive reaction, Sanjaya uttered the last verse of the Gita and gave his opinion about the victory of Pāṇḍavas candidly without any question from King Dhṛtarāṣṭra or without any regard for his reaction.

One may wonder why there was no impact on Dhṛtarāṣṭra like the one that was seen on Sanjaya and Arjuna after listening to the same remarkable philosophy of the Bhagavad-Gita. The answer to this question can be derived when we study the very first verse of the Gita:

**धर्मक्षेत्रे कुरुक्षेत्रे समवेता युयुत्सवः ।**
**मामकाः पाण्डवाश्चैव किमकुर्वत सञ्जय ॥ १.१ ॥**

*Dharmakṣetre kurukṣetre samavetā yuyutsavaḥ* ।
*Māmakāḥ pāṇḍavāś caiva kim akurvata sañjaya* ॥ *1.1* ॥

"O Sanjaya! Tell me what did 'my sons' and the 'sons of Pāṇḍu' do when they assembled on the holy field of Kurukṣetra to fight the war." The land of **Kurukṣetra** is also known as the land of war, duty, history, and as a place where people seek spiritual awakening. It is a 'historical land' since it is mentioned in the history named 'Jaya'. It is a 'religious land' since the war for the establishment of Dharma was fought on it. [Note: The word Dharma indicates many meanings: righteousness, morality, prescribed duty, or Religion. In this context, it specifically means Sanātana Vedic Hindu Dharma.] It is a 'spiritual land' since the Bhagavad-Gita, specifically the portion having the teachings of Vedānta, was taught on it. On this epic land, Kauravas, whom Dhṛtarāṣṭra addressed as 'mine,' and Pāṇḍavas, whom he considered his 'enemies,' were assembled for the war.

The answer to the question – "Why Dhṛtarāṣṭra was not affected after listening to the Gita?" – lies in the sense of 'mineness' in Dhṛtarāṣṭra's mind and consequent demarcation made by him. Dhṛtarāṣṭra considered Duryodhana, Duhśāsana, and Śakuni as 'mine,' and Arjuna, Bhīma and Yudhiṣṭhīra as 'enemies.' These six people are not mere individuals. Each one of them symbolizes a specific collection of vices and virtues. Duryodhana is greedy, conceited, and unjust by nature. Duhśāsana is lustful, reckless, and thoughtless. Śakuni is diabolic. Dhṛtarāṣṭra considered these flawed people to be 'mine.' Arjuna has virtuous mind, pure intellect, firm obedience, and the trait of not condemning anyone unnecessarily. Yudhiṣṭhīra is truthful, modest, and upright. Bhīma has immense power and affinity to Dharma. Dhṛtarāṣṭra considered them his 'enemies.' In other words, he accepted the vices of Kauravas and rejected the virtues of Pāṇḍavas. As a result, he was completely unaffected by the teachings of the Gita. For him, the Gita was a mere collection of syllables when he listened to the words of Lord Kṛṣṇa.

The implication of this event for us in the present age is that a person may read the Gita, listen to it, memorize its verses, or may even write articles or give discourses about it. But if he adheres to such vices as that of Kauravas, he will not reap the desired benefit from the study of the Gita. On the contrary, if he embodies such virtues as those of Pāṇḍavas, he will soak up the profound teachings of Lord Kṛṣṇa. This reality has been explained in the Bhagavad-Gita itself. Duryodhana did not have the divine qualities like humility, modesty, and unpretentiousness. Duhśāsana was full of desire, lust, and anger, the traits that represent Rajoguṇa (*3.37*). Śakuni did not have even a trace of honesty and uprightness. On the contrary, he was devious and fraudulent. Dhṛtarāṣṭra considered these malicious qualities to be his own, and hence, the teachings of the Gita did not bear him any fruits.

Arjuna, on the other hand, possessed all the divine qualities, and he was dearly loved by Lord Kṛṣṇa. He thus attained the desired effect of the teachings of the Gita. Lord Kṛṣṇa Himself addresses Arjuna as His 'loved one' (*10.1*). Therefore, He guides Arjuna towards his real, lasting welfare by imparting the knowledge of the Gita. Bhīma and Yudhiṣṭhīra, just like Arjuna, had profound faith in Lord Kṛṣṇa, and they, too, were bestowed with many divine qualities. But Dhṛtarāṣṭra considered them his enemies; therefore, he was eager to defeat them in the war. St. Jñāneśwara has made insightful remarks about this disparity between Dhṛtarāṣṭra and Pāṇḍavas in his renowned treatise Jñāneśwari *(9.522)* and devotional poetry Haripāṭha (*1.4*). He says, "A male buffalo relaxing in the mud remains rigidly passive in that sludge and does not move even a bit. Similarly, Dhṛtarāṣṭra was mired in the mud of vicious qualities and entangled in the web of delusion and attachment; therefore, he was unmoved and untouched by the teachings of the Bhagavad-

Gita. Arjuna, however, soaked up the teachings and attained liberation from his temptations and delusion."

The very first verse of the Gita mentions two words: **Dharmakṣetra** and **Kurukṣetra**. These words can be better understood in the light of the Gita itself. In the 13th chapter Lord Kṛṣṇa says –

**इदं शरीरं कौन्तेय क्षेत्रमित्यभिधीयते । (१३.१)**

*Idaṃ śarīraṃ kaunteya kṣetram ity abhidhīyate* ॥ *(13.1)*

"The word **Kṣetra** (क्षेत्र) means the body." The term 'Dharmakṣetra' indicates the human body since only humans have the capacity to understand and follow the precepts of Dharma, act according to them, and obtain the results. Other Kṣetras do not have this ability. Lord Kṛṣṇa says that He will be born in every age for the establishment of Dharma. Lord Kṛṣṇa's expectations from this Dharmakṣetra – the human body or human birth – are evidently outlined in the philosophy of the Bhagavad-Gita. The word **Kuru** indicates an order to perform an action. The body which is a Dharmakṣetra is also a Kurukṣetra since the body can be ordered to perform prescribed actions, it can perform the ordered actions and bear the fruits of those actions. In this body or Kṣetra, man has a natural tendency to embrace the traits of Kauravas which give instant gratification. He finds it difficult to nurture the divine virtues of Pāṇḍavas. Human beings have an inherent choice to follow any path of action. Such a free will is known as Kriyamāṇa Karma Swātantrya in scriptures. They can choose to tread on either the divine path or the evil path. There is a verse in Ṛgveda that says,

**सच्चासच्च वचसि पस्पृधाते ।**

*Saccāsacca vacasi paspṛdhāte* ॥

"True and false contest on the ground of the speech (Vāṇi)." This simply means that a person can speak either what is true or what is false. In this contest, if he chooses to tell the truth, then he finds lasting happiness. And if he chooses to speak what is false, then he continually oscillates between the duality of joy and grief.

## The cause of delusion (*Moha*) and its effects

It is popularly believed that the Bhagavad-Gita is a melodious song of the Lord. People who perceive Lord Kṛṣṇa merely as an extraordinary human being do not necessarily understand the primacy of this remarkable divine song. Lord Kṛṣṇa says about Himself –

**अवजानन्ति मां मूढा मानुषीं तनुमाश्रितम् ।**
**परं भावमजानन्तो मम भूतमहेश्वरम् ॥ ९.११ ॥**

*Avajānanti māṃ mūḍhā mānuṣīṃ tanum āśrītam* ।
*Paraṃ bhāvam ajānanto mama bhūtamaheśvaram* ॥ *9.11* ॥

"Deluded people merely behold Me as a human body, so they cannot recognize Me as Īśvara – the owner, governor of this world. Those who do not know My Divine Nature disregard Me when I descend in the human form and consider Me an ordinary human just like them."

**अव्यक्तं व्यक्तिमापन्नं मन्यन्ते मामबुद्धयः ।**
**परं भावमजानन्तो ममाव्ययमनुत्तमम् ॥ ७.२४ ॥**

*Avyaktaṃ vyaktim āpannaṃ manyante māmabuddhayaḥ* ।
*Paraṃ bhāvam ajānanto mamāvyayam anuttamam* ॥ *7.24* ॥

"Deluded people do not understand My Highest, imperishable nature. Being unintelligent, they cannot comprehend the real Me through their mind or senses. They regard Me, the unmanifested, as having come into existence just like them."

**त्रिभिर्गुणमयैर्भावैरेभिः सर्वमिदं जगत् ।**
**मोहितं नाभिजानाति मामेभ्यः परमव्ययम् ॥ ७.१३ ॥**

*Tribhir guṇamāyāir bhāvair ebhiḥ sarvam idaṃ jagat* ।
*Mohitaṃ nābhijānāti mām ebhyaḥ param avyayam* ॥ *7.13* ॥

"All beings in this world are deluded by the three Guṇas: Sattva, Rājas, and Tāmas. Therefore, they do not understand the real Me who is immutable, and who transcends the three Guṇas." Guṇas are the cause of dispositions in each being. These above verses underscore the fact that humans are deluded by nature, and they do not necessarily understand what lies in their best interest.

The entire Bhagavad-Gita is meant for the ultimate, lasting welfare of all human beings, and it is wise to accept the teachings of the Gita without challenging them. If it is difficult for a person to learn the teachings of the Gita himself, he should learn them from the luminary sages like Ādi Śaṅkarācārya or St. Jñāneśwara. These saints were born for the very reason of spreading the message of the Gita. St. Nāmadeva, Samartha Rāmadāsa, St. Kabira, and St. Tukārāma did not write direct commentaries on the Gita, but they, too, did similar eminent, selfless work of taking the Vedānta to masses. The seeker should follow these enlightened saints who are beyond doubt or question.

## The Puṣpikā (concluding line) of the Gita

Every chapter of the Bhagavad-Gita ends with a Puṣpikā which is the customary concluding line for each chapter. For all 18 chapters, this Puṣpikā is the same, except for the sequential number and name of each chapter. E.g. The Puṣpikā of the first chapter of the Gita is as follows –

**ॐ तत्सदिति श्रीमद्भगवद्गीतासूपनिषत्सु ब्रह्मविद्यायां योगशास्त्रे श्रीकृष्णार्जुनसंवादे अर्जुनविषादयोगोनाम प्रथमोऽध्यायः ॥**

*Om tatsaditi Śrimadbhagvadgitāsūpaniṣatsu Brahmavidyāyāṃ Yogaśāstre Śrīkṛṣṇārjunasaṅvāde Arjunaviṣādayogonāma Prathamo'dhyāyaḥ* ॥

"In the Upaniṣad of the Bhagavad-Gita, regarding the Knowledge of Brahman, in the Yogaśāstra, and in the dialogue between Śrīkṛṣṇa and Arjuna, **ArjunaViṣādaYoga** is the **first** chapter." The same Puṣpikā is found at the end of each chapter with the particular *name* and *number* of that chapter. [Note: Yogaśāstra means the philosophy of the union of Jiva and Brahman.]

This concluding Puṣpikā is deeply meaningful and pivotal in the study of the Gita. By learning the profundity of this succinct concluding line, students can find the specific direction for their study which is intended to be given by the creator of this treatise. The Gita should be regarded as **Śruti** (Upaniṣad) and studied with meticulous adherence to philosophy. Ādi Śaṅkarācārya has addressed the Gita as **Smṛti** in his commentary as it is a part of the Mahābhārata Smṛti. The word Śruti stands for the Vedas and Upaniṣads since they were as if heard by ancient luminary sages when they were in deep meditation. The verses of Śrutis are not explicitly written by humans. Rather they were revealed to the sages having highly pure and steady intellect when they were meditating. Hence, Śrutis are considered the most authentic texts available to mankind given that they are not tainted by the faults of the human intellect. The word Smṛti indicates the text written from memory. Mahābhārata is an epic treatise written by sage Vyāsa; hence, it is considered a Smṛti. Leaving aside this technical detail, the Gita should be regarded as Śruti as expressed in the word 'Upaniṣatsu' in the concluding Puṣpikā of each chapter.

There is a famous invocation verse, which is usually recited before studying the Gita –

**सर्वोपनिषदो गावो दोग्धा गोपालनन्दनः ।**
**पार्थो वत्सः सुधीर्भोक्ता दुग्धं गीतामृतं महत् ॥**

*Sarvopaniṣado gāvo dogdhā Gopālanandanaḥ* ।
*Pārtho vatsaḥ sudhirbhoktā dugdhaṃ gītāmṛtaṃ mahat* ॥

"All the Upaniṣads are the cows, which are milked by Gopala (Kṛṣṇa), the son of Nanda. Arjuna (Pārtha), a man of wise intellect, is the calf who enjoys the milk – the supreme, eternal nectar of the philosophy of the Gita." Ādi Śaṅkarācārya has explained the word Upaniṣad by decompounding it and analyzing its roots –

- **Upa** (उप) – Sit close to
- **Ni** (नि) – To propel, escort, give direction to
- **Sad** (सद्) – To loosen the clasp or destroy (ignorance)

**Analysis of Puṣpikā: Upaniṣad – (Upa)**

The prefix **Upa** from the word **Upa-ni-ṣad** means sit close to. In spiritual pursuit, Sadguru (a Self-realized saint or Spiritual Master) is the true well-wisher of every seeker. The seeker should sit close to his Sadguru with utmost humility, surrender to him, and serve him unconditionally. Lord Kṛṣṇa says –

**तद्विद्धि प्रणिपातेन परिप्रश्नेन सेवया ।**
**उपदेक्ष्यन्ति ते ज्ञानं ज्ञानिनस्तत्त्वदर्शिनः ॥ ४.३४ ॥**

*Tad viddhi praṇipātena paripraśnena sevayā ।*
*Upadekṣyanti te jñānaṃ jñāninas tattvādarśinaḥ ॥ 4.34 ॥*

"First, a disciple should bow down very politely and prostrate before the feet of his Sadguru, render services to him honestly and modestly, and ask insightful questions to him. Then the enlightened Sadguru imparts the spiritual knowledge to him." Arjuna surrendered to his Sadguru, Lord Kṛṣṇa, in the same manner, and said –

**यच्छ्रेयः स्यान्निश्चितं ब्रूहि तन्मे शिष्यस्तेऽहं शाधि मां त्वां प्रपन्नम् ॥ २.७ ॥**

*Yac chreyaḥ syān niścitaṃ brūhi tan me*
*Śiṣyaste'haṃ śādhi māṃ tvāṃ prapannam ॥ 2.7 ॥*

"I request you to tell me what is definitely in my best interest (Śreya). I have surrendered to You as Your disciple. Kindly guide me." The word **Śreya** used by Arjuna in his request is originally explained in Kaṭha Upaniṣad –

**श्रेयो हि धीरोऽभि प्रेयसो वृणीते प्रेयो मन्दो योगक्षेमाद् वृणीते ॥ (१.२.२)**

*Śreyo hi dhīro'bhi preyaso vṛṇīte preyo*
*mando yogakśemādvṛṇīte ॥ (1.2.2)*

"The prudent, thoughtful people prefer spiritual welfare (Śreya) that leads to liberation and lasting happiness. On the contrary, ignorant people embrace worldly welfare (Preya) that leads to the progress in worldly life."

After Arjuna's request, Lord Kṛṣṇa did not directly say to Arjuna, "I am your Guru, and I accept you as my disciple." Instead, He started imparting His actual teaching from verse *2.11*. He taught the essence of the philosophy in two subsequent verses to Arjuna:

**नासतो विद्यते भावो नाभावो विद्यते सतः ।**
**उभयोरपि दृष्टोऽन्तस्त्वनयोस्तत्त्वदर्शिभिः ॥ २.१६ ॥**

*Nāsato vidyāte bhāvo nābhāvo vidyāte sataḥ* ।
*Ubhayorapi dṛṣṭo'antas tvanayos tattvādarśibhiḥ* ॥ *2.16* ॥

"The unreal (*Asat*) has no real existence, and it is never the case that the real (*Sat*) does not exist. The enlightened people who are knowers of the Truth see the reality in both these cases."

**अविनाशि तु तद्विद्धि येन सर्वमिदं ततम् ।**
**विनाशमव्ययस्यास्य न कश्चित्कर्तुमर्हति ॥ २.१७ ॥**

*Avināśi tu tad viddhi yena sarvam idaṃ tatam* ।
*Vināśam avyayasyāsya na kaścit kartum arhati* ॥ *2.17* ॥

"Know that Pure Existence (*Sat*), which permeates the entire world, is indestructible. No one can ever destroy that *Sat* which is imperishable." Lord Kṛṣṇa, who is a kind-hearted well-wisher and Sadguru, has thus described the essence of Upaniṣads in the Bhagavad-Gita. This same philosophy is repeatedly explained in the Upaniṣads in greater detail.

## Analysis of Puṣpikā: Upaniṣad – (Ni)

The prefix **Ni** from the word **Upa-ni-ṣad** means to propel or to give direction or to take towards the goal. The Gita is considered an Upaniṣad since Lord Kṛṣṇa has given directions to Arjuna and propelled him towards his highest benefit or ultimate goal. The philosophy of the Gita propels (drives) not just Arjuna but also other seekers – even today – in multiple ways. The directions given in the Gita are discussed below –

1. From *ignorance* to *Self-Knowledge*

   **इदं तु ते गुह्यतमं प्रवक्ष्याम्यनसूयवे ।**
   **ज्ञानं विज्ञानसहितं यज्ज्ञात्वा मोक्ष्यसेऽशुभात् ॥ ९.१ ॥**

   *Idaṃ tu te guhyatamaṃ pravakṣyāmy anasūyave* ।
   *Jñānaṃ vijñānasahitaṃ yaj jñātvā mokṣyase'śubhāt* ॥ *9.1* ॥

   "I will impart this most confidential, profound, mysterious Knowledge of the true Self to you and also teach a way to realize it and make it a living reality since you are neither envious nor caviler by nature. You have a divine disposition. Having known this Knowledge, you shall be liberated from depraved ignorance."

2. From the *duality of joy-sorrow* to *Pure Bliss*

   **मात्रास्पर्शास्तु कौन्तेय शीतोष्णसुखदुःखदाः ।**
   **आगमापायिनोऽनित्यास्तांस्तितिक्षस्व भारत ॥ २.१४ ॥**

   *Mātrāsparśās tu kaunteya śītoṣṇasukhaduḥkhadāḥ* ।
   *Āgamāpāyino'nityās tāṃs titikṣasva bhārata* ॥ *2.14* ॥

   "O Arjuna! The contact of the senses with objects and their subsequent separation cause joy and grief, respectively. Favorable experiences lead to joy, and unfavorable experiences lead to grief. These joy and sufferings are subject to creation and destruction, and thus impermanent. It is best to brave them out calmly." The next verse in this chapter says that the seeker who shows such fortitude is eligible for liberation i.e. Mokṣa. The body or the mind may be inflicted with many sufferings or adversities, but Ātman, the true Self, is not attached to or encaged by them.

3. From *identification with body* to *identification with Ātman*

   **योगी युञ्जीत सततमात्मानं रहसि स्थितः ।**
   **एकाकी यतचित्तात्मा निराशीरपरिग्रहः ॥ ६.१० ॥**

   *Yogī yuñjīta satatam ātmānaṃ rahasi sthitaḥ* ।
   *Ekākī yatacittātmā nirāśīr aparigrahaḥ* ॥ *6.10* ॥

   "The seeker who practices meditation should conquer his mind and body, stay in solitude, and strive to remain steadily absorbed in Kuṭastha Caitanya i.e. Ātman or Pure Consciousness."

4. From *the world is real* to *Brahman alone is real*

**गामाविश्य च भूतानि धारयाम्यहमोजसा ।**
**पुष्णामि चौषधीः सर्वाः सोमो भूत्वा रसात्मकः ॥ १५.१३ ॥**

*Gām āviśya ca bhūtāni dhārayāmy aham ojasā* ।
*Puṣṇāmi cauṣadhīḥ sarvāḥ somo bhūtvā rasātmakaḥ* ॥ *15.13* ॥

"And permeating the earth, I provide sustenance to all beings through My power. And being the essence (nectar) of the moon, I nourish all herbs and plants." Therefore, instead of being attached to earthly objects, the seeker should be attached to Īśvara who permeates the earth.

5. From *I am the doer* to *Īśvara is the doer*

**तस्मात्त्वमुत्तिष्ठ यशो लभस्व जित्वा शत्रून् भुङ्क्ष्व राज्यं समृद्धम् ।**
**मयैवैते निहताः पूर्वमेव निमित्तमात्रं भव सव्यसाचिन् ॥ ११.३३ ॥**

*Tasmāt tvam uttiṣṭha yaśo labhasva*
*jitvā śatrūn bhuṅkṣva rājyaṃ samṛddham* ।
*Māyāivaite nihatāḥ pūrvam eva*
*nimittamātraṃ bhava savyasācin* ॥ *11.33* ॥

"Therefore, get ready for the war! Conquer the enemy and enjoy the prosperous kingdom. Your enemies as well as friends have been already killed by Me. Be only a medium or an instrument to kill them!" All events in the world are predestined and pre-planned in the scheme of Īśvara. They merely occur through someone acting as a medium. The person acting as a medium should not consider himself as the doer of those events.

6. From *complacent and passive* to *dynamic and active*

**तस्मादसक्तः सततं कार्यं कर्म समाचर ।**
**असक्तो ह्याचरन्कर्म परमाप्नोति पूरुषः ॥ ३.१९ ॥**

*Tasmād asaktaḥ satataṃ kāryaṃ karma samācara* ।
*Asakto hy ācaran karma param āpnoti pūruṣaḥ* ॥ *3.19* ॥

"Therefore, constantly and meticulously perform prescribed actions and duties without attachment to the potential fruits or rewards of work; since, by performing actions without attachment, one realizes the true nature of the Self as Supreme Ātman."

7. From being *attached* to *non-attachment*

   The prior verse describes detachment while performing actions. This verse mentions the importance of not being attached to worldly affairs:

   **अश्वत्थमेनं सुविरूढमूलं असङ्गशस्त्रेण दृढेन छित्त्वा ॥ (१५.३)**

   *Aśvatthāmenaṃ suvirūḍhamūlaṃ*

   *asaṅgaśastreṇa dṛḍhena chittvā* ॥ *(15.3)*

   "The holy fig (*Aśvattha*) tree of the world is firmly rooted in attachment. Cut it completely with the sharp ax of detachment." The reason for the emphasis on dispassion or detachment is that the true Self is distinct from the body, mind, and all worldly creations. Here in this verse, the Lord asks us not to remain attached to any worldly matter which is analogous to the Aśvattha tree that is in a constant state of flux.

8. From *bondage* to *liberation*

   **सर्वधर्मान्परित्यज्य मामेकं शरणं व्रज ।**
   **अहं त्वा सर्वपापेभ्यो मोक्षयिष्यामि मा शुचः ॥ १८.६६ ॥**

   *Sarvadharmān parityajya mām ekaṃ śaraṇaṃ vraja* ।
   *Ahaṃ tvā sarvapāpebhyo mokṣyayiṣyāmi mā śucaḥ* ॥ *18.66* ॥

   "Relinquish the binding thought that 'I am the doer' while performing all duties and surrender exclusively unto Me. I will liberate you from the cycle of sins and virtues. Do not despair."

Those listed above are certainly not the only directions in which Kṛṣṇa has propelled Arjuna. A conscientious reader can construe several more directions of guidance from the Bhagavad-Gita.

## Analysis of Puṣpikā: Brahmavidyā

The word Brahmavidyāyāṃ in the concluding Puṣpikā denotes that the core topic of the Bhagavad-Gita is Brahmavidyā i.e. the knowledge propounded in Upaniṣads. All other topics are contextual, incidental, secondary, and inconsequential. If the seeker chooses to focus on the other peripheral topics, he will disregard the core topic in the course of study. The result of Brahmavidyā is liberation i.e. Mokṣa. The student of the Gita needs to be eligible for Mokṣa, and attaining such eligibility is an arduous process. It is imperative to nurture dispassion towards the world for this purpose. Many a time, the study of the Gita becomes only an academic pursuit. The reader gets interested only in its theoretical comprehension. A true seeker should make himself aware of the ultimate goal of 'Mokṣa' while studying or reading the word 'Brahmavidyā' in the Puṣpikā at the end of each chapter. St. Jñāneśwara has written an epic commentary in Marathi on the Bhagavad-Gita which is called Jñāneśwari. In his commentary (*18.1750*), he states, "The Gita is a treatise that is centered on the 'philosophy of the true Self' (Adhyatmaśāstra). The seeker who studies the core gist of this philosophy and attains Mokṣa is its rightful student. Others find pleasure in studying the peripheral factors like poetry, simile, metaphors, and other literary aspects." This is true both for the Bhagavad-Gita and Jñāneśwari. It is possible to digress from the core purpose of Mokṣa and get engaged in other incidental aspects stated in the Gita such as discussing the system of Karma, emphasizing on performing duties, trying to find instances of communism, and thinking about the obsolete system of the Four Social Orders (Chaturvarṇas), etc. But the genuine seeker should focus on Mokṣa alone while studying the Gita.

The words Brahmavidyā and Ātmavidyā mean the Knowledge of Brahman and the Knowledge of Ātman, respectively, and they are synonyms of each other. Self-realization is the firm, unchanging, direct realization of the Jiva that "I am Brahman." It is essential to understand that Ātman is not attached to the body, and Brahman is not attached to the world. The theoretical understanding of Brahman is incomplete without a clear understanding of the terms Jiva, Īśvara, Ātman, and Brahman. These terms are explained in the Gita in the following manner –

1. The concept of *Jiva*

**वासांसि जीर्णानि यथा विहाय नवानि गृह्णाति नरोऽपराणि ।**
**तथा शरीराणि विहाय जीर्णान्यन्यानि संयाति नवानि देही ॥ २.२२ ॥**

*Vāsāṃsi jīrṇāni yathā vihāya navāni gṛhṇāti naro'parāṇi* ।
*Tathā śarīrāṇi vihāya jīrṇāni anyāni saṅyāti navāni dehī* ॥ *2.22*॥

"Ātman permeates the body, yet it is not attached to the body. In other words, it is separate from the body. Therefore, omnipresent Ātman does not get new bodies. Jiva exists in association with the intellect. Just as new clothes replace old clothes, so also every Jiva gets a new body in the place of the old body after his death." The Jiva who abides in the Kṣetra of his body is known as the 'Kṣetrajña.'

**इदं शरीरं कौन्तेय क्षेत्रमित्यभिधीयते ।**
**एतद्यो वेत्ति तं प्राहुः क्षेत्रज्ञ इति तद्विदः ॥ १३.१ ॥**

*Idaṃ śarīraṃ kaunteya kṣetram ity abhidhīyate* ।
*Etad yo vetti taṃ prāhuḥ kṣetrajña iti tadvidaḥ* ॥ *13.1* ॥

"The body is called the Kṣetra. One who knows activities of the Kṣetra is called the Kṣetrajña (Jiva)."

2. The concept of Īśvara

**ईश्वरः सर्वभूतानां हृद्देशेऽर्जुन तिष्ठति ।**
**भ्रामयन्सर्वभूतानि यन्त्रारूढानि मायया ॥ १८.६१ ॥**

*Īśvaraḥ sarvabhūtānāṃ hṛdde'śerjuna tiṣṭhati* ।
*Bhrāmāyān sarvabhūtāni yantrārūḍhāni māyayā* ॥ *18.61* ॥

"Īśvara dwells in the hearts (Antaḥkaraṇa) of all beings. He causes all beings who identify themselves with the body, and who are mounted by their ego on the machine of His scheme of things, to revolve in the cycle of birth and death through the power of His Yogamāyā." Īśvara is the ultimate governor (orchestrator). Every Jiva is governed by Him. Īśvara creates, maintains, and destroys both insentient entities and sentient beings in the world. Brahman accompanied by Māyā is known as Īśvara. This relationship between Brahman and Māyā is imaginary; however, it is perceived as real due to the power of Māyā. Īśvara is the Knower and Witness of everything (Sarvajñā, Sarvasakṣi). He is all-powerful, and His power works in three different ways:

a. *Kartum*: Īśvara has the power to do anything. He can create and govern the entire universe through His mere wish. The sun rises and sets on time; nature changes its seasons cyclically every year; an ocean never crosses its boundaries, etc. These are all examples of Īśvara's power to govern the universe.
b. *Akartum*: Īśvara also has the power to do nothing. He will not create a universe if he wishes to do so.
c. *Anyathākartum*: There are two meanings of this term:
    - Īśvara can do what is not meant to be, do something differently, or undo what is already done. E.g. He appeared through a wooden pole to protect His devotee Prahlāda; He reversed the effects of the poison that was given to St. Mirābai and saved her from dying. He uses this power only as per His wish to help his ardent devotees in exceptional cases.
    - The term 'Anyathā' also means 'in other manner.' Īśvara's power is the ultimate. Once He says or decides something, it takes place in exactly the same manner, not in any other manner. This simply means that Īśvara's system cannot be challenged or altered in any way.

Īśvara governs all manifestations of power and energy in the world. There is a verse in the 10th chapter of the Gita that describes Īśvara –

**अहं सर्वस्य प्रभवो मत्तः सर्वं प्रवर्तते । (१०.८)**

*Ahaṃ sarvasya prabhavo mattaḥ sarvaṃ pravartate । (10.8)*

"I am the source of all; everything originates from Me." Akṣara and Adhidaiva are the alternate names for Īśvara. Lord Kṛṣṇa states:

**गतिर्भर्ता प्रभुः साक्षी निवासः शरणं सुहृत् ।**
**प्रभवः प्रलयः स्थानं निधानं बीजमव्ययम् ॥ ९.१८ ॥**

*Gatir bhartā prabhuḥ sākṣī nivāsaḥ śaraṇaṃ suhṛt ।*
*Prabhavaḥ pralayaḥ sthānaṃ nidhānaṃ bījam avyam ॥ 9.18 ॥*

"All entities of the visible world merge in Me as I am the ultimate goal – Gati. I am the nourisher, the Lord, the Witness, the abode, the shelter, the true friend, the supporter, the imperishable, and the very root of creation, preservation, and dissolution. I am the reservoir in which everything merges in a subtle form to become the seed for the next round of formation. I am Īśvara." [For more details, check Brahmasūtra *1.3.11*]

3. The concept of *Ātman*

**अहमात्मा गुडाकेश सर्वभूताशयस्थितः ।**
**अहमादिश्च मध्यं च भूतानामन्त एव च ॥ १०.२० ॥**

*Aham ātmā guḍākeśa sarvabhūtāśayasthitaḥ ।*
*Aham ādiś ca madhyaṃ ca bhūtānām anta eva ca ॥ 10.20 ॥*

"I, as Ātman, pervade the hearts of all beings." This Ātman is also known as ***Kuṭastha* Caitanya** which is the Witness of all actions of the Jiva. All-pervasive Brahman is called Ātman in the context of an individual body. The words Ātman, Brahman, and Īśvara are used interchangeably in many places in the Vedāntic texts. The seeker should accept their meanings as per the context of that discussion. [Note: In Vedānta, the word heart (Hṛdaya) does not mean the body organ. It indicates 'inner instrument' or *Antaḥkaraṇa* also known as the subtle body comprising of the mind, intellect, memory, and ego.]

### 4. The concept of *Brahman*

The word **Bṛhat** in Sanskrit means vast or all-pervasive. Brahman is vast regardless of any limits. It is all-pervasive, formless, beginningless, endless, perpetual, and primordial. It is Absolute and Pure Existence, Consciousness, Bliss (*Sat-Cit-Ānanda*). It is the transcendental, Eternal Truth (Satya). Brahman, Ātman, Īśvara are not nouns; rather, they are the spiritual, philosophical concepts in Vedānta. Name and form go hand-in-hand. Therefore, the formless concepts like Ātman, Brahman, and Īśvara cannot have names. They can only be indirectly described. The names Brahman, Īśvara, etc. are given just as references for facilitating the description of these concepts. Even the concepts are useful only till the seeker attains enlightenment. "I am Brahman" or 'I am not Jiva, I am Brahman' – all of these thoughts disappear in Self-realization. Upaniṣad says –

**यतो वाचो निवर्तन्ते अप्राप्य मनसा सह ।**

*Yato vāco nivartante aprāpya manasā saha* I *(Tai. Up. 2.9.1)*

"Mind and speech (Vāṇī) cannot realize Ātman; therefore, they retire entirely at the time of Self-realization."

**यन्मनसा न मनुते येनाहुर्मनो मतम् ।**

*Yanmanusā na manute yenāhurmano matam* I *(Kena. Up. 1.6)*

"That, which cannot be thought of with the mind, but which is the substratum on which the mind thinks, is one all-pervasive Brahman." Jiva, Īśvara are mere words used to indicate the corresponding concepts. Brahman is birthless, ageless, and deathless. The Jiva believes that he is subject to birth, aging, and death so long as he identifies himself with the body. He is liberated from the birth and death cycle when he realizes that "I am Brahman."

5. The world is a false appearance seen on Brahman

**मयाध्यक्षेण प्रकृतिः सूयते सचराचरम् ।**
**हेतुनानेन कौन्तेय जगद्विपरिवर्तते ॥ ९.१० ॥**

*Mayādhyakṣeṇa prakṛtiḥ sūyate sacarācaram* ।
*Hetunānena kaunteya jagad viparivartate* ॥ *9.10* ॥

"Māyā (Prakṛti) as if creates the sentient and insentient world on Me (Brahman) as substratum. As a result, the beginningless lifecycle of the world keeps revolving."

6. Jiva is a part of Brahman

**ममैवांशो जीवलोके जीवभूतः सनातनः ।**
**मनःषष्ठानीन्द्रियाणि प्रकृतिस्थानि कर्षति ॥ १५.७ ॥**

*Mamaivāṃśo jīvaloke jīvabhūtaḥ sanātanaḥ* ।
*Manaḥṣaṣṭhānīndriyāṇi prakṛtisthāni karṣati* ॥ *15.7* ॥

"Every Jiva, who resides in the body, is a part or fraction of Me. The Jiva regulates actions of the mind and five senses." Technically, Brahman has no parts, divisions, subdivisions, or separations of any kind. The concepts like 'a part' or 'parts of the whole' are not applicable to Brahman or valid in Brahman. However, Jiva appears to be created as a part of Brahman due to the Upādhi, which is the limiting adjunct of the body. The eternal light of Brahman is reflected in an individual mind. The reflected light is known as Cidābhāsa, and it governs all activities of the body.

7. Brahman is birthless

**अजोऽपि सन्नव्ययात्मा भूतानामीश्वरोऽपि सन् ।**
**प्रकृतिं स्वामधिष्ठाय सम्भवाम्यात्ममायया ॥ ४.६ ॥**

*Ajo'pi sann avyayātmā bhūtānām īśvaro'pi san* ।
*Prakṛtiṃ svām adhiṣṭhāya saṃbhavāmy ātmamāyayā* ॥ *4.6* ॥

"Although I am birthless, imperishable, immutable, and the governor of all beings, yet I manifest in this world through the power of My own Māyā."

8. Ātman is imperishable

**अन्तवन्त इमे देहा नित्यस्योक्ताः शरीरिणः ।**
**अनाशिनोऽप्रमेयस्य तस्माद्युध्यस्व भारत ॥ २.१८ ॥**

*Antavanta ime dehā nityasyoktāḥ śarīriṇaḥ* ।
*Anāśino 'prameyasya tasmād yudhyasva bhārata* ॥ *2.18* ॥

"Ātman is indestructible and eternal. It is devoid of the triad of knower-knowable-knowledge. Imperishable Ātman resides in these bodies which are perishable in nature. O Arjuna! Bear this in your mind and fight the war."

9. Brahman is unmanifested, imperceptible, immutable

**अव्यक्तोऽयमचिन्त्योऽयमविकार्योऽयमुच्यते ।**
**तस्मादेवं विदित्वैनं नानुशोचितुमर्हसि ॥ २.२५ ॥**

*Avyakto 'yamacintyo 'yamavikaryo 'yamucyate* ।
*Tasmādevaṃ viditvainaṃ nānuśocitumarhasi* ॥ *2.25* ॥

"Brahman is the most subtle and formless principle; therefore, it can never manifest in any form. Only that which is perceivable through the five senses and mind can be thought about and reflected upon. Brahman is 'Self-cognizant' (*Swasaṃvedya*)." It cannot be comprehended by the conventional epistemic sources of knowledge (Pramāṇas) but can be realized only by being One with it. It is Self-effulgent (*Swayaṃprakāśa*), and it illumines the senses and the mind. The Jiva cannot reflect on Brahman like he reflects on the other worldly objects. Anything which is born or created is subject to further changes like growth, decay, and death. Brahman is eternal, and the Absolute Truth; therefore, it is not subject to any change, hence immutable in nature.

## Analysis of Puṣpikā: Yogaśāstre

The term Yogaśāstre in the concluding Puṣpikā indicates that the entire Gita is a philosophical treatise on Yoga. **Yoga** means to join, to unite, or to come together. In the context of spiritual knowledge, Yoga means an imaginary reunion of Jiva and Brahman. In fact, every Jiva is originally Brahman, but he is ignorant about it. Yoga helps him reunite with his own nature; thus, it is just an *imaginary reunion* after *imaginary separation.* For this reunion, the prescribed practices or paths are:

- **Action** (*Karma*): executing prescribed duties without thinking that "I am the doer" and without desiring fruits of those actions.
- **Worship** (*Upāsanā*): worshipping God, unconditionally surrendering to Him, following His orders.
- **Meditation** (*Dhyāna*): meditating on the fact that "I am Brahman."
- **Knowledge** (*Jñāna*): knowing, contemplating, and realizing the true Self as Brahman.

These practices are the tools meant to help in achieving the imaginary reunion of Jiva and Brahman.

The union of Jiva with Brahman is obstructed due to many reasons, which may be named in the following manner as per the teachings of the Gita:

- **अर्जुनविषादयोग** *Arjunaviṣādayoga* – grieving like Arjuna
- **आसुरीसंपदायोग** *Āsurisampadāyoga* – possessing demoniac qualities
- **त्रिगुणबंधनयोग** *Triguṇabandhanayoga* – being influenced by 3 Guṇas

The union of a Jiva with grief or demoniac qualities is a bad union (*Kuyoga*) since it is detrimental to his spiritual pursuit. E.g. when 'the Jiva is in union with disbelief,' which arises from ignorance and lack of faith, he cannot realize that he is One with Brahman. The Gita says:

**अज्ञश्चाश्रद्दधानश्च संशयात्मा विनश्यति ।**
**नायं लोकोऽस्ति न परो न सुखं संशयात्मनः ॥ ४.४० ॥**

*Ajñaścāśraddadhānaśca saṃśayātmā vinaśyati* ।
*Nāyaṃ loko 'sti na paro na sukhaṃ saṃśayātmanaḥ* ॥ *4.40* ॥

"One who is ignorant, faithless, and full of doubts is destroyed from a spiritual perspective. A skeptical person neither achieves success nor happiness in this or the other world." According to a verse in Kaṭha Upaniṣad (2.2.6), "Ignorant people only believe in the existence of this world, and they absolutely do not believe in the existence of any other world. How can then they possibly find Pure Bliss of Ātman?" They only crave for pleasures which are transient and derived from worldly objects of pleasure. They do not believe in the next world like heaven since it cannot be substantiated with the direct, absolute epistemic sources of knowledge (Pratyakṣa *Pramāṇa*). They reject the happiness in heaven and disregard the eternal, Pure Bliss of Ātman. Similarly, the Jiva, who is heavily influenced by the powerful and impure Rajoguṇa, remains in the detrimental union with insatiable cravings and fierce anger. This impels him towards sinful behavior and does not allow him to acquire Self-Knowledge.

The very first chapter, '*Arjunaviṣādayoga*', describes many shades of grief (Viṣāda). The next chapter also touches upon some of them. Every seeker should wipe out grief and suffering from his mind to realize his union with Ātman. The intellect which is perturbed and deluded by grief does not allow the Jiva to realize his Oneness with Brahman. The famous Indian poet Bhavabhūti has described the effect of grief on human mind in his composition –

**विषादे कर्तव्ये विदधति जडाः प्रत्युत मुदं ।**

*Viṣāde kartavye vidadhati jaḍāh pratyuta mudaṃ* ।

"Due to grief, an ignorant fool runs away from duties instead of happily fulfilling them." In another famous poetic treatise Raghuvaṅśam, the poet says –

**विषादलुप्तप्रतिपत्ति सैन्यं ।**

*Viṣādaluptapratipatti sainyaṃ* ।

"The entire army was in dilemma due to grief, and they did not know what the right thing to do was." Arjuna himself was suffering in many detrimental unions (*Kuyoga*) due to his grief. The effects of those bad unions were as follows:

1) **कृपया परयाविष्ट योग** *Krupayā Parayāviṣṭa Yoga (1.28)* – Arjuna was deeply anguished due to needless sympathy.
2) **मनभ्रमण योग** *Manabhramaṇa Yoga (1.28 to 1.30)* – Trembling of the body, drying up of the mouth, sweating, hair standing on the end, loosening of grip on the bow, burning sensation in the skin, imbalance and inability to stand properly.
3) **श्रेयाश्रेयभ्रम योग** *Śreyāśreyabhrama Yoga (1.31)* – Mistaking that which is beneficial to be detrimental
4) **पुरुषार्थच्युती योग** *Puruṣārthacyuti Yoga (1.32)* – Victory, power, kingdom, and prosperity are the real goals for a warrior (Kṣatriya). However, Arjuna started feeling reluctant to work toward the same goals.
5) **विपरीत कृतज्ञता योग** *Viparita Krutajñatā Yoga (1.33 to 35)* – Being grateful is an essential virtue. However, gratefulness towards unjust and evil people is perverse and abnormal.
6) **अन्यायक्षमा योग** *Anyāyakṣamā Yoga (1.38 to 39)* – Kauravas were doing injustice due to excessive greed and ego. Despite knowing this well, Arjuna was ready to forgive these unlawful people unnecessarily.
7) **धर्माधर्ममोह योग** *Dharmādharmamoha Yoga (1.40 to 45)* – Giving more importance to aspects like eradication of the lineage and intermingling of castes and social order; sidelining the critical issues of being just, righteous, and executing prescribed duties.
8) **शोकसंविग्नमानस योग** *Śokasaṃvignamānasa Yoga (1.47)* – Being mournful and heartbroken in advance due to potential future grief.
9) **कश्मल योग** *Kaśmala Yoga (2.2)* – Being trapped in the mud of ignorance. This is the very root of all detrimental unions mentioned so far from the first chapter.
10) **अनार्यजुष्ट, अस्वर्ग्य, अकीर्तिकर योग** *Anāryajuṣṭa, Aswargya, Akīrtikara Yoga (2.2)* – Arjuna's thoughts were disgraceful and incongruous for a brave warrior. They would keep him away

from attaining heaven and eradicate his glory of being a great archer.

11) क्षुद्रहृदयदौर्बल्य योग *Kśudrahṛdayadaurbalya Yoga (2.3)* – Fragility of the mind that leads to pettiness, tendency to yield to impotence, and weakening of the courage.
12) कार्पण्यदोषोपहृत योग *Kārpaṇyadoṣopahata Yoga (2.7)* – The intellect corrupted by meekness and thoughtlessness.
13) मोहकलिल योग *Mohakalila Yoga (2.52)* – Considering the impermanent to be permanent and perishable to be imperishable due to delusion.
14) मनोगतकाम योग *Manogatakama Yoga (2.55)* – Being attached to many desires in mind.
15) शुभाशुभचिंतन योग *Śubhāśubhacintana Yoga (2.57)* – Clinging to the worldly ideas of piousness and impiousness in day-to-day life.
16) इंद्रीयप्रमाथिनी योग *Indriyapramāthini Yoga (2.60)* – Uncontrolled organs running amuck, not remaining calm and stable.

The Bhagavad-Gita teaches that every seeker must consciously wipe out these bad or detrimental unions (Kuyoga) from his mind to realize the desired union (Suyoga) of the Jiva with Brahman.

## Analysis of Puṣpikā: Śrīkṛṣṇārjunasaṃvāde

Śrīkṛṣṇārjunasaṃvāde is the fourth part of the concluding Puṣpikā of each chapter. The two main people – Lord Kṛṣṇa and Arjuna – engaged in this dialogue are both divine. Lord Kṛṣṇa says that Arjuna is His own Divine Glory (Vibhūti). Arjuna has various alternate names which indicate his extraordinary qualities. The name 'Bhārata' means the one who revels in knowledge or the one who has affinity for knowledge. Arjuna appreciated knowledge, and he was keen to follow the teachings of spiritual wisdom, hence he was called Bhārata. 'Guḍākeśa' means the one who has complete control over his sleep.

'Anasūya' means the one who is neither jealous nor a caviler. Arjuna is an exceptional person and an eligible, authentic listener. Although deluded by Māyā before the war, he was originally a very distinguished, eminent, remarkable person. St. Jñāneśwara has given an excellent description of Arjuna's qualities in the $9^{th}$ chapter of his treatise Jñāneśwari (*9.36*, *9.40*). He says that Arjuna was bestowed with many excellent virtues such as the pure mind, the intellect that is in line with the precepts of scriptures, the tendency to not condemn anyone, firm loyalty to Lord Kṛṣṇa, brilliant intelligence, obedience, and empathy for others. This is precisely why Lord Kṛṣṇa chose to tell him the most profound, confidential, and royal the Knowledge of Ātman.

Lord Kṛṣṇa's appearance in the human form, actions, and disappearance (Tirodhana) in the end are all divine and mysterious. Lord Kṛṣṇa is formless Nirguṇa Brahman. Even then, He manifested Himself through a divine body, performed glorious actions, and disappeared in a magnificent manner in the end. He is the sublime, Supreme Lord. Kṛṣṇa Himself states in verse 4.9 that His entire life from birth to disappearance is incredible and transcendental. His own maternal uncle killed His six older siblings. He was born in a prison. He was transferred to a different place amid torrential rains, and He was raised by a different mother. He faced enormous adversities as a child, but He easily managed to overcome all of them, thus manifesting His divine nature. Later He killed His own maternal uncle Kaṅsa, coronated His grandfather Ugrasena as the King of Mathurā, and established another kingdom in Dwāraka. For most of His life, He fought with king Jarāsandha and the like. He finished his formal education in the Āśrama of Sāndipani Muni. He fought wars even for marriage. Before the epic battle of Mahābhārata started, He provided timeless guidance to Arjuna in the form of the Gita and impelled him to fight the battle with an equanimous mind. To convince Arjuna, He projected the picture that all warriors on both sides – except 5 Pāṇḍavas, Sātyaki, Kṛtavarmā, Dhṛtarāṣṭra, Kṛpācārya, and Aśvatthāmā – are already slain by Him. Towards the end, after destroying His own lineage of frenetic Yādavas, He imparted guidance to His great devotee Uddhava and disappeared with His body. Even Brahmadeva and other gods – who considered themselves omniscient – could not understand the secret behind His sudden disappearance. His biography continues to enchant and influence millions of people to date. Even today, people feel immense love and attraction for Kṛṣṇa.

The Bhagavad-Gita is the glorious dialogue between these two eminent personalities. It has been translated into many languages. Even in this age, people all over the world continue to study the Gita and reflect upon its teachings. Here, the speaker is an incarnation of God, while the listener is surrendered to the Lord. Arjuna's questions are based on the doubts about justice, righteousness, and Religion (Sanātana Vaidic Dharma). His questions are not asked for any personal gain or profit.

The Bhagavad-Gita, being a dialogue between two divine people, does not have the four taints found in the texts which are composed by an ordinary human intellect. Human intellect is tainted with the following four types of faults:

1) <u>Delusion</u> (*Bhrama*, **भ्रम**) – Human intellect considers unreal to be more appropriate than real due to ignorance, selfishness, and ego. It believes what is delusive to be real and enjoyable. The true Self, Ātman, is eternal Pure Bliss, yet people seek external pleasure in material objects. It is the Jiva who likes or dislikes objects, but the liking or disliking is wrongly attributed to Ātman due to delusion.

2) <u>Error or Blunder</u> (*Pramāda*, **प्रमाद**) – There is a famous saying: "To err is human." Human intellect is prone to

wrongdoing, deterioration, inattentiveness, and ignorance; therefore, incorrect decisions are often made by human beings. Any text created by the flawed intellect is bound to be incorrect. Implausible text cannot be accepted as the ultimate guide.

3) Imperfect senses (*Karaṇāpāṭava*, **करणापाटव**) – 'Karaṇa' means an instrument or a bodily organ. 'Apaṭutā' means incompetency. Incompetency of the organs is known as Karaṇāpāṭava. Some people have organ disorders right from birth. For others, organs gradually weaken due to aging, genetic disorders, diseases, heedlessness, etc. Organs in a human body are not as efficient as they appear to be. Eyes or ears cannot always sense or perceive flawlessly. E.g. while reading, we may read a word which is not in the text but still grasp its meaning. Only when re-reading do we realize that the word is not actually in the text. This is a good example of the incompetence of organs. The mind that we rely so highly upon fails to work as expected many times. The text written with the help of the imperfect mind and flawed senses is bound to be unauthoritative and unreliable. Lord Kṛṣṇa is an incarnation of Īśvara; He has a divine body and flawless organs. His words can never be unreliable due to the incompetence of the organs.

4) Cheating propensities for personal gain (*Vipralipsā*, **विप्रलिप्सा**) – Vipralipsā stands for excessive greed, selfishness, and mean tendency. Humans are innately selfish in nature. Greediness depends on Vāsanās; therefore, everyone is greedy in a different way. Human birth is a result of past Karma, hence it is known as Karmavigraha (vigraha = body). The text authored by a person having the greedy mind can never be fully accurate, so it is not trustworthy. Lord Kṛṣṇa's birth is known as 'Līlavigraha' which is a mere play of Īśvara. His body is acquired by Himself per His own wish, so it is not affected by Vāsanās. Lord Kṛṣṇa states in verse *4.14* that He is neither bound by actions nor does He aspire for fruits. He also says, "There is nothing unattained in the three worlds that should be attained by

Me, yet I engage Myself in actions. (*3.22*)" These verses help us understand the real divinity of Lord Kṛṣṇa.

Thus, by analyzing the concluding *Puṣpikā* at the end of each chapter, seekers can progress in the right direction in their spiritual pursuit.

## The Synopsis of each chapter of the Gita

All eighteen chapters in the Bhagavad-Gita are named in a specific manner as per the content of each chapter. Let us now reflect on the correlation between the name and topic of each chapter and analyze the specific relation or sequential link among all these chapters.

**1.** Arjunaviṣādayoga **(अर्जुनविषादयोग)** – This is the first chapter of the Bhagavad-Gita. It is the very foundation of the doctrine of the Gita. All humans experience grief and despair in some form. The nature of problems and grief may vary from person to person. Arjuna was suffering from Viṣāda due to the impending crisis at that time. The word Viṣāda (grief or lamentation) is already explained in this preface before. *Sāṅkhyayoga*, in the next chapter, was told only to pull out Arjuna from his distressed state of mind and remove his suffering. Arjuna's ignorance was manifested in these notions: "The world is real, I am the potential killer, the enemy would be killed by me, and Ātman (Self) dies with the death of the body." Lord Kṛṣṇa imparts the Knowledge of the true Self in the next chapter to eradicate his ignorance.

**2.** *Sāṅkhyayoga* **(साङ्ख्ययोग)** – This chapter does not depict the famous philosophy of Sāṅkhya Darśana. It describes the philosophy of Jñānayoga which explains how to develop the unswerving resolve of the intellect that "I am Ātman." Verses 11 to 30 outline the core principles of this philosophy of Self-Knowledge. Verse 29 explains the importance of Jñānayoga and says that the person who speaks about Ātman, listens about

Ātman, and realizes Ātman is indeed very rare. Kaṭha Upaniṣad has a similar verse (*1.2.7*) that states the same fact. From 31 to 46, there is the description of Dharma, fame, duties, the concept of sins and merits (Pāpa and *Puṇya*), the intellect groomed by the Sāṅkhya philosophy, and the fruit born of such intellect. Verses 47 to 61 outline the characteristics of a person having steady wisdom, *Sthitaprajña*, who is absorbed in Yoga and the way he performs actions. "A person has right only to perform actions, and not to decide what the result of those actions should be" – this famous teaching of the Gita is expressed in verse 47. Verses 58 to 68 narrate various spiritual practices to help the seeker abide in Yoga and attain equanimity. Attainment of Brahman, i.e. realizing "I am Brahman", is the ultimate result of these practices.

3. <u>Karmayoga</u> **(कर्मयोग)** – Arjuna is confused by Lord Kṛṣṇa's speech made earlier, which he thought to be contradictory. Arjuna was deeply affected by grief. Despite being supremely intelligent, faithful, Sāttvic, and despite his unconditional surrender to Lord Kṛṣṇa, he could not understand the essence of Kṛṣṇa's teaching when Kṛṣṇa said, "Do not be attached to passivity or actionlessness (*2.47*)." Arjuna heard, "One should perform actions (*2.48*)," but he overlooked the other half of this verse, "Be steady in Yoga and perform actions without attachment." Arjuna heard, "The Path of Action is inferior to the Path of Knowledge (*2.49*)," but he did not recognize the fact that "Those who expect fruits of actions are even more inferior." He was influenced by the teaching, "Devote yourself to Yoga (*2.50*)," but he neglected that "A person who performs actions with equanimous mind frees himself from merits and sins alike." None of the Lord's teachings in the second chapter is contradictory or perplexing. Arjuna's confusion was in-fact caused by his own lamentation, but he blamed it upon Kṛṣṇa.

Lord Kṛṣṇa, however, refuted his blame squarely in the same instant. Kṛṣṇa said, "I have described two faiths (paths) in the past." He clarified that not doing actions or abandoning actions is not the prescribed practice for attaining the Knowledge of Brahman. Thereafter Kṛṣṇa explained many ways to correctly perform actions so that they are not binding for the seeker. He said, "It is impossible to remain without action even for a second. Forcing the organs to remain static and motionless is just a façade. It is essential to perform prescribed actions. Perform actions in a detached manner and offer the fruits to Īśvara. Give others their due share from fruits generated by actions. Take care of the elemental cycle of nature. An enlightened person should continue actions even when they are not necessary for himself and be an exemplary role-model for society. Do not disorient ordinary people by telling them the importance of taking the vows of monastic life (Saṁnyāsa). Understand the sinful nature of desires as well as anger and renounce them. Know for sure that the three Guṇas manifest themselves through the body, and as a result, the behavior of every person can be attributed to the three Guṇas." These are the teachings of Karmayoga that Kṛṣṇa imparted to Arjuna in this chapter.

**4.** Jñānakarmasaṁnyāsayoga **(ज्ञानकर्मसंन्यासयोग)** – The tradition of teachings of Jñānayoga (*Sāṅkhyayoga*) in the 2nd chapter and Karmayoga in the 3rd chapter is very ancient. This tradition was broken in the interim. Lord Kṛṣṇa revived the same knowledge and imparted it to Arjuna on the battlefield. The Path of Knowledge (*Jñānayoga*) and the Path of Renunciation of Actions (*Karmasaṁnyāsayoga*) are complementary to each other. Jñānayoga alone is a mere intellectual exercise. Actions are inevitable for all humans; therefore, the seeker should perform actions by knowing the true Self and renounce the fruits of actions. From verses 4 to 9, Lord Kṛṣṇa has described his own nature as Īśvara, which reflects why His teachings are considered flawless and venerable. From verses 10 to 22, Kṛṣṇa teaches various tactics for performing actions and explains in greater detail the idea that "The real skillful talent is being equanimous in results while executing actions (*2.50*)." From verses 23 to 33, there is a description of various kinds of Yajñas (offerings in fire) which are considered 'actions' and which make a seeker eligible for realizing Self-Knowledge. In verse 34, Kṛṣṇa explains the relationship between disciples and Sadguru. He says that by following the guidance of the Sadguru, Karma becomes the same as Saṁnyāsa, and it builds the foundation for Self-Knowledge. The 41st verse says that actions cannot bind those who have renounced (results of) actions as per Karmayoga and also those who have resolved all doubts through the Knowledge of the Jiva-Brahman union. All remaining doubts and uncertainties about Karma are addressed in the 5th chapter of the Gita.

5. Karmasaṁnyāsayoga **(कर्मसंन्यासयोग)** – In the last verse of the previous chapter, Kṛṣṇa encouraged Arjuna to let go of all doubts and get ready to fight the war with a clear, assured mind. However, Arjuna is not yet fully sure and doubt-free. He is still deluded by the notion that renunciation (Saṁnyāsa) is superior to action (Karma). Arjuna asks Kṛṣṇa a question at the beginning of this chapter with a faint hope that Kṛṣṇa will ask him to renounce everything and recommend him to not fight the war. However, Kṛṣṇa clearly answers Arjuna's question. In the first 5 verses, the Lord says that those who differentiate between *desireless work* (*Niṣkāma Karma*) and *renunciation* (Saṁnyāsa) are indeed immature and childish. Kṛṣṇa says that taking the vows of formal monasticism or Saṁnyāsa is more complicated than performing desireless work. However, both these approaches lead to the same result. The remaining chapter expounds on the same topic.

6. Ātmasaṁyamayoga **(आत्मसंयमयोग)** – Acting in a desireless manner (*Niṣkāma Karma*) is possible only if a person performs actions while knowing his true nature. Intellectual understanding of the philosophy may impel the person towards 'desireless actions' to some extent. However, the tendency to 'desire fruits' can never fully subside until the person gets a glimpse of Pure Bliss of his own nature. The person who does not have an equanimous vision cannot find inner peace in favorable as well as unfavorable conditions (*6.8*). Without renouncing the desire for worldly pleasures, the duality of joy and grief cannot be erased (*6.22*). Without destroying sins (*5.25*), one cannot be established in the true Self, Ātman (*6.25*). By attaining Knowledge of the Self, one can conquer organs, develop an even vision, and be content in the true Self (*6.8*). From 9 to 26, Lord Kṛṣṇa explains how to practice continuous deep meditation (*Nididhyāsana*) and the result of such meditation i.e. enlightenment. The state of an enlightened person is described with the following three words: Brahmabhūta (ब्रह्मभूत) – one who becomes Brahman himself (*6.27*), Brahmasaṅsparśa (ब्रह्मसंस्पर्श) – one who attains Pure Bliss after Self-realization (*6.28*), and Sarvabhūtasthamātmānam (सर्वभूतस्थमात्मानम्) – one who sees his Self abiding in all beings (*6.28*). Arjuna later complains that, "The mind is very wavering and turbulent." Lord Kṛṣṇa agrees with him and teaches him a way to conquer the mind. He assures Arjuna that even if one's spiritual pursuit of Mokṣa remains incomplete in the present birth, his future births provide him with a necessary environment to progress on the spiritual path. The chapter ends with Kṛṣṇa's statement, "According to Me, one who completely surrenders to Me and worships Me with utmost faith is superior amongst all Yogis." The next chapter 7 describes in detail the word Māṃ (मां) – '(to) Me,' which appears in the last verse of this chapter.

7. Jñānavijñānayoga **(ज्ञानविज्ञानयोग)** – In the first verse, the word **Jñāna** indicates the 'characteristics of Īśvara (Saguṇa Brahman),' while the word ***Vijñāna*** suggests the 'knowledge of worldly matters.' In Vedānta, the term *Taṭastha Lakṣana* (तटस्थ लक्षण) implies the characteristics of Īśvara. The term *Swarūpa Lakṣana* (स्वरूप लक्षण) implies the description of Pure Brahman. Knowing the Lord in entirety involves knowing about His strength, opulence, prosperity (Bala, Aishwarya, Vibhūti), which are the characteristics of Īśvara and not of Pure Brahman. The 3rd verse states that "Only one in thousands knows Me as Brahman." Kṛṣṇa also says that it is extremely difficult to recognize Him as Brahman. In the 12th verse, He says, "I pervade all sentient beings and insentient objects in this world, yet I am not attached to them. But those deluded by Māyā think of Me to be encaged in all beings and objects." In the 15th verse, Kṛṣṇa discusses the kind of people who can never know His real nature. In verses 16 to 26, He describes the kind of people who can know Him. In the end, He says, "To comprehend My real nature fully, the seeker needs to know the terms Adhyātma, Adhidaiva, Adhibhūta, etc." and thus paves the way for the eighth chapter.

8. Akṣarabrahmayoga **(अक्षरब्रह्मयोग)** – In this chapter, Lord Kṛṣṇa defines the terms *Adhyātma*, *Adhidaiva*, *Adhibhūta*, and further explains *Adhiyajña* and *Karma* (actions) in the same frame of reference. Adhiyajña (Viṣṇu) is the real Me described by the word 'Māṃ' **(मां)** in earlier chapters. Further, until verse 22, Kṛṣṇa explains the ultimate place attained by the seeker who remembers Kṛṣṇa's true nature (Brahman) at the time of his death. From verse 24 onwards, there is a description of the person who follows Aṣṭāngayoga and his life after death.

9. Rājavidyārājaguhyayoga **(राजविद्याराजगुह्ययोग)** – Lord Kṛṣṇa says in the 1st verse that He will now explain the terms *Jñāna* and *Vijñāna* from the 7th chapter. The terms Adhyātma, Adhibhūta, etc. were explained in the 8th chapter, and now Kṛṣṇa

resumes the thread of Jñāna and *Vijñāna* here. The highly confidential philosophy, which is profound and hence mysterious, is described in this chapter. It is essential to carefully discern the seemingly contradictory statements such as 'All beings exist in Me' (4), and 'All beings do not exist in me' (5). After understanding them, it is easy to know the relationship between the sentient and insentient world and Brahman in the form of Kṛṣṇa. Without knowing this relation, it is indeed a mere farce to worship the Lord indicated by the word 'Māṃ' (मां) (11). Later, Lord Kṛṣṇa describes various ways to perform worship (Upāsanā) and explains His all-pervasiveness as Brahman (13 to 19). In the end, the transience of heaven is explained along with the concept of real devotion (22 to 34). In the Vārkari cult (Sampradāya), the chapters 9 and 12 are of prime importance.

**10.** Vibhūtiyoga **(विभूतियोग)** – In the 9th chapter, the nature of real Me (God) is explained with the help of the verses: "I am the sacrifice, and I am the Yajña (*9.16*)". The explanation that "Kṛṣṇa is Brahman" is properly concluded in this chapter. In all previous chapters, Lord Kṛṣṇa's Divine Glories were shown, in glimpses, on different occasions. In the 18th verse of this chapter, Arjuna requests Lord Kṛṣṇa to describe His Divine Glories in more detail. Kṛṣṇa approves Arjuna's wish and describes His important Glories. Afterward, Kṛṣṇa asks, "What is the necessity, O Arjuna, for this detailed knowledge and so many examples? (*42*)." He suggests Arjuna to identify His Glory everywhere in a generic manner –

**यद्यद्विभूतिमत्सत्त्वं श्रीमदूर्जितमेव वा ।**
**तत्तदेवावगच्छ त्वं मम तेजोंऽशसम्भवम् ॥ १०.४१ ॥**

*Yadyadvibhūtimat sattvaṃ Śrīmad ūrjitam eva vā* ।
*Tattadevāvagaccha tvaṃ mama tejo'ṃśasaṃbhavam* ॥ *10.41* ॥

"Everything which is opulent, majestic, and powerful, you must know that to arise from but a fraction of My glory." Lastly, Kṛṣṇa says, "I support the manifestation of the entire world with the help of a single fraction of Myself," and helps us understand the puniness of endless multiverses and insignificance of all worldly matters.

11. Viśvarūpadarśanayoga (**विश्वरूपदर्शनयोग**) – Arjuna agrees right at the outset that his intellect is now free from delusion due to Kṛṣṇa's guidance so far. He hesitantly expresses a wish to see Kṛṣṇa's Divine Cosmic Form mentioned in the 10th chapter. Lord Kṛṣṇa then shows His Divine Cosmic Form to his loving friend Arjuna. It was certainly impossible for Arjuna to behold the terrifying and astonishing form of the Lord for a long time, so he requested the Lord to show him His previous form having four arms again (*46*). The prime and central message of this chapter is given in the 33rd verse, where Kṛṣṇa teaches Arjuna to perform all duties merely as an instrument or as a medium. In the 54th verse, Kṛṣṇa says that it is possible to know Him through utmost, single-minded devotion, and thus He leads us into the next 12th chapter.

12. Bhaktiyoga (**भक्तियोग**) – Arjuna asks Kṛṣṇa, "Is it easier to worship the unmanifested formless Nirguṇa Brahman, or the manifested Saguṇa Brahman having form? Which worship is superior to the other?" Kṛṣṇa answers that the worship of Saguṇa is superior to that of Nirguṇa. Kṛṣṇa further explains variations in worship as per the eligibility of the worshipper. St. Rāmadāsa has said, "A true Bhakta is not Vibhakta from God i.e. a true devotee is not separate from God (Brahman)." Lord Kṛṣṇa describes the characteristics of those who are One with God and further says that they are His most beloved and cherished devotees.

13. Kṣetrakṣetrajñavibhāgayoga (**क्षेत्रक्षेत्रज्ञविभागयोग**) – It seems as if a completely new topic is introduced in this chapter. But this misunderstanding is removed when we think about it in two ways. Madhusūdana Saraswati, a distinguished academic and philosopher, has divided the chapters of the Bhagavad-Gita

in three conceptual parts based on the Vedāntic Mahāvākya '**Thou art that**' (*Tat-Tvam-Asi*). According to him –

- Chapters 1 – 6: describe **Tvam** word (**Thou** / you / Jiva)
- Chapters 7 – 12: describe **Tat** word (**That** / Brahman / Ātman / *Kuṭastha* Caitanya / Pure Consciousness)
- Chapters 13 – 18: describe **Asi** word (**Art** / are / Oneness of Jiva and Brahman)

After describing *Tvam* and *Tat* in the previous 12 chapters, this 13th chapter describes how to join *Tvam* and *Tat* with *Asi*. Some aspects are helpful in the union of Jiva (Tvam) and Brahman (Tat), while some are obstructing. The five verses from 13 to 17 in the 13th chapter articulate both the helpful and obstructing aspects in detail. The most significant obstruction in the union of Jiva and Brahman is the strong identification of the Jiva with his body – the belief that "I am the body." To remove this obstruction, Lord Kṛṣṇa has named the insentient body as the Kṣetra (field) and the sentience in the body as the Kṣetrajña (Jiva, knower of the field). This chapter is specifically told for ignorant people who firmly believe "I am the body." The insentient body is bound to die, while the true Self, Ātman, dwelling in the body, is deathless. This teaching is concluded in the 24th verse, "A person who thus knows the underlying principle of Puruṣa and Prakṛti is not born again despite performing all kinds of actions." The same thought is also explained in the 2nd chapter.

Also, the topic of Jñāna and *Vijñāna* was not really concluded at the end of the 12th chapter. Lord Kṛṣṇa discussed an easy way to realize "I am Brahman" in Bhaktiyoga, but He did not teach philosophy to eradicate the wrong notion that "I am the body." To address this issue, in 13.2, Kṛṣṇa describes Jñāna as the knowledge of the Kṣetra and Kṣetrajña. He concludes His teaching in the last verse by saying, "Those who can distinguish between the Kṣetra and the Kṣetrajña through the 'eye of wisdom' achieve the supreme principle, Brahman."

**14.** Guṇatrayavibhāgayoga **(गुणत्रयविभागयोग)** – The three Guṇas were previously discussed in the Gita in the following verses: "Transcend the three Guṇas (*2.45*)" and "This is a mere play of the Guṇas amongst each other (*3.28*)." Rājas and Tāmas Guṇas are significant obstacles for the Jiva in realizing "Thou art that," which is the primary teaching of Sadguru. Sattvaguṇa facilitates Self-realization, but only to some extent. Lord Kṛṣṇa concludes the chapter with this statement: "One who worships Me with utmost devotion and transcends the three Guṇas is qualified for Self-realization (I am Brahman)."

**15.** Puruṣottamayoga **(पुरुषोत्तमयोग)** – In the 13th chapter, the word Kṣetra indicates an individual body, while the sentience in it is known as Kṣetrajña. In this chapter, we may say that the cosmic body i.e. world is known as a tree, while the sentience in it is known as Īśvara. The tree of the material world is created through God's imagination. So, it is a mere false appearance. It is nourished by the water of the past Vāsanās of Jivas, hence ever-green in nature. The nests of various planes reside on its branches. An ignorant person considers this illusory tree as real. Every individual Jiva in this worldly tree is Kṣara Puruṣa which means he is 'perishable'. Īśvara – sentience that pervades the Jiva and the world – is Akṣara Puruṣa; He is 'relatively imperishable' since He has much longer life (many eons) than an individual Jiva. Brahman is Uttam Puruṣa, and it is 'absolutely imperishable.' Jiva comes to an end in a few years. Īśvara comes to an end at the end of Mahākalpa, which is a very long period of time. Brahman is not subject to creation and destruction; it is timeless. A person who understands this deeply mysterious philosophy is a qualified seeker. He performs the worship of the Lord and attains Self-realization.

**16.** Daivāsurasampadvibhāgayoga **(दैवासुरसम्पद्विभागयोग)** – Divine qualities help the union of Jiva and Brahman. In contrast, demoniac qualities create enormous hurdles in this union.

Divine qualities arise from Sattvaguṇa, while demoniac qualities arise from Rājas and Tāmas Guṇas. The identification that "I am the body" is very feeble in people who have divine qualities. On the contrary, it is very firm in those who possess Rājas and Tāmas Guṇas. The consequences of Rajoguṇa and Tamoguṇa are indeed dreadful. E.g. 'The lack of excessive pride' (नातिमानिता) is a divine quality. A person who has this quality thinks minimally about his body, intelligence, fame, and wealth. On the contrary, worldly thoughts are highly dominant in people who have arrogance, which is a demoniac trait. All demoniac traits are governed by Rajoguṇa and Tamoguṇa. Liberating oneself from the heavy influence of the demoniac traits like greed, anger, and desires is the first step in spiritual pursuit. After that, when a person performs his duties as prescribed by scriptures, he can rapidly progress on the path of Mokṣa.

**17.** Śraddhātrayavibhāgayoga **(श्रद्धात्रयविभागयोग)** – This chapter is the second half of the 16th chapter. When a seeker executes actions like fire sacrifice (*Yajña*), donation (*Dāna*), austerities (*Tapas*), etc. through Sāttvic faith, they purify his mind and eventually lead him to unite with Brahman. However, actions executed through Rājas or Tāmas faith become obstacles in the path of liberation.

**18.** MokṣaSaṅnyāsayoga **(मोक्षसंन्यासयोग)** – This chapter is popularly known as the 'One-chapter Gita.' Initially, there is a discussion on the primary difference between abandonment and renunciation (Tyāga and Saṅnyāsa). There is also an articulation of various opinions on this topic. Secondly, the chapter describes the Sāttvic, Rājas, and Tāmas manifestations of actions like Yajña, Dāna, and Tapas. Later it talks about the five reasons behind each action. A person who executes actions and deludes himself with the notion that "I am the doer" is essentially said to be an ignorant person. The triads like knower-knowable-knowledge, doer-instrument-action are different according to the three Guṇas. Furthermore, the intellect, the ability to ingrain knowledge in mind, and Sukha happiness are classified according to the Guṇas. Next, there is a discussion on the characteristics and duties of the four Social Orders (Varṇas) and the guidance that "Everyone should meticulously follow his prescribed duties." There is a question that is commonly associated with social orders – "Is the social order determined by one's birth or by his virtues or characteristics?" The answer to this question is given in a Sanskrit verse –

**जन्मना जायते शूद्रः संस्कारात् भवेत् द्विजः ।**
**वेद-पाठात् भवेत् विप्रः ब्रह्म जानातीति ब्राह्मणः ॥**

*Janmanā jāyate sūdrah sanskārāt bhavet dvijah* ।
*Veda-pāthat bhavet viprah brahma jānātiti brāhmanah* ॥

"By birth, a person may belong to the lower social order Śūdra, who are onsidered not knowledgeable, but by spiritual conditioning, one can become knowledgeable i.e. Dvija. A person who learns or teaches the Vedas is a Vipra, and one who knows his true Self as Brahman is a Brāhmin." The word Dvija literally means borned twice. It is based on the belief that a person is first born physically, and later, he is born for the second time spiritually, usually when he undergoes the 'Thread Ceremony (Upanayana)' that initiates him for spiritual studies of the Vedas. If a person undergoes the Thread Ceremony merely as a ritual, without taking to the intended spiritual studies, would it be right to call him a Dvija? How can a person who is not conditioned to spiritual life be a Dvija, and why can a person who is conditioned to spiritual life not be a Dvija?

At the end of the 18th chapter, the Lord elaborates upon the attainment of Self-Knowledge through the Path of Devotion and the Path of Knowledge. There is also a discussion about "Who is qualified to study the Bhagavad-Gita?" Lastly, Lord Kṛṣṇa issues a command to Arjuna: "Fix your mind on Me alone, devote yourself to Me, bow down and surrender to Me alone."

He assures that a person who follows this order will be liberated from all sins and be led to Mokṣa. After Kṛṣṇa's teaching, Arjuna clearly states that his delusion and consequent grief are eradicated. Kṛṣṇa started imparting his actual teaching of the philosophy from verse 2.11, where he said, "Wise people do not lament." The same teaching comes full circle in 18.66, where Kṛṣṇa concludes his teachings, "Do not lament."

## The first reason for conflict:

This preface mentions conflict-free and struggle-free life right at the outset. Conflict may arise on any of the four levels: the individual, familial, social, or national level. It is impossible to eradicate conflicts or avoid them or escape from them. Social thinkers, intellectuals, or philosophers may come up with many ideologies, but the ground reality shows that disagreements and fights are unavoidable, and they are integral part of social life. Every seeker has to interact with his relatives, spouse, brothers, sisters, cousins, children, neighbors, colleagues, acquaintances, seniors, juniors, owners, servants, friends, aggressive leaders of caste or religion, sellers, buyers, and politicians. The seeker has to struggle and face a dispute or conflict in some manner while dealing with these people. Selfishness, greed, competition, pride, envy, resentment, jealousy, comparison, success, failure, power, wealth, fame, status, etc. give rise to the conflict. Many people may also face a constant battle within themselves. No matter what the apparent cause of conflict is, all conflicts can be traced to some person (Jiva). Knowing the true nature of each Jiva and systematically dealing with him through a proper mindset is the only way to face a dispute or a conflict effectively and maintain one's inner peace in the process. It is also essential for the seeker to fully understand the nature of the surrounding world – where all humans (Jivas) live and transact with each other – and remember it at all times. The seeker should accept on faith the power of Īśvara which creates, governs, and ultimately destroys this world. Through all these actions, the seeker can recognize and know his true Self, just as Arjuna remembered it after listening to Lord Kṛṣṇa's guidance (*18.73*). By abiding in his true Self, the seeker can become the person of steady wisdom i.e *Sthitaprajña*, or a Yogi, or a devotee, and lead a peaceful, joyous life himself, despite living in the world full of disputes, conflicts, and disagreements. For being happy amid all struggles, the seeker has to realize that he himself is Pure Bliss through the philosophy taught in the Gita. But much before Self-realization, he can use spiritual discrimination, which evolves from the study of philosophy and start living the conflict-free, stress-free, happy life on a daily basis. With that, even the journey towards Pure Bliss of Self-realization will become pleasant for him.

The Bhagavad-Gita and other scriptures help us better understand the true nature of the individual person and world who are integral parts of all conflicts. According to Vedānta, human life involves the following three aspects: Jiva, Īśvara, and Brahman. A seeker should get clear idea of these concepts with the help of the Gita or other scriptures to eliminate conflicts from life.

1) A person lives his life as a Jiva in this world.
2) The Jiva and the world are both regulated by Īśvara as per His scheme of governance.
3) Both Jiva and Īśvara exist on the substratum of *Sat-Cit-Ānanda* Brahman.

These three aspects are not explained directly in any one verse or a particular group of verses in the Gita. But they can be logically inferred from the Gita in the following manner –

1. Worldly life of a Jiva involving actions

**नियतं कुरु कर्म त्वं कर्म ज्यायो ह्यकर्मणः ।**
**शरीरयात्रापि च ते न प्रसिद्ध्येदकर्मणः ॥ ३.८ ॥**

*Niyataṃ kuru karma tvaṃ karma jyāyo hy akarmaṇaḥ* ।
*Śarīrayātrāpi ca te na prasidhyed akarmaṇaḥ* ॥ *3.8* ॥

"Perform the duties prescribed to you. It is far superior to perform actions than not doing anything. If you do not work, you will not even be able to earn a livelihood."

2. <u>Īśvara's governance of sentient and insentient entities</u>

**ईश्वरः सर्वभूतानां हृद्देशेऽर्जुन तिष्ठति ।**
**भ्रामयन्सर्वभूतानि यन्त्रारूढानि मायया ॥ १८.६१ ॥**

*Īśvaraḥ sarvabhūtānāṃ hṛddeśe'rjuna tiṣṭhati* ।
*Bhrāmāyān sarvabhūtāni yantrārūḍhāni māyayā* ॥ *18.61* ॥

"Īśvara resides in hearts of all beings. He causes all those who consider themselves as doers, and who are mounted by their ego on the machine of His scheme of things, to revolve in the cycle of birth and death through the power of His Māyā."

**गामाविश्य च भूतानि धारयाम्यहमोजसा ।**
**पुष्णामि चौषधीः सर्वाः सोमो भूत्वा रसात्मकः ॥ १५.१३ ॥**

*Gām āviśya ca bhūtāni dhārayāmy aham ojasā* ।
*Puṣṇāmi cauṣadhīḥ sarvāḥ somo bhūtvā rasātmakaḥ* ॥ *15.13* ॥

"Permeating the earth, I maintain all beings by My potency. Having become the essential nectar of the moon, I nourish all plants and herbs."

3. <u>Braman that permeates everything yet remains untouched</u>

**मया ततमिदं सर्वं जगदव्यक्तमूर्तिना ।**
**मत्स्थानि सर्वभूतानि न चाहं तेष्ववस्थितः ॥ ९.४ ॥**

*Mayā tatam idaṃ sarvaṃ jagad avyaktamūrtinā* ।
*Matsthāni sarvabhūtāni na cāhaṃ teṣv avasthitaḥ* ॥ *9.4* ॥

"I, as Nirguṇa Nirakara Brahman, permeate the entire world. All beings exist on My substratum. However, I am not attached to or encaged by them." This thought is indirectly reflected in other verses as well, but at times it is not readily apparent and needs to be carefully sought out. E.g. –

**बुद्धियुक्तो जहातीह उभे सुकृतदुष्कृते ।**
**तस्माद्योगाय युज्यस्व योगः कर्मसु कौशलम् ॥ २.५० ॥**

*Buddhiyukto jahātīha ubhe sukṛtaduṣkṛte* ।
*Tasmād yogāya yujyasva yogaḥ karmasu kauśalam* ॥ 2.50 ॥

"Good and bad actions refer to the worldly life of a Jiva. The desire to do good or bad actions in the Jiva is governed by Īśvara. The equanimous intellect of the Jiva is the result of him realizing his true Self." Thus, actions belong to the Jiva, motivation for good or bad comes from Īśvara, and the philosophy of *Sāṅkhyayoga* is pertinent to the Self-realization that "I am Brahman."

Every Jiva goes through the cycle of birth and death until he is liberated. Vāsanā is the primary cause of rebirth in the cycle of life. The disposition of each Jiva is different due to different Vāsanās which are unfulfilled desires from past births residing in him.

**स्वभावजेन कौन्तेय निबद्धः स्वेन कर्मणा ।**
**कर्तुं नेच्छसि यन्मोहात्करिष्यस्यवशोऽपि तत् ॥ १८.६० ॥**

*Svabhāvajena kaunteya nibaddhaḥ svena karmaṇā* ।
*Kartuṃ necchasi yan mohāt kariṣyasy avaśo'pi tat* ॥ 18.60 ॥

"O son of Kunti! You are bound by your disposition created by your own blend of Guṇas and past actions. Hence, you will helplessly perform even those actions which you may not desire to do since you will be influenced by your delusion." Lord Kṛṣṇa gives an excellent direction to lead a conflict-free life through this verse. Vāsanā leads to delusion, delusion creates disposition, and disposition gives rise to behavior, thoughts, and speech. This is a chain. It is possible to relate Vāsanās with genes in the modern scientific paradigm. Predispositions of people to certain habits and behaviors can be traced to their genetic makeup, which in turn can be traced to Vāsanās. When the seeker understands the root cause of why people behave the way they behave or speak the way they speak, then he can respond appropriately as the situation calls. But since the seeker's response will be in perspective of the root cause of the situation or the conflict, it will not disturb his inner peace and joy. Likewise, he can also avoid unnecessary thoughts about people when they are not around or after they part.

The disposition of each person is created from the three Guṇas as well as his Vāsanās. In fact, Guṇas act like a 'coupler' between the Vāsanās and the disposition of a person. The Bhagavad-Gita gives an elaborate description of the three Guṇas, and as such, this coupler should be studied in its own right. All the three Guṇas are classified in two ways: pure and impure. According to verse 14.18, Rajoguṇa is instinctively dominant in most humans. Pure Rajoguṇa is more akin to Sattvaguṇa. Impure Rajoguṇa is a storehouse of all bad traits described in the Gita. Desire, anger, and greed are the three hallmarks of impure Rajoguṇa. They impel the person to perform an action, even if it is against his own wishes (*3.36, 37*). Lord Kṛṣṇa says –

**तत्त्ववित्तु महाबाहो गुणकर्मविभागयोः ।**
**गुणा गुणेषु वर्तन्त इति मत्वा न सज्जते ॥ ३.२८ ॥**

*Tattvavit tu mahābāho guṇakarmavibhāgayoḥ* ।
*Guṇā guṇeṣu vartanta iti matvā na sajjate* ॥ *3.28* ॥

"A wise person, who understands the principle or profundity (influence) of the three Guṇas and actions, knows that Guṇas constantly interplay with each other. So, he doesn't get drawn into obsessing over them." This verse clearly states that Guṇas influence the disposition and behavior of every person. The influence may rise or wane from time to time. E.g. a Sāttvic person is predominantly influenced by Sattvaguṇa. Still, he may occasionally yield to the impetus of Rajoguṇa or Tamoguṇa. An addicted person is influenced by the object of his addiction, an insatiable person is influenced by greed, an enraged person is influenced by anger, a child is influenced by ignorance, and an amorous person is influenced by lust. So long as the person is under any influence, he continues to think, behave, and speak in that way. Knowing this, the seeker can calmly embrace any situation, protect his self-interests, remain unaffected by the impetus of the Guṇas, and thereby minimize conflicts in his life.

**The second reason for conflict:**

Every action is associated with fruits or results. A person may expect a particular fruit, but he may or may not get the fruit of his action in the desired form or quantity. This difference between what or how much of something is desired and what or how much is actually achieved is another cause of incessant conflict in life. There may be no limits to human ambitions, but ambitions are certainly constrained by reality. The limits of practical reality are manifested in the form of stiff competition, adverse circumstances, unforeseen events, and difficult people. E.g. it is necessary to compete with people in the same field. Situations like war are created by political people. Accidents are usually caused by the careless or rash behavior of other humans. Some individuals hold unnecessary grudge or enmity and create obstacles in one's path. Human ambitions and desires are often destroyed or partially fulfilled due to various reasons such as physical ailments, natural calamities, social revolutions, familial feuds, etc. Amid this commotion, how to retain one's inner peace largely depends on how the seeker perceives these conflicts, and the Gita provides excellent guidance precisely in this regard.

**योगस्थः कुरु कर्माणि सङ्गं त्यक्त्वा धनञ्जय ।**
**सिद्ध्यसिद्ध्योः समो भूत्वा समत्वं योग उच्यते ॥ २.४८ ॥**
**दूरेण ह्यवरं कर्म बुद्धियोगाद्धनञ्जय ।**
**बुद्धौ शरणमन्विच्छ कृपणाः फलहेतवः ॥ २.४९ ॥**

*Yogasthaḥ kuru karmāṇi saṅgaṃ tyaktvā dhanañjaya* ।
*Siddhyasiddhyoḥ samo bhūtvā samatvaṃ yoga ucyate* ॥ *2.48* ॥
*Dūreṇa hy avaraṃ karma buddhiyogād dhanañjaya* ।

*Buddhau śaraṇam anviccha kṛpaṇāḥ phalahetavaḥ* II *2.49* II

"O Dhananjaya! Perform your duties by renouncing attachment to fruits of actions. Be equanimous in success and failure. This equanimity is known as Yoga. Perform your duties by being firmly resolved on Self-Knowledge that "I am Ātman (*Sāṅkhyabuddhi*)." Gainful actions performed by desiring fruits are inferior. On the contrary, actions performed while being firmly resolved on the true Self, Atman, are superior. Hence, take refuge in *Sāṅkhyabuddhi* and firmly abide in your true Self. People who are impelled by fruits towards actions are contemptible indeed."

There is a tremendous emphasis on positive thinking these days, which is the result of aggressive attitude in industrial and other professional fields. It is certainly necessary to be persistent, courageous, and patient to overcome obstacles and make progress in any field. However, the emphasis on positivity has clearly taken an abnormal turn in the modern world. E.g. To win at any cost, a sportsman sometimes consumes drugs to enhance his capability and thus defames himself and the nation. A person may go to the extent of contract murder to get rid of his enemies and pervert the judicial and government systems in the process. Witnesses are bought in. Policemen convict an innocent person with false charges to meet their annual target. The list of such cases is potentially endless. There is only one takeaway from these instances. The spiritual seeker should consciously stay away from pervert practices while trying to progress in his worldly life. Undoubtedly, it is essential for the seeker to enhance and expand his individual strengths and capabilities, use them judiciously, give the necessary time to his work, learn new knowledge and technologies, hone the professional skills, and continue to work devotedly in his field. If the seeker is running a business, he should plan for profit and honestly strive to achieve it. Some people may object that planning for profit is equivalent to expecting some fruit, but it is necessary for the success in business. However, professional ambition should not be a mere daydream nor an unrealistic hope nor a demoniac desire.

Conflict or struggle grows in mind when a person works with the feeling that "I am the doer." Generally, there is a natural tendency to seek, demand, or snatch credit when a person completes a task. But the same perosn faces a conflict when someone else takes the credit of his well-done job. The feeling of doership also leads to other unproductive thoughts in mind: "The job is done because of me," "What would have happened in my absence?," and "What will happen after my death?" These thoughts can degrade to become ugly and perverted when the person stoops down to thinking, "I will not allow the work to complete in my absence." Conflict, struggle, hatred, and disquietude is the ensuing chain of events, which culminate in grief. Therefore, the Gita says –

**नैव किञ्चित्करोमीति युक्तो मन्येत तत्त्ववित् । (५.८)**

*Naiva kiṃcit karomīti yukto manyeta tattvavit* ॥ *(5.8)*

**इन्द्रियाणीन्द्रियार्थेषु वर्तन्त इति धारयन् ॥ (५.९)**

*Indriyāṇīndriyārtheṣu vartanta iti dhārayan* ॥ *(5.9)*

**मयैवैते निहताः पूर्वमेव निमित्तमात्रं भव सव्यसाचिन् ॥ (११.३३)**

*Māyāivaite nihatāḥ pūrvameva nimittamātraṃ bhava savyasācin*

"One who has realized his true Self as Ātman knows that his true Self does not do anything. He recognizes that all organs perform their respective duties as dictated by his Jiva and remains certain that his true Self does nothing at all. Lord Kṛṣṇa also reveals to Arjuna that whoever is going to die in the war has already been slain by Him i.e. his death is prearranged by the Lord's will. Arjuna will only have to serve as an instrument for their death." Thus, what is meant to happen – happens in any case, and it occurs according to the governance of Īśvara. The person is just an instrument or a medium for the occurrence of that event. In the process, he may or may not get credit or punishment as dictated by the local law, international judiciary system, government regulations, or state ordinances. E.g. Vedic scriptures state that the one who dies fighting a war for the nation goes to heaven. However, today if a soldier is taken in as a prisoner of war by the enemy, he may face incessant cruel torture in prison, and he may suffer if he is in hell. Wars take place according to the governance of Īśvara. Fighting war for power, wealth, or other issues has been a human necessity for ages. Lord Kṛṣṇa states, "I am the war-strategy in desirers of victory (*10.38*)." Thus, the winning war-strategy is a Divine Glory (Vibhūti) of Īśvara. War offers a platform to earn the victory, so war itself may be considered a Divine Glory of Īśvara. St. Jñāneśwara describes 'war' as a divine tool to reduce the burden of humans and other animals on the earth.

## The third reason for conflict

The eternal quest for happiness is the third reason for conflict and struggle in human life. Svetasvetara Upaniṣad explains how to attain constant, lasting Bliss and get rid of suffering –

**यदा चर्मवदाकाशं वेष्टयिष्यन्ति मानवाः ।**
**तदा देवमविज्ञाय दुःखस्यान्तो भविष्यति ॥ ६.२० ॥**

*Yadā carmavadākāśaṃ veṣṭayiṣyanti mānavāḥ*
*Tadā devamavijñaya duḥkhasyānto bhaviṣyati* ॥ *6.20* ॥

"If a person can figure out how to wrap the entire sky with a skin-like cover, only then it may be possible to overcome suffering in life without knowing who is real God." This simply means, it is impossible to find lasting Bliss without knowing 'I am God' or without the direct realization (*Aparokṣānubhūti*) that "I am Brahman." People experience both joy and grief while dealing with the objects of pleasure in this world. The Bhagavad-Gita has classified them as the Kṣetra (*13.6*). Joy and grief are subject to a beginning, a state, and an end. The experiences of joy and grief involves the triad of three distinct aspects –

- Experiencer – one who is happy
- Experienced – the object of happiness
- Experience – enjoying the object through sense organs

Eternal, Pure Bliss of Ātman is not dependent on the triad above as there is no duality or triad in it. It is Self-cognizant (*Swasaṃvedya*). Each of the three Guṇas gives rise to happiness in its own way. Of the three Guṇas, the joy arising from Sattvaguṇa is captivating or binding, and Sattvaguṇa also makes the seeker gravitate towards such joy. However, Lord Kṛṣṇa says in the Gita (*14.6*, *14.9*) that the Sāttvic pleasure is transient as well. This is precisely why Kṛṣṇa asks Arjuna to transcend the three Guṇas (*2.45*). Pure Bliss of Brahman is beyond the influence of the three Guṇas. Lord Kṛṣṇa clearly states –

**ब्रह्मणो हि प्रतिष्ठाहममृतस्याव्ययस्य च ।**
**शाश्वतस्य च धर्मस्य सुखस्यैकान्तिकस्य च ॥ १४.२७ ॥**

*Brahmaṇo hi pratiṣṭhāham amṛtasyāvyayasya ca ।*
*Śāśvatasya ca dharmasya sukhasyaikāntikasya ca ॥ 14.27 ॥*

"Being Pure Bliss myself, I am the substratum of all pleasures." This direct and unchangeable realization can alone lead the seeker to lasting and uninterrupted happiness.

Struggle or conflict is inevitable for the seeker who continues to depend on pleasures derived from objects. To understand this better, we can examine the happiness derived from love or touch. All of us experience love through many relationships like mother and children, husband and wife, siblings, friends, neighbors, relatives, etc. We also love political or social leaders, actors-actresses, players, authors, or spiritual personalities. Love is manifested in many forms, such as faith, respect, ideology, and love. Everyone routinely experiences ups and downs in these relationships. These experiences may vary from extreme love to extreme hate. The experience which is desired or favorable leads to love, undesired or unfavorable leads to hatred. Love or hate lasts so long as the person or object continues to be favorable or unfavorable, respectively. The key fact to note here is that every person is extremely selfish for his or her own happiness. Upaniṣad firm states a fundamental principle of life in this regard –

**आत्मनस्तु कामाय सर्वं प्रियं भवति ।**

*Ātmanastu kāmāya sarvam priyam bhavati* । *(Bṛ.Up. 2.4.5)*

"The feeling of love for others is ultimately for one's own happiness, not for the happiness of others." This principle is not stated explicitely in the Gita; however, it is a harsh reality of life. Enlightened sages and saints live by the same principle even when they abide in a highly evolved, sublime state. St. Tukārāma expresses his deep concern for mankind in his poetry, "I am unable to watch people drowning themselves in this ocean of material pursuits." St. Samartha says, "The one who knows how to float and survive in the ocean of worldly life should also save others from drowning." This simply means that the enlightened sages help others because doing so makes them happy. An ordinary man donates money to charity only to derive pleasure for himself, even though the donation involves his financial loss. The Gita explains the same mindset in this verse

**यक्ष्ये दास्यामि मोदिष्य ॥ (१६.१५)**

*Yakṣye dāsyāmi modiṣya* ॥ *(16.15)*

It is commonly seen that a mother feels happy by fulfilling the duty of tending her child. But even a notable lady like Kunti left her newborn son Karṇa in the river as she was more concerned about her own disgrace than the well-being of her child. A person quickly discards his or her previous love for the sake of new love relationship. If a son turns out to be dreadful, his parents even wish that he were born a dead child. St. Tukārāma effectively portrays the reality of human nature in this devotional poetry, where he says, "Even a sister adores and loves her brother only when he is doing well in his professional life and helping her financially." Two brothers, who love each other dearly, part ways after marriage. The business started enthusiastically by two partners is broken down due to selfish desires. Patients who worship a doctor as God are the same people who denounce him after he fails a surgery. There are many such examples in real life. Therefore, the Gita states definitively –

**यत्र चैवात्मनात्मानं पश्यन्नात्मनि तुष्यति ॥ (६.२०)**

*Yatra caivātmanātmānaṃ paśyann ātmani tuṣyati* ॥ *(6.20)*

"The subtle and pure mind realizes 'I am Supreme Ātman' and remains absorbed in Pure Bliss of the Self. There is no gain more significant than this in the world." Enlightened sages who have realized Ātman know this for sure (*6.22*). It is common to face a situation where people or relatives around us do not fulfill our expectations. This often leads to misery, agony, conflict, and grief in life. Even the joy of fulfilled expectations does not last long. But Pure Bliss of Self-realization lasts forever, and therefore, superior to all.

An Ignorant person does not understand that there is more to the world than what meets the eye. His life is selfish and naïve, and it is bound to be full of struggles and conflicts. Purely materialistic life is replete with anguish and grief; seeking happiness in such life verily leads to suffering. There is for sure some pleasure associated with worldly objects. But such pleasure inevitably leads to pain. The person who mindlessly pursues worldly pleasures experiences both joy and suffering and other subsequent dualities. Many learned people think that this is a pessimistic and discouraging thought-process that demeans the merits of worldly life. Nonetheless, objective evaluation of the underlying reality of the surrounding world reflects what St. Tukārāma portrays in his poem. He says, "One may find only a tinge of happiness in life mostly filled with pain and suffering." He also says, "It is foolish to expect happiness in worldly life, just the way it is foolish to expect sound sleep in a bed full of bedbugs." Some people think that St. Tukārāma personally experienced very little happiness in the world, which is why he wrote devotional poetry in a dejected manner. However, that is not the case. Lord Kṛṣṇa says in the Gita –

**तं विद्याद् दुःखसंयोगवियोगं योगसञ्ज्ञितम् ॥ (६.२३)**

*Taṃ vidyād duḥkhasaṅyogaviyogaṃ yogasaṃjñitam* ॥ *(6.23)*

"Yoga is dissociation from the association-with-grief. This Yoga should be known and realized by seekers." The grief associated with birth, aging, and death is routinely experienced in the world. People (parents) are constantly worried about a baby who is still in the mother's womb. After birth, they are concerned about possible diseases or psychological disorders affecting the child. As the child grows, they feel anxious about his education, job, business, competition, success-failure, and so on. Towards the end, there is distress associated with growing age, familial tensions, old-age ailments, etc., and the person feels scared of his impending death. For most people, death is the inescapable reality of life, and it is the biggest fear of all. In 12.7, Lord Kṛṣṇa says that worldly life is the 'ocean of death.' This is the very nature of human life, and it will be so for ages to come. Although human life in this world will always be replete with suffering, the philosophy in the Gita helps to wipe out all kinds of grief and fear from the mind. As a result, man can find happiness and inner peace while living his life amid challenges, conflict, and struggle in the external world.

**The world is not real the way it seems**

**अश्वत्थमेनं सुविरूढमूलं असङ्गशस्त्रेण दृढेन छित्त्वा ॥ (१५.३)**

*Aśvatthāmenaṃ suvirūḍhamūlaṃ asaṅgaśastreṇa dṛḍhena chittvā* ॥

"The firmly rooted Aśvattha tree of the transient world can be severed with a sharp weapon (ax) of detachment." The word **Aśvattha** in Sanskrit means dynamic and ever-changing – now it is there, then soon it is not. Although worldly life is momentary, yet it seemingly continues to have robust, rigid existence due to our deep-rooted Vāsanās and ego. Einstein, too, has famously said, "The world is an illusion." He was neither a pessimist nor a hopeless loser. He worked arduously for the highest scientific research mankind has ever seen. We should note the fact that even such a distinguished scholar has addressed the world as an illusion. The seeker can uproot this worldly tree by leading his life in a detached manner since the detached mind can understand that the world is not real the way it seems.

When the seeker transcends the duality of joy and grief and remains immersed in unqualified Pure Bliss, he does not face any conflict in his life. Causes of conflict in the surrounding world continue to exist as before, but the seeker who realizes Pure Bliss of Ātman perceives the same situation differently and does not see it as a conflict. There is a famous saying which states, "You cannot clap with one hand alone." Akin to this, an enlightened person can never experience a conflict since he can deal with any situation – even adverse – without any contention from his side. The Bhagavad-Gita earnestly explains the importance of peace in life. Life without any contention or struggle is peaceful in a true sense. Such peacefulness is not dependent on one's physical health or general well-being. As mentioned in the Gita (*6.8*), such a person is content due to realizing Self-Knowledge; he is truly at peace. He has consciously conquered his mind (*6.7*) by transcending all dualities.

**प्रसादे सर्वदुःखानां हानिरस्योपजायते ।**
**प्रसन्नचेतसो ह्याशु बुद्धिः पर्यवतिष्ठते ॥ २.६५ ॥**

*Prasāde sarvaduḥkhānāṃ hānir asyopajāyate* ।
*Prasannacetaso hy āśu buddhiḥ paryavatiṣṭhate* ॥ *2.65* ॥

"When the mind is filled with Absolute, Pure Bliss of Self-realization, all external causes lose their capacity to cause grief." Thereafter, nothing is grievous, and nothing can cause suffering in life. Only such an enlightened, happy person having steady intellect can be truly at peace. The Gita (*2.66*) asks a question, "How can a disquiet or perturbed person ever be happy?" Peace and happiness are two sides of the same coin. They cannot exist without one another. Lord Kṛṣṇa explains how to attain peace in this verse –

> **विहाय कामान्यः सर्वान्पुमांश्चरति निःस्पृहः ।**
> **निर्ममो निरहङ्कारः स शान्तिमधिगच्छति ॥ २.७१ ॥**
>
> *Vihāya kāmān yaḥ sarvān pumāṃś carati niḥspṛhaḥ* ।
> *Nirmamo nirahaṃkāraḥ sa śāntim adhigacchhati* ॥ *2.71* ॥

"A person who lives without selfish motives and gives up the desires of all fruits transcends the ego and attachment and thus attains total peace." As a result of realizing the Knowledge of Ātman, he attains 'supreme peace' (Parā Shanti) (*4.39*). Here the adjective 'supreme' is used deliberately. St. Jñāneśwara addresses his Guru Nivṛttinātha as the 'personification of supreme peace.' Lord Kṛṣṇa says in verse *6.22* that an enlightened person does not ever lose his peace and does not get perturbed even when inflicted with massive calamities in life. An unperturbed, serene mind indicates supreme peace.

The term **Mokṣa** means the liberation from all kinds of bondages which eventually lead to suffering. The traditional and popular concept of liberation from the birth-death cycle is just a trivial byproduct of Mokṣa, but it is given undue importance by many alike. For liberation from all griefs, it is necessary to see how many walls or bondages the seeker creates around himself, how he constrains himself in these walls, and analyze how these walls can be demolished in the light of the Gita.

1. **The physical body** is the obvious first wall around the true Self. It exists right from birth and is explicitly seen by one and all. The strong identification that 'I am my body' is the very reason why the body becomes a wall around the true Self. The wall gets stronger when one feels, "I am fair or

black, tall or short, beautiful or ugly, healthy or sick," etc. Identification with the body becomes more rigid with passing time. However, the body is not perpetual. It inches towards death every moment and changes in every new birth. Lord Kṛṣṇa explains the transient nature of the body by equating it with an old cloth (*2.22*) and stating that the Jiva transmigrates to another body after his death (*2.13*).

2. **The subtle body** (Antaḥkaraṇa) is the second wall around the true Self. It gets stronger and taller when one feels, "I am intelligent or dumb, I like this, I want that, I cannot focus," etc. It creates a sheath around the true Self and conceals one's real identity. Intelligence or dumbness is the characteristic of the intellect (Buddhi); focus and adherence are the characteristics of the memory (Citta). These are not the characteristics of Ātman, the true Self. In the 13th chapter of the Gita, it is said that the subtle body is a part of the insentient Kṣetra (Field) since it can be perceived separately from oneself. The mind is perceived as 'my mind.' Everything that can be perceived is insentient. Thus, the mind is insentient since it can be perceived. The insentient mind cannot possibly be the sentient 'I' or Self.
3. **The ego** is a part of the subtle body as mentioned in (*13.5*). However, it is the toughest wall to break. One cannot even dream of attaining Mokṣa without transcending the wall of ego around the true Self. Lord Kṛṣna says in the Gita –

   **अहङ्कारविमूढात्मा कर्ताहमिति मन्यते ॥ (३.२७)**

   *Ahaṃkāravimūḍhātmā kartāham iti manyate ॥ (3.27)*

   "A person who is deluded by the ego believes himself to be the doer and experiencer (Kartā and Bhoktā)." He behaves in a childish manner (from the spiritual perspective) and suffers due to constant comparison, boasting, etc. Some people even boast of the lineage they belong to. Following fine family traditions like worship, welcoming visitors, etc.

set forth by ancestors is one thing, but having pompous pride about one's ancestry is another thing. Lord Kṛṣṇa says –

**समोऽहं सर्वभूतेषु । (९.२९)**

*Samohaṃ sarvabhūteṣu* ॥ *(9.29)*

"I, as Brahman, am the same in all beings." In a way, Kṛṣṇa proved this when He staged complete destruction of Yadavas – His own family members – who had acquired demonic qualities and then observed the destruction of his family in an unperturbed, detached manner. Arjuna, on the other hand, was distressed due to the mere thought of annihilation of his clan (*1.39*).

Human beings create many other walls like fame, wealth, prestige, caste, religion, language, and country around them, and they entrap themselves inside those walls. Undoubtedly these are natural aspects of human life. But for the greater good of achieving liberation, the spiritual seeker should only entertain what is needed to live a basic, minimalistic, normal life and quietly let go of what is superfluous. People find themselves working and living in different streams of life. These streams may even be useful for spiritual pursuit. But the true seeker should self-evaluate the purpose of each aspect (job or duty) of his life and gently withdraw from unnecessary duties to free himself from the mundane flow of life. To this end, Lord Kṛṣṇa says –

**श्रेयान्स्वधर्मो विगुणः । (१८.४७)**

*Śreyān svadharmo viguṇaḥ* ॥ *(18.47)*

"It is important to follow one's own Dharma (duty), even though it is of less importance or of inferior social grade." At the same time, He also says –

**सर्वधर्मान्परित्यज्य मामेकं शरणं व्रज ॥ (१८.६६)**

*Sarvadharmān parityajya mām ekaṃ śaraṇaṃ vraja* ॥ *(18.66)*

"Relinquish all ideas of Dharma (duties, righteousness, morality, etc.) and surrender unto Me exclusively." It is essential to note the spirit of both these verses in the right context.

**The pursuit of happiness**

The pursuit of happiness is a never-ending quest for all human beings. However, most people do not necessarily understand that they need to abandon a few things and embrace some things to find lasting happiness in life. Even if they know this theoretically, they cannot put it into practice. Ordinary humans succumb to incessant and abundant desires, wishes, resolutions, hopes, ambitions, and daydreams, which need to be renounced for attaining lasting happiness since such desires hamper spiritual progress. This is precisely the reason why some people accuse the spiritual path of inducing passivity and cutting the wings of ambition from human life. But the same spiritual philosophy as laid out by Lord Kṛṣṇa in the Gita also guides all humans to engage in actions continually –

**तस्मादसक्तः सततं कार्यं कर्म समाचर ॥ (३.१९)**

*Tasmād asaktaḥ satataṃ kāryaṃ karma samācara* ॥ *(3.19)*

**कर्मणैव हि संसिद्धिमास्थिता जनकादयः ॥ (३.२०)**

*Karmaṇaiva hi saṃsiddhim āsthitā janakādayaḥ* ॥ *(3.20)*

**न मे पार्थास्ति कर्तव्यं त्रिषु लोकेषु किञ्चन ।**
**नानवाप्तमवाप्तव्यं वर्त एव च कर्मणि ॥ ३.२२ ॥**

*Na me pārthāsti kartavyaṃ triṣu lokeṣu kiṃcana* ।
*Nānavāptam avāptavyaṃ varta eva ca karmaṇi* ॥ *3.22* ॥

Here, the idea is not to run away from actions; rather, the emphasis is on executing them in the best possible manner. A person who performs actions judiciously is bound to get the designated fruits. For example, King Janaka attained Supreme Brahman through meticulous execution of his duties and adherence to actions. The world-cup tournament in cricket is also a great example in this regard. A player can only improve his own game and play to the best of his ability, but he cannot control the end-result of the game. If the purpose of the Bhagavad-Gita were to propound inactive and passive life, why would Lord Kṛṣṇa constantly encourage Arjuna – who was ready to renounce the battleground and take the vows of monastic life – to get ready and fight the war? The Bhagavad-Gita opposes mindless wealth acquisition which is done without ever being conscientious about the real purpose of human life. The Gita also does not support impractical and demoniac ambitions, and it does not advocate bowing down to injustice. Furthermore, the Gita does not endorse excessive attachment to worldly matters where a person does not think of retiring from worldly life by passing his baton to the next generation. Traditional religion propounds doing social work (Pūrta Karma) such as creating gardens, hospitals, refugee shelters, educational institutes, orphanages, etc. However, the seeker is not expected to spend his entire life doing only the social work or engaging in charity. It is essential to perform these social duties selflessly and pass the baton to the next generation at the right time. Such execution of duties purifies the mind and helps the process of Self-realization.

The science of spiritual philosophy (Adhyātmaśāstra) in the Bhagavad-Gita is meant for evolved humans, while the paths of action and worship are typically prescribed for ordinary humans. From the perspective of the Gita, a person is not considered evolved by his caste, gender, title, wealth, power, etc. Rather, he is seen as evolved person due to his noble actions, good thoughts, selfless work, selfless worship, and finally, his ability to think about the prime purpose of human life. The Gita says –

**मनुष्याणां सहस्रेषु कश्चिद्यतति सिद्धये ।**
**यततामपि सिद्धानां कश्चिन्मां वेत्ति तत्त्वतः ॥ ७.३ ॥**

*Manuṣyāṇāṃ sahasreṣu kaścid yatati siddhaye* ।
*Yatatām api siddhānāṃ kaścin māṃ vetti tattvataḥ* ॥ *7.3* ॥

"Out of many thousands of people, hardly one strives for Self-realization; out of those so striving, hardly one actually achieves self-realization and knows My true nature Brahman." Every person may read and understand the verses in the Gita. But rarely may anyone achieve the ultimate result i.e. the union of Jiva with Brahman propounded by the Gita. If the message of the Gita is taught to less evolved or premature people, they are likely to only suffer losses as they are not sufficiently evolved to understand the true spirit behind those teachings. Lord Kṛṣṇa says –

**न बुद्धिभेदं जनयेदज्ञानां कर्मसङ्गिनाम् ।**
**जोषयेत्सर्वकर्माणि विद्वान्युक्तः समाचरन् ॥ ३.२६ ॥**

*Na buddhibhedaṃ janayed ajñānāṃ karmasaṃginām* ।
*Joṣayet sarvakarmāṇi vidvān yuktaḥ samācaran* ॥ *3.26* ॥

"No wise man should create discord in the minds of ignorant people, who are attached to action. He should not tell them stories of monastic life and discuss the Knowledge of Brahman with them. He should earnestly perform all actions himself and impel all others to engage in actions enthusiastically." In the end, Kṛṣṇa explains when the Gita should not be taught –

**इदं ते नातपस्काय नाभक्ताय कदाचन ।**
**न चाशुश्रूषवे वाच्यं न च मां योऽभ्यसूयति ॥ १८.६७ ॥**

*Idaṃ te nātapaskāya nābhaktāya kadācana* ।
*Na cāśuśrūṣave vācyaṃ na ca māṃ yo'bhyasūyati* ॥ *18.67* ॥

"The philosophy in the Gita should neither be disclosed to a person devoid of austerities, nor to the one who is not faithful towards Īśvara and saints, nor to the one who is reluctant to learn the Gita, and nor to the one who is envious of Me i.e. who considers Me as an ordinary human being." Those having receptive and evolved minds should certainly be taught the knowledge of the Gita. This verse clearly states that the Gita should not be taught to atheists and to those who are not eligible to be its listeners. However, a person who is not eligible for the Gita may genuinely seek a higher life for himself. In this case, he may engage in austerities, nurture faith in Īśvara and enlightened saints, and worship Lord Kṛṣṇa. Even the most malicious person has a chance to redeem himself with the Gita, so it is no wonder that an atheist, too, has an opportunity for redemption. Kṛṣṇa says –

**अपि चेत्सुदुराचारो भजते मामनन्यभाक् ।**
**साधुरेव स मन्तव्यः सम्यग्व्यवसितो हि सः ॥ ९.३० ॥**

*Api cet sudurācāro bhajate mām ananyabhāk* ।
*Sādhur eva sa mantavyaḥ samyag vyavasito hi saḥ* ॥ *9.30* ॥

"If even the most sinful person worships Me with utmost devotion, then he, too, should be regarded as saintly or righteous, because his intellect is awakened towards spiritual pursuit and correctly resolved."

**The Description of Yajñas:**

The description of many Yajñas in the 4th chapter indicates the wide variety of spiritual practices available to seekers. These are approved by Lord Kṛṣṇa and lead the seeker towards Mokṣa. These Yajñas are entirely different from those defined in Pūrva-Mīmāṃsā, which is the part of the Vedas that describes in detail the traditional ritualistic system of offering oblations in the fire. Right at the outset, the Gita describes the qualifications necessary for a seeker to perform Brahmayajña –

**गतसङ्गस्य मुक्तस्य ज्ञानावस्थितचेतसः ।**
**यज्ञायाचरतः कर्म समग्रं प्रविलीयते ॥ ४.२३ ॥**

*Gatasaṅgasya muktasya jñānāvasthitacetasaḥ* ।
*Yajñayācarataḥ karma samagraṃ pravilīyate* ॥ *4.23* ॥

"One who remains absorbed in the Pure Knowledge of Brahman by being dispassionate about worldly matters may engage externally in Yajña or other similar actions, but his actions are considered destroyed, in principle, since they do not yield fruits. A Self-realized person does not consider himself as a doer, and thereby, he is freed from the effects of accrued Karma or ongoing Karma." How his actions are freed from the bondage of fruits by performing various Yajñas is described below:

1. ब्रह्मार्पणं ब्रह्म हविर्ब्रह्माग्नौ ब्रह्मणा हुतम् ।
ब्रह्मैव तेन गन्तव्यं ब्रह्मकर्मसमाधिना ॥ ४.२४ ॥

*Brahmārpaṇaṃ brahma havir brahmāgnau brahmaṇā hutam* ।
*Brahmaiva tena gantavyaṃ brahmakarmasamādhinā* ॥ *4.24* ॥

The Knower of Brahman knows that the tool which is used for offering oblation in Yajña is Brahman. He knows that every offering is Brahman, fire is Brahman, one who performs the ritual is Brahman, and the result of Yajña is Brahman as well. As he sees Brahman in all objects, the whole universe is Brahman for him. Thus, all actions of sacrifice become Brahman for him, and they get destroyed or nullified in effect without giving worldly results of any kind.

2. दैवमेवापरे यज्ञं योगिनः पर्युपासते ॥ (४.२५)

*Daivamevāpare yajñaṃ yoginaḥ paryupāsate* ॥ *(4.25)*

Ādi Śaṅkara has equated the word **Daiva** with God in the commentary of this verse, and he has said that the worship of God is a form of Yajña. In this Yajña, one is supposed to fix his mind steadily on God alone, thus surrender the mind and unite with God. If the meaning of the word Daiva is taken as destiny (Prārabdha), then this Yajña can be considered a process of offering one's entire life, which is bound by Prārabdha, to Īśvara who is the ultimate governor. St. Tukārāma describes this Yajña in a devotional poem where he says, "The seeker should remain content and composed in whichever situation granted by God." This does not mean that St. Tukārāma is fostering passive attitude among people. The spirit of this Yajña is that the seeker should first execute any action to the best of his ability and then be content with whichever result comes his way.

3. ब्रह्माग्नावपरे यज्ञं यज्ञेनैवोपजुह्वति ॥ (४.२५)

*Brahmāgnāvapare yajñaṃ yajñenaivopajuvhati* ॥ *(4.25)*

In every Yajña, offerings are made in fire. This verse states that Brahman itself is the fire. Ātman is also called Yajña. Therefore everything, including knowledge, can be seen as offering to

Brahman and so can be sacrificed as an oblation in Brahman. Therefore, the Knowledge of Brahman should be sacrificed in fire of Brahman. Mind, intellect, etc. are considered the Upādhi of Ātman on account of ignorance. All Upādhi of the Jiva should be offered in the fire of Brahman. In other words, when all Upādhi of the Jiva are sacrificed in Brahman, the Jiva becomes One with Brahman.

**4. श्रोत्रादीनीन्द्रियाण्यन्ये संयमाग्निषु जुह्वति ॥ (४.२६)**

*Śrotrādīnīndriyāṇy anye saṁyamāgniṣu juvhati* ॥ *(4.26)*

Some practitioners offer the oblation of organs in the fire of self-restraint. This simply means that they strive to restrain their organs from pursuing worldly objects and immerse their minds in Ātman. They do not allow the mind to digress through organs in different directions. Kena Upaniṣad says that Ātman is the 'ear of ears.' Seekers, here, try to make their organs disappear in Ātman i.e. they strive to stop activities of their organs and rest them in Ātman.

**5. शब्दादीन्विषयानन्य इन्द्रियाग्निषु जुह्वति ॥ (४.२६)**

*Śabdādīn viṣayān anya indriyāgniṣu juvhati* ॥ *(4.26)*

Some seekers offer the oblation of objects-of-senses in the fire-of-senses. E.g. ears hear words. So, in this Yajña, the seekers sacrifice the words in the ears themselves. This means that they try to disregard words – whether praise or criticism – and thus do not react after hearing good or bad words. Here, sacrificing the act of enjoyment itself is known as a Yajña. Such a sacrifice helps in purification of the mind and ultimately in the union of the Jiva with Brahman. [This does not mean that one should completely refrain from eating good food or seeing good places of nature, etc., but the objects of pleasure should be approved by scriptures, and they should be enjoyed as prescribed by scriptures. This automatically curbs the process of enjoying worldly pleasures.]

6. सर्वाणीन्द्रियकर्माणि प्राणकर्माणि चापरे ।
आत्मसंयमयोगाग्नौ जुह्वति ज्ञानदीपिते ॥ ४.२७ ॥

*Sarvāṇīndriyakarmāṇi prāṇakarmāṇi cāpare* ।
*Ātmasaṅyamayogāgnau juvhati jñānadīpite* ॥ 4.27 ॥

Some seekers offer all actions of all organs and functioning of the Prāṇas in the fire of self-restraint. Fire is ignited when oil or butter is added to it. Similarly, seekers offer their actions to the fire-of-Ātman which is ignited by the fuel of spiritual discrimination between real and unreal. They practice discrimination in various ways –

- I am Ātman, not the body.
- The world is not real but just a false appearance.
- The body goes through changes and ailments, Ātman is immutable.
- The world, including my body, is impermanent.

When this discrimination is strengthened, it is declared as *Vijñāna*. When the seeker remains naturally immersed in this firm *Vijñāna*, he does not feel that "I am the doer." The feeling of doership is a sign of ignorance. It is offered as an oblation in this Yajña.

**7 to 12.**

द्रव्ययज्ञास्तपोयज्ञा योगयज्ञास्तथापरे ।
स्वाध्यायज्ञानयज्ञाश्च यतयः संशितव्रताः ॥ ४.२८ ॥

*Dravyayajñas tapoyajña yogayajñas tathāpare* ।
*Svādhyāyajñanayajñaśca yatayaḥ saṃśitavratāḥ* ॥ 4.28 ॥

a. Yajña of wealth (***Dravyayajña***) – Offering financial wealth for the development of temples or holy places with a sense of sacrifice without expecting any benefits is the Yajña of wealth. It also includes the construction of buildings for devotees who come to visit holy places, creating facilities for visitors, donating food, running hospitals and free dormitories, etc.

b. Yajña of austerities (***Tapoyajña***) – Resolutely practicing physical, mental, and verbal austerities for spiritual pursuit.
c. Yajña of Yoga (***Yogayajña***) – Practicing the stages of Aṣṭānga-Yoga such as Yama and Niyamas.
d. Yajña of self-study (***Swādhyaya***) – Intently studying the ancient scriptures such as the Vedas, Upaniṣads, Gita, etc., memorizing and reciting their verses.
e. Yajña of Knowledge (***Jñānayajña***) – Knowing the in-depth meaning of the doctrine presented in the Vedas and Upaniṣads and discussing it with others.
f. Yajña of arduous rituals (***Saṅśitavrata* Yajña**) – Practicing arduous rituals, pious observances, or religious rituals like bathing in cold water before sunrise in winter, eating only one meal per day, strict celibacy, etc.

**13 to 15.**

**अपाने जुह्वति प्राणं प्राणेऽपानं तथापरे ।**
**प्राणापानगती रुद्ध्वा प्राणायामपरायणाः ॥ ४.२९ ॥**

*Apāne juvhati prāṇaṃ prāṇe'pānaṃ tathāpare* ।
*Prāṇāpānagatī ruddhvā prāṇāyāmaparāyaṇāḥ* ॥ *4.29* ॥

a. Some seekers sacrifice Prāṇavāyu (in-coming breath) in Apānavāyu (out-going breath). They perform the Pūraka Prāṇāyāma where Prāṇas are inhaled gradually and quietly with specific counts.
b. Some perform the sacrifice of Apāna in Prāṇa, which is the Recaka Prāṇāyāma where they exhale in a specific way for a specific time.
c. Some seekers hold the flow of both Prāṇa and Apāna for some time and perform Kumbhaka. They surrender entirely to the process of Prāṇāyāma. This Yajña is more difficult than the two Yajñas mentioned above and more effective as well. The primary purpose of these three Yajñas is to awaken the power of Kunḍalini, which is the invisible inner power in every being.

16. अपरे नियताहाराः प्राणान्प्राणेषु जुह्वति ।
सर्वेऽप्येते यज्ञविदो यज्ञक्षपितकल्मषाः ॥ ४.३० ॥
*Apare niyatāhārāḥ prāṇān prāṇeṣu juvhati* ।
*Sarve'pyete yajñavido yajñakṣapitakalmaṣāḥ* ॥ *4.30* ॥

Some seekers who have strictly regulated their food intake sacrifice the four auxiliary Prāṇas one by one into the main Prāṇa. It means, they sequentially conquer each Prāṇa and rest it in the main Prāṇa. All differentiations among Prāṇas thus disappear in the main Prāṇa.

All sins are eradicated for seekers who practice the above Yajñas, and they are liberated in sequential steps in due course. However, enlightened people who have firm, unchanging, direct realization that "I am Brahman" are instantly liberated in the same birth while they are still alive. Lord Kṛṣṇa says that the Yajña of Knowledge (*Jñānayajñā*) is superior to all other Yajñas and all actions culminate in Self-Knowledge at the end (*4.32-33*).

## Worship of Lord Kṛṣṇa:

There are many ways to worship Lord Kṛṣṇa. The key principle behind the worship can be recognized through the following verse in the Bhagavad-Gita. Kṛṣṇa explains the very reason for His birth in the fourth chapter –

यदा यदा हि धर्मस्य ग्लानिर्भवति भारत ।
अभ्युत्थानमधर्मस्य तदात्मानं सृजाम्यहम् ॥ ४.७ ॥
*Yadā yadā hi dharmasya glānir bhavati bhārata* ।
*Abhyutthānam adharmasya tadātmānaṃ sṛjāmy aham* ॥ *4.7* ॥

"O Bhārata! Whenever the influence of Dharma i.e. adherence to duty, righteousness, morality, and Religion declines, I manifest Myself personally to reinstate Dharma."

परित्राणाय साधूनां विनाशाय च दुष्कृताम् ।
धर्मसंस्थापनार्थाय सम्भवामि युगे युगे ॥ ४.८ ॥
*Paritrāṇāya sādhūnāṃ vināśāya ca duṣkṛtām* ।
*Dharmasaṃsthāpanārthāya saṃbhavāmi yuge yuge* ॥ *4.8* ॥

"For the protection of those treading the noble path, for the destruction of the evil, and for reinstating the waning Dharma, I am born in every Yuga. [Yuga is an era, a part of four-age cycle mentioned in Hinduism.]"

All those who worship Lord Kṛṣṇa or His other incarnations should participate in the execution of duties mentioned explicitly by Lord Kṛṣṇa in the above verses. Abiding by these duties is a form of worship. Seekers should understand the significance of these three duties for which formless Lord Kṛṣṇa was compelled to incarnate Himself in a form. If Lord Kṛṣṇa indeed nurtures so much affection for Dharma, then His worshippers should equally love Dharma. Especially in the current state of affairs in India, one must nurture genuine love for righteous living. Dharma has extrinsic and intrinsic aspects, both of which should be fostered with equal emphasis. We should at least cultivate the cultural aspect of Dharma with faith and enthusiasm. People in southern India still put a dot of vermilion powder or apply sandalwood paste on forehead, despite being dressed in modern fashion. Today, we can keep ambiance in the home conducive for worshipping God, so that we can easily teach the lessons of culture and morality to the new generation.

For most ordinary people, a simple step to abide in Dharma would be to disregard evil and immoral people and not hold them in high esteem. Seekers can always avoid taking any kind of help from immoral people and avoid being in their company. In today's age, people who want to annihilate the evil forces may themselves get destroyed in turn. Such is the pathetic condition of governance in society. Newspapers regularly expose the reality of those who make false propaganda that they work for the protection of good and destruction of bad. Therefore, it becomes necessary that the devotees of Lord Kṛṣṇa conscientiously practice rituals like fasting, going on pilgrimages, visiting temples, chanting, wearing the necklace of pious beads, reading scriptures, etc. It may be easy for a devotee to simply offer flowers, fruits, etc. to his beloved deity, but it is far from being a full form of worship. If the devotee really loves God, and God loves Dharma, then the devotee is obviously supposed to love Dharma and embrace it as a way of life. Otherwise, wouldn't we mandate God to manifest Himself again by behaving in an unrighteous manner like Kaṅsa or Rāvaṇa?

## Cyclic nature of worldly life

The Bhagavad-Gita has made us aware of the cyclic and dynamic nature of the world and worldly life. By carefully reflecting on this dynamic cycle of the world, the seeker can easily cultivate dispassion for worldly life.

**अन्नाद्भवन्ति भूतानि पर्जन्यादन्नसम्भवः ।**
**यज्ञाद्भवति पर्जन्यो यज्ञः कर्मसमुद्भवः ॥ ३.१४ ॥**
**कर्म ब्रह्मोद्भवं विद्धि ब्रह्माक्षरसमुद्भवम् ।**
**तस्मात्सर्वगतं ब्रह्म नित्यं यज्ञे प्रतिष्ठितम् ॥ ३.१५ ॥**
**एवं प्रवर्तितं चक्रं नानुवर्तयतीह यः ।**
**अघायुरिन्द्रियारामो मोघं पार्थ स जीवति ॥ ३.१६ ॥**

*Annād bhavanti bhūtāni parjanyād annasaṃbhavaḥ* ।
*Yajñad bhavati parjanyo yajñaḥ karmasamudbhavaḥ* ॥ *3.14* ॥
*Karma brahmodbhavaṃ viddhi brahmākṣarasamudbhavam* ।
*Tasmāt sarvagataṃ brahma nityaṃ yajñe pratiṣṭhitam* ॥ *3.15* ॥
*Evaṃ pravartitaṃ cakraṃ nānuvartayatīha yaḥ* ।
*Aghāyur indriyārāmo moghaṃ pārtha sa jīvati* ॥ *3.16* ॥

"Beings are created from food, food is produced from rain, rain is produced from Yajña, Yajña is originated from actions, actions are prescribed by the Vedas, and the Vedas were revealed from Brahman; therefore, all-pervasive Brahman is ever-present in Yajñas. A person who lives without knowing this cyclic nature of human life and without knowing that his own life is momentary wastes his life in a sinful manner by only indulging in worldly objects." In this cycle of life, everything has a momentum. Various cycles are stated and classified in scriptures as follows –

- The cycle of life (*Bhūtacakra*) – Beings are created and nourished from food, later they rest and merge in the food itself (Tai. Up.)
- The cycle of food (*Annacakra*) – Crop seeds are sown in a specific season, they grow, and later perish in the end (Sasyamiva jāyate, Kaṭha Up.)
- The cycle of rain (*Parjanyacakra*) – Seasons change in the cycle of summer, rains, and winter.
- The cycle of Yajña (*Yajñacakra*) – Qualified practitioners perform particular Yajñas periodically at a specific time.
- The cycle of action (*Karmacakra*) – Human beings engage in actions by thinking that "I am the doer"; therefore, they get trapped in the cycle of birth-life-death, which is an intricate and mysterious cycle of doing actions and bearing their results. (4.17)
- The cycle of the Vedas (*Vedacakra*) – The same Vedas get created over and over again at the time of recreation of the universe which takes place after its destruction in the previous Kalpa.

From these descriptions, it can be deduced that whatever is dynamic or changing, it is impermanent in nature. When the seeker recognizes this fact, he finds it easy to detach from the world and worldly transactions. Lord Kṛṣṇa says about Yajña –

**सहयज्ञाः प्रजाः सृष्ट्वा पुरोवाच प्रजापतिः ।**
**अनेन प्रसविष्यध्वमेष वोऽस्त्विष्टकामधुक् ॥ ३.१० ॥**

*Sahayajñaḥ prajāḥ sṛṣṭvā purovāca prajāpatiḥ* ।
*Anena prasaviṣyadhvam eṣa vo'stviṣṭa kāmadhuk* ॥ *3.10* ॥

"The creator (Prajāpati) created mankind at the beginning of a Kalpa along with Yajña and said, 'By doing this Yajña, you will prosper. This Yajña will give you what is good for you.'" We have already seen the synopsis of these Yajñas from the 4th chapter. Chāndogya Upaniṣad (*5.4.1*, *5.5.1*) explains a form of worship where the rain is considered the fire, and the wind is a type of fuel for the fire.

| Verse 5.4.1 - | Verse 5.5.1 - |
|---|---|
| Fire: Heavenly World | Fire: Rain |
| Offering: Sun | Offering: Wind |
| Smoke: Rays | Smoke: Clouds |
| Flames: Days | Flames: Lightning |
| Glow: Moon | Glow: Thunderbolt |
| Sparks: Constellations | Sparks: Cloud Thunder |

The concept put forth here is that Īśvara is Himself a highly evolved Jiva; therefore, we may think that He also performs Yajñas to run these cycles of nature (rain, etc.) properly. The ingredients of His Yajña are also cosmic and grand like Him, as listed in the aforementioned verses of Chāndogya. This can be one possible explanation of how Yajñas executed by Him result in rains, as mentioned in verse *3.14* of the Gita. The actual ingredients of the Īśvara's Yajña are outlined in verses *5.4.1* and *5.5.1* of Chāndogya Upaniṣad stated above.

## Śraddhā (spiritual faith)

In the last 50 years, social workers and philosophical intellectuals have comprehensively examined the blind-faith practices in society. Many efforts to eradicate the blind-faith practices are still going on. Some examples of popular blind beliefs are: 'Hanging lemon and chillies at the door wards off evil' or 'A cat crossing one's path is a bad omen', etc. Careful reflection on this issue reveals that such practices are not blind practices. On the contrary, they ought to be called 'distorted practices'. The work done by social well-wishers or intellectuals has certainly helped to eradicate these distorted practices to some extent.

The belief that the true Self is Brahman is initially just blind faith. It later evolves into the direct realization and firm conviction that "I am Brahman" by following the teachings of enlightened saints, serving the Sadguru, and performing spiritual practices as taught by the Guru. All other distortions of faith take the seeker further away from the spiritual path, and they are detrimental to both worldly as well as spiritual wellbeing of the seeker. Many Rajas and Tamas practices are described in the 17th chapter of the Gita, all of which are distorted practices, not blind practices. Kṛṣṇa says that the faiths that originate from the three Guṇas exist innately in each Jiva since birth (*17.2*). Vāsanā is the cause of the birth of a Jiva. Disposition of the Jiva is formed according to his past Vāsanās. Sāttvic people worship God, Rājas people worship Yakṣa and demons, while Tāmas people worship dead-bodies and ghosts (*17.4*). Even though the Gita mentions these three faiths, it only approves the Sāttvic faith. People who nurture Rājas and Tāmas faiths are pretentious and egoistic, and they neglect the scriptures and nurture demoniac ambitions (*17.5*). Their faith is perverted. People having pervert faith do not pay heed to the consequences of their pervert actions, losses incurred due to their acts, violence or cruelty in those actions, or the limitations of their own power (*18.25*).

Kṛṣṇa clearly states that the direct Self-realization (*Aparokṣānubhūti*) "I am Ātman" can be gained only by those who have faith in Ātman, scriptures, and Sadguru (*4.39*). This simply means that the end goal of faith is Self-realization. For that, the seeker must nurture unwavering faith in the teachings of the Gita, Upaniṣads, Sadguru, and enlightened saints like Kabira, Jñāneśwara, etc. St. Rāmadāsa has described the characteristics of an authentic Sadguru in detail in his treatise Dāsabodha, and there is no trace of ambiguity in it. Foolish, ignorant, wishful, and greedy people are tricked by cheaters in day-to-day life. E.g. It is common to see people getting duped by cheaters who promise to create two bills from one. The same people get bluffed by imposter spiritual Gurus as well. They also get tricked and robbed by politicians who give fake promises about money, jobs, etc. The field of spirituality is not at fault here. The onus is on those greedy, foolish people who do not understand the essence of spiritual pursuit. They interact with God and Guru only to resolve their worldly problems, overcome obstacles, or to gain power, wealth, success, fame, status in society. Such people are spiritual encroachers or robbers.

In the beginning, faith in the spiritual philosophy is essentially a blind faith, since the seeker must believe in the teachings of the enlightened saints, scriptures (the Gita, Upaniṣads), Sadguru, and the concepts of Ātman, Jiva, etc. without knowing much about them. Gradually the seeker understands their direct relevance in his life and sees them in the light of logic and his own experience. Once he clearly learns the harmony and correlation between spiritual and worldly life, his faith in the teachings of saints, scriptures, Sadguru, etc. does not remain a mere blind-faith. Rather it evolves into a great spiritual practice.

It is also essential to note that spiritual faith is just a practice (tool). Initially, the seeker is supposed to keep faith primarily in Ātman. After Self-realization, Śraddhā (faith) – the tool – is no longer required since he realizes "I am Ātman" in a firm, direct, permanent manner. Thereafter faith automatically retires. As a novice seeker, it may be fine to pray to Īśvara for helping through grave difficulties in life, especially when the seeker does not clearly understand the concepts of Mokṣa, dispassion, etc. However, it is incorrect when he succumbs to practices such as wearing black threads, using stones, practicing sorcery, or trying to appease planets, etc. for a trouble-free life. Lord Kṛṣṇa Himself says –

**चतुर्विधा भजन्ते मां जनाः सुकृतिनोऽर्जुन ।**
**आर्तो जिज्ञासुरर्थार्थी ज्ञानी च भरतर्षभ ॥ ७.१६ ॥**

*Caturvidhā bhajante māṃ janāḥ sukṛtino'rjuna ।*
*Ārto jijñāsur arthārthī jñānī ca bharatarṣabha ॥ 7.16 ॥*

Four kinds of virtuous people worship Me. They are –

1) Distressed (***Ārta***) – One who prays to God in the times of personal, familial, social trouble or a national calamity and promises to offer God something in return if the crisis is removed from his life.
2) Desirer of wealth (***Arthārthi***) – One who worships God for worldly gain, progress, and upliftment.
3) Inquisitive (***Jijñasu***) – One who worships God to understand Him and learn more about the nature of the world, the purpose of life, scriptures, spiritual practices, Guru, Jiva, Ātman, etc.
4) Wise (***Jñāni***) – One who lovingly worships God even after learning spiritual philosophy and attaining Self-Knowledge.

The Bhagavad-Gita explicitly says that mere faith (in God or scriptures) is not sufficient.

**श्रद्धावाँल्लभते ज्ञानं तत्परः संयतेन्द्रियः ।**
**ज्ञानं लब्ध्वा परां शान्तिमचिरेणाधिगच्छति ॥ ४.३९ ॥**

*Śraddhāvāṃl labhate jñānaṃ tatparaḥ saṅyatendriyaḥ ।*
*Jñānaṃ labdhvā parāṃ śāntim acireṇādhigacchati ॥ 4.39 ॥*

The seeker who is faithful can gain the theoretical knowledge of Brahman. But he should also strive to attain Self-realization (*Aparokṣānubhūti*) that "I am Brahman," which is the very purpose of spiritual faith. It is also necessary for him to have faith in Saguṇa and Nirguṇa forms of God, the scriptures of the Vedānta and Gita, and Sadguru. Moreover, he should strive to conquer his senses. Such a seeker can quickly attain the supreme peace after realizing the Knowledge of the true Self. Lord Kṛṣṇa also says that such faith needs to be accompanied by the abandonment of desires –

**श्रद्धया परया तप्तं तपस्तत्त्रिविधं नरैः ।**
**अफलाकाङ्क्षिभिर्युक्तैः सात्त्विकं परिचक्षते ॥ १७.१७ ॥**

*Śraddhayā parayā taptaṃ Tapas tat trividhaṃ naraiḥ* ।
*Aphalākāṅkṣibhir yuktaiḥ sāttvikaṃ paricakṣate* ॥ *17.17* ॥

Austerity practiced with utmost faith and selflessness without expectation of specific fruits is Sāttvic in nature. Here, too, it is mentioned that the devotees – who worship God to escape from distress or who are desirers of wealth – are not eligible for Mokṣa until they become unselfish, desireless, and unconditional worshippers. After significant accumulation of merits from past and present births, they can first become inquisitive seekers and then become the highest enlightened devotees.

**Teachings on four levels**

Lord Kṛṣṇa has taught the philosophy of the Gita on four levels –

1) Worldly advice (***Laukika***)

**अकीर्तिं चापि भूतानि कथयिष्यन्ति तेऽव्ययाम् ।**
**सम्भावितस्य चाकीर्तिर्मरणादतिरिच्यते ॥ २.३४ ॥**

*Akīrtiṃ cāpi bhūtāni Kaṭhayiṣyanti te'vyayām* ।
*Saṃbhāvitasya cākīrtir maraṇād atiricyate* ॥ *2.34* ॥

"Arjuna, if you do not perform your duty in this war, people will recount your infamy for ages to come. Infamy or disgrace is more agonizing than death for a respected and honored person."

**भयाद्रणादुपरतं मंस्यन्ते त्वां महारथाः ।**
**येषां च त्वं बहुमतो भूत्वा यास्यसि लाघवम् ॥ २.३५ ॥**

*Bhayād raṇād uparataṃ maṃsyante tvāṃ mahārathāḥ*
*Yeṣāṃ ca tvaṃ bahumato bhūtvā yāsyasi lāghavam* ॥ *2.35* ॥

"The mighty warriors, who hold you in high regard and esteem, will look down upon you. They will consider you have retreated from the battlefield out of fear."

2) Ethical advice (***Naitika***)

**यदृच्छया चोपपन्नं स्वर्गद्वारमपावृतम् ।**
**सुखिनः क्षत्रियाः पार्थ लभन्ते युद्धमीदृशम् ॥ २.३२ ॥**

*Yadṛcchayā copapannaṃ svargadvāram apāvṛtam* ।
*Sukhinaḥ kṣatriyāḥ pārtha labhante yuddhamīdṛśam* ॥ *2.32* ॥

The tactics of war have been prescribed for all Kṣatriyas i.e. warriors. The real warrior is born with an innate instinct to protect the weak and fight for justice. He instinctively follows the war tactics. Ethical war for the protection of good is a boon as well as a challenge for a hardcore warrior. One may find it strange to associate happiness with fighting the war. However, this verse points to the sheer enthusiasm felt by a warrior at the time of fighting a battle. In this verse, Lord Kṛṣṇa indicates that this war is imposed unjustly and wrongfully by Kauravas. It is being fought for justice, and so it is a must-win situation for Arjuna and other Pāṇḍavas.

3) Religious advice (***Dhārmika***)

Heaven and hell, merit and sin, prescribed actions and forbidden actions, etc. belong to the realm of Dharma. Lord Kṛṣṇa entices Arjuna to fight by saying that if he wins this war, he will go to heaven as per the precepts of Dharma. He says –

**हतो वा प्राप्स्यसि स्वर्गं जित्वा वा भोक्ष्यसे महीम् ॥ (२.३७)**

*Hato vā prāpsyasi svargaṃ jitvā vā bhokṣyase mahīm* ॥ *(2.37)*

Thus, even from the traditional Religious perspective, Arjuna is required to fight this battle for the protection of what is good and righteous.

4) Spiritual advice (***Paramarthika***)

**नासतो विद्यते भावो नाभावो विद्यते सतः ।**
**उभयोरपि दृष्टोऽन्तस्त्वनयोस्तत्त्वदर्शिभिः ॥ २.१६ ॥**

*Nāsato vidyāte bhāvo nābhāvo vidyāte sataḥ* ।
*Ubhayor api dṛṣto'antas tvanayos tattvādarśibhiḥ* ॥ *2.16* ॥

Bodies of soldiers from both sides of the war are unreal (*Asat*). They do not have real existence (*Sat*). However, Ātman – the true Self –in all warriors is real and eternal; it can never be destroyed.

Therefore, from all these four perspectives, fighting the war and executing the duty is imperative and unavoidable. Arjuna's idea of Dharma conformed to some ordinary aspects such as not rebelling against Guru or elders in the family, not killing and thus circumventing the execution of postmortem rituals for his kin, and avoiding complete destruction of his lineage, etc. However, fighting for justice and protection of good is a far higher dimension of Dharma than these ordinary aspects. If the seeker follows the higher dimensions of Dharma through the discipline of spiritual bearing, his actions cannot be labeled as sins or unrighteous behavior. The Gita says –

**य एनं वेत्ति हन्तारं यश्चैनं मन्यते हतम् ।**
**उभौ तौ न विजानीतो नायं हन्ति न हन्यते ॥ २.१९ ॥**

*Ya enaṃ vetti hantāraṃ yaś cainaṃ manyate hatam* ।
*Ubhau tau na vijānīto nāyaṃ hanti na hanyate* ॥ *2.19* ॥

"He who thinks that Ātman, the true Self, dies, and he who thinks he can slay Ātman, both are ignorant. Since Ātman neither dies nor can it be slain."

## Divine glories (Vibhūti) of Lord Kṛṣṇa

Not many people pay careful attention to the 10th chapter of the Bhagavad-Gita. After describing all His glories in great detail, Lord Kṛṣṇa states the very quintessence of all verses in the end –

**यद्यद्विभूतिमत्सत्त्वं श्रीमदूर्जितमेव वा ।**
**तत्तदेवावगच्छ त्वं मम तेजोंऽशसम्भवम् ॥ १०.४१ ॥**

*Yadyadvibhūtimat sattvaṃ Śrīmad ūrjitam eva vā* ।
*Tattadevāvagaccha tvaṃ mama tejoṃ'śasaṃbhavam* ॥ *10.41* ॥

"Whichever entity is opulent, majestic, or powerful, know that it arises from but a fraction of My glory." The world is comprised of many sentient and insentient entities. Sentient Jivas include royal animals like lions; nimble, swift, and fast animals like horses; and birds having razor-sharp vision like eagles, etc. Insentient entities include the vast and deep sky, seemingly boundless ocean, shimmering jewels, and enchanting play of colors in a rainbow. Influential human beings span from the likes of Emperor Śivāji to other distinguished luminaries like Ādi Śaṅkara, Einstein, Rāmānujan, Rājā Ravi Varmā, and Tānasena. Even today, many notable personalities bedeck society. Wherever the seeker sees these remarkable qualities, he should recognize and behold them as the Divine Glory (Vibhūti) of Lord Kṛṣṇa and heartily accept them in that divine form. Such acceptance will help remove the negative traits of jealousy, hostility, envy, and resentfulness from the mind, and thus cleanse and purify his mind. The seeker who has a pure mind becomes eligible for higher spiritual pursuit.

The seeker – who acknowledges that both birth and death are the Glories of the Lord – learns to see that both these events are a mere play of God, and thus, he does not experience joy or grief due to them. The Lord says in verse 10.34 –

**मृत्युः सर्वहरश्चाहमुद्भवश्च भविष्यताम् । (१०.३४)**

*Mṛtyuḥ sarvaharaś cāham udbhavaś ca bhaviṣyatām । (10.34)*

"I am the death that destroys everyone and the cause of creation too." Furthermore, Lord Kṛṣṇa says that the deceptive game of gambling is His own glory (*10.36*). This explains why humans have an inescapable attraction towards that game. Also, the letter 'a or A' is naturally intertwined in every letter, and it is a Glory of Īśvara. The Sattvaguṇa in all Sāttvic people is a Glory of Īśvara. Both these facts indicate that all Sāttvic literature is a manifestation of Īśvara himself. Even a destructive weapon like the thunderbolt is a manifestation of Lord Kṛṣṇa, which means all other lethal weapons and missiles are Him as well. Thus, we can conclude that destruction is a part of His governance. Destruction, however atrocious it may be, is unavoidable. The charming season of spring is Him, and the cruel animal crocodile is Him as well. Both policemen and army personnel are meant to repress evil forces. If we recognize that they are manifestations of the Lord, no trace of corruption will be left in society. Intelligence, philosophy, forgiveness, truth, control of the organs, restraint of the mind, pleasure, pain, creation, and destruction are all Divine Glories of Kṛṣṇa. A person who can behold them in that manner is liberated from all sins (*10.3*).

The Lord says that those who worship Him lovingly by recognizing and being aware of all His glories attain outstanding results in their spiritual pursuit. He promises to bestow spiritual disposition – the intellect that can abide in Ātman – upon all devotees so that they can unite with the true Self (*10.10*). An earnest devotee strives to see his beloved Kṛṣṇa everywhere and knows that the Lord is all-pervasive. The Lord then bestows upon him Pure Knowledge of his true Self. In other words, He makes an arrangement through which the devotee attains Self-realization. Eminent saints of Mahārāṣṭra like St. Gorā Kumbhāra, Nāmadeva Mahārāja, Tukārāma Mahārāja, etc. had no formal degree or education in any monastery, and they did not have any spiritual lineage to guide them. However, they were all liberated by attaining the highest Self-Knowledge that "I am Brahman." We can infer that they must have gotten their enlightenment through their devotion alone as mentioned above. Even incarnations of Īśvara like Lord Kṛṣṇa and Lord Rāma had to earn their knowledge from their respective Gurus *Ṛṣi* Sāndipani and Sage Vasiṣṭha.

The 11th chapter of the Gita presents a crucial thought for the seeker. It is a fact that human faces, bodies, colors may be very beautiful, ugly, cheerless, grim, dismal, attractive, or detestable.

All of them are the same Ātman. This chapter is mainly meant to reveal and portray the Divine Cosmic Form of Lord Kṛṣṇa. However, no other seeker will get to see the complete Cosmic Form of Kṛṣṇa like Arjuna saw it. Therefore, the seeker should learn to see the Lord in every being with the help of teachings presented in the 11$^{th}$ chapter. The core message of this chapter is given in *11.33* when Kṛṣṇa asks Arjuna to execute actions by thinking of himself as a mere tool, medium, or instrument to do those actions. Every seeker should consciously remember this message while performing actions.

The indication of Om, Tat, and *Sat* (*17.23*) is one more special characteristic of the Gita. If these words are conscientiously pronounced before beginning and after completion of each action, the act is offered to God. It does not yield a fruit that needs to be borne later in the future. Kaṭha Upaniṣad states that **Om** indicates the substratum Brahman. 'Om' encompasses the three states of Jiva and Īśvara (individual and cosmos), as well as the three Guṇas. The word **Tat** indicates Brahman. The term ***Sat*** indicates that Brahman transcends both space and time. Pure Brahman is all-pervasive and beyond the three times of past, present, and future.

**ॐ तत्सदिति निर्देशो ब्रह्मणस्त्रिविधः स्मृतः ।**
**ब्राह्मणास्तेन वेदाश्च यज्ञाश्च विहिताः पुरा ॥ १७.२३ ॥**

*Oṃ tat sad iti nirdeśo brahmaṇas trividhaḥ smṛtaḥ* ।
*Brāhmaṇās tena vedāś ca Yajñaś ca vihitāḥ purā* ॥ *17.23* ॥

"Brahman is described with the help of the three words Om, Tat, and *Sat*. Brāhmins, Yajñas, and the Vedas were created from this Om alone." The Vedas are divided into three sections: Action (Karma), worship (Upāsanā), and Knowledge (Jñāna). These three are integral parts of human life, so the entire life is pervaded with the Vedas. Therefore, it is felicitous to remember Brahman before and after each action by pronouncing **Om-Tat-*Sat***.

After teaching the entire philosophy in the Bhagavad-Gita, Lord Kṛṣṇa does not enforce Arjuna to act as per His wish. He gives Arjuna the freedom to act according to his wish (*18.63*). Kṛṣṇa suggests that Arjuna should carefully reflect on these teachings from all angles and do what is deemed right by him. In return, Arjuna bows to Kṛṣṇa and says that he will exactly do as guided by Lord Kṛṣṇa (*18.73*). An important takeaway from this is that a teacher should not enforce his teachings on students after he has taught them. Imposing, coercion, compelling, or dictation of any kind has no place in this process.

**Addendum:**

Many eminent scholars have written commentaries to date on the Bhagavad-Gita, which is a universally acclaimed scripture with extraordinary philosophy. These commentaries present different interpretations of the Gita's philosophy, and some also address the social and political needs of each era. Mr. Amartya Sen, a Nobel Prize winning economist, has raised a question whether the destruction of millions of humans and animals initiated by Pāṇḍavas for their own welfare was valid and justifiable. He has apparently raised this question by keeping in mind the plight of ordinary humans. The picture of mass-destruction painted by Arjuna before the war was actualized as a reality after the war. Hence, Mr. Sen has also subtly questioned the appropriateness of Kṛṣṇa's persistent motivation and philosophical guidance to Arjuna for fighting the war. These points may have been raised under the influence of socialism and communism. His questions never seem to refer to the Pāṇḍavas who were ready to compromise and be content in exchange of ownership of five towns. Also, the author has not even cognized the role of the duty of a warrior i.e. Kṣātradharma, which was a characteristic feature of that era. It was imperative in those times for a warrior to participate in war once it was commenced. The Bhagavad-Gita may continue to garner such unfair and one-sided objections even in the future.

As mentioned in this preface by the present commentator, Arjuna is a representative of spiritual seekers. From his personal perspective, it was his prime duty to fight the impending war. The decision to fight the war was imposed by the then circumstances and not a personal choice of either Arjuna or Lord Kṛṣṇa. Noble and conscientious Arjuna found it very hard to accept the decision to fight the war. He was caught in a dilemma whether it was right to fight against his own kinsmen. Despite being on the lawful side, if a person succumbs – just like Arjuna – to unwarranted pity or wrong notions of morality due to his agreeable nature and withdraws from war or from taking action, evil people can freely walk away with malicious intents. The history of Hindus is full of many such incidents. Mahābhārata gives the message: "Evil people can also be strong and formidable in themselves. Many other valiant warriors may prefer to join the evil side for their own reasons. However, to fight these evil forces, a warrior can adapt the path of untruth or diplomacy if required." St. Rāmadāsa says, "The reason maliciousness proliferates in society is that virtuous people fear vicious people and do not engage strategically in the game of politics." St. Tukārāma says, "Real mercy has two aspects: first, taking care of good and noble beings, and second, completely eradicating the vicious forces."

All genuine spiritual seekers are conscientious and noble-minded by nature. The dilemma faced by Arjuna is every seeker's dilemma. The Bhagavad-Gita has given excellent resolution to this commonly faced dilemma. Political strategists may spin the teachings of the Gita to their advantage, progressive patrons may opine about the Gita in any way, intellectuals may regard whatever they wish about it, mere academicians produced by marketing mediums may think in any direction, opposition masterminds may nurture whichever notion, or modern alleged spiritual leaders may distort the teachings of the Gita in a way that suits their purpose. Regardless of it all, the Bhagavad-Gita will continue to show the right path to all genuine spiritual seekers for ages to come.

Now, to realize the goal of the Gita, it is essential to consider certain aspects of the Vedānta philosophy. There should be no ambiguity while learning vital concepts in spiritual texts. The reader should know that the same word can be used in different contexts, and its meaning should be understood within that context. For example, St. Rāmadāsa and St. Tukārāma have used the word **Upādhi** in different contexts in their texts. The term Upādhi typically means a limiting adjunct. Upādhi is known to show one object separately from the other. St. Rāmadāsa states that "The real seeker is the one who discards the Upādhi of his body, strives to achieve the unachievable Ātman, and remains firmly steady in the thought that 'I am Ātman' (*Dāsabodha 5.9.23*)." St. Tukārāma Mahārāja says, "A seeker should have a neutral (equanimous) mind, and he should not be associated with Upādhi of any kind." St. Rāmadāsa has used the word Upādhi in the light of Vedānta where he means that "The Upādhi of the body separates a seeker from his true nature i.e. Ātman." St. Tukārāma has used the word Upādhi to mean "Unnecessary identification of the Jiva with any internal or external object. (e.g. I am rich, I am beautiful, I am brilliant, I am emotional, I am forgetful, etc.)" Even if the word Upādhi is the same in both the cases, their meanings are different. The body is the Upādhi of a Jiva, while the universe is the Upādhi of Īśvara. When both Upādhis are removed, the seeker can realize Brahman – which is beyond Upādhi – as his true Self. Self-realization in this manner is extremely difficult; therefore, St. Rāmadāsa calls it unachievable. In other words, Brahman is ever-available and ever-attained. Therefore, it cannot be achieved like a separate goal. However, Self-realization is perceived as a goal due to ignorance, and the seeker has to perform spiritual practice for attaining it. In this process, the seeker may see a glimpse of his Self as Brahman, but that experience is not firm and constant. The seeker is supposed to consistently strive to train himself to meditate on the fact that "I am Brahman." St. Tukārāma says that, for Self-realization, the seeker is supposed to consciously discard superfluous external Upādhis and get rid of unnecessary thoughts in his mind. He should purposefully give up all unwarranted wishes and strive to remain in this neutral state. Such a seeker can attain Mokṣa by consistently practicing in this manner.

The term **Mokṣa** means liberation from all bondages. It also means liberation from illusions due to which one considers the bondage as real, freedom from dualities like joy and grief, freedom from life filled with the triads like knower-knowable-knowledge, and liberation from the cycle of life and death. Ordinary people are constrained by many bondages. The notable bondages are as follow:

- I am the body, and the world is mine.
- I am subject to birth, aging, and death.
- Happiness is found in worldly objects.
- The world is real the way it seems.
- I am the doer and enjoyer.
- I am happy or distressed.
- The divisions and differences in the surrounding world are real.

The Gita provides timeless guidance for liberation from all the above bondages. It teaches us how futile it is to grieve or suffer in life.

Some significant questions may arise in the seeker's mind at this stage. What would happen if one does not attain Mokṣa in this life? What difference does it make if one is not liberated?

What is that glory of enlightenment for which an ordinary person is expected to strive by deprioritizing his other worldly chores? Why run after the seemingly abstract or mirage-like illusory Bliss of Mokṣa when one can experience tangible happiness from many objects in the world? Why make a mountain out of a molehill while discussing griefs in human life and toil so much to avoid them? When there is no explicit splendor or grandeur in Mokṣa, why make an effort to conquer the mind and organs, and why deny oneself the readily available worldly luxuries? What is the proof that the concept of the cycle of birth-life-death-rebirth is real when it based on mere faith? Does the path of spirituality maliciously mask the traits like laziness, lethargy, and poverty? Is Mokṣa meant to be the goal for losers or pessimists?

These and similar questions have been systematically answered in the Bhagavad-Gita, Upaniṣads, and other texts composed by the enlightened saints. All these answers can be found by starting with an observation stated by St. Jñāneśwara. He says, "If one doesn't understand the importance of something, it becomes boring or uninteresting for him (*Jñāneśwari 18.1627*)." This fact holds true even in day-to-day life. E.g. an unaesthetic person has no interest in poetry, literature, or no affinity in any form of art. A person who arduously loves one sport may totally dislike the other. A simplistic person hates decorative or ornamental get-up. One who loves being at home dislikes traveling. A reticent person is repulsed by chatty or talkative people. Exactly analogous to this, many worldly people are reluctant to tread the spiritual path. The Bhagavad-Gita has accepted this inevitable reality of human life

**मनुष्याणां सहस्रेषु कश्चिद्यतति सिद्धये ।**
**यततामपि सिद्धानां कश्चिन्मां वेत्ति तत्त्वतः ॥ ७.३ ॥**

*Manuṣyāṇāṃ sahasreṣu kaścid yatati siddhaye* ।
*Yatatām api siddhānāṃ kaścin māṃ vetti tattvataḥ* ॥ *7.3* ॥

"(Lord Kṛṣṇa says) Out of many thousands of people hardly one strives for Self-realization; out of those so striving, hardly one attains Self-realization and knows My true nature, Brahman." St. Rāmadāsa says in his treatise Dāsabodha that it is rare to find a person with a conscientious, subtle, and Sāttvic mind. Most others are wavering, fickle, and superficial in nature. It is pointless to argue with them (*14.8.46*). The Gita says, "No wise man should create discord in the minds of ignorant people who are attached to action. He should not teach them about renunciation and the Knowledge of Brahman (*3.26*)."

Arjuna has many divine qualities; therefore, Lord Kṛṣṇa said that He would teach Arjuna many profound and mysterious secrets in the path of spirituality (*9.1*). It is hard to answer why some people like a game of football, and some don't. However, enlightened saints and God answer in their texts why some people like the path of spirituality and some don't. St. Tukārāma says, "Genuine interest in Lord Viṭṭhala or the path of spirituality is developed only as a result of benevolent and good deeds from many past births." Lord Kṛṣṇa says in the holy text Śrīmad Bhāgavatam –

**नरानां क्षीणपापानां कृष्णे भक्तिः प्रजायते ।**

*Narānāṃ kṣīṇapāpānāṃ Kṛṣṇe bhaktiḥ prajāyate* ।

"People – whose sins are attenuated – gradually start reveling in the devotion of Lord Kṛṣṇa." Thus, it can be deduced that a person who has not accumulated merits and whose sins are not attenuated will not revel in the devotion of Kṛṣṇa nor will he desire Mokṣa.

Man is the only animal in all sentient beings whose intellect is completely evolved. He is the epitome of the evolution of sentient life. It is evident that the intellectual development is not the same in all humans. Some men have plain animal instincts, while some are exceptionally brilliant. Some examples of supremely evolved people are Einstein in the field of science,

Shakespeare or Rabindranatha Tagore in the field of literature, Bach or Pt. Ravi Shankar in the field of music, Wordsworth or Kalidasa in the field of poetry, and Ādi Śaṅkara in the field of spirituality. At the same time, primitive people having animal-like instincts can still be found in the dense forests of Africa. Which intellect can be declared as the evolved intellect? Inquisitiveness is the hallmark of the human intellect. What kind of inquisitiveness can be considered the most sublime? Is it the curiosity about the surrounding world, or the curiosity about how to lead a happy life in this world, or the curiosity about knowing 'Who am I?' St. Tukārāma says, "The quest to know the true nature of the Self or 'I' is the most fundamental and complex quest of human life." The scriptures which teach the philosophy of Mokṣa have accepted this challenge. The question "Who am I?" has been settled long ago in the era of Upaniṣads. Extrovert people, who are merely curious about the external universe or who seek objects of pleasure, do not find it necessary to realize the primal question of human life – "Who am I?" Thomas Edison invented electricity and enabled mankind to see even in the night. The Gita, however, showed mankind their inner light which is the very substratum of all kinds of knowledge. People – who are enchanted and captivated by the external shine and glory – do not even remotely think about the inner Self-effulgence that is ever-available in the form of eternal, Pure Knowledge. It is, in fact, impossible to survive without this inner light even for a moment. However, most people are still bewitched only by the external extravaganza.

St. Tukārāma, the renowned enlightened aint from Maharashtra, says, "The deep cove of the world is full of Bliss, and the ripples of actions and reactions in it are Bliss themselves. I am immersed in this cove; my body is Bliss itself." A seeker has to have his intellect at least evolved to the extent where he can understand the vast divinity in this experience of St.

Tukārāma. Only then, he may appreciate what St. Tukārāma achieved by taking a backseat from the ephemeral worldly life and abandoning the short-lived pleasures. This is similar to the case where some unfortunate people, who could not even dream of going to the moon, thought that the video of man's epic voyage to the moon was fabricated. People who are accustomed to the constant game of actions and reactions cannot imagine the quality of peaceful life. They perceive peaceful life as insipid, dull, tasteless, boring, unexciting, and passive. They can hardly see that the life which is quiet and peaceful can be truly happy and joyous. People who have an affinity towards the busy, hurried, and bustling life may find it challenging to live in a minimalistic and measured manner.

After listening to the philosophy of the Gita, even Arjuna says, "By Lord Kṛṣṇa's grace My delusion is eradicated, and I have regained memory about my true nature and my duties (*18.73*)." The true nature of every Jiva is Pure Bliss. Towards the end, Arjuna was able to not only learn that his true Self is Brahman which pervades the body and beyond, but he also wholeheartedly accepted his duty – as an embodied being in the role of a warrior – to fight the righteous war.

Happiness derived from worldly objects is so enticing and captivating that it does not let a person even think about the shortcomings of such happiness and get an insight about the very root of its origin. The Gita (*2.14*) says that objects of pleasure are transient; they are created, sustained for some time, and eventually destroyed. There are five types of sense perceptions: sound, touch, form, taste, and smell (***Pañca-Viṣayas**: śabda, sparśa, rūpa, rasa,* and *gandha*). A flower has a scent, which only exists for some time. The scent vanishes the moment the flower dries up. The flower itself dies. Even when the flower is fresh, an old or weak person is unable to smell it due to his weak senses. Also, it is boring for any person to smell the same flower repeatedly. People who are allergic to pollens cannot enjoy the smell despite having efficient senses. All of these are the shortcomings of the pleasure derived from the senses. Another example is that of sound. Ears can hear words. Praise makes a person happy, while criticism causes grief. Even if other people ignore the person and remain silent, the negligence can cause distress to the person. The other three senses i.e. eyes, skin, tongue, and their respective objects can be analyzed in the same manner.

Before enjoying objects of pleasure, one must endure some discomfort, irritation, or even pain due to the effort required to acquire that object, but not many people pay heed to that suffering. E.g. to attend a music concert, a person needs to spend money prior to the event and get the tickets. On the day of the show, he has to drive through heavy traffic, find a parking lot, and make efforts to reach the venue on time. Staying up late in the night and enjoying soft-drinks or coffee in the intermission may cause acidity the next day. The person who wants to derive pleasure from that concert has to sit tightly in a closed space for three hours. He has to pretend he likes the concert even if he is not familiar with the music. If he gets the seat in a back row with a lower value ticket, it brings a shade of inferiority to his mind. If the orchestra is not performing well, or not playing his favorite songs, he feels bored and repents why he bought the tickets in the first place. This musical evening affects his efficiency and productivity the next day. These are various kinds of discomforts and sufferings associated with the so-called joyful event of attending a music concert. In short, such pleasure cannot be considered lasting, unadulterated, unqualified Pure Bliss.

There are five more objects of pleasure: power, wealth, success, fame, and prestige. In Sanskrit, they are called ***Viṣaya***. The root Viṣa (विष) in Sanskrit means bondage. Viṣaya is that which binds a person, mandates him to depend on the object, and gets him addicted in a gradual manner. All humans are more or less bound or confined by the ten objects mentioned so far. All people get their own share of objects; some get more while some get less. This gives rise to suffering born out of comparison, competition, envy, jealousy, anguish, criticism, and hatred.

The doctrine of Vedānta states that the mind (*Añtaḥkaraṇa*) becomes quiet and completely disappears in Ātman when a person is experiencing an object of his liking. As a result, Pure Bliss of Ātman gets manifested. The person mistakenly assumes that he felt happy by enjoying the external object; however, it is nothing but the manifestation of ever-existent and ever-available Pure Bliss which is the very nature of every being. Enlightened people know it. Those who do not understand the very gist or source of happiness spend their entire life chasing external objects and accumulating them with the hope and impression that more objects will bring more happiness.

There is no question of glorifying suffering in life. Every Jiva invariably gets his share of suffering as dictated by his destiny (Prārabdha). Many factors like injuries, diseases, death, poverty, dishonor, anger, loss, fear, worry, envy, resentment, failure, revenge, bitterness, etc. cause grief in life. There are many more reasons for suffering, such as disputes in house, an irresponsible son, a daughter having a failed marriage, selfish relatives, demanding or troublesome judiciary system, annoying neighbor, deficiency of objects, repairs in house, etc. The Bhagavad-Gita gives excellent guidance to handle distress in these situations with the help of a composed mind.

**रागद्वेषवियुक्तैस्तु विषयानिन्द्रियैश्चरन् ।**
**आत्मवश्यैर्विधेयात्मा प्रसादमधिगच्छति ॥ २.६४ ॥**

*Rāgadveṣavimuktais tu viṣayān indriyaiś caran* ।
*Ātmavaśyair vidheyātmā prasādam adhigacchati* ॥ *2.64* ॥

"Complete satisfaction and peace is attained by the one who feels neither attachment nor hatred towards material objects and conquers his organs from seeking objects even when surrounded by objects." Every person, knowingly or unknowingly, seeks to be happy because Pure Bliss of Ātman is his very nature. Grief is like a visitor, so nobody desires it. But when a person associates himself with the body and the world, it invariably gives rise to suffering in his mind. Bṛhadāraṇyaka Upaniṣad has mentioned a key principle of life –

**आत्मनस्तु कामाय सर्वं प्रियं भवति ।**

*Atmanastu kāmāya sarvaṃ priyaṃ bhavati* । *(Bru. 2.4.5)*

"The feeling of love for others is ultimately for one's own happiness, not for the pleasure of others." Everyone tries to be happy in his or her own way. This trait inevitably leads to conflict with others since everyone has a different take on happiness. Such conflict gives rise to many subsequent griefs. A person can only minimize the chances of conflict from his side in such situations. The Gita says –

**आपूर्यमाणमचलप्रतिष्ठं समुद्रमापः प्रविशन्ति यद्वत् ।**
**तद्वत्कामा यं प्रविशन्ति सर्वे स शान्तिमाप्नोति न कामकामी ॥ २.७० ॥**

*Āpūryamāṇam acalapratiṣṭhaṃ Samudrām āpaḥ praviśanti yadvat* ।
*Tadvatkāmā yaṃ praviśantisarve Sa śāntimāpnoti na kāmakāmī* ॥2.70

"Water enters the ocean from many sides, but the ocean remains unaffected and does not ever cross its boundaries. Likewise, only that person can revel in Pure Bliss and true serenity whose inner peace is unaffected even when many objects of pleasure enter his life." On the contrary, a person who chases the objects of pleasure does not attain that kind of perpetual inner peace.

Indeed, the attainment of Mokṣa does not depend on whether one has a prosperous, wealthy life or not. St. Tukārāma Mahārāja was penniless for most of his life. St. Ekanātha Mahārāja was a landlord, and King Janaka was an emperor. All of them were enlightened saints. They denied the very necessity of worldly objects for their happiness. St. Tukārāma found lasting Bliss in his beloved Lord Viṭṭhala. Emperor Janaka definitively knew that the joy derived from objects is Pure Bliss of Ātman, his true Self.

Every seeker needs to conquer his mind and organs. Without that, he feels no inclination to explore and pursue the eternal, Pure Bliss of Ātman i.e. *Ānanda*. The seeker is supposed to disregard the trivial gains in day-to-day life to achieve higher goals. If he gets caught in mundane pleasures derived from objects, he does not feel any desire to attain higher, better, and lasting happiness.

The concept of rebirth should be accepted through faith and logic. Faith in scriptures can help us establish belief in the concept of rebirth. The Gita (*2.22*) and Kaṭha Upaniṣad (*2.1.10*) explicitly state the concept of rebirth. Faith is an essential virtue in the spiritual path. The seeker must accept the concepts of Jiva, Ātman, Īśvara, Brahman and Mokṣa through faith initially and continue his spiritual pursuit. When the seeker attains firm, direct Self-realization, he does not need to accept the concepts above on mere faith. The fact that "I am Brahman" becomes a living reality for him. Similarly, he can initially accept the concept of rebirth by keeping faith in scriptures. He can also logically deduce the possibility of rebirth just by observing human life even without taking the support of scriptures. Twin brothers are conceived, born, and brought up in the same circumstances, but both of them grow up to be completely different personalities. The only reason for this must be different actions executed by them in past births. Dr. Ian Stevenson, a Canadian born US psychiatrist, has established the fact of reincarnation based on scientific study and evidence.

At times, dejected, lost, lazy, hopeless, incompetent, thoughtless, and inefficient people take refuge in the shelter of spirituality; however, this is not the fault of spiritual scriptures. When powerful, wealthy people enter the field of academics, criminals enter politics, selfish people enter cooperative departments, and ruthless people enter the medical profession, it is not the fault of that profession. People who are afflicted by calamities and those who are matured by the awakening of ability to discriminate between real and unreal due to past merits – both tread the path of spirituality. There are examples of both attaining the highest goal of Mokṣa. E.g. St. Tukārāma has described his extreme poverty in some of his compositions. On the other side, the six seekers of Mokṣa in Praśnopaniṣada were successful and well-established in their life. These examples substantiate the fact that the field of spirituality is open for one and all.

This text is an effort to write a commentary on this timeless, magnificent scripture which is called the Bhagavad-Gita. It is intentional not to script this text like a discourse or a lecture. The core purpose of this commentary is to describe the verses of the Gita purely from the perspective of helping seekers get ready for spiritual pursuit and implement the teachings of the Gita in day-to-day life. Many other eminent scholars have written detailed commentaries on each verse of the Gita. This text does not intend to add to them. Still, most verses are addressed in this book. I sincerely hope that this commentary will be useful to genuine seekers of Mokṣa.

**Dr. Shrikrishna Deshmukh**

Chapter 1

# Arjuna's dilemma and lamentation

## ॥ अर्जुनविषादयोगः (Arjunaviṣādayogaḥ) ॥

Arjuna's dilemma and lamentation have been described in the preface of this commentary. The essence of the first verse, '*Dharmakṣetre Kurukṣetre*,' has been discussed from a seeker's perspective in the same section. Most seekers lead a worldly life, just like Pāṇḍavas. Very few are celibates or monks. The cousins of the Kuru Dynasty – Kauravas and Pāṇḍavas – fought an epic battle for two reasons: first, Yudhiṣṭhīra lost the game of dice and his kingdom due to treachery; and second, Duryodhana and Duhśāsana harbored insatiable greed for sovereign power over the kingdom. They refused to return the kingdom to Yudhiṣṭhīra even when the conditions laid down in the game were fulfilled. Even today, people fight or even kill each other for many domestic reasons and end up going to court. Such fights are inescapable especially when members in a family share the same profession, business, or property. If by chance, a genuinely righteous and Sāttvic seeker is a part of such a group of people, he is not supposed to fall prey to treachery like Yudhiṣṭhīra. If indeed such a situation arises where he must face a conflict with his clan, he should not be inclined to renounce his worldly life like Arjuna. Instead, he is expected to garner support from those who can fight on his side for justice. He should attempt every strategy to defeat the unjust side.

St. Gondavalekara, the well-known saint from Mahārāṣṭra, contested a court-case against his brother who had wrongfully encroached his land. But, on a personal level, he continued being affectionate to his brother even when the case was being actively debated in court. This is a great example to keep in mind for dealing with injustice. When conflict arises, a person should not succumb to the pressure but instead rise to the occasion. He should not pay heed to who is favoring the unjust side. The second chapter discusses in detail the spiritual perspective required for dealing with such situations.

**Dhṛtarāṣtra's question about the war**

*धृतराष्ट्र उवाच ।*
**धर्मक्षेत्रे कुरुक्षेत्रे समवेता युयुत्सवः ।**
**मामकाः पाण्डवाश्चैव किमकुर्वत सञ्जय ॥ १ ॥**

*Dhṛtarāṣṭra uvāca* ।
*Dharmakṣetre kurukṣetre samavetā yuyutsavaḥ* ।
*Māmakāḥ pāṇḍavāś caiva kim akurvata sañjaya* ॥ *1* ॥

**Meaning:** (Dhṛtarāṣṭra said) O Sanjaya! Tell me, what did my sons and the sons of Pāṇḍu do when they assembled on the holy field of Kurukṣetra to fight the war?

**Sanjaya's description of the setting of the battlefield**

*सञ्जय उवाच ।*
**दृष्ट्वा तु पाण्डवानीकं व्यूढं दुर्योधनस्तदा ।**
**आचार्यमुपसङ्गम्य राजा वचनमब्रवीत् ॥ २ ॥**

*Sañjaya uvāca* ।
*Dṛṣṭvā tu pāṇḍavānīkaṃ vyūḍhaṃ duryodhanas tadā* ।
*Ācāryam upasaṅgamya rājā vacanam abravīt* ॥ *2* ॥

**Meaning:** (Sanjaya said) After seeing the army of Pāṇḍavas arranged in a battle phalanx, King Duryodhana approached his teacher Droṇācārya and spoke the following words –

**Duryodhana's request to Droṇācārya**

**पश्यैतां पाण्डुपुत्राणामाचार्य महतीं चमूम् ।**
**व्यूढां द्रुपदपुत्रेण तव शिष्येण धीमता ॥ ३ ॥**

*Paśyaitāṃ pāṇḍuputrāṇām ācārya mahatīṃ camūm* ।
*Vyūḍhāṃ drūpadaputreṇa tava śiṣyeṇa dhīmatā* ॥ *3* ॥

**Meaning:** (Duryodhana said) O respected teacher! Behold the mighty army of Pāṇḍavas arranged in a military phalanx by your brilliant disciple, the son of Dṛpada!

Here Duryodhana tried to incite Droṇācārya for war in two ways: first, by mentioning the name 'Dṛpada', he reminded Droṇācārya that Droṇācārya's personal enemy is against him; and second, by stating that Dṛpada's son – who is Droṇācārya's disciple – is also fighting against Droṇācārya.

**The description of the main warriors in Pāṇḍava's army**

अत्र शूरा महेष्वासा भीमार्जुनसमा युधि ।
युयुधानो विराटश्च द्रुपदश्च महारथः ॥ ४ ॥
धृष्टकेतुश्चेकितानः काशिराजश्च वीर्यवान् ।
पुरुजित्कुन्तिभोजश्च शैब्यश्च नरपुङ्गवः ॥ ५ ॥
युधामन्युश्च विक्रान्त उत्तमौजाश्च वीर्यवान् ।
सौभद्रो द्रौपदेयाश्च सर्व एव महारथाः ॥ ६ ॥

*Atra śūrā maheṣvāsā bhīmārjunasamā yudhi* ।
*Yuyudhāno virāṭaśca drūpadaś ca mahārathaḥ* ॥ *4* ॥
*Dhṛṣṭaketuś cekitānaḥ kāśirājaś ca vīryavān* ।
*Purujit kuntibhojaś ca śaibyaś ca narapuṅgavaḥ* ॥ *5* ॥
*Yudhāmanyuś ca vikrānta uttamaujāś ca vīryavān* ।
*Saubhadro draupadeyāś ca sarva eva mahārathāḥ* ॥ *6* ॥

**Meaning:** In this army, there are mighty bowmen like Arjuna, Bhīma, powerful warriors like Sātyaki, Virāṭa, Dṛpada, Dhṛṣṭaketu, Cekitāna, the valiant Kāśiraja, Purujita, Kuntibhoja, the indomitable Śaibya, the dauntless Yudhāmanyu, the tenacious Uttamaujā, Subhadrā's son Abhimanyu, and stalwarts like Draupadi's five sons.

**Duryodhana's recount of the special warriors in his army**

अस्माकं तु विशिष्टा ये तान्निबोध द्विजोत्तम ।
नायका मम सैन्यस्य सञ्ज्ञार्थं तान्ब्रवीमि ते ॥ ७ ॥
भवान्भीष्मश्च कर्णश्च कृपश्च समितिञ्जयः ।
अश्वत्थामा विकर्णश्च सौमदत्तिस्तथैव च ॥ ८ ॥
अन्ये च बहवः शूरा मदर्थे त्यक्तजीविताः ।
नानाशस्त्रप्रहरणाः सर्वे युद्धविशारदाः ॥ ९ ॥

*Asmākaṃ tu viśiṣṭā ye tān nibodha dvijottama* ।
*Nāyakā mama sainyasya saṃjñārthaṃ tān bravīmi te* ॥ *7* ॥
*Bhavān bhīṣmaś ca karṇaś ca kṛpaś ca samitiñjayaḥ* ।
*Aśvatthāmā vikarṇaś ca saumadattis tathaiva ca* ॥ *8* ॥
*Anye ca bahavaḥ śūrā madarthe tyaktajīvitāḥ* ।
*Nānāśastrapraharaṇāḥ sarve yuddhaviśāradāḥ* ॥ *9* ॥

**Meaning:** O best of Brāhmins! Also, note the specially qualified leaders in our army. I will recount the names of those courageous warriors for your information. Yourself, Bhīṣma, Karṇa, the always victorious Kṛpa, Vikarṇa, Aśvatthāma, and Somadatta's son Bhūriśrava are great warriors. Many other brave fighters are proficient in war tactics, equipped with various weapons, and ready to risk their lives for my sake.

**Duryodhana's comparison of his army with Pāṇḍava's army**

अपर्याप्तं तदस्माकं बलं भीष्माभिरक्षितम् ।
पर्याप्तं त्विदमेतेषां बलं भीमाभिरक्षितम् ॥ १० ॥

*Aparyāptaṃ tad asmākaṃ balaṃ bhīṣmābhirakṣitam* ।
*Paryāptaṃ tvidam eteṣāṃ balaṃ bhīmābhirakṣitam* ॥ *10* ॥

**Meaning:** Our army is brilliantly protected by commander Bhīṣma from all sides, and it is invincible. Pāṇḍava's army protected by Bhīma is limited, and it is easy to conquer.

**Duryodhana's appeal**

अयनेषु च सर्वेषु यथाभागमवस्थिताः ।
भीष्ममेवाभिरक्षन्तु भवन्तः सर्व एव हि ॥ ११ ॥

*Ayaneṣu ca sarveṣu yathābhāgam avasthitāḥ* ।
*Bhīṣmam evābhirakṣantu bhavantaḥ sarva eva hi* ॥ *11* ॥

**Meaning:** All of you must be stationed in your respective formations as per the designated divisions of the army to give full protection to Bhīṣma alone.

**The loud blow of the conch and other war instruments**

तस्य सञ्जनयन्हर्षं कुरुवृद्धः पितामहः ।
सिंहनादं विनद्योच्चैः शङ्खं दध्मौ प्रतापवान् ॥ १२ ॥
ततः शङ्खाश्च भेर्यश्च पणवानकगोमुखाः ।
सहसैवाभ्यहन्यन्त स शब्दस्तुमुलोऽभवत् ॥ १३ ॥

*Tasya sañjanayan harṣaṃ kuruvṛddhaḥ pitāmahaḥ* ।
*Siṃhanādaṃ vinadyocchaiḥ śaṅkhaṃ dadhmau pratāpavān* ॥*12*॥
*Tataḥ śaṅkhāś ca bheryaś ca paṇavānakagomukhāḥ* ।
*Sahasaivābhyahanyanta sa śabdas tumulo'bhavat* ॥ *13* ॥

**Meaning:** The elderly and valiant grandsire of Kauravas – Bhīṣma – loudly blew the conch roaring like a lion due to which Duryodhana became joyful. Thereafter, conch-shells, bugles, cow-horns, trumpets, and drums were resounded simultaneously, creating a tumultuous sound together.

**The loud blow of the conch by Pāṇḍavas and their warriors**

ततः श्वेतैर्हयैर्युक्ते महति स्यन्दने स्थितौ ।
माधवः पाण्डवश्चैव दिव्यौ शङ्खौ प्रदध्मतुः ॥ १४ ॥
पाञ्चजन्यं हृषीकेशो देवदत्तं धनञ्जयः ।
पौण्ड्रं दध्मौ महाशङ्खं भीमकर्मा वृकोदरः ॥ १५ ॥
अनन्तविजयं राजा कुन्तीपुत्रो युधिष्ठिरः ।
नकुलः सहदेवश्च सुघोषमणिपुष्पकौ ॥ १६ ॥
काश्यश्च परमेष्वासः शिखण्डी च महारथः ।
धृष्टद्युम्नो विराटश्च सात्यकिश्चापराजितः ॥ १७ ॥
द्रुपदो द्रौपदेयाश्च सर्वशः पृथिवीपते ।
सौभद्रश्च महाबाहुः शङ्खान्दध्मुः पृथक्पृथक् ॥ १८ ॥

*Tataḥ śvetair hayair yukte mahati syandane sthitau ।*
*Mādhavaḥ pāṇḍavaś caiva divyau śaṅkhau pradaghmatuḥ ॥ 14 ॥*
*Pāñcajanyaṃ hṛṣīkeśo devādattaṃ dhanañjayaḥ ।*
*Pauṇḍraṃ dadhmau mahāśaṅkhaṃ bhīmakarmā vṛkodaraḥ ॥15॥*
*Anañtavijayaṃ rājā kuntīputro yudhiṣṭhiraḥ ।*
*Nakulaḥ sahadevaś ca sughoṣamaṇipuṣpakau ॥ 16 ॥*
*Kāśyaś ca parameṣvāsaḥ śikhaṇḍī ca mahārathaḥ ।*
*Dhṛṣṭadyumno virāṭaś ca sātyakiś cāparājitaḥ ॥ 17 ॥*
*Drūpado draupadeyāś ca sarvaśaḥ pṛthivīpate ।*
*Saubhadraś ca mahābāhuḥ śaṅkhān dadhmuḥ pṛthakpṛthak ॥18॥*

**Meaning:** Thereafter, Lord Kṛṣṇa and Arjuna, seated in a magnificent chariot harnessing white horses, blew their divine conches. Śrīkṛṣṇa, the Lord of the mind and senses, blew the Pañcajanya; Arjuna blew the Devadutta; and Bhīma, the doer of incredible actions, blew the conch named Pouṇḍra. King Yudhiṣṭhīra, the son of Kunti, blew the Anantavijaya; Nakula blew the Sughośa; and Sahadeva blew the Maṇipuṣpaka conch-shell. Similarly, the expert archer King of Kāśi, resolute Śikhanḍi, Dhṛṣṭadyumna, Virāṭa, the invincible Sātyaki, Dṛpada, Abhimanyu – the mighty armed son of Subhadrā, the five sons of Draupadi, and Arjuna – all blew their respective conch-shells from different positions.

## The impact of roaring conch sounds on the Kaurava's army

स घोषो धार्तराष्ट्राणां हृदयानि व्यदारयत् ।
नभश्च पृथिवीं चैव तुमुलो व्यनुनादयन् ॥ १९ ॥

*Sa ghoṣo dhārtarāṣṭrāṇāṃ hṛdayāni vyadārayat ।*
*Nabhaś ca pṛthivīṃ caiva tumulo vyanunādayan ॥ 19 ॥*

**Meaning:** The uproarious sound reverberating through the sky and earth pierced the hearts of Kauravas, the sons of Dhṛtarāṣṭra.

## Arjuna's request to Śrīkṛṣṇa

अथ व्यवस्थितान्दृष्ट्वा धार्तराष्ट्रान् कपिध्वजः ।
प्रवृत्ते शस्त्रसम्पाते धनुरुद्यम्य पाण्डवः ॥ २० ॥

हृषीकेशं तदा वाक्यमिदमाह महीपते ।
*अर्जुन उवाच ।*
सेनयोरुभयोर्मध्ये रथं स्थापय मेऽच्युत ॥ २१ ॥
यावदेतान्निरीक्षेऽहं योद्धुकामानवस्थितान् ।
कैर्मया सह योद्धव्यमस्मिन्रणसमुद्यमे ॥ २२ ॥
योत्स्यमानानवेक्षेऽहं य एतेऽत्र समागताः ।
धार्तराष्ट्रस्य दुर्बुद्धेर्युद्धे प्रियचिकीर्षवः ॥ २३ ॥

*Atha vyavasthitān dṛṣṭvā dhārtarāṣṭrān.h kapidhvajaḥ* ।
*Pravṛtte śastrasampāte dhanur udyamya pāṇḍavaḥ* ॥ *20* ॥
*Hṛṣīkeśaṃ tadā vākyam idam āha mahīpate* ।
*Arjuna uvāca* ।
*Senayor ubhayor madhye rathaṃ sthāpaya me'cyuta* ॥ *21* ॥
*Yāvad etān nirikṣe'haṃ yoddhukāmān avasthitān* ।
*Kair mayā saha yoddhavyam asmin raṇasamudyame* ॥ *22* ॥
*Yotsyamānān avekṣe'haṃ ya ete'tra samāgatāḥ* ।
*Dhārtarāṣṭrasya durbuddher yuddhe priyacikīrṣavaḥ* ॥ *23* ॥

**Meaning:** (Sanjaya said) O King, the sons of Dhṛtarāṣṭra are all geared up to commence the war, and the time has come to fight with weapons. Seeing that, Arjuna, whose banner was ensigned with Lord Hanumāna, lifted his bow and said these words to Śrīkṛṣṇa, "O Acyuta! Please place my chariot in the center of the two armies. Station it there as long as I wish to behold the warriors arrayed on battlefield and decide with whom I must wage this war. I will inspect the warriors who have assembled here intent on pleasing the evil-minded Duryodhana."

## The dialogue between Lord Kṛṣṇa and Arjuna

*सञ्जय उवाच ।*
एवमुक्तो हृषीकेशो गुडाकेशेन भारत ।
सेनयोरुभयोर्मध्ये स्थापयित्वा रथोत्तमम् ॥ २४ ॥
भीष्मद्रोणप्रमुखतः सर्वेषां च महीक्षिताम् ।
उवाच पार्थ पश्यैतान् समवेतान्कुरूनिति ॥ २५ ॥

*Sañjaya uvāca* ।
*Evam ukto hṛṣīkeśo guḍākeśena bhārata* ।
*Senayor ubhayor madhye sthāpayitvā rathottamam* ॥ *24* ॥
*Bhīṣmadroṇapramukhataḥ sarveṣāṃ ca mahīkṣitām* ।
*Uvāca pārtha paśyaitān samavetān kurūn iti* ॥ *25* ॥

**Meaning:** Thus, being addressed by Arjuna, Lord Kṛṣṇa drew up that finest chariot in the center of both the armies and placed it in front of Bhīṣma, Droṇa, and other rulers. Thereafter, Kṛṣṇa said, "Arjuna, carefully behold these Kauravas assembled here for this war."

**Arjuna's lamentation after observing his close relatives**

तत्रापश्यत्स्थितान्पार्थः पितॄनथ पितामहान् ।
आचार्यान्मातुलान्भ्रातॄन्पुत्रान्पौत्रान्सखींस्तथा ॥ २६ ॥
श्वशुरान्सुहृदश्चैव सेनयोरुभयोरपि ।
तान्समीक्ष्य स कौन्तेयः सर्वान्बन्धूनवस्थितान् ॥ २७ ॥
कृपया परयाविष्टो विषीदन्निदमब्रवीत् ।
*अर्जुन उवाच ।*
दृष्ट्वेमं स्वजनं कृष्ण युयुत्सुं समुपस्थितम् ॥ २८ ॥
सीदन्ति मम गात्राणि मुखं च परिशुष्यति ।
वेपथुश्च शरीरे मे रोमहर्षश्च जायते ॥ २९ ॥
गाण्डीवं स्रंसते हस्तात्त्वक्चैव परिदह्यते ।
न च शक्नोम्यवस्थातुं भ्रमतीव च मे मनः ॥ ३० ॥
निमित्तानि च पश्यामि विपरीतानि केशव ।
न च श्रेयोऽनुपश्यामि हत्वा स्वजनमाहवे ॥ ३१ ॥

*Tatrāpaśyat sthitān pārthaḥ pitṛn atha pitāmahān* ।
*Ācāryān mātulān bhrātṛn putrān pautrān sakhīṃs tathā* ॥ *26* ॥
*Śvaśurān suhṛdaś caiva senayor ubhayor api* ।
*Tān samīkṣya sa kaunteyaḥ sarvān bandhūn avasthitān* ॥ *27* ॥
*Kṛpayā parayāviṣṭo viṣīdann idamabravīt* ।
*Arjuna uvāca* ।
*Dṛṣṭvemaṃ svajanaṃ kṛṣṇa yuyutsuṃ samupasthitam* ॥ *28* ॥
*Sīdanti mama gātrāṇi mukhañ ca pariśuṣyati* ।
*Vepathuś ca śarīre me romaharṣaś ca jāyate* ॥ *29* ॥

*Gāṇḍīvaṃ straṃsate hastāt tvak caiva paridahyate* ।
*Na ca śaknomy avasthātuṃ bhramatīva ca me manaḥ* ॥ *30* ॥
*Nimittāni ca paśyāmi viparītāni keśava* ।
*Na ca śreyo'nupaśyāmi hatvā svajanam āhave* ॥ *31* ॥

**Meaning:** Thereafter, Arjuna observed his uncles, grandfathers, teachers, maternal uncles, brothers, sons, grandsons, friends, fathers-in-law, acquaintances, and well-wishers. Overwhelmed with deep compassion and stricken with grief, Arjuna, the son of Kunti, said, "O Kṛṣṇa! Seeing these people assembled in the battleground with a desire to fight the war, my mouth is getting dry, my body is trembling, my organs are weakening, and this scene is making my hair stand on end. My bow Gāṇḍīva is slipping from these hands, and my skin is burning all over. I am unable to stand here in a composed manner. My mind is in a delusional state. O Keśava! I see ominous indicators everywhere. I don't see any good in killing my kinsmen in this battle."

**Arjuna lost his desire for kingdom, victory, and happiness**

**न काङ्क्षे विजयं कृष्ण न च राज्यं सुखानि च ।**
**किं नो राज्येन गोविन्द किं भोगैर्जीवितेन वा ॥ ३२ ॥**

*Na kāṅkṣe vijayaṃ kṛṣṇa na ca rājyaṃ sukhāni ca* ।
*Kiṃ no rājyena govinda kiṃ bhogair jīvitena vā* ॥ *32* ॥

**Meaning:** O Kṛṣṇa! I do not desire victory nor the kingdom nor even happiness. O Govinda! What would I gain by acquiring the kingdom? Of what avail are all materialistic pleasures? What is the use of life itself?

**Arjuna's reluctance to destroy his clan**

**येषामर्थे काङ्क्षितं नो राज्यं भोगाः सुखानि च ।**
**त इमेऽवस्थिता युद्धे प्राणांस्त्यक्त्वा धनानि च ॥ ३३ ॥**
**आचार्याः पितरः पुत्रास्तथैव च पितामहाः ।**
**मातुलाः श्वशुराः पौत्राः श्यालाः सम्बन्धिनस्तथा ॥ ३४ ॥**

एतान्न हन्तुमिच्छामि घ्नतोऽपि मधुसूदन।
अपि त्रैलोक्यराज्यस्य हेतोः किं नु महीकृते ॥ ३५ ॥

*Yeṣām arthe kāṅkṣitaṃ no rājyaṃ bhogāḥ sukhāni ca ।*
*Ta ime 'vasthitā yuddhe prāṇāṃs tyaktvā dhanāni ca ॥ 33 ॥*
*Ācāryāḥ pitaraḥ putrās tathaiva ca pitāmahāḥ ।*
*Mātulāḥ śvaśurāḥ pautrāḥ śyālāḥ sambandhinas tathā ॥ 34 ॥*
*Etān na hantum icchhāmi ghnato 'pi madhusūdana ।*
*Api trailokyarājyasya hetoḥ kiṃ nu mahīkṛte ॥ 35 ॥*

**Meaning:** Our own people for whom we desire this kingdom, enjoyments, and worldly pleasures stand here on the battleground without the slightest concern for their life and wealth. Our teachers, uncles, sons, grandfathers, maternal uncles, fathers-in-law, grandsons, brothers-in-law, and many other relatives are present here in this place. They are ready to kill me, but O Madhusūdana! I have no desire to kill them even for the rulership of the three planes, much less for the sake of ruling the earth.

## Arjuna's arguments for not fighting the war

निहत्य धार्तराष्ट्रान्नः का प्रीतिः स्याज्जनार्दन।
पापमेवाश्रयेदस्मान्हत्वैतानाततायिनः ॥ ३६ ॥
तस्मान्नार्हा वयं हन्तुं धार्तराष्ट्रान्स्वबान्धवान्।
स्वजनं हि कथं हत्वा सुखिनः स्याम माधव ॥ ३७ ॥
यद्यप्येते न पश्यन्ति लोभोपहतचेतसः।
कुलक्षयकृतं दोषं मित्रद्रोहे च पातकम् ॥ ३८ ॥
कथं न ज्ञेयमस्माभिः पापादस्मान्निवर्तितुम्।
कुलक्षयकृतं दोषं प्रपश्यद्भिर्जनार्दन ॥ ३९ ॥
कुलक्षये प्रणश्यन्ति कुलधर्माः सनातनाः।
धर्मे नष्टे कुलं कृत्स्नमधर्मोऽभिभवत्युत ॥ ४० ॥
अधर्माभिभवात्कृष्ण प्रदुष्यन्ति कुलस्त्रियः।
स्त्रीषु दुष्टासु वार्ष्णेय जायते वर्णसङ्करः ॥ ४१ ॥
सङ्करो नरकायैव कुलघ्नानां कुलस्य च।
पतन्ति पितरो ह्येषां लुप्तपिण्डोदकक्रियाः ॥ ४२ ॥

**दोषैरेतैः कुलघ्नानां वर्णसङ्करकारकैः ।**
**उत्साद्यन्ते जातिधर्माः कुलधर्माश्च शाश्वताः ॥ ४३ ॥**
**उत्सन्नकुलधर्माणां मनुष्याणां जनार्दन ।**
**नरकेऽनियतं वासो भवतीत्यनुशुश्रुम ॥ ४४ ॥**

*Nihatya dhārtarāṣṭrān naḥ kā prītiḥ syājanārdana* ।
*Pāpam evāśrayed asmān hatvaitān ātatāyinaḥ* ॥ *36* ॥
*Tasmān nārhā vayaṃ hantuṃ dhārtarāṣṭrān svabāndhavān* ।
*Svajanaṃ hi kathaṃ hatvā sukhinaḥ syāma mādhava* ॥ *37* ॥
*Yadyapyete na paśyanti lobhopahatacetasaḥ* ।
*Kulakṣayakṛtaṃ doṣaṃ mitradrohe ca pātakam* ॥ *38* ॥
*Kaṭhaṃ na jñeyam asmābhiḥ pāpād asmān nivartitum* ।
*Kulakṣayakṛtaṃ doṣaṃ prapaśyadbhir janārdana* ॥ *39* ॥
*Kulakṣaye praṇaśyanti kuladharmāḥ sanātanāḥ* ।
*Dharme naṣṭe kulaṃ kṛtsnam adharmo'bhibhavaty uta* ॥ *40* ॥
*Adharmābhibhavāt kṛṣṇa praduṣyanti kulastriyaḥ* ।
*Strīṣu duṣṭāsu vārṣṇeya jāyate varṇasaṅkaraḥ* ॥ *41* ॥
*Saṅkaro narakāyaiva kulaghnānāṃ kulasya ca* ।
*Patanti pitaro hy eṣāṃ luptapiṇḍodakakriyāḥ* ॥ *42* ॥
*Doṣair etaiḥ kulaghnānāṃ varṇasaṅkarakārakaiḥ* ।
*Utsādyante jātidharmāḥ kuladharmāś ca śāśvatāḥ* ॥ *43* ॥
*Utsannakuladharmāṇāṃ manuṣyāṇāṃ janārdana* ।
*Narake'niyataṃ vāso bhavatīty anuśuśruma* ॥ *44* ॥

**Meaning:** What good would we achieve by slaying Duryodhana and the likes? We would only incur sins by killing these aggressors. O Mādhava, how can we ever be happy by killing our own brothers? This is why it is not appropriate to kill them. The minds of these people are corrupted by the greed of the kingdom. They are unable to see the demerit in destruction of their lineage and the sin in betraying their friends. O Janārdana! Why should we not refrain from sinning despite seeing the clear crime in destroying our lineage? If the dynasty is destroyed, it results in perishing of the ancient spiritual and religious traditions of the clan. Then Adharma i.e. unrighteousness, sin, and immorality spread through the entire family. O Kṛṣṇa! Thus, with the proliferation of sins, women in the family become degraded, and that leads to the intermingling of castes due to which undesirable progeny comes into existence. This leads the family and destroyers of the family to hell. The ancestors also go to hell due to such progeny. They are deprived of the post-death rituals like offerings of food and water. Such evil deeds result in the destruction of the religious rites pertaining to the caste and nobility of the lineage. And O Janārdana! We have heard that people for whom the spiritual family traditions are destroyed perish in hell for an unknown period.

## It is better to get slain than to perform such sinful acts

अहो बत महत्पापं कर्तुं व्यवसिता वयम् ।
यद्राज्यसुखलोभेन हन्तुं स्वजनमुद्यताः ॥ ४५ ॥
यदि मामप्रतीकारमशस्त्रं शस्त्रपाणयः ।
धार्तराष्ट्रा रणे हन्युस्तन्मे क्षेमतरं भवेत् ॥ ४६ ॥

*Aho bata mahat pāpaṃ kartuṃ vyavasitā vayam* ।
*Yad rājyasukhalobhena hantuṃ svajanam udyatāḥ* ॥ *45* ॥
*Yadi mām apratīkāram aśastraṃ śastrapāṇayaḥ* ।
*Dhārtarāṣṭrā raṇe hanyus tan me kṣemataraṃ bhavet* ॥ *46* ॥

**Meaning:** Alas! How distressful it is that we have resolved to kill our kin due to the greed of ruling the kingdom and enjoying pleasures, and thereby we are bent on committing a colossal sin. If the sons of Dhṛtarāṣṭra armed with many weapons in hand slay me – unarmed and unresisting – in battle, it will still be highly beneficial for me.

## The renunciation of weapons by grieved Arjuna

*सञ्जय उवाच ।*
एवमुक्त्वार्जुनः सङ्ख्ये रथोपस्थ उपाविशत् ।
विसृज्य सशरं चापं शोकसंविग्नमानसः ॥ ४७ ॥

*Sañjaya uvāca* ।
*Evam uktvārjunaḥ saṅkhye rathopastha upāviśat* ।
*Visṛjya saśaraṃ cāpaṃ śokasaṃvignamānasaḥ* ॥ *47* ॥

**Meaning:** (Sanjaya said) Having spoken thus at the time of the battle, Arjuna, overwhelmed with deep despair, abandoned his weapons, got out of the chariot, and sat down there.

**ॐ तत्सदिति श्रीमद्भगवद्गीतासूपनिषत्सु ब्रह्मविद्यायां योगशास्त्रे श्रीकृष्णार्जुनसंवादे अर्जुनविषादयोगोनाम प्रथमोऽध्यायः ॥**

*Om Tatsaditi Śrimadbhagvadgitāsūpaniṣatsu Brahmavidyāyāṃ Yogaśāstre Śrīkṛṣṇārjunasaṅvāde Arjunaviṣādayogonāma Prathamo'dhyāyaḥ* ॥

Chapter 2

# The Yoga of Self-Knowledge

॥ साङ्ख्ययोगः (Sāṅkhyayogaḥ) ॥

This chapter describes Vedic **Sāṅkhyayoga** or **Buddhiyoga** which is immensely important. It sets up the background score for the doctrine of Karmayoga. This Sāṅkhyayoga is different from Sāṅkhya Darśana established by Ṛṣi Kapila. In the 10th chapter, Lord Kṛṣṇa says that He is the Vaidic Kapila in all Ṛṣis. However, Ādi Śaṅkara – in his commentary on Brahmasūtra – says that Vaidic Kapila is different from Ṛṣi Kapila of the Sāṅkhya School of Philosophy.

Arjuna was a Kṣatriya, so fighting a battle was his sacred duty and responsibility. War has been a fundamental need of mankind for ages, however destructive, devastating, and dreadful it may be. The lives of Śrirāma, Śrīkṛṣṇa, and Śivāji were replete with wars. Even today, the world superpowers are all set for war through and through. Fighting in battle may not be the prescribed duty for most ordinary people. However, they, too, need to deal with one or the other conflict in day-to-day situations. This chapter is essential for all those who struggle and face conflicts – whether big or small – in their lives.

**Sanjaya narrates Kurukṣetra's reality to Dhṛtarāṣṭra**

*सञ्जय उवाच ।*

तं तथा कृपयाविष्टमश्रुपूर्णाकुलेक्षणम् ।
विषीदन्तमिदं वाक्यमुवाच मधुसूदनः ॥ १ ॥

*Sañjaya Uvāca* ।

*Taṃ tathā kṛpayāviṣṭamaśrupūrṇākulekṣaṇam* ।
*Viṣīdantamidaṃ vākyam uvāca madhusūdanaḥ* ॥ *1* ॥

**Meaning:** (Sanjaya said) Thus, seeing that Arjuna was deeply overwhelmed with compassion, his eyes full of tears, his mind agitated and grief-stricken, Lord Madhusūdana spoke these words –

**Guidance to lamenting Arjuna**

*श्रीभगवानुवाच ।*
**कुतस्त्वा कश्मलमिदं विषमे समुपस्थितम् ।**
**अनार्यजुष्टमस्वर्ग्यमकीर्तिकरमर्जुन ॥ २ ॥**
**क्लैब्यं मा स्म गमः पार्थ नैतत्त्वय्युपपद्यते ।**
**क्षुद्रं हृदयदौर्बल्यं त्यक्त्वोत्तिष्ठ परन्तप ॥ ३ ॥**

*Śrībhagavān uvāca* ।
*Kutas tvā kaśmalam idaṃ viṣame samupasthitam* ।
*Anāryajuṣṭam asvargyam akīrtikaram arjuna* ॥ *2* ॥
*Klaibyaṃ mā sma gamaḥ pārtha naitat tvayyupapadyate* ।
*Kṣudraṃ hṛdayadaurbalyaṃ tyaktvottiṣṭha paraṃtapa* ॥ *3* ॥

**Meaning:** (Śrībhagavān said) How can you be deluded at this time of crucial emergency? This delusion does not befit a brave warrior; it deprives him of heaven and brings disgrace. O Arjuna! Do not succumb to this meek impotence. It does not beseem you. O Arjuna, the castigator of enemy! Cast off this petty fragility of heart and arise!

While counseling Arjuna, Lord Kṛṣṇa did not delve into the spiritual philosophy right at the outset. Instead, his initial guidance conforms to a simple code of conduct for everyday life, and it includes the precepts of Dharma which prescribe duties and responsibilities. That implies, in simple terms, that one should at least be able to abide by one's own Dharma i.e. duty by following the appropriate code of conduct. It is a deplorable situation when a great mighty warrior is afflicted with unnecessary compassion and sheds tears due to grief. When such a valiant warrior is condemned by someone, it is bound to shatter his self-belief. The very life of a warrior is laden with wars. If he shows unwarranted mercy or courteousness to his enemies, he will be unable to fulfill his warrior duties and fail to protect society. 'Humanitarian perspective' often encourages inhuman atrocities, and ordinary people suffer in the process. Lord Kṛṣṇa has reprimanded Arjuna from all three perspectives: the responsibility of his lineage, Dharma, and the social code of conduct. Kṛṣṇa has given guidance from the perspective of worldly life as well as Dharma here. A person is expected to live a sublime, noble, and honorable life. Arjuna was a brave, distinguished warrior. Meek and cowardly behavior did not befit him in any way. The Vedic scriptures of Dharma state that the person who dies while fighting in war attains heaven. Fighting the war for justice is the chief duty i.e. Dharma of a Kṣatriya. If every person conscientiously follows his Dharma, he, too, will follow the same path and attain heaven. A person who is a famous leader finds infamy or disgrace to be more painful than death. The word 'impotent' used by Kṛṣṇa here is the greatest disgrace for a warrior. Arjuna, who is the incarnation of 'Nara' (Man, the name of a famous ancient sage), must have been deeply afflicted by that disgrace. A person who is disillusioned about his duties can neither execute worldly actions nor follow his prescribed Dharma.

Arjuna was not able to even recognize the grave danger in front of Pāṇḍavas since his mind was deluded. Fighting war to destroy threats or dangers is considered the prime duty of every warrior. Even Lord Kṛṣṇa was surprised to see Arjuna's delusion in this crucial situation. Arjuna was not aware of the grim long-term consequences of his vulnerability that arose from his momentary thoughtlessness. However, Lord Kṛṣṇa understood them well. Arjuna was familiar with the eminent life and biography of Lord Kṛṣṇa. Even then, he chose to disregard the profundity of His command and posed his doubts as well as questions to Kṛṣṇa again.

**Arjuna's skepticism**

*अर्जुन उवाच ।*

**कथं भीष्ममहं सङ्ख्ये द्रोणं च मधुसूदन ।**
**इषुभिः प्रति योत्स्यामि पूजार्हावरिसूदन ॥ ४ ॥**
**गुरूनहत्वा हि महानुभावान् श्रेयो भोक्तुं भैक्ष्यमपीह लोके ।**
**हत्वार्थकामांस्तु गुरूनिहैव भुञ्जीय भोगान् रुधिरप्रदिग्धान् ॥ ५ ॥**
**न चैतद्विद्मः कतरन्नो गरीयो यद्वा जयेम यदि वा नो जयेयुः ।**
**यानेव हत्वा न जिजीविषामस्तेऽवस्थिताः प्रमुखे धार्तराष्ट्राः ॥ ६ ॥**
**कार्पण्यदोषोपहतस्वभावः पृच्छामि त्वां धर्मसम्मूढचेताः ।**
**यच्छ्रेयः स्यान्निश्चितं ब्रूहि तन्मे शिष्यस्तेऽहं शाधि मां त्वां प्रपन्नम् ॥ ७ ॥**
**न हि प्रपश्यामि ममापनुद्याद् यच्छोकमुच्छोषणमिन्द्रियाणाम् ।**
**अवाप्य भूमावसपत्नमृद्धं राज्यं सुराणामपि चाधिपत्यम् ॥ ८ ॥**

*Arjuna uvāca ।*
*Kaṭhaṃ bhīṣmam ahaṃ sāṅkhye droṇaṃ ca madhusūdana ।*
*Iṣubhiḥ prati yotsyāmi pūjārhāv arisūdana ॥ 4 ॥*
*Gurūn ahatvā hi mahānubhāvān*
*śreyo bhoktuṃ bhaikṣyam apīha loke ।*
*Hatvārthakāmāṃstu gurunihaiva*
*Bhuñjīya bhogān rudhirapradigdhān ॥ 5 ॥*
*Na caitad vidmaḥ kataran no garīyo*
*yad vā jayema yadi vā no jayeyuḥ ।*
*Yān eva hatvā na jijīviṣāmas te'*
*vasthitāḥ pramukhe dhārtarāṣṭrāḥ ॥ 6 ॥*
*Kārpaṇyadoṣopahatasvabhāvaḥ*
*pṛcchāmi tvāṃ dharmasaṃmūḍhacetāḥ ।*
*Yacchreyaḥ syānniścitaṃ brūhi tanme*
*Śiṣyaste'haṃ śādhi māṃ tvāṃ prapannam ॥ 7 ॥*
*Na hi prapaśyāmi mamāpanudyād*
*Yac chokam ucchoṣaṇam indriyāṇām ।*
*Avāpya bhūmāv asapatnam ṛddhaṃ*
*Rājyaṃ surāṇām api cādhipatyam ॥ 8 ॥*

**Meaning:** (Arjuna said) O Madhusūdana! O destroyer of enemies! O Śrīkṛṣṇa! How shall I fight against Bhīṣma and Droṇa in the war with the help of arrows? They are worthy of my worship. These teachers are superior to all in studies and austerities. It would be better to live in this world even by begging alms than to slay my most noble teachers. Even if I kill these teachers who live off Duryodhana's riches, our worldly pleasures and enjoyments will be tainted by their blood. We do not understand which is better: to conquer them or be conquered by them. We do not wish to live after defeating Kauravas who are now standing before us. I have lost my power of discrimination due to the weakness of my mind. Not being able to differentiate between Dharma and Adharma, I am asking you to tell me with utmost certainty what is most beneficial for me. I am totally surrendering to you as a disciple. Please instruct me. Even if I win a prosperous, unrivaled kingdom on earth or sovereignty in heaven, I do not see a way to wipe out this grief that is weakening my senses.

Being deluded, Arjuna was unable to differentiate between duty and nonduty, virtue and sin, Dharma and Adharma, etc. A seeker today may face the same dilemma in his life. It is his duty to use spiritual discrimination and resolve this confusion through the guidance of enlightened saints and scriptures. If the seeker does not clearly understand the difference between right and wrong, he may continually face inner turmoil as to whether he is indeed doing the right thing, and such turmoil can disturb his spiritual practice. It is a sign of delusion when the seeker becomes anxious about success or failure after performing his duty in the best possible manner. To think that "The victory of an unjust enemy may be a good thing" is a delusion. The lack of desire to stand up against injustice is a sign of delusion as well. Bhīṣma and Droṇa were surely worthy of reverence and worship. However, since they were fighting on the side of injustice, it was imperative to retribute them with full power and capacity. Arjuna was the dearest disciple of Droṇācārya. He felt immense gratitude for his teacher, and so he was unable to digest the idea of fighting against his revered teacher. Droṇācārya was a teacher of Kauravas as well, and he had also taken refuge in their shelter; hence he was morally obligated to fight on their side. Bhīṣma was Arjuna's grandfather. He too decided to embrace the side of Kauravas since he believed the adage: 'Man is enslaved by wealth. *Arthasya Puruṣo Dasaḥ.*' In Bhīṣma's case, he was enslaved by his political duties. He considered he was obliged to serve and protect the throne of Hastinapur due to the vow taken by him when he was young. Arjuna found it utterly wrong to fight against these stalwarts. He felt it was disgraceful to enjoy the kingdom and other pleasures after defeating these luminaries. He was deluded by the notion that it was indeed fine for tyrant Kauravas to be victorious in war. He was unable to see any glory in killing Kauravas and continue living after that.

One should have at least accumulated enough merits (*Puṇya*) to recognize by himself that he is enmeshed in a delusion. Arjuna, while narrating his state of mind to Kṛṣṇa, was clearly introspecting himself. He could see his immense strength and warrior instincts were crippled at the time. He realized that he had lost even the ability to distinguish between Dharma and Adharma. Under the circumstances, Arjuna, whose Sattvaguṇa was alive, surrendered to the Lord. He became Kṛṣṇa's disciple. He felt that his profound grief and lamentation would not disappear despite winning absolute sovereignty over the earth as well as heaven. There are two kinds of suffering: one is for events in the past, while the second is for events in the future. Lamenting for either creates utter confusion in mind.

Consumed by grief, Arjuna declared that "I will not fight" and remained silent. Thereafter, Lord Kṛṣṇa started imparting knowledge to him. Arjuna was undoubtedly brilliant but not headstrong. He was aware that he needed guidance at that moment. Arjuna knew that the one who could guide was right there in front of him, and he was sensible enough to surrender to Him. He was ready to be reproached by the teacher in this process. Every seeker should have at least this much Sattvaguṇa to progress on the spiritual path.

**Lord Kṛṣṇa's reaction to Arjuna's condition**

*सञ्जय उवाच ।*

**एवमुक्त्वा हृषीकेशं गुडाकेशः परन्तप ।**
**न योत्स्य इति गोविन्दमुक्त्वा तूष्णीं बभूव ह ॥ ९ ॥**
**तमुवाच हृषीकेशः प्रहसन्निव भारत ।**
**सेनयोरुभयोर्मध्ये विषीदन्तमिदं वचः ॥ १० ॥**

*Sañjaya uvāca* ।

*Evam uktvā hṛṣīkeśaṃ guḍākeśaḥ paraṃtapaḥ* ।
*Na yotsya iti govindam uktvā tūṣṇīṃ babhūva ha* ॥ *9* ॥
*Tam uvāca hṛṣīkeśaḥ prahasann iva bhārata* ।
*Senayor ubhayor madhye viṣīdantam idaṃ vacaḥ* ॥ *10* ॥

**Meaning:** (Sanjaya said) O, King! After addressing Śrīkṛṣṇa, Arjuna – the chastiser of enemies and conqueror of sleep – said, "I will not fight" and fell silent. O descendant of Bharata, King Dhṛtarāṣṭra! At the time, Lord Kṛṣṇa, standing amid both armies, laughed a little and spoke the following words to forlorn Arjuna.

Arjuna abandoned his prescribed duty by putting down the bow and remained silent in delusion. Seeing Arjuna in this meek state, Kṛṣṇa was amused and smiled at him even in that grave situation. A seeker should remember that a wise man having a spiritually discriminating mind remains composed and does not abandon his duties under any circumstances.

**Spiritual discrimination to overcome suffering in life**

*श्रीभगवानुवाच ।*

**अशोच्यानन्वशोचस्त्वं प्रज्ञावादांश्च भाषसे ।**
**गतासूनगतासूंश्च नानुशोचन्ति पण्डिताः ॥ ११ ॥**

न त्वेवाहं जातु नासं न त्वं नेमे जनाधिपाः ।
न चैव न भविष्यामः सर्वे वयमतः परम् ॥ १२ ॥
देहिनोऽस्मिन्यथा देहे कौमारं यौवनं जरा ।
तथा देहान्तरप्राप्तिर्धीरस्तत्र न मुह्यति ॥ १३ ॥
मात्रास्पर्शास्तु कौन्तेय शीतोष्णसुखदुःखदाः ।
आगमापायिनोऽनित्यास्तांस्तितिक्षस्व भारत ॥ १४ ॥

*Śrībhagavān uvāca* ।

*Aśocyān anvaśocas tvaṃ prajñāvādāṃś ca bhāṣase* ।
*Gatāsūn agatāsūṃś ca nānuśocanti paṇḍitāḥ* ॥ *11* ॥
*Natv evāhaṃ jātu nāsaṃ na tvaṃ neme janādhipāḥ* ।
*Na caiva na bhaviṣyāmaḥ sarve vayam ataḥ param* ॥ *12* ॥
*Dehino'smin yathā dehe kaumāraṃ yauvanaṃ jarā* ।
*Tathā dehāntaraprāptir dhīras tatra na muhyati* ॥ *13* ॥
*Mātrāsparśās tu kaunteya śītoṣṇasukhaduḥkhadāḥ* ।
*Āgamāpāyino'nityās tāṃs titikṣasva bhārata* ॥ *14* ॥

**Meaning:** (Śrībhagavān said) You are grieving for those who should not be grieved for, yet you speak the language of wisdom. The wise lament neither the dead nor the living. There was never any time in the past when I, you, or these kings did not exist and nor shall any of us cease to exist in the future. The body of every Jiva goes through the stages of childhood, youth, and old age. Likewise, it is just a stage to receive another body after death. Wise men are not disturbed by this fact. The contact of the senses with objects and their subsequent separation cause joy and suffering, respectively. These pleasures and pains are transient and perishable. It is best to brave them out.

Wise and discerning men do not lament for people who are dead or still alive. Arjuna himself was consumed with delusion and deep agony. Yet, he was making hollow arguments pretending to be a wise, thoughtful person. The cycle of birth and death continues without interruption for all Jivas. Therefore, those who are born are undoubtedly subject to death and rebirth. This cycle is beginningless. It is not possible to conclusively determine the time when it started. Even those who will die in the future were alive at some point in this cycle of life. There is no exception to this rule. Ordinary people can only understand that one dies after getting old. The fact that there is to be a rebirth after death has to be explained by a wise person. These deep, mysterious concepts in the realm of Īśvara can be only learnt if taught by Īśvara Himself. Wise people accept these facts on faith. They know that every Jiva is bound to get a new body in the future, regardless of the reason or stage of life in which he dies. Thus, they do not suffer due to the idea of their own death or someone else's death. The theory of rebirth is applicable until one attains liberation. After Mokṣa, the Jiva becomes One with Brahman. He ceases to exist as a separate Jiva, so he is not subject to rebirth. As such, the body and the external world that affects the body are continuously subject to changes. Therefore, the seeker should endure them while maintaining his inner peace. If the seeker can practice discrimination by recognizing this spiritual reality, nothing will cause delusion or suffering in his life.

As a matter of fact, being victorious and enjoying a kingdom are supposed to give pleasure to a person. However, Arjuna was lamenting even over them due to his sheer thoughtlessness. Arjuna could not choose between right and wrong due to the delusions in his mind. In reality, all worldly pleasures and sorrows are impermanent. When the sense-organs come in contact with favorable objects, their union leads to joy. When the senses come in contact with unfavorable objects, their union leads to grief. Objects – whether favorable or unfavorable – come and go; therefore, one cannot depend on them for finding pure, lasting happiness. The seeker should see such sensory experiences in a detached, impassive manner. The seeker who is not afflicted by the arrival and separation of worldly objects is rightly eligible for Mokṣa. For him, worldly pleasures and pains are the same. Being untouched by them, he remains absorbed in his true Self, Ātman. As a result, he does not ruminate on the cause of good or bad events in life. In his mind, there is a total acceptance of every situation since he knows it to be a fleeting experience. However, as mentioned in the commentary of the first chapter in this text, if any situation in day-to-day life necessitates a strong reaction, the seeker should react in a thoughtful, calculated manner to achieve the desired effect while ensuring that he is totally at peace from within.

**As a result of endurance, attaining Mokṣa becomes easier**

**यं हि न व्यथयन्त्येते पुरुषं पुरुषर्षभ ।**
**समदुःखसुखं धीरं सोऽमृतत्वाय कल्पते ॥ १५ ॥**

*Yaṃ hi na vyathayanty ete puruṣaṃ puruṣarṣabha* ।
*Samaduḥkhasukhaṃ dhīraṃ so'mṛtatvāya kalpate* ॥ *15* ॥

**Meaning:** O best among men! The wise person who is equanimous in both joy and grief is not distressed by worldly objects. He is eligible for Mokṣa.

Lord Kṛṣṇa explains to Arjuna, "A person who maintains his composure in the polarities of joy and grief, respect and disrespect, etc. and who adheres – without disturbance – to his true Self, Ātman, is rightfully eligible for Mokṣa." In this regard, Lord Kṛṣṇa will now state the essential spiritual reality of the Eternal Truth, which a seeker should always remember and keep in mind.

**The Eternal Spiritual Truth**

**नासतो विद्यते भावो नाभावो विद्यते सतः ।**
**उभयोरपि दृष्टोऽन्तस्त्वनयोस्तत्त्वदर्शिभिः ॥ १६ ॥**

*Nāsato vidyāte bhāvo nābhāvo vidyāte sataḥ* ।
*Ubhayor api dṛṣṭo' ntas tvanayos tattvādarśibhiḥ* ॥ *16* ॥

**Meaning:** That which is unreal (*Asat*) has no existence. The real (*Sat*) can never be non-existent. The seers of the Truth have arrived at a conclusion regarding both of these.

Ordinary human intellect cannot comprehend the Supreme Truth which is veiled by sentient and insentient entities in the universe. Ancient Ṛṣis in the era of Upaniṣads had pure and pious minds. As a result, they had developed highly subtle intellect which could delve deep into the Truth. These Ṛṣis were enlightened with the Supreme Truth themselves, and they later expressed it in words. The distinguished luminaries such as Ādi Śaṅkarācārya, St. Jñāneśwara, St. Tukārāma could experience and explain this Truth. The world is subject to creation, existence, and destruction. However, the Truth underlying the world is beginningless, eternal, and the most primeval (*Anādi, Nitya, Ādya*). That Truth can never be non-existent, and the world which deceptively appears on the Truth can never exist. The concepts of 'existence' and 'non-existence' are relative to each other, and underlying them both is the unqualified Pure Truth – Brahman. Both the existence and non-existence of the world depend on this Truth. The Truth, however, does not depend on either one of them. This Eternal Truth is called ***Sat*** or Pure Existence from which the concepts of existence and non-existence are derived.

In this verse, the word ***Asat*** indicates *Sat-Asat-Vilakṣaṇa-Anirvacaniya* ***Mithyā***. This simply means that *Asat* is neither real nor unreal, hence indescribable and illusory. *Sat* is the Truth that remains constant and changeless through past, present, and future. It is (Pure) Existence, Consciousness, Bliss itself. It is formless, attributeless, and highly subtle. That which can be known by the senses or the nine epistemic sources of knowledge (Pramāṇas), is considered illusory. The Truth is Self-cognizant (*Swasaṃvedya*); it cannot be comprehended by the senses or other instruments. Even the most honest seeker is perplexed by this seemingly ambiguous language in the beginning. According to Kaṭha Upaniṣad (*2.3.13*) *Asti Iti Upalabdhavyo*, the seeker should initially accept the fact that "This Eternal Truth exists" on utmost, unswerving faith. Whatever is known by the senses is not the Truth – even this needs to be accepted on faith in the beginning.

*Sat* or Ātman is not born of anything else as it is the most primeval principle. *Sat* is birthless, ageless, and deathless. It is eternal; therefore, it transcends the concept of time – past, present, future – conceived by the human intellect. This fact should be taken on faith in the beginning until one learns the Truth by Self-realization.

The world is perceived through our ego. Before any thought or action, 'I' has to be active. When a person says, "I perceive," or "I do," there has to be 'I' behind each of his thought or action. Everything in the world is with respect to 'I' or in the context of 'I.' Without 'I,' the world does not exist. This 'I' or ego is wholly manifested in the waking state, partially manifested in the dreaming state, and disappears during the deep-sleep. Therefore, it is generally believed that the world exists on account of ego.

This phenomenal world is subject to creation, state, and destruction; hence it is unreal (*Asat*), so it is not wise to be attached to it. Even the little world i.e. the immediate circle of the seeker is bound by these three states. It is unreal. The seeker should first learn to see ephemerality in his own little world that includes his body, house, estate, relatives, family, business, hobby, skills, knowledge, friends, neighbors, etc. This simply means that he should know for sure that his near and dear ones are impermanent, and he should not depend on those relationships for his happiness. This knowledge or resolve of impermanence should not give way to dispirited, dry, caustic, abrupt, or bitter interactions. While being aware of his true Self,

Ātman, the seeker is supposed to perform all the duties in life gladly without any expectation or attachment. Lord Kṛṣṇa has instructed in the Gita that one must perform the duties prescribed for him *Tvaṃ niyataṃ kuru karma* (*3.8*). Kṛṣṇa has also mentioned in the Gita that He resides in the hearts of all beings *Sarvasya cāhaṃ hṛdi saṃniviṣṭomattaḥ* (*15.15*). Thus, the seeker should interact with every being as just a form of Kṛṣṇa or Īśvara and perform all duties towards everyone happily, without any complaint.

**Ātman is imperishable, the world is perishable**

अविनाशि तु तद्विद्धि येन सर्वमिदं ततम् ।
विनाशमव्ययस्यास्य न कश्चित्कर्तुमर्हति ॥ १७ ॥
अन्तवन्त इमे देहा नित्यस्योक्ताः शरीरिणः ।
अनाशिनोऽप्रमेयस्य तस्माद्युध्यस्व भारत ॥ १८ ॥
य एनं वेत्ति हन्तारं यश्चैनं मन्यते हतम् ।
उभौ तौ न विजानीतो नायं हन्ति न हन्यते ॥ १९ ॥

*Avināśi tu tad viddhi yena sarvam idaṃ tatam* ।
*Vināśam avyayasyāsya na kaścit kartum arhati* ॥ *17* ॥
*Antavanta ime dehā nityasyoktāḥ śarīriṇaḥ* ।
*Anāśino 'prameyasya tasmād yudhyasva bhārata* ॥ *18* ॥
*Ya enaṃ vetti hantāraṃ yaś cainaṃ manyate hatam* ।
*Ubhau tau na vijānīto nāyaṃ hanti na hanyate* ॥ *19* ॥

**Meaning:** Know that the world – permeated by Ātman – is perishable, but nobody can destroy that imperishable Ātman. The Vedas, scriptures, and enlightened saints state that these bodies, permeated by Ātman, are subject to an end. Ātman itself is eternal, indestructible, and incomprehensible by the epistemic sources of knowledge (Pramāṇas). Therefore, fight the battle, O Arjuna! A person who thinks that Ātman is the 'slayer' and one who thinks that Ātman is 'slain' are both ignorant about Ātman. This is because, Ātman, the true Self, neither slays anyone nor is slain by anyone else.

These verses are the concluding part of the previous $16^{th}$ verse. A seeker should remain detached and dispassionate towards his own body as well as the surrounding world. He should verily remember that his own body is ultimately a part of the world. One theory in Vedānta states that the world is created by Īśvara. The second theory states that the world is a false appearance seen on the substratum of God. Another theory suggests that the world is pervaded by God, and every entity is God. One more theory says that the world was never created. Scriptures thus describe the relationship between the world and God in many ways. No matter how they are related, each theory states that Brahman or God alone is real, and it is the essence of everything in the world. On the contrary, the world is unreal and nonessential or peripheral. The takeaway for the seeker is that he should remain firm on his spiritual resolve and use it in his day-to-day life. He can dwell on it in the following ways:

1. The world belongs to Īśvara, so it is not mine; therefore, I should not be attached to it.
2. The world is just a deceptive appearance; hence, there is no point in being attached to it.
3. If everything in the world is verily Brahman, then the one who is attached to the world and the object of attachment are all Brahman. Therefore, attachment is not possible.
4. If the world was never created, attachment to it is out of question.

These philosophical concepts can help develop a new perspective of the surrounding world. The seeker is supposed to see them as steps in spiritual evolution rather than examining their intricate theoretical details. Being dispassionate or detached from worldly matters is the prime goal here, irrespective of how it is achieved.

Dispassion for the world is needed ultimately for Self-realization. The true Self, Ātman, permeates the body and the world; it is indestructible. The body and the world are mere apparent Upādhis i.e. limiting adjuncts of Brahman. All Jivas are originally Ātman; however, they do not know it due to ignorance. Ignorant Jivas firmly identify themselves with the body. As a result, when the body is killed, they misconceive that their true Self, Ātman, is being killed. They also mistakenly think that Ātman in one body kills or gets killed by Ātman in the other body, when in fact, Ātman is not bound by, identified with, or encaged by any body. Ātman is all-pervasive, omnipresent, and non-attached, so it can neither slay anyone nor be slain by anyone. The seeker is supposed accept this Eternal Truth proclaimed by Lord Kṛṣṇa on utmost, unswerving faith so he can achieve what is most beneficial for him. The Jivātma i.e. embodied soul is, however, considered to leave his first body upon death and enter another body subsequently. Lord Kṛṣṇa insists that by recognizing these facts, Arjuna should assuredly fight the war using his complete prowess and with sheer enthusiasm since fighting evil is his prime duty in day-to-day transactional life.

## The nature of Ātman

न जायते म्रियते वा कदाचिन् नायं भूत्वा भविता वा न भूयः ।
अजो नित्यः शाश्वतोऽयं पुराणो न हन्यते हन्यमाने शरीरे ॥ २० ॥
वेदाविनाशिनं नित्यं य एनमजमव्ययम् ।
कथं स पुरुषः पार्थ कं घातयति हन्ति कम् ॥ २१ ॥
वासांसि जीर्णानि यथा विहाय नवानि गृह्णाति नरोऽपराणि ।
तथा शरीराणि विहाय जीर्णान्यन्यानि संयाति नवानि देही ॥ २२ ॥
नैनं छिन्दन्ति शस्त्राणि नैनं दहति पावकः ।
न चैनं क्लेदयन्त्यापो न शोषयति मारुतः ॥ २३ ॥
अच्छेद्योऽयमदाह्योऽयमक्लेद्योऽशोष्य एव च ।
नित्यः सर्वगतः स्थाणुरचलोऽयं सनातनः ॥ २४ ॥
अव्यक्तोऽयमचिन्त्योऽयमविकार्योऽयमुच्यते ।
तस्मादेवं विदित्वैनं नानुशोचितुमर्हसि ॥ २५ ॥
अथ चैनं नित्यजातं नित्यं वा मन्यसे मृतम् ।

**तथापि त्वं महाबाहो नैवं शोचितुमर्हसि ॥ २६ ॥**
**जातस्य हि ध्रुवो मृत्युर्ध्रुवं जन्म मृतस्य च ।**
**तस्मादपरिहार्येऽर्थे न त्वं शोचितुमर्हसि ॥ २७ ॥**
**अव्यक्तादीनि भूतानि व्यक्तमध्यानि भारत ।**
**अव्यक्तनिधनान्येव तत्र का परिदेवना ॥ २८ ॥**

*Na jāyate mriyate vā kadācin*
*Nāyaṃ bhūtvā bhavitā vā na bhūyaḥ* ।
*Ajo nityaḥ śāśvato'yaṃ purāṇo*
*Na hanyate hanyamāne śarīre* ॥ *20* ॥

*Vedāvināśinaṃ nityaṃ ya enam ajam avyayam* ।
*Kaṭhaṃ sa puruṣaḥ pārtha kaṃ ghātayati hanti kam* ॥ *21* ॥
*Vāsāṃsi jīrṇāni yathā vihāya Navāni gṛhṇāti naro'parāṇi* ।
*Tathā śarīrāṇi vihāya jīrṇāni Anyāni saṅyāti navāni dehī* ॥ *22* ॥
*Nainaṃ chindanti śastrāṇi nainaṃ dahati pāvakaḥ* ।
*Na cainaṃ kledayanty āpo na śoṣayati mārutaḥ* ॥ *23* ॥
*Acchedyo'yam adāhyo'yam akledyo'śoṣya eva ca* ।
*Nityaḥ sarvagataḥ sthāṇur acalo'yaṃ sanātanaḥ* ॥ *24* ॥
*Avyakto'yam acintyo'yam avikaryo'yam ucyate* ।
*Tasmādevaṃ viditvainaṃ nānuśocitumarhasi* ॥ *25* ॥
*Atha cainaṃ nityajātaṃ nityaṃ vā manyase mṛtam* ।
*Tathāpi tvaṃ mahābāho naivaṃ śocitum arhasi* ॥ *26* ॥
*Jātasya hi dhruvo mṛtyur dhruvaṃ janma mṛtasya ca* ।
*Tasmād aparihārye'rthe na tvaṃ śocitum arhasi* ॥ *27* ॥
*Avyaktādīni bhūtāni vyaktamadhyāni bhārata* ।
*Avyaktanidhanāny eva tatra kā paridevanā* ॥ *28* ॥

**Meaning:** There is neither birth nor death of Ātman at any time. It is not that Ātman came into being before and will not be born later. It is also not that it did not exist before and will be born later. Ātman is birthless, changeless, ancient, and eternal. Ātman is not destroyed when the body is killed. O Pārtha! How can a person – who knows Ātman to be eternal, indestructible, birthless, and immutable – think that he will kill anyone or get someone killed? Just as a man discards his old, worn-out clothes and puts on new clothes, so also Jivātma casts off his old bodies and acquires new bodies. Weapons cannot sever Ātman, fire does not burn it, water does not wet it, and wind cannot dry it up. This Ātman can never be severed nor burnt nor moistened nor dried up. It is all-pervading, immovable, actionless, ancient, and eternally the same. Ātman is also formless and unmanifested. It is unthinkable and inconceivable as it cannot be comprehended by the intellect [Ātman is formless and attributeless, so the intellect cannot think about it.] It is immutable and not subject to any change. Knowing Ātman to be such, it is improper for you to lament about it. O mighty Arjuna! Even if you think that Ātman is always subject to birth and death just like the body, even then, you should not grieve. For, death is indeed inevitable for anyone who is born, and birth is certain for anyone who has died. Hence, it is not right for you to mourn over the inevitable. These beings, Jivas having bodies, are unmanifested in the beginning, manifest in the interim state, and disappear again in the unmanifested at the end of the universe. Why then lament for these beings?

Both the killer and the killed have bodies. A body is made up of millions of cells, so it acquires shape and a form. This form can be destroyed. Cells are micro-organs of the body. Ātman is organless; it does not have a form. Ātman is the most subtle principle, and it is formless and organless. Therefore, it cannot be severed, burnt, moistened, or dried up. Bodies can be cut to pieces during a war, but Ātman can neither be burnt nor be cut.

Ātman is changeless. It is not subject to these six changes –

1 Existence (*Asti* – **अस्ति**)
2 Birth (*Jāyate* – **जायते**)
3 Growth (*Vardhate* – **वर्धते**)
4 Change (*Vipariṇamate* – **विपरिणमते**)
5 Decay (*Apakṣīyate* – **अपक्षीयते**)
6 Death (*Mriyate* – **म्रियते**)

The body, on the other hand, undergoes these six changes. It is a law of nature that the body is subject to birth and death in a cyclic manner. Ātman is eternal, endless, and organless. Therefore, it is unmanifested, and it is beyond thought or comprehension of the senses. By knowing it as such, one need not mourn for any changes in the body and the inevitable death. It is a stark reality that every Jiva is subject to the cycle of birth and death, but the true Self, Ātman, – neither attached to nor limited by nor encaged by the body – is not subject to that cycle. Reality can neither be good nor bad; rather, it is just a reality. It is man who labels 'birth' to be good and 'death' to be bad due to ignorance and loses his inner peace and contentment. A seeker who thinks thus cannot perform high-quality spiritual practice.

In these verses, Lord Kṛṣṇa is also counseling Arjuna from the perspective of simple day-to-day life. Whatever is created is bound to be destroyed. Jiva, who is born, is bound to die. Similarly, rebirth is inevitable after death. When the seeker grieves for what is inevitable, his joyousness is unnecessarily compromised, and he is unable to even think about Ātman, his true Self.

That which does not exist before and after may seem to exist in the interim state; however, it is neither real nor the permanentTruth. The interim existence is just an illusory, transient, false appearance. The mirage exists neither in the morning nor in the evening. Even if it seems to be real in the afternoon, it certainly is an illusion. Therefore, there is no reason to grieve for the mirage, whether it appears, disappears, or ceases to exist. It is easy to understand this fact about the deceptive appearance of the mirage in the desert. However, it is indeed difficult to be convinced of the same point about the body and the world. Therefore, the seeker should learn, reflect, and contemplate in many ways to convince himself of this fact. Scriptures state that the body is a collection of 25, 36, or 82 elements. [Different scriptures state different numbers of elements, and the numbers depend on how the elements are divided. Essentially all elements are part of one body.] Ādi Śaṅkara says –

न मे बुद्ध्यहंकार चित्तानिनाहं ।

*Na me buddhyahaṅkāra cittāninā ham* ।

"I am neither mind nor the intellect nor the memory." Likewise, I am none of the other elements in the body nor the body itself. This is an excellent thought-process for the seeker. By contemplating in this manner, the seeker can dissociate himself from strong identification with the body. One more technique that helps in Self-realization is the theory that "Ātman pervades the three states of waking, dreaming, and deep-sleep, yet it is dissociated or detached from the body in each of these states." There is another theory that explains the systems of four bodies or five sheaths and Ātman as the illuminator of them all. Thus, many techniques can help the seeker liberate himself from the bondage of the deceptive world and the thought that "I am the body."

**Lord Kṛṣṇa describes the incredible nature of Ātman**

आश्चर्यवत्पश्यति कश्चिदेनम्
आश्चर्यवद्वदति तथैव चान्यः ।
आश्चर्यवच्चैनमन्यः शृणोति
श्रुत्वाप्येनं वेद न चैव कश्चित् ॥ २९ ॥

*Āścaryavat paśyati kaścid enam*
*Āścaryavad vādati tathaiva cānyaḥ* ।
*Āścaryavac cainam anyaḥ śṛṇoti*
*Śrutvāpy enaṃ veda na caiva kaścit* ॥ *29* ॥

**Meaning 1:** Some see this Ātman as an incredible wonder; some describe it as an astonishing wonder; some listen to it as an incredible wonder. Yet, having heard about it, nobody can know it in entirety.

**Meaning 2:** Knowing Ātman is a wonder, describing it is a wonder, listening about it is a wonder, and not realizing Ātman – despite hearing about it – is a real wonder as well.

This verse describes the four wonders regarding Ātman. The word ***Paśyati*** in Sanskrit means seeing. However, in the context of Ātman, *Paśyati* does not mean 'seeing,' instead, it means 'realizing' Ātman. The realization of Ātman is a matter of great astonishment since it cannot be known through the five senses of ears, eyes, skin, nose, and tongue. Ātman cannot also be known with the help of the Pramāṇas. Pramāṇas are the nine epistemic sources of gaining knowledge. The non-dual school of Vedānta states that there are a total of nine Pramāṇas as stated below, but Ātman cannot be known through any one of them.

- *Pratyakṣa* (**प्रत्यक्ष**): Direct perception through the five senses. Ātman is formless and unmanifested, so it cannot be known through Pratyakṣa *Pramāṇa.*
- *Anumāna* (**अनुमान**): Inference; e.g. observing smoke far away and inferring the presence of fire. Ātman is non-dual, so there is no second entity from which one can infer its presence.
- *Upamāna* (**उपमान**): Knowing with the help of comparison and analogy; e.g. knowing about a tiger by drawing its analogy with a cat. Ātman is non-dual, so it cannot be compared with anything else.
- *Śabda* (**शब्द**): Relying on the words of scriptures and the testimony of enlightened sages who have realized the true Self. It is possible to gain the theoretical knowledge i.e. *Parokṣa Jñana* of Ātman by reading authentic words from the Upaniṣads and other saintly scriptures. But one cannot achieve direct realization i.e. *Aparokṣa Jñāna* of Ātman through words since Ātman is beyond language and speech.
- *Arthāpatti* (**अर्थापत्ती**): Postulation or derivation from circumstances, circumstantial implication. E.g. if "A person

is healthy and obese" and "He does not eat in the day," it implies that "He stealthily eats at night." Ātman cannot be known in this manner as it is only one, non-dual principle, so there is no one else who can derive or postulate about Ātman.

- *Anupalabdhi* (अनुपलब्धी): Cognitive proof using non-availability or non-existence. E.g. if "Himālaya is present in India," we can know that "It is not present in China." Ātman cannot be known in this manner because it is omnipresent and all-pervasive.
- *Śakya* (शक्य): Possible existence of a part known from the whole. E.g. If "A person has ₹5 bill," then we can know that "He possibly has 50 paisa." Ātman cannot be known in this manner because there are no parts in it. It is the one, monolithic principle that is beyond the concepts of part and whole.
- *Aitihya* (ऐतिह्य): Known through a shared belief or a historical tradition. E.g. "A temple in an old village is believed to be built by a certain king." Even though there is no scriptural evidence to support this, the belief exists to date, and people can learn from that belief. Ātman cannot be realized in this manner as it is timeless. It transcends time, so there is no history from which we can learn about Ātman.
- *Cesṭā* (चेष्टा): Learning through body language or certain gestures. E.g. a person who eats the food can indicate with gestures like 'thumbs up' or 'thumbs down' whether the food is good or not. Ātman cannot be learnt through such indicators since there is no duality in it, and being formless, it cannot be pointed to.

Apart from these nine Pramāṇas, one cannot experience Ātman by doing experiments in a laboratory or mathematical calculations. During meditation, Ātman does not 'come' when eyes are closed. It does not 'go away' by opening the eyes.

Ātman is Self-luminous, ever-substantiated, ever-existent, and the true Self.

Ātman is Self-effulgent (*Swayaṃprakāśa*); all objects are illumined only in the light of Ātman. The word 'illumination' means 'knowledge' in Vedānta. The Jiva knows objects by seeing or touching them or by using other senses on the substratum of Ātman, which is Pure Knowledge. External objects are illumined (*Prakāśya*). They are knowable, while Ātman is their illuminator (*Prakāśaka*). Ātman is the substratum of the process of knowing. The sense organs themselves are mere instruments for knowing, and they too function on the substratum of Ātman, the Pure Knowledge. The transactional knowledge in everyday life is of two kinds –

- Objective knowledge, which is descriptive
- Subjective knowledge, which is reflective

Ātman is formless. It can neither be described like an object nor be reflected upon from the perspective of a knower. Ātman is the very nature of all Jivas. It cannot be known by anyone or anything. There is no procedure, tool, or method to know Ātman. The only way to know or realize Ātman is to remove all reasons which veil Ātman and keep it hidden. Therefore, the experience or realization of Ātman is a matter of great wonder indeed.

The second wonder is the fact that the eminent, luminary sages describe Ātman. While revealing "What is not Ātman" sequentially step-by-step, they escort the seeker right to the doorstep of Self-realization that "I am Ātman." The terms – beginningless, endless, ageless, deathless – describe Ātman in this manner. Even the word ***Sat*** denotes that Ātman is *not Asat*. The term ***Cit*** denotes there is no ignorance in Ātman. The term ***Ānanda*** denotes that there is no grief in Ātman.

The third wonder is that some people realize "I am Ātman" after hearing such unusual, remarkable descriptions. Such a realization is only possible if a wise sage instructs genuine and qualified listeners.

The fourth wonder is that even after listening about Ātman in many ways, many people cannot even surmise what it is all about.

There are many astounding, unusual, and remarkable objects in the world surrounding us. However, none come close to Ātman in any way. Ātman is one of the most perplexing mysteries for many alike. Ātman is not a traditional name as it does not have a form. A formless entity cannot have a figure and name. Therefore, Ātman is just a concept until one realizes "I am Ātman." That which is *Sat* is not *Asat*; that which is *Cit* is not *Acit*; that which is *Ānanda* is not even remotely touched by grief – such principle is known as Ātman. ***Sat*** is that which is never non-existent. ***Cit*** is that which has no trace of ignorance. ***Ānanda*** is that which is totally untouched by grief.

In the word 'white paper,' the paper is the object, while whiteness is its characteristic property. However, *Sat-Cit-Ānanda* are not properties or characteristics of Ātman. The sun is round, hot, and shining, all at the same time. The three features together make up the sun. Similarly, *Sat-Cit-Ānanda* together indicate Ātman. That Ātman, which is *Sat*, is itself *Cit*, and it is itself *Ānanda* as well.

Ātman is birthless, thus consequently ageless and deathless. It is beginningless (*Anādi*) as it is eternal and unqualified Pure Existence. It is the Truth (Satya) as it transcends time. It is eternal (*Nitya*) as it is never non-existent. It is the most primeval (*Ādya*) as it exists before everything else regardless of time. It is endless (*Ananta*) as it has no end at any point in the future. It is omnipresent (*Vibhu*). It permeates all entities everywhere in the world uniformly. Yet, it is not attached to anything in any way. There is a misconception that Ātman is less in smaller objects. This perception is due to the difference amongst Upādhis i.e.

names and forms of objects. Ātman evenly pervades a tiny ant and a giant elephant. This is conceptually similar to the fact that space pervades pots of all sizes evenly. The pots, in-turn, are themselves created in space. Space is not injected into the pots after their creation, like air is injected in a balloon. A stone sinks in water; however, 'Brahman in the stone' does not sink in 'Brahman in water.' Brahman is the only one, universal, non-dual principle.

Ātman is not artificial. It is not created by anyone. Therefore, it cannot be realized by doing any action. Whatever is created is bound to get destroyed. The world, which is replete with many names and forms, is created. It is bound to get destroyed, hence impermanent. Every object having a name and form has three aspects:

- Existence (*Asti*, **अस्ति**)
- Cognizance (*Bhāti*, **भाति**)
- Likeability (*Priya*, **प्रिय**).

An object 'exists,' it is 'cognized,' and it can be 'liked' or 'disliked.' Even though there is a massive variation in names and forms, the three factors of existence, cognizance, and likeability are common amongst all of them. They are manifestations of *Sat-Cit-Ānanda* Brahman as stated below:

- Existence is manifested from Pure Existence (*Sat*),
- Cognizance is manifested from Pure Knowledge (*Cit*)
- Likeability is manifested from Pure Bliss (*Ānanda*)

These aspects correspond to different realms as stated below:

- Name and form belong to the realm of Māyā
- *Asti*, *Bhāti*, and *Priya* belong to the realm of Īśvara
- *Sat*, *Cit*, *Ānanda* together indicate Brahman

'Pure Awareness' or 'Pure Consciousness' is the very nature of Ātman. When one becomes aware of attributes like color, height, weight, etc. it is 'qualified awareness' (**सविशेष जाणीव**). When awareness is mixed with the knowledge acquired by the senses, it becomes 'qualified awareness'. Pure Awareness (शुद्ध जाणीव) without any specific distinction, characteristic, or property is the very nature of Ātman. It resides in and permeates through the body as Pure Consciousness, which is the true Self of every being.

Ātman, as discussed, is nothing short of incredible astonishment. It is ever-attained (*Nityaprāpta*), yet one strives to know and attain it, which is again a wonder. The entire life continues on the substratum of Pure Consciousness, yet nobody is conscious of it; isn't that a sheer wonder? Every Jiva lives in the world. Ātman is the very life of every Jiva; however, the fact that the Jiva is ignorant about his own life, his true Self, is an amazement for sure.

**Lord Kṛṣṇa's guidance to Arjuna**

**देही नित्यमवध्योऽयं देहे सर्वस्य भारत ।**
**तस्मात्सर्वाणि भूतानि न त्वं शोचितुमर्हसि ॥ ३० ॥**
**स्वधर्ममपि चावेक्ष्य न विकम्पितुमर्हसि ।**
**धर्म्याद्धि युद्धाच्छ्रेयोऽन्यत्क्षत्रियस्य न विद्यते ॥ ३१ ॥**
**यदृच्छया चोपपन्नं स्वर्गद्वारमपावृतम् ।**
**सुखिनः क्षत्रियाः पार्थ लभन्ते युद्धमीदृशम् ॥ ३२ ॥**
**अथ चेत्त्वमिमं धर्म्यं सङ्ग्रामं न करिष्यसि ।**
**ततः स्वधर्मं कीर्तिं च हित्वा पापमवाप्स्यसि ॥ ३३ ॥**
**अकीर्तिं चापि भूतानि कथयिष्यन्ति तेऽव्ययाम् ।**
**सम्भावितस्य चाकीर्तिर्मरणादतिरिच्यते ॥ ३४ ॥**
**भयाद्रणादुपरतं मंस्यन्ते त्वां महारथाः ।**
**येषां च त्वं बहुमतो भूत्वा यास्यसि लाघवम् ॥ ३५ ॥**
**अवाच्यवादांश्च बहून्वदिष्यन्ति तवाहिताः ।**
**निन्दन्तस्तव सामर्थ्यं ततो दुःखतरं नु किम् ॥ ३६ ॥**
**हतो वा प्राप्स्यसि स्वर्गं जित्वा वा भोक्ष्यसे महीम् ।**
**तस्मादुत्तिष्ठ कौन्तेय युद्धाय कृतनिश्चयः ॥ ३७ ॥**

*Dehī nityam avadhyo'yaṃ dehe sarvasya bhārata* ।
*Tasmāt sarvāṇi bhūtāni na tvaṃ śocitum arhasi* ॥ *30* ॥

*Svadharmam api cāvekṣya na vikampitum arhasi* ।
*Dharmyād dhi yuddhāc chreyo 'nyat kṣatriyasya na vidyāte* ॥ *31*॥
*Yadṛcchayā copapannaṃ svargadvāram apāvṛtam* ।
*Sukhinaḥ kṣatriyāḥ pārtha labhante yuddham īdṛśam* ॥ *32* ॥
*Atha cet tvam imaṃ dhārmyaṃ saṅgrāmaṃ na kariṣyasi* ।
*Tataḥ svadharmaṃ kīrtiṃ ca hitvā pāpam avāpsyasi* ॥ *33* ॥
*Akīrtiṃ cāpi bhūtāni Kaṭhayiṣyanti te 'vyayām* ।
*Saṃbhāvitasya cākīrtir maraṇād atiricyate* ॥ *34* ॥
*Bhayād raṇād uparataṃ maṃsyante tvāṃ mahārathāḥ*
*Yeṣāṃ ca tvaṃ bahumato bhūtvā yāsyasi lāghavam* ॥ *35* ॥
*Avācyavādāṃś ca bahūn vadiṣyanti tavāhitāḥ* ।
*Nindantas tava sāmarthyaṃ tato duḥkhataraṃ nu kim* ॥ *36* ॥
*Hato vā prāpsyasi svargaṃ jitvā vā bhokṣyase mahīm* ।
*Tasmād uttiṣṭha kaunteya yuddhāya kṛtaniścayaḥ* ॥ *37* ॥

**Meaning:** Ātman pervades the body of every being, and it can never be destroyed. Therefore, it is not right for you to grieve for any being. Moreover, considering your duty as a warrior (*Kṣatriya*), it is not right for you to turn your back on the battle. Indeed, there is no better endeavor for a warrior than the battle based on Dharma. O Arjuna! This war is a wide door effortlessly opened for you to go to heaven! Only fortunate warriors are called upon to fight such battles. Despite this, if you refuse to fight this war which is meant for the establishment of Dharma, then you will certainly incur sins and lose your reputation as a warrior. Also, people will recount your disgrace for ages to come. For a respectable person, dishonor is more painful and unbearable than death. Those who held you in high esteem before will think that you have bailed out of the war due to fear and look down on you. Your enemies will discredit the very prowess for which you are well-known among the masses and will denounce you with bad words. Alas! What could be more painful than that? Moreover, O son of Kunti! Either you will be slain on the battlefield and attain heaven, or you will conquer and enjoy the kingdom of the earth. Therefore, stand up with a firm resolve to fight this war!

While imparting the spiritual knowledge about the realization of Ātman, Lord Kṛṣṇa also advises Arjuna to fight the war from the perspective of executing his duty as a Kṣatriya. Indeed, for every human being, there is no better Dharma than following his prescribed duty. For a brave, valiant, fearless warrior, an opportunity to fight the war for the establishment of Dharma is a matter of the highest fortune and honor. Had Arjuna missed this opportunity, he would have incurred the sin of not executing his duty, and his spotless reputation would have been tarnished at the same time. The more famous a person is, the more infamy or disgrace ensues when he performs wrong actions. Thus, Arjuna would have faced great dishonor in society by not fighting in the war. The word 'timid warrior' is a paradox. Arjuna would have lost his eminence, integrity, and esteem in this situation.

Lord Kṛṣṇa is trying to awaken Arjuna to execute his duty in many ways. He is describing various advantages of performing duties and disadvantages of renouncing duties in a language that ordinary people can understand and relate to. As St. Jñāneśwara says, Lord Kṛṣṇa is teaching the entire world by engaging Arjuna as a 'medium' in this process. "A seeker should never turn away from his duties" – this is the essence of these verses.

**The guidance for executing actions**

सुखदुःखे समे कृत्वा लाभालाभौ जयाजयौ ।
ततो युद्धाय युज्यस्व नैवं पापमवाप्स्यसि ॥ ३८ ॥
एषा तेऽभिहिता साङ्ख्ये बुद्धिर्योगे त्विमां श्रृणु ।
बुद्ध्या युक्तो यया पार्थ कर्मबन्धं प्रहास्यसि ॥ ३९ ॥
नेहाभिक्रमनाशोऽस्ति प्रत्यवायो न विद्यते ।
स्वल्पमप्यस्य धर्मस्य त्रायते महतो भयात् ॥ ४० ॥

व्यवसायात्मिका बुद्धिरेकेह कुरुनन्दन ।
बहुशाखा ह्यनन्ताश्च बुद्धयोऽव्यवसायिनाम् ॥ ४१ ॥

*Sukhaduḥkhe same kṛtvā lābhālābhau jayājayau* ।
*Tato yuddhāya yujyasva naivaṃ pāpam avāpsyasi* ॥ *38* ॥
*Eṣā te'bhihitā sāṅkhye buddhir yoge tv imāṃ śṛṇu* ।
*Buddhyā yukto yayā pārtha karmabandhaṃ prahāsyasi* ॥ *39* ॥
*Nehābhikramanāśo'sti pratyavāyo na vidyāte* ।
*Svalpam apy asya dharmasya trāyate mahato bhayāt* ॥ *40* ॥
*Vyavasāyātmikā buddhir ekeha kurunandana* ।
*Bahuśākhā hy anantāś ca buddhayo'vyavasāyinām* ॥ *41* ॥

**Meaning:** O Arjuna! Engage in the battle by being equanimous in joy and grief, gain and loss, and victory and defeat. By doing so, you shall not incur sin. Arjuna! So far, I have explained the Knowledge of Ātman to you. Now, for realizing "I am Ātman," listen to the knowledge of '**desireless actions**' (*Niṣkāma Karmayoga*). Contemplating persistently on it, you shall release yourself from the bondage of actions [Ātman is actionless or a non-doer. So, this contemplation i.e. ***Buddhiyoga*** involves abiding in the thought that "The true Self is the non-doer."]. The Karma that is commenced by following this Karmayoga is not ruined without fruits [In other words, such Karma is bound to get appropriate worldly fruits.] And it is not censured by Dharma. It is faultless. Even a little practice of this Dharma – doing duties as per Karmayoga – will protect a person from the greatest fear of the birth and death cycle. O Arjuna! The intellect must be resolute and single-pointed in this pursuit. The intellect of those who are unable to resolve in this manner is distracted.

Every Jiva experiences the duality of joy and grief, victory and defeat, etc. The Jiva is impermanent, and the world in which dualities are experienced is impermanent as well. The objects that give rise to joy and grief are present in this world. Even the causes of victory and defeat, as well as winners and losers, are part of this world. Therefore, they are all impermanent and illusory or Māyic in nature. Without giving them undue attention, the seeker should execute his duties to the best of his abilities. Such execution of duties does not incur merits or sins. Rather than dwelling on what can be attained through merits or sins, the seeker should focus on the realization that "I am Ātman that is beyond merits and sins." Duties which are performed without desiring fruits according to the principle of *Buddhiyoga* are not bound by merits or sins. This simply means that duties performed by abiding in the thought – "I, as Ātman, am not the doer" – do not create any bondage for the seeker. Such actions are not ruined or considered futile without worldly fruits, and they are not censured by Dharma as well. These actions do give fruits as per the 'Law of Prārabdha' but are blameless from the perspective of Īśvara's 'Law of action.' Actions like Yajña, which are essentially paired with specific desires, may be interrupted by obstacles or ruined completely. Desireless actions also may be interrupted for some reason. Still they cannot be called 'ruined' or 'futile' as there were no desires associated with them. The doer remains at peace whether the action is completed or interrupted and whether he gets any fruits or not. When an action is executed as per Lord Kṛṣṇa's guidance and philosophy as stated in the Gita, it cannot be incorrect or defective. So, the doer who is desireless does not become restless despite any obstacles, interruptions, or complete destruction of his actions. So, he can dwell on the fact that "I am Ātman." A devotee of Saguṇa Kṛṣṇa can also dwell on his beloved Lord while executing all actions in this manner.

It is necessary to have a firmly resolved, constant, single-pointed intellect to absorb the spiritual philosophy in the journey towards Mokṣa. For executing any work, first one needs to have the firm resolve and then act accordingly. It is also necessary to persistently stick to this resolve, for which Sattvaguṇa is essential. The very nature of Rajoguṇa is 'wavering' or 'unsteadiness,' so it does not allow the intellect to hold on to a firm decision. For many seekers, the mind remains engrossed in business, money, family, society, politics, art, sport, entertainment, addictions, television, literature, movies, and theater, etc. Such a preoccupied mind can never be steady or focused on one goal. Being versatile and taking pleasure in these diverse aspects of life, at least to some extent, is considered a sign of eminent, evolved, progressive, aesthetic, and well-rounded life in society. Such a person is held in high esteem, so naturally, many people tend to live in the same fashion. However, the intellect which is thus distracted in many ways cannot be channelized and focused in one direction for spiritual pursuit. The intellect can be distracted even for the seeker who is engaged in many religious activities. Many rituals give way to scattered emotions. The seeker is deceived into thinking that he is doing something religious or spiritual, but in reality, he does not progress on the spiritual path. The seeker must gather all scattered emotions, channel them in one direction, and focus them on one goal. Without this, the intellect cannot resolve that "I am Brahman," and even if it resolves, it cannot stick to that resolution. The seeker has to change his entire lifestyle to adhere to the decision that "I am Ātman." The intellect that is immersed in mundane worldly thoughts of "I, me, and mine" cannot persevere in the efforts to maintain the resolve that "I am Ātman." Many distracted seekers are unable to think resolutely in this manner, and they often do not find the right people who can steer them in the necessary direction for spiritual pursuit.

**Discussion on scattering of the intellect**

यामिमां पुष्पितां वाचं प्रवदन्त्यविपश्चितः ।
वेदवादरताः पार्थ नान्यदस्तीति वादिनः ॥ ४२ ॥
कामात्मानः स्वर्गपरा जन्मकर्मफलप्रदाम् ।
क्रियाविशेषबहुलां भोगैश्वर्यगतिं प्रति ॥ ४३ ॥

**भोगैश्वर्यप्रसक्तानां तयापहृतचेतसाम् ।**
**व्यवसायात्मिका बुद्धिः समाधौ न विधीयते ॥ ४४ ॥**

*Yām imāṃ puṣpitāṃ vācaṃ pravādanty avipaścitaḥ* ।
*Vedavādaratāḥ pārtha nānyad astīti vādinaḥ* ॥ *42* ॥
*Kāmātmānaḥ svargaparā janmakarmaphalapradām* ।
*Kriyāviśeṣabahulāṃ bhogaiśvaryagatiṃ prati* ॥ *43* ॥
*Bhogaiśvaryaprasaktānāṃ tayāpahṛtacetasām* ।
*Vyavasāyātmikā buddhiḥ samādhau na vidhīyate* ॥ *44* ॥

**Meaning:** Ignorant, ritualistic people, who do not understand the gist of the Vedas, take pleasure in the Vedic verses that glorify fruitive or gainful actions. Their language is ornamental and pretentious. They believe that the attainment of heaven is the highest joy. They do not acknowledge the presence of the 'Section of Knowledge' (*Jñānakāṇḍa*) which is separate and independent of the 'Section of Actions' (*Karmakāṇḍa*) in the Vedas. People, whose minds are filled with worldly desires, and who revel in pleasures and opulence that result in birth, actions, pleasure, and pain, are verily drawn in the same direction. Their intellect can never be steady in deep, absorbed, steady meditation i.e. Samādhi.

These three verses are based on the context of the ancient Vedic culture of performing Yajñas and desiring the attainment of heavenly pleasures. Today, there is no reason to dwell on the traditional rituals of Yajñas and their fruits. Yajña-yāgās are described in the Pūrva-Mīmāṅsā section of the Vedas. By performing them properly, one can enjoy plush pleasures in heaven. Currently, there is a proliferation of newer forms of enjoyment and luxuries. Even though there is no belief in the concept of heaven, the fundamental craving for pleasures is the same in most people. The tendency to luxuriate in plush objects in an unconstrained manner is explicitly seen in society today. There is also a propensity towards refusing the theory that propounds performing actions and worship without desiring any fruits. People even refuse the principles of *Sāṅkhyayoga* to make way for purely materialistic life. Most people tend to prefer instant gratification over Eternal, Pure Bliss. This tendency is mostly a result of Rajoguṇa and Tamoguṇa. Such people engage happily in the *Karmakāṇḍa* and they get increasingly attached to the desire of plush heavenly pleasures. Their intellect can never remain resolute in the true Self, Ātman. It is important to note a Śruti in Śvetāśvetar Upaniṣad in this regard –

**यदा चर्मवदाकाशं वेष्टयिष्यन्ति मानवाः ।**
**तदा देवमविज्ञाय दुःखस्यान्तो भविष्यति ॥ (६.२०)**

*Yadā carmavadākāśaṃ veṣṭayiṣyanti mānavāḥ*
*Tadā devamavijñaya duḥkhasyānto bhaviṣyati* ॥ *(6.20)*

"If a person can figure out how to wrap the entire sky with a skin-like cover, only then it may be possible to eradicate grief in life without knowing who real God is." This simply means, it is impossible to find lasting Bliss without knowing "I am God" or without the direct realization that "I am Brahman." The happiness derived from worldly objects is illusory, impermanent, and it diminishes with time. It enslaves men to depend on those objects. It is not possible to find true and lasting happiness through such worldly objects.

## The value of the Vedas in today's world

**त्रैगुण्यविषया वेदा निस्त्रैगुण्यो भवार्जुन ।**
**निर्द्वन्द्वो नित्यसत्त्वस्थो निर्योगक्षेम आत्मवान् ॥ ४५ ॥**
**यावानर्थ उदपाने सर्वतः सम्प्लुतोदके ।**
**तावान्सर्वेषु वेदेषु ब्राह्मणस्य विजानतः ॥ ४६ ॥**

*Traiguṇyaviṣayā vedā nistraiguṇyo bhavārjuna* ।
*Nirdvandvo nityasatvastho niryogakṣema ātmavān* ॥ *45* ॥
*Yāvān artha udapāne sarvataḥ saṃplutodake* ।
*Tāvān sarveṣu vedeṣu brāhmaṇasya vijānataḥ* ॥ *46* ॥

**Meaning:** All the four Vedas deal with the characteristic tendencies of Sattva, Rājas, and Tāmas Guṇas. O Arjuna! Transcend the three Guṇas and free yourself from all dualities.

Acquire the traits of Sattvaguṇa. Be intent on your real Self, Ātman, without rejoicing in the mundane life of acquiring and preserving objects. The 'Section of Actions' (*Karmakāṇḍa*) in the Vedas, is of little value to the Knower of Brahman, just as a small pond is of little value when there is water everywhere in the surroundings.

The Vedas consist of the following three sections:

- The Section of Action (*Karmakāṇḍa*) – the theory that deals with the execution of actions and bearing their fruits
- The Section of Worship (*Upāsanākāṇḍa*) – the theory that deals with various forms of worship and their results
- The Section of Knowledge (*Jñānakāṇḍa*) – the theory that deals with the realization of Ātman, the true Self

These three sections are influenced by the characteristics of Sāttva, Rājas, and Tāmas Guṇas. Among them, the 'Section of Action' has fruit-driven gainful rituals which create desires to obtain and enjoy luxuries. However, Kṛtayuga, Tretāyuga, and Dwāpārayuga each had their own peculiarities. The first two sections of the Vedas that dealt with actions and worship were prominent in the earlier Yugas. They are not so prevalent in today's Kaliyuga. Today, the system of Yajña-Yaga propounded in the 'Section of Action' has been mostly replaced by actions based on Karmayoga, the third chapter of the Gita. The worship of deities like Indra, Agni stated in the 'Section of Worship' is now replaced by the worship of Lord Rāma and Lord Kṛṣṇa, etc. However, the 'Section of Knowledge,' the third section of the Vedas, is as relevant today as it was in the past. While studying the 'Section of Knowledge,' it is advisable to abstain from the play of the Guṇas pertinent to the actions and worship taught in the Vedas and adhere to Ātman by nurturing Sattvaguṇa alone. A large lake may have a huge reservoir of water; however, a person only needs as much water as is required to quench his thirst. Likewise, the Vedas may prescribe many rituals in actions and worship; however, studying the Upaniṣads in 'Section of Knowledge,' is enough for a seeker to attain liberation. St. Tukārāma says in this regard, "The Vedas may discuss many topics in detail. But their gist is that we should surrender completely to Viṭṭhala. We should chant His Mantra with utmost love, devotion, and unswerving faith that 'I am Brahman.'"

Brahman, the true Self, is beyond the three Guṇas. The seeker who is under the influence of the three Guṇas cannot realize that he is Brahman. Therefore, one who seeks the Knowledge of Brahman should not dwell on fruitive or gainful actions and gainful worship. When the seeker strives to gain fruits from actions and worship, it creates the dualities of success or failure, less or more fruits, etc. in his mind. These dualities pertain to worldly matters, so he succumbs to worldly influences even more by the day. It is necessary for the seeker to consciously dismiss them. Lord Kṛṣṇa says that the seeker who mainly has Sāttvaguṇa attains a higher plane of gods and other deities (*14.8*). However, Sattvaguṇa also creates bondage (*14.6*). The desirer of Mokṣa should not be proud of his Sattvic disposition since it is an instrument for spiritual practice, not the ultimate goal.

All worldly people must perform some job or business for their subsistence. Each person becomes rich or poor in accordance with the earnings from his work. It is a stark reality that even if people work honestly and arduously to the best of their abilities, their financial status varies from one to another. No political philosophy has been able to change or avoid this reality. St. Rāmadāsa says, "A person should be engaged happily in his material life, but, at the same time, strive to progress on the spiritual path." It is necessary for the seeker to lead a steady, secure worldly life, but this doesn't mean he is supposed to constantly mull over it or be influenced by it. First, he should ascertain the scope and draw a boundary around his day-to-day worldly life. If the seeker feels obliged to cater to the needs of all relatives, extended family members, old friends, professional colleagues, and neighbors, then he will not be left with any time for spiritual pursuit. The main problem for every worldly seeker is being preoccupied with unnecessary thoughts, worry, and anxiety about daily life and interactions. This anxiousness arises from incomplete actions or duties performed half-heartedly or the expectation of fruits. "I should have done this," "I should not have done this," "Not sure why I did that or didn't do that" – these are some superfluous thoughts which usually occupy the mind. If the seeker follows all dos and don'ts as stated in scriptures, then the meticulous and timely execution of duties will leave no room for anxiousness in his mind. The expectation of results, various desires, constant comparison, competition, and jealousy are some other causes of anxiousness and worry in life. The sense of insecurity also leads to worry and anxiety. The seeker should consciously wipe out these thoughts and tendencies from his mind.

## The analysis of actions and fruits of actions

**कर्मण्येवाधिकारस्ते मा फलेषु कदाचन ।**
**मा कर्मफलहेतुर्भूर्मा ते सङ्गोऽस्त्वकर्मणि ॥ ४७ ॥**
**योगस्थः कुरु कर्माणि सङ्गं त्यक्त्वा धनञ्जय ।**
**सिद्ध्यसिद्ध्योः समो भूत्वा समत्वं योग उच्यते ॥ ४८ ॥**
**दूरेण ह्यवरं कर्म बुद्धियोगाद्धनञ्जय ।**
**बुद्धौ शरणमन्विच्छ कृपणाः फलहेतवः ॥ ४९ ॥**
**बुद्धियुक्तो जहातीह उभे सुकृतदुष्कृते ।**
**तस्माद्योगाय युज्यस्व योगः कर्मसु कौशलम् ॥ ५० ॥**

*Karmaṇy evādhikāras te mā phaleṣu kadācana* ।
*Mā karmaphalahetur bhūr mā te saṅgo'stv akarmaṇi* ॥ *47* ॥
*Yogasthaḥ kuru karmāṇi saṅgaṃ tyaktvā dhanañjaya* ।
*Siddhyasiddhyoḥ samo bhūtvā samatvaṃ yoga ucyate* ॥ *48* ॥

*Dūreṇa hy avaraṃ karma buddhiyogād dhanañjaya* ।
*Buddhau śaraṇam anviccha kṛpaṇāḥ phalahetavaḥ* ॥ *49* ॥
*Buddhiyukto jahātīha ubhe sukṛtaduṣkṛte* ।
*Tasmād yogāya yujyasva yogaḥ karmasu kauśalam* ॥ *50* ॥

**Meaning:** You only have the right to perform your prescribed duty, but never at any time, are you entitled to its fruits. Neither should you be the desirer of the fruits of action nor should you be obstinate about non-action. Perform your duties by being firm in Yoga. Renounce the attachment to fruits of action. Be equanimous in success as well as failure. This equanimity is known as Yoga. Fruitive or gainful actions, as described in the Karmakāṇḍa of the Vedas, are far inferior to the equanimity in *Buddhiyoga* – the Yoga of Self-Knowledge. Hence, establish yourself in *Buddhiyoga*. Those who engage in actions by keeping an eye on fruits are contemptible indeed. All merits and sins are worn off for people who execute actions with an equanimous mind. Therefore, embrace the Yoga of Equanimity. The real talent is being equanimous in results while performing actions.

These verses present a great, prominent principle of the Indian Vaidic philosophy. There is an inviolable relationship between man and actions. Actions and expectation of their fruits go hand in hand. Precisely here, man engages in conflict with Īśvara's governance and thus becomes discontent himself. Evidently, a person cannot decide how much success he should get for whichever activity he performs. St. Rāmadāsa, who strongly propounds utmost efforts in every action, says that human beings cannot control the results. He states in Dāsabodha (*20.4.11*), "Sometimes, Īśvara engulfs a person with ignorance to let him fail. And sometimes, Īśvara propels a person towards knowledge so that he becomes successful. Only Īśvara knows why and how He does it." Therefore, the seeker should put exhaustive efforts in every action but not be worried about its fruits. Everyone has a right to execute actions. In other words, every person must engage in some action, one way or the other, since it is the order of Lord Kṛṣṇa. However, there is no guarantee that the action will yield the fruits which are desired by the doer. Every action is naturally bound to get its prearranged fruits according to the doer's past Prārabdha as per the governance of Īśvara. Knowing this, the seeker should not expect specifically customized fruits for his actions and thus lock horns with Īśvara's scheme of governance. Whether he expects fruits or not, his actions are bound to yield designated fruits. These fruits may be less than, more than, or the same as his expectations, but they are always as per Īśvara's scheme. Expecting a fruit is invariably associated with suffering. When the seeker does not recognize or embrace this fact quietly, his life becomes restless, perturbed, and polluted due to unnecessary comparison, competition, jealousy, and greed. He feels angry at adverse circumstances and, in turn, feels helpless. Even if he gets expected fruits or success, it inflates his ego. Boasting about success brings restlessness in his life. In today's world, every person should certainly plan for profit, properly organize work, judiciously execute all actions, and in the end, be content with the results granted by Īśvara.

The word **Yoga** has many different meanings. Being equanimous in the fruits of actions – whether completed or left incomplete – is known as Yoga. A person who has an equanimous mind in the fruit, be it success or failure, is known as **Yogastha** – established in Yoga. After performing the actions in the best possible manner, the seeker should unconditionally accept the prearranged fruits of his actions. Thereafter, He is supposed to remain content in whichever circumstances come his way and continue the spiritual practices of chanting, meditation, studying scriptures, etc. The Yogic state of equanimity is compromised when the seeker mulls over or gets attached to the fruits and becomes restless as a result. The restless, wavering mind can neither chant a Mantra nor think about Ātman.

An action performed by being proud that "I am the doer" and by desiring fruits is far inferior to the desireless actions performed as per *Niṣkāma Karmayoga* – this is explained in *Buddhiyoga*. **Buddhiyoga**, the Yoga of Self-Knowledge, states that Ātman is the true nature of each Jiva. Ātman is actionless and non-doer. Hence, the true Self is a non-doer as well. Therefore, the seeker should strive to abide in *Buddhiyoga* – the thought that "I am Ātman" – and perform actions without seeking fruits. People who perform actions by seeking fruits suffer in many ways. Desiring fruits often leads to the feelings of hope and despair, gain and loss, jealousy, malice, and anguish that ensues from them.

The real nature of every Jiva is Pure Bliss. But he forgets his real nature and experiences dejection. The world may hold ambitious people in high esteem. But they are contemptible from the spiritual perspective. They have to rotate continuously in the cycle of birth and death. The seeker is himself responsible for the fruits if he performs actions seeking fruits. When he considers himself as the 'doer of actions' and 'enjoyer of fruits', he verily gets stuck in the birth and death cycle. Every Jiva is tied by Prārabdha. He is impelled to act accordingly. Sometimes, the seeker may strive to perform a good deed but still end up performing an evil deed. If he can steadily adhere to the thought that "I am not the doer," he will not incur the merits of good actions or sins of bad actions. This simply means he will not be bound by the fruits of those actions. Such a seeker will not be deluded by thinking of himself as virtuous or sinful. This argument is not meant to give leeway to evil actions, but rather it is only meant to throw light on what may happen due to powerful Prārabdha. Scriptures state that a person may experience fruits of actions in different planes. However, all planes are ultimately perishable. That Yoga is considered 'Supreme' following which man attains his lasting benefit and welfare.

The tendency of not doing any action to avoid the trouble of bearing its fruits or repercussions indicates cowardly behavior. Only the seeker who takes the vows monastic life for Self-realization is eligible for the formal renouncement of worldly duties prescribed for him. For a vast majority of other worldly seekers, their mind is purified when they perform actions without seeking fruits.

The word **Sāṅkhya** in Sanskrit means 'Samyak + Ā + Khyā,' which means the appropriate decision. The decision on "How to best execute actions" in this chapter is proclaimed directly by Lord Kṛṣṇa; so, it is flawless. When this Sāṅkhya is assimilated by the intellect, it is known as ***Sāṅkhyabuddhi*** or ***Yogabuddhi***. This simply means that the person having *Sāṅkhyabuddhi* can decide the best course of doing actions as directed by Lord Kṛṣṇa. The real talent, expertise, or skill lies in living a dynamic, active life while performing all actions through such appropriately decisive intellect.

## The result of Buddhiyoga

**कर्मजं बुद्धियुक्ता हि फलं त्यक्त्वा मनीषिणः ।**
**जन्मबन्धविनिर्मुक्ताः पदं गच्छन्त्यनामयम् ॥ ५१ ॥**
**यदा ते मोहकलिलं बुद्धिर्व्यतितरिष्यति ।**
**तदा गन्तासि निर्वेदं श्रोतव्यस्य श्रुतस्य च ॥ ५२ ॥**
**श्रुतिविप्रतिपन्ना ते यदा स्थास्यति निश्चला ।**
**समाधावचला बुद्धिस्तदा योगमवाप्स्यसि ॥ ५३ ॥**

*Karmajaṃ buddhiyuktā hi phalaṃ tyaktvā manīṣiṇaḥ* ।
*Janmabandhavinirmuktāḥ padaṃ gacchhanty anāmāyām* ॥ *51* ॥
*Yadā te mohakalilaṃ buddhir vyatitariṣyati* ।
*Tadā gantāsi nirvedaṃ śrotavyasya śrutasya ca* ॥ *52* ॥

*Śrutivipratipannā te yadā sthāsyati niścalā* ।
*Samādhāv acalā buddhis tadā yogam avāpsyasi* ॥ *53* ॥

**Meaning:** Wise people, who practice *Buddhiyoga*, renounce the fruits arising from actions and thus liberate themselves from the bondage of the birth and death cycle. They attain eternal Pure Bliss beyond all sufferings. When your intellect is cleansed from the mire of delusion, you shall be disinterested in all worldly pleasures that have been heard to date, and all that are yet to be heard. When your intellect remains steady, and it is no longer disturbed or influenced by the Vedic verses which describe glorious fruits of actions, it shall attain *Buddhiyoga*.

Wise men attain *Buddhiyoga* and thus live life by abiding in the true Self. They liberate themselves from the birth-death cycle by not seeking fruits of actions. They become One with their true Self, Brahman, where they are not troubled by the bondage of ignorance, actions, and Vāsanā. On the contrary, people who are closely attached to their body, actions, and the world are engulfed by ignorance. Ignorance leads to Vāsanā, Vāsanā leads to more actions, and the chain continues further. This chain can be broken only by Self-realization. Actions performed by abiding in the philosophical tenets of the 'Yoga of Self-Knowledge' free the intellect from the mire of delusion. There are three kinds of delusion: "I am the body," "The world is real," "I am the doer and enjoyer." When these delusions are wiped out, the mind is freed from desires to discuss, listen, or dwell on worldly matters. A large part of human life is wasted in reminiscing about the memories of past life and achievements. A lot of time is also spent worrying about the future. Dwelling in such memories, worries, etc. is a waste of time and mental energy. These thoughts bind humans in the life and death cycle. When the intellect deluded by such thoughts is freed from delusions, the liberated Jiva loses interest in fruits of actions. He becomes dispassionate about worldly matters and attains lasting inner peace.

Actions can be good or bad, auspicious or inauspicious, or virtuous or sinful. However, their fruits do not disturb the one who selflessly executes actions without desiring fruits. The onus of actions that are performed according to the precepts of scriptures is on scriptures themselves. In general, good actions generate **merit** (*Puṇya*). However, the same actions performed without any desires generate **pure merit** (*Śuddha Puṇya*), which helps in the attainment of Mokṣa. It is the pure merit due to which the seeker is graced by the Lord, and in due course, he is graced by the blessings of some enlightened sage.

There are three kinds of actions in human life –

1 ***Sañciṭa karma***: Accumulated actions of a Jiva from all past human births. Every person has to endure the fruits of all actions – good or bad – at some point in time. Only after Self-realization, these accumulated actions are fully wiped out.

2 **Prārabdha *karma***: A slice of actions from Sañciṭa karma which are ripe and fructescent, on account of which the Jiva gets his body in the current birth. The body of the Jiva lasts so long as his Prārabdha Karma is not exhausted.

3 ***Kriyamāṇa karma***: Fresh new actions performed by the Jiva. If new actions are done with "I am the doer" mindset and by desiring results, they get added to the Sañciṭa of that Jiva.

When Kriyamāṇa karma is performed without expectations, it does not get added to Sañcita. Prārabdha comes to an end when it is fully endured. After Self-realization, Sañcita Karma is burnt in the same birth or in rare cases after many births. Such a Yogi who practices the principles of the Yoga of Self-Knowledge is liberated. He realizes Pure Bliss of Ātman where there is not a trace of grief.

Actions and their attractive fruits are commonly discussed in the Vedas to a great extent. The intellect becomes fickle while repetitively hearing about actions and seeking their glorious fruits. When the same intellect becomes quiet, stops seeking fruits, and remains equanimous in fruits, it attains the desired effect of *Buddhiyoga*.

There are many theories in Upaniṣads that are seemingly contradictory or incongruent with each other. E.g. one theory in Taittiriya Upaniṣad suggests that the universe is created from the Five Great Elements. In contrast, another theory in Chāndogya. Upaniṣad suggests that it is created from the Three Great Elements. The seeker who stumbles upon these contradictions can resolve them and put his doubts to rest in the company of enlightened saints. He then gets convinced about the authenticity of scriptures, and he understands the gist of philosophy. When such a seeker, whose intellect is steadied by doing desireless actions, continually strives to abide in Ātman, he becomes One with his true Self, Ātman. Thereafter, he is known as *Sthitaprajña*.

## Arjuna's question about the person of steady wisdom

**अर्जुन उवाच ।**

**स्थितप्रज्ञस्य का भाषा समाधिस्थस्य केशव ।**
**स्थितधीः किं प्रभाषेत किमासीत व्रजेत किम् ॥ ५४ ॥**

*Arjuna uvāca* ।

*Sthitaprajñasya kā bhāṣā samādhisthasya keśava* ।
*Sthitadhīḥ kiṃ prabhāṣeta kim āsīta vrajeta kim* ॥ *54* ॥

**Meaning:** (Arjuna said) O Keśava! What are the characteristics of the man of steady wisdom who uninterruptedly remains absorbed in Samādhi? How does he speak, how does he sit, and how does he walk?

A person of steady wisdom whose intellect is firmly immersed in his true Self, Ātman, is known as ***Sthitaprajña***. It is the very nature of his intellect to remain steady in its own Self. The word ***Sthita*** in Sanskrit does not mean being stuck, paused, or stopped. There are many misconceptions about the word *Sthitaprajña* in society. In fact, misconceptions are much more, and only a few understand what the word really means. Ātman is Absolute, Pure Bliss, and one who realizes "I am Ātman" also becomes Pure Bliss himself. He continues to revel in Pure Bliss regardless of all other factors. People who do not comprehend this fact create misconceptions about Ātman. Stories of many enlightened, ascetic sages in the remote Himālayas only augment these misbeliefs. Ordinary people feel nervous about the idea that the life of an enlightened person may be substantially different from normal human life. Some even question, "What is the point of living such insensitive, passive life?" However, Arjuna's question in this verse reflects that *Sthitaprajña* – the man of steady wisdom – lives, speaks, and performs actions like everyone else. He does not live in the state of actionless Samādhi for years together. How can he guide large groups of people, travel to holy places, or write spiritual texts in the state of actionless Samādhi?

**Lord Kṛṣṇa's answer**

*श्रीभगवानुवाच ।*
प्रजहाति यदा कामान्सर्वान्पार्थ मनोगतान् ।
आत्मन्येवात्मना तुष्टः स्थितप्रज्ञस्तदोच्यते ॥ ५५ ॥
दुःखेष्वनुद्विग्नमनाः सुखेषु विगतस्पृहः ।
वीतरागभयक्रोधः स्थितधीर्मुनिरुच्यते ॥ ५६ ॥
यः सर्वत्रानभिस्नेहस्तत्तत्प्राप्य शुभाशुभम् ।
नाभिनन्दति न द्वेष्टि तस्य प्रज्ञा प्रतिष्ठिता ॥ ५७ ॥

*Śrībhagavān uvāca* ।
*Prajahāti yadā kāmān sarvān pārtha manogatān* ।
*Ātmany evātmanā tuṣṭaḥ sthitaprajñas tadocyate* ॥ 55 ॥
*Duḥkheṣv anudvignamanāḥ sukheṣu vigataspṛhaḥ* ।
*Vītarāgabhayakrodhaḥ sthitadhīr munir ucyate* ॥ 56 ॥

*Yaḥ sarvatrānabhisnehas tattatprāpya śubhāśubham* ।
*Nābhinandati na dveṣṭi tasya prajñā pratiṣṭhitā* ॥ 57 ॥

**Meaning:** When that wise person completely renounces all desires in mind and remains satisfied in Pure Bliss by being One with his true Self, *Sat-Cit-Ānanda*, he is called the ***Sthitaprajña***. A person whose mind is neither perturbed due to distress nor elated with joy and free from attachment, fear, and anger is called the ***Muni***.A person who has no attachment to any worldly objects, and who neither rejoices nor becomes unhappy due to whatever good or bad things he receives in life, his intellect is said to be steady in Ātman.

There are many desires in a seeker's mind without him being aware of them. Ranging from mere daydreams to everyday responsibilities, a multitude of desires and thoughts throng his mind. He also wishes for the presence or absence of certain things on a familial, social, and political level. It is necessary for the seeker to classify his desires or wishful thoughts conscientiously. He can classify them in two ways:

- Practical and useful
- Impractical and useless

A desire should be practical i.e. feasible to fulfill. After fulfillment, it should not cause trouble but rather be useful in life. A novice seeker who is just starting on a spiritual path should – at the least – earnestly give up all impractical, unproductive, and useless desires. By removing such desires, the seeker may get a glimpse of Pure Bliss of his true Self, Ātman. Once he is captivated by such Bliss, even the supposedly productive and useful desires recede from his mind and exert less influence on him. Thereafter, only bare minimum desires necessary for a basic, simplistic life remain in his mind. In the enlightened stage, even basic needs are taken care of by Prārabdha. Such an evolved seeker is always satisfied in life. He, as if, plays with his Self (*Ātmakrīḍa*) and rejoices in Pure Bliss of his Self (*Ātmarati*). In the realm of devotion, he plays with and rejoices in Lord Kṛṣṇa in every action. St. Mirabai, the renowned devotee of Kṛṣṇa, says –

**तोरी प्रीत छोडू कृष्णा कौन संग जोडू?**

*Tori prit chodu Kṛṣṇa kaun sanga jodu*?

"If I renounce loving you, who else is left for me to love?" This is the real state of a person of steady wisdom. Once he learns to see Ātman everywhere and revel in Pure Bliss of Ātman, he doesn't grieve even during tragic, unfortunate situations. Being Pure Bliss himself, he does not feel the need for objects of pleasure even if he obtains them. Ordinary people mistakenly assume that he must be happy or sad when he encounters good or bad situations. But that is not the case.

The feeling of love for other people or objects is ultimately for one's own happiness, not for the happiness of others. Most people fear potential obstacles in the path of happiness, or they fear death as they strongly identify themselves with the body. They also feel angry at people or circumstances that obstruct their happiness. However, the one having steady wisdom has no reason to be angry at anyone for any reason since he is Bliss himself. The attachment felt by a person for his body and the world is for his own pleasure. These pleasures are impermanent. The person of steady wisdom remains detached and dispassionate at all times since he realizes the perpetual, never-receding Pure Bliss of his true Self. The concepts of good or bad and auspicious or inauspicious become inconsequential for him. Whether auspicious or inauspicious, everything is merged in Lord Rāma for him. He is neither elated by auspicious events nor dejected by ominous events. When he is steadily absorbed in Self-realization of Ātman, inauspiciousness and auspiciousness both cease to exist for him. Everything is verily Brahman in this stage.

When a wise person who is perfected in the teachings of *Buddhiyoga* – the firm resolve that "I am Atman" – renounces desires of all kinds and remains content in Ātman, he is known as the *Sthitaprajña*. Such a person may not necessarily be only from a warrior background like Arjuna. He may as well be a businessman, industrialist, farmer, or a professional in any other field. It is necessary for him to organize, plan, and think about making a profit while working in his industry, business, agriculture, or profession. Being engaged in work is not detrimental from the spiritual perspective. However, indulging in obsessive analysis of finances, sense of insecurity, unrealistic ambitions, and succumbing to hope or dejection are detrimental for any seeker.

Every person should certainly plan and execute his daily duties and responsibilities to the best of his abilities. But when he becomes anxious or restless about the outcome after meticulous execution of his action, such desire for result is called *Kāmanā*, which is detrimental. Arjuna says at the beginning of this chapter, "We do not understand which is better: to conquer them or be conquered by them (*2.6*)." While fighting a war, these thoughts about potential victory or loss indicate mulling over its result right from the outset. After a warrior takes all necessary steps and efforts to be victorious, nurturing the desire in mind to be victorious takes the form of a *Kāmanā*. Such a desire is detrimental, and it causes restlessness. It may even affect his judgment while fighting the war.

Even the person having steady wisdom is compelled to look for food, clothing, and shelter to protect his body. There is a story of St. Jñāneśwara, where he roasted an Indian bread on his back through the power of Yoga to appease his hunger. Enlightened saints like Śri Gondavalekara loved to eat sorghum bread with a special curry, and Gādage Mahārāja loved to eat onions with sorghum bread. These preferences in food are not detrimental desires. However, being preoccupied with food delicacies, taking fascination for branded and fashionable clothes, and aiming for king-size life are harmful desires. They should be wiped out from the mind. St. Ekanātha belonged to a prosperous, wealthy background. It is said that his daily meals consisted of classic Indian desserts. King Janaka lived in a magnificent palace. Both were renowned as enlightened luminaries. However, the prosperity in their lives did not stem from their desires; rather, it was a result of their Prārabdha. When the seeker renounces all superfluous desires and executes actions with a content mind while reveling in Pure Bliss of Ātman, he is known as the ***Sthitaprajña***. The Gita says that, "He is content in all situations (*12.19*)."

A person who has wiped away love, fear, and anger, who does not feel despondent even in somber incidents, and who does not crave for joy is called the *Sthitaprajña* or Muni. Vedānta states that when both merits and sins from past lives are suddenly balanced for a Jiva, he is born as a human. Thus, every person inevitably faces both joyful and painful incidents in his life, which result from his past merits and sins, respectively. The person may face a joyful event such as promotion at work or a painful event such as death in his family. But it is not mandatory for him to become happy or sad in such situations. Events may themselves necessitate love, fear, or anger. However, the seeker can entirely use his discretion and react appropriately. Events or circumstances cannot mandate the seeker to be attached, angry, or frightened in any way. In this verse, the term 'Raga or love' indicates attachment. Everyone naturally has an instinct to love and be loved. However, love is converted to excessive attachment due to ignorance. Attachment gives way to an intense craving (*Īṣṇa*) for money, appreciation, wife, children, objects of pleasure, mastering scriptures, and long life. Grief is a natural reaction to adverse circumstances, and it is manifested in many ways. E.g. a person *fears* adversities while enjoying money, health, status, power, fame, success, etc. At the same time, he feels *angry* at those who create adversities. However, an enlightened person of steady wisdom is not disturbed by grief nor does he have any superfluous desires, so he is not frightened at any time for any reason. Prārabdha brings certain situations in life, but it cannot compel a person to feel happy or sad about them. One who continually adheres to this philosophy and renounces the negative traits of desire, anger, and attachment is called the Muni. There is more discussion on this topic in the upcoming 62nd verse.

A person who is dispassionate in all aspects of life, who remains unperturbed in good and bad situations, and who maintains equanimity in joy and grief is known as the *Sthitaprajña.* He remains unruffled in victory and defeat, profit and loss, respect and disrespect, praise and reproach, fame and disgrace, success and failure, and all such dualities. His intellect is ever equanimous in all circumstances.

**The relation between organs, objects and the seeker**

**यदा संहरते चायं कूर्मोऽङ्गानीव सर्वशः ।**
**इन्द्रियाणीन्द्रियार्थेभ्यस्तस्य प्रज्ञा प्रतिष्ठिता ॥ ५८ ॥**
**विषया विनिवर्तन्ते निराहारस्य देहिनः ।**
**रसवर्जं रसोऽप्यस्य परं दृष्ट्वा निवर्तते ॥ ५९ ॥**
**यततो ह्यपि कौन्तेय पुरुषस्य विपश्चितः ।**
**इन्द्रियाणि प्रमाथीनि हरन्ति प्रसभं मनः ॥ ६० ॥**
**तानि सर्वाणि संयम्य युक्त आसीत मत्परः ।**
**वशे हि यस्येन्द्रियाणि तस्य प्रज्ञा प्रतिष्ठिता ॥ ६१ ॥**

*Yadā saṃharate cāyaṃ kūrmo 'ṅgānīva sarvaśaḥ* ।
*Indriyāṇīndriyārthebhyas tasya prajñā pratiṣṭhitā* ॥ *58* ॥
*Viṣayā vinivartante nirāhārasya dehinaḥ* ।
*Rasavarjaṃ raso 'pyasya paraṃ dṛṣṭvā nivartate* ॥ *59* ॥
*Yatato hy api kaunteya puruṣasya vipaścitaḥ* ।
*Indriyāṇi pramāthīni haranti prasabhaṃ manaḥ* ॥ *60* ॥

*Tāni sarvāṇi saṅyamya yukta āsīta matparaḥ* ।
*Vaśe hi yasyendriyāṇi tasya prajñā pratiṣṭhitā* ॥ *61* ॥

**Meaning:** The tortoise withdraws its limbs from all sides into the shell. Analogous to this, a seeker who withdraws his senses from sense-objects has his intellect steadied in the Self. The person may restrict his senses from seeking worldly objects, but the longing for enjoyment remains in his mind. However, even this longing comesto an end after realizing "I am Brahman." O Arjuna! While a wise person is striving hard to restrain himself, his strong and disruptive senses forcefully impel his mind towards objects. Therefore, the seeker should quieten his mind, restrain his organs, and be My devotee exclusively. The seeker whose senses are completely restrained is said to have his intellect firmly steady in Ātman.

A tortoise is known to retract its limbs from all sides. Likewise, when a seeker withdraws his senses from worldly objects and rests his intellect in Ātman, the true Self, his intellect is said to be firmly steady. At this stage, he has restrained his senses which usually stray in all directions seeking happiness. When the senses cease to take in or be influenced by their respective objects, the seeker loses his very interest in those objects. Even if he experiences any pleasure due to Prārabdha, he doesn't voluntarily seek or enjoy objects for happiness. Rather, objects are enjoyed naturally without him being an enjoyer. The seeker sees all objects as petty, inconsequential pleasures.

The senses are naturally drawn towards objects due to imprints and conditioning in mind from many past births. The outward attraction of the senses is a part of the governance of Īśvara. The pull of the outside world – whether more or less – exists according to the specific mix of Sattva, Rājas, or Tāmas Guṇa in the seeker. The seeker should make a note of this and firmly attempt to restrain his organs without being dejected. At the same time, he need not feel constantly guilty and lose his confidence if he is unable to conquer his organs or curb his desires.

The seeker is required to observe careful discretion to detach himself from worldly objects. All objects of pleasure like praise, touch, power, fame, etc. are insentient. Objects cannot think 'to whom they should go to,' or 'by whom they should be acquired.' They do not have the power and freedom to give happiness since they are insentient. We can use a simple logic in this regard. If the happiness derived from objects is indeed 'objective', then everyone should feel equally happy while enjoying the same object. E.g. some people need hot water for bathing, but some like cold water. Thus, the hot or cold touch does not have an intrinsic power or freedom to make anyone happy. Happiness depends on the Jiva, the experiencer, hence it is 'subjective' in nature. The sentient experiencer may be pleased or unhappy while experiencing the same object. An insentient object is that which neither knows itself nor understands the other. E.g. yellow color belongs to a form (like a flower), and it is seen by the eyes. The object itself neither understands that "I am yellow" nor does the object like or dislike its own color. However, the experiencer Jiva knows that the object is yellow. The Jiva likes or dislikes it. The Jiva may like being a famous himself but may dislike someone else's fame, or he may even like it when another person faces infamy or disgrace in society. Other people may be resentful towards a person when he becomes famous for some reason. Therefore, even fame cannot provide any person with absolute, unadulterated, and lasting happiness. It is thus evident that happiness derived from worldly objects is superficial and delusional. This fact is clearly seen in objects of all kinds. When the seeker learns this theory, reflects upon it, and assimilates it, he can restrain his senses from objects of pleasure relatively easily.

The seeker can experience happiness in deep-sleep even when there are no objects. The experiencer disappears in his true Self in deep-sleep, and thus he realizes Pure Bliss of his Self, Brahman. But imprints of ignorance are restored when he wakes up from deep-sleep. Therefore, happiness in deep-sleep does not sustain in the waking state. The seeker is supposed to meditate on the Vedāntic Mahāvākya **'Thou art that'** (*Tat-Tvam-Asi*), which means 'You are Brahman', to experience the same lasting Pure Bliss of his Self in the state of waking. He needs to learn this Mahāvākya first from his Sadguru, and then deeply meditate on it. Only then the veil of ignorance can be removed from his mind. For that, he must restrain his organs from going out to objects. After restraining organs, his intellect remains steady in Ātman by discriminating between real and unreal, transient and permanent, core and peripheral, truth and illusion, and perishable and imperishable. The seeker eventually becomes One with his true Self, Ātman.

Despite many earnest efforts from the seeker to restrain his mind, his organs forcefully impel the mind towards worldly objects. Therefore, first he has to try to curb the organs at least until he gets a glimpse of Pure Bliss of Ātman. As such, it is possible to somehow restrain the organs from seeking objects, but the mental longing for objects is fully wiped out only after Self-realization. Between restraining the organs (*Dama*) and conquering the mind (*Śama*), it is relatively easy to restrain the organs through discretion and forceful self-control. However, it is extremely difficult to conquer the mind. The obstinate mind cannot be conquered due to its inherent attachment to objects. Between 'experiencing the objects' and the 'desire to experience the objects', one may let go of the experience, but letting go of the desire to experience is much harder. When the seeker attains the firm, unchanging, direct realization that "I am Pure Bliss myself," only then his desire for pleasure comes to an end, and his delusion that "Objects provide happiness" is destroyed.

The senses are naturally attracted towards external objects due to many deep-rooted Vāsanās, unfulfilled desires from past births, regarding the body, world, and objects. Kaṭha Upaniṣad says –

**पराञ्चि खानि व्यतृणत् स्वयम्भूस्तस्मात्पराङ्पश्यति नान्तरात्मन् ॥**

*Parāñci khāni vyatṛṇat svayambhūs*
*Tasmāt parāṅpaśhyati nāntarātman* ॥

"Brahmadeva, the original Creator, has designed all sense organs to be innately extrovert." Outgoing organs find it challenging to turn inwards and detach from the outside world. It is the seeker's responsibility to resolutely turn them inwards to the true Self, Ātman. He has the innate freedom to do so. St. Tukārāma gives clear guidance to the seeker. He says, "The organs should be controlled from running out towards pleasures. The mind should be controlled so that desires do not emerge in mind. Vāsanās should be decayed gradually. As a result, when the mind becomes pure and calm, the inner, ever-present, Pure Bliss of the Self manifests automatically." [In a way, these actions are all interdependent. If organs and mind are controlled, it becomes easy to experience Pure Bliss of the Self. If one gets even a glimpse of Pure Bliss of his Self, he realizes that the source of happiness is inside. He learns that he is Bliss himself and tries to control his mind and withdraw from worldly objects.]

St. Jñāneśwara says, "Real happiness is experienced when the Jiva or Cidābhāsa disappears and becomes One with his own Self Brahman. (*Jñāneśwari 13.131*)" Even enlightened people experience external happiness from worldly objects. However, they know that the source of happiness is not outside. Such worldly pleasure is just a manifestation of the ever-available inner Bliss of the true Self which is experienced through the medium of that object. Therefore, they neither crave for objects nor are they attached to the world. Objects of pleasure are considered crucial in today's world. A status symbol is assigned to them, and massive marketing campaigns are conducted to thrust luxury objects into a common man's life. This emphasis on luxurious lifestyle is indeed a great challenge for all conscientious seekers. Every seeker should continue all prescribed spiritual practices like chanting, meditation, worship, learning scriptures with Sadguru's grace, and proceed on the spiritual path.

Lord Kṛṣṇa states in this verse that one should discipline and restrain all organs and surrender the mind exclusively to Him. When the senses are conquered, the intellect naturally remains steady and anchored. Here Lord Kṛṣṇa has asked the devotee to surrender to His Saguṇa form and not surrender to formless Nirguṇa Brahman. This is a better interpretation of the verse, although the word *Matpara* can be interpreted to mean both: surrender to **Saguṇa God** and surrender to **Nirguṇa Brahman**. It is easier for the extrovert mind to worship the Saguṇa God having a beautiful form. Many enlightened saints have prescribed the worship of Saguṇa God, e.g. seeing His divine form, chanting His Mantra, and hearing stories of His glory. This eventually leads to a firm, steadfast mind established in Brahman, the true Self.

## The debacle of a seeker due to incessant thinking of objects

ध्यायतो विषयान्पुंसः सङ्गस्तेषूपजायते ।
सङ्गात्सञ्जायते कामः कामात्क्रोधोऽभिजायते ॥ ६२ ॥
क्रोधाद्भवति सम्मोहः सम्मोहात्स्मृतिविभ्रमः ।
स्मृतिभ्रंशाद् बुद्धिनाशो बुद्धिनाशात्प्रणश्यति ॥ ६३ ॥
रागद्वेष वियुक्तैस्तु विषयानिन्द्रियैश्चरन् ।
आत्मवश्यैर्विधेयात्मा प्रसादमधिगच्छति ॥ ६४ ॥
प्रसादे सर्वदुःखानां हानिरस्योपजायते ।
प्रसन्नचेतसो ह्याशु बुद्धिः पर्यवतिष्ठते ॥ ६५ ॥

नास्ति बुद्धिरयुक्तस्य न चायुक्तस्य भावना ।
न चाभावयतः शान्तिरशान्तस्य कुतः सुखम् ॥ ६६ ॥
इन्द्रियाणां हि चरतां यन्मनोऽनुविधीयते ।
तदस्य हरति प्रज्ञां वायुर्नावमिवाम्भसि ॥ ६७ ॥
तस्माद्यस्य महाबाहो निगृहीतानि सर्वशः ।
इन्द्रियाणीन्द्रियार्थेभ्यस्तस्य प्रज्ञा प्रतिष्ठिता ॥ ६८ ॥

*Dhyāyato viṣayān puṃsaḥ saṅgas teṣūpajāyate* ।
*Saṅgāt sañjāyate kāmaḥ kāmāt krodho 'bhijāyate* ॥ *62* ॥
*Krodhād bhavati saṃmohaḥ saṃmohāt smṛtivibhramaḥ* ।
*Smṛtibhraṃśād buddhināśo buddhināśāt praṇaśyati* ॥ *63* ॥
*Rāgadveṣavimuktais tu viṣayān indriyaiś caran* ।
*Ātmavaśyair vidheyātmā prasādam adhigacchati* ॥ *64* ॥
*Prasāde sarvaduḥkhānāṃ hānir asyopajāyate* ।
*Prasannacetaso hy āśu buddhiḥ paryavatiṣṭhate* ॥ *65* ॥
*Nāsti buddhir ayuktasya na cāyuktasya bhāvanā* ।
*Na cābhāvayataḥ śāntir aśāntasya kutaḥ sukham* ॥ *66* ॥
*Indriyāṇāṃ hi caratāṃ yan mano 'nuvidhīyate* ।
*Tad asya harati prajñāṃ vāyur nāvam ivāmbhasi* ॥ *67* ॥
*Tasmād yasya mahābāho nigṛhītāni sarvaśaḥ* ।
*Indriyāṇīndriyārthebhyas tasya prajñā pratiṣṭhitā* ॥ *68* ॥

**Meaning:** When the mind dwells continuously on objects of pleasure, it gets attached to objects. Attachment leads to craving. When the craving is not fulfilled, it creates anger. Due to anger, the intellect is unable to discriminate between real and unreal. As a result, the seeker forgets the very goal of spiritual pursuit, which is being even-minded in all circumstances and attaining Self-realization. Thus, when the intellect loses its one-pointed focus, the seeker perishes completely from the spiritual perspective. But a seeker who has conquered his mind remains content, even while enjoying worldly objects, as he is free from attachment and aversion. When his mind is content and fulfilled, his suffering comes to an end. The intellect of a joyful person can be quickly steadied in Ātman. [A dismal, desolate, and thoughtless person does not have a steady intellect.] A person of unsteady intellect cannot even have faith in the existence of Ātman. Such a person finds no peace anywhere, and how can the person who is not at peace find happiness in life? When the senses of a person are chasing their respective objects, his mind yields to the senses. The mind drags the intellect with itself in the wrong direction, just like wind drags a boat in the wrong direction in water. Therefore, O Arjuna! That person is said to have a steady intellect whose mind and senses are completely conquered.

The debacle of the human mind has been portrayed in an evidential manner here. These verses state that the very root of the downfall of the human mind lies in its continuous dwelling on objects. A person dwells on objects due to the delusion that objects provide happiness. He seeks happiness in external objects as he has forgotten the spiritual reality that Pure Bliss is his nature. For the person who strongly identifies that "I am the body" instead of "I am Ātman", the main goal of human life – Mokṣa – is totally sidelined. The worldly life of such a person may be prosperous or poor. But when he is caught in the vortex of worldly pleasures and the ensuing dualities of pleasure and pain, he disregards the goal of Mokṣa.

St. Tukārāma says, "The birth takes place due to many unfulfilled desires, Vāsanās, from past birth." According to this rule, Vāsanās are attached to a person right from his birth. They reside in his intellect and compel him to make decisions that are necessary for fulfilling the Vāsanās. Most ordinary people are extroverted for the same reason. A person who is an extrovert i.e. not true to his real Self can neither conquer his mind nor keep his intellect steady in Ātman nor even think of God. In other words, he can never be the one of steady wisdom. St. Rāmadāsa says, "Those who are true to their real Self transcend worldly life, while those who seek external objects of pleasure sink in worldly life." While a seeker strives very hard to turn his mind inward and be intent on his Self, his mind subjugated by Vāsanās is pulled outside towards worldly objects. Despite trying to restrain the mind with Yama-Niyama, etc., it evades all constraints and flees out towards objects.

The person who has conquered his organs remains at peace, even when he is surrounded by objects since he can use his organs without attachment and aversion. There is a tight coupling between the organs and objects. E.g. *a form* is an object (*Viṣaya*) of the *eyes*. Every person is bound to see forms as soon as he opens his eyes. He is bound to hear sound whenever there is noise in his surroundings. It is not practical to physically distance oneself from objects (form, sound, smell, touch, taste) or abandon them completely. While it is technically possible to avoid objects of touch, there is no point in making this near-impossible effort of abandoning objects altogether. It is more important to control the actions, reactions, and responses while interacting with objects.

Strong attachment and strong aversion are both reactions. Attachment leads to dependency, expectation, and extreme agony due to the mere idea of separation from objects. The interplay of hope and despair ensues after attachment. Aversion also leads to constant dwelling on objects due to which the mind is polluted. These reactions are indeed discouraging for the seeker who genuinely strives to restrain his mind and turn it inward. There is an intense struggle in his mind between his old Vāsanās and the new desire for Mokṣa. If the seeker indeed wants to subjugate his Vāsanās and continue on the path to Mokṣa, he should quietly seek the support of God and surrender exclusively to God. Here, it is recommended that the seeker should continually try to contemplate on the real nature Lord Kṛṣṇa, Ātman, without giving undue importance to the technical details of Saguṇa vs. Nirguṇa. Contemplation is the nature of the mind, so it is necessary to provide the mind with at least one topic of contemplation. The best option for the seeker is to contemplate on God alone. For that purpose, he must withdraw his mind from worldly matters. But the seeker should be aware that withdrawing from worldly affairs is an arduous task and diligently continue his effort without being dejected or lost in between. St. Tukārāma describes the state of wise men, "Enlightened people realize only one God through all objects experienced by the five senses. So they do not feel attached to their relatives, parents, wealth, or other worldly matters."

The person who thinks only about worldly objects remains constantly immersed in objects. His incessant thinking gradually transforms into attachment and further becomes an obsession that leads to an intense craving to obtain those objects. If he is unable to fulfill his craving, he feels extremely angry at people or circumstances that obstruct his path. The seeker who thus yields to anger disregards all teachings of the scriptures and Sadguru completely. His intellect succumbs to delusion. Delusion is a characteristic of Tamoguṇa, so his mind is ruled by thoughtlessness or indiscretion. His ability to discriminate on the transactional, moral, religious as well as spiritual level (*Viveka*) is destroyed at this stage. The seeker, whose power to think is thus destroyed, is on his way to complete destruction from the spiritual perspective. However, if he understands the gravity of these issues, he can get his act together and lead his life back on a meaningful path. For attaining lasting satisfaction, it is imperative to control the organs. It is totally detrimental for the seeker if he lets his organs run amuck for attaining trivial, temporary pleasures.

When the mind runs behind organs which chase mundane pleasures, the mind drags the intellect with itself, just like the storm that drags a boat in an ocean. Therefore, the person who can control his organs and withdraw them from objects develops a steady intellect. The light of Ātman i.e. Pure Bliss is manifested in such pure, calm, and steady intellect. After realizing "I am Ātman" in this manner, the seeker enjoys serenity, stability, and lasting joy.

The word ***Samādhāna*** generally means composure or satisfaction. In Sanskrit, the word Samādhāna stands for '*Samyak Ādhāna*,' which means the mind that constantly resolves on the true Self, Ātman. The seeker whose mind remains content in Ātman is able to overcome all suffering. The intellect of such a seeker remains steady. The seeker whose intellect is not resolved on the Knowledge of Ātman also cannot firmly abide in equanimity. His intellect cannot resolve on the true Self, so his organs chase worldly pleasures. On the other hand, the intellect cannot resolve on the true Self as long as organs chase worldly pleasures. Thus, they are interdependent. A person who has consciously withdrawn his mind and senses from objects can adhere to the Knowledge of Ātman.

One who is unable to internalize the principles of *Sāṅkhyayoga* cannot adhere to the Knowledge of Ātman. Such a seeker cannot find peace in life, and one who is not at peace can never be happy. Not many people quite understand the direct relationship between the lack of peace and grief. These people suffer in many ways by living a life that is far from peaceful. Worry, fear, anger, greed, jealousy, desire, competition, envy, comparison, etc. are some reasons for losing peace in life. A lifestyle that encourages excitement also has no peace in it. A life full of excitement has wide recognition and acceptance in today's society. A person who stays away from excitement is cast aside by society. Travel, tourism, TV serials based on familial or social problems, sports, parties, discussions, drinking, socializing are all avenues for excitement. They eventually create disquietude in the mind. Some people even need to be treated with tranquilizers to regain peace after wild excitement. This means that peace is necessary for happiness. So what is the point of being excited first and then adapting artificial, superficial measures to regain peace? Modern life seemingly has no answer to this question.

The seeker who finds a way through all aforementioned hurdles can regulate and conquer his mind. He frees himself from the duality of attachment and aversion. He continues to live life as dictated by Prārabdha – the world may see it as good or bad – but his contentment is untouched through all experiences. His joyfulness does not depend on the presence or absence of anything. Just because he is seen experiencing or enjoying objects, it is not right to say that he is dependent on those objects for happiness. St. Ekanātha Maharaj says, "An enlightened person who sees one Brahman everywhere may seem soaked in objects of pleasure and reveling in them, but his enlightenment is not tainted by them. (Bhāgavata. 6.207)." This is because there is no pleasure in objects from his perspective. When a person always revels in uninterrupted joy, he does not experience any suffering. He can soon be One with his true Self, Ātman. Therefore, every seeker should learn to be joyful, cheerful even in his routine life. A grim, dejected, hopeless, complaining, negative, and antagonistic person can never be a true seeker. Dejection is associated with the world. A person whose joy depends on whether or not he obtains worldly objects is bound to have a restless mind.

Every seeker is required to develop intent devotion (Niṣṭhā) towards the spiritual philosophy of Self-realization. For that purpose, it is necessary to engage in the following three practices consistently:

- ***Śravaṇa*** (**श्रवण**) – Intent listening
- ***Manana*** (**मनन**) – Contemplation
- ***Nididhyāsana*** (**निदिध्यासन**) – Deep, meditative reflection

The seeker who has realized Self-Knowledge does not lose his inner peace in any situation. Peace and happiness are the two sides of the same coin. The experience of pure, unqualified peace is coupled with Pure Bliss of Ātman. Inner peace is a key criterion to assess the spiritual progress of a seeker. The mind that craves for objects compels the organs to go out and seek happiness. There are many objects of pleasure, and they are all transient. So, the mind and organs which chase these objects always remain in a distracted or scattered state. They do not allow the intellect to remain steady in wisdom. It is not possible to truly conquer the mind and senses as long as the seeker delusively thinks that happiness is derived from objects.

**The difference in perspectives**

**या निशा सर्वभूतानां तस्यां जागर्ति संयमी ।**
**यस्यां जाग्रति भूतानि सा निशा पश्यतो मुनेः ॥ ६९ ॥**

*Yā niśā sarvabhūtānāṃ tasyāṃ jāgarti saṅyamī* ।
*Yasyāṃ jāgrati bhūtāni sā niśā paśyato muneḥ* ॥ *69* ॥

**Meaning:** A person of steady wisdom, *Sthitaprajña*, is awake in that which is the night for all beings. And when all beings are awake, it is the night for an introspective sage (Muni).

This is a well-known and peculiar verse in the Bhagavad-Gita. The words 'waking' and 'sleep' *(night)* indicate 'knowledge' and 'ignorance,' respectively. Ignorant people are wide awake about the senses and their objects. However, enlightened people are passively unconcerned about them. A wise person who is intent on his true Self Brahman, and who has attained firm, direct, steady Self-realization that "I am Brahman", is as if asleep while thinking about all worldly objects. He disregards them. When all ignorant people are awake or alert about obtaining more objects, the enlightened one is asleep. The *Sthitaprajña* is equanimous in both the joy and grief that are derived from objects. Worldly objects are completely unimportant and irrelevant from his perspective. Those who have not realized Ātman seek to derive happiness from objects. They become elated when they find joy and depressed when they find grief in life. Their entire life is spent in experiencing the duality of joy and grief as imposed by Prārabdha. However, the man of steady wisdom enjoys the life of lasting, unqualified, Pure Bliss. St. Tukārāma clearly says, "There is only an iota of happiness in a life filled mostly with suffering." Ignorant people do not stop their blind pursuit of objects, even when they find very little and impermanent happiness in those objects. However, an enlightened sage rejoices in Pure Bliss of his true Self while being indifferent to the pleasures and pains imposed by Prārabdha.

**An Example of ocean to explain the greatness of a wise sage**

**आपूर्यमाणमचलप्रतिष्ठं समुद्रमापः प्रविशन्ति यद्वत् ।**
**तद्वत्कामा यं प्रविशन्ति सर्वे स शान्तिमाप्नोति न कामकामी ॥ ७० ॥**

*Āpūryamāṇam acalapratiṣṭhaṃ*
*Samudrām āpaḥ praviśanti yadvat* ।
*Tadvat kāmā yaṃ praviśanti sarve*
*Sa śāntim āpnoti na kāmakāmī* ॥*70*॥

**Meaning:** Water enters an ocean from all sides, but the ocean remains unaffected and does not ever cross its boundaries. Similarly, a wise person who is not perturbed by the incessant flow of incoming worldly desires from all sides in his mind can alone find peace. A person who seeks worldly pleasures can never be peaceful.

Even an enlightened person of steady wisdom faces many experiences in life – both good and bad – as dictated by Prārabdha. However, since he has attained equanimity in joy and grief, his peace is never compromised. An ignorant person, on the other hand, experiences peace and disturbance in a cyclic manner.

**A desireless person can experience peace**

विहाय कामान्यः सर्वान्पुमांश्चरति निःस्पृहः ।
निर्ममो निरहङ्कारः स शान्तिमधिगच्छति ॥ ७१ ॥

*Vihāya kāmān yaḥ sarvān pumāṃś carati niḥspṛhaḥ* ।
*Nirmamo nirahaṃkāraḥ sa śāntim adhigacchhati* ॥ *71* ॥

**Meaning:** A person who abandons all desires and executes his prescribed duties unacquisitively without ego and mineness can alone attain real peace.

A person desires for objects in two ways –

- When an object is newly encountered, he wishes to acquire it.
- By remembering an object due to past Vāsanā, he desires it.

E.g. a form (*Rūpa*) is an object (*Viṣaya*) for the eyes. When a person of steady wisdom opens his eyes, he, too, has no choice but to see all forms around him. But he has a firm understanding that all forms are bound to give both pleasure and pain, and it is not possible to derive lasting, unqualified, Pure Bliss from any form . As a result, his mind and organs do not chase those forms.

Every person has no choice but to smell and hear the respective objects surrounding him. Even the person of steady wisdom experiences smell, sound, etc., but he does not expect happiness from them. He enjoys many pleasurable objects, but he knows that it is his own inner Pure Bliss of Ātman that is manifested through those pleasures. Thus, he is not attached to any object. Even if he seems surrounded by various objects, his peace is unperturbed as he is completely detached from his body and the world. He has no desire, acquisitiveness, mineness, or unwarranted ego. He is never disturbed in either the presence or absence of sensory pleasures. He has no desires left in mind. As he does not yearn for objects, he feels no mineness or attachment for avenues through which objects can be obtained. When desires and mineness are not present, there is no ego of being the enjoyer or experiencer of objects. When all these qualities are wiped out from his mind, what else may he experience other than complete peace and happiness?

**Conclusion**

एषा ब्राह्मी स्थितिः पार्थ नैनां प्राप्य विमुह्यति ।
स्थित्वास्यामन्तकालेऽपि ब्रह्मनिर्वाणमृच्छति ॥ ७२ ॥

*Eṣā brāhmī sthitiḥ pārtha naināṃ prāpya vimuhyati* ।
*Sthitvāsyām antakāle'pi brahmanirvāṇa mṛcchati* ॥ *72* ॥

**Meaning:** O Pārtha! This is verily known as the Brāhmi state i.e. complete absorption in Brahman. After attaining this, the seeker is never deluded. He remains in the same state even at the time of death and attains Oneness with Brahman.

ॐ तत्सदिति श्रीमद्भगवद्गीतासूपनिषत्सु ब्रह्मविद्यायां योगशास्त्रे श्रीकृष्णार्जुनसंवादे साङ्ख्ययोगो नाम द्वितीयोऽध्यायः ॥

*Om Tatsaditi Śrimadbhagvadgitāsūpaniṣatsu Brahmavidyāyāṃ Yogaśāstre Śrīkṛṣṇārjunasaṅvāde Sāṅkhyayogo Nāma Dvitīyo'dhyāyaḥ* ॥

When the seeker remains naturally immersed in Brahman, it is known as the **Brāhmi** state. Jivanmukti, Sadyomukti, Sayujyamukti are some other names for it. When the body dies in this state, the seeker is known as **Videhamukta**. The Brāhmi state is a firm, naturally assimilated, and irreversible stage. In this state, there is the direct realization (*Aparokṣānubhūti*) of 'I am Brahman.' The very nature of an enlightened person is Pure Bliss in this state, so he is not enticed to strive for happiness separately. He is Pure Existence himself, so there is no fear of death in his mind. He is Pure Knowledge himself, so he is not deluded that 'I am ignorant.' Brahman is all-pervasive and without divisions or seperations of any kind. So, he is not deluded by diverse appearances around him. Brahman is changeless, so he is not deceived into thinking that he is subject to changes like birth, aging, and death. His state of mind remains constant at the time of death; ultimately, he merges in Brahman. This is the supreme epitome of human life, as portrayed in the Indian scriptures of Vedānta. It is the only wish of scriptures and Lord Kṛṣṇa that the seeker should focus all efforts in this direction to attain Self-realization.

## Chapter 3

# The Yoga of Action

**॥ कर्मयोगः (Karmayogaḥ) ॥**

Lord Kṛṣṇa explained the philosophy of being equanimous in actions in the 2nd chapter. Now, he will describe the philosophical system of Karma in detail. The discussion starts with a question in Arjuna's mind.

**Arjuna's dilemma**

*अर्जुन उवाच ।*

**ज्यायसी चेत्कर्मणस्ते मता बुद्धिर्जनार्दन ।**
**तत्किं कर्मणि घोरे मां नियोजयसि केशव ॥ १ ॥**
**व्यामिश्रेणेव वाक्येन बुद्धिं मोहयसीव मे ।**
**तदेकं वद निश्चित्य येन श्रेयोऽहमाप्नुयाम् ॥ २ ॥**

*Arjuna uvāca* ।

*Jyāyasī cet karmaṇas te matā buddhir janārdana* ।
*Tat kiṃ karmaṇi ghore māṃ niyojayasi keśava* ॥ *1* ॥
*Vyāmiśreṇeva vākyena buddhiṃ mohayasīva me* ।
*Tad ekaṃ vāda niścitya yena śreyo'ham āpnuyām* ॥ *2* ॥

**Meaning:** (Arjuna said) O Keśava! If you think that the Yoga of Knowledge (*Buddhiyoga*) is superior to Karma, why then do you urge me towards this gruesome action like war? You are only confusing me with your perplexing speech. Therefore, tell me with certainty which one Yoga will be the most beneficial for me.

The preface of this text states that no words of Lord Kṛṣṇa are perplexing or contradictory in nature. Arjuna was influenced by the thought of renouncing the battle. So, he listened only to that part of Kṛṣṇa's teaching which was convenient for his renunciation. The already deluded Arjuna felt that Lord Kṛṣṇa was only increasing his confusion. But he was Sāttvic in nature. Even in this situation, his discrimination ability was intact to some extent. So, he requested Lord Kṛṣṇa to help him choose the correct path which would be in his best interest. Arjuna did not understand the relation between the Path of Karma and the Path of Knowledge. So, he asked Kṛṣṇa whether it would be more beneficial for him to perform the horrendous action of fighting the war or strive for attaining Self-Knowledge as prescribed in *Buddhiyoga*. The crux of Buddhiyoga is that one should meticulously execute his prescribed actions without thinking about the fruits, whether good or bad.

**Lord Kṛṣṇa answers**

श्रीभगवानुवाच ।
लोकेऽस्मिन् द्विविधा निष्ठा पुरा प्रोक्ता मयानघ ।
ज्ञानयोगेन साङ्ख्यानां कर्मयोगेन योगिनाम् ॥ ३ ॥

*Śrībhagavān uvāca* ।
*Loke 'smin dvividhā niṣṭhā purā proktā mayānagha* ।
*Jñānayogena sāṅkhyānāṃ karmayogena yogināṃ* ॥ *3* ॥

**Meaning:** (Śrībhagavān said) O sinless Arjuna! I have previously described a twofold path in this world. One is the Path of Knowledge of the Sāṅkhyās, and the second is the Path of Action of the ritualistic people.

Lord Kṛṣṇa knows that there is no sin or guile in Arjuna's mind when he asks this question. Arjuna genuinely considered it to be a big flaw or sin to fight against his kinsmen and teachers. As a result, he was unable to remember his extraordinary strength, sense of justice, and failure of all reconciliation efforts which were taken before the war. In verse *2.38*, there is a clear discussion of the relation between the Path of Action *(Karmayoga)* and the Path of Knowledge (*Buddhiyoga*). Later,

Lord Kṛṣṇa also declares his final decision, "By continually reflecting on the knowledge of desireless actions (*Niṣkāma Karmayoga*), the seeker will be liberated from the bondage of actions (*2.39*)."

**Actions should not be renounced**

न कर्मणामनारम्भान्नैष्कर्म्यं पुरुषोऽश्नुते ।
न च संन्यसनादेव सिद्धिं समधिगच्छति ॥ ४ ॥

*Na karmaṇām anārambhān naiṣkarmyaṃ puruṣo'śnute* ।
*Na ca saṃnyasanād eva siddhiṃ samadhigacchati* ॥ *4* ॥

**Meaning:** One cannot achieve *Naiṣkarmyasiddhi* (freedom from the cycle of actions and fruits) merely by abstaining from actions or by renouncing actions.

The word ***Naiṣkarmyasiddhi*** in Sanskrit literally means 'actionlessness' or 'total inaction.' But the meaning of Naiṣkarmyasiddhi is different in the context of this verse. When actions are performed without thinking that "I am the doer," they do not yield any fruits – this is the real nature of Naiṣkarmyasiddhi. The term Naiṣkarmyasiddhi also indicates that when a doer of actions is unconcerned about the fruits, actions become fruitless for him for all practical purposes. Swāmi Prajñānananda defines the word Naiṣkarmyasiddhi as the attainment of actionless Brahman in his treatise Naiṣkarmyasiddhi. The word **Naiṣkarmya** mainly means Brahman. The central topic of his treatise is the realization of Brahman. However, there is a relation between Karma and the realization of Brahman. This relation is not real, rather it is falsely-attributed (*Adhyāropa*) until the seeker is enlightened with the Knowledge of Brahman. St. Tukārāma Mahārāja explains his own enlightenment where he says, "The system of bearing fruits of Karmas has now become moot for me after Self-realization. All my actions and their fruits are now One with Nārāyana (God)." To attain such enlightenment, the seeker needs to invest in various spiritual practices such as conquering the mind and organs, being dispassionate from worldly objects, and subtle contemplative meditation that "I am Brahman." He may be tempted to evade actions altogether to avoid having to go through these arduous practices. He may even think that by abstaining from actions he will not have to bear any fruits. However, both these notions are improper and incorrect.

**Reason why actions cannot be renounced**

न हि कश्चित्क्षणमपि जातु तिष्ठत्यकर्मकृत् ।
कार्यते ह्यवशः कर्म सर्वः प्रकृतिजैर्गुणैः ॥ ५ ॥

*Na hi kaścit kṣaṇam api jātu tiṣṭhaty akarmakṛt* ।
*Kāryate hy avaśaḥ karma sarvaḥ prakṛtijair guṇaiḥ* ॥ 5 ॥

**Meaning:** No one can ever remain without engaging in action, even for a moment. All beings are under the influence of the three Guṇas of Prakṛti (material nature), and the three Guṇas impel a person to perform actions.

The 18th chapter of the Bhagavad-Gita (*23–28*) has a detailed discussion of the three types of doers pertaining to the three Guṇas and their respective actions. In short, there is a firm, inviolable bonding between the doer, actions, and three Guṇas. Therefore, it is futile to wish or think, "I will not execute any action not to bear the fruit."

**The difference between authentic and pretentious seekers**

कर्मेन्द्रियाणि संयम्य य आस्ते मनसा स्मरन् ।
इन्द्रियार्थान्विमूढात्मा मिथ्याचारः स उच्यते ॥ ६ ॥
यस्त्विन्द्रियाणि मनसा नियम्यारभतेऽर्जुन ।
कर्मेन्द्रियैः कर्मयोगमसक्तः स विशिष्यते ॥ ७ ॥

*Karmendriyāṇi saṁyamya ya āste manasā smaran* ।
*Indriyārthān vimūḍhātmā mithyācāraḥ sa ucyate* ॥ 6 ॥
*Yas tv indriyāṇi manasā niyamyārabhate'rjuna* ।
*Karmaindriyaiḥ karmayogam asaktaḥ sa viśiṣyate* ॥ 7 ॥

**Meaning:** A foolish person who forcefully restrains the organs of action but whose mind continually dwells on the objects of pleasure is certainly pretentious. Mere thinking about pleasures without doing any action is just like daydreaming. It spoils both worldly life and spiritual practice. On the other hand, a person who controls his organs with the help of his mind, remains dispassionate, and executes all actions by following Karmayoga is superior in a unique sense.

Actions are unavoidable in human life. The seeker who wants to perform actions without any bondage is required to first conquer his organs by resolving on Self-Knowledge (*Sāṅkhyabudddhi*). St. Jñāneśwara says, "One should perform all prescribed duties, avoid all prohibited or unrighteous actions, and detach from the fruits by offering them to Īśvara." Many other enlightened saints give similar guidance in their texts. When a seeker evolves to a higher spiritual plane, he has no wish to enjoy even those pleasures that are approved by the scriptures, let alone the pleasures that are prohibited. The main problem in spiritual pursuit is unnecessary dwelling on worldly objects, and not so much in enjoying them. The reason for dwelling on objects is the expectation of pleasure. When a person does not know that he himself is Pure Bliss, he expects pleasure from external objects. The treatise of Pañcadashi states that one may seek worldly pleasures even after Self-realization –

**समेऽपि भोगे व्यसनं भ्रान्तो गच्छेन्न बुद्धिमान् ।**
**अशक्यार्थस्य सङ्कल्पाद्भ्रान्तस्य व्यसनं बहु ॥ (७.१६९) ॥**

*Same'pi bhoge vyasanaṃ bhrānto gacchenna buddhimān* ।
*Aśakyārthasya sankalpādbhrāntasya vyasanaṃ bahu* ॥ *7.169* ॥

An ignorant person and an enlightened person both encounter objects of enjoyment. However, the ignorant person is bound while enjoying them, but the enlightened person remains detached and liberated. The ignorant and deluded person craves for worldly objects beyond his reach and thus enmeshes and jeopardizes himself in many ways.

**Execute the prescribed actions**

**नियतं कुरु कर्म त्वं कर्म ज्यायो ह्यकर्मणः ।**
**शरीरयात्रापि च ते न प्रसिद्ध्येदकर्मणः ॥ ८ ॥**

*Niyataṃ kuru karma tvaṃ karma jyāyo hy akarmaṇaḥ* ।
*Śarīrayātrāpi ca te na prasidhyed akarmaṇaḥ* ॥ *8* ॥

**Meaning:** O Arjuna! Perform the actions prescribed for you, since doing so is more beneficial than not doing any action. You will not be able to support even your day-to-day sustenance without performing actions.

Arjuna was a valorous, resolute warrior from a royal lineage. His warrior instincts would have never left him, even if he had decided to renounce them. Also, had he forcefully abandoned his warrior duties, there would have been no other avenue for him to earn his living in that era. Even today, a passive person who does not do any action cannot earn or support his living. The person has to perform at least the actions of sitting on a roadside and begging to support himself. Being born as a human, every seeker should either perform his duties that are traditionally prescribed by the Vedic scriptures or execute duties voluntarily accepted by him as per the demands of modern social setup.

**Perform action in a detached manner**

**यज्ञार्थात्कर्मणोऽन्यत्र लोकोऽयं कर्मबन्धनः ।**
**तदर्थं कर्म कौन्तेय मुक्तसङ्गः समाचर ॥ ९ ॥**

*Yajñarthāt karmaṇo'nyatra loko'yaṃ karmabandhanaḥ* ।
*Tadarthaṃ karma kaunteya muktasaṅgaḥ samācara* ॥ *9* ॥

**Meaning:** A person gets bound by those actions which he performs for any reason other than sacrifice *(Yajña)*. Therefore,

O son of Kunti, perform all actions without being attached to them.

The core part of a traditional Yajña is 'sacrificing' or 'offering oblation in the fire'. Doing our own action with a spirit of sacrifice means sharing some part of the fruit with others. This point is explained further in the 12th verse. The seeker should give the due share of his earnings to God, ancestors, king, guests, family, and other needy people. Even this sharing should be done without thinking, "I am the doer," "I will accumulate merits by doing this action," or "I will gain appreciation, gratitude, respect from others," etc.

**Humans and the creator of the universe**

सहयज्ञाः प्रजाः सृष्ट्वा पुरोवाच प्रजापतिः ।
अनेन प्रसविष्यध्वमेष वोऽस्त्विष्टकामधुक् ॥ १० ॥
देवान्भावयतानेन ते देवा भावयन्तु वः ।
परस्परं भावयन्तः श्रेयः परमवाप्स्यथ ॥ ११ ॥

*Sahayajñaḥ prajāḥ sṛṣṭvā purovāca prajāpatiḥ* ।
*Anena prasaviṣyadhvameṣa vo'stviṣṭakāmadhuk* ॥ *10* ॥
*Devān bhāvayatānena te devā bhāvayantu vaḥ* ।
*Parasparaṃ bhāvayantaḥ śreyaḥ param avāpsyatha* ॥ *11* ॥

**Meaning:** At the beginning of the universe, having created Yajñas along with humankind, the creator Brahmadeva said to humans, "May you evolve and prosper in the material life by performing these actions of sacrifice. This Yajña will fulfill all your desires. May you please the deities with theese acts of sacrifice, and in-turn, the deities will also propitiate you. Thus, by mutually pleasing each other, may you attain supreme welfare."

The word ***Arthavāda*** means usage of inflated praising statements that are unrelated to the practical facts or actual philosophy but are made to entice a person into performing a particular action. Even if these two verses are considered

Arthavāda, their gist is evident. If we indeed please Īśvara residing in hearts of family members, guests, the king, and other needy people, Īśvara will be naturally pleased with that service (*4.11*). St. Rāmadāsa says, "One should worship the omnipresent Īśvara by pleasing and serving at least one human being every day."

**Many shareholders in the results of Yajña**

**इष्टान्भोगान्हि वो देवा दास्यन्ते यज्ञभाविताः ।**
**तैर्दत्तानप्रदायैभ्यो यो भुङ्क्ते स्तेन एव सः ॥ १२ ॥**
**यज्ञशिष्टाशिनः सन्तो मुच्यन्ते सर्वकिल्बिषैः ।**
**भुञ्जते ते त्वघं पापा ये पचन्त्यात्मकारणात् ॥ १३ ॥**

*Iṣṭān bhogān hi vo devā dāsyante yajñabhāvitāḥ* ।
*Tair dattān apradāyaibhyo yo bhuṅkte stena eva saḥ* ॥ *12* ॥
*Yajñaśiṣṭāśinaḥ santo mucyante sarvakilbiṣaiḥ* ।
*Bhuñjate te tv aghaṃ pāpā ye pacanty ātmakāraṇāt* ॥ *13* ॥

**Meaning:** The deities, pleased by the sacrifices, will bestow desired necessities upon you. A person who enjoys the received gifts without offering them in return to others is indeed a thief. Those who first share the results of Yajñas with others and then enjoy the remaining portion are freed from all sins. But those who cook food only for their own sake are sinful.

The Indian way of life has extensively thought about repaying debts (*ṛna*, ऋण) – more than individual rights – on the social, familial, religious, and national levels. People are encouraged to repay their debts in one or the other form. The act of sharing cooked food in these verses is symbolic. The same holds true even for sharing one's knowledge with others. When a seeker shares his earnings with others with a sense of repaying his debts, there is no expectation of appreciation or recognition associated with that sharing. As a result, he earns the fruit which is the 'purification of his mind'.

## The cycle of nature and sacrifice

अन्नाद्भवन्ति भूतानि पर्जन्यादन्नसम्भवः ।
यज्ञाद्भवति पर्जन्यो यज्ञः कर्मसमुद्भवः ॥ १४ ॥
कर्म ब्रह्मोद्भवं विद्धि ब्रह्माक्षरसमुद्भवम् ।
तस्मात्सर्वगतं ब्रह्म नित्यं यज्ञे प्रतिष्ठितम् ॥ १५ ॥
एवं प्रवर्तितं चक्रं नानुवर्तयतीह यः ।
अघायुरिन्द्रियारामो मोघं पार्थ स जीवति ॥ १६ ॥

*Annād bhavanti bhūtāni parjanyād annasaṃbhavaḥ* ।
*Yajñad bhavati parjanyo yajñaḥ karmasamudbhavaḥ* ॥ *14* ॥
*Karma brahmodbhavaṃ viddhi brahmākṣarasamudbhavam* ।
*Tasmāt sarvagataṃ brahma nityaṃ yajñe pratiṣṭhitam* ॥ *15* ॥
*Evaṃ pravartitaṃ cakraṃ nānuvartayatīha yaḥ* ।
*Aghāyur indriyārāmo moghaṃ pārtha sa jīvati* ॥ *16* ॥

**Meaning:** Living beings come into existence from food, food itself is produced from rains, rains are created from sacrifices (Yajñas), and sacrifices are born of actions. Actions originate from the Vedas, and the Vedas are directly manifested from imperishable Īśvara. Therefore, all-pervading Īśvara continually resides in the acts of sacrifice. A person who does not nurture the cycle of nature in this world and himself indulges in sensory pleasures lives a meaningless life.

Īśvara is the governor of the world. Unless one accepts this fact whole-heartedly and with full faith, these three verses cannot be put in context. The verses above state that it rains when humans offer sacrifices in Yajñas. This statement is especially difficult to accept if one does not have faith in the Vedas. Skeptical people should know that human-being is the most evolved of all animals. If humans nurture the elements of nature, animals, and take care of other humans with a sense of selfless sacrifice or offering, then the intrinsic cycle of nature will continue to subsist without any friction. The environmental science, which is very popular in today's era, advocates the same standpoint. When the nature is adequately nourished, the rainy season and other seasons will continue as a natural response to that nourishment. The prevalent problems of global warming, irregular and disparate rains, blocking the rivers with enormous dams, deforestation, etc. are verily the result of not taking care of the intrinsic cycle of nature. The thoughts mentioned in these verses are indeed highly useful for most people leading ordinary lives.

**Real detachment**

यस्त्वात्मरतिरेव स्यादात्मतृप्तश्च मानवः ।
आत्मन्येव च सन्तुष्टस्तस्य कार्यं न विद्यते ॥ १७ ॥
नैव तस्य कृतेनार्थो नाकृतेनेह कश्चन ।
न चास्य सर्वभूतेषु कश्चिदर्थव्यपाश्रयः ॥ १८ ॥
तस्मादसक्तः सततं कार्यं कर्म समाचर ।
असक्तो ह्याचरन्कर्म परमाप्नोति पूरुषः ॥ १९
कर्मणैव हि संसिद्धिमास्थिता जनकादयः ।
लोकसङ्ग्रहमेवापि सम्पश्यन्कर्तुमर्हसि ॥ २० ॥
यद्यदाचरति श्रेष्ठस्तत्तदेवेतरो जनः ।
स यत्प्रमाणं कुरुते लोकस्तदनुवर्तते ॥ २१॥

*Yas tv ātmaratir eva syād ātmatṛptaś ca mānavaḥ* ।
*Ātmany eva ca saṃtuṣṭas tasya kāryaṃ na vidyāte* ॥ *17* ॥
*Naiva tasya kṛtenārtho nākṛteneha kaścana* ।
*Na cāsya sarvabhūteṣu kaścid arthavyapāśrayaḥ* ॥ *18* ॥
*Tasmād asaktaḥ satataṃ kāryaṃ karma samācara* ।
*Asakto hy ācaran karma param āpnoti pūruṣaḥ* ॥ *19* ॥
*Karmaṇaiva hi saṃsiddhim āsthitā janakādayaḥ* ।
*Lokasaṃgraham evāpi saṃpaśyan kartum arhasi* ॥ *20* ॥
*Yadyad ācarati śreṣṭhas tattad evetaro janaḥ* ।
*Sa yat pramāṇaṃ kurute lokas tad anuvartate* ॥ *21* ॥

**Meaning:** But there is no duty to be done for the one who revels in Pure Bliss of Ātman and remains fully satiated in the Self. He gains nothing whatsoever by doing or not doing any action, nor does he depend on any being for obtaining anything for himself. Therefore, you should consistently perform actions without attachment. One who performs actions without attachment attains liberation. For example, King Janaka and others reached the Supreme goal by following scriptural commands. You should engage in actions to represent what is ideal in front of society. Whichever action a great man performs, ordinary people imitate him. Whatever he sets up as the standard with his exemplary actions, the world merely follows that.

A person for whom duties are no longer necessary due to being enlightened has no expectations of any kind. However, a person who expects fruits but evades duties is selfish and deceitful. All expectations are related to happiness. A liberated person revels in Pure Bliss of Ātman all the time. Therefore, he has no expectations of any kind. Lord Kṛṣṇa says in these verses that Arjuna should understand this fact and perform his prescribed duty of fighting the war without any expectations in mind. If Arjuna could act in this manner, he, too, would not incur the sin – as per his own opinion – of killing his kin, since he would fight the war without being attached to it. King Janaka was a sovereign ruler. It was his duty to perform gruesome actions like fighting wars and punishing criminals. Despite that, he was liberated due to his detached state of mind. After liberation, wise men should meticulously fulfill their duties and should not misdirect ordinary people. There should be no spiritual arrogance of any kind in their minds. They should not have the wrong notion that they are not answerable to anyone anymore. St. Jñāneśwara says, "Enlightened saints should tread on the path shown by scriptures and also encourage ordinary people to do so. They should not behave in any unusual or queer manner when they are present amongst people in public life. (*Jñāneśwari 3.169*)"

**Lord Kṛṣṇa narrates His own example**

न मे पार्थास्ति कर्तव्यं त्रिषु लोकेषु किञ्चन ।
नानवाप्तमवाप्तव्यं वर्त एव च कर्मणि ॥ २२ ॥

यदि ह्यहं न वर्तेयं जातु कर्मण्यतन्द्रितः ।
मम वर्त्मानुवर्तन्ते मनुष्याः पार्थ सर्वशः ॥ २३ ॥
उत्सीदेयुरिमे लोका न कुर्यां कर्म चेदहम् ।
सङ्करस्य च कर्ता स्यामुपहन्यामिमाः प्रजाः ॥ २४ ॥
सक्ताः कर्मण्यविद्वांसो यथा कुर्वन्ति भारत ।
कुर्याद्विद्वांस्तथासक्तश्चिकीर्षुर्लोकसङ्ग्रहम् ॥ २५ ॥
न बुद्धिभेदं जनयेदज्ञानां कर्मसङ्गिनाम् ।
जोषयेत्सर्वकर्माणि विद्वान्युक्तः समाचरन् ॥ २६ ॥

*Na me pārthāsti kartavyaṃ triṣu lokeṣu kiṃcana ।*
*Nānavāptam avāptavyaṃ varta eva ca karmaṇi ॥ 22 ॥*
*Yadi hy ahaṃ na varteyaṃ jātu karmaṇy atandritaḥ ।*
*Mama vartmānuvartante manuṣyāḥ pārtha sarvaśaḥ ॥ 23 ॥*
*Utsīdeyur ime lokā na kuryāṃ karma ced aham ।*
*Saṃkarasya ca kartā syām upahanyām imāḥ prajāḥ ॥ 24 ॥*
*Saktāḥ karmaṇy avidvāṃso yathā kurvanti bhārata ।*
*Kuryād vidvāṃs tathāsaktaś cikīrṣur lokasaṃgraham ॥ 25 ॥*
*Na buddhibhedaṃ janayed ajñānāṃ karmasaṃginām ।*
*Joṣayet sarvakarmāṇi vidvān yuktaḥ samācaran ॥ 26 ॥*

**Meaning:** O Pārtha! There is no duty prescribed for Me in the three worlds since there is nothing that is unattained by Me, yet I engage Myself in actions. If I ever fail to perform actions unwearyingly, all people will undoubtedly follow My path in every respect. If I do not execute actions, all these worlds will perish. I will be the cause of confusion between liberated and non-liberated people, and I will be responsible for their destruction. Ignorant people perform actions by being attached to them. The wise person should perform all actions but without attachment to establish what is ideal in society. By abandoning actions altogether, the wise person should not unsettle the minds of ignorant people who are attached to action. Moreover, he should impel them all to execute actions and himself fulfill all his duties while internally abiding in the true Self, Ātman.

Lord Kṛṣṇa is the owner of the entire universe. There is no question of Him needing or wishing anything for Himself. All objects in the world may be owned by different owners in a worldly sense; but they are all ultimately owned by Him. Even then, Lord Kṛṣṇa engages in actions earnestly, tirelessly as if He is required to attain many objectives. He dwells in the hearts of all beings and impels them to work. Hence, if He remains passive Himself, all beings will imitate Him and cease to perform actions. It is a spiritual truth that actions are not binding for enlightened sages since they act without attachment while being steady in Yoga i.e. by being constantly aware that "I am Brahman". But such wise people are scarce. If millions of other ordinary people follow suit and conveniently stop working, it would create disaster in the world. Lord Kṛṣṇa will be ultimately responsible for that disaster. To avoid this, even wise people should follow His footsteps and meticulously perform actions as if showcasing that they are attached to actions. They should not misguide and lead ignorant people astray. On the contrary, they should set the highest standards for society by their exemplary behavior and persistently impel everyone towards actions. The word 'Saṅkara' in the 24th verse does not refer to hybridization of castes. It refers to the confusion between knowing who is wise and who is ignorant.

**Characteristics of ignorant people and the duty of wise men**

प्रकृतेः क्रियमाणानि गुणैः कर्माणि सर्वशः ।
अहङ्कारविमूढात्मा कर्ताहमिति मन्यते ॥ २७ ॥
तत्त्ववित्तु महाबाहो गुणकर्मविभागयोः ।
गुणा गुणेषु वर्तन्त इति मत्वा न सज्जते ॥ २८ ॥
प्रकृतेर्गुणसम्मूढाः सज्जन्ते गुणकर्मसु ।
तानकृत्स्नविदो मन्दान्कृत्स्नविन्न विचालयेत् ॥ २९ ॥

*Prakṛteḥ kriyamāṇāni guṇaiḥ karmāṇi sarvaśaḥ* ।
*Ahaṃkāravimūḍhātmā kartāham iti manyate* ॥ 27 ॥

*Tattvavit tu mahābāho guṇakarmavibhāgayoḥ* ।
*Guṇā guṇeṣu vartanta iti matvā na sajjate* ॥ *28* ॥
*Prakṛter guṇasaṃmūḍhāḥ sajjante guṇakarmasu* ।
*Tān akṛtsnavido mandān kṛtsnavin na vicālayet* ॥ *29* ॥

**Meaning:** In reality, all actions are executed by the impetus of the three Guṇas of Prakṛti. A person deluded by ego mistakenly thinks that "I am the doer." However, O valiant Arjuna! The wise person, who knows that Guṇas and actions are different from Ātman also understands that "This is merely an interplay of Guṇas amongst each other." Hence he is not attached to them. People who are deluded by the Guṇas of Prakṛti get attached to Guṇas and actions. The wise i.e. Self-realized person should not renounce his actions and thus mislead the spiritually ignorant and feeble-minded people on the path of self-destruction. [He should continue to work diligently like King Janaka.]

All actions are executed by a person due to the influence of the three Guṇas on him. Sattvaguṇa impels towards peace and happiness, Rajoguṇa impels towards activity, Tamoguṇa impels towards lethargy. Every Jiva engages in actions as per the influence of the Guṇa dominant in him at the time. An ignorant person does not recognize that a particular action is done by the influence of the Guṇa, so he is deluded by the notion, "I am the doer." Guṇas create a trait or disposition in a person and impel him to execute actions. But Guṇas and actions are not even remotely related to the true Self, Ātman, which itself is not attached to anything. Guṇas are insentient and falsely superimposed (*Adhyasta*). They are not associated with the substratum Ātman in any of the following three ways –

1 ***Saṅyoga Saṃbandha*** – A temporary contact between two objects, e.g. a bird sitting on a branch.
2 ***Samavaya Saṃbandha*** – A constant relation between two objects, e.g. threads woven together to form a fabric.

3 ***Tādātmya Saṃbandha*** – The delusive perception that two objects are the same, e.g. a hot red iron-ball looks like it is a ball of fire itself.

The relation between Guṇas and Ātman does not fall under any of these three categories. Their relation is purely a false superimposition (*Ādhyāsika Sambandha*). It is delusive in nature. An enlightened person knows for sure that all worldly transactions are solely a play of Guṇas amongst each other.

Māyā evolves in the universe in the following three stages –

- ***Mūlamāyā***: The most primeval wish surfaced on Brahman, "I am one, and I shall manifest in many forms."
- ***Guṇamāyā***: Creation of the three Guṇas.
- ***Jaḍamāyā***: Creation of the five Great Elements.

Māyā itself manifests progressively in the form of the three Guṇas and the five Great Elements. Together these eight constitute the Aṣtadhā Prakṛti, the eightfold nature of sentient beings. It is as if the three Guṇas play with the Five Great Elements through the medium of the body. In other words, the three Guṇas and the Five Great Elements together constitute the body. Actions executed by the body are part of the three Guṇas. The wise person understands this principle and remains detached from the Guṇas, body, organs, and actions. Ordinary people do not recognize this extremely rare, precious state. They can neither imagine nor have the faintest idea about it. If ignorant people become passive or cease to perform actions, they lose out on many benefits of actions such as earning a livelihood, engaging in religious activities, purifying the mind through selfless actions, and attaining Mokṣa. They indeed incur hefty losses due to inactivity in life.

**Fighting war is a duty for warriors**

मयि सर्वाणि कर्माणि संन्यस्याध्यात्मचेतसा ।
निराशीर्निर्ममो भूत्वा युध्यस्व विगतज्वरः ॥ ३० ॥

ये मे मतमिदं नित्यमनुतिष्ठन्ति मानवाः ।
श्रद्धावन्तोऽनसूयन्तो मुच्यन्ते तेऽपि कर्मभिः ॥ ३१ ॥
ये त्वेतदभ्यसूयन्तो नानुतिष्ठन्ति मे मतम् ।
सर्वज्ञानविमूढांस्तान्विद्धि नष्टानचेतसः ॥ ३२ ॥
सदृशं चेष्टते स्वस्याः प्रकृतेर्ज्ञानवानपि ।
प्रकृतिं यान्ति भूतानि निग्रहः किं करिष्यति ॥ ३३ ॥
इन्द्रियस्येन्द्रियस्यार्थे रागद्वेषौ व्यवस्थितौ ।
तयोर्न वशमागच्छेत्तौ ह्यस्य परिपन्थिनौ ॥ ३४ ॥
श्रेयान्स्वधर्मो विगुणः परधर्मात्स्वनुष्ठितात् ।
स्वधर्मे निधनं श्रेयः परधर्मो भयावहः ॥ ३५ ॥

*Mayi sarvāṇi karmāṇi saṁnyasyādhyātmacetasā* ।
*Nirāśīr nirmamo bhūtvā yudhyasva vigatajvaraḥ* ॥ 30 ॥
*Ye me matam idaṃ nityam anutiṣṭhanti mānavāḥ* ।
*Śraddhāvanto'nasūyanto mucyante te'pi karmabhiḥ* ॥ 31 ॥
*Ye tv etad abhyasūyanto nānutiṣṭhanti me matam* ।
*Sarvajñānavimūḍhāṃs tān viddhi naṣṭān acetasaḥ* ॥ 32 ॥
*Sadṛśaṃ ceṣṭate svasyāḥ prakṛter jñānavān api* ।
*Prakṛtiṃ yānti bhūtāni nigrahaḥ kiṃ kariṣyati* ॥ 33 ॥
*Indriyasyendriyasyārthe rāgadveṣau vyavasthitau* ।
*Tayor na vaśam āgacchhet tau hy asya paripanthinau* ॥ 34 ॥
*Śreyān svadharmo viguṇaḥ paradharmāt svanuṣṭhitāt* ।
*Svadharme nidhanaṃ śreyaḥ paradharmo bhayāvahaḥ* ॥ 35 ॥

**Meaning:** O Arjuna! Execute actions by being firmly intent on Ātman and surrender the actions to Me. By abandoning mineness (*Mamatva*) and the hope of fruits, engage in war without troubling yourself. All those who faithfully embrace and follow this teaching without caviling at Me are freed from the bondage of actions. However, those who nurture an erroneous perception of Me and do not follow My teachings are deluded about Self-Knowledge. Know them to be completely doomed to destruction. Even an enlightened person behaves in accordance with his Prakṛti i.e. nature, and all beings follow their instincts as dictated by Prakṛti; what is the use of obstinacy here?

Attraction or aversion of the organs towards objects exists from time immemorial; one should not get caught in their flow, for they are his enemies on the path of supreme welfare. Engaging in one's own duty (Dharma) – that may seem inferior from a worldly perspective – is better than doing the duty of another that may seem superior and joyous. Even if death comes while doing one's own duty, it is better than performing the duty of another as it ultimately leads to destruction.

*Viveka*, consistent discrimination between real and unreal, is a great spiritual tool that can be used to make the mind intent on Ātman and keep it that way. Discriminating between core and peripheral, real and illusory, permanent and impermanent are different forms of *Viveka*. One should firmly know that actions are peripheral, illusory, and impermanent, yet execute them as if they are essential and permanent and offer them to Lord Kṛṣṇa. St. Rāmadāsa has asked all disciples to offer all impermanent objects to their Sadguru, but he also clarifies the purpose of such offering. The Sadguru does not need anything from his disciples. Still, disciples are asked to offer objects so they get detached from those objects which may impede their path of Self-realization. Lord Kṛṣṇa also has nothing whatsoever to gain from actions or objects offered to Him. The primary purpose here is that the seeker should renounce the "I am the doer" attitude and remain detached from the fruits of his actions.

Lord Kṛṣṇa is guiding Arjuna that he should abandon the feeling that "Bhīṣma, Droṇa, etc. are mine" and fight his enemies without attachment to the results of the impending war. Kṛṣṇa further says that there is no reason for Arjuna to feel distressed about engaging in violence, committing sin, ruining traditional Dharma, and being disloyal to his teacher or relatives in war. This is the ultimate pinnacle of adhering to the prescribed duties. Lord Rāma's life is replete with exemplary actions of fulfilling duties.

People who wholeheartedly accept orders of Lord Kṛṣṇa and lead life by conforming to them are eventually freed from the bondage of actions. However, some people erroneously perceive Lord Kṛṣṇa as a mere human. They disregard His orders since they see no point in obeying orders of another man. Such people are skeptical, suspicious, or disapproving of the knowledge imparted by Him. Lord Kṛṣṇa reveals His true nature in the upcoming chapter of the Gita (*10.8*). The 18th chapter of the Gita also addresses such erroneous perception of Lord Kṛṣṇa and the resultant lack of faith in Him (*67 to 71*). Ignorant people ruin their lives from a spiritual standpoint due to such lack of faith, even though they may be leading a prosperous, successful, well-organized worldly life according to their Prārabdha.

In spiritual pursuit, even a seeker who theoretically knows that "I am Brahman" behaves under the influence of the three Guṇas of Prakṛti. Mere theoretical knowledge is of no use for the seeker. Lord Kṛṣṇa later explains the dreadfulness of the enemy named 'desire' (*Kāma*), and the importance of keeping it under control (*3.41*). Here we should only note that all beings are influenced by the three Guṇas, and they behave according to their Vāsanās which stem from the Guṇas. As such, there is no use insisting that people should change their intrinsic behavior.

The senses are attracted to some objects and aversive towards others; this system exists since eternity. Every person wants to acquire what is favorable and discard what is unfavorable to him. Favorable objects lead to joy, and unfavorable objects lead to grief. However, every Jiva gets both joyous and grievous experiences as designated by his Prārabdha – this system, too, exists since eternity. Every person has a choice to accept this system or obstinately fight with it. Rather than trying to challenge the system of Prārabdha, one should take it on faith. No person has the freedom to change the imminent situations in a life imposed by his Prārabdha, but he certainly has the freedom to react in an even, neutral, impassive manner to both joyous and grievous incidents. By doing so, he can earn an equanimous vision of *Buddhiyoga* – the firm resolve that "I am Brahman" – required for his spiritual progress. A person who does not have an equanimous mind gets carried away in the currents of dualistic feelings such as "I like this" or "I dislike this." He remains immersed in the vast ocean of worldly life. Therefore, Lord Kṛṣṇa tells Arjuna that though he is seeing faults like violence, killing others, etc. in his own warrior duty and merits in the duties of other classes – e.g. forgiving is a duty of Brāhmins or serving is a duty of Vaiśya – he should continue to perform his own prescribed duty, even if it is a gruesome action like war. Society needs all kinds of activities conducted by people in all classes. They must be executed by someone or the other. It is later said in the Gita that all actions are associated with one or the other fault (*18.48*). Therefore, if a person continues to perform prescribed actions and duties selflessly and dies while doing so, this death leads to his highest welfare i.e. Mokṣa. On the contrary, if a person delusively performs duties meant for others, it leads to the dire consequence of being repeatedly caught in the cycle of birth and death.

In the 33rd verse, it is said that a person having just theoretical knowledge of Brahman may also be impelled by the influence of the three Guṇas of Prakṛti. The acclaimed treatise of Pañcadashi goes further and says that it is possible even for a wise, enlightened person to be influenced by the three Guṇas. The author of Pañcadashi says –

**नैष दोषो यतोऽनेकविधं प्रारब्धमीक्ष्यते ।**
**इच्छानिच्छा परेच्छा च प्रारब्धं त्रिविधं स्मृतम् ॥ ७.१५२ ॥**

*Naiṣā doṣo yato'nekavidhaṃ prārabdhamīkśyate* ।
*Icchānicchā parecchā cha prārabdhaṃ trividhaṃ smṛtam* ॥ *7.152* ॥

"Even if an enlightened person gets caught in the current of the three Guṇas, it is not his fault. Very strong Prārabdha can impel the person in that manner." There are examples of King Nala, Yudhiṣṭhīra, and Lord Śrirāma in this regard. This is not meant to justify the erroneous behavior of enlightened people. It is just another explanation of the last line of the 33rd verse which states that there is indeed no use insisting that one should disregard the influence of the Guṇas. Ādi Śaṅkara also says in one of his hymns (Bhaja Govindam), "Whether treading the path of Yoga or enjoying the material world, the one who is absorbed in Ātman revels in Supreme Bliss."

**Arjuna's question**

*अर्जुन उवाच ।*
अथ केन प्रयुक्तोऽयं पापं चरति पूरुषः ।
अनिच्छन्नपि वार्ष्णेय बलादिव नियोजितः ॥ ३६ ॥

*Arjuna uvāca* ।
*Atha kena prayukto'yaṃ pāpaṃ carati pūruṣaḥ* ।
*Anicchann api vārṣṇeya balād iva niyojitaḥ* ॥ *36* ॥

**Meaning:** (Arjuna says) But impelled by what does a man commit prohibited actions or sins? Although he himself is unwilling, why does he behave as if he is forced to do it?

**Answer**

*श्रीभगवानुवाच ।*
काम एष क्रोध एष रजोगुणसमुद्भवः ।
महाशनो महापाप्मा विद्ध्येनमिह वैरिणम् ॥ ३७ ॥
धूमेनाव्रियते वह्निर्यथादर्शो मलेन च ।
यथोल्बेनावृतो गर्भस्तथा तेनेदमावृतम् ॥ ३८॥
आवृतं ज्ञानमेतेन ज्ञानिनो नित्यवैरिणा ।
कामरूपेण कौन्तेय दुष्पूरेणानलेन च ॥ ३९॥
इन्द्रियाणि मनो बुद्धिरस्याधिष्ठानमुच्यते ।
एतैर्विमोहयत्येष ज्ञानमावृत्य देहिनम् ॥ ४०॥
तस्मात्त्वमिन्द्रियाण्यादौ नियम्य भरतर्षभ ।

पाप्मानं प्रजहि ह्येनं ज्ञानविज्ञाननाशनम् ॥ ४१॥
इन्द्रियाणि पराण्याहुरिन्द्रियेभ्यः परं मनः ।
मनसस्तु परा बुद्धिर्यो बुद्धेः परतस्तु सः ॥ ४२॥
एवं बुद्धेः परं बुद्ध्वा संस्तभ्यात्मानमात्मना ।
जहि शत्रुं महाबाहो कामरूपं दुरासदम् ॥ ४३॥

*Śrībhagavān uvāca* ।

*Kāma eṣa krodha eṣa rajoguṇasamudbhavaḥ* ।
*Mahāśano mahāpāpmā viddhy enam iha vairiṇam* ॥ *37* ॥
*Dhūmenāvriyate vanhir yathādarśo malena ca* ।
*Yatholbenāvṛto garbhas tathā tenedam āvṛtam* ॥ *38* ॥
*Āvṛtaṃ jñānam etena jñānino nityavairiṇā* ।
*Kāmarupeṇa kaunteya duṣpūreṇānalena ca* ॥ *39* ॥
*Indriyāṇi mano buddhir asyādhiṣṭhānam ucyate* ।
*Etair vimohayaty eṣa jñānam āvṛtya dehinam* ॥ *40* ॥
*Tasmāt tvam indriyāṇy ādau niyamya bharatarṣabha* ।
*Pāpmānaṃ prajahi hy enaṃ jñānavijñānanāśanam* ॥ *41* ॥
*Indriyāṇi parāṇy āhur indriyebhyaḥ paraṃ manaḥ* ।
*Manasas tu parā buddhir yo buddheḥ paratas tu saḥ* ॥ *42* ॥
*Evaṃ buddheḥ paraṃ buddhvā saṃstabhyātmānam ātmanā* ।
*Jahi śatruṃ mahābāho kāmarūpaṃ durāsadam* ॥ *43* ॥

**Meaning:** (Śrībhagavān says) **Desire** and **anger** (*Kāma, Krodha*) born of Rajoguṇa are the main culprits that impel a person towards sinful actions, and they cannot be satiated by anything. [The Jiva performs sinful actions due to the inescapable force exerted by desire and anger.] Know them to be your enemies in this world. Fire is enveloped by smoke, a mirror is covered by dust, and a thin sac veils an embryo. Analogous to these, Knowledge of the true Self is concealed by desire and anger. Pure Knowledge is covered by the enemy called the insatiable fire of desire. It is said that desire sustains on the support of the organs, mind, and intellect, and desire deludes a person by veiling his knowledge and wisdom. Therefore, O eminent descendant of the Bharatas! First, you should conquer your organs and destroy the desire which ruins knowledge and wisdom. The organs (senses) are said to be subtler than the worldly objects; the mind is subtler than the organs; the intellect is subtler than the mind; and (one meaning –) Ātman is subtler than the intellect, (alternate meaning –) desire is subtler than the intellect. Thus, O valiant Arjuna! Destroy the enemy called desire, which is extremely difficult to conquer, with the help of the conquered mind and the intellect which is made subtler through spiritual practice.

**ॐ तत्सदिति श्रीमद्भगवद्गीतासूपनिषत्सु ब्रह्मविद्यायां योगशास्त्रे श्रीकृष्णार्जुनसंवादे कर्मयोगो नाम तृतीयोऽध्यायः ॥**

*Om Tatsaditi Śrimadbhagvadgitāsūpaniṣatsu Brahmavidyāyāṃ Yogaśāstre Śrīkṛṣṇārjunasaṅvāde Karmayogo Nāma Tṛtīyo'dhyāyaḥ*॥

A seeker who is a mere academic scholar of Vedānta can frequently engage in a prohibited action or erroneous behavior. An enlightened person may also do so in a rare case. The seeker can practice spiritual discrimination that "Brahman alone is real; the world is unreal," and also know that "Brahman is Pure Bliss." Knowing it as such, the seeker is not supposed to seek happiness from objects in the unreal and impermanent world. But the seeker who is a mere academic scholar may be defeated by desires which awaken in his mind due to past Vāsanās. An enlightened person revels in Pure Bliss of the true Self; however, he, too, may rarely be seen performing incongruous actions.

The incongruous behavior is due to the mighty power of desire that stems from Rajoguṇa. For most people, Rajoguṇa is generally dominant, while Sattva and Tāmas are stronger only once in a while. Therefore, the traits of **desire** and **anger** are naturally present in most people. Desire and anger work in a cyclic manner. They compel people to engage in many erroneous, prohibited actions. As a result, their minds become impure, unsteady, and their behavior become even more indiscriminate. So long as this cycle continues, Vāsanās do not decay; and such seekers keep revolving in the cycle of life and death. St. Rāmadāsa describes Rajoguṇa as the one that compels a person to engage in jealousy and fraudulent behavior, to crave for the wealth of others, to indulge in indiscriminate behavior, to wish for the downfall of others, to dislike virtues like devotion and detachment, and to like glamour and pompousness (*Dāsabodha 2.5*). If Rajoguṇa becomes dominant, the person is soon destroyed from the spiritual perspective. Therefore, desire and anger – the products of Rajoguṇa – are the real enemies of a person. They pollute and unsettle the mind.

The mind is tainted with two faults –

- Impurity (*Mala*)
- Unstability (*Vikṣepa*)

Due to these faults, one cannot experience the light of Pure Knowledge of Ātman. St. Rāmadāsa describes a solution to gradually free oneself from the clutches of Rajoguṇa. He says, "No matter how hard one strives to fulfill desires in mind, they become stronger by the day. Therefore, instead of trying to fulfill desires, one should lovingly worship God and sing His praises. One should also donate to others in whatever manner possible. Also, it is important not to hold anybody else responsible for the joy or suffering in life and remember God in all situations. (*Dāsabodha 2.5.36, 38*)" As a result, the influence of Rajoguṇa will gradually recede and Sattvaguṇa will rise to become more influential.

The 42$^{nd}$ verse of this chapter states –

**यो बुद्धेः परतस्तु सः ।**

*Yo buddheḥ paratas tu saḥ* ।

This statement has two alternate meanings. It can be said that "Desire is subtler than or superior to the intellect" since desire

(*Kāmā*) is the central topic of this verse. However, the Knowledge of Ātman is the main objective for any seeker. Kaṭha Upaniṣad states that Ātman is subtler than the intellect. Therefore, this verse may also mean that "Ātman is subtler than or superior to the intellect." The seeker may accept either or both meanings, conquer desires in his mind, and lead himself to Self-realization of Ātman.

Desire exists due to the support of the mind, organs, and intellect. St. Ekanātha states in his devotional poetry Haripāṭha, "Birth takes place due to the past unfulfilled desires i.e. Vāsanās." These past Vāsanās generate desires, and Rajoguṇa strengthens them. Vāsanās reside in the intellect. The intellect makes a decision as per the Vāsanās and conveys the decision to act in a certain manner to action-organs through the mind as an intermediary. Therefore, desire pervades the mind, the organs, as well as the intellect. As a result, Cidābhāsa in the intellect has no way of practicing *Viveka*. It is unable to discriminate between real Ātman and unreal Anātman. Cidābhāsa remains constantly preoccupied with desires, and so it cannot adhere to the true Self. Desires delude the mind and impel it towards the external world. Therefore, the seeker cannot attain the highest goal unless he conquers desires in his mind. The theoretical knowledge of Brahman or the realized Self-Knowledge i.e. wisdom of an enlightened person can easily succumb to powerful desires in their mind due to strong Prārabdha. So powerful is this desire that it can deceptively trick even a wise person who has attained clear, doubtless Self-Knowledge.

Lord Kṛṣṇa narrates the subtle nature of desire and explains the immense difficulty in controlling it. Although we have discussed this topic before, let us revisit it here in detail. All worldly objects are perceived with the help of the senses. E.g. a stone is seen with eyes. It is important to note that eyes can 'see' an object, but they cannot 'know' the object. When a stone is seen, its image is conveyed to Cidābhāsa in the intellect via the mind as an intermediary, and Cidābhāsa knows the object as "This is a stone." Desires reside in the intellect in the form of Vāsanās. Therefore, Vāsanās are subtler than the intellect and extremely difficult to conquer. St. Tukārāma says that the seeker should first control his organs and conquer his senses to debilitate his Vāsanās. Lord Kṛṣṇa says the same thing here. Practicing discrimination between real Ātman and unreal Anātman, being devoted to God, engaging in actions as prescribed by scriptures, and meditating are some ways to conquer the senses.

Lord Kṛṣṇa says to Arjuna that one should restrain, stabilize, organize, and balance oneself and then conquer the most difficult enemy i.e. desire. For this purpose, know that desire is subtler than intellect. It is important to learn how one can possibly restrain, stabilize, and organize himself in this process. It is necessary to learn the exact role played by the mind, the intellect, the memory, and the ego in the process of controlling Kāmā.

St. Jñāneśwara gives various solutions on how to control each one of them.

**Controlling the mind** (*Jñāneśwari 9.517*) –

The mind is responsible for making a wish or generating a desire. One should center all his wishes and desires in God, lovingly worship God with intent devotion, and bow down to omnipresent God.

**Controlling the memory** (*Jñāneśwari 12.95*) –

The memory is responsible for firmly adhering to the object of desire. When a seeker adheres to God steadily in his memory, only then his worship can be labeled as real devotion.

**Controlling the intellect** (*Jñāneśwari 5.87*) –

The intellect is responsible for making a decision. One should decide that "I am Brahman" with the help of the intellect and remain firmly steady in Brahman.

**Controlling the ego** (*Jñāneśwari 6.71*) –

The seeker who understands the precise nature of the ego knows that it is merely a false superimposition (Adhyāsa). He focuses his attention solely on the substratum Brahman and meditates on the fact: "I am that Brahman." He thus leads himself to the highest goal of liberation.

Thus, when all four manifestations of the Antaḥkaraṇa steadily adhere to God, they can be controlled, and the seeker can thus conquer all kinds of desires.

## Chapter 4

# Renunciation of Action in Knowledge

**॥ ज्ञानकर्मसंन्यासयोगः (Jñānakarmasaṁnyāsayogaḥ) ॥**

In the last verse of the 3rd chapter, Lord Kṛṣṇa summoned Arjuna to dismiss all uncertainties and get ready for the war with a firm, decisive mind. However, Arjuna is not yet convinced. He is still inclined towards embracing the formal monastic way of life (*Saṁnyāsa*). He still has a ray of hope that Lord Kṛṣṇa will support him for being a monk rather than ask him to do worldly actions. He asks a clear question in this regard, and Kṛṣṇa gives a clear answer in response to it. Kṛṣṇa also chides those who differentiate between 'renouncing actions' and 'doing desireless actions' by calling them childish, since both these practices lead to the same result. The rest of this chapter sheds light on the same concept and also describes various aspects of engaging in desireless actions (*Niṣkāma Karma*).

**<u>The tradition of the knowledge of Karmayoga</u>**

*श्रीभगवानुवाच ।*

इमं विवस्वते योगं प्रोक्तवानहमव्ययम् ।
विवस्वान्मनवे प्राह मनुरिक्ष्वाकवेऽब्रवीत् ॥ १ ॥
एवं परम्पराप्राप्तमिमं राजर्षयो विदुः ।
स कालेनेह महता योगो नष्टः परन्तप ॥ २ ॥
स एवायं मया तेऽद्य योगः प्रोक्तः पुरातनः ।
भक्तोऽसि मे सखा चेति रहस्यं ह्येतदुत्तमम् ॥ ३ ॥

*Śrībhagavān uvāca* ।

*Imaṃ vivasvate yogaṃ proktavān aham avyayam* ।
*Vivasvān manave prāha manur ikṣvākave 'bravīt* ॥ *1* ॥

*Evaṃ paramparāprāptam imaṃ rājarṣayo viduḥ* ।
*Sa kāleneha mahatā yogo naṣṭaḥ paraṃtapa* ॥ *2* ॥
*Sa evāyaṃ mayā te 'dya yogaḥ proktaḥ purātanaḥ* ।
*Bhakto 'si me sakhā ceti rahasyaṃ hy etad uttamam* ॥ *3* ॥

**Meaning:** (Śrībhagavān said) This Karmayoga explained so far describes timeless values. I taught it to Vivasvāna before. Vivasvāna taught it to Manu, and Manu taught it to Ikṣvāku. This tradition of knowledge was passed down from father to son in succession and was known by royal seers. However, later it disappeared over time. I have taught the same ancient Karmayoga to you today. I have shared this supreme secret with you since you are My great devotee and a dear friend.

Vivasvāna is one of the names of the sun. Purāṇas, the ancient holy Indian scriptures, describe that Manu is the very first human being. He is considered the author of the treatise Manusmṛti. He was the very first emperor and a warrior. Ikṣvāku, his son, was also a valiant emperor. All of them were highly efficient and active people. Lord Kṛṣṇa first taught the 'philosophy of desireless actions' (*Niṣkāma Karmayoga*) to the sun. A verse in Ṛgveda states –

**ॐ स्वस्ति पन्थामनुचरेम सूर्यचन्द्रमसामिव ।**
**किं पुनर्जानता अघ्नता ददता सङ्गमेमहि ॥ (५.५१.१५)**

*Om Swasti panthāmanucarema sūryacandramasāmiva* ।
*Kim punarjānatā agnatā dadatā sangamemahi* ॥ *(5.51.15)*

"Let us all walk together on the path of welfare, just like the sun and the moon. Acquiring knowledge, not distressing anyone, and sharing what we have with others, let us walk together." This verse explains the nature of Karmayoga followed by the sun. The text of Manusmṛti explains actions prescribed under Karmayoga, which were taught by Vivasvāna to Manu. Later, Manusmṛti faded with time, and Parāśarasmṛti came to light. This fact is mentioned in the very first verse of Parāśarasmṛti. Lord Rāma was born in the lineage of the sun. Ikṣvāku is the primordial person of the same lineage. The execution of Karmayoga was one of the significant ideals for Lord Rāma.

The doctrine of Karmayoga disappeared over time. There was nobody left on the earth who could abide by the principles of Karmayoga. There is a saying in Sanskrit that states: "Kālāya tasmai namaḥ". It means, "We have to surrender to time eventually." Time – that rules our lives – has both evolution and devolution going on cyclically in it. This simply means that every person and his circumstances are bound to evolve and devolve in a cyclic manner. The spiritual seeker should make an effort in his own capacity to prevent himself and his conditions from devolution, but without desiring fruits of that effort. St. Jñāneśwara says in this regard, "Ignorance or delusion has grown unknowingly in the human mind and consequently, a lot of time has been wasted without knowing this traditional philosophy of Yoga (*Karmayoga*) (*Jñāneśwari 4.26*)." We should make a note that this process has happened unknowingly so far. Lord Kṛṣṇa revived and re-explained Karmayoga to eradicate the delusion in Arjuna's mind. He chose Arjuna because Arjuna was his childhood friend and a great devotee, and they were dear to each other. Besides, it was imperative for Arjuna to fight the war. Also, he was eminently eligible to listen to philosophy. In reality, Arjuna was a mere instrument or medium, and the precious doctrine of the Gita has been made available to all human beings through Arjuna. Later, St. Rāmadāsa, other enlightened sages, and saints organized the tenets of Karmayoga in a way synchronous with the modern times.

## Arjuna's question and its answer

*अर्जुन उवाच ।*

**अपरं भवतो जन्म परं जन्म विवस्वतः ।**
**कथमेतद्विजानीयां त्वमादौ प्रोक्तवानिति ॥ ४ ॥**

*Arjuna uvāca* ।

*Aparaṃ bhavato janma paraṃ janma vivasvataḥ* ।
*Kaṭham etad vijānīyāṃ tvam ādau proktavān iti* ॥ *4* ॥

श्रीभगवानुवाच ।

**बहूनि मे व्यतीतानि जन्मानि तव चार्जुन ।**
**तान्यहं वेद सर्वाणि न त्वं वेत्थ परन्तप ॥ ५ ॥**
**अजोऽपि सन्नव्ययात्मा भूतानामीश्वरोऽपि सन् ।**
**प्रकृतिं स्वामधिष्ठाय सम्भवाम्यात्ममायया ॥ ६ ॥**
**यदा यदा हि धर्मस्य ग्लानिर्भवति भारत ।**
**अभ्युत्थानमधर्मस्य तदात्मानं सृजाम्यहम् ॥ ७ ॥**
**परित्राणाय साधूनां विनाशाय च दुष्कृताम् ।**
**धर्मसंस्थापनार्थाय सम्भवामि युगे युगे ॥ ८ ॥**
**जन्म कर्म च मे दिव्यमेवं यो वेत्ति तत्त्वतः ।**
**त्यक्त्वा देहं पुनर्जन्म नैति मामेति सोऽर्जुन ॥ ९ ॥**

*Śrībhagavānuvāca* ।

*Bahūni me vyatītāni janmāni tava cārjuna* ।
*Tāny ahaṃ veda sarvāṇi na tvaṃ vettha paraṃtapa* ॥ *5* ॥
*Ajo'pi sann avyayātmā bhūtānām īśvaro'pi san* ।
*Prakṛtiṃ svām adhiṣṭhāya saṃbhavāmy ātmamāyayā* ॥ *6* ॥
*Yadā yadā hi dharmasya glānir bhavati bhārata* ।
*Sbhyutthānam adharmasya tadātmānaṃ sṛjāmy aham* ॥ *7* ॥
*Paritrāṇāya sādhūnāṃ vināśāya ca duṣkṛtām* ।
*Dharmasaṃsthāpanārthāya saṃbhavāmi yuge yuge* ॥ *8* ॥
*Janma karma ca me divyam evaṃ yo vetti tattvataḥ* ।
*Tyaktvā dehaṃ punarjanma naiti mām eti so'rjuna* ॥ *9* ॥

**Meaning:** (Arjuna said) O Kṛṣṇa! Your birth is recent, while the birth of Vivasvāna is ancient. So, how am I to understand that You taught this Karmayoga to him?

(Śrībhagavān said) O distresser of enemies, Arjuna! I have taken many births so far, and so have you. I know all of them, but you do not know them. In reality, I am birthless, changeless, and governor of the universe. Yet, I take birth through an illusory body with the help of My Prakṛti. Whenever there is the decay of Dharma, I manifest Myself to free everyone from Adharma. For the protection of the good, for the destruction of the evil, and for the establishment of Dharma, I am born age after age. Thus, a person who recognizes the philosophy behind My divine births and divine actions is not born again after the death of his body and comes unto Me in the end.

These six verses can be best understood and taken only on utmost faith. For the total acceptance of Dharma, Saguṇa God worship, and the teachings of the Gita, it is necessary to have unswerving faith in them. Spiritual life is based on the three pillars: righteous living according to Dharma, worshipping Saguṇa God, and careful contemplation on the Vedānta doctrine. These pillars offer great support to every seeker. Lord Kṛṣṇa gives immense importance to the establishment of Dharma, the protection of the good, and the destruction of evil in society. So much so, that he is willing to be born in every age for these duties. Thus, every genuine devotee of Lord Kṛṣṇa, who wishes to please Him through worship, should also attach great importance to these three duties. A devotee will evidently be able to do these monumental duties only within his individual capacity. Even then, he should not just passively wait for God to incarnate and save or uplift the world. Inertia or complacent devotion is not coherent with love for God and faith in Him. If God loves a particular cause or duty, then the devotee must like the same cause or duty as well.

The devotee can only love Saguṇa God who has a form. Saguṇa God, when incarnated in the form of a human being, may look and transact like other ordinary people. However, His body is illusory in nature. This is stated in the 14 verses of Śrīmad Bhāgavatam which describe the disappearance (*Niryāṇa*) of Lord Kṛṣṇa's incarnation. Every seeker should remember that his own body is illusory as well, though not in the same way as the Lord's body. Lord Kṛṣṇa's birth is called **Līlāvigraha** i.e.

acceptance of a body voluntarily to conduct the play of this universe. On the contrary, every seeker's birth is called **Karmavigraha** i.e. the result of actions. Nevertheless, it is essential to understand that they are both illusory. The term Līlāvigraha means embodiment with choice, while Karmavigraha means the body given to the Jiva as a result of his past actions. The body born of Līlāvigraha can be seen coming into existence but not going out of existence. The body born of Karmavigraha is seen after birth and death as well. If the Jiva is not liberated, he gets the next body. Actions in the life of Līlāvigraha are not executed by thinking, "I am the doer." One who can act without the feelng of doership also does not think that he is the enjoyer of the fruits. Actions performed in the life of Līlāvigraha are divine since they are mainly meant for the establishment of Dharma and spirituality. Every seeker should see this as an ideal way of action and strive to perform his duties in the same manner. If he is indeed able to do his prescribed duties without any desires, he becomes eligible for the Knowledge of Ātman and attains liberation after death. He becomes One with Brahman; he becomes Brahman himself. [Note: Kṛṣṇa's body was not visible after he left it. He disappeared along with his body, while the ordinary Jiva leaves his physical body behind after death. The birth and death of Kṛṣṇa were both extraordinary and divine. Lord Rāma adapted a more human way of life, since Rāvaṇa, the ten-headed demon king, could only be killed by a human being.]

## The method for execution of actions

**वीतरागभयक्रोधा मन्मया मामुपाश्रिताः ।**
**बहवो ज्ञानतपसा पूता मद्भावमागताः ॥ १० ॥**
**ये यथा मां प्रपद्यन्ते तांस्तथैव भजाम्यहम् ।**
**मम वर्त्मानुवर्तन्ते मनुष्याः पार्थ सर्वशः ॥ ११ ॥**
**काङ्क्षन्तः कर्मणां सिद्धिं यजन्त इह देवताः ।**
**क्षिप्रं हि मानुषे लोके सिद्धिर्भवति कर्मजा ॥ १२ ॥**

**चातुर्वर्ण्यं मया सृष्टं गुणकर्मविभागशः ।**
**तस्य कर्तारमपि मां विद्ध्यकर्तारमव्ययम् ॥ १३ ॥**
**न मां कर्माणि लिम्पन्ति न मे कर्मफले स्पृहा ।**
**इति मां योऽभिजानाति कर्मभिर्न स बध्यते ॥ १४ ॥**
**एवं ज्ञात्वा कृतं कर्म पूर्वैरपि मुमुक्षुभिः ।**
**कुरु कर्मैव तस्मात्त्वं पूर्वैः पूर्वतरं कृतम् ॥ १५ ॥**

*Vītarāgabhayakrodhā manmayā mām upāŚrītāḥ* ।
*Bahavo jñānatapasā pūtā madbhāvam āgatāḥ* ॥ *10* ॥
*Ye yathā māṃ prapadyante tāṃs tathaiva bhajāmy aham* ।
*Mama vartmānuvartante manuṣyāḥ pārtha sarvaśaḥ* ॥ *11* ॥
*Kāṃkṣantaḥ karmaṇāṃ siddhiṃ yajanta iha devatāḥ* ।
*Kṣipraṃ hi mānuṣe loke siddhir bhavati karmajā* ॥ *12* ॥
*Cāturvarṇyaṃ mayā sṛṣṭaṃ guṇakarmavibhāgaśaḥ* ।
*Tasya kartāram api māṃ viddhy akartāram avyayam* ॥ *13* ॥
*Na māṃ karmāṇi limpanti na me karmaphale spṛhā* ।
*Iti māṃ yo'bhijānāti karmabhir na sa badhyate* ॥ *14* ॥
*Evaṃ jñātvā kṛtaṃ karma pūrvair api mumukṣubhiḥ* ।
*Kuru karmaiva tasmāt tvaṃ pūrvaiḥ pūrvataraṃ kṛtam* ॥ *15* ॥

**Meaning**: By freeing themselves from attachment, fear, and anger, and being absorbed in Me, the seekers who constantly think of Me are purified through austerity of Self-Knowledge. They become One with My real nature. With whatever intent men approach me, I grant them results accordingly. However, in reality, all human beings follow only that path through which they can attain Me. People who desire specific fruits worship the respective deities that grant them those fruits. This is because fruits of actions are promptly granted to humankind on this plane of earth. I have given the necessary Guṇas to perform four different types of duties to respective people in the fourfold Social Orders (Varṇas). I – as Īśvara – may be known as the creator of the fourfold Social Orders; but know that I – as imperishable Brahman – am not the doer of anything. I do not desire fruits of actions, so the bondage of actions does not tie me. Actions do not bind a person who knows Me thus and worships Me accordingly. Knowing this, many people have engaged in actions to date. Therefore, you, too, should perform actions as done traditionally by ancient people.

The desire to be happy gives rise to attachment. A person feels attached to objects that make him happy. He fears losing those objects and also fears the death of the body which is a tool to enjoy objects. When objects are snatched, or the body is harmed, he is angry at those who cause this distress. Attachment, fear, and anger can be removed only by knowing that Lord Kṛṣṇa is Absolute, Pure Bliss and by abiding in Him. To abide in God, the seeker can initially worship a deity and constantly think about Saguṇa God. As he evolves, he should take arduous efforts to know the real nature of God i.e. Nirguṇa Brahman. By the grace of Sadguru, he should engage in austere practices to meditate on Nirguṇa Brahman. These practices purify the seeker and eventually, he can realize Oneness with real Lord Kṛṣṇa i.e. Brahman. Meditation on Nirguṇa is the last and the highest form of spiritual practice; however, many people do not take a note of it. Even if they note, they do not understand its significance, or they are unable to meditate in that manner. Therefore, people worship Lord Kṛṣṇa while desiring various implicit or explicit fruits in their mind. Lord Kṛṣṇa, as Īśvara, bestows fruits upon them according to their wishes, faith, intent, longing, and commitment. People desire fruits only for happiness. They seek Kṛṣṇa alone through all their desires – knowingly or unknowingly – as Kṛṣṇa is Pure Bliss himself. But they don't understand that they are seeking Brahman in the form of Kṛṣṇa and hence worship other deities for fulfilling their desires. It is a part of Īśvara's governance that actions done on this earth get the expected fruits relatively soon.

Īśvara created the system of Fourfold Social Orders. He specified and distributed actions in each of these social classes.

1 ***Brāhmin*** (ब्राह्मण): Priestly class mainly responsible for teaching and religious activities
2 ***Kṣatriya*** (क्षत्रिय): Warrior class mainly responsible for ruling, security, and administration
3 ***Vaiśya*** (वैश्य): Business class mainly meant to produce goods and commercial progress
4 ***Śūdra*** (शूद्र): Service class mainly meant for all kinds of assistance, cleaning, and laborious jobs.

In ancient times, the Indian way of life was based on these four Varṇas. People in each Varṇa are bestowed with the required qualities to execute actions prescribed for them. Society runs appropriately when the respective classes perform all four types of actions. All humans in the world execute at least one of the four types of aforementioned actions. The discussion – whether one should inherit his duties by birth or by actions – has become meaningless in today's age. Enlightened sages and seers have embraced the new-age reality. The changed modern perspective towards Dharma is a part of Lord Kṛṣṇa's (Īśvara's) governance; Lord Kṛṣṇa as Brahman is completely detached from it.

The term **Glāni** indicates 'decay of Dharma' or 'lethargy in following Dharma' in verse 7. This phrase evidently proves that the system established by Īśvara is bound to decay with time. Many people in society work to pervert and distort the system of Īśvara. From the perspective of Brahman, the world, society, and the system are all illusory or unreal. Brahman is not attached or related to them in any way. Īśvara, too, is ever-liberated (*Nityamukta*). However, He is subject to birth and death. Īśvara is not imperishable. Brahman is imperishable. Saguṇa Kṛṣṇa may engage in many actions, but He is not bound by them. Every spiritual seeker should assimilate these facts and engage in actions by knowing that his true Self is neither the doer of actions nor the enjoyer of fruits. His life can become truly meaningful through this thought-process. It is indeed challenging to understand the Law of Karma, but the seeker can greatly benefit from knowing its essence and doing his duties in the right way.

## The Law of Karma

किं कर्म किमकर्मेति कवयोऽप्यत्र मोहिताः ।
तत्ते कर्म प्रवक्ष्यामि यज्ज्ञात्वा मोक्ष्यसेऽशुभात् ॥ १६ ॥
कर्मणो ह्यपि बोद्धव्यं बोद्धव्यं च विकर्मणः ।
अकर्मणश्च बोद्धव्यं गहना कर्मणो गतिः ॥ १७ ॥
कर्मण्यकर्म यः पश्येदकर्मणि च कर्म यः ।
स बुद्धिमान्मनुष्येषु स युक्तः कृत्स्नकर्मकृत् ॥ १८ ॥

*Kiṃ karma kimakarmeti kavayo'py atra mohitāḥ* ।
*Tat te karma pravakṣyāmi yaj jñātvā mokṣyase'śubhāt* ॥ *16* ॥
*Karmaṇo hy api boddhavyaṃ boddhavyaṃ ca vikarmaṇaḥ* ।
*akarmaṇaś ca boddhavyaṃ gahanā karmaṇo gatiḥ* ॥ *17* ॥
*Karmaṇy akarma yaḥ paśyed akarmaṇi ca karma yaḥ* ।
*Sa buddhimān manuṣyeṣu sa yuktaḥ kṛtsnakarmakṛt* ॥ *18* ॥

**Meaning:** Even wise sages cannot decisively state 'what action is' and 'what inaction is.' Now I shall teach you the principle of performing actions, knowing which you shall be liberated from the unholy cycle of birth and death. It is essential to understand the nature of the right action, forbidden action, and inaction. The knowledge of actions is indeed profound and unfathomable. He who recognizes 'inaction in action' and 'action in inaction' is the wisest amongst all men; he is a true equanimous Yogi even while performing all actions.

Any physical, verbal, or mental activity is termed as a **Karma** or an action. Men are expected to engage in actions as prescribed by the scriptures of Dharma, or in a way taught by Lord Kṛṣṇa or enlightened sages. In ancient times, scriptures such as Pūrva-Mīmāṃsā, Paraśarasmṛti, and Dharmasindhu were considered authoritative and were followed by people. Nowadays people who abide by the teachings of these scriptures are close to none. Today, it is possible as well as necessary to engage in actions in a newer way taught by Lord Kṛṣṇa in the Gita or as guided by enlightened saints like Rāmadāsa, Kabira, and Tukārāma in their texts. Actions which are not propounded by Lord Kṛṣṇa or other enlightened saints are termed as **Vikarma** (prohibited actions). The state of not doing any action is known as **Akarma** (inaction). The repercussions of doing or not doing these actions are best understood only with the help of scriptures. The worldly results of actions are different from extraordinary results like purification of the mind and accumulating merits, which are gained through desireless actions (*Niṣkāma Karma*). Therefore, it is not very easy to gauge the profundity of actions. Only if a person executes prescribed actions in a selfless or desireless manner, or while remembering God and offering the fruits of actions to Him, then such actions do not create bondage for him, and they can be considered **non-action** (action unexecuted). The 3rd chapter describes this philosophy in detail. Even the statement, "I will not perform any action" involves a verbal/mental action. One who clearly understands this philosophy and acts accordingly is a wise Sāṅkhya-Karmayogi since he performs actions by following the principles of Karmayoga while abiding in the Knowledge of the true Self. In other words, he performs all actions without the feeling of doership knowing that his true Self, Ātman, is non-doer.

## Characteristics of a Karmayogi

यस्य सर्वे समारम्भाः कामसङ्कल्पवर्जिताः ।
ज्ञानाग्निदग्धकर्माणं तमाहुः पण्डितं बुधाः ॥ १९ ॥
त्यक्त्वा कर्मफलासङ्गं नित्यतृप्तो निराश्रयः ।
कर्मण्यभिप्रवृत्तोऽपि नैव किञ्चित्करोति सः ॥ २० ॥
निराशीर्यतचित्तात्मा त्यक्तसर्वपरिग्रहः ।
शारीरं केवलं कर्म कुर्वन्नाप्नोति किल्बिषम् ॥ २१ ॥

**यदृच्छालाभसन्तुष्टो द्वन्द्वातीतो विमत्सरः ।**
**समः सिद्धावसिद्धौ च कृत्वापि न निबध्यते ॥ २२ ॥**
**गतसङ्गस्य मुक्तस्य ज्ञानावस्थितचेतसः ।**
**यज्ञायाचरतः कर्म समग्रं प्रविलीयते ॥ २३ ॥**

*Yasya sarve samārambhāḥ kāmasaṃkalpavarjitāḥ* ।
*Jñānāgnidagdhakarmāṇaṃ tam āhuḥ paṇḍitaṃ budhāḥ* ॥ *19* ॥
*Tyaktvā karmaphalāsaṅgaṃ nityatṛpto nirāśrayaḥ* ।
*Karmaṇy abhipravṛtto'pi naiva kiṃcit karoti saḥ* ॥ *20* ॥
*Nirāśīr yatacittātmā tyaktasarvaparigrahaḥ* ।
*Śārīraṃ kevalaṃ karma kurvan nāpnoti kilbiṣam* ॥ *21* ॥
*Yadṛcchālābhasaṃtuṣṭo dvandvātīto vimatsaraḥ* ।
*Samaḥ siddhāv asiddhau ca kṛtvāpi na nibadhyate* ॥ *22* ॥
*Gatasaṅgasya muktasya jñānāvasthitacetasaḥ* ।
*Yajñayācarataḥ karma samagraṃ pravilīyate* ॥ *23* ॥

**Meaning:** When a person appropriately commences his actions and performs them without any desire for fruits, his actions are burnt in the fire of the Knowledge of Ātman. Hence, he is known as the **wise** by sages. He is ever-content since he has abandoned attachment to the fruits of actions. He neither acts as a refuge to anyone else nor does he seek refuge in anyone else. Although ready to perform actions, he does not do anything, in essence. He does not hope for anything; his mind and intellect are under control, and he has mentally renounced all possessions. Even if such a Yogi performs actions by the body, he incurs no bondage or sin. He is content with what comes to him through Prārabdha. He is free from the duality of joy and grief and devoid of envy or jealousy. Being equanimous in success and failure alike, this enlightened person is not bound by actions despite executing them. He is free from all attachments, and his mind remains steady due to the knowledge of equanimity (*Sāmyabuddhi*). His life itself becomes Yajña, so all his actions disappear in Brahman [He does not have to bear fruits of those actions, and thus they merge or disappear in Brahman.]

The word **Samāraṃbha** means *Samyak Āraṃbha* i.e. rightly-begun. This Karmayogi, who has earned equanimity in actions, performs every action appropriately as prescribed by scriptures. His actions are not added to his Sañcita; rather, they disappear in the fire of Self-Knowledge which is manifested from equanimous execution of duties. As he is detached from the fruits due to spiritual discrimination, he remains naturally content.

Ātman i.e. Pure Consciousness neither needs a shelter nor does it act as a refuge for anyone else. Therefore, an enlightened person, who has realized Ātman, also acts in the same manner. Ātman is only one, non-dual principle, so how can there be the duality of a refugee and a shelter in it? A seeker may seek refuge or offer shelter in day-to-day life, but the same is not possible from the spiritual perspective in the realm of Ātman. Being constantly aware of this fact, the seeker can remain detached from all people in his life.

The tree of worldly life flourishes with the water of hope. So long as there is hope for worldly attainments, the delusion that "The world is real" cannot be removed, and attachment to worldly affairs cannot subside. But if the mind and intellect are conquered, then one can practice spiritual discrimination i.e. *Viveka* and wipe out all worldly hopes from his mind. This does not connote that such a seeker becomes hopeless or dejected, as it is commonly understood; rather, he consciously wipes out desires which manifest as hope from his mind. The seeker can also mentally disconnect from people and objects that were previously gathered for pleasure. Thereafter, actions done through his gross body and subtle body as per Prārabdha are not added to his Sañcita. He has to endure his Prārabdha while his body is alive, even if he is enlightened with the Knowledge of Ātman. However, after enlightenment, he remains content with whichever benefits he gets or does not get as per his Prārabdha.

He is liberated from the duality of joy and suffering that arises from desiring results. He is not jealous of any other person who owns more or better objects of pleasure. Neither does he feel happy with success nor does he feel distressed with failure. Any action does not bind this equanimous Karmayogi. All his actions are equivalent to Yajña (sacrifice), and they become Brahman.

**Types of Yajñas**

ब्रह्मार्पणं ब्रह्म हविर्ब्रह्माग्नौ ब्रह्मणा हुतम् ।
ब्रह्मैव तेन गन्तव्यं ब्रह्मकर्मसमाधिना ॥ २४ ॥
दैवमेवापरे यज्ञं योगिनः पर्युपासते ।
ब्रह्माग्नावपरे यज्ञं यज्ञेनैवोपजुह्वति ॥ २५ ॥
श्रोत्रादीनीन्द्रियाण्यन्ये संयमाग्निषु जुह्वति ।
शब्दादीन्विषयानन्य इन्द्रियाग्निषु जुह्वति ॥ २६ ॥
सर्वाणीन्द्रियकर्माणि प्राणकर्माणि चापरे ।
आत्मसंयमयोगाग्नौ जुह्वति ज्ञानदीपिते ॥ २७ ॥
द्रव्ययज्ञास्तपोयज्ञा योगयज्ञास्तथापरे ।
स्वाध्यायज्ञानयज्ञाश्च यतयः संशितव्रताः ॥ २८ ॥
अपाने जुह्वति प्राणं प्राणेऽपानं तथापरे ।
प्राणापानगती रुद्ध्वा प्राणायामपरायणाः ॥ २९ ॥
अपरे नियताहाराः प्राणान्प्राणेषु जुह्वति ।
सर्वेऽप्येते यज्ञविदो यज्ञक्षपितकल्मषाः ॥ ३० ॥
यज्ञशिष्टामृतभुजो यान्ति ब्रह्म सनातनम् ।
नायं लोकोऽस्त्ययज्ञस्य कुतोऽन्यः कुरुसत्तम ॥ ३१ ॥
एवं बहुविधा यज्ञा वितता ब्रह्मणो मुखे ।
कर्मजान्विद्धि तान्सर्वानेवं ज्ञात्वा विमोक्ष्यसे ॥ ३२ ॥

*Brahmārpaṇaṃ brahma havir brahmāgnau brahmaṇā hutam* ।
*Brahmaiva tena gantavyaṃ brahmakarmasamādhinā* ॥ 24 ॥
*Daivam evāpare yajñaṃ yoginaḥ paryupāsate* ।
*Brahmāgnāv apare yajñaṃ yajñenaivopajuvhati* ॥ 25 ॥
*Śrotrādīnīndriyāṇy anye saṅyamāgniṣu juvhati* ।
*Śabdādīn viṣayān anya indriyāgniṣu juvhati* ॥ 26 ॥
*Sarvāṇīndriyakarmāṇi prāṇakarmāṇi cāpare* ।
*Ātmasaṅyamayogāgnau juvhati jñānadīpite* ॥ 27 ॥

*DravyaYajñas tapoYajña yogaYajñas tathāpare* ।
*SvādhyāYajñanaYajñaś ca yatayaḥ saṃśitavratāḥ* ॥ 28 ॥
*Apāne juvhati prāṇaṃ prāṇe'pānaṃ tathāpare* ।
*Prāṇāpānagatī ruddhvā prāṇāyāmaparāyaṇāḥ* ॥ 29 ॥
*Apare niyatāhārāḥ prāṇān prāṇeṣu juvhati* ।
*Sarve'pyete yajñavido yajñakṣapitakalmaṣāḥ* ॥ 30 ॥
*Yajñaśiṣṭāmṛtabhujo yānti brahma sanātanam* ।
*Nāyaṃ loko'sty ayajñasya kuto'nyaḥ kurusattama* ॥ 31 ॥
*Evaṃ bahuvidhā* Yajña *vitatā brahmaṇo mukhe* ।
*Karmajān viddhi tān sarvān evaṃ jñātvā vimokṣyase* ॥ 32 ॥

**Meaning:** One who knows himself as Brahman sees all elements of sacrifice (clarified butter, rice, etc.) as Brahman, offers them in the fire that is Brahman, and his act of oblation is also Brahman; he verily becomes Brahman himself by being intent on Brahman in all his actions. Some ritualistic people perform traditional Yajnas by offering the chanting of the Veda-Mantras to the fire-of-Vedas to worship the Lord of Yajña. Wise people perform the Yajña-of-Knowledge by offering their limited self (Jiva) to the fire of Brahman, the true Self. [This simply means they become One with Brahman.] Some offer the sense-organs like ears etc. in the fire-of-restraint, while some offer sound and other objects-of-senses in the fire-of-senses. Others offer the organs and Prāṇas in the fire of self-restraint kindled by knowledge. Others who practice strong austerities offer wealth, austerity, Yoga, the study of scriptures, execution of prescribed duties, and knowledge as sacrifice. Those who are experts in breath control restrain the flow of outgoing and incoming breaths and offer the outgoing breath (Apāna) as a sacrifice in the incoming breath (Prāṇa) and the incoming breath in the outgoing breath. Others – with a well-regulated diet – offer the sacrifice of the incoming breath in its function. All those who execute such Yajñas and consume the nectar of Yajña attain Eternal Brahman. Those who do not perform any such acts of sacrifice do not find success even in this world, so how may they attain any other world? Many other similar Yajñas are manifested from the Vedas. Knowing them all as born of action, you shall be liberated from the bondage of action.

These Yajñas are unlike traditional Yajñas in which actual fire is ignited, and offerings are made in the fire while chanting appropriate hymns from the Vedas. Yajñas described in these verses may vary greatly in rituals, though they are mostly done through the mind, the intellect, and the Prāṇas. However, all of these are equally qualified as acts of sacrifice. The seeker does not need to know the technical, minute details of all Yajñas. The upcoming 33rd verse states that all Yajñas need a deity, organs, Prāṇas (life-forces), and self-restraint. Various Yajñas can be practiced through different actions. But all these actions and their results are ultimately perishable. They are all subjective i.e. dependent on being done by someone. But Self-effulgent Ātman is ever-established by itself, so it does not need to be established, proved, or attained through any action. Ātman, the true Self, is ever-existent regardless of anything else. The seeker who understands this fact is liberated from all kinds of bondages born out of actions. In other words, he does not attach any importance in gaining anything in this world that can be achieved through actions. He does not think that life is all about actions and their fruits. He does not feel proud that "I am the doer of actions"; for him, actions are naturally executed through his body and mind as per Prārabdha. He does not bother about the fruits of actions that are performed as prescribed by scriptures. He attains Mokṣa since actions cannot bind him anymore. This philosophy has a significant implication in Arjuna's case of fighting war.

**<u>The seeker should perform the Yajña of Knowledge</u>**

श्रेयान्द्रव्यमयाद्यज्ञाज्ज्ञानयज्ञः परन्तप ।
सर्वं कर्माखिलं पार्थ ज्ञाने परिसमाप्यते ॥ ३३ ॥

तद्विद्धि प्रणिपातेन परिप्रश्नेन सेवया ।
उपदेक्ष्यन्ति ते ज्ञानं ज्ञानिनस्तत्त्वदर्शिनः ॥ ३४ ॥
यज्ज्ञात्वा न पुनर्मोहमेवं यास्यसि पाण्डव ।
येन भूतान्यशेषेण द्रक्ष्यस्यात्मन्यथो मयि ॥ ३५ ॥
अपि चेदसि पापेभ्यः सर्वेभ्यः पापकृत्तमः ।
सर्वं ज्ञानप्लवेनैव वृजिनं सन्तरिष्यसि ॥ ३६ ॥
यथैधांसि समिद्धोऽग्निर्भस्मसात्कुरुतेऽर्जुन ।
ज्ञानाग्निः सर्वकर्माणि भस्मसात्कुरुते तथा ॥ ३७ ॥

*Śreyān dravyamayād Yajñaj jñānayajñaḥ paramtapa* ।
*Sarvaṃ karmākhilaṃ pārtha jñāne parisamāpyate* ॥ *33* ॥
*Tad viddhi praṇipātena paripraśnena sevayā* ।
*Upadekṣyanti te jñānaṃ jñāninas tattvādarśinaḥ* ॥ *34* ॥
*Yaj jñātvā na punar moham evaṃ yāsyasi pāṇḍava* ।
*Yena bhūtāny aśeṣeṇa drakṣyasy ātmany atho mayi* ॥ *35* ॥
*Api ced asi pāpebhyaḥ sarvebhyaḥ pāpakṛttamaḥ* ।
*Sarvaṃ jñānaplavenaiva vṛjinaṃ saṃtariṣyasi* ॥ *36* ॥
*Yathaidhāṃsi samiddho'gnir bhasmasāt kurute'rjuna* ।
*Jñānāgniḥ sarvakarmāṇi bhasmasāt kurute tathā* ॥ *37* ॥

**Meaning:** O Arjuna, the distresser of enemies! The Yajña for attaining Self-Knowledge (*Jñānayajña*) is superior to the Yajña done with any other kind of worldly elements. All actions facilitate Knowledge. To attain this Self-Knowledge, bow down and prostrate in front of the enlightened sages, serve them with humility, and ask them questions about the supreme achievement of life. Know that they will then impart the highest Knowledge of Ātman to you. You will not be deluded again after attaining this Self-Knowledge. Thereafter, you will see that just like Me, you, too, are the substratum of the whole of creation. Even if you are the most sinful of all sinners, you shall cross the ocean of all sins by this raft of Self-Knowledge. O Arjuna! The blazing fire reduces all its fuel and wood into ashes. Similarly, the fire of Self-Knowledge burns all bondages of actions into ashes.

People are accustomed to performing actions in the following sequence. The desire for attaining some fruit first arises in mind. The person then collects the needed material. He executes that action and lastly gets the fruit. This sequence works well in routine life. Each worldly result has the '**cause and effect'** principle behind it. However, the Knowledge of Ātman is not based on the 'cause and effect' theory. Any worldly object is first non-existent and later comes into existence after its creation. Ātman is ***Sat*** i.e. Pure Existence. It is ever-existent, so it cannot be created, attained, or altered at all. This means that the the Knowledge of Ātman cannot be attained, created, or altered like any other worldly qualified knowledge. A person who knows this fact performs actions in such a way that they are not binding for him. He is not attached to actions or their impermanent results.

Actions, when performed as instructed in the Gita or texts authored by the enlightened saints, lead to purification of the mind. Purified mind pines for the supreme purity of Ātman. The seeker should surrender to the wise, enlightened sages to fulfill his pining for liberation, eradicate his ignorance, and attain the ever-attained Self-Knowledge, which is merely hidden due to ignorance. He should serve the wise sages with utmost humility and ask them questions – at the right time – about supreme welfare (goal) of human life. These wise sages then impart the Knowledge of Ātman to him and other such seekers. The seeker should consistently practice spiritual discrimination between real and unreal, discard all unreal elements, and overcome the obstacle of Śūnya – the stage of void – in meditation. After this, he can realize, "I am the ever-shining Self-effulgent light of Ātman." Thereafter, he is not deluded by the world or bound by actions or their results anymore.

All sentient beings reside in the insentient world, and they are bound by action. Both sentient and insentient entities subsist on the substratum of Brahman. An enlightened person knows that his true Self (Brahman) is the very substratum of the entire universe.

**स विद्वान्पुण्यपापे विधूय परमसाम्यमुपैति ।**

*Sa vidvānpuṇyapāpe vidhūya paramasāmyamupaiti* ।

*(Muṇḍak. Up 3.1.3)*

According to this verse, even if he is a great sinner in day-to-day life, he transcends his sins and leads a glorious life. Merits and sins are created when one considers himself a limited being with a name and form. The knowledge that "I am Brahman" transcends all merits and sins. All past actions executed in delusion and their fruits – merits and sins – are burnt to ashes for a Self-realized person.

## The importance of the Knowledge of Brahman

**न हि ज्ञानेन सदृशं पवित्रमिह विद्यते ।**
**तत्स्वयं योगसंसिद्धः कालेनात्मनि विन्दति ॥ ३८ ॥**

*Na hi jñānena sadṛśaṃ pavitram iha vidyāte* ।
*Tat svayaṃ yogasaṃsiddhaḥ kālenātmani vindati* ॥ *38* ॥

**Meaning:** There is nothing pure and pious like Knowledge (of Ātman) in this world. He who has pure mind attains Knowledge in due time by being perfected in Karmayoga.

Muṇḍaka Upaniṣad has classified knowledge in two parts: **Parā** (superior) and **Aparā** (inferior). The knowledge related to world is inferior, while the Knowledge of Ātman is declared as superior or the ultimate. The 32nd and 33rd verse in this chapter state that everything produced or created by action is ultimately perishable. The universe created by Īśvara, and the small world created by each Jiva – I, mine, and all ensuing desires – are both perishable. All knowledge pertinent to them is perishable, and thus inferior. Pure Knowledge of Ātman is the epitome of the evolution of the human intellect. It is the most pious of all kinds of knowledge. The worldly knowledge is certainly necessary in day-to-day transactions; however, the Knowledge of Ātman is superior to it. A seeker who follows the principles of Karmayoga, and who has equanimous mind, attains steady spiritual knowledge that "I am Brahman" in due course of time.

## Importance of faith in the Knowledge of Ātman

श्रद्धावाँल्लभते ज्ञानं तत्परः संयतेन्द्रियः ।
ज्ञानं लब्ध्वा परां शान्तिमचिरेणाधिगच्छति ॥ ३९ ॥
अज्ञश्चाश्रद्दधानश्च संशयात्मा विनश्यति ।
नायं लोकोऽस्ति न परो न सुखं संशयात्मनः ॥ ४० ॥
योगसंन्यस्तकर्माणं ज्ञानसञ्छिन्नसंशयम् ।
आत्मवन्तं न कर्माणि निबध्नन्ति धनञ्जय ॥ ४१ ॥
तस्मादज्ञानसम्भूतं हृत्स्थं ज्ञानासिनात्मनः ।
छित्त्वैनं संशयं योगमातिष्ठोत्तिष्ठ भारत ॥ ४२ ॥

*Śraddhāvāṃl labhate jñānaṃ tatparaḥ saṅyatendriyaḥ* ।
*Jñānaṃ labdhvā parāṃ śāntim acireṇādhigacchati* ॥ *39* ॥
*Ajñaścāśraddadhānaśca saṃśayātmā vinaśyati* ।
*Nāyaṃ loko'sti na paro na sukhaṃ saṃśayātmanaḥ* ॥ *40* ॥
*Yogasaṃnyastakarmāṇaṃ jñānasaṃchinnasaṃśayam* ।
*Ātmavantaṃ na karmāṇi nibadhnanti dhanaṃjaya* ॥ *41* ॥
*Tasmād ajñānasañbhūtaṃ hṛtsthaṃ jñānāsinātmanaḥ* ।
*Chittvainaṃ saṃśayaṃ yogam ātiṣṭhottiṣṭha bhārata* ॥ *42* ॥

**Meaning:** A seeker who is Sāttvic, full of faith, master of his senses, and who has longing for the Knowledge of Ātman attains that Self-Knowledge and thereby enjoys supreme peace. He who is ignorant, faithless, and full of doubts deteriorates from the spiritual perspective. A skeptical person neither achieves success and happiness in this world nor in the other. Actions do not bind the Self-realized person who acts with equanimous intellect, and whose doubts are eradicated completely by Self-Knowledge. Therefore, O Arjuna! Severe the ignorance-born uncertainties and doubts in your mind with Self-Knowledge. Engage in actions with the equanimous mind and get ready for your duty as a warrior.

**ॐ तत्सदिति श्रीमद्भगवद्गीतासूपनिषत्सु ब्रह्मविद्यायां योगशास्त्रे श्रीकृष्णार्जुनसंवादे ज्ञानकर्मसंन्यासयोगो नाम चतुर्थोऽध्यायः ॥**

*Om Tatsaditi Śrimadbhagvadgitāsūpaniṣatsu Brahmavidyāyāṃ Yogaśāstre Śrīkṛṣṇārjunasaṅvāde Jñānakarmasaṅnyāsayogo Nāma Caturtho'dhyāyaḥ* ॥

Sāttvic faith is of immense importance in spiritual pursuit. If perverted faith – like black magic – proliferates in society, it discredits and maligns even the path of true, beneficial faith. The true faith should evolve in four stages: tradition, logic, the experience of other people, and self-experience. If traditions of thousands of years were futile or meaningless, they indeed would have been abandoned much earlier. Enlightened saints are completely selfless, so we can easily trust their teachings. These wise saints have recorded their experiences of Self-realization and described ways to realize those teachings. Man is bound to attain Self-Knowledge if he follows the guidelines and teachings of enlightened saints. When a person catches even a glimpse of Self-Knowledge himself, his faith in spiritual philosophy is strengthened. The initial faith in Ātman should evolve into the firm realization that "I am Ātman." For this purpose, the seeker should conquer his senses and the mind and nurture intense longing for attainment of Self-Knowledge. The seeker who is fully centered in his Sadguru and his teachings, and who abides by all prescribed spiritual practices, attains Self-realization and revels in Supreme Bliss. A faithless and ignorant person deteriorates from the spiritual perspective. He may be successful in worldly life. However, even in day-to-day life, he cannot perform any transaction properly if he has no faith in any system. Such a person does not even remotely think of the next world like heaven, etc.

If the seeker follows the tenets of Karmayoga by being firmly intent on the true Self, he realizes "I am Ātman. " Thereafter, all his doubts about what is real and unreal, perpetual and nonperpetual, etc. are resolved. Actions do not bind an enlightened person. Therefore, Lord Kṛṣṇa says, "O Arjuna! If you engage in this so-called gruesome action of war with the equanimous mind, you will not be bound by it. Remove the delusion in your mind which is born of ignorance and uncertainty. Get enthusiastically ready for your duty of fighting war."

In the Second World War, the American pilots who dropped the atom-bomb on Hirośima and Nāgāsāki felt guilty after seeing the results of their action. Had they listened to the spiritual teachings of the Gita, they would not have felt this guilt. The responsibility of the attack belonged to their higher authorities. The pilots were merely instruments who carried out their assigned duties. Similarly, Arjuna was merely an instrument in the epic battle of Mahābhārata who was expected to annihilate the evil forces.

Chapter 5

# Renunciation of Actions

॥ कर्मसंन्यासयोगः (Karmasaṁnyāsayogaḥ) ॥

A person may have a very sharp, subtle, penetrating, and Sāttvic intellect, yet if it is clouded by delusion, it is extremely difficult for him to comprehend the doctrine of Vedānta. Arjuna's question demonstrates this fact. He was skeptical about the perplexing teaching of Lord Kṛṣṇa at the beginning of the third chapter. His mind is still doubtful and uncertain about Śrīkṛṣṇa's guidance. Therefore, he had to listen quietly when Kṛṣṇa addressed him as a person with childish, immature intellect (*5.4*).

**Arjuna's question**

**अर्जुन उवाच ।**
**संन्यासं कर्मणां कृष्ण पुनर्योगं च शंससि ।**
**यच्छ्रेय एतयोरेकं तन्मे ब्रूहि सुनिश्चितम् ॥ १ ॥**

*Arjuna uvāca* ।
*Saṃnyāsaṃ karmaṇāṃ kṛṣṇa punar yogaṃ ca śaṃsasi* ।
*Yac chreya etayor ekaṃ tan me brūhi suniścitam* ॥ *1* ॥

**Meaning:** (Arjuna said) O Kṛṣṇa! First, You praise the renunciation of actions (*Karmasaṁnyāsa*), and yet again You praise the performance of actions according to Karmayoga then and there. So, tell me conclusively which is better of the two.

In verse 4.15, Kṛṣṇa instructed Arjuna to perform actions. This instruction is creating uncertainty in Arjuna's mind. He is still mulling over Kṛṣṇa's words which were spoken earlier in *2.45*: "Abide in Ātman without dwelling on the thoughts of worldly gains and preservation." All subsequent teachings of Kṛṣṇa are kind of erased from Arjuna's mind.

## The superiority of Karmayoga

*श्रीभगवानुवाच ।*
संन्यासः कर्मयोगश्च निःश्रेयसकरावुभौ ।
तयोस्तु कर्मसंन्यासात्कर्मयोगो विशिष्यते ॥ २ ॥
ज्ञेयः स नित्यसंन्यासी यो न द्वेष्टि न काङ्क्षति ।
निर्द्वन्द्वो हि महाबाहो सुखं बन्धात्प्रमुच्यते ॥ ३ ॥
साङ्ख्ययोगौ पृथग्बालाः प्रवदन्ति न पण्डिताः ।
एकमप्यास्थितः सम्यगुभयोर्विन्दते फलम् ॥ ४ ॥
यत्साङ्ख्यैः प्राप्यते स्थानं तद्योगैरपि गम्यते ।
एकं साङ्ख्यं च योगं च यः पश्यति स पश्यति ॥ ५ ॥
संन्यासस्तु महाबाहो दुःखमाप्तुमयोगतः ।
योगयुक्तो मुनिर्ब्रह्म नचिरेणाधिगच्छति ॥ ६ ॥

*Śrībhagavān uvāca* ।
*Saṃnyāsaḥ karmayogaś ca niḥśreyasakarāv ubhau* ।
*Tayos tu karmaSaṅnyāsāt karmayogo viśiṣyate* ॥ *2* ॥
*Jñeyaḥ sa nityaSaṅnyāsī yo na dveṣṭi na kāṅkṣati* ।
*Nirdvandvo hi mahābāho sukhaṃ bandhāt pramucyate* ॥ *3* ॥
*Sāṃkhyayogau pṛthag bālāḥ pravādanti na paṇḍitāḥ* ।
*Ekam apy āsthitaḥ samyag ubhayor vindate phalam* ॥ *4* ॥
*Yat sāṃkhyaiḥ prāpyate sthānaṃ tad yogair api gamyate* ।
*Ekaṃ sāṃkhyaṃ ca yogaṃ ca yaḥ paśyati sa paśyati* ॥ *5* ॥
*Saṃnyāsas tu mahābāho duḥkham āptum ayogataḥ* ।
*Yogayukto munir brahma nacireṇādhigacchati* ॥ *6* ॥

**Meaning:** (Śrībhagavān said) Renunciation of actions (*Karmasaṅnyāsa*) and execution of actions according to Karmayoga both lead to the highest goal i.e. Self-realization. But of the two, execution of actions as per Karmayoga is superior to renunciation of actions. A Karmayogi who does not hate anyone and desires nothing is a real monk (Saṅnyāsin). This is because he is freed from the duality of attachment and aversion. Wise people do not consider the **Path of Self-Knowledge**

(*Sāṅkhyayoga*) followed by Saṅnyāsins to be different from the **Path of Desireless-Actions** (*Niṣkāma Karmayoga*). Those who consider them to be separate are indeed childish and immature. A person who is perfected in any one of these two paths attains the results of both. The state reached by following the Path of Knowledge is also reached by following the Path of Action. He is the real seer who sees *Sāṅkhyayoga* and *Karmayoga* as the same for Self-realization. It is tough to perfect the renunciation of actions without the help of Karmayoga. It does not take long for a contemplative Karmayogi to realize the Knowledge of Brahman.

Kaṭha Upaniṣad states that worldly life is *Preya*, and spiritual pursuit for Mokṣa is *Śreya*. A person who is fully engaged in day-to-day duties and content with fruits that comes his way through Prārabdha is indeed free from both attachment and aversion. He feels no resentment or anger since there is no comparison, competition, or jealousy in his mind. He is not greedy since there are no expectations in his mind. As there is no greed or anger in his mind, he is not troubled by any action. Thus, he naturally attains the renunciation of actions. A person who is troubled by actions needs to go through specific rituals to embrace the path of formal Saṅnyāsa and become a monk. But a Karmayogi who executes actions by knowing the true Self has no reason to adapt formal Saṅnyāsa. A Saṅnyāsin – who takes formal vows of monastic life and follows its rules meticulously – also obtains the same results as a Karmayogi. A Saṅnyāsin does not get anything more or different than a Karmayogi. A seeker who knows the gist and spirit of this philosophy is a true seer.

Despite this fact, it is difficult to practice formal Saṅnyāsa in real life without following Karmayoga. In today's world, it is indeed more beneficial to follow the Path of Action according to Karmayoga due to various reasons: inescapable tendency towards action, imperative need for action, no chance of earning livelihood without action, the perverted image of Saṁnyāsa in the modern times, and possibility of not being able to brave through the challenges of formal Saṁnyāsa. As a result, it is better to selflessly execute actions without desiring fruits and by knowing the true Self. If such a seeker consistently practices *Viveka* and discriminates between Ātman and Anātman, he soon realizes "I am Ātman" and attains liberation.

## Spiritual practices for Mokṣa

योगयुक्तो विशुद्धात्मा विजितात्मा जितेन्द्रियः ।
सर्वभूतात्मभूतात्मा कुर्वन्नपि न लिप्यते ॥ ७ ॥
नैव किञ्चित्करोमीति युक्तो मन्येत तत्त्ववित् ।
पश्यञ्शृण्वन्स्पृशञ्जिघ्रन्नश्नन्गच्छन्स्वपञ्श्वसन् ॥ ८ ॥
प्रलपन्विसृजन्गृह्णन्नुन्मिषन्निमिषन्नपि ।
इन्द्रियाणीन्द्रियार्थेषु वर्तन्त इति धारयन् ॥ ९ ॥
ब्रह्मण्याधाय कर्माणि सङ्गं त्यक्त्वा करोति यः ।
लिप्यते न स पापेन पद्मपत्रमिवाम्भसा ॥ १० ॥
कायेन मनसा बुद्ध्या केवलैरिन्द्रियैरपि ।
योगिनः कर्म कुर्वन्ति सङ्गं त्यक्त्वात्मशुद्धये ॥ ११ ॥

*Yogayukto viśuddhātmā vijitātmā jitendriyaḥ* ।
*Sarvabhūtātmabhūtātmā kurvann api na lipyate* ॥ 7 ॥
*Naiva kiṃcit karomīti yukto manyeta tattvavit* ।
*Paśyañ śṛṇvan spṛśañ jighrann aśnan gacchan svapañ śvasan* ॥8
*Pralapan visṛjan gṛhṇann unmiṣan nimiṣann api* ।
*Indriyāṇīndriyārtheṣu vartanta iti dhārayan* ॥ 9 ॥
*Brahmaṇy ādhāya karmāṇi saṅgaṃ tyaktvā karoti yaḥ* ।
*Lipyate na sa pāpena padmapatram ivāmbhasā* ॥ 10 ॥
*Kāyena manasā buddhyā kevalair indriyair api* ।
*Yoginaḥ karma kurvanti saṅgaṃ tyaktvātmaśuddhaye* ॥ 11 ॥

**Meaning:** One who constantly adheres to the principles of Karmayoga, who is not inclined towards prohibited actions, who has conquered his mind and controlled his senses, and who realizes his Self as the Self in all beings (*Yasmin Sarvāṇi*

*Bhūtāni – Iśāvāsya. Up. 6*), such a seeker is not bound by actions even though he is immersed in actions. A wise person who has realized Self-Knowledge should think that "I do nothing." Even while seeing, listening, touching, smelling, eating, walking, sleeping, breathing, etc. he should think the same. Similarly, though speaking, taking, abandoning, opening and closing the eyes, he should know that his senses are engaged in their duties and think with certainty, "I do nothing at all." A person who performs actions offering them to Brahman and renounces attachment to actions and fruits alike remains free from merits and sins, just as a lotus leaf remains untouched by water. A Karmayogi, who performs all actions for the purification of the mind, knows for certain that actions are performed at the level of the body, mind, intellect, and organs.

These thoughts have been discussed many times so far. Action-organs like hands and feet are drawn towards their respective actions. Sense-organs like nose, eyes are drawn towards their respective objects. Ātman, the true Self, is totally unaware of these activities. Every Jiva goes through the three states of waking, dreaming, and deep-sleep; yet the true Self, Ātman, is completely unrelated to these states. All states belong to the Jiva. The real I, Ātman, is not attached to or encaged by anything. A Karmayogi offers all actions in the world to Brahman which is the very substratum of the world. This is his spiritual practice. He calmly and contentedly accepts the results which come his way through Prārabdha, the system of Īśvara's governance.

**The characteristics of a Karmayogi**

युक्तः कर्मफलं त्यक्त्वा शान्तिमाप्नोति नैष्ठिकीम् ।
अयुक्तः कामकारेण फले सक्तो निबध्यते ॥ १२ ॥
सर्वकर्माणि मनसा संन्यस्यास्ते सुखं वशी ।
नवद्वारे पुरे देही नैव कुर्वन्न कारयन् ॥ १३ ॥

न कर्तृत्वं न कर्माणि लोकस्य सृजति प्रभुः ।
न कर्मफलसंयोगं स्वभावस्तु प्रवर्तते ॥ १४ ॥
नादत्ते कस्यचित्पापं न चैव सुकृतं विभुः ।
अज्ञानेनावृतं ज्ञानं तेन मुह्यन्ति जन्तवः ॥ १५ ॥
ज्ञानेन तु तदज्ञानं येषां नाशितमात्मनः ।
तेषामादित्यवज्ज्ञानं प्रकाशयति तत्परम् ॥ १६ ॥
तद्बुद्धयस्तदात्मानस्तन्निष्ठास्तत्परायणाः ।
गच्छन्त्यपुनरावृत्तिं ज्ञाननिर्धूतकल्मषाः ॥ १७ ॥
विद्याविनयसम्पन्ने ब्राह्मणे गवि हस्तिनि ।
शुनि चैव श्वपाके च पण्डिताः समदर्शिनः ॥ १८ ॥
इहैव तैर्जितः सर्गो येषां साम्ये स्थितं मनः ।
निर्दोषं हि समं ब्रह्म तस्माद् ब्रह्मणि ते स्थिताः ॥ १९ ॥
न प्रहृष्येत्प्रियं प्राप्य नोद्विजेत्प्राप्य चाप्रियम् ।
स्थिरबुद्धिरसम्मूढो ब्रह्मविद् ब्रह्मणि स्थितः ॥ २० ॥
बाह्यस्पर्शेष्वसक्तात्मा विन्दत्यात्मनि यत्सुखम् ।
स ब्रह्मयोगयुक्तात्मा सुखमक्षयमश्नुते ॥ २१ ॥
ये हि संस्पर्शजा भोगा दुःखयोनय एव ते ।
आद्यन्तवन्तः कौन्तेय न तेषु रमते बुधः ॥ २२ ॥

*Yuktaḥ karmaphalaṃ tyaktvā śāntim āpnoti naiṣṭhikīm* ।
*Ayuktaḥ kāmakāreṇa phale sakto nibadhyate* ॥ *12* ॥
*Sarvakarmāṇi manasā saṃnyasyāste sukhaṃ vaśī* ।
*Navadvāre pure dehī naiva kurvan na kārayan* ॥ *13* ॥
*Na kartṛtvaṃ na karmāṇi lokasya sṛjati prabhuḥ* ।
*Na karmaphalasaṅyogaṃ svabhāvas tu pravartate* ॥ *14* ॥
*Nādatte kasyacit pāpaṃ na caiva sukṛtaṃ vibhuḥ* ।
*Ajñānenāvṛtaṃ jñānaṃ tena muhyanti jantavaḥ* ॥ *15* ॥
*Jñānena tu tad ajñānaṃ yeṣāṃ nāśitam ātmanaḥ* ।
*Teṣām ādityavaj jñānaṃ prakāśayati tat param* ॥ *16* ॥
*Tadbuddhayas tadātmānas tanniṣṭhās tatparāyaṇāḥ* ।
*Gacchanty apunarāvṛttiṃ jñānanirdhūtakalmaṣāḥ* ॥ *17* ॥
*Vidyāvinayasaṃpanne brāhmaṇe gavi hastini* ।
*Śuni caiva śvapāke ca paṇḍitāḥ samadarśinaḥ* ॥ *18* ॥
*Ihaiva tair jitaḥ sargo yeṣāṃ sāmye sthitaṃ manaḥ* ।
*Nirdoṣaṃ hi samaṃ brahma tasmād brahmaṇi te sthitāḥ* ॥ *19* ॥

*Na prahṛṣyet priyaṃ prāpya nodvijet prāpya cāpriyam* ।
*Sthirabuddhir asaṃmūḍho brahmavid brahmaṇi sthitaḥ* ॥ *20* ॥
*Bāhyasparśeṣv asaktātmā vindaty ātmani yat sukham* ।
*Sa brahmayogayuktātmā sukham akṣayam aśnute* ॥ *21* ॥
*Ye hi saṃsparśajā bhogā duḥkhayonaya eva te* ।
*Ādyantavantaḥ kaunteya na teṣu ramate budhaḥ* ॥ *22* ॥

**Meaning:** A Karmayogi seeker offers fruits of actions to Brahman and thereby attains supreme peace (Parā Shanti). However, one who is not a Karmayogi gets bound due to the attachment to actions and fruits. The seeker who has conquered his senses mentally offers all actions to Īśvara. Such a seeker is liberated from thoughts such as "I act, or I impel others to act." He dwells happily in the city of nine gates which is his gross body. Ātman, Supreme God, does not induce the feeling of doership in the Jiva nor impels him to actions nor grants the fruits for actions. It is Prakṛti (Nature) that does all of this. All-pervading Brahman does not impel anyone towards merits or sins. Self-Knowledge is veiled by ignorance, and hence all Jivas are deluded. But for those whose ignorance is destroyed by the Knowledge of Ātman, Knowledge illumines their minds just like the sunlight. For the seekers who constantly abide in Ātman by focusing their mind, intellect, and faith on Ātman, their sins are completely wiped out, and they are freed from the cycle of birth and death. A learned and humble scholar, a cow, an elephant, a dog, and an outcaste – enlightened sages see them all with even vision. People who are steady in such equanimity transcend the cycle of rebirth in this world itself, as they are steadfast in Pure Brahman which permeates everywhere. A wise and discriminating Knower of Brahman does not rejoice when he gets what he wants and does not lament when he gets what he does not want. He thus remains steady in his true Self, Brahman. In this state of being dispassionate about external objects, the Knower of Brahman revels in Supreme Bliss of the Self. Being absorbed in the Self, he always enjoys Pure Bliss of Ātman. Pleasures born out of the contact of the senses with their objects consequently give rise to grief. Worldly pleasures are subject to a beginning and an end, so wise people do not rejoice in them.

The body is a city which has nine doors: two eyes, two ears, two nostrils, a mouth, a genital, and a rectum. Every Jiva has to reside in this city for some duration as decided by his Prārabdha. The Karmayogi lives peaceful life filled with Bliss in this city.

Ātman, the true Self, is a non-doer. It neither gives nor receives anything from anyone. Ātman does not impel anyone towards right actions (merits) or wrong actions (sins). It neither grants fruits nor does it receive fruits in return. Īśvara executes these transactions through His power of Māyā in a systematic, organized manner. Lord Kṛṣṇa has given a conclusive judgment on merits and sins in His Gita. As a Saguṇa God, He has the power to liberate people (like Arjuna) – who obey His orders – from their sins (*18.66*). Every Jiva is deluded due to ignorance, and he feels that God has urged him to do a good or bad action. In reality, it is his own Vāsanā that impels him to decide to act in a particular manner. Scriptures like the Gita are authoritative texts which teach us the exact nature of Vāsanā. Īśvara is the one who grants the fruits to the Jiva as per his behavior. But an enlightened person frees himself from the system of bearing fruits of actions. He does not rejoice in impermanent worldly pleasures. The person who becomes happy is bound to become sad at some or the other time. He does not find absolute, lasting, supreme peace. One who is Pure Bliss himself does not feel happy or dejected in a worldly sense.

**Conclusion**

**शक्नोतीहैव यः सोढुं प्राक्शरीरविमोक्षणात् ।**
**कामक्रोधोद्भवं वेगं स युक्तः स सुखी नरः ॥ २३ ॥**

योऽन्तःसुखोऽन्तरारामस्तथान्तर्ज्योतिरेव यः ।
स योगी ब्रह्मनिर्वाणं ब्रह्मभूतोऽधिगच्छति ॥ २४ ॥
लभन्ते ब्रह्मनिर्वाणमृषयः क्षीणकल्मषाः ।
छिन्नद्वैधा यतात्मानः सर्वभूतहिते रताः ॥ २५ ॥
कामक्रोधवियुक्तानां यतीनां यतचेतसाम् ।
अभितो ब्रह्मनिर्वाणं वर्तते विदितात्मनाम् ॥ २६ ॥
स्पर्शान्कृत्वा बहिर्बाह्यांश्चक्षुश्चैवान्तरे भ्रुवोः ।
प्राणापानौ समौ कृत्वा नासाभ्यन्तरचारिणौ ॥ २७ ॥
यतेन्द्रियमनोबुद्धिर्मुनिर्मोक्षपरायणः ।
विगतेच्छाभयक्रोधो यः सदा मुक्त एव सः ॥ २८ ॥
भोक्तारं यज्ञतपसां सर्वलोकमहेश्वरम् ।
सुहृदं सर्वभूतानां ज्ञात्वा मां शान्तिमृच्छति ॥ २९ ॥

*Śaknotīhaiva yaḥ soḍhuṃ prāk śarīravimokṣaṇāt* ।
*Kāmakrodhodbhavaṃ vegaṃ sa yuktaḥ sa sukhī naraḥ* ॥ 23 ॥
*Yo'ntaḥsukho'ntarārāmas tathāntarjyotir eva yaḥ* ।
*Sa yogī brahmanirvāṇaṃ brahmabhūto'dhigacchati* ॥ 24 ॥
*Labhante brahmanirvāṇam ṛṣayaḥ kṣīṇakalmaṣāḥ* ।
*Chinnadvaidhā yatātmānaḥ sarvabhūtahite ratāḥ* ॥ 25 ॥
*Kāmakrodhaviyuktānāṃ yatīnāṃ yatacetasām* ।
*Abhito brahmanirvāṇaṃ vartate viditātmanām* ॥ 26 ॥
*Sparśān kṛtvā bahir bāhyāṃś cakṣuś caivāntare bhruvoḥ* ।
*Prāṇāpānau samau kṛtvā nāsābhyantaracāriṇau* ॥ 27 ॥
*Yatendriyamanobuddhirmunir mokṣaparāyaṇaḥ* ।
*Vigatecchābhayakrodho yaḥ sadā mukta eva saḥ* ॥ 28 ॥
*Bhoktāraṃ yajñatapasāṃ sarvalokamaheśvaram* ।
*Suhṛdaṃ sarvabhūtānāṃ jñātvā māṃ śāntim ṛcchati* ॥ 29 ॥

**Meaning:** A person who can resist the impulses of desire and anger even here in this world before he leaves the body is a real renunciate of Karma; he is happy in a true sense. A renunciate Yogi whose happiness is Ātman, whose relaxation is Pure Bliss of Ātman, and whose light is the eternal light of Ātman realizes that "I am Brahman" and attains Mokṣa. Enlightened Ṛṣis whose sins are destroyed, who are free of all doubts, whose minds are controlled, and who are earnest about the welfare of all beings attain Mokṣa of Self-realization. A renunciate who is free from the impulses of desire and anger, who has conquered his mind and realized "I am Brahman," is liberated naturally. A sage whose goal is liberation shuts out all external objects and steadies the mind by fixing his gaze in between the eyebrows. He equalizes the outward and inward breaths in the nostrils; controls the mind, intellect, and senses with high vigilance; and dispels Vāsanā, fear, and anger from his mind. He is liberated forever. My devotee realizes, "I am the enjoyer of all sacrifices (Yajñas) and austerities (*Tapas*), the Lord of all three worlds like heaven, etc., and a selfless friend of all beings." Knowing this, he attains supreme peace.

**ॐ तत्सदिति श्रीमद्भगवद्गीतासूपनिषत्सु ब्रह्मविद्यायां योगशास्त्रे श्रीकृष्णार्जुनसंवादे कर्मसंन्यासयोगो नाम पञ्चमोऽध्यायः ॥**

*Om Tatsaditi Śrimadbhagvadgitāsūpaniṣatsu Brahmavidyāyāṃ Yogaśāstre Śrīkṛṣṇārjunasaṁvāde Karmasaṁnyāsayogo Nāma Pañcamo'dhyāyaḥ* ॥

After declaring that the *execution of Karmayoga* is easier than renunciation of Karma, Lord Kṛṣṇa explains the nature of **true renunciation**. The impulses of attachment for a favorable object and aversion for an unfavorable object come to an end for a renunciate person. He is able to stay free from desire and anger until the end of his life. Every person has to perform actions for fulfilling his desires. If the desire itself is eliminated, it becomes easier to renounce actions, and then the desire for fruits does not arise in mind. When desires, actions, and fruits are not present, attachment and aversion also come to an end as there is nothing favorable or unfavorable anymore. Thereafter, such a seeker experiences lasting peace and happiness. He strives to rejoice in Pure Bliss of his Self and ultimately realizes "I am Brahman."

As a result of self-restraint and resolution of all doubts in his mind, he begins to see his own Self everywhere around him and attains liberation. He begins to think about the welfare of others more than his personal progress. This enlightened *Ṛṣi* spreads joy everywhere around him. This muni who practices *Viveka* between Ātman and Anātman attains liberation naturally. He does not pursue unreal and transient material objects anymore, instead he strives to conquer his mind, and he abides in the thoughts of Ātman. He spends some time for spiritual practice in solitude and spends the rest of the time amongst people helping them on the path of welfare (*Dāsabodha 19.8.29*).

His meditation begins by focusing the mind on the center of his eyebrows. To support this practice, he fixes his gaze in between the eyebrows and restrains the mind in this manner. He regulates the speed of Prāṇa and Apāna by equalizing incoming and outgoing breaths. He does not do uneven breathing or doesn't make use of just one nostril. Here, the usage of eyes is essential. [It is even possible to focus the mind on the center of eyebrows, instead of fixing the physical gaze there.] By practicing renunciation of Karma, he can conquer his mind and organs. Eventually, Vāsanās, fear, and anger are wiped out from his mind, and he is steadily established in Self-realization. These concluding verses are a prelude to the sixth chapter.

After attaining Mokṣa, he can realize the highest state of the Self as described in Taittiriya Upaniṣad –

**अहं वृक्षस्य रेरिवा। कीर्तिः पृष्ठं गिरेरिव। (१.१०)**

*Ahaṃ vṛkṣasya rerivā। kīrtiḥ pṛṣṭham gireriva। (Taitti. 1.10)*

"I am the mover of the tree of worldly life. My glory is like the lofty peak of a mountain."

Chapter 6

# The Yoga of Meditation

## ॥ आत्मसंयमयोगः (Ātmasaṁyamayogaḥ) ॥

The fifth chapter comes to an end with a prelude to the sixth chapter i.e. the Path of Meditation. This chapter provides the guidance to fix the mind on the tip of the nose instead of fixing it on the center of the brows. It describes in more detail the posture, place, and sitting arrangement for meditation. It also mentions the regulatory practices needed for meditation. Chapters 2 to 5 of the Gita are summarized and concluded in the first nine verses of the sixth chapter. These nine verses describe the philosophy of desireless actions, ***Niṣkāma Karmayoga***, while abiding in the Knowledge of Atman. Even if chapters 2 to 5 are named differently, their central theme – executing actions without desiring fruits while abiding in the true Self – is the same. They may seem to shed light on different topics in specific contexts but their core subject remains the same. The perceived blend of various topics is mainly meant to show the great significance of the core subject of Karmayoga and Sāṅkhyayoga and repeat those teachings. From the tenth verse onwards, there is the description of Dhyānayoga.

### Karmayoga and Karmasaṅnyāsa are the same

*श्रीभगवानुवाच।*
अनाश्रितः कर्मफलं कार्यं कर्म करोति यः।
स संन्यासी च योगी च न निरग्निर्न चाक्रियः ॥ १ ॥
यं संन्यासमिति प्राहुर्योगं तं विद्धि पाण्डव।
न ह्यसंन्यस्तसङ्कल्पो योगी भवति कश्चन ॥ २ ॥

आरुरुक्षोर्मुनेर्योगं कर्म कारणमुच्यते ।
योगारूढस्य तस्यैव शमः कारणमुच्यते ॥ ३ ॥
यदा हि नेन्द्रियार्थेषु न कर्मस्वनुषज्जते ।
सर्वसङ्कल्पसंन्यासी योगारूढस्तदोच्यते ॥ ४ ॥
उद्धरेदात्मनात्मानं नात्मानमवसादयेत् ।
आत्मैव ह्यात्मनो बन्धुरात्मैव रिपुरात्मनः ॥ ५ ॥
बन्धुरात्मात्मनस्तस्य येनात्मैवात्मना जितः ।
अनात्मनस्तु शत्रुत्वे वर्तेतात्मैव शत्रुवत् ॥ ६ ॥
जितात्मनः प्रशान्तस्य परमात्मा समाहितः ।
शीतोष्णसुखदुःखेषु तथा मानापमानयोः ॥ ७ ॥
ज्ञानविज्ञानतृप्तात्मा कूटस्थो विजितेन्द्रियः ।
युक्त इत्युच्यते योगी समलोष्टाश्मकाञ्चनः ॥ ८ ॥
सुहृन्मित्रार्युदासीनमध्यस्थद्वेष्यबन्धुषु ।
साधुष्वपि च पापेषु समबुद्धिर्विशिष्यते ॥ ९ ॥

*Śrībhagavān uvāca* ।

*Anāśrītaḥ karmaphalaṃ kāryaṃ karma karoti yaḥ* ।
*Sa Sannyāsī ca yogī ca na niragnir na cākriyaḥ* ॥ *1* ॥
*Yaṃ Sannyāsam iti prāhur yogaṃ taṃ viddhi pāṇḍava* ।
*Na hy asaṃnyastasaṃkalpo yogī bhavati kaścana* ॥ *2* ॥
*Āruruksor muner yogaṃ karma kāraṇam ucyate* ।
*Yogārūḍhasya tasyaiva śamaḥ kāraṇam ucyate* ॥ *3* ॥
*Yadā hi nendriyārtheṣu na karmasv anuṣajjate* ।
*SarvasaṃkalpaSannyāsī yogārūḍhas tadocyate* ॥ *4* ॥
*Uddhared ātmanātmānaṃ nātmānam avasādayet* ।
*Ātmaiva hy ātmano bandhur ātmaiva ripur ātmanaḥ* ॥ *5* ॥
*Bandhur ātmātmanas tasya yenātmaivātmanā jitaḥ* ।
*Anātmanas tu śatrutve vartetātmaiva śatruvat* ॥ *6* ॥
*Jitātmanaḥ praśāntasya paramātmā samāhitaḥ* ।
*Śītoṣṇasukhaduḥkheṣu tathā mānāpamānayoḥ* ॥ *7* ॥
*Jñānavijñānatṛptātmā kūṭastho vijitendriyaḥ* ।
*Yukta ity ucyate yogī samaloṣṭāśmakāñcanaḥ* ॥ *8* ॥
*Suhṛnmitrāryudāsīnamadhyasthadveṣyabandhuṣu* ।
*Sādhuṣv api ca pāpeṣu samabuddhir viśiṣyate* ॥ *9* ॥

**Meaning:** (Śrībhagavān said) He is a Saṅnyāsin and he verily is a Yogi who performs his prescribed duty without seeking its fruits. A person who abandons the rituals like Yajña or does not perform actions is neither a Saṅnyāsin nor a Yogi. O Arjuna! That which is Saṅnyāsa is the same as Karmayoga, for no one becomes a true Karmayogi without renouncing desires in his mind. **Action** (Karma) is stated as the means or practice for the one who wishes to become a Yogi. **Equanimous peace** or quiescence is stated as the means for the one who is established as a Yogi. When a person is not attached to objects or actions, and he renounces desires, then alone he is said to be established in Yoga. Man should raise himself by his self alone and not degrade himself by destroying his own welfare, for he is his own friend and his own enemy as well. One who has controlled himself is his own friend. One who does not know his true Self – Ātman – becomes his own enemy. A Yogi who has controlled his mind and focused it on one place attains supreme peace. As a result, he is liberated from the dualities of cold and heat (season), honor and dishonor, joy and grief, etc. Having known and realized Self-Knowledge (*Vijñāna*), being ever-satiated, remaining unshaken, and having conquered his senses, the Yogi considers a clod, gold, and a stone to be of the same value, as he knows them all to be impermanent. A man – who has equal regard for well-wishers, friends, strangers, mediators, hateful people, family members, saints, and sinners – has a unique standing as an enlightened person.

The traditional way of living according to the Social Orders and Stages of life (*Varṇa* and *Āśrama*) is not prevalent in today's age. So also, maintaining a holy thread or crest and performing religious rituals, special worships, acts of atonement, and other actions prescribed and prohibited by the Vedas have become mostly obsolete nowadays. In such circumstances, the principles of Karmayoga need to be reinstituted and followed in the right spirit. In the present times, the seeker can follow the tenets of Karmayoga by categorizing and performing actions in the following manner:

1) Actions pertaining to the body (***Deha-Karma***) – Keeping the body clean and healthy, maintaining optimistic outlook, nourishing the mind with virtuous thoughts, being ready for hard-work, striving to sit in a specific posture (Āsana) for a considerable time, etc.
2) Actions pertaining to the job / business (***Vyavasāya-Karma***) – Engaging in professional work or running a business for earning livelihood, being skillful and meticulous in the chosen work, maintaining strong work ethic, executing the job in a righteous and efficient manner, chosing a job or business that is not rooted in deceiving, looting, defrauding, or manipulating others, etc.
3) Actions pertaining to the Religious rituals (***Dharma-Karma***) – Performing traditional rituals prescribed by Dharma such as worship, fasting, pilgrimage, festival celebration, pious observance (Vrata), Yajña, etc. whenever possible; those who cannot abide by such rituals can chant the Mantra of a deity earnestly since chanting is much easier to practice everyday, and it is prescribed by enlightened saints.
4) Actions pertaining to Personal Duties (***Kartavya-Karma***) – Executing personal duties towards friends, neighbors, society, parents, teachers, children, nation, and other acquaintances selflessly without any expectations from them, prioritizing adherence to the duty over traditional dictums (E.g. Arjuna was asked to do his duty of fighting against his grandfather and Guru, instead of the traditional idea that he should serve them), disregarding the emotional aspect or conventional values of righteousness while fulfilling the duties which support justice and truth. (E.g.

Lord Kṛṣṇa encouraged Yudhiṣṭhīra to *lie* on the battlefield to enable Dṛṣtadyumna to kill Droṇācārya.)

5) Actions pertaining to Spiritual pursuit (***Adhyātma-Karma***) – Striving to know and realize the true Self, seeking the company of enlightened saints, following at least one Path of Yoga (Action, Devotion, Meditation, Knowledge), and serving Sadguru in every which way with utmost faith, devotion, and humility.

The categorization of actions as mentioned herein can help the seeker follow the teachings of scriptures, even in today's age. Not all the actions mentioned above can be done in a desireless or selfless manner. Professional work includes job, farming, business, trading, etc. These activities are associated with earning money and livelihood. It is not possible to execute them selflessly without expecting fruits. In spiritual pursuit, there is an expectation of liberation i.e. Mokṣa. The very word **Mumukṣu** states the expectation of Mokṣa. In actions pertaining to the body, there is an expectation that the body continues to work well. Bodily actions like bathing, cleaning, exercising, eating food, rest, traveling in nature, etc. prepare the body to achieve the fourfold achievements of human life (Dharma, Artha, Kāma, Mokṣa). Religious rituals such as pious observances, worship, singing holy songs, pilgrimages, reading sacred scriptures, etc. should be done without any expectation of blessings or favors from God. Duties are also known as **Dharma**. The seeker should follow his duty as a son, daughter, mother, father, neighbor, etc. in a completely selfless manner. St. Jñāneśwara has outlined three specific duties pertaining to spiritual pursuit that every seeker should follow for Self-realization: living in the company of enlightened saints, following at least one path of Yoga, and being detached from worldly affairs. By learning about the Law of Karma and performing these three duties, the seeker's ego merges or disappears in the true Self, Ātman.

Duties, jobs, and businesses are associated with their own rules. A Karmayogi who acts by following the necessary rules is essentially a monk i.e. Karmasaṁnyāsi. Lawyers, doctors, contractors, teachers, and businessmen are all bound by their professional ethics. One who follows the work-ethics is a Karmayogi. All working people are bound by regulations, policies, leeways, and boundaries. One who abides by them is a Karmayogi. No one becomes a Yogi or even a Saṁnyāsin by not working properly or disregarding the work ethics. Saṁnyāsa is accomplished when there is no greediness about any object in mind. Such a Saṁnyāsin is verily a Karmayogi and vice-a-versa. The seeker who yearns for the realization that "I am Brahman" through Yoga should accomplish the Karmayoga as described here.

For evolving and remaining steady in Yoga, the seeker needs peacefulness or quiescence that can only be attained when his mind his stable. The mind can be stabilized when the seeker performs actions without desiring their fruits. By performing actions in this way, he can sustain in his worldly life. His mind can remain stable as it abides in the true Self amid all actions. As a result, his senses are not attached to worldly pleasures. Even though Lord Kṛṣṇa has given an order to perform actions, a Karmayogi is not attached to actions. All his desires and doubts come to an end. This state is verily known as being established in Yoga (*Yogārūḍha*). The seeker should attain this state and thereby raise himself to his supreme welfare. He should avoid his destruction (ignorance) that comes by disregarding the tenets of Karmayoga. He should avoid being his own enemy and instead become his own friend. The seeker who conquers his past Vāsanās is superior to any other great conqueror in the world. The seeker who realizes the true Self by conquering

Vāsanās becomes his own well-wisher. Otherwise, he becomes his own enemy since he incurs the sin of not using his precious human body for Self-realization, which is the very reason why Īśvara gave it to him. Kaṭha Upaniṣad has explained the importance of an organized, stable, and single-pointed mind. When the seeker is able to conquer his mind, it becomes calm, collected, and single-pointed. Such a seeker develops a state of equanimity in all dualities. This equanimity leads to him to Self-realization of Ātman. He feels content and develops an even vision for all sentient-insentient entities. Thereafter, he feels no attachment or aversion towards any object.

**The practice of meditation as per Dhyānayoga**

योगी युञ्जीत सततमात्मानं रहसि स्थितः ।
एकाकी यतचित्तात्मा निराशीरपरिग्रहः ॥ १० ॥
शुचौ देशे प्रतिष्ठाप्य स्थिरमासनमात्मनः ।
नात्युच्छ्रितं नातिनीचं चैलाजिनकुशोत्तरम् ॥ ११ ॥
तत्रैकाग्रं मनः कृत्वा यतचित्तेन्द्रियक्रियः ।
उपविश्यासने युञ्ज्याद्योगमात्मविशुद्धये ॥ १२ ॥
समं कायशिरोग्रीवं धारयन्नचलं स्थिरः ।
सम्प्रेक्ष्य नासिकाग्रं स्वं दिशश्चानवलोकयन् ॥ १३ ॥
प्रशान्तात्मा विगतभीर्ब्रह्मचारिव्रते स्थितः ।
मनः संयम्य मच्चित्तो युक्त आसीत मत्परः ॥ १४ ॥
युञ्जन्नेवं सदात्मानं योगी नियतमानसः ।
शान्तिं निर्वाणपरमां मत्संस्थामधिगच्छति ॥ १५ ॥

*Yogī yuñjīta satatam ātmānaṃ rahasi sthitaḥ* ।
*Ekākī yatacittātmā nirāśīr aparigrahaḥ* ॥ 10 ॥
*Śucau deśe pratiṣṭhāpya sthiram āsanam ātmanaḥ* ।
*Nātyucchritaṃ nātinīcaṃ cailājinakuśottaram* ॥ 11 ॥
*Tatraikāgraṃ manaḥ kṛtvā yatacittendriyakriyaḥ* ।
*Upaviśyāsane yuñjyād yogam ātmaviśuddhaye* ॥ 12 ॥
*Samaṃ kāyaśirogrīvaṃ dhārayann acalaṃ sthiraḥ* ।
*Saṃprekṣya nāsikāgraṃ svaṃ diśaś cānavalokayan* ॥ 13 ॥

*Praśāntātmā vigatabhīr brahmacārivrate sthitaḥ* ।
*Manaḥ saṅyamya maccitto yukta āsīta matparaḥ* ॥ *14* ॥
*Yuñjann evaṃ sadātmānaṃ yogī niyatamānasaḥ* ।
*Śāntiṃ nirvāṇaparamāṃ matsaṃsthām adhigacchati* ॥ *15* ॥

**Meaning:** A Yogi should practice focusing his mind on Ātman by living in solitude, conquering his mind, removing desires, and renouncing possessions. On a clean, pious ground, he should first spread grass, a deer-skin, and a soft cloth, one over the other, and thus prepare the place where he can sit in comfort. The seat should neither be too high nor too low. By sitting steady on this seat, regulating movements of his mind and organs, focusing the mind on one point, he should study for realizing the Knowledge of Ātman. Having stabilized himself firmly in a comfortable posture, he should sit straight while holding the back, neck, and head erect in one line and fix the gaze on the tip of his nose without looking around. With a serene and fearless mind, by being firm in the vow of celibacy, and having controlled the mind completely, he should contemplate on Me and be intent on Me alone. Thus, while consistently studying Yoga, the Yogi who conquers his mind attains the supreme peace of liberation by being One with My real nature.

These six verses do not mention Yama, Niyama, Prāṇāyāma, etc. from Patanjali Yogasūtras. Verse *5.27* states that it is necessary to regulate the speed of Prāṇa and Apāna by equalizing incoming and outgoing breaths. It does not mention the count or speed of Prāṇa; instead, it is only states that Prāṇa and Apāna are equalized in this process. The word ***Yatacitta*** (यतचित्त) literally means temporarily blocking the movements of the mind or the stillness of the mind. However, in this verse, Lord Kṛṣṇa gives an order – "Fix the mind on Me alone." Here the word '**Me**' means Ātman. Thus, it is congruous to say here that the word Yatacitta means fixing the mind on Ātman and merging it in Ātman or Pure Consciousness. In a way, Yatacitta can be considered a spiritual practice for attaining Self-Knowledge.

These verses also mention celibacy and possessionlessness i.e. not collecting or hoarding more than what is essential for a living. We may also say that celibacy and possessionlessness indicate the practice of Yama and Niyama which are part of Aṣṭāngayoga in an indirectly inferential manner (*Adhyāhāra*). Whether a seeker physically renounces his possessions or just mentally detaches from them, the renunciation certainly helps his spiritual practice. Even if he is unable to renounce them physically, he should mentally detach from them and not dwell on them in his mind. If the seeker has practiced Karmayoga without desiring fruits and by being resolved on the true Self, he becomes dispassionate about the material world. Worldly ambitions and a strong desire to conquer or surpass others (killer instinct) are deterrent factors for any spiritual seeker.

The place for practicing meditation should be clean and pious. The surrounding ambience should be calm and pious as it helps in concentration. The sites where enlightened saints led their lives are considered pious. However, in today's world, such sites are usually very crowded, full of activities and noise. So instead of practicing in a crowded place, the seeker may choose a not-so-famous temple in a nearby secluded area. Today it is considered illegal to use deer-skin for any purpose, let alone for meditation. Therefore, he may select new customized sitting mats, which are neither too soft nor too rough, created specifically for meditation. Rather than giving undue importance to these external factors, the seeker should strive – most importantly – to conquer his senses and focus the mind. The posture with straight back and head-neck-back in one straight line helps the seeker to stabilize his body in the chosen posture. A comfortable, strain-free posture helps in the concentration of the mind. [There is no mention of awakening the Kuṇḍalini in these verses.] In fact, this posture is also helpful in chanting the name of Saguṇa God. Here, it is mentioned that one should fix his mind on the tip of the nose, which is an excellent way to stabilize the movements of the mind. Having steadied his mind, the seeker should strive to focus it solely on Lord Kṛṣṇa, think only about Him, and remain centered in Him alone. For that purpose, St. Rāmadāsa says that the seeker should seek the guidance of the Sadguru, practice meditation, avoid the intermediate stage of a void (*Śūnya*), and strive to center his mind solely in Ātman. When the effort to meditate in this manner succeeds, the seeker attains Mokṣa in the form of supreme peace. The Pure Bliss of Ātman is supreme peace itself. It is indeed a great fortune if the seeker can attain it. This supreme peace is absolute and unqualified; it is not dependent on anything or anyone. Any ignorant Jiva cannot even remotely think about it.

**Regulatory rules of Dhyānayoga**

**नात्यश्नतस्तु योगोऽस्ति न चैकान्तमनश्नतः ।**
**न चातिस्वप्नशीलस्य जाग्रतो नैव चार्जुन ॥ १६ ॥**
**युक्ताहारविहारस्य युक्तचेष्टस्य कर्मसु ।**
**युक्तस्वप्नावबोधस्य योगो भवति दुःखहा ॥ १७ ॥**

*Nātyaśnatas tu yogosti na caikāntam anaśnataḥ* ।
*Na cātisvapnaśīlasya jāgrato naiva cārjuna* ॥ *16* ॥
*Yuktāhāravihārasya yuktaceṣṭasya karmasu* ।
*Yuktasvapnāvabodhasya yogo bhavati duḥkhahā* ॥ *17* ॥

**Meaning:** O Arjuna! Yoga cannot be practiced by him who overeats nor by him who fasts for a long time nor by one who sleeps too much or too little. For a person who eats, sleeps, works, moves, and stays awake in moderation, the practice of Yoga is not painful in any way.

St. Tukārāma states, "One who wishes to take the medicine of chanting Viṭṭhala's name should also follow its prescribed dos and don'ts." Like chanting and other spiritual practices, meditation, too, is associated with a set of regulations. Even though the regulations are explained differently here, most of them are analogous to the reglations prescribed for chanting. Overall health and well-being of the body are vital for the practice of meditation. Therefore, these verses specifically call out the rules such as eating in moderation, sleeping in moderation, etc. which need to be followed for good health. They are self-explanatory and do not need elaborate descriptions. Kṛṣṇa has also mentioned the execution of actions in these verses as a reminder for readers.

**The process of meditation**

यदा विनियतं चित्तमात्मन्येवावतिष्ठते ।
निःस्पृहः सर्वकामेभ्यो युक्त इत्युच्यते तदा ॥ १८ ॥
यथा दीपो निवातस्थो नेङ्गते सोपमा स्मृता ।
योगिनो यतचित्तस्य युञ्जतो योगमात्मनः ॥ १९ ॥
यत्रोपरमते चित्तं निरुद्धं योगसेवया ।
यत्र चैवात्मनात्मानं पश्यन्नात्मनि तुष्यति ॥ २० ॥
सुखमात्यन्तिकं यत्तद् बुद्धिग्राह्यमतीन्द्रियम् ।
वेत्ति यत्र न चैवायं स्थितश्चलति तत्त्वतः ॥ २१ ॥
यं लब्ध्वा चापरं लाभं मन्यते नाधिकं ततः ।
यस्मिन्स्थितो न दुःखेन गुरुणापि विचाल्यते ॥ २२ ॥
तं विद्याद् दुःखसंयोगवियोगं योगसञ्ज्ञितम् ।
स निश्चयेन योक्तव्यो योगोऽनिर्विण्णचेतसा ॥ २३ ॥
सङ्कल्पप्रभवान्कामांस्त्यक्त्वा सर्वानशेषतः ।
मनसैवेन्द्रियग्रामं विनियम्य समन्ततः ॥ २४ ॥
शनैः शनैरुपरमेद् बुद्ध्या धृतिगृहीतया ।
आत्मसंस्थं मनः कृत्वा न किञ्चिदपि चिन्तयेत् ॥ २५ ॥
यतो यतो निश्चरति मनश्चञ्चलमस्थिरम् ।
ततस्ततो नियम्यैतदात्मन्येव वशं नयेत् ॥ २६ ॥
प्रशान्तमनसं ह्येनं योगिनं सुखमुत्तमम् ।
उपैति शान्तरजसं ब्रह्मभूतमकल्मषम् ॥ २७ ॥

युञ्जन्नेवं सदात्मानं योगी विगतकल्मषः ।
सुखेन ब्रह्मसंस्पर्शमत्यन्तं सुखमश्नुते ॥ २८ ॥

*Yadā viniyataṃ cittam ātmany evāvatiṣṭhate* ।
*Niḥspṛhaḥ sarvakāmebhyo yukta ity ucyate tadā* ॥ *18* ॥
*Yathā dīpo nivātastho neṅgate sopamā smṛtā* ।
*Yogino yatacittasya yuñjato yogam ātmanaḥ* ॥ *19* ॥
*Yatroparamate cittaṃ niruddhaṃ yogasevayā* ।
*Yatra caivātmanātmānaṃ paśyann ātmani tuṣyati* ॥ *20* ॥
*Sukham ātyantikaṃ yat tad buddhigrāhyam atīndriyam* ।
*Vetti yatra na caivāyaṃ sthitaś calati tattvataḥ* ॥ *21* ॥
*Yaṃ labdhvā cāparaṃ lābhaṃ manyate nādhikaṃ tataḥ* ।
*Yasmin sthito na duḥkhena guruṇāpi vicālyate* ॥ *22* ॥
*Taṃ vidyād.h duḥkhasaṅyogaviyogaṃ yogasaṃjñitam* ।
*Sa niścayena yoktavyo yogo'nirviṇṇacetasā* ॥ *23* ॥
*Saṅkalpaprabhavān kāmāṃs tyaktvā sarvān aśeṣataḥ* ।
*Manasaivendriyagrāmaṃ viniyamya samantataḥ* ॥ *24* ॥
*Śanaiḥ śanair uparamed buddhyā dhṛtigṛhītayā* ।
*Ātmasaṃsthaṃ manaḥ kṛtvā na kiṃcid api cintayet* ॥ *25* ॥
*Yato yato niścarati manaś cañcalam asthiram* ।
*Tatas tato niyamyaitad ātmany eva vaśaṃ nayet* ॥ *26* ॥
*Praśāntamanasaṃ hy enaṃ yoginaṃ sukham uttamam* ।
*Upaiti śāntarajasaṃ brahmabhūtam akalmaṣam* ॥ *27* ॥
*Yuñjann evaṃ sadātmānaṃ yogī vigatakalmaṣaḥ* ।
*Sukhena brahmasaṃsparśam atyantaṃ sukham aśnute* ॥ *28* ॥

**Meaning:** When a seeker having firmly disciplined mind remains steady in Ātman and becomes free from all desires, he is known as a **Yogi** i.e. absorbed in Yoga. A flame of a lamp placed in a place where there is no wind remains steady without flickering. Analogous to this, the Yogi should practice concentration on the light of Ātman (*Ātmajyoti*) in his pure and steady mind where there are no desires. When his mind controlled by the practice of Yoga remains steady and quiet, the light of Ātman manifests in it, and consequently, the Yogi realizes that he himself is Bliss. This Absolute, Pure Bliss – which is always present regardless of anything else – may be gauged by the intellect, but it cannot be experienced through the intellect or senses. While reveling in this Bliss, the Yogi does not move away – even a little – from his true Self. Thereafter, he thinks that there is no gain superior to Self-realization, and the greatest affliction does not perturb him. This is known as the Yoga of severance from pain. It should be practiced with unflinching resolve. Relinquishing all desires in mind, retracting all senses from their objects, supporting the mind with patience, fortitude, and resolve – the seeker should gradually rest his mind in his true Self, Ātman. All other thoughts should be completely ceased. The naturally wavering mind should be curbed and brought back from wherever it goes, and it should be steadied in Ātman. The seeker whose mind is thus conquered, and whose Rajoguṇa is abated, attains Self-realization and becomes Pure Bliss himself. In this way, the Yogi who becomes sinless and steadies his mind revels effortlessly in ever-existent, Absolute, Pure Bliss of Self-realization that "I am Brahman."

Antaḥkaraṇa is the inner, subtle organ which is present in every sentient being. It has four aspects: mind, intellect, memory, and ego (Manas, Buddhi, Citta, Ahaṅkāra). It is imperative to restrain and conquer them all so that they can be made to disappear and merge in the true Self, Ātman. The mind and its aforementioned four aspects or movements disappear when Cidābhāsa becomes One with Ātman in meditation. The execution of Karmayoga while being resolved in the true Self assists significantly in this process. The mind which is at peace and not pierced by repentance or guilt can easily disappear in Ātman. The familiar awareness of one's limited self -- 'I or I exist' -- goes into oblivion when the mind and its movements disappear in Ātman during meditation. Some seekers fear being disconnected from their familiar feeling of the self pertaining to the body. It is necessary to have patience or fortitude to not fear this obliviousness of the self.

The realization that "I am Ātman and Pure Bliss myself" cannot be known through the intellect or the senses, as Ātman is Self-cognizant and Self-effulgent. The seeker can intellectually ponder on the scriptures of Vedānta and estimate Pure Bliss of Ātman by logical thinking. St. Jñāneśwara and St. Rāmadāsa have explained the process of attaining the Knowledge of Ātman in their treatises in an exemplary manner (*Jñāneśwari 6.366, Dāsabodha 5.6.1*). In the process of meditation, Cidābhāsa (Reflected Consciousness) turns back from the intellect, sees its own Self Ātman (Pure Consciousness), realizes "I am that Ātman," and disappears in Ātman in the same moment. This experience of one's own true Self by the apparent self is called the Knowledge of Ātman. **Cidābhāsa** is a concept or a system instituted by those who created the Vedāntic scriptures. Cidābhāsa is the reflection of the light of Ātman in a pure, Sāttvic intellect. This reflection is not like the one in a mirror. Instead, it is like the light that permeates through a clean, transparent glass sphere. The intellect becomes quiet and retires or disappears for a while during meditation. As a result, the light of Ātman which is reflected or permeated in the intellect turns back and disappears in its origin Ātman. The practitioner self, Cidābhāsa, disappears in the true Self, Ātman. Cidābhāsa is the main reason why we see multiplicity in the surrounding world. When Cidābhāsa disappears in Ātman, the practitioner realizes non-duality and Oneness with Ātman.

## The state of a Yogi who practices meditation

सर्वभूतस्थमात्मानं सर्वभूतानि चात्मनि ।
ईक्षते योगयुक्तात्मा सर्वत्र समदर्शनः ॥ २९ ॥
यो मां पश्यति सर्वत्र सर्वं च मयि पश्यति ।
तस्याहं न प्रणश्यामि स च मे न प्रणश्यति ॥ ३० ॥

सर्वभूतस्थितं यो मां भजत्येकत्वमास्थितः ।
सर्वथा वर्तमानोऽपि स योगी मयि वर्तते ॥ ३१ ॥
आत्मौपम्येन सर्वत्र समं पश्यति योऽर्जुन ।
सुखं वा यदि वा दुःखं स योगी परमो मतः ॥ ३२ ॥

*Sarvabhūtastham ātmānaṃ sarvabhūtāni cātmani* ।
*Īkṣate yogayuktātmā sarvatra samadarśanaḥ* ॥ *29* ॥
*Yo māṃ paśyati sarvatra sarvaṃ ca mayi paśyati* ।
*Tasyāhaṃ na praṇaśyāmi sa ca me na praṇaśyati* ॥ *30* ॥
*Sarvabhūtasthitaṃ yo māṃ bhajaty ekatvam āsthitaḥ* ।
*Sarvathā vartamāno'pi sa yogī mayi vartate* ॥ *31* ॥
*Ātmaupamyena sarvatra samaṃ paśyati yo'rjuna* ।
*Sukhaṃ vā yadi vā duḥkhaṃ sa yogī paramo mataḥ* ॥ *32* ॥

**Meaning:** Being perfected in Yoga and thus seeing only one principle everywhere, this seeker sees himself in all beings and all beings in himself. One who sees Me everywhere and sees all in Me never becomes ignorant of Me nor do I become ignorant of him. A Yogi who worships Me abiding in all beings by being One with Me – he abides in Me alone regardless of his mode of living. That Yogi who sees equanimity everywhere and knows the pleasure and pain of others – just as he knows of himself – is regarded as superior to all.

"I am not the body; I am not the mind; I am not the intellect, etc." – these thoughts constitute the spiritual practice of **Vyatireka** (negation). By pondering on "Who I am not," the seeker comes to the realization of Oneness. He is able to think, "I am Ātman, and everything around me is Ātman as well." This is known as an experience of **Anvaya**, which is seeing the same Brahman pervading uniformly everywhere in the surroundings. Enlightened sages like St. Tukārāma, Kabira, and Vivekānanda were able to see their own Self in all beings. Therefore, they always strived for the welfare of all beings. This is the result of the disappearance of duality and the experience of Oneness in the universe. It is an incredible journey from the ignorance that

"There is no Ātman" to the firm belief that "Ātman is present everywhere."

## Arjuna's complaint about restlessness of the mind

अर्जुन उवाच ।
योऽयं योगस्त्वया प्रोक्तः साम्येन मधुसूदन ।
एतस्याहं न पश्यामि चञ्चलत्वात्स्थितिं स्थिराम् ॥ ३३ ॥
चञ्चलं हि मनः कृष्ण प्रमाथि बलवद् दृढम् ।
तस्याहं निग्रहं मन्ये वायोरिव सुदुष्करम् ॥ ३४ ॥

*Arjuna uvāca* ।
*Yo'yaṃ yogas tvayā proktaḥ sāmyena madhusūdana* ।
*Etasyāhaṃ na paśyāmi cañcalatvāt sthitiṃ sthirām* ॥ *33* ॥
*Cañcalaṃ hi manaḥ kṛṣṇa pramāthi balavad dṛḍham* ।
*Tasyāhaṃ nigrahaṃ manye vāyor iva suduṣkaram* ॥ *34* ॥

**Meaning:** (Arjuna said) O Kṛṣṇa! I don't think that the Yoga of equanimity taught by You can be sustained since the mind is wavering. O Kṛṣṇa! This mind is extremely wavering, turbulent, strong, and obstinate. I feel it is difficult to control the mind, just as it is difficult to control the wind.

The topic of controlling the mind and senses has been discussed many times so far. It is of immense importance in the pursuit of Mokṣa. St. Rāmadāsa has authored 205 poetic verses (Manobodha) which famously converse with the mind to stabilize it and calm it down. Ādi Śaṅkara has also authored a dialogue between Ātman and the mind in his text 'Upadeśa Sāhasri' to make the mind see the Truth. Upaniṣad says –

मन एव मनुष्याणां कारणं बंधमोक्षयोः ॥

*Mana eva manuśyāṇam kāraṇam bandhamokṣayoḥ* ॥

"The mind is responsible for both bondage and liberation of a human being." In fact, according to a verse in Kaṭha Upaniṣad (1.3.3), the mind is equivalent to reins. The intellect is a charioteer that uses the reins-of-mind to control the horses-of-organs. The intellect takes decisions according to Vāsanās, which are subtle unfulfilled desires from past lives. Therefore, the best way to control the mind is to abate the Vāsanās gradually. St. Tukārāma states the same in his devotional poetry, "One should first conquer the senses, attenuate his Vāsanās, and then ensure that no desire arises in the mind."

**Lord Kṛṣṇa's answer**

*श्रीभगवानुवाच ।*
असंशयं महाबाहो मनो दुर्निग्रहं चलम् ।
अभ्यासेन तु कौन्तेय वैराग्येण च गृह्यते ॥ ३५ ॥
असंयतात्मना योगो दुष्प्राप इति मे मतिः ।
वश्यात्मना तु यतता शक्योऽवाप्तुमुपायतः ॥ ३६ ॥

*Śrībhagavān uvāca* ।
*Asañśayaṃ mahābāho mano durnigrahaṃ calam* ।
*Abhyāsena tu kaunteya vairāgyeṇa ca gṛhyate* ॥ 35 ॥
*Asaṅyatātmanā yogo duṣprāpa iti me matiḥ* ।
*Vaśyātmanā tu yatatā śakyo'vāptum upāyataḥ* ॥ 36 ॥

**Meaning:** (Śrībhagavān said) O Arjuna! No doubt that the mind is extremely wavering and difficult to control. But it can be disciplined through consistent practice and detachment. In My opinion, for a person who cannot conquer the mind, it is tough to accomplish Dhyānayoga i.e. Self-realization through meditation. However, it can be attained by a seeker who can restrain his mind and take appropriate efforts.

The word **Abhyāsa** in Sanskrit means doing the same thing persistently over and over again. Constant effort to control the mind is required in spiritual pursuit. It is imperative to support this effort with **Vairāgya** i.e. detachment. The mind which is not detached from the materialistic world cannot be quietened or stabilized. The crux of all spiritual practices lies in detachment. A predominantly Rajoguṇi person cannot become detached or dispassionate. So, the seeker should necessarily take to Sāttvic food, thoughts, company, and reading to reduce the influence of

Rajoguṇa in his life. This topic is further explained in more detail in chapters 14 and 18. The spiritual practices like unconditional worship, desireless actions, and the attainment of Self-Knowledge cannot be strengthened and advanced without detachment. Lord Kṛṣṇa says in the 15th chapter that one should use the weapon of detachment to reduce the strong clutch of the world on him. Upaniṣad states –

असंगोऽह्ययं पुरुषः ।

*Asańgo'hyayam Puruṣaḥ* । *(Bṛh. Up. 4.3.15)*

"This Puruṣa (Brahman) is unattached." Ātman is not attached to anything. Therefore, the seeker should also not be attached to anything to realize that "I am Ātman."

**Arjuna's question**

*अर्जुन उवाच ।*

अयतिः श्रद्धयोपेतो योगाच्चलितमानसः ।
अप्राप्य योगसंसिद्धिं कां गतिं कृष्ण गच्छति ॥ ३७ ॥
कच्चिन्नोभयविभ्रष्टश्छिन्नाभ्रमिव नश्यति ।
अप्रतिष्ठो महाबाहो विमूढो ब्रह्मणः पथि ॥ ३८ ॥
एतन्मे संशयं कृष्ण छेत्तुमर्हस्यशेषतः ।
त्वदन्यः संशयस्यास्य छेत्ता न ह्युपपद्यते ॥ ३९ ॥

*Arjuna uvāca* ।

*Ayatiḥ śraddhayopeto yogāc calitamānasaḥ* ।
*Aprāpya yogasaṃsiddhiṃ kāṃ gatiṃ kṛṣṇa gacchati* ॥ 37 ॥
*Kacchin nobhayavibhraṣṭaś chinnābhram iva naśyati* ।
*Apratiṣṭho mahābāho vimūḍho brahmaṇaḥ pathi* ॥ 38 ॥
*Etan me saṃśayaṃ kṛṣṇa chettum arhasy aśeṣataḥ* ।
*Tvādanyaḥ saṃśayasyāsya chettā na hy upapadyate* ॥ 39 ॥

**Meaning:** (Arjuna said) O Kṛṣṇa! If a faithful person abandons his spiritual practice halfway before attaining perfection in Yoga, to what end does he go to? On the path of Self-Knowledge, if he is unable to remain established in Yoga (**Yogārūḍha**) due to delusion, then having degraded from both the spiritual and worldly life, does he perish like the cloud that disperses without giving the rain? Please remove this doubt from my mind completely, as no one but you may answer this question.

This doubt in Arjuna's mind is the representative of doubts in our minds. All seekers who tread the spiritual path face this question. It is accepted here that even for the most faithful seeker, his detachment and practice may fall short of what is requisite for Mokṣa. The answer to Arjuna's question in this verse is deeply profound and mysterious. Therefore, acceptance of the answer is dependent on faith. The creation of the universe by Īśvara and His scheme of governance of living beings are beyond the scope of the human intellect. Only an incarnation of Īśvara can explain it, and humans should take it on total faith.

**Lord Kṛṣṇa's answer**

*श्रीभगवानुवाच ।*

पार्थ नैवेह नामुत्र विनाशस्तस्य विद्यते ।
न हि कल्याणकृत्कश्चिद् दुर्गतिं तात गच्छति ॥ ४० ॥
प्राप्य पुण्यकृतां लोकानुषित्वा शाश्वतीः समाः ।
शुचीनां श्रीमतां गेहे योगभ्रष्टोऽभिजायते ॥ ४१ ॥
अथवा योगिनामेव कुले भवति धीमताम् ।
एतद्धि दुर्लभतरं लोके जन्म यदीदृशम् ॥ ४२ ॥
तत्र तं बुद्धिसंयोगं लभते पौर्वदेहिकम् ।
यतते च ततो भूयः संसिद्धौ कुरुनन्दन ॥ ४३ ॥
पूर्वाभ्यासेन तेनैव ह्रियते ह्यवशोऽपि सः ।
जिज्ञासुरपि योगस्य शब्दब्रह्मातिवर्तते ॥ ४४ ॥
प्रयत्नाद्यतमानस्तु योगी संशुद्धकिल्बिषः ।
अनेकजन्मसंसिद्धस्ततो याति परां गतिम् ॥ ४५ ॥
तपस्विभ्योऽधिको योगी ज्ञानिभ्योऽपि मतोऽधिकः ।
कर्मिभ्यश्चाधिको योगी तस्माद्योगी भवार्जुन ॥ ४६ ॥
योगिनामपि सर्वेषां मद्गतेनान्तरात्मना ।
श्रद्धावान्भजते यो मां स मे युक्ततमो मतः ॥ ४७ ॥

*Śrībhagavān uvāca* ।
*Pārtha naiveha nāmutra vināśas tasya vidyāte* ।
*Na hi kalyāṇakṛt kaścid durgatiṃ tāta gacchati* ॥ *40* ॥
*Prāpya puṇyakṛtāṃ lokān uṣitvā śāśvatīḥ samāḥ* ।
*Śucīnāṃ Śrīmatāṃ gehe yogabhraṣṭo'bhijāyate* ॥ *41* ॥
*Athavā yoginām eva kule bhavati dhīmatām* ।
*Etad dhi durlabhataraṃ loke janma yad īdṛśam* ॥ *42* ॥
*Tatra taṃ buddhisaṅyogaṃ labhate paurvadehikam* ।
*Yatate ca tato bhūyaḥ saṃsiddhau kurunandana* ॥ *43* ॥
*Pūrvābhyāsena tenaiva hriyate hyavaśo'pi saḥ* ।
*Jijñāsur api yogasya śabdabrahmātivartate* ॥ *44* ॥
*Prayatnād yatamānas tu yogī saṃśuddhakilbiṣaḥ* ।
*Anekajanmasaṃsiddhas tato yāti parāṃ gatim* ॥ *45* ॥
*Tapasvibhyo'dhiko yogī jñānibhyo'pi mato'dhikaḥ* ।
*Karmibhyaś cādhiko yogī tasmād yogī bhavārjuna* ॥ *46* ॥
*Yoginām api sarveṣāṃ madgatenāntarātmanā* ।
*Śraddhāvān bhajate yo māṃ sa me yuktatamo mataḥ* ॥ *47* ॥

**Meaning:** (Śrībhagavān said) O Arjuna! His spiritual practice is neither destroyed in this world nor the next. This is because the person who engages in right actions can never degrade. A seeker who has fallen from Yoga goes to the next world like heaven, which is attainable by people who have accumulated merits (*Puṇya*). He resides there for many years, and later, he is reborn in the house of a pure and wealthy family. Alternatively, he is reborn in the family of a wise Yogi, which indeed is very difficult to obtain in this world. In the new birth, he regains the knowledge earned in his former birth. He strives more than before for being perfected in Yoga. That very practice in the previous birth urges him to start over the study of Yoga. The Yogi who is genuinely eager about practicing meditation is superior to the scholar having mere theoretical knowledge of Brahman. [It is said in the Gita (*12.12*) that meditation is superior to theoretical knowledge of Brahman.] By consistently striving to be perfected in Yoga, he becomes sinless and attains Mokṣa after many births. The Yogi – who takes to the Path of Meditation – is superior to the one who engages in austerities or who is a mere theoretical scholar. Also, one who adheres to the 'philosophy of desireless actions' (*Niṣkāma Karmayoga*) is superior to the one who performs actions desiring fruits. Therefore, O Arjuna! You should strive to be a Yogi who engages in desireless actions while being aware of the true Self. In my opinion, amongst all these Yogis, one who completely surrenders his mind to Me and worships Me with utmost faith is superior to all.

**ॐ तत्सदिति श्रीमद्भगवद्गीतासूपनिषत्सु ब्रह्मविद्यायां योगशास्त्रे श्रीकृष्णार्जुनसंवादे आत्मसंयमयोगो नाम षष्ठोऽध्यायः ॥**

*Om Tatsaditi Śrimadbhagvadgitāsūpaniṣatsu Brahmavidyāyāṃ Yogaśāstre Śrīkṛṣṇārjunasaṁvāde Ātmasaṁyamayogo Nāma Ṣaṣṭho'dhyāyaḥ* ॥

There is some ambiguity associated with the usage of the word **Yoga** in many places in the Gita. The meaning should be inferred based on the context and the spirit of each chapter. There may be genuine disagreements while interpreting the term Yoga. The word **Yogi** means Dhyānayogi, i.e the Yogi who primarily engages in meditation, in the 45th verse. The word Yogi in the first line of the 46th verse means Dhyānayogi again since a comparison is intended there. There is a term *Karmibhih* in the second line of 46th verse; so here, the meaning is inferred as the one who engages in actions of Karmakāṇḍa and desires fruits. Lord Kṛṣṇa has concluded verse 46 by saying, "Tasmād yogī bhavārjuna." The meaning of the word Yogi in this line is taken as one who performs Karmayoga by being aware of his true Self, and this meaning is based on Lord Kṛṣṇa's consistent teaching of the importance of desireless actions. People who practice austerities may do so for accumulating merits, earning fruits, or achieving power. A mere scholar may study scriptures for theoretical expertise, debating, or making money. Compared to them, a detached seeker, who has conquered his mind and senses, and who strives to practice meditation in solitude, is certainly superior. However, this kind of meditation requires arduous, painstaking efforts from the seeker. For this reason, Karmayoga, which is much easier for many people to practice, is considered superior to meditation. Lord Kṛṣṇa concludes this chapter by saying that the devotee who nurtures utmost faith in God and who remains intently devoted to God alone is the supreme amongst all Yogis.

꧁ Chapter 7 ꧂

# Spiritual Knowledge and Worldly Knowledge

॥ ज्ञानविज्ञानयोगः (Jñānavijñānayogaḥ) ॥

The term **Vijñāna** means steady absorption in the Knowledge of Ātman. The second meaning of the word Vijñāna is worldly knowledge. According to the 1st verse of this chapter, the first meaning seems accurate. However, the 4th verse mentions the details of the eightfold Prakṛti; therefore, the second meaning may be considered accurate. The name of this chapter can be taken as **The Knowledge of Self-realization** as per the first meaning. Alternatively, the name of this chapter may also be taken as **Spiritual Knowledge and Worldly Knowledge** as per the second meaning. As stated by St. Jñāneśwara in his treatise Jñāneśwarī (*7.6*), it will be more appropriate to take the meaning of the name of this chapter as 'Spiritual Knowledge and Worldly Knowledge.'

## Spiritual Knowledge and worldly knowledge

*श्रीभगवानुवाच ।*

मय्यासक्तमनाः पार्थ योगं युञ्जन्मदाश्रयः ।
असंशयं समग्रं मां यथा ज्ञास्यसि तच्छृणु ॥ १ ॥
ज्ञानं तेऽहं सविज्ञानमिदं वक्ष्याम्यशेषतः ।
यज्ज्ञात्वा नेह भूयोऽन्यज्ज्ञातव्यमवशिष्यते ॥ २ ॥
मनुष्याणां सहस्रेषु कश्चिद्यतति सिद्धये ।
यततामपि सिद्धानां कश्चिन्मां वेत्ति तत्त्वतः ॥ ३ ॥
भूमिरापोऽनलो वायुः खं मनो बुद्धिरेव च ।
अहङ्कार इतीयं मे भिन्ना प्रकृतिरष्टधा ॥ ४ ॥

अपरेयमितस्त्वन्यां प्रकृतिं विद्धि मे पराम् ।
जीवभूतां महाबाहो ययेदं धार्यते जगत् ॥ ५ ॥
एतद्योनीनि भूतानि सर्वाणीत्युपधारय ।
अहं कृत्स्नस्य जगतः प्रभवः प्रलयस्तथा ॥ ६ ॥

*Śrībhagavān uvāca* ।

*Mayy āsaktamanāḥ pārtha yogaṃ yuñjan madāśrayaḥ* ।
*Asaṃśayaṃ samagraṃ māṃ yathā jñāsyasi tac chṛṇu* ॥ *1* ॥
*Jñānaṃ te'haṃ savijñānam idaṃ vakṣyāmy aśeṣataḥ* ।
*Yaj jñātvā neha bhūyo'anyaj jñātavyam avaśiṣyate* ॥ *2* ॥
*Manuṣyāṇāṃ sahasreṣu kaścid yatati siddhaye* ।
*Yatatām api siddhānāṃ kaścin māṃ vetti tattvataḥ* ॥ *3* ॥
*Bhūmir āpo'nalo vāyuḥ khaṃ mano buddhir eva ca* ।
*Ahaṃkāra itīyaṃ me bhinnā prakṛtir aṣṭadhā* ॥ *4* ॥
*Apareyam itas tvanyāṃ prakṛtiṃ viddhi me parām* ।
*Jīvabhūtāṃ mahābāho yayedaṃ dhāryate jagat* ॥ *5* ॥
*Etadyonīni bhūtāni sarvāṇīty upadhāraya* ।
*Ahaṃ kṛtsnasya jagataḥ prabhavaḥ pralayas tathā* ॥ *6* ॥

**Meaning:** (Śrībhagavān said) O Arjuna! Keeping your mind focused steadily on Me, taking refuge in Me, and practicing Karmayoga, you will know My true nature in entirety, without any doubt or uncertainty. I shall teach you this Knowledge comprehensively and also a way to realize it and make it a living reality. Once it is realized, nothing more remains to be known in this world. Out of many thousands of people, hardly one strives for Self-realization; and out of those so striving, scarcely one attains Self-realization and knows My real nature, Brahman. My Prakṛti is eightfold: the earth, water, fire, air, space or sky, mind, intellect, and ego. O Arjuna! This is my inferior or insentient Aparā Prakṛti, but different from it is my superior Parā Prakṛti due to which the world is upheld. It is the world of all sentient beings. Know that all entities are produced from My Parā and Aparā Prakṛti; therefore, I am verily the place of origin and dissolution of the whole world.

In the last verse of the sixth chapter, Lord Kṛṣṇa said –

**श्रद्धावान् भजते यो मां ।**

*Śraddhāvān bhajate yo mām̩* ।

"Those who worship Me with utmost faith ultimately attain Me." Kṛṣṇa is now revealing the real nature of **Me** (Māṃ) that needs to be worshipped. In other words, he is explaining His own nature. This same topic will be discussed in more detail until the end of the 12th chapter. Verse 9.1 reiterates that the seeker should gain the Knowledge of Ātman and learn how to make it a living reality. The devotee should have clear, comprehensive knowledge of God to whom he is supposed to surrender, and he should also know what the benefit of such surrender is. Lord Kṛṣṇa has explained the sheer rarity of Self-Knowledge, as well as its exceptional importance in human life. Even enlightened saints insist that one should conscientiously execute all actions by understanding its philosophical nuances. The insentient world is created from the Five Great Elements (Pañcamahābhūta). This creation takes place after the process of Quintuplication (Pañcikaraṇa), where each element is mixed with the remaining four in a particular proportion. The sentient world is created from the Five Great Elements and Antaḥkaraṇa having Cidābhāsa. Īśvara is the owner and governor of the entire universe. Even though He is in the same category as the sentient Jiva, He is the creator, governor, and the destroyer of the world. Lord Kṛṣṇa, as Brahman, is not attached to or encaged by anything. He is the very nature of all Jivas. The world is superimposed (*Adhyasta*) on the substratum (*Adhiṣṭhāna*) of Brahman. The seeker who has realized the substratum Brahman is known as omniscient or all-knowing (*Sarvajña*). St. Rāmadāsa states in his treatise Dāsabodha that, "A person who can read someone else's mind, or who can tell details of the money in someone else's pocket, or who can narrate the events in the past or future – he is not really omniscient from the spiritual perspective."

**The real nature of 'Me' (Lord Krṣṇa)**

मत्तः परतरं नान्यत्किञ्चिदस्ति धनञ्जय ।
मयि सर्वमिदं प्रोतं सूत्रे मणिगणा इव ॥ ७ ॥
रसोऽहमप्सु कौन्तेय प्रभास्मि शशिसूर्ययोः ।
प्रणवः सर्ववेदेषु शब्दः खे पौरुषं नृषु ॥ ८ ॥
पुण्यो गन्धः पृथिव्यां च तेजश्चास्मि विभावसौ ।
जीवनं सर्वभूतेषु तपश्चास्मि तपस्विषु ॥ ९ ॥
बीजं मां सर्वभूतानां विद्धि पार्थ सनातनम् ।
बुद्धिर्बुद्धिमतामस्मि तेजस्तेजस्विनामहम् ॥ १० ॥
बलं बलवतां चाहं कामरागविवर्जितम् ।
धर्माविरुद्धो भूतेषु कामोऽस्मि भरतर्षभ ॥ ११ ॥
ये चैव सात्त्विका भावा राजसास्तामसाश्च ये ।
मत्त एवेति तान्विद्धि न त्वहं तेषु ते मयि ॥ १२ ॥

*Mattaḥ parataraṃ nānyat kiṃcid asti dhanaṃjaya* ।
*Mayi sarvam idaṃ protaṃ sūtre maṇigaṇā iva* ॥ *7* ॥
*Raso'hamapsu kaunteya prabhāsmi śaśisūryayoḥ* ।
*Praṇavaḥ sarvavedeṣu śabdaḥ khe pauruṣaṃ nṛṣu* ॥ *8* ॥
*Puṇyo gandhaḥ pṛthivyāṃ ca tejaś cāsmi vibhāvasau* ।
*Jīvanaṃ sarvabhūteṣu tapaś cāsmi tapasviṣu* ॥ *9* ॥
*Bījaṃ māṃ sarvabhūtānāṃ viddhi pārtha sanātanam* ।
*Buddhir buddhimatām asmi tejas tejasvinām aham* ॥ *10* ॥
*Balaṃ balavatāṃ cāhaṃ kāmarāgavivarjitam* ।
*Dharmāviruddho bhūteṣu kāmo'asmi bharatarṣabha* ॥ *11* ॥
*Ye caiva sātvikā bhāvā rājasās tāmasāś ca ye* ।
*Matta eveti tān viddhi na tv ahaṃ teṣu te mayi* ॥ *12* ॥

**Meaning:** O Arjuna! There is nothing whatsoever subtler than Me or different from Me anywhere at any time. This world is connected by My thread, just as beads are strung together in a string. I am the sapidity in water, the radiance in the moon, the splendor in the sun, the syllable Om in all the four Vedas, sound in sky (space), and valiance in men. I am the sweet fragrance in earth, brilliance in fire, the life in all beings, and austerity in the austere. I am the eternal seed of all living beings in the world. I am the intelligence of the intelligent, the splendor of the splendid. I am the strength of the strong who are devoid of desire and attachment. I am the desire, which is in accordance with Dharma in all beings. Apart from these, I am all beings or entities which are Sāttvic, Rājas, and Tāmas (pure, active, and inert). They are all created from Me, yet I am not in them.

The 10th chapter specifically describes various Divine Glories (Vibhūtis) of God. Kṛṣṇa says, "I am the sun in many confluences of stars, the moon in asterisms, the mind in all organs, consciousness in all beings, ocean in water-reservoirs, Himālaya in all immovable things, lion in animals, and eagle in birds, etc. (*10.21*, *10.30*)" Lord Kṛṣṇa has also described His Glories in many other places. One can find the essence of broad, inclusive, expansive worship along with the teachings of scriptures and the values of righteousness in these Glories. All Jivas feel an innate attraction for the opposite gender for the creation of progeny. However, this attraction is constrained by the boundaries of Dharma and righteousness in human beings. If a strong and powerful man has uncontrolled desires, ordinary people in society are troubled by them. Hence, the power and strength devoid of uncontrolled desires is a Glory of the Lord. Everything that can be known by its existence is a form of Kṛṣṇa, and it is pervaded by Kṛṣṇa. A devotee should be able to see Lord Kṛṣṇa everywhere: as sapidity while drinking water, as luminosity while seeing light, as sweet fragrance while smelling a flower, as intelligence, as splendor, etc. Seeing His omnipresence in this manner is a form of broad, expansive worship of God.

## The reason for not recognizing the omnipresent Lord Kṛṣṇa

**त्रिभिर्गुणमयैर्भावैरेभिः सर्वमिदं जगत् ।**
**मोहितं नाभिजानाति मामेभ्यः परमव्ययम् ॥ १३ ॥**
**दैवी ह्येषा गुणमयी मम माया दुरत्यया ।**
**मामेव ये प्रपद्यन्ते मायामेतां तरन्ति ते ॥ १४ ॥**

न मां दुष्कृतिनो मूढाः प्रपद्यन्ते नराधमाः ।
मााययापहृतज्ञाना आसुरं भावमाश्रिताः ॥ १५ ॥

*Tribhir guṇamāyāir bhāvair ebhiḥ sarvam idaṃ jagat* ।
*Mohitaṃ nābhijānāti mām ebhyaḥ param avyayam* ॥ *13* ॥
*Daivī hy eṣā guṇamayī mama māyā duratyayā* ।
*Mām eva ye prapadyante māyām etāṃ taranti te* ॥ *14* ॥
*Na māṃ duṣkṛtino mūḍhāḥ prapadyante narādhamāḥ* ।
*Māyayāpahṛtajñānā āsuraṃ bhāvam āśrītāḥ* ॥ *15* ॥

**Meaning:** The entire world is filled with the three Guṇas. [Guṇa is the cause of individual disposition or inclination.] People deluded by the Guṇas do not know the imperishable Me who is beyond the three Guṇas. This divine Māyā of Mine is made up of the three Guṇas, and it is extremely difficult to cross over it. They alone can cross over Māyā who seek refuge in Me. People who are deluded and engaged in evil activities, and whose spiritual discrimination is destroyed due to Māyā, do not seek refuge in Me due to their demoniac nature.

The philosophy of Vedānta states that the world is created in the following sequence –

- **Mūlamāyā** – The very first will which surfaced on the substratum of Brahman *(Chān. Up. 6.2.3)* – "I am one and I shall manifest in many forms."
- **Guṇamāyā** – Mūlamāyā and the three Guṇas
- **Jaḍamāyā** – Guṇamāyā and the Five Great Elements

Later, from Jaḍamāyā, the world is created, which is why the world as a whole is permeated by the three Guṇas. The effect of Tamoguṇa is delusion and lethargy; the effect of Rajoguṇa is constant movement, wavering, or fickleness; and the effect of Sattvaguṇa is happiness. As a result, people get immersed in these Guṇas. Their behavior in day-to-day life is influenced by the Guṇa which is dominant at that time. Hence, they do not know Me who transcends the three Guṇas and whose very nature is unqualified Pure Bliss.

Māyā is made up of the three Guṇas, and it manifests in three ways mentioned above: Mūlamāyā, Guṇamāyā, Jaḍamāyā. Its power is divine and unfathomable. Every other power in this world can be seen or felt, and it is manifested in some way. But the power of Māyā – though it underlies all worldly powers – is unmanifested. Therefore, it is difficult to recognize the power of unmanifested Māyā and remain separate from it. Īśvara owns and governs the insentient Māyā. The seeker who recognizes that "Īśvara is originally Brahman" and becomes One with Brahman can alone transcend the influence of Māyā. Due to the overpowering impact of Māyā, people tend to disregard the values of Dharma, righteousness, and justice, and they succumb to delusion, foolishness, and sinful behavior. As a result, they are not even remotely aware of the presence of Īśvara. The word **Asura**, which means demon or devil in Sanskrit, is defined as follow –

**असुषु रमते इति असुरः ।**

*Asushu ramate iti asurah* ।

"A person who is engrossed in his body and strongly identifies that 'I am the body' is verily known as an Asura."

## The types of devotees who worship God

**चतुर्विधा भजन्ते मां जनाः सुकृतिनोऽर्जुन ।**
**आर्तो जिज्ञासुरर्थार्थी ज्ञानी च भरतर्षभ ॥ १६ ॥**
**तेषां ज्ञानी नित्ययुक्त एकभक्तिर्विशिष्यते ।**
**प्रियो हि ज्ञानिनोऽत्यर्थमहं स च मम प्रियः ॥ १७ ॥**
**उदाराः सर्व एवैते ज्ञानी त्वात्मैव मे मतम् ।**
**आस्थितः स हि युक्तात्मा मामेवानुत्तमां गतिम् ॥ १८ ॥**
**बहूनां जन्मनामन्ते ज्ञानवान्मां प्रपद्यते ।**
**वासुदेवः सर्वमिति स महात्मा सुदुर्लभः ॥ १९ ॥**

*Caturvidhā bhajante māṃ janāḥ sukṛtino'rjuna* ।
*Ārto jijñāsur arthārthī jñānī ca bharatarṣabha* ॥ *16* ॥
*Teṣāṃ jñānī nityayukta ekabhaktir viśiṣyate* ।
*Priyo hi jñānino'tyartham ahaṃ sa ca mama priyaḥ* ॥ *17* ॥

*Udārāḥ sarva evaite jñānī tv ātmaiva me matam* ।
*Āsthitaḥ sa hi yuktātmā mām evānuttamāṃ gatim* ॥ *18* ॥
*Bahūnāṃ janmanām ante jñānavān māṃ prapadyate* ।
*Vāsudevaḥ sarvam iti sa mahātmā sudurlabhaḥ* ॥ *19* ॥

**Meaning:** Four kinds of virtuous men worship Me: men afflicted by grief; seekers who wish to know God; men who are desirers of wealth, success, etc.; and enlightened devotees who are One with God. Of these four, the enlightened devotee who knows Me, who is desireless, and who constantly contemplates on Me is superior amongst all. This is because I am dear to him, and he is dear to Me. All four kinds of devotees are indeed noble; however, I deem the enlightened devotee as My own form. This is because he regards Me alone as the supreme goal, contemplates on Me, and takes refuge in Me alone. (He is totally dependent on Me). Having performed My worship in many previous births, he comes to Me at the end. Having realized that this entire world is God Vāsudeva, the enlightened devotee unites with Me. However, it is extremely rare to find such a wise, great soul.

Lord Kṛṣṇa – who is very benevolent Himself – embraces all four kinds of devotees. All these devotees are virtuous; therefore, they connect with God for their own reasons and fulfillment of their desires. Amongst all of them, the enlightened devotee who worships God even after attaining Self-Knowledge is exceedingly dear to God. Every seeker should remember this liking of God and strive to evolve from the prior three categories to become the fourth – enlightened devotee. In spiritual pursuit, ***Anvaya*** is the practice of seeing the same God everywhere. e.g. "My body is God, my mind is God, every being is God, every object is God, etc.' ***Vyatireka*** is a practice where one distinguishes the true Self or true God using the method of negation. E.g. "I am not my body, I am not my mind, I am not my emotions, etc." After all knowable objects are negated in this way, the Pure Existence which remains is the nature of God and "That is who I am." When the seeker realizes that "I am God or Ātman" in this manner, he is also able to see the same God everywhere around him. This is when he is said to have developed the vision of *Anvaya*. God loves the devotional practice of *Anvaya* more than the preliminary practice of *Vyatireka*. His fourth devotee, an enlightened sage, can see everything as God, which is why he is dear to God. However, it is certainly challenging to develop this vision of *Anvaya* i.e. seeing the same God everywhere around us.

**<u>Disloyal, faithless devotion</u>**

कामैस्तैस्तैर्हृतज्ञानाः प्रपद्यन्तेऽन्यदेवताः ।
तं तं नियममास्थाय प्रकृत्या नियताः स्वया ॥ २० ॥
यो यो यां यां तनुं भक्तः श्रद्धयार्चितुमिच्छति ।
तस्य तस्याचलां श्रद्धां तामेव विदधाम्यहम् ॥ २१॥
स तया श्रद्धया युक्तस्तस्याराधनमीहते ।
लभते च ततः कामान्मयैव विहितान्हि तान् ॥ २२ ॥
अन्तवत्तु फलं तेषां तद्भवत्यल्पमेधसाम् ।
देवान्देवयजो यान्ति मद्भक्ता यान्ति मामपि ॥ २३ ॥
अव्यक्तं व्यक्तिमापन्नं मन्यन्ते मामबुद्धयः ।
परं भावमजानन्तो ममाव्ययमनुत्तमम् ॥ २४ ॥
नाहं प्रकाशः सर्वस्य योगमायासमावृतः ।
मूढोऽयं नाभिजानाति लोको मामजमव्ययम् ॥ २५ ॥
वेदाहं समतीतानि वर्तमानानि चार्जुन ।
भविष्याणि च भूतानि मां तु वेद न कश्चन ॥ २६ ॥
इच्छाद्वेषसमुत्थेन द्वन्द्वमोहेन भारत ।
सर्वभूतानि सम्मोहं सर्गे यान्ति परन्तप ॥ २७ ॥

*Kāmais tais tair hṛtajñānāḥ prapadyante 'nyadevatāḥ* ।
*Taṃ taṃ niyamam āsthāya prakṛtyā niyatāḥ svayā* ॥ 20 ॥
*Yo yo yāṃ yāṃ tanuṃ bhaktaḥ śraddhayārcitum icchati* ।
*Tasya tasyācalāṃ śraddhāṃ tām eva vidadhāmy aham* ॥ 21 ॥
*Sa tayā śraddhayā yuktas tasyārādhanam īhate* ।
*Labhate ca tataḥ kāmān māyāivaḥ vihitān hi tān* ॥ 22 ॥

*Antavat tu phalaṃ teṣāṃ tad bhavaty alpamedhasām* ।
*Devān devayajo yānti madbhaktā yānti mām api* ॥ 23 ॥
*Avyaktaṃ vyaktim āpannaṃ manyante māmabuddhayaḥ* ।
*Paraṃ bhāvam ajānanto mamāvyayam anuttamam* ॥ 24 ॥
*Nāhaṃ prakāśaḥ sarvasya yogamāyāsamāvṛtaḥ* ।
*Mūḍho'yaṃ nābhijānāti loko mām ajam avyayam* ॥ 25 ॥
*Vedāhaṃ samatītāni vartamānāni cārjuna* ।
*Bhaviṣyāṇi ca bhūtāni māṃ tu veda na kaścana* ॥ 26 ॥
*Icchādveṣasamutthena dvandvamohena bhārata* ।
*Sarvabhūtāni saṃmohaṃ sarge yānti paraṃtapa* ॥ 27 ॥

**Meaning:** The seekers – whose discrimination (intellect) is destroyed due to desires arising in their minds as per their dispositions – go to their favored deities and worship them. Such seekers follow and execute the rules and rituals specific to those deities. Whichever form of a deity a devotee wishes to worship, I reinforce his faith in the same deity. The devotee worships that deity with unswerving faith and consequently gets fruits which are ultimately prescribed by My scheme. But worldly fruits obtained by those foolish worshippers are perishable. (In the end) The worshippers of those deities unite with them, and they are not liberated from the birth and death cycle; however, My devotees unite with Me. People who are deluded do not understand My subtle, sublime, transcendent, and imperishable nature; therefore, they think of Me – the unmanifested – as having come to manifestation. My subtle, sublime nature is as if covered with the veil of Yogamāyā, so I am not revealed to all in My true nature. The deluded people do not know Me to be birthless and imperishable. I, as Īśvara, know all beings of the past, present, and future, but no one knows Me. Many desires and aversions create duality and delusion in mind; as a result, all Jivas are subject to illusion right from their birth.

There is a verse in Sanskrit, which says –

**बुद्धिः कर्मानुसारिणी ।** *Buddhih karmānusāriṇi* ।

"The intellect works as dictated by the imprints of past actions." According to this rule, many desires arise in a seeker's mind due to the imprints of his past actions i.e. Vāsanās, and they do not permit his intellect to practice spiritual discrimination (*Viveka*). The seeker has the freedom to curb and gradually cease the awakening of desires in his mind, and he is also free to practice discrimination. He is free to choose which actions he should perform in human life. Every seeker has the freedom to be consciously aware of the decision taken by his intellect under the influence of Vāsanās, to evaluate it, and to change it with the help of discrimination. He is supposed to learn 'how to practice discrimination' with the help of spiritual scriptures written by enlightened saints. In the beginning, the seeker may make mistakes while practicing discrimination; however, he must take the practice to completion by improvising and correcting his mistakes.

All desires that can be fulfilled by worshipping deities are ultimately perishable. It is far better to live a more sublime life of lasting peace, happiness, contentment, fearlessness, and satisfaction that exists regardless of any situation in life. This also includes liberation from the life and death cycle. For that, it is imperative to nurture spiritual discrimination in mind. St. Tukārāma states, "There are different kinds of petty deities: some have grotesque faces; some are merely painted with orange color, and some are known to fulfill the wish of a devotee only in exchange of some offering. These petty deities have very limited and trivial powers." It is essential that seekers recognize the true spirit of this statement and differentiate between such deities and real God. In Śrīmad Bhāgavatam, Lord Kṛṣṇa has stated to Uddhava that His own incarnated body is illusory. His real Nirguṇa nature cannot be comprehended by people who live under the influence of Yogamāyā. Māyā which is deemed to have imaginary union with Brahman should be known as

Yogamāyā. The relation between real Brahman and unreal Māyā is imaginary and incomprehensible. (Brahmasūtra Śānkarabhāshya states: *Satyānrute Mithunikṛtvā*, which means the union between real Brahman and unreal Māyā is a mere illusion.) Formless Lord Kṛṣṇa has manifested Himself through the power of His Māyā as Saguṇa Kṛṣṇa. The seeker should worship Saguṇa Kṛṣṇa by knowing His true nature, and thus unite with the real Kṛṣṇa – Brahman – who transcends the Māyā. Petty deities in this illusory world should not be worshipped by true devotees who desire only Oneness with God.

**Real worshipper**

**येषां त्वन्तगतं पापं जनानां पुण्यकर्मणाम् ।**
**ते द्वन्द्वमोहनिर्मुक्ता भजन्ते मां दृढव्रताः ॥ २८ ॥**
**जरामरणमोक्षाय मामाश्रित्य यतन्ति ये ।**
**ते ब्रह्म तद्विदुः कृत्स्नमध्यात्मं कर्म चाखिलम् ॥ २९ ॥**
**साधिभूताधिदैवं मां साधियज्ञं च ये विदुः ।**
**प्रयाणकालेऽपि च मां ते विदुर्युक्तचेतसः ॥ ३० ॥**

*Yeṣāṃ tv antagataṃ pāpaṃ janānāṃ puṇyakarmaṇām* ।
*Te dvandvamohanirmuktā bhajante māṃ dṛḍhavratāḥ* ॥ 28 ॥
*Jarāmaraṇamokṣāya mām āśrītya yatanti ye* ।
*Te brahma tad viduḥ kṛtsnam adhyātmaṃ karma cākhilam* ॥29 ॥
*Sādhibhūtādhidaivaṃ māṃ sādhiyajñaṃ ca ye viduḥ* ।
*Prayāṇakāle'pi ca māṃ te vidur yuktacetasaḥ* ॥ 30 ॥

**Meaning:** People who have given up sinful actions while continuously performing virtuous deeds, and whose sins have come to an end through practices such as chanting are verily liberated from the duality of joy and grief which arises due to delusion. They take to My worship by remaining firm in their vows. They strive to find My refuge to liberate themselves from the grief of old-age and death. Thereby, they attain complete knowledge of the principle of Karma, Adhyātma, and Brahman. They know with certainty that it is Me who is present everywhere along with Adhibhūta, Adhidaiva, and Adhiyajña.

As they continuously contemplate on Me, they realize only My Knowledge at the time of death.

**ॐ तत्सदिति श्रीमद्भगवद्गीतासूपनिषत्सु ब्रह्मविद्यायां योगशास्त्रे श्रीकृष्णार्जुनसंवादे ज्ञानविज्ञानयोगो नाम सप्तमोऽध्यायः ॥**

*Om Tatsaditi Śrimadbhagvadgitāsūpaniṣatsu Brahmavidyāyāṃ Yogaśāstre Śrīkṛṣṇārjunasaṅvāde Jñānavijñānayogo Nāma Saptamo'dhyāyaḥ* ॥

St. Jñāneśwara assures us in his devotional poetry Haripāṭha that all sins of past births are burnt away by consistently chanting the Mantra of the Lord. The life of such a seeker becomes pious, clean, and devoid of all sins. By surrendering completely to Lord Kṛṣṇa, his delusion and its effects -- joy and grief, etc. -- are destroyed. His delusion that "I am the doer" is eradicated, his ability to discriminate remains intact, and he can practice the thought that "Lord Kṛṣṇa is the ultimate doer." He understands the Law of Karma and accepts the system of Prārabdha. These worshippers engage in the worship of Lord Kṛṣṇa and remain firm in their vows of worship. To surrender the body and its states to Śrīkṛṣṇa, they remain in His refuge alone. They seek Śrīkṛṣṇa's refuge by seeing Him as their Sadguru since Śrīkṛṣṇa Himself is Pure Knowledge, and He Himself is the personification of the teachings of this philosophy. By being in His shelter, they gain a clear understanding of the doctrine of Karma, Adhyātma, and Brahman. These terms are explained further in the next chapter. It is a part of Īśvara's governance that one who worships Him and takes refuge in Him is given the necessary spiritual disposition and intelligence through which he can know Him.

## Chapter 8

# The Imperishable Brahman

॥ अक्षरब्रह्मयोगः (Akṣarabrahmayogaḥ) ॥

At the end of the 7th chapter, there is a description of devotees whose minds are absorbed in Yoga. It is stated that these devotees understand the principles of Adhibhūta, Adhyātma, Adhiyajña, and the tenets of Karmayoga. They are aware of the true nature of Lord Kṛṣṇa at the time of their death. This chapter presents a detailed discussion on these topics.

**<u>Arjuna's question about Adhibhūta, Adhidaiva, etc.</u>**

*अर्जुन उवाच ।*

**किं तद्ब्रह्म किमध्यात्मं किं कर्म पुरुषोत्तम ।**
**अधिभूतं च किं प्रोक्तमधिदैवं किमुच्यते ॥ १ ॥**
**अधियज्ञः कथं कोऽत्र देहेऽस्मिन्मधुसूदन ।**
**प्रयाणकाले च कथं ज्ञेयोऽसि नियतात्मभिः ॥ २ ॥**

*Arjuna uvāca*

*Kiṃ tad brahma kim adhyātmaṃ kiṃ karma puruṣottama* ।
*Adhibhūtaṃ ca kiṃ proktam adhidaivaṃ kim ucyate* ॥ *1* ॥
*Adhiyajñaḥ Kaṭhaṃ ko'tra dehe'smin madhusūdana* ।
*Prayāṇakāle ca Kaṭhaṃ jñeyo'si niyatātmabhiḥ* ॥ *2* ॥

**Meaning:** (Arjuna said) What is Brahman? What is the nature of Adhyātma? What is known as Karma? What is the nature of Adhibhūta? What is known as Adhidaiva? What is the nature of Adhiyajña? How does he reside in this body? How can You be known at the time of death by those seekers who have conquered their minds?

**Lord Kṛṣṇa's answer**

*श्रीभगवानुवाच ।*

अक्षरं ब्रह्म परमं स्वभावोऽध्यात्ममुच्यते ।
भूतभावोद्भवकरो विसर्गः कर्मसंज्ञितः ॥ ३ ॥
अधिभूतं क्षरो भावः पुरुषश्चाधिदैवतम् ।
अधियज्ञोऽहमेवात्र देहे देहभृतां वर ॥ ४ ॥
अन्तकाले च मामेव स्मरन्मुक्त्वा कलेवरम् ।
यः प्रयाति स मद्भावं याति नास्त्यत्र संशयः ॥ ५ ॥
यं यं वापि स्मरन्भावं त्यजत्यन्ते कलेवरम् ।
तं तमेवैति कौन्तेय सदा तद्भावभावितः ॥ ६ ॥
तस्मात्सर्वेषु कालेषु मामनुस्मर युध्य च ।
मय्यर्पितमनोबुद्धिर्मामेवैष्यस्यसंशयम् ॥ ७ ॥
अभ्यासयोगयुक्तेन चेतसा नान्यगामिना ।
परमं पुरुषं दिव्यं याति पार्थानुचिन्तयन् ॥ ८ ॥

*Śrībhagavān uvāca* ।

*Akṣaraṃ brahma paramaṃ svabhāvo'dhyātmam ucyate* ।
*Bhūtabhāvodbhavakaro visargaḥ karmasaṃjñitaḥ* ॥ *3* ॥
*Adhibhūtaṃ kṣaro bhāvaḥ puruṣaś cādhidaivatam* ।
*Adhiyajño'hamevātra dehe dehabhṛtāṃ vara* ॥ *4* ॥
*Antakāle ca mām eva smaran muktvā kalevaram* ।
*Yaḥ prayāti sa madbhāvaṃ yāti nāsty atra saṃśayaḥ* ॥ *5* ॥
*Yaṃ yaṃ vāpi smaran bhāvaṃ tyajaty ante kalevaram* ।
*Taṃ tam evaiti kaunteya sadā tadbhāvabhāvitaḥ* ॥ *6* ॥
*Tasmāt sarveṣu kāleṣu mām anusmara yudhya ca* ।
*Mayy arpitamanobuddhir mām evaiṣyasy asaṃśayam* ॥ *7* ॥
*Abhyāsayogayuktena cetasā nānyagāminā* ।
*Paramaṃ puruṣaṃ divyaṃ yāti pārthānucintayan* ॥ *8* ॥

**Meaning:** (Śrībhagavān said) Supreme **Brahman** is imperishable. Individual body or Swabhāva is known as **Adhyātma**. That by which many beings are brought into existence is known as **Karma**. Perishable entities that are the effects are named as **Adhibhūta**. Puruṣa that dwells inside these perishable entities like body is called **Adhidaiva**, and I alone am the **Adhiyajña** in them. When a seeker leaves his body at the time of his death while remembering Me alone, he undoubtedly attains My real nature, Brahman. Whichever entity a person thinks of while leaving his body, he will go to and attain the same entity, since he continually contemplates on that one entity alone. Therefore, always contemplate on Me and fight the battle! Let your mind desire Me, and let your intellect firmly believe in Me or My existence alone. By doing so, you will doubtlessly meet Me and unite with Me. When a seeker does not think about anything else, steadies his mind, and contemplates on the divine nature of that Supreme Puruṣa, he goes to the Supreme Puruṣa and attains Him alone.

In the union of the Jiva and Brahman, only Brahman is imperishable this fact is reinstated here. One can see the glimpses of the Yoga of conquering the mind (मनःसंयमयोग) from the 6th and 7th chapters here as well. Through this Yoga, the practitioner clearly decides that the body and the world are perishable and meditates on imperishable Brahman. Lord Kṛṣṇa is now answering questions asked in this regard. The word **Swabhāva** means *Swasya Bhāvaḥ* (स्वस्य भावः), which indicates that Ātman seems to come into existence i.e. born as a Jiva through a body. Therefore, the body may be called **Adhyātma**, and afflictions pertaining to the body may be called **Ādhyātmika Tapa**. The body is known as the **Upādhi**, limiting adjunct, in Vedāntic scriptures. St. Jñāneśwara says that Pure Consciousness is subtle and concealed. It pervades the Upādhi of the body through and through (*Jñāneśwari 2.126*). The philosophy of the realization that "I am Pure Consciousness pervading the body," is known as *Adhyatmaśāstra*. There are three words in Sanskrit as follow –

***Śarira***: the body
***Śariri***: indweller of the body
***Śariraka***: Consciousness that resides in the body

Thus, the commentary by Ādi Śaṅkara on the Brahmasūtras is known as Śāriraka Bhāśya. It is pertinent to the doctrine of Adhyātma alone. The word **Karma** in the 3rd verse indicates the action of creating the universe as per the very first conscientious will (Ikṣana/Ādisaṅkalpa) evoked on Brahman.

**एकोऽहम् बहुस्याम् ।**

*Eko'ham bahusyām* । *(Cāndogya Upaniṣad 6.2.3)*

"I am one, and I shall manifest in many forms." Thereafter, the universe was created which is divided in two parts: sentient and insentient. The insentient world, made up of the Five Great Elements, is known as **Adhibhūta**. It is perishable.

The **Karma** of creation of the universe is the very first main action in the universe. All actions executed by the Jiva are essentially sub-actions that are part of the main action of the creation of the universe. A seeker should reflect on the main action and abandon his pride in being the doer, agent, or executor of sub-actions in his day-to-day life. No matter how many and whatsoever actions are performed in the perishable world of Adhibhūta, they are bound to perish at some point. Thus, even if one performs truly meaningful and great work, it should be done for the purification of the mind and not for earning fame or wealth. St. Rāmadāsa states that "One should perform such magnificent work that it immortalizes him even after his death." The same St. Rāmadāsa also prays to Lord Rāma, "Let all that is mine be destroyed and let all that is Yours remain." St. Tukārāma has made an insightful observation that "All Brāhmins have become insolent by wrongly being proud of executing Karma as described in the Vedas and by being ardent followers of so-called religious rituals." St. Tukārāma also says that "We (enlightened sages) understand that all actions, duties, and Dharmas are ultimately perishable." Nowhere is there a wrong signal in these statements that one should neglect his duties. Every person should strive to work in the best possible manner but not be proud of those actions. Such pride disturbs his inner peace and happiness. The mortal Jiva may perform any action with the help of Adhibhūta, but the action itself and its fruit are ultimately bound to end. The action may be used in different causes and may be praised by people until it comes to an end one day. E.g. the action of researching an antibiotic for a disease is of use only until germs develop immunity towards them. Afterward, that particular antibiotic is of no use for that disease. This means antibiotics are destroyed along with research that went into their creation. All actions will naturally be destroyed at the end of the world. It may take millions of years for the world to end, but the theorem that "Actions are perishable" still remains intact. Every seeker has a finite life in which he should get rid of the ego of being the doer, live happily, and not squander his precious life in any manner – this is the only learning one should take from these verses.

Īśvara resides in the body and the world as **Adhidaiva** and governs them. This simply means that He is Antaryāmi in Adhyātma and Adhibhūta – the body and the world – , and He is omniscient. Lord Kṛṣṇa, as Ātman, resides in the body in the supreme form of **Adhiyajña**. All actions performed by the body are offered to Him. All actions should be performed with a goal to attain Him. If a person is proud that he is the doer of actions, then actions create bondage for him. The Yajña of the entire life should be offered to Lord Kṛṣṇa. The seeker should perform all actions by the body, speech, and mind for Him and while remembering Him. Only by doing so, he can remember Kṛṣṇa as Adhiyajña at the time of death, and thereby he can become One with real Lord Kṛṣṇa i.e. Brahman. If, however, the seeker thinks about a perishable person or object at the time of death, he needs to be born again to acquire and enjoy that object or person. It is the law of Īśvara that the Jiva is reborn for that object or person whom he holds in his mind at the time of death. There is a Sanskrit verse which states –

अन्ते मतिः सा गतिः ।

*Ante matih sa gatih* ।

"Jiva ensues the direction of the last thought in his mind at the time of death." Therefore, Lord Kṛṣṇa has ordered Arjuna that he should perform his duty and fight the battle while mentally adhering to Lord Kṛṣṇa. If a seeker conquers his mind and adheres to the Divine Puruṣa alone, then he meets Him in the end.

**The nature of the Divine Puruṣa**

कविं पुराणमनुशासितारमणोरणीयांसमनुस्मरेद्यः ।
सर्वस्य धातारमचिन्त्यरूपमादित्यवर्णं तमसः परस्तात् ॥ ९ ॥

*Kaviṃ purāṇam anuśāsitāraṃ*
*Aṇor aṇīyāṃsam anusmared yaḥ* ।
*Sarvasya dhātāram acintyarūpaṃ*
*Ādityavarṇaṃ tamasaḥ parastāt* ॥ 9 ॥

**Meaning:** (The Divine Puruṣa) is omniscient, beginningless, subtler than the subtlest, inconceivable, radiant like the sun, the primordial, the governor, the supporter of all, and beyond the darkness of ignorance.

Being omniscient is a *Taṭastha Lakṣaṇa* of Brahman. In other words, it is a characteristic of Īśvara. Being the creator of the world, He has an innate understanding of the world. Also, since He resides in the hearts of all beings (18.61), He naturally has all the knowledge known by all beings. He is aware of all actions performed by all sentient beings in the world and governs them accordingly.

The word *Purāṇa* means very ancient, beginningless, and primordial. This is a *Swarūpa Lakṣaṇa* of Brahman. "Since when does Brahman exist?" – in this question, the 'when' is not answerable. Brahman is ever-existent in the form of ***Sat***. "It was," "it is," and "it will be" – these expressions pertinent to the past, present, or future are not applicable to Brahman. Even the expression of negation – "It was not," "it is not," and "it will not be" – does not apply to Brahman. It is primordial (*Ādya*), which means it exists from the beginning of the universe. The regular meaning of the word primordial cannot be applied here in the context of Brahman. The primordial person in a lineage is documented and presented in some cases. Such a person is called the very first in a family because his predecessor is not known. But that is not the case in the realm of Brahman.

Brahman is the pinnacle of subtlety. Pure Consciousness or Pure Awareness is its very nature. The words like molecule, atom, subatomic particle, process, field, and uncertainty are used in the context of insentient objects; these words cannot represent the subtleness of Brahman. Brahman is not something which manifests with sentient and insentient entities, permeates them, and which is destroyed with them. Scientists in today's world are taking enormous efforts to investigate this Pure Awareness. However, the awareness that tries to investigate itself through the intellect is baffled when it needs to know itself, and thereby it is unable to know anything at that stage. Pure Awareness is beyond the awareness that works through the intellect, so it cannot be known in an objective manner. Pure Awareness is not an object, so it cannot even be known in a subjective manner. Therefore, Brahman or Pure Awareness is Self-cognizant (*Swasaṃvedya*) and Pure Knowledge itself (*Jñānarūpa*). Brahman is inconceivable, incomprehensible, and unknowable. Not being an object, it cannot be thought of in a traditional, objective manner. There is no tool available for experiencing it. It cannot be logically inferred by the intellect. It is not a knowable object, so it cannot be known by any epistemic sources of knowledge.

Brahman is ever-existent as ***Sat***. The world exists and appears to be real on the substratum of Brahman. Thus, Brahman supports the world as a whole. The word *Ādityavarṇa* means effulgent as the sun. However, effulgence is a property of the fire, which is itself an insentient element. So here we should infer the meaning of *Ādityavarṇa* as Brahman that is the resplendence of Pure Knowledge. Being Pure Knowledge itself, Brahman has no awareness or non-awareness in it. In other words, there is neither qualified knowledge (*Vṛttijñāna*) that includes the triad of knowable-instrument-knower nor a trace of ignorance (*Ajñāna*) in Brahman.

## The method to be One with the Divine Puruṣa

**प्रयाणकाले मनसाचलेन भक्त्या युक्तो योगबलेन चैव ।**
**भ्रुवोर्मध्ये प्राणमावेश्य सम्यक् स तं परं पुरुषमुपैति दिव्यम् ॥ १० ॥**
**यदक्षरं वेदविदो वदन्ति विशन्ति यद्यतयो वीतरागाः ।**
**यदिच्छन्तो ब्रह्मचर्यं चरन्ति तत्ते पदं सङ्ग्रहेण प्रवक्ष्ये ॥ ११ ॥**
**सर्वद्वाराणि संयम्य मनो हृदि निरुध्य च ।**
**मूर्ध्न्याधायात्मनः प्राणमास्थितो योगधारणाम् ॥ १२ ॥**
**ओमित्येकाक्षरं ब्रह्म व्याहरन्मामनुस्मरन् ।**
**यः प्रयाति त्यजन्देहं स याति परमां गतिम् ॥ १३ ॥**
**अनन्यचेताः सततं यो मां स्मरति नित्यशः ।**
**तस्याहं सुलभः पार्थ नित्ययुक्तस्य योगिनः ॥ १४ ॥**

*Prayāṇakāle manasācalena*
*Bhaktyā yukto yogabalena caiva* ।
*Bhruvor madhye prāṇam āveśya samyak*
*Sa taṃ paraṃ puruṣam upaiti divyam* ॥ *10* ॥
*Yad akṣaraṃ vedavido vādanti*
*Viśanti yad yatayo vītarāgāḥ* ।
*Yad icchanto brahmacaryaṃ caranti*
*Tat te padaṃ saṃgraheṇa pravakṣye* ॥ *11* ॥
*Sarvadvārāṇi saṅyamya mano hṛdi nirudhya ca* ।
*Mūrdhny ādhāyātmanaḥ prāṇam āsthito yogadhāraṇām* ॥ *12* ॥

*Om ity ekākṣaraṃ brahma vyāharan mām anusmaran* ।
*Yaḥ prayāti tyajan dehaṃ sa yāti paramāṃ gatim* ॥ *13* ॥
*Ananyacetāḥ satataṃ yo māṃ smarati nityaśaḥ* ।
*Tasyāhaṃ sulabhaḥ pārtha nityayuktasya yoginaḥ* ॥ *14* ॥

**Meaning:** At the time of his own death, having fixed his Prāṇa with the power of Yoga in the middle of the two eyebrows, the seeker who has a serene mind full of utmost devotion, and who remains steady in this state (*Yogārūḍha*), attains the Divine Puruṣa and unites with Him. I will now explain the goal which knowers of the Vedas call imperishable. To attain that goal, Saṅnyāsins become dispassionate, and to unite with it, they remain celibate. Having controlled all gates of the body such as eyes, ears, etc. and having ceased their activities, having fixed Prāṇas in the crown of the head, a person who leaves his body by repeatedly remembering and chanting the one-syllable-Brahman **Om** attains the supreme goal. I am easily attainable to that Yogi who constantly adheres to Me in his thoughts and remains intently devoted to Me.

In these verses, Lord Kṛṣṇa describes His real nature to the one who takes to the Path of Meditation to attain imperishable Brahman. He also explains a way to realize "I am Brahman." There is an explanation of four aspects of human life here: the body, world, Īśvara, Brahman, and their relationship with each other. The following Mantra of Muṇḍaka Upaniṣad (*1.2.11*) has been retold here in an alternate way:

**तपःश्रद्धे ये ह्युपवसन्त्यरण्ये शान्ताविद्वांसो भैक्ष्यचर्यां चरन्तः।**
**सूर्यद्वारेण ते विरजाः प्रयान्ति यत्रामृतः स पुरुषो ह्यव्ययात्मा ॥**

*Tapaḥśraddhe ye hyupavasantyaraṇye śāntāvidvāṃso bhaikṣyacaryāṃ carantaḥ* । *Sūryadvāreṇa te virajāḥ prayānti yatrāmṛtaḥ sa puruṣo hyavyayātmā* ॥

Lord Kṛṣṇa explains the prior readiness for spiritual pursuit such as controlling senses, being dispassionate, etc. in these verses. The fixing of Prāṇas on eyebrows is a mysterious concept, and one should get guidance from an expert Yoga teacher before practicing it. Focusing the mind on a specific part of the body like the center of the eyebrows may lead to the same effect that is achieved by focusing the Prāṇas. After this, the seeker who leaves his body remembering Me and steadily chanting the syllable Prāṇava – Om, the highest symbol of Brahman – attains the supreme goal, Brahman.

Here, Lord Kṛṣṇa has asked the seeker to engage in three practices at the same time. The Yogic Dhāraṇā of fixing the Prāṇas on the crown of the head, chanting of Om – the one-syllable Brahman, and remembering God. The word **Dhāraṇā** means concentrating the mind on any one point like an object, breath, or sound, etc. After Dhāraṇā is steadied, chanting of Om is equivalent to remembering God. Such a seeker can easily attain God in His true nature. Remembering one God and chanting the Mantra of some other deity is a discrepancy, which can only disrupt the mind. Therefore, one may either chant Om while remembering Brahman or chant the Mantra of a deity with a firm knowledge that the deity is Brahman.

## The effect of attaining God

मामुपेत्य पुनर्जन्म दुःखालयमशाश्वतम् ।
नाप्नुवन्ति महात्मानः संसिद्धिं परमां गताः ॥ १५ ॥
आब्रह्मभुवनाल्लोकाः पुनरावर्तिनोऽर्जुन ।
मामुपेत्य तु कौन्तेय पुनर्जन्म न विद्यते ॥ १६ ॥
सहस्रयुगपर्यन्तमहर्यद् ब्रह्मणो विदुः ।
रात्रिं युगसहस्रान्तां तेऽहोरात्रविदो जनाः ॥ १७ ॥
अव्यक्ताद् व्यक्तयः सर्वाः प्रभवन्त्यहरागमे ।
रात्र्यागमे प्रलीयन्ते तत्रैवाव्यक्तसञ्ज्ञके ॥ १८ ॥
भूतग्रामः स एवायं भूत्वा भूत्वा प्रलीयते ।
रात्र्यागमेऽवशः पार्थ प्रभवत्यहरागमे ॥ १९ ॥
परस्तस्मात्तु भावोऽन्योऽव्यक्तोऽव्यक्तात्सनातनः ।
यः स सर्वेषु भूतेषु नश्यत्सु न विनश्यति ॥ २० ॥

*Māṃ upetya punarjanma duḥkhālayam aśāśvatam* ।
*Nāpnuvanti mahātmānaḥ saṃsiddhiṃ paramāṃ gatāḥ* ॥ *15* ॥
*Ā brahmabhuvanāl lokāḥ punarāvartino'rjuna* ।
*Māṃ upetya tu kaunteya punarjanma na vidyāte* ॥ *16* ॥
*Sahasrayugaparyantam ahar yad brahmaṇo viduḥ* ।
*Rātriṃ yugasahasrāntāṃ te'horātravido janāḥ* ॥ *17* ॥
*Avyaktād vyaktayaḥ sarvāḥ prabhavanty aharāgame* ।
*Rātryāgame pralīyante tatraivāvyaktasaṃjñake* ॥ *18* ॥
*Bhūtagrāmaḥ sa evāyaṃ bhūtvā bhūtvā pralīyate* ।
*Rātryāgame 'vaśaḥ pārtha prabhavaty aharāgame* ॥ *19* ॥
*Paras tasmāt tu bhāvo 'nyo 'vyakto 'vyaktāt sanātanaḥ* ।
*Yaḥ sa sarveṣu bhūteṣu naśyatsu na vinaśyati* ॥ *20* ॥

**Meaning:** Having attained Oneness with Brahman, these great souls come to Me and unite with Me. They are not subject to rebirth that is impermanent and filled with suffering. All worlds, including that of Brahmaloka, are subject to creation and resurrection over and over again. But these great souls are not reborn to go to the other worlds after being united with Me. Those who understand the secret of day and night know that one day of Brahmadeva lasts a thousand Yugas (eons), and His night is the same. At the dawn of Brahmadeva's day, the universe and all its sentient and insentient entities are created from the **Avyakta**, an unmanifested storehouse of all beings in a seed-form. At the start of Brahmadeva's night, they merge again in the same *Avyakta*. This entire universe is created and destroyed again and again. It is completely non-autonomous. However, much subtler than this Avyakta, there is eternal, unmanifested Pure Existence which is not destroyed even after the destruction of all beings and entities.

The narrative in these verses is dependent on faith, and it can assist significantly in strengthening the resolve to attain Mokṣa. An individual body and all entities in the universe continuously undergo enormous changes like creation, sustenance, and destruction. Despite that, Ātman – which is formless, immutable, imperishable, and *Sat-Cit-Ānanda* – is not subject to even the slightest change. The seeker should strive to focus on this changeless principle. Brahmadeva's day and night are relative to the universe; similarly, a person, too, has days-nights in his extremely short life-span in which his little world disappears and reappears. Man cannot possibly see the creation and destruction of the vast universe in his lifetime; however, he is expected to reflect on the fact that even his little world is certainly going to end someday. It is necessary for the seeker to decisively know that the little world of every person – which consists of his body, home, family, profession, city, relatives, acquaintances, neighbors, friends, etc. – is unreal and illusory. Otherwise, the seeker may just fall into the trap of thinking that the vast universe may be unreal as mentioned in scriptures, but his own little world is certainly real. This delusional trap is a deterrent for every seeker in his spiritual pursuit.

**The nature of the supreme goal (path)**

अव्यक्तोऽक्षर इत्युक्तस्तमाहुः परमां गतिम् ।
यं प्राप्य न निवर्तन्ते तद्धाम परमं मम ॥ २१ ॥
पुरुषः स परः पार्थ भक्त्या लभ्यस्त्वनन्यया ।
यस्यान्तःस्थानि भूतानि येन सर्वमिदं ततम् ॥ २२ ॥

*Avyakto 'kṣara ity uktas tam āhuḥ paramāṃ gatim* ।
*Yaṃ prāpya na nivartante tad dhāma paramaṃ mama* ॥ *21* ॥
*Puruṣaḥ sa paraḥ pārtha bhaktyā labhyas tv ananyayā* ।
*Yasyāntaḥsthāni bhūtāni yena sarvam idaṃ tatam* ॥ *22* ॥

**Meaning:** That which is unmanifested and imperishable is known as the supreme goal (path). Having attained that goal, one is not born again; it is My highest abode. That highest *Puruṣa* (goal) in whom all beings reside, and who pervades the whole world, can be attained by unswerving devotion to Him.

The words 'goal' (*Gati*) and 'abode' (*Dhāma*) are used here only to facilitate the conceptual understanding of seekers. The term 'supreme goal' (*Parama Gati*) is respective to the debacle of being caught in the birth and death cycle. One can walk on a regular path. But in this case, Brahman – the supreme goal or the highest path – cannot be walked upon like an ordinary path or achieved like a regular goal. Brahman is ever-attained, but most seekers are ignorant about it. The word *Mokṣadhāma* – the abode of Mokṣa – is respective to the places like heaven. Mokṣa is neither a place nor abode. It is not even a state of freedom. One only discusses Mokṣa as a state of liberation with respect to the state of being bound. By mentioning the highest Puruṣa where all beings reside, it is reinforced that the phenomenal world is not separate from Him.

**The path received by a Dhyānayogi is dependent on time**

**यत्र काले त्वनावृत्तिमावृत्तिं चैव योगिनः ।**
**प्रयाता यान्ति तं कालं वक्ष्यामि भरतर्षभ ॥ २३ ॥**
**अग्निर्ज्योतिरहः शुक्लः षण्मासा उत्तरायणम् ।**
**तत्र प्रयाता गच्छन्ति ब्रह्म ब्रह्मविदो जनाः ॥ २४ ॥**
**धूमो रात्रिस्तथा कृष्णः षण्मासा दक्षिणायनम् ।**
**तत्र चान्द्रमसं ज्योतिर्योगी प्राप्य निवर्तते ॥ २५ ॥**
**शुक्लकृष्णे गती ह्येते जगतः शाश्वते मते ।**
**एकया यात्यनावृत्तिमन्ययावर्तते पुनः ॥ २६ ॥**

*Yatra kāle tv anāvṛttim āvṛttiṃ caiva yoginaḥ ।*
*Prayātā yānti taṃ kālaṃ vakṣyāmi bharatarṣabha ॥ 23 ॥*
*Agnir jotir ahaḥ śuklaḥ ṣaṇmāsā uttarāyaṇam ।*
*Tatra prayātā gacchanti brahma brahmavido janāḥ ॥ 24 ॥*
*Dhūmo rātris tathā kṛṣṇaḥ ṣaṇmāsā dakṣiṇāyanam ।*
*Tatra cāndramasaṃ jyotir yogī prāpya nivartate ॥ 25 ॥*
*Śuklakṛṣṇe gatī hy ete jagataḥ śāśvate mate ।*
*Ekayā yāty anāvṛttim anyayāvartate punaḥ ॥ 26 ॥*

**Meaning:** O Arjuna! Now I shall tell about the time in which if Dhyānayogis die, they will not be reborn; and the time in which if they die, they will be reborn. Fire, daytime, the bright fortnight from no moon to full moon, and the six months of the northern solstice – enlightened yogis practicing the Path of Meditation who die at this specified time attain Brahman. Smoke, nighttime, the dark fortnight from full moon to no moon, and the six months of the southern solstice – enlightened yogis practicing the Path of Meditation who die at this specified time go to the plane of the moon and return to the earth. These two paths – the bright path (*Śuklamārga*) and the dark path (*Kṛṣṇamārga*) – are considered constant in this world. If one follows the first path, he attains liberation from the life and death cycle; and one who follows the other path is stuck in the cycle of birth and death.

The words *jagataḥ ete śāśvate mate* (जगतः एते शाश्वते मते) should be inferred to mean that these paths are traditionally accepted. Even here, only faith is the tool to accept this narrative. The term *Śuklamārga* can mean the Path of Knowledge, while the term *Kṛṣṇamārga* may mean the Path of Ignorance.

**The characteristic feature of Karmayoga**

**नैते सृती पार्थ जानन्योगी मुह्यति कश्चन ।**
**तस्मात्सर्वेषु कालेषु योगयुक्तो भवार्जुन ॥ २७ ॥**
**वेदेषु यज्ञेषु तपःसु चैव**
**दानेषु यत्पुण्यफलं प्रदिष्टम् ।**
**अत्येति तत्सर्वमिदं विदित्वा**
**योगी परं स्थानमुपैति चाद्यम् ॥ २८ ॥**

*Naite sṛtī pārtha jānan yogī muhyati kaścana* ।
*Tasmāt sarveṣu kāleṣu yogayukto bhavārjuna* ॥ *27* ॥
*Vedeṣu yajñeṣu tapaḥsu caiva*
*dāneṣu yat puṇyaphalaṃ pradiṣṭam* ।
*Atyeti tat sarvam idaṃ viditvā*
*yogī paraṃ sthānam upaiti cādyam* ॥*28*॥

**Meaning:** A Karmayogi who understands the gist of these two paths is not subject to delusion ever. Therefore, practice

Karmayoga at all times. By engaging in the study of the Vedas and performing fire-sacrifices, austerities, and donations (Yajña, *Tapas*, *Dāna*), the seeker accumulates merits; however, the Karmayogi goes beyond all of this. He gains the theoretical Knowledge of Ātman (*Jñāna*) and also realizes "I am Ātman" (*Vijñāna*); thus, he reaches the supreme goal.

There are no such restrictions about the time of death for the one who practices *Sāṅkhyayoga* – the Path of Knowledge or *Karmayoga* – the Path of Action. It is said that Bhīṣma waited till the beginning of the northern solstice for his death; from this, we may infer that he followed the Path of Meditation. Even if the one who meditates is subject to rebirth, he is born in a condition that is conducive for his spiritual pursuit and attainment of Mokṣa (*6.42*). The Karmayogi, who understands these details, always follows the principle of Karmayoga and does not get caught in the bondage of time for attaining good death. Actions such as fire-sacrifice and donation are performed; hence, they are bound to end someday. Artificial or unreal tools or practices cannot attain what is real, eternal, and natural. A wise and enlightened devotee becomes One with the timeless, real nature of God, Brahman, as mentioned in the 7th chapter.

**ॐ तत्सदिति श्रीमद्भगवद्गीतासूपनिषत्सु ब्रह्मविद्यायां योगशास्त्रे श्रीकृष्णार्जुनसंवादे अक्षरब्रह्मयोगो नामाष्टमोऽध्यायः ॥**

*Om Tatsaditi Śrimadbhagvadgitāsūpaniṣatsu Brahmavidyāyāṃ Yogaśāstre Śrīkṛṣṇārjunasaṅvāde Akṣarabrahmayogo Nāma Aṣṭamo'dhyāyaḥ* ॥

Chapter 9

# The Supreme Knowledge and Profound Secret

॥ राजविद्याराजगुह्ययोगः (Rājavidyārājaguhyayogaḥ) ॥

श्रीभगवानुवाच ।
इदं तु ते गुह्यतमं प्रवक्ष्याम्यनसूयवे ।
ज्ञानं विज्ञानसहितं यज्ज्ञात्वा मोक्ष्यसेऽशुभात् ॥ १ ॥
राजविद्या राजगुह्यं पवित्रमिदमुत्तमम् ।
प्रत्यक्षावगमं धर्म्यं सुसुखं कर्तुमव्ययम् ॥ २ ॥

*Śrībhagavān uvāca* ।
*Idaṃ tu te guhyatamaṃ pravakṣyāmy anasūyave* ।
*Jñānaṃ vijñānasahitaṃ yaj jñātvā mokṣyase'śubhāt* ॥ *1* ॥
*Rājavidyā rājaguhyaṃ pavitram idam uttamam* ।
*Pratyakṣāvagamaṃ dharmyaṃ susukhaṃ kartum avyayam* ॥ *2* ॥

**Meaning:** (Śrībhagavān said) O Arjuna! I shall explain the most mysterious, profound Knowledge of Brahman (Jñāna) to you, and I shall also give the relevant details to realize it and make it a living reality (*Vijñāna*) since you are neither envious nor a caviler. Having known this Knowledge, you shall be free from miserable ignorance. This Knowledge is the sovereign of all kinds of knowledge, the highest secret of all secrets, the purest of all, and the one that gives excellent results. It can be directly realized. It is authenticated by scriptures, imperishable, and easy to put into practice.

Arjuna is devoid of envy and cavil, which is the reason why Lord Kṛṣṇa revealed the Knowledge of Brahman to him. When a person's mind is polluted by jealousy, antipathy, disgust, hatred, or hostility, this spiritual Knowledge slips from his mind even if he listens to it many times. By addressing Arjuna as

**Anasuya** – one who is not envious or a caviler – in this verse, Lord Kṛṣṇa deliberately gives a message that "The seeker should constantly strive to keep himself away from envy and other such negative traits."

The seeker may feel envious of others due to three factors: strong identification with the body, half-hearted acceptance of Prārabdha, and obliviousness of the all-pervasive God residing in every being. The seeker who strongly identifies himself with the body has a turmoil of thoughts in his mind pertinent to 'I, me, and mine.' Competition, comparison, and envy dominate such a seeker, and they further fuel jealousy in his mind. As per Prārabdha – Īśvara's scheme of governance – every person gets what he is bound to get in life according to his past actions. So, if the seeker feels envious when someone else gets more wealth or respect, or if he feels superior while seeing an inferior or less fortunate person and develops disgust for him, these feelings indicate that he has not accepted Īśvara's governance and not surrendered to Him. We commonly hear the fact that "God pervades equally in the hearts of all beings." So, if the seeker feels jealous of any other person despite knowing that "God resides in him," it indicates jealousy for God Himself. Most seekers do not understand the gravity of this issue. St. Tukārāma has said that not being envious of anyone is the very gist of worshipping Īśvara. Kaṭha Upaniṣad describes Ātman as God in every being –

**गूढमनुप्रविष्टं गुहाहितं ।**

*Gūḍhamanupraviṣṭaṃ guhāhitaṃ* । (*1.2.12*)

"(This Ātman is) hidden and lodged mysteriously in the cave of the mind (of every being)."

Lord Kṛṣṇa says that the Knowledge of Ātman is the most profound and supreme of all kinds of knowledge, and it is His Divine Glory (Vibhūti). Ātman is Self-effulgent, which means it cannot be known through any epistemic sources of knowledge.

Ātman is the illuminator of the intellect. The human intellect, which is itself illumined or known by the presence of Ātman, is unable to know its illuminator Ātman. In fact, no light is available or necessary for the illumination of Self-effulgent Ātman. This is the reason why the Knowledge of Ātman is profound and mysterious. Human life cannot be meaningful and glorious without this Self-Knowledge; therefore, it is the highest of all. When a person is liberated from the duality of joy and grief and becomes Pure Bliss himself, his life is said to be meaningful in a true sense. The worldly knowledge of material sciences is essential for living a comfortable worldly life, but the same knowledge may also lead to destruction. This is not a fault of that knowledge; rather, it is a fact that all kinds of worldly knowledge are dependent on people who may have faulty dispositions. The spiritual Knowledge of Ātman does not provide any material comforts, but it enables the seeker to know that he himself is unqualified Pure Bliss, which is eternally available to him regardless of anything else. Happiness derived from worldly comforts can only be restrictively enjoyed through one's body or mind, and such happiness is disrupted when comforts are disrupted. A qualified person like Arjuna is eligible to attain Pure Bliss of Ātman, which is never disrupted or destroyed for any reason. A person who does not have a pure mind is not qualified for spiritual pursuit. He cannot revel in Pure Bliss of his true Self since Self-Knowledge is not subservient to him.

Ātman is pure; it has no impurities (Mala) of any kind. So, the Knowledge of Ātman is pure and pious as well. It liberates the Jiva from impious, ominous impurities of the three bodies (gross, subtle, causal), the three states (waking, dreaming, deep-sleep), the three Guṇas (Sattva, Rājas, Tāmas), all dualities (joy-grief, success-failure, etc.), and the cycle of birth and death. It unites the Jiva with his original nature i.e. pure and pious Ātman.

It purifies the Jiva along with his body. Muṇḍak Upaniṣad testifies this fact –

ब्रह्मवेद ब्रह्मैव भवति ।

*Brahmaved Brahmaiva Bhavati* । *(3.2.9)*

"One who realizes Brahman becomes Brahman himself." St. Tukārāma has attested to the fact that the speech and body are purified by chanting the Mantra of God. A devotional poem written for St. Tukārāma states that he himself became Brahman after Self-realization.

Such is the description of the Knowledge of Ātman. Lord Kṛṣṇa has used two adjectives for it: **supreme** and **excellent**. It is the supreme of all kinds of knowledge and one that gives excellent results. By acquiring this Self-Knowledge, the seeker realizes that "I am imperishable Ātman," hence, this Self-Knowledge is imperishable as well. The scriptures state that **Mokṣa** is the highest of the Fourfold Achievements (*Caturvidha Puruṣārtha*) of human life. Thus, this Self-Knowledge, which leads to Mokṣa, is approved by and included in Dharma. It is authenticated whole-heartedly by Dharma. A seeker can attain the direct Self-realization that "I am Ātman" by pursuing this Knowledge. Any Qualified Knowledge (*Vṛttijñāna*) can be gained through the five senses or direct perception; however, true Self-Knowledge cannot be known through the senses or mind in the same way. Direct realization is the very nature of the Knowledge of Ātman. Ātman can never be indirect (*Parokṣa*) or far away. It is always direct (*Aparokṣa*); in fact, it is the very nature of each Jiva.

The sovereign Knowledge of Ātman described in this chapter is easy to learn and put into practice. It is neither arduous nor painful. The words easy and difficult need to be used very carefully and contextually for the Knowledge of Ātman. The Path of Renunciation of Actions involves renouncing all worldly possessions, and the Path of Meditation involves conquering the mind. As compared to these two, the qualified seeker – one having an unenvious mind – may find it easier to practice Jñānayoga described here which involves thinking, reflecting, and contemplating on Self-Knowledge.

## The effect of not nurturing faith

अश्रद्दधानाः पुरुषा धर्मस्यास्य परन्तप ।
अप्राप्य मां निवर्तन्ते मृत्युसंसारवर्त्मनि ॥ ३ ॥

*Aśraddadhānāḥ puruṣā dharmasyāsya paraṃtapa* ।
*Aprāpya māṃ nivartante mṛtyusaṃsāravartmani* ॥ *3* ॥

**Meaning:** People devoid of faith cannot attain this Knowledge, which is included in the scriptures of Dharma and authenticated by Dharma. Such people are not liberated from the cycle of life-death since they are unable to attain Me.

This part is already explained in verses *2.39* and *2.40*. The seeker who nurtures faith in scriptures and who is devoid of jealousy is described later in verse *18.71*.

## The realization of the Knowledge of Ātman

मया ततमिदं सर्वं जगदव्यक्तमूर्तिना ।
मत्स्थानि सर्वभूतानि न चाहं तेष्ववस्थितः ॥ ४ ॥
न च मत्स्थानि भूतानि पश्य मे योगमैश्वरम् ।
भूतभृन्न च भूतस्थो ममात्मा भूतभावनः ॥ ५ ॥
यथाकाशस्थितो नित्यं वायुः सर्वत्रगो महान् ।
तथा सर्वाणि भूतानि मत्स्थानीत्युपधारय ॥ ६ ॥
सर्वभूतानि कौन्तेय प्रकृतिं यान्ति मामिकाम् ।
कल्पक्षये पुनस्तानि कल्पादौ विसृजाम्यहम् ॥ ७ ॥
प्रकृतिं स्वामवष्टभ्य विसृजामि पुनः पुनः ।
भूतग्राममिमं कृत्स्नमवशं प्रकृतेर्वशात् ॥ ८ ॥

*Mayā tatam idaṃ sarvaṃ jagad avyaktamūrtinā* ।
*Matsthāni sarvabhūtāni na cāhaṃ teṣv avasthitaḥ* ॥ *4* ॥
*Na ca matsthāni bhūtāni paśya me yogam aiśvaram* ।
*Bhūtabhṛn na ca bhūtastho mamātmā bhūtabhāvanaḥ* ॥ *5* ॥

*Yathākāśasthito nityaṃ vāyuḥ sarvatrago mahān* ।
*Tathā sarvāṇi bhūtāni matsthānīty upadhāraya* ॥ *6* ॥
*Sarvabhūtāni kaunteya prakṛtiṃ yānti māmikām* ।
*Kalpakṣaye punas tāni kalpādau visṛjāmy aham* ॥ *7* ॥
*Prakṛtiṃ svām avaṣṭabhya visṛjāmi punaḥ punaḥ* ।
*Bhūtagrāmam imaṃ kṛtsnam avaśaṃ prakṛter vaśāt* ॥ *8* ॥

**Meaning:** I am inexpressible and unmanifested, yet this manifested world is entirely permeated by Me. All beings exist in Me, yet I do not dwell in them. In reality, beings also do not exist in Me. This is the grandeur of My Divine Yoga; know and behold it. I am not attached to beings, yet I am their creator. Just as the mighty wind exists everywhere in space, know that all beings dwell in Me. At the end of every Kalpa, all beings rest in My Prakṛti. I recreate them at the beginning of the next Kalpa again. Through the medium of My Prakṛti, I create them again and again. This entire world of beings is completely controlled by Prakṛti. [Kalpa is a very long period mentioned in ancient Hindu scriptures, and it is measured in millions of years.]

The real nature of Lord Kṛṣṇa is Brahman which has no attributes. Brahman is not made up of particles or components, hence it is formless and unmanifested. It has no divisions or subdivisions of any kind. The world has many components, divisions, and subdivisions. It is manifested, and it has a visible form. The Pure Existence (***Sat***) aspect of Brahman appears to be manifested in the existence (***Astitva***) of worldly entities due to the power of Prakṛti or Māyā. This simply means *Sat* is the underlying principle of the existence of worldly objects; however, these objects do not exist in *Sat*. Māyā is of different nature than *Sat* (***Sat-vilakṣaṇa***) and of different nature than *Asat* (***Asat-vilakṣaṇa***). Ignorant people mistakenly see the world as real due to the influence of Māyā. Enlightened people do not see the world as real as they have sublated it in their minds.

The seekers may face a question, "How and why does the unreal world appear to be real on the substratum of Brahman?" Formless Brahman does not have an exact analogy or representative in day-to-day life. Hence, it is necessary to answer this question with the example of ice and water. E.g. water exists in ice, yet ice does not exist in the water. Only due to the cold temperature, ice is seen instead of water. This is not an example of *Pariṇamavāda*, rather it explains *Vivartavāda* in a more understandable way. More specifically, this is an example of *Anadhyasta Vivarta*, which means that the external form changes without any change in the nature of an object.

[Note:

- ***Pariṇamavāda*** is a theory of real transformation. It states, "A cause transforms itself into an effect." E.g. milk (cause) gets transformed into curd (effect). Similarly, Brahman gets transformed into the world. The Sāṅkhya and Yoga schools of philosophy have accepted this theory.
- ***Vivartavāda*** is a theory of illusory transformation where "A cause appears as an effect." E.g. In dim light, a rope appears as a snake due to ignorance of rope. Similarly, non-dual Brahman merely appears to be the world of plurality due to the ignorance of Brahman. The Advaita Vedānta school of philosophy has accepted this theory.]

Seeing ice but knowing it to be water is known as sublation (बाध) of the ice. Similarly, seeing the world but knowing it to be Brahman is known as sublation of the world. On the other hand, if one only sees ice and completely disregards water, it is known as ignorance. It may seem as if water is trapped in ice. But ice cannot be seen once it is melted, yet water remains even after melting. Cold temperature is an 'instrumental cause' (*Nimitta Kāraṇa*) in the process of creation of the ice. Water is not dependent on ice, but ice cannot exist without water. Analogous to this, Brahman is not dependent on the world, but the world cannot exist without Brahman.

The example of 'rope and snake' and different philosophical doctrines (*Khyātis*) may be grand theories in themselves, but they are difficult for most people to learn. The seeker is supposed to take many intellectual efforts to understand the fact that the body and world are impermanent and illusory, because this understanding helps him in being dispassionate about his body and other worldly matters. Vedānta uses the term ***Sat-Asat-Vilakṣaṇa-Anirvacaniya*** to explain the illusory appearance of the world.

- The word ***Sat*** means Absolute, Pure Existence without past, present, or future. *Sat* is the one that stays unaltered in all three times. But the world changes with time. It did not exist millions of years ago, it exists now, and it will cease to exist sometime in the future. Existence of the world is pertinent to time. Hence it is not *Sat*; it is of different nature than *Sat* - ***Sat-Vilakṣaṇa***.
- The word ***Asat*** means Absolute Non-existence. ***Asat*** or *Asatya* means that which has no existence at any given time. *Asat* can never be seen or perceived by anyone. Vedānta gives three famous examples to understand the concept of *Asat*: a flower on the vine of the sky (*khapuṣpa*), horns of a hare (*śaśaśṛṅga*), and a son of a sterile woman (*vandhyā-putra*). The world is not *Asat* like these examples since the world seems to exist in the present time. Hence, it is not ***Asat***; it is of different nature than *Asat*. In other words, it is ***Asat-Vilakṣaṇa***.

The world is neither *Sat* nor *Asat*, hence indescribable and illusory. All enlightened people decisively know that "The world is not real." They are able to sublate the world when others see it as real. When a seeker is able to see the world as unreal, his attachment to the body and the world comes to an end. His body continues to exist as per Prārabdha, but he revels in Pure Bliss of his true Self for the rest of his life.

The wind (air) pervades and dwells in some portion of the vast space. Similarly, all sentient beings dwell in Brahman. Space is vast and more expansive than air, and it exists much beyond the layer of air. Similarly, Brahman pervades all beings, yet exists far beyond them. Īśvara governs all beings; He creates and destroys them as per His scheme of things. As per the theory of false-attribution (*Adhyāropa*), when seeing the world as real, intially one should accept that the formless, attributeless Brahman creates the world with the help of Prakṛti. Without this theory, it is difficult to construe the creation of the world by actionless Brahman. Scriptures have presented examples like this to ascertain the fact that Ātman is not attached to anything or encaged by anything. It is actionless or neutral.

**The real nature of Lord Kṛṣṇa**

**न च मां तानि कर्माणि निबध्नन्ति धनञ्जय ।**
**उदासीनवदासीनमसक्तं तेषु कर्मसु ॥ ९ ॥**
**मयाध्यक्षेण प्रकृतिः सूयते सचराचरम् ।**
**हेतुनानेन कौन्तेय जगद्विपरिवर्तते ॥ १० ॥**
**अवजानन्ति मां मूढा मानुषीं तनुमाश्रितम् ।**
**परं भावमजानन्तो मम भूतमहेश्वरम् ॥ ११ ॥**

*Na ca māṃ tāni karmāṇi nibadhnanti dhanaṃjaya* ।
*Udāsīnavad āsīnam asaktaṃ teṣu karmasu* ॥ *9* ॥
*Mayādhyakṣeṇa prakṛtiḥ sūyate sacarācaram* ।
*Hetunānena kaunteya jagad viparivartate* ॥ *10* ॥
*Avajānanti māṃ mūḍhā mānuṣīṃ tanum āŚrītam* ।
*Paraṃ bhāvam ajānanto mama bhūtamaheśvaram* ॥ *11* ॥

**Meaning:** Despite being engaged in these actions, I am not bound by them, because I am unattached and neutral regarding all actions. Prakṛti creates all sentient and insentient entities in the world due to the seed of My will. The world keeps revolving in this manner only due to Me. Deluded people merely behold Me as a human body, so they cannot recognize Me as the owner and governor of this world. Those who do not know My Divine Nature disregard Me and do not listen to My teachings.

It is better to take the meaning of **I** or **Me** as Īśvara (not Brahman) in these verses. Īśvara incarnates Himself in the three well-known forms of Brahmadeva, Viṣṇu, and Maheśa. Īśvara Himself is said to be created through the very first will that surfaced on Brahman – "I am one, I shall be many". The world is said to be created through deep meditation by Īśvara. The statement that the world is created is just an *Adhyaropa* i.e. false attribution which is meant for seekers who believe the world to be real.. Īśvara is a witness of all activities in the world (*Muṇḍaka Up. 3.1.1*). He resides in the hearts of all beings and governs them in an impersonal manner (*18.61*).

**The state of those who disregard Me**

मोघाशा मोघकर्माणो मोघज्ञाना विचेतसः ।
राक्षसीमासुरीं चैव प्रकृतिं मोहिनीं श्रिताः ॥ १२ ॥

*Moghāśā moghakarmāṇo moghajñānā vicetasaḥ* ।
*Rākṣasīm āsurīṃ caiva prakṛtiṃ mohinīṃ Śrītāḥ* ॥ *12* ॥

**Meaning:** People with pervert intellects behave by being servile to demoniac, devilish, and delusive nature. Therefore, their hopes, knowledge, and actions cannot be fulfilled and go in vain.

**Great souls having divine disposition**

महात्मानस्तु मां पार्थ दैवीं प्रकृतिमाश्रिताः ।
भजन्त्यनन्यमनसो ज्ञात्वा भूतादिमव्ययम् ॥ १३ ॥
सततं कीर्तयन्तो मां यतन्तश्च दृढव्रताः ।
नमस्यन्तश्च मां भक्त्या नित्ययुक्ता उपासते ॥ १४ ॥
ज्ञानयज्ञेन चाप्यन्ये यजन्तो मामुपासते ।
एकत्वेन पृथक्त्वेन बहुधा विश्वतोमुखम् ॥ १५ ॥

*Mahātmānas tu māṃ pārtha daivīṃ prakṛtim āŚrītāḥ* ।
*Bhajanty ananyamanaso jñātvā bhūtādim avyayam* ॥ *13* ॥

*Satataṃ kīrtayanto māṃ yatantaś ca dṛḍhavratāḥ* ।
*Namasyantaś ca māṃ bhaktyā nityayuktā upāsate* ॥ *14* ॥
*Jñānayajñena cāpy anye yajanto mām upāsate* ।
*Ekatvena pṛthaktvena bahudhā viśvatomukham* ॥ *15* ॥

**Meaning:** The great souls (*Mahātmā*) – having divine disposition – know Me as the imperishable source of all beings and worship Me with unswerving devotion. Always striving by being firm in vows, they prostrate before Me in devotion, glorify Me through singing, focus their mind on Me, and worship Me. Many others worship Me – who resides in all forms and thus sees everywhere – by being One with Me, or by remaining separate from Me, or by performing various Yajñas of Knowledge (*Jñānayajña*).

Some great souls like Arjuna are born with divine qualities which eventually lead them to liberation (*16.5*). They worship God by knowing His real nature and by believing that they are not separate from Him. Such great souls are naturally very rare. St. Tukārāma says that only after accumulating pure merits of many past lives, the seeker can worship God by being One with Him. Such seekers persistently engage in spiritual practices due to Sattvaguṇa. Their spiritual practice mainly consists of the Path of Devotion. They also sing praises of God and glorify Him through devotional songs (*Kirtana*). Kirtana has many forms, such as singing in a Sāmpradāyic manner as per the spiritual cult, saying devotional songs, reading the biography of God, and discussing His glory through dialogues. Those who engage in these practices can fully focus their minds on God. They are always immersed in God; they contemplate on Him and eventually evolve to realize direct Oneness with Him. St. Rāmadāsa has stated an excellent worship for experiencing Oneness everywhere. He says, "The act of not deliberately hurting a person belonging to a lower cast or inferior standing is a form of social worship (*Bhajana*)."

Lord Kṛṣṇa is directly available as the **light of Pure Knowledge** to one and all. He is constantly present in the three states of waking, dreaming, and deep-sleep. In the state of waking, God is the substratum of all kinds of qualified knowledge gained by the senses. In the state of dreaming, objects – even when not actually present – are known in the light of God alone. [Deep sleep is also known as the causal body, and one goes to dreaming and waking states from it. Even in a deep-sleep, the 'light of Pure Knowledge' is present. When a person wakes up from the deep-sleep, he remembers that there was a period of blankness in his sleep. He can remember this because it was his experience of absence (knowledge of blankness) in that state.] From the state of deep-sleep, the person goes to a dream. All objects in the dream state are created in an inexplicable manner. But the knowledge in the dream is neither created with the creation of that object nor does it enter the mind in any way. It is ever-present as Ātman. Some seekers practice the thought, "I am that light of Ātman." Some seekers discriminate between Ātman and Anātman in the beginning and later realize Oneness with Ātman by discarding all that is Anātman. Some seekers practice discrimination between real and unreal, perishable and imperishable, transient and perpetual, etc. All these practices are based on the same principle, yet some practices may be emphasized more according to the Sampradāya or individual disposition.

## Some Divine Glories of Lord Kṛṣṇa

अहं क्रतुरहं यज्ञः स्वधाहमहमौषधम् ।
मन्त्रोऽहमहमेवाज्यमहमग्निरहं हुतम् ॥ १६ ॥
पिताहमस्य जगतो माता धाता पितामहः ।
वेद्यं पवित्रमोङ्कार ऋक्साम यजुरेव च ॥ १७ ॥
गतिर्भर्ता प्रभुः साक्षी निवासः शरणं सुहृत् ।
प्रभवः प्रलयः स्थानं निधानं बीजमव्ययम् ॥ १८ ॥

तपाम्यहमहं वर्षं निगृह्णाम्युत्सृजामि च ।
अमृतं चैव मृत्युश्च सदसच्चाहमर्जुन ॥ १९ ॥

*Ahaṃ kratur ahaṃ yajñaḥ svadhāham aham auṣadham* ।
*Mantro'aham aham evājyam aham agnir ahaṃ hutam* ॥ *16* ॥
*Pitāham asya jagato mātā dhātā pitāmahaḥ* ।
*Vedyaṃ pavitram oṃkāra ṛk sāma yajur eva ca* ॥ *17* ॥
*Gatir bhartā prabhuḥ sākṣī nivāsaḥ śaraṇaṃ suhṛt* ।
*Prabhavaḥ pralayaḥ sthānaṃ nidhānaṃ bījam avyam* ॥ *18* ॥
*Tapāmy aham ahaṃ varṣaṃ nigṛṇhāmy utsṛjāmi ca* ।
*Amṛtaṃ caiva mṛtyuś ca sad asac cāham arjuna* ॥ *19* ॥

**Meaning:** Śrauta and Smārta Yajñas, food offered to ancestors in Śrāddha, medicinal herbs, Mantras, offerings like clarified butter, and oblations in the fire are all Me. I am the father, the mother, the grandfather, and the support of the world. I am all that is knowable, the pious syllable Om, Ṛgveda, Yajurveda, and Sāmaveda. I am the final goal, the nourisher, owner, witness, residence, shelter, friend, origin, sustenance, dissolution, and the imperishable seed of all. I alone give heat, withhold water, and send forth the rain. Immortality and death, existence and non-existence – all of these are Me alone.

Lord Kṛṣṇa pervades the cause, state, dissolution, and actions of all beings. Religious rituals such as paying annual homage to dead ancestors, Yajñas, Yāgas, their tools, and ingredients are all forms of God. He alone is the following three:

- ***Kārya-Brahma*** – Brahman as the effect in the form of the world
- ***Kāraṇa-Brahma*** – Brahman as the cause
- ***Kārya-Kāraṇatita Śuddha Brahma*** – Pure Brahman that transcends both cause and effect

Om, which is created from the Vedas, and all the Vedas are forms of God. God Himself executes all transactions in the world. The duality of immortality and death is not separate from Him. Śruti declares that God alone pervades everywhere in the world and beyond. He is omnipresent. St. Tukārāma says that he is accompanied by God everywhere, and it is God alone who supports him in all his endeavors. His realization is a proof of this spiritual reality. St. Rāmadāsa says that there is no place where his beloved Lord Rāma is not present. St. Tukārāma says that whenever one speaks about anything, that speech verily points to Viṭṭhala alone. [Any speech normally pertains to a Jiva or the world or Īśvara or Ātman or Brahman. All of these are Viṭṭhala, in principle. Therefore, whatever may manifest through any speech, it is Viṭṭhala Himself.]

God gives birth and nourishes all beings. He is the friend and owner of all. So, men should completely surrender to God alone as no one else is worthy of it. Surrendering to God is not the same as surrendering to the enemy after losing the war. It is also not the same as surrendering to a lender after one goes bankrupt. God is the principal director of all events in life. The very nature of the surrender to God is that the seeker should be happy in life that with whatever comes his way as per God's scheme or His direction and not complain in any manner. In this life governed by Him, the seeker should listen to His commands, worship Him, and realize Oneness with Him; this is the glory of the true surrender. The seeker should know that both joyous and grievous experiences in life are part of Blissful life. Both sides of the duality are God Himself. Lord Kṛṣṇa talks about equanimity in many places in the Gita: "One should be equanimous in joy-grief" (*2.15*), "Transcend the duality and remove jealousy from mind" (*4.22*), "One who is born is bound to die" (*2.27*), etc. Birth and death, joy and grief, etc. are part of Īśvara's governance, so they are all pervaded by God. They are pertinent to the body of a Jiva, not his true Self (Ātman). To experience this lasting, Absolute, Pure Bliss in life, the Gita teaches that "One should seek refuge in *Buddhiyoga* i.e. adhere to the firm resolve of the intellect that 'I am Brahman'(*2.49*)."

## One who only performs rituals goes to the inferior path

त्रैविद्या मां सोमपाः पूतपापा यज्ञैरिष्ट्वा स्वर्गतिं प्रार्थयन्ते ।
ते पुण्यमासाद्य सुरेन्द्रलोकमश्नन्ति दिव्यान्दिवि देवभोगान् ॥ २० ॥
ते तं भुक्त्वा स्वर्गलोकं विशालं क्षीणे पुण्ये मर्त्यलोकं विशन्ति ।
एवं त्रयीधर्ममनुप्रपन्ना गतागतं कामकामा लभन्ते ॥ २१ ॥

*Traividyā māṃ somapāḥ pūtapāpā*
*Yajñair iṣṭvā svargatiṃ prārthayante* ।
*Te puṇyam āsādya surendralokaṃ*
*Aśnanti divyān divi devabhogān* ॥ *20* ॥
*Te taṃ bhuktvā svargalokaṃ viśālaṃ*
*Kṣīṇe puṇye martyalokaṃ viśanti* ।
*Evaṃ trayīdharmam anuprapannā*
*Gatāgataṃ kāmakāmā labhante* ॥ *21* ॥

**Meaning:** The ritualistic people engage in actions as described in the three Vedas, drink juice of a plant named Soma, worship Me with Yajñas, and thereby become sinless. They then nurture the desire for heaven, attain heaven of Indra based on their accumulated merits, and enjoy the divine pleasure meant for deities. Having enjoyed heavenly pleasures, when their stock of merits comes to an end, they are reborn on the earth. Thus, by engaging in gainful or fruitive actions (Kāmya Karma) described in the Vedas, they fulfill their desires and get caught in the cycle of life and death.

This topic is explained in verses *2.42* to *2.44* earlier in the Gita. All enlightened sages and saints have discarded the idea of enjoyment of heavenly pleasures. They have ensured that the concept of heaven is merely a matter of theoretical discussion in today's world.

## The glory of a single-minded devotee

अनन्याश्चिन्तयन्तो मां ये जनाः पर्युपासते ।
तेषां नित्याभियुक्तानां योगक्षेमं वहाम्यहम् ॥ २२ ॥

*Ananyāś cintayanto māṃ ye janāḥ paryupāsate* ।
*Teṣāṃ nityābhiyuktānāṃ yogakṣemaṃ vahāmy aham* ॥ 22 ॥

**Meaning:** Some devotees constantly worship Me alone through unswerving devotion and surrender to Me. I provide them with that which they do not possess and secure for them what they already possess.

To attain that which is unattained is **Yoga** and to secure that which is obtained is ***Kṣema***. In an exceptional case, God provides for the subsistence and security of his devotee to enable him to worship God. There is a famous tale in Mahārāṣṭra where king Śivāji sent money and gifts to St. Tukārāma who was suffering in poverty. This was God alone who offered help to his great devotee Tukārāma for his day-to-day sustenance through king Śivāji as a medium. But St. Tukārāma refused to accept the gift and stayed away from the security (*Kṣema*) sent by God. Even then, his wife continued to manage their family life. St. Tukārāma has himself narrated the stories of his damaged family life in his devotional poetry. St. Jñāneśwara and his siblings sustained on the support given by society. St. Rāmadāsa worked his entire life on alms given by society, even though he was a spiritual Guru of King Śivāji.

These are worldly aspects of God's help; however, there is a far bigger spiritual side to this help. The realization that "I am Ātman" (*Yoga*) and remaining immersed in that Self-realization (*Kṣema*) are immensely important for a devotee. For spiritual *Yoga* and *Kṣema*, the devotee needs sacred Knowledge of his true Self (*4.38*). All actions come to an end in the Pure Knowledge of the true Self (*4.33*). This Self-Knowledge is attained by those who nurture unconditional faith in Lord Kṛṣṇa. Nothing needs to be attained or obtained after one realizes "I am Ātman." In the end –

तेषां सततयुक्तानां भजतां प्रीतिपूर्वकम् ।
ददामि बुद्धियोगं तं येन मामुपयान्ति ते ॥ १०-१० ॥

*Teṣāṃ satatayuktānāṃ bhajatāṃ prītipūrvakam* ।
*dadāmi buddhiyogaṃ taṃ yena mām upayānti te* ॥ *10-10* ॥

This is the Yoga of lasting spiritual welfare conferred by God. He may directly or indirectly offer worldly help to a devotee. However, He confers the spiritual Yoga – union of Jiva-Brahman – upon His devotees through His own divine power or in the form of Sadguru. St. Tukārāma has said that his beloved Viṭṭhala loves him so much that He guides Him as a Guru despite being God Himself. Lord Śrirāma graced St. Rāmadāsa by being his Guru. St. Jñāneśwara states that God considers enlightened saints as His own forms, and He Himself grants Self-Knowledge to them. God Himself ensures that His devotee – who bows down to Him, serves Him, and asks questions for spiritual welfare (*4.34*) – attains the Yoga of Self-realization. He also ensures that such a devotee remains immersed in Self-realization. The Lord says –

**सर्वधर्मान्परित्यज्य मामेकं शरणं व्रज ।**
**अहं त्वा सर्वपापेभ्यो मोक्षयिष्यामि मा शुचः ॥ १८.६६ ॥**

*Sarvadharmān parityajya mām ekaṃ śaraṇaṃ vraja* ।
*Ahaṃ tvā sarvapāpebhyo mokṣyayiṣyāmi mā śucaḥ* ॥ *18.66* ॥

The Lord takes complete care of a true devotee until he attains the highest goal of Mokṣa.

## Devotees who do not worship the incarnations of God

**येऽप्यन्यदेवता भक्ता यजन्ते श्रद्धयान्विताः ।**
**तेऽपि मामेव कौन्तेय यजन्त्यविधिपूर्वकम् ॥ २३ ॥**
**अहं हि सर्वयज्ञानां भोक्ता च प्रभुरेव च ।**
**न तु मामभिजानन्ति तत्त्वेनातश्च्यवन्ति ते ॥ २४ ॥**
**यान्ति देवव्रता देवान्पितॄन्यान्ति पितृव्रताः ।**
**भूतानि यान्ति भूतेज्या यान्ति मद्याजिनोऽपि माम् ॥ २५ ॥**

*Ye'pyanyadevatābhaktā yajante śraddhayānvitāḥ* ।
*Te'pi mām eva kaunteya yajanty avidhipūrvakam* ॥ *23* ॥
*Ahaṃ hi sarvayajñanāṃ bhoktā ca prabhur eva ca* ।
*Na tu mām abhijānanti tattvenātaś cyavanti te* ॥ *24* ॥

*Yānti devavratā devān pitṛn yānti pitṛvratāḥ* ।
*Bhūtāni yānti bhūtejyā yānti madyājino 'pi mām* ॥ *25* ॥

**Meaning:** Even those devotees who worship other deities through complete faith – although their methods are wrong – worship Me alone. For, I alone am the owner and enjoyer of all Yajñas. But these people do not understand My real nature, so they fall from their own best interest. Those who worship deities, dead ancestors, and other beings go to their planes, respectively; My worshippers verily come to Me and unite with Me.

As mentioned in verses *16-19* of this chapter, those who worship other deities like Śani, Indra, Varuṇa, etc. worship Lord Kṛṣṇa alone. This is because Kṛṣṇa alone is all deities, in essence, though they seem to be different from Him in appearances. There is a famous tale of how Kṛṣṇa stopped the worship of Indra in Gokula in His childhood. All devotees who worship other deities have worldly desires in their mind, and they worship God by remaining separate from Him. They are never curious to know the real nature of God whom they worship. In the Indian way of living, it is believed that there are 33 types (*Koṭi*) of deities in total. They are as follows: Vasu – 8, Āditya – 12, Rudra – 11, Indra – 1, Prajāpati – 1. Their powers are very limited, minimal, and trivial. So, the fruit of worshipping a deity with limited power is limited as well. These deities belong to the realm of Īśvara; worshipping them means indirectly worshipping Īśvara Himself. Even then, the worshipper gets the fruit of his worship only in accordance with his faith, devotion, and surrender (*4.11*). Such worship does not culminate in Mokṣa.

## The distinctiveness of worship of Lord Kṛṣṇa

**पत्रं पुष्पं फलं तोयं यो मे भक्त्या प्रयच्छति ।**
**तदहं भक्त्युपहृतमश्नामि प्रयतात्मनः ॥ २६ ॥**

यत्करोषि यदश्नासि यज्जुहोषि ददासि यत्।
यत्तपस्यसि कौन्तेय तत्कुरुष्व मदर्पणम् ॥ २७ ॥
शुभाशुभफलैरेवं मोक्ष्यसे कर्मबन्धनैः।
संन्यासयोगयुक्तात्मा विमुक्तो मामुपैष्यसि ॥ २८ ॥

*Patraṃ puṣpaṃ phalaṃ toyaṃ yo me bhaktyā prayacchati* ।
*Tad ahaṃ bhaktyupahṛtam aśnāmi prayatātmanaḥ* ॥ *26* ॥
*Yat karoṣi yad aśnāsi yaj juhoṣi dadāsi yat* ।
*Yat tapasyasi kaunteya tat kuruṣva madarpaṇam* ॥ *27* ॥
*Śubhāśubhaphalair evaṃ mokṣyase karmabandhanaiḥ* ।
*Saṃnyāsayogayuktātmā vimukto mām upaiṣyasi* ॥ *28* ॥

**Meaning:** If a devotee of a pure heart offers Me a leaf, a flower, a fruit, or even water with utmost devotion, I accept that holy offering. Whatever you eat, offer in sacrifice, donate, everything that you do, or whichever austerity you practice, offer it to Me. As a result, you will be freed from the bondage of actions which yield good or bad results. By practicing the yoga of renunciation of actions, you shall unite with Me and thereby be liberated.

Most people offer leaves, flowers, fruits, and water to God while worshipping. However, there is a very special significance attached to the leaf offered by Draupadi, the flower offered by Gajendra, the fruits offered by Śabari, and the water offered by Rantideva. These offerings were done with remarkable and exceptional devotion. When Pāṇḍavas were spending 12 years of exile in the forest, Draupadi was once deeply worried as sage Durvāsa could have possibly cursed her family for not feeding a large group of sages traveling with him. So, she ardently prayed to Lord Kṛṣṇa by thinking of Him as her only savior in that crucial time and lovingly offered him a little leaf stuck to the plate in her house. Kṛṣṇa saved her from that emergency due to her wholehearted, earnest devotion. Gajendra was scared for his life when he was being pulled by the crocodile under water. None of his family members helped him in this emergency. So, he prayed to Lord Viṣṇu with great intensity and offered Him a lotus available nearby. Seeing his intense devotion at that time, God liberated him. Śabari was pining to see Lord Rāma for many years as that was the only aim of her life. When He came, she offered Him simple fruits from the jungle with loving devotion. Rantideva gave the water that he owned to a thirsty traveler in a terrible drought condition, knowing that he himself may die due to lack of water. He did this as he was seeing God in every being and considered it his duty to serve God in the form of the traveler. These profound emotions are supremely valuable. Leaves, flowers are ordinary tools used to manifest the emotion and devotion inside the devotee.

There is one more perspective to look at the ritual of worship. The beauty and sweet fragrance of flowers offered to a sculpture please the God residing in the worshipper himself. If the worshipper has indeed made his offerings with great love and single-minded focus, the Lord residing in his own heart heartily accepts those offerings. In other words, the devotee himself becomes happy by offerings to God, which is one of the main objectives of the worship.

These verses also mention offering everything in life to God without any reserve. The seeker performs many actions through his mind as well as his body which is regulated by the mind. If he offers all these actions to God, it is the Yoga of natural offering (*Sahajārpaṇayoga*). As a result, he unites with the internal God, Ātman. In this state, the actions done by the seeker may be good or bad; but since they are offered to God, they do not have the capacity to yield fruits. St Jñāneśwara says in his poetry Haripāṭha that by chanting regularly, all sins are eradicated. This is because when chanting is done with devotion while performing actions, all actions are automatically offered to God. By engaging in worship of this kind, the seeker achieves everything that can be attained by formal Saṅnyāsa without actually taking the vows of monastic life.

## The evenness of God

समोऽहं सर्वभूतेषु न मे द्वेष्योऽस्ति न प्रियः ।
ये भजन्ति तु मां भक्त्या मयि ते तेषु चाप्यहम् ॥ २९ ॥

*Samo'haṃ sarvabhūteṣu na me dveṣyo'sti na priyaḥ* ।
*Ye bhajanti tu māṃ bhaktyā mayi te teṣu cāpy aham* ॥ *29* ॥

**Meaning:** I am the same to all beings. No one is dear or hateful to Me. However, those who worship Me with utmost devotion are in Me, and I am in them.

This speech of Lord Kṛṣṇa is highly assuring and comforting for all seekers. One should not behold God as if He is a human being. God is never partial to anyone. The joy and grief experienced by people are results of their own past deeds; God only confers those results upon them in an impartial manner. The Lord has said many times to Arjuna, "You are dear to Me," "You are My friend," etc. Arjuna is a true devotee; therefore, he resides in the Lord's heart, and the Lord resides in his heart. One who is a real devotee will become similar to Arjuna. The devotion of the devotee is of utmost importance, and God is not partial towards anyone in any manner.

## Even an evil person has a chance to redeem himself

अपि चेत्सुदुराचारो भजते मामनन्यभाक् ।
साधुरेव स मन्तव्यः सम्यग्व्यवसितो हि सः ॥ ३० ॥
क्षिप्रं भवति धर्मात्मा शश्वच्छान्तिं निगच्छति ।
कौन्तेय प्रतिजानीहि न मे भक्तः प्रणश्यति ॥ ३१ ॥
मां हि पार्थ व्यपाश्रित्य येऽपि स्युः पापयोनयः ।
स्त्रियो वैश्यास्तथा शूद्रास्तेऽपि यान्ति परां गतिम् ॥ ३२ ॥
किं पुनर्ब्राह्मणाः पुण्या भक्ता राजर्षयस्तथा ।
अनित्यमसुखं लोकमिमं प्राप्य भजस्व माम् ॥ ३३ ॥

*Api cet sudurācāro bhajate mām ananyabhāk* ।
*Sādhur eva sa mantavyaḥ samyag vyavasito hi saḥ* ॥ *30* ॥
*Kṣipraṃ bhavati dharmātmā śaśvacchāntiṃ nigacchhati* ।
*Kaunteya pratijānīhi na me bhaktaḥ praṇaśyati* ॥ *31* ॥

*Māṃ hi pārtha vyapāśrītya ye'pi syuḥ pāpayonayaḥ* ।
*Striyo vaiśyās tathā śūdrās te'pi yānti parāṃ gatim* ॥ 32 ॥
*Kiṃ punar brāhmaṇāḥ puṇyā bhaktā rājarṣayas tathā* ।
*Anityam asukhaṃ lokam imaṃ prāpya bhajasva mām* ॥ 33 ॥

**Meaning:** If a person – no matter how sinful he is – worships Me with single-minded devotion, he should be treated as righteous and pure since his intellect is rightly resolved. In such cases, he soon becomes a noble man and attains lasting peace. Know for certain that My devotee never degrades or perishes. People who surrender to Me attain the supreme goal, even if they are of inferior birth like women, Vaiśya, Śūdra, etc. Needless to say, holy Brāhmins and royal sages shall attain the same supreme goal if they, too, are virtuous in nature. Therefore, being born in this transient and joyless world, you should wholeheartedly worship Me. [Note: People from Śūdra (service), Vaiśya (business) classes and women are generally called inferior because most of them have Rajoguṇa and Tamoguṇa in abundance and less Sattvaguṇa that is required for worship.]

There is no reason to hold any grudge against a malicious, sinful person and disdain him. Even he has an equal chance to reform himself completely, engage in the worship of God, and lead himself to his lasting welfare. Vālya, the dacoit, was transformed into the famous sage Vālmiki by surrendering to God and continuously chanting His Mantra. This is not a mere fancy-tale, but a reality. Due to the sheer influence of worshipping the Lord, imprints of the past life of a person are eradicated, and a new chapter of life begins. A person who was a destroyer of Dharma in the past becomes the greatest follower of Dharma and attains eternal peace. Any seeker who worships God attains the supreme goal in due course of time.

It is also necessary to think about the four social classes (Varṇas), women, and sinful people mentioned in this verse in the context of the social setting in Mahābhārata's era. Women still need to follow some constraints in today's world due to their femininity, or else, they become vulnerable to attacks. This is a stark reality of today's life, even though it is gruesome. It should be taken into consideration while defining the spiritual path for women as well. The gist of this discussion is that any person with good disposition can wholeheartedly surrender to God and attain the highest goal with single-minded devotion, even in today's social setup.

**The essence of the chapter**

मन्मना भव मद्भक्तो मद्याजी मां नमस्कुरु ।
मामेवैष्यसि युक्त्वैवमात्मानं मत्परायणः ॥ ३४ ॥

*Manmanā bhava madbhakto madyājī māṃ namaskuru* ।
*Māṃ evaiṣyasi yuktvaivam ātmānaṃ matparāyaṇaḥ* ॥ *34* ॥

**Meaning:** Think about Me alone, be My devotee, offer everything to Me, and worship Me. Being thus absorbed in Me in every which way, if you contemplate on Me alone, you shall come and unite with Me.

ॐ तत्सदिति श्रीमद्भगवद्गीतासूपनिषत्सु ब्रह्मविद्यायां योगशास्त्रे श्रीकृष्णार्जुनसंवादे राजविद्याराजगुह्ययोगो नाम नवमोऽध्यायः ॥

*Om Tatsaditi Śrimadbhagvadgitāsūpaniṣatsu Brahmavidyāyāṃ Yogaśāstre Śrīkṛṣṇārjunasaṅvāde Rājavidyārājaguhyayogo Nāma Navamo'dhyāyaḥ* ॥

This verse is the key to live a life by being immersed in Lord Kṛṣṇa. It is the prime aphorism of the philosophy of the Gita. It is also the meaning of the conclusion of Kṛṣṇa's teaching in verse 18.65. The Lord refers to Himself as '***Māṃ*** (Me)' six times in this last verse. The seeker should seek God through all his desires. God is only one, so there are no options to Him. The seeker's mind should remain steady in God. All offerings in the

Yajña of life should go to God, and He alone should be worshipped in different ways. The seeker should surrender to Kṛṣṇa instead of surrendering to worldly life. Such a seeker whose life is filled with Kṛṣṇa can externally engage in his duties while internally remaining immersed in Kṛṣṇa. This can be best understood with the example of dancing which is performed on the rhythm of the background score. People in the audience are focused on that dance; however, the dancer is more focused on the rhythm. Likewise, a driver can drive a vehicle despite all distractions around him. A woman and a man can lead their lives without explicitly being aware that "I am a woman" or "I am a man," respectively. Femininity or masculinity comes naturally to a person. In the same way, divine awareness that "I am God" can be steadily internalized, and one can even fight a giant war with this awareness. The specific awareness that "I am a man" or "I am a woman" awakens in particular situations. Likewise, a devotee can realize his own divinity while beholding God, worshipping Him, chanting His Mantra, listening to His stories, or learning the scriptures of Vedānta. The rest of the time, he can perfectly lead his worldly life while being aware of his own divine nature in the mind. Lord Kṛṣṇa has not given importance to meditating 24x7 or remaining immersed in God and thus disregarding one's worldly life, or being established in non-duality and thus losing the awareness of the surrounding duality. God does not consider such life as an ideal form of human life.

Chapter 10

# Divine Glories

## ॥ विभूतियोगः (Vibhūtiyoga) ॥

Lord Kṛṣṇa is teaching the philosophy in this chapter which is in Arjuna's best interest. In general, the entire Gita is focused on the lasting welfare of human beings. The true God is subtle, formless, attributeless, and as such, He cannot be known even by deities or great Ṛṣis. The tenth chapter brings forth imperceivable God in a perceivable form for all seekers. Any manifestation which is glorious, divine, sublime, and stunning in any manner is the Glory (Vibhūti) of the Lord. We can even see these glorious forms in today's world. E.g. Einstein in scientists, atomic bomb in weapons, Kohinoor in diamonds, emperor Śivāji in kings, Himālaya in mountains, Vallabhbhai Patel in ministers, Don Bradman in cricket, Kalidāsa in poets, Niagara in waterfalls, Tirupati in holy places, Śrīmad Bhāgavatam in Purāṇas, Martin Luther King in reformers, Grand Canyon in canyons, and Tājamahal in architecture are all divine manifestations of the Lord. The seeker should also know that the dreadful forms described in the 11th chapter are His Glories as well. Knowing with certainty that beauty and atrociousness are both Him, the seeker can tone down his reactions and respond to all situations with a steady mind in a calm, appropriate manner. In today's hypercompetitive world, the seeker can think, "Anyone who is better than me or superior to me is a manifestation of the Lord." Such thinking can assist him in being composed and content. This thought-process is not meant to repress or inhibit the seeker; rather, it is meant to prevent his futile efforts to outperform others. Any person – who is meant to excel – is bound to proceed on his path without waiting for anyone else. The teaching above that "One should see another superior or better person as the manifestation of the Lord" is mainly meant for those who don't have the capacity to rise higher through their own efforts. There are millions of such people in the world.

**Knowledge of Lord Kṛṣṇa and its influence**

*श्रीभगवानुवाच ।*

भूय एव महाबाहो श्रृणु मे परमं वचः ।
यत्तेऽहं प्रीयमाणाय वक्ष्यामि हितकाम्यया ॥ १ ॥
न मे विदुः सुरगणाः प्रभवं न महर्षयः ।
अहमादिर्हि देवानां महर्षीणां च सर्वशः ॥ २ ॥
यो मामजमनादिं च वेत्ति लोकमहेश्वरम् ।
असम्मूढः स मर्त्येषु सर्वपापैः प्रमुच्यते ॥ ३ ॥

*Śrībhagavānuvāca* ।

*Bhūya eva mahābāho śṛṇu me paramaṃ vacaḥ* ।
*Yatte'haṃ prīyamāṇāya vakṣyāmi hitakāmyayā* ॥ *1* ॥
*Na me viduḥ suragaṇāḥ prabhavaṃ na maharṣayaḥ* ।
*Aham ādir hi devānāṃ maharṣīṇāṃ ca sarvaśaḥ* ॥ *2* ॥
*Yo mām ajam anādiṃ ca vetti lokamaheśvaram* ।
*Asaṃmūḍhaḥ sa martyeṣu sarvapāpaiḥ pramucyate* ॥ *3* ॥

**Meaning:** (Śrībhagavān said) O valiant Arjuna! Listen to My priceless spiritual teachings one more time. I am teaching what is in your best interest since you love Me immensely. Even the greatest of Ṛṣis and deities cannot comprehend My real nature and My Saguṇa form through which I manifest Myself as a mere play (Līlā). This is because I am the primordial source (cause) of them all. A wise person who knows Me as birthless, beginningless, and the governor of all worlds – he amongst all men is liberated from all sins.

To know the true nature of Lord Kṛṣṇa, one needs to feel immense love for Him. Love alone helps the seeker attain the supreme goal of Mokṣa. Just as a baby in a womb cannot know his mother, all humans, deities, and great Ṛṣis in the universe cannot know Brahman – the true nature of Kṛṣṇa. A mother is the cause of the baby in her womb. Similarly, Brahman is the imaginary cause of the world as it is the substratum of the world. Brahman itself manifests as Īśvara and thereafter incarnates in many ways merely as a play, none of which may be imagined by any being. In Śrīmad Bhāgavatam, chapter 31 of the 11th section beautifully describes the glorious way in which Lord Kṛṣṇa left the earth and disappeared along with his body. By the grace of the Sadguru, the seeker can gain comprehensive knowledge of spiritual concepts like Brahman, Īśvara, incarnations of God, the illusionary nature of the world, the Jiva, and his union with Brahman. Such a wise seeker is liberated from ignorance which itself is a sin.

**The manifestations of various qualities from the Lord**

बुद्धिर्ज्ञानमसम्मोहः क्षमा सत्यं दमः शमः ।
सुखं दुःखं भवोऽभावो भयं चाभयमेव च ॥ ४ ॥
अहिंसा समता तुष्टिस्तपो दानं यशोऽयशः ।
भवन्ति भावा भूतानां मत्त एव पृथग्विधाः ॥ ५ ॥
महर्षयः सप्त पूर्वे चत्वारो मनवस्तथा ।
मद्भावा मानसा जाता येषां लोक इमाः प्रजाः ॥ ६ ॥

*Buddhir jñānam asaṃmohaḥ kṣamā satyaṃ damaḥ śamaḥ* ।
*Sukhaṃ duḥkhaṃ bhavo'bhāvo bhayaṃ cābhayam eva ca* ॥ 4 ॥
*Ahiṃsā samatā tuṣṭis tapo dānaṃ yaśo'yaśaḥ* ।
*Bhavanti bhāvā bhūtānāṃ matta eva pṛthagvidhāḥ* ॥ 5 ॥
*Maharṣayaḥ sapta pūrve catvāro manavas tathā* ।
*Madbhāvā mānasā jātā yeṣāṃ loka imāḥ prajāḥ* ॥ 6 ॥

**Meaning:** Intellect, knowledge, non-attachment, forgiveness, truth, controlling the senses and the mind, joy, grief, existence, non-existence, fear, fearlessness, non-violence, evenness, satisfaction, austerities, donation, success, failure – these and other similar qualities of beings arise from Me. The seven great Ṛṣis, the four sons of Brahmadeva – Sanaka, Sanandana, Sanātana, and Sanatkumara – who were created prior to the Ṛṣis, and the fourteen Manus are My glories. They are born from My resolve. All beings in today's world have come forth from them. [Manu is the archetypal man or the progenitor of humanity as per the early texts of Hinduism.]

**The result of this knowledge**

एतां विभूतिं योगं च मम यो वेत्ति तत्त्वतः ।
सोऽविकम्पेन योगेन युज्यते नात्र संशयः ॥ ७ ॥

*Etāṃ vibhūtiṃ yogaṃ ca mama yo vetti tattvataḥ* ।
*So'vikampena yogena yujyate nātra saṃśayaḥ* ॥ 7 ॥

**Meaning:** Whosoever knows the underlying principle of My Divine Glories (Vibhūtis) and My power of Yoga, he undoubtedly attains My real nature through his unswerving devotion.

The verses 4-7 mentioned above teach us the practice of seeing Lord Kṛṣṇa permeated in all aspects of life. Every seeker needs traits like the ability to control his mind and senses for his spiritual progress, and he receives these good qualities from Kṛṣṇa. He also receives success and failure, fame and infamy, etc., which are part of his routine worldly life, from Kṛṣṇa. Thus, all these aspects – whether spiritual or worldly – are forms of Kṛṣṇa. The seeker should worship Lord Kṛṣṇa for his spiritual progress, and, at the same time, peacefully deal with all worldly situations as His wish. Every seeker is constantly faced with obstacles and difficulties in worldly life. To remove these obstacles, He should directly worship Lord Kṛṣṇa and pray to Him to attain His grace. Kṛṣṇa resides in the hearts of all beings. He instantly listens to the prayers and confers the results upon the seeker at the right time. Whatever the seeker receives after praying to Kṛṣṇa is the fruit of his prayer. Ordinary people invariably feel helpless in many political situations in a country like India. The rulers in power who are responsible for justice are often unjust to ordinary people. However, the seeker should know for certain that the ultimate supreme power belongs to Lord Kṛṣṇa. Despite knowing this, he should continue to take utmost efforts in all actions pertaining to day-to-day life, and, at the same time, continue praying to the Lord in his mind.

St. Rāmadāsa says that "Intelligence is the gift of God." St. Tukārāma says that "A person can sharpen his intellect by chanting a Mantra of God, and then he can comprehend the incomprehensible." Lord Kṛṣṇa assures his devotees that He bestows spiritual disposition – the intellect that can abide in the true Self, Ātman – upon those devotees who surrender to Him completely so they can unite with His real nature (*10.10*). The creation and destruction of the universe as well as the birth and death of every individual originate from Him. Thus, these events are verily Kṛṣṇa just the way they are. Equanimous mind and traits like satisfaction, composure are also God, and hence the seeker should remember Him when he recognizes these traits in him. He should remember God alone in moments of fear and grief. The seeker who can conquer his mind and control his senses is not supposed to take pride in his ability to do so; instead, he should learn that these traits are none other than Kṛṣṇa.

All beings in the world are born of the seven great Ṛṣis and great sages, and these originators themselves belong to Kṛṣṇa. Therefore, all beings are owned by the Lord the way they are. The relationships such as husband and wife, brother and sister, friend and enemy, local and foreigner, etc. are created only according to His governance. The seeker is expected to nurture these relationships in day-to-day life and also confront the relatives where necessary, while being aware in mind that all his relatives and relationships are Kṛṣṇa, in essence. He should also abandon attachment to worldly matters and the feeling of doership. The seeker who understands the real nature of Śrīkṛṣṇa, learns the philosophical gist of His incarnation, recognizes the incredible power of His Yogamāyā, and constantly worships Him with intent devotion, will certainly be One with Kṛṣṇa in due course. There is no need to question it or be astonished about it.

**The glory of Krsna's devotees**

अहं सर्वस्य प्रभवो मत्तः सर्वं प्रवर्तते ।
इति मत्वा भजन्ते मां बुधा भावसमन्विताः ॥ ८ ॥
मच्चित्ता मद्गतप्राणा बोधयन्तः परस्परम् ।
कथयन्तश्च मां नित्यं तुष्यन्ति च रमन्ति च ॥ ९ ॥
तेषां सततयुक्तानां भजतां प्रीतिपूर्वकम् ।
ददामि बुद्धियोगं तं येन मामुपयान्ति ते ॥ १० ॥
तेषामेवानुकम्पार्थमहमज्ञानजं तमः ।
नाशयाम्यात्मभावस्थो ज्ञानदीपेन भास्वता ॥ ११ ॥

*Ahaṃ sarvasya prabhavo mattaḥ sarvaṃ pravartate* ।
*Iti matvā bhajante māṃ budhā bhāvasamanvitāḥ* ॥ *8* ॥
*Maccittā madgataprāṇā bodhayantaḥ parasparam* ।
*Kaṭhayantaś ca māṃ nityaṃ tuṣyanti ca ramanti ca* ॥ *9* ॥
*Teṣāṃ satatayuktānāṃ bhajatāṃ prītipūrvakam* ।
*dadāmi buddhiyogaṃ taṃ yena māṃ upayānti te* ॥ *10* ॥
*Teṣām evānukampārtham aham ajñānajaṃ tamaḥ* ।
*nāśayāmy ātmabhāvastho jñānadīpena bhāsvatā* ॥ *11* ॥

**Meaning:** I am the origin (cause) of many multiverses. They are activated to function due to Me alone. Knowing this, the wise devotees constantly worship Me with utmost faith. Such devotees contemplate on Me, take arduous efforts to attain Me, discuss My real nature with each other, and tell glories of My incarnations to others. Being content in this way, they revel in Me. To those people whose mind is attached to Me through love, I grant the intelligence to comprehend My real nature. As a result, they come to Me and become One with Me. I, who continuously dwell in their hearts, illumine the lamp of Knowledge to grace them and destroy the darkness of ignorance in them.

These four verses are essential for a worldly seeker. The glory of Lord Kṛṣṇa – with and without form (*Saguṇa* and *Nirguṇa*) – is indeed worth knowing and describing to others. There is a remarkable confluence of emotion and intelligence i.e. faith in God and knowledge of His real nature in these verses. For example, St. Tukārāma asks an upfront question to his beloved deity Viṭṭhala, "We are the same in essence. So why cannot I be just like You?" The mystery behind this question is revealed in these verses. Just like Viṭṭhala, St. Tukārāma is both Saguṇa and Nirguṇa. Every seeker should make a resolve that he, too, is God or Brahman and constantly adhere to the resolve. The seeker who may not have a natural inclination to love God can learn to love Him only by His grace. To earn God's grace, he should behold His Saguṇa form, describe stories from His life, sing praises of His bravery, relish His affection for devotees, visit holy places, and engage in His worship every day. The seeker, who thus seeks God with increasing love, will have intelligence conferred upon him by God through His power of *Yogamāyā*.

The devotee can attain Self-Knowledge only by the grace of God. This can happen through a specific sequence of events mentioned in Chapter 2. The tale of St. Nāmadeva is famous in this regard. By the grace of Viṭṭhala, certain events happened in Nāmadeva's life through the medium of St. Goroba. As a result, Nāmadeva found his Guru in St. Visobā Khecara; and thereafter, he learnt about all-pervasive, omnipresent God, Brahman. Nāmadeva was known for his friendship with Saguṇa Viṭṭhala and total devotion to Viṭṭhala. He was known to converse daily with the idol of Viṭṭhala. From that stage, he evolved to learn the real Nirguṇa nature of Viṭṭhala who is beyond speech or conversation. He became One with God.

God does not confer intelligence upon the devotee through some external experiment; rather, it is God Himself dwelling in the heart of every being who – in the form of *Sadguru* – sets in motion a chain of events that leads the devotee towards spiritual disposition or spiritual intelligence (*Buddhiyoga*). This simply means that God helps the devotee abide in the firm resolve that "I am Brahman." Sadguru is himself Brahman. He is famously described as:

**तत्त्वमस्यादि लक्ष्यं ।**

*Tattvamasyādi Lakśyaṃ* ।

In the Vedāntic Mahāvākya *Tat-Tvam-Asi*, Sadguru is the core meaning of the word **Tat**, Brahman.

## Lord Kṛṣṇa as known by Arjuna

***अर्जुन उवाच ।***

**परं ब्रह्म परं धाम पवित्रं परमं भवान् ।**
**पुरुषं शाश्वतं दिव्यमादिदेवमजं विभुम् ॥ १२ ॥**
**आहुस्त्वामृषयः सर्वे देवर्षिर्नारदस्तथा ।**
**असितो देवलो व्यासः स्वयं चैव ब्रवीषि मे ॥ १३ ॥**
**सर्वमेतदृतं मन्ये यन्मां वदसि केशव ।**
**न हि ते भगवन्व्यक्तिं विदुर्देवा न दानवाः ॥ १४ ॥**
**स्वयमेवात्मनात्मानं वेत्थ त्वं पुरुषोत्तम ।**
**भूतभावन भूतेश देवदेव जगत्पते ॥ १५ ॥**

*Arjuna uvāca* ।

*Paraṃ brahma paraṃ dhāma pavitraṃ paramaṃ bhavān* ।
*Puruṣaṃ śāśvataṃ divyam ādidevam ajaṃ vibhum* ॥ 12 ॥
*Āhus tvām ṛṣayaḥ sarve devarṣir nāradas tathā* ।
*Asito devalo vyāsaḥ svayaṃ caiva bravīṣi me* ॥ 13 ॥
*Sarvam etad ṛtaṃ manye yan māṃ vādasi keśava* ।
*Na hi te bhagavan vyaktiṃ vidur devā na dānavāḥ* ॥ 14 ॥
*Svayam evātmanātmānaṃ vettha tvaṃ puruṣottama* ।
*Bhūtabhāvana bhūteśa devadeva jagatpate* ॥ 15 ॥

**Meaning:** (Arjuna said) O Lord! You are supreme Brahman, supreme abode, and supremely pious. All Ṛṣis address you as the Divine Puruṣa, the primeval God, eternal, birthless, and omnipresent. Great sages like Nārada, Asita, Devala, and Vyāsa acclaim the same fact. Now You Yourself say the same to me. I firmly believe that these statements are true in entirety. O Lord! Neither gods nor demons know your Divine birth (*Līlāvigraha*). O creator of all beings! O owner of all beings, the Supreme God of all gods, and governor of the world! O the best of all beings! You alone know Yourself.

Incarnated Saguṇa Kṛṣṇa can be seen in a human form, yet He is birthless. This is the glory of His Divine birth. One needs a great fortune to understand this fact. His incarnation, life, and disappearance are indeed highly mysterious. He is all-pervasive despite being in a form. His birth and actions are divine. All noted Ṛṣis acclaim these facts. Lord has also said the same things about Himself. Other than Himself, there is no one else who knows His true nature.

## Arjuna's prayer to Lord Kṛṣṇa

वक्तुमर्हस्यशेषेण दिव्या ह्यात्मविभूतयः ।
याभिर्विभूतिभिर्लोकानिमांस्त्वं व्याप्य तिष्ठसि ॥ १६ ॥
कथं विद्यामहं योगिंस्त्वां सदा परिचिन्तयन् ।
केषु केषु च भावेषु चिन्त्योऽसि भगवन्मया ॥ १७ ॥
विस्तरेणात्मनो योगं विभूतिं च जनार्दन ।
भूयः कथय तृप्तिर्हि शृण्वतो नास्ति मेऽमृतम् ॥ १८ ॥

*Vaktum arhasy aśeṣeṇa divyā hy ātmavibhūtayaḥ* ।
*Yābhir vibhūtibhir lokān imāṃs tvaṃ vyāpya tiṣṭhasi* ॥ *16* ॥
*Kaṭhaṃ vidyām ahaṃ yogiṃs tvāṃ sadā paricintayan* ।
*Keṣu keṣu ca bhāveṣu cintyo'si bhagavan mayā* ॥ *17* ॥
*Vistareṇātmano yogaṃ vibhūtiṃ ca janārdana* ।
*bhūyaḥ Kaṭhaya tṛptir hi śṛṇvato nāsti me'mṛtam* ॥ *18* ॥

**Meaning:** You have permeated all these worlds through many Divine Glories (Vibhūti). You alone are eligible to describe these Divine Glories to me. O Lord of the Yoga! How may I know you by constantly thinking about You? And O Lord! Which different forms of Yours are right for me to contemplate on? O Lord! Tell me in detail Your power of Yogamāyā and Divine Glories. For, I am not yet satiated by Your speech – as sweet as nectar – despite hearing it over and over again.

Lord Kṛṣṇa was not available all the time in person even for Arjuna to directly behold Him. For ordinary people like us in today's age, He certainly is not available for direct contact, nor will He be available in the future. So, to constantly think about Him, it is necessary to learn about His many manifestations, forms, and their whereabouts and other details. If a seeker learns to see many forms of God, he is more likely to contemplate on God through those forms. If a devotee who is separate from God is indeed able to see Divine Glories of God in many places in many forms, then it will be easy for him to unite with God.

## The Divine Glories of Lord Kṛṣṇa

श्रीभगवानुवाच
हन्त ते कथयिष्यामि दिव्या ह्यात्मविभूतयः ।
प्राधान्यतः कुरुश्रेष्ठ नास्त्यन्तो विस्तरस्य मे ॥ १९ ॥
अहमात्मा गुडाकेश सर्वभूताशयस्थितः ।
अहमादिश्च मध्यं च भूतानामन्त एव च ॥ २० ॥
आदित्यानामहं विष्णुर्ज्योतिषां रविरंशुमान् ।
मरीचिर्मरुतामस्मि नक्षत्राणामहं शशी ॥ २१ ॥
वेदानां सामवेदोऽस्मि देवानामस्मि वासवः ।
इन्द्रियाणां मनश्चास्मि भूतानामस्मि चेतना ॥ २२ ॥

*Śrībhagavān uvāca* ।
*Hanta te Kaṭhayiṣyāmi divyā hy ātmavibhūtayaḥ* ।
*Prādhānyataḥ kuruśreṣtha nāsty anto vistarasya me* ॥ *19* ॥
*Aham ātmā guḍākeśa sarvabhūtāśayasthitaḥ* ।
*Aham ādiś ca madhyaṃ ca bhūtānām anta eva ca* ॥ *20* ॥

*Ādityānām ahaṃ viṣṇur jyotiṣāṃ ravir aṃśumān* ।
*Marīcir marutām asmi nakṣatrāṇām ahaṃ śaśī* ॥ *21* ॥
*Vedānāṃ sāmavedo'smi devānām asmi vāsavaḥ* ।
*Indriyāṇāṃ manaś cāsmi bhūtānām asmi cetanā* ॥ *22* ॥

**Meaning:** (Śrībhagavān said) It would have been nice if it were indeed possible to narrate all My Divine Glories. I shall describe the most prominent and divine Glories to you now since there is no end to My expanse and manifestations. I am Ātman, the Self, dwelling in the hearts of all beings. So also, I am the beginning, the middle, and the end of all beings. Among the twelve Ādityas, I am Viṣṇu; among many confluences of stars, I am the sun; among Maruts, I am Marici; and among asterisms, I am the moon. I am Sāmaveda in the Vedas, Indra in all gods, the mind in all organs, and consciousness in all beings.

These verses mention many familiar objects in human life. One may recognize that they are Glories of Lord Kṛṣṇa in specific contexts. E.g. my own mind and the knowledge in it are the Glories of Kṛṣṇa. The game of creation, sustenance, and destruction – constantly seen in surroundings – is His Glory as well. The sun, the moon, the wind, the verses of Sāmaveda, the mind, consciousness, and Indra are frequently encountered in day-to-day life. These Glories pertaining to an individual and the world are all Lord Kṛṣṇa Himself. There are many ways of worshipping His Glories: worshipping the sun and the moon on festival days; worshipping Indra and Vāyu for rain and wind, respectively; not hurting anyone's feelings; and singing the verses of Sāmaveda. [Indra is the king of gods who is also the deity of rain. Worshipping Indra, Vāyu, etc. was prevalent in the era of Mahābhārata.]

## Some more Divine Glories

रुद्राणां शङ्करश्चास्मि वित्तेशो यक्षरक्षसाम् ।
वसूनां पावकश्चास्मि मेरुः शिखरिणामहम् ॥ २३ ॥

पुरोधसां च मुख्यं मां विद्धि पार्थ बृहस्पतिम् ।
सेनानीनामहं स्कन्दः सरसामस्मि सागरः ॥ २४ ॥
महर्षीणां भृगुरहं गिरामस्म्येकमक्षरम् ।
यज्ञानां जपयज्ञोऽस्मि स्थावराणां हिमालयः ॥ २५ ॥

*Rudrāṇāṃ śaṃkaraś cāsmi vitteśo yakṣarakṣasām ।*
*Vasūnāṃ pāvakaś cāsmi meruḥ śikhariṇām aham ॥ 23 ॥*
*Purodhasāṃ ca mukhyaṃ māṃ viddhi pārtha bṛhaspatim ।*
*Senānīnām ahaṃ skāṇḍaḥ sarasām asmi sāgaraḥ ॥ 24 ॥*
*Maharṣīṇāṃ bhṛgur ahaṃ girām asmy ekam akṣaram ।*
*Yajñanāṃ japayajño'smi sthāvarāṇāṃ himālayaḥ ॥ 25 ॥*

**Meaning:** Among the eleven Rudras, I am Śaṅkara; among Yakṣas and Rakṣasas, I am Kubera; among the eight Vasus, I am fire; and among mountains, I am Himālaya. I am Bṛhaspati in priests, Skanda in generals of the army, and ocean in water-reservoirs. I am Bhṛgu in all great Ṛṣis, the syllable Om in words, the Yajña of chanting (Japa) in all Yajñas, and Himālaya in all immovable things.

There are numerous holy places of Lord Śaṅkara and Lord Viṣṇu in India. They are all Glories of Lord Kṛṣṇa. Seeing an ocean is the same as beholding Lord Kṛṣṇa. The syllable Om, which is implicitly a part of all words, is verily a form of Kṛṣṇa. Therefore, one beholds Lord Kṛṣṇa every time he reads, writes, or listens to scriptures. There are many forms of Yajña, but chanting a Mantra of a deity is superior to all of them. Due to chanting, the seeker unites with the Lord whose Mantra is chanted. The great sage Bhṛgu who was qualified to evaluate gods is a Divine manifestation of Kṛṣṇa. Similarly, one feels joy upon seeing Himālaya since Himālaya is nothing but Kṛṣṇa.

## More Divine Glories

अश्वत्थः सर्ववृक्षाणां देवर्षीणां च नारदः ।
गन्धर्वाणां चित्ररथः सिद्धानां कपिलो मुनिः ॥ २६ ॥
उच्चैःश्रवसमश्वानां विद्धि माममृतोद्भवम् ।

ऐरावतं गजेन्द्राणां नराणां च नराधिपम् ॥ २७ ॥
आयुधानामहं वज्रं धेनूनामस्मि कामधुक् ।
प्रजनश्चास्मि कन्दर्पः सर्पाणामस्मि वासुकिः ॥ २८ ॥

*Aśvatthaḥ sarvavṛkṣāṇāṃ devarṣīṇāṃ ca nāradaḥ* ।
*Gandharvāṇāṃ citrarathaḥ siddhānāṃ kapilo muniḥ* ॥ 26 ॥
*Uccaiḥśravasam aśvānāṃ viddhi māṃ amṛtodbhavam* ।
*Airāvataṃ gajendrāṇāṃ narāṇāṃ ca narādhipam* ॥ 27 ॥
*Āyudhānām ahaṃ vajraṃ dhenūnām asmi kāmadhuk* ।
*Prajanaś cāsmi kāṇḍarpaḥ sarpāṇām asmi vāsukiḥ* ॥ 28 ॥

**Meaning:** Among all trees, I am the Aśvattha tree; among divine sages, I am Nārada; among Gandharvas, I am Citraratha – the king of Gandharvas; and amongst all enlightened people, I am Kapila. I am the horse named Ucchaiḥśravā in horses, Airāvata in elephants, and king in all men. I am Vajra in weapons, Kāmadhenu in cows, and Vāsuki in serpents. I am Kāmadeva who is responsible for creating progeny. [Ucchaiḥśravā and Airāvata rose along with Amṛta from the churning of the milk-ocean]

The tree of Aśvattha (Sacred Fig) is always laden with leaves, Nārada is renowned for indirectly helping in Īśvara's work, Citraratha Gandharva was known for defeating Karṇa and Kauravas, and Kapila muni was a famous follower of the Vedas. They are Divine forms of Lord Kṛṣṇa. The horse Ucchaiḥśravā and the elephant Airāvata in heaven and the king who governs his people are all Kṛṣṇa Himself. The weapon 'Vajra' was created from the extraordinary offering of sage Dadhichi; the Kāmadhenu cow is known for fulfilling all desires; Kāmadeva is the god who creates natural attraction between a male and a female, and he resides in all beings; and the serpent Vāsuki was used by gods as a rope at the time of churning the ocean – they are all Divine Glories of Kṛṣṇa. [Sage Dadhichi is mainly known for sacrificing his life and offering his bones to the Devas who could make the weapon called Vajra from his bones; The devas then defeated the Asuras with this Vajra and reclaimed their place in heaven.]

## More Divine Glories

अनन्तश्चास्मि नागानां वरुणो यादसामहम् ।
पितृणामर्यमा चास्मि यमः संयमतामहम् ॥ २९ ॥
प्रह्लादश्चास्मि दैत्यानां कालः कलयतामहम् ।
मृगाणां च मृगेन्द्रोऽहं वैनतेयश्च पक्षिणाम् ॥ ३० ॥
पवनः पवतामस्मि रामः शस्त्रभृतामहम् ।
झषाणां मकरश्चास्मि स्रोतसामस्मि जाह्नवी ॥ ३१ ॥

*Anantaś cāsmi nāgānāṃ varuṇo yādasām aham* ।
*Pitṛṇām aryamā cāsmi yamaḥ saṅyamatām aham* ॥ *29* ॥
*Pralhādaś cāsmi daityānāṃ kālaḥ kalayatām aham* ।
*Mṛgāṇāṃ ca mṛgendro'haṃ vainateyaś ca pakṣiṇām* ॥ *30* ॥
*Pavanaḥ pavatām asmi rāmaḥ śastrabhṛtām aham* ।
*Jhaṣāṇāṃ makaraś cāsmi strotasām asmi jāhnavī* ॥ *31* ॥

**Meaning:** Among serpents, I am the Śeṣa, the resting place of Viṣṇu; I am Varuṇa, the lord of water, who gives life to aquatic animals; among dead ancestors, I am Āryama; and among those who punish others, I am Yama, the lord of death. I am Prahlāda in demons, time (fortnight, month, etc.) in time reckoners, lion in animals, and eagle in birds. They are My Divine Glories. In speedy entities, I am wind; in warriors, I am Lord Rāma; in aquatic animals, I am crocodile; and in rivers, I am Ganga.

Prahlāda was born in a family of demons. Despite that, he is acclaimed for being an ardent devotee of Lord Viṣṇu. The plant of Tulasi, a type of Basil, is known to be sacred even if it grows among narcotic plants by chance. Similarly, Prahlāda is considered a Divine Glory of Kṛṣṇa, even though he was born among demons. Units of time such as seconds, minutes, hours, days, etc. are His Glories as well. The entire human life is pervaded with the Glory of time. A bird like the eagle is also qualified for being the Glory of Kṛṣṇa since he serves Śriviṣṇu by being His vehicle. Also, eagle is known for being the strongest amongst all birds and is known as the king of birds in ancient literature. Wind is superior to all other speedy objects, Lord Rāma is superior to all other warriors, and they are both Glories of the Lord.

**More Divine Glories**

सर्गाणामादिरन्तश्च मध्यं चैवाहमर्जुन ।
अध्यात्मविद्या विद्यानां वादः प्रवदतामहम् ॥ ३२ ॥
अक्षराणामकारोऽस्मि द्वन्द्वः सामासिकस्य च ।
अहमेवाक्षयः कालो धाताहं विश्वतोमुखः ॥ ३३ ॥
मृत्युः सर्वहरश्चाहमुद्भवश्च भविष्यताम् ।
कीर्तिः श्रीर्वाक्च नारीणां स्मृतिर्मेधा धृतिः क्षमा ॥ ३४ ॥

*Sargāṇām ādir antaś ca madhyaṃ caivāham arjuna* ।
*Adhyātmavidyā vidyānāṃ vādaḥ pravādatām aham* ॥ 32 ॥
*Akṣarāṇām akāro'smi dvandvaḥ sāmāsikasya ca* ।
*Aham evākṣayaḥ kālo dhātāhaṃ viśvatomukhaḥ* ॥ 33 ॥
*Mṛtyuḥ sarvaharaś cāham udbhavaś ca bhaviṣyatām* ।
*Kīrtiḥ Śrīr vāk ca nārīṇāṃ smṛtir medhā dhṛtiḥ kṣamā* ॥ 34 ॥

**Meaning:** I am the beginning, the middle, and the end of the universe. I am Self-Knowledge (*Adhyatmavidyā*) in all kinds of knowledge, rational discussion in all debates, syllable A in all letters, the copulative-compound in word-compounds, the inexhaustible time of time, the one who has faces from all sides (who can see everything), and also the one who nourishes all. So also, I am death that destroys everyone and the very cause of creation too. Fame, wealth, speech, memory, intelligence, firmness, fortitude, and forgiveness – these qualities expressed in feminine Sanskrit words are verily My own Divine Glories.

Everything that exists, existed, or will exist can be addressed as Kṛṣṇa's form. The day-to-day bits of knowledge may be necessary for transactional life. But the Absolute, Pure Knowledge of Ātman is superior to all of them since it leads a seeker to his highest, lasting welfare. There were various forms of debate in ancient India such as Jalpa, Vitanḍa, and Vāda for agreeing on a principle. The kind of debate, where there is a discussion and conclusion only about the Truth (*Satya*), is known as Vāda, and it is the Glory of Kṛṣṇa. Compound words adorn a language; amongst them, the copulative-compound is superior to all. E.g. the Sanskrit word 'Jñānayoga' can be decompounded in two ways:

- ***Jñānashcha Yogashcha***: Knowledge and Yoga
- ***Jñāna eva Yoga***: Knowledge itself is Yoga

The universe is regulated by time. Lord Kṛṣṇa is the regulator of time. Creation, sustenance, and destruction are His Glories as well. Fame is a unique characteristic Glory of Lord Kṛṣṇa. The qualities on which human life is dependent such as speech, memory are His Glories too. They should be seen in the same manner.

**More Divine Glories**

**बृहत्साम तथा साम्नां गायत्री छन्दसामहम् ।**
**मासानां मार्गशीर्षोऽहमृतूनां कुसुमाकरः ॥ ३५ ॥**
**द्यूतं छलयतामस्मि तेजस्तेजस्विनामहम् ।**
**जयोऽस्मि व्यवसायोऽस्मि सत्त्वं सत्त्ववतामहम् ॥ ३६ ॥**
**वृष्णीनां वासुदेवोऽस्मि पाण्डवानां धनञ्जयः ।**
**मुनीनामप्यहं व्यासः कवीनामुशना कविः ॥ ३७ ॥**
**दण्डो दमयतामस्मि नीतिरस्मि जिगीषताम् ।**
**मौनं चैवास्मि गुह्यानां ज्ञानं ज्ञानवतामहम् ॥ ३८ ॥**

*Bṛhatsāma tathā sāmnāṃ gāyatrī chandasām aham* ।
*Māsānāṃ mārgaśīrṣo'ham ṛtūnāṃ kusumākaraḥ* ॥ *35* ॥
*Dyutaṃ chalayatām asmi tejas tejasvinām aham* ।
*Jayo'smi vyavasāyo'smi sattvaṃ sattvavatām aham* ॥ *36* ॥
*Vṛṣṇīnāṃ vāsudevo'smi pāṇḍavānāṃ dhanaṃjayaḥ* ।
*Munīnām apy ahaṃ vyāsaḥ kavīnām uśanā kaviḥ* ॥ *37* ॥
*Daṇḍo damāyātām asmi nītir asmi jigīṣatām* ।
*Maunaṃ caivāsmi guhyānāṃ jñānaṃ jñānavatām aham* ॥ *38* ॥

**Meaning:** Among Vaidic hymns that can be sung, I am Bṛhatsāma Stotra; among meters i.e. rhythmic syllabic patterns of poetic verses, I am Gāyatri; among months, I am Mārgaśīrṣa; and among seasons, I am the spring. I am the game of gambling played by deceitful people, splendor in shining objects, victory in winners, decisiveness in intellect, and Sattvaguṇa in Sāttvic people. I am Vāsudeva in the lineage of Vriṣnis, Arjuna in Pāṇḍ avas, Vyāsa in sages, and Śukrācārya in poets. I am the power (scepter) of punishers, the war-strategy in desirers of victory, the silence necessary to maintain secrecy in secrets, and the knowledge of enlightened people.

Melody enhances the presentation of poetry. Of them, Bṛhatsāma is a great example of poetry. Jagati, Gāyatri are various meters in poetry; the Gāyatri meter is well-known and pious amongst them. In the era of Mahābhārata, the counting of months used to start from Mārgaśīrṣa month as per Hindu calendar. The Mārgaśīrṣa is a month with a pleasant ambience that comes around November-December in Gregorian calendar; it is neither too cold like Aśvina or Kārtika month nor too hot like Vaiśākha or Pauṣa or Māgha month. Mārgaśīrṣa usually marks the time when harvesting and reaping of crops are finished. People feel much satisfied and joyous when they can see grains, which symbolize the prosperity of life, in their stores. The season of spring is loved by one and all due to the blooming of flowers and fruits. All these manifestations are Kṛṣṇa Himself. Irresistible tendency to gamble and deceive others is an ancient necessity of human life. This power of irresistibility comes from God. The splendor of shiny objects like diamond belongs to Him. A strategy of war is crucial for warriors to win the war. Also, the mind needs enormous power to keep a secret. These are all Glories of Kṛṣṇa. The Knowledge in Upaniṣads is not created by humans, it is divine and belongs to Lord Kṛṣṇa alone.

## The gist of learning the Yoga of Divine Glories

यच्चापि सर्वभूतानां बीजं तदहमर्जुन ।
न तदस्ति विना यत्स्यान्मया भूतं चराचरम् ॥ ३९ ॥
नान्तोऽस्ति मम दिव्यानां विभूतीनां परन्तप ।
एष तूद्देशतः प्रोक्तो विभूतेर्विस्तरो मया ॥ ४० ॥
यद्यद्विभूतिमत्सत्त्वं श्रीमदूर्जितमेव वा ।
तत्तदेवावगच्छ त्वं मम तेजोंऽशसम्भवम् ॥ ४१ ॥
अथवा बहुनैतेन किं ज्ञातेन तवार्जुन ।
विष्टभ्याहमिदं कृत्स्नमेकांशेन स्थितो जगत् ॥ ४२ ॥

*Yac cāpi sarvabhūtānāṃ bījaṃ tad aham arjuna* ।
*Na tad asti vinā yat syān mayā bhūtaṃ carācaram* ॥ *39* ॥
*Nānto 'sti mama divyānāṃ vibhūtīnāṃ paraṃtapa* ।
*Eṣa tūddeśataḥ prokto vibhūter vistaro mayā* ॥ *40* ॥
*Yadyadvibhūtimat sattvaṃ Śrīmad ūrjitam eva vā* ।
*Tattadevāvagaccha tvaṃ mama tejo 'ṃśasaṃbhavam* ॥ *41* ॥
*Athavā bahunaitena kiṃ jñātena tavārjuna* ।
*Viṣṭabhyāham idaṃ kṛtsnam ekāṃśena sthito jagat* ॥ *42* ॥

**Meaning:** I alone am the cause of the creation of all beings. There is no being, whether sentient or insentient, without Me in this entire universe. There is no end to My Divine Glories. I have briefly explained these extensive manifestations to you. Apart from these, whatever is prosperous, resplendent, or powerful, know that it is a manifestation of a part of My splendor. However, what is the use of this detailed knowledge to you? I support the whole world by a mere small part of Myself, but I exist beyond all this.

Lord Kṛṣṇa as Brahman is vast, omnipresent, and all-pervasive irrespective of anything else. In this chapter, his expansive presence has been described with respect to some objects. Human life is replete with Glories of Kṛṣṇa. His presence is so extensive that He can be seen everywhere, frequently, and at all times. The Lord has described 70 Glorious manifestations of Himself in approximately 29 verses. We can even think of new Divine Glories in today's world. The new manifestations may be slightly less in terms of divinity, but they can be highly useful to nurture the vision of seeing Him everywhere around us.

**ॐ तत्सदिति श्रीमद्भगवद्गीतासूपनिषत्सु ब्रह्मविद्यायां योगशास्त्रे श्रीकृष्णार्जुनसंवादे विभूतियोगो नाम दशमोऽध्यायः ॥**

*Om Tatsaditi Śrimadbhagvadgitāsūpaniṣatsu Brahmavidyāyāṃ Yogaśāstre Śrīkṛṣṇārjunasaṅvāde Vibhūtiyogo Nāma Daśamo'dhyāyaḥ* ॥

1. **Maharṣi (महर्षि):** They are the great Ṛṣis who are majestic, produced themselves (sons born to Brahmadeva by His mere wish), all-pervasive yet incarnated in the body, and One with God. They are considered superior as they are born by mere wish of the Lord. There are many Maharṣis. Amongst them, following 10 are considered prominent: Bhṛgu, Marici, Atri, Angirā, Pulaha, Kratu, Manu, Dakśa, Vasiṣṭha, and Pulastya.
2. **The Seven Sages or Saptarṣi (सप्तर्षि):** Longevity; creators of the Mantras; majestic; having divine vision; precedential by virtues, knowledge, and age; seers of Dharma, and those who carry forward the lineage – only those Maharṣis who possess these seven qualities are known as Saptarṣis. The framework of Dharma continues due to them. They are different in every Manvantara (age of Manu – the progenitor of humanity).
   a. Saptarṣis in current Manvantara: Kaśyapa, Atri, Bhāradwaja, Viśwāmitra, Gautama, Jamadagni, Vasiṣṭha
   b. Saptarṣis in Swāyambhuva Manvantara: Marici, Atri, Angirā, Pulastya, Pulaha, Ṛtu, Vasiṣṭha
3. **Twelve Āditya (१२ आदित्य):** They are all the sons of Kaśyapa and Aditi. Their names are mentioned differently in two places:

a. Śakra, Viṣṇu, Āryama, Dhātā, Tvaṣṭa, Pusha, Viśvāvasu, Mitra, Varuṇa, Anśuman, Bhaga, Atiteja
b. Dhātā, Mitra, Aryama, Rudra, Varuṇa, Sūrya, Bhaga, Vivasvata, Pushan, Savitru, Tvaṣṭa, Viṣṇu

4. **Marut (मरुत्)**:
   a. The Lord of the Wind
   b. Marudgana: There are total 49 Maruts, who are the sons of Diti and Kaśyapa. Diti had practiced an arduous austerity to have a son that would destroy Indra. Indra entered her womb at an opportune time. He divided the baby in her womb into 49 (7*7) pieces, but still he could not kill them due to sheer intensity of Diti's relentless practice. Then, Indra removed the demoniac nature from those 49 babies and made them eligible for consuming Soma (only gods and sages are eligible for this).
   c. God in Vaivasvata Manvantara
5. **Deva (देव):** A birth (species) superior to mankind. These are differentiated in this way: Viśvadeva, Sādhyadeva, Kṛtakadeva, Mūladeva, etc.
6. **Devarṣi (देवर्षि):** Ṛṣis akin to gods residing in the Devaloka (plane of gods). They are knowers of the three times: past, present, and future; speakers of the truth; knowledgeable; ascetic; majestic; those who have ability to move in the three Lokas (Swarga, Bhu, Pātāla); and those who are surrounded by Ṛṣis. Devarṣis are present amongst all Devas, Brāhmins and Kṣatriyas. E.g. Nara, Nārāyaṇa, Vālākhilya, Asita, Atri, Angirasa, etc. Devas are controlled by them.
7. **Gandharva (गंधर्व)**:
   a. Special beings in gods (Devas)
   b. Singers for gods
   c. The state of Jiva from the death till he is reborn
8. **Siddha (सिद्ध)**:
   a. One who has earned all special powers in the gross and subtle world; one who is endowed with Dharma,

knowledge, grandeur, dispassion, etc.; and who is filled with gratitude and contentment

b. That which is proved by the epistemic sources of knowledge (Pramāṇas)

9. **Sarpa (सर्प)**:
   a. Snake, a snake named Vāsuki was the king of all snakes
   b. One of the Gurus of Avadhūta
   c. The name of a Rudra

10. **Vidyā (विद्या):** There are total 14 kinds of knowledge (Vidyā). Their counting is done in different ways:
    a. Brahmajñāna, Rasāyana, Svaradhara, Veda, Jyotiṣa, Vyākaraṇa, Dhanurvidyā, Jalataraṇa, Nyāya, Koka, Aśvarohaṇa, Naṭa, Kṛshi, Vaidya
    b. The four Vedas, 4 Upavedas, and Six schools of thoughts (Śāstras)
    c. The four Vedas, six Vedāngas, two Meemānsas, one Dharmaśāstra, one Purāṇa (all Purāṇas)

    Vidyā is also believed to be of 18 kinds: The four Vedas, four Upavedas, six Vedāngas, Purāṇas, Nyāya, Mīmānsa, and Dnarmaśāstra

11. **Chanda (छंद):** Composition conforming to specific letter-patterns (Vruttas). As per the count of specific letter, there are total 7 Chandas (meters) in the Vedas: Gāyatri (24 letters, each next Chanda has increasingly 4 extra letters.) Uṣnik, Anuṣtup, Bṛhati, Pankti, Triṣṭupa, and Jagati (48 letters).

12. **Fourteen Manu (१४ मनु):** Svayambhuva, Svārociṣa, Uttama, Tāmas, Raivata, Cākśuṣa, Vaivasvata, Sāvarṇi, Dakśasāvarṇi, Brahmasāvarṇi, Dharmasāvarṇi, Rudrasāvarṇi, Devasāvarṇi, and Indrasāvarṇi.

## Chapter 11

# Beholding the Cosmic Divine Form

**॥ विश्वरूपदर्शनयोगः (Viśvarūpadarśanayogaḥ) ॥**

This is the remaining half of the 10th chapter. Arjuna was intrigued by the Divine Glories of the Lord. He requested, albeit hesitantly, a desire to behold the manifestation of Kṛṣṇa that has faces in all directions (*10.33*). Having listened to many Glories of Kṛṣṇa, Arjuna initially said to Him, "My ignorance is now removed" and "I have heard about the creation and destruction of all beings." However, he was still intrigued by those Glories. This chapter describes how Lord Kṛṣṇa fulfilled Arjuna's wishes and how that affected Arjuna in the end. The importance of being a loving devotee of God can be understood in this chapter alone.

**Arjuna's preface**

*अर्जुन उवाच*

मदनुग्रहाय परमं गुह्यमध्यात्मसञ्ज्ञितम् ।
यत्त्वयोक्तं वचस्तेन मोहोऽयं विगतो मम ॥ १ ॥
भवाप्ययौ हि भूतानां श्रुतौ विस्तरशो मया ।
त्वत्तः कमलपत्राक्ष माहात्म्यमपि चाव्ययम् ॥ २ ॥
एवमेतद्यथात्थ त्वमात्मानं परमेश्वर ।
द्रष्टुमिच्छामि ते रूपमैश्वरं पुरुषोत्तम ॥ ३ ॥
मन्यसे यदि तच्छक्यं मया द्रष्टुमिति प्रभो ।
योगेश्वर ततो मे त्वं दर्शयात्मानमव्ययम् ॥ ४ ॥

*Arjuna uvāca* ।
*Madanugrahāya paramaṃ guhyam adhyātmasaṃjñitam* ।
*Yat tvayoktaṃ vacas tena moho'yaṃ vigato mama* ॥ *1* ॥

*Bhavāpyayau hi bhūtānāṃ śrutau vistaraśo mayā* ।
*Tvattaḥ kamalapatrākṣa māhātmyam api cāvyayam* ॥ *2* ॥
*Evam etad yathāttha tvam ātmānaṃ parameśvara* ।
*Draṣṭum icchāmi te rūpam aiśvaraṃ puruṣottama* ॥ *3* ॥
*Manyase yadi tac chakyaṃ mayā draṣṭum iti prabho* ।
*Yogeśvara tato me tvaṃ darśayātmānam avyayam* ॥ *4* ॥

**Meaning:** (Arjuna said) You have conferred upon me this profound Knowledge of the Self and immensely graced me; as a result, my delusion is now removed. I have heard in detail the process of creation, sustenance, and destruction of beings. O lotus-eyed Kṛṣṇa! I have also heard about Your imperishable grandness. O Lord! Now, as You have described Yourself, I wish to see Your Glorious, Divine Form in person. O Lord of Yoga! If you think it is possible for me to see it, then show me Your eternal Self.

Humans can know and think about objects which have forms and attributes. But they cannot comprehend that which is formless and unmanifested. This is the reason why Self-Knowledge has become elusive and mysterious for almost all people, and they are ignorant of their true Self. Ignorance is a part of Īśvara's system, so one has to learn Self-Knowledge from Īśvara alone. 'Self-Knowledge' and 'Knowledge of the real God' are one and the same. Kṛṣṇa, the Lord of Yoga, has Himself hidden Knowledge of His true nature by a veil of ignorance. He has also made a provision to remove this veil with the help of scriptures and by making Himself available to devotees in the form of a Sadguru. This is a mere game, pastime (Līlā) for Him, and wise men of discrimination are able to know His real nature through His teaching alone. As such, for wise men, there is no mystery in Self-Knowledge or Knowledge of the real God. So, we have to say that the mystery is solely felt by an ignorant Jiva who is seeking to resolve that mystery. If

Self-Knowledge or Knowledge of the real God were indeed mysterious, no Jiva would ever have attained it in reality.

**Lord Kṛṣṇa's answer**

*श्रीभगवानुवाच ।*
पश्य मे पार्थ रूपाणि शतशोऽथ सहस्रशः ।
नानाविधानि दिव्यानि नानावर्णाकृतीनि च ॥ ५ ॥
पश्यादित्यान्वसून्रुद्रानश्विनौ मरुतस्तथा ।
बहून्यदृष्टपूर्वाणि पश्याश्चर्याणि भारत ॥ ६ ॥
इहैकस्थं जगत्कृत्स्नं पश्याद्य सचराचरम् ।
मम देहे गुडाकेश यच्चान्यद् द्रष्टुमिच्छसि ॥ ७ ॥
न तु मां शक्यसे द्रष्टुमनेनैव स्वचक्षुषा ।
दिव्यं ददामि ते चक्षुः पश्य मे योगमैश्वरम् ॥ ८ ॥

*Śrībhagavān uvāca ।*
*Paśya me pārtha rūpāṇi śataśo'tha sahastraśaḥ ।*
*Nānāvidhāni divyāni nānāvarṇākṛtīni ca ॥ 5 ॥*
*Paśyādityān vasūn rudrān aśvinau marutas tathā ।*
*Bahūny adṛṣṭapūrvāṇi paśyāścaryāṇi bhārata ॥ 6 ॥*
*Ihaikasthaṃ jagat kṛtsnaṃ paśyādya sacarācaram ।*
*Mama dehe guḍākeśa yac cānyad draṣṭum icchasi ॥ 7 ॥*
*Na tu māṃ śakyase draṣṭum anenaiva svacakṣuṣā ।*
*Divyaṃ dadāmi te cakṣuḥ paśya me yogam aiśvaram ॥ 8 ॥*

**Meaning:** (Śrībhagavān said) O Arjuna! Behold My many manifestations of different kinds, various colors, many shapes, and hundreds and thousands of Divine forms. Behold Āditya, Vasu, Rudra, Marut, and many other astonishing forms never seen before. See the whole sentient and insentient world united in My body. And see whatever else you desire as well. But you will never be able to behold My Cosmic Divine Form with your own eyes. Therefore, I will give you the divine sight with which you can behold the Glory of My Yoga and its power.

Today Lord Kṛṣṇa does not exist in person. Also, we are not His beloved devotees like Arjuna. Therefore, we will have to be content just by hearing the description of what was seen by Arjuna through his divine sight. We may be able to imagine the same Divine Form within our minds or thoughts. Even that is enough for us to get an idea of Lord's Divine power of Yoga and thus abandon our ego. It will help us surrender entirely to Him.

## The Cosmic Divine Form of Kṛṣṇa

सञ्जय उवाच ।
एवमुक्त्वा ततो राजन्महायोगेश्वरो हरिः ।
दर्शयामास पार्थाय परमं रूपमैश्वरम् ॥ ९ ॥
अनेकवक्त्रनयनमनेकाद्भुतदर्शनम् ।
अनेकदिव्याभरणं दिव्यानेकोद्यतायुधम् ॥ १० ॥
दिव्यमाल्याम्बरधरं दिव्यगन्धानुलेपनम् ।
सर्वाश्चर्यमयं देवमनन्तं विश्वतोमुखम् ॥ ११ ॥

*Sañjaya uvāca* ।
*Evam uktvā tato rājan mahāyogeśvaro hariḥ* ।
*Darśayām āsa pārthāya paramaṃ rūpam aiśvaram* ॥ *9* ॥
*Anekavaktranayanam anekādbhūtadarśanam* ।
*Anekadivyābharaṇaṃ divyānekodyatāyudham* ॥ *10* ॥
*Divyamālyāmbaradharaṃ divyagandhānulepanam* ।
*Sarvāścaryamāyāṃ devam anantaṃ viśvatomukham* ॥ *11* ॥

**Meaning:** (Sanjaya said) O King Dhṛtarāṣṭra! Then Hari, the Supreme Yogi and destroyer of ignorance, showed Arjuna His Supreme, Glorious Divine Cosmic Form. Arjuna saw the Supreme God having many faces and many eyes, with countless extraordinary sights, adorned with many ethereal ornaments, holding multiple divine weapons in hands, wearing divine garlands and clothes, anointed with celestial perfumes, filled with numerous amazing sights, resplendent, endless, and having a myriad of mouths on all sides.

Arjuna was incredibly fortunate to behold this enthralling, captivating, awe-inspiring, and Divine Cosmic Form of the Lord. He was filled with respect and fright. He was aware that the Cosmic Form belonged to Lord Śrīkṛṣṇa. Along with celestial perfumes, garlands, and ethereal ornaments, the Lord had numerous weapons, and He also had faces on all sides. As a result, Arjuna's fear increased manifold.

**The magnificence of the Divine Cosmic Form**

**दिवि सूर्यसहस्रस्य भवेद्युगपदुत्थिता ।**
**यदि भाः सदृशी सा स्याद्भासस्तस्य महात्मनः ॥ १२ ॥**
**तत्रैकस्थं जगत्कृत्स्नं प्रविभक्तमनेकधा ।**
**अपश्यद्देवदेवस्य शरीरे पाण्डवस्तदा ॥ १३ ॥**

*Divi sūryasahastrasya bhaved yugapad utthitā* ।
*Yadi bhāḥ sadṛśī sā syād bhāsas tasya mahātmanaḥ* ॥ *12* ॥
*Tatraikasthaṃ jagat kṛtsnaṃ pravibhaktam anekadhā* ।
*Apaśyad devadevasya śarīre pāṇḍavas tadā* ॥ *13* ॥

**Meaning:** If the resplendence of a thousand suns were to blaze in the sky all at once, then that may be somewhat like the splendor of the Cosmic Form. Arjuna saw the world – divided in countless ways – all resting together in the body of the Supreme Lord.

The father of the atomic bomb, Robert Oppenheimer, voluntarily remarked after seeing the nuclear explosion that it brought to his mind the words of this verse *11.12* of the Bhagavad-Gita. The shining radiance in this endless world belongs to Him. He is not radiance Himself because radiance is the very nature of fire, but the radiance exists because of Him.

Īśvara's body is known as the universe or Brahmāṅḍa. Arjuna saw it directly with his divine eyes. Man sees the universe divided in many different ways. There may be huge distances between places; however, it seemed as if they were merged in one place in the Cosmic Form.

## Description of the Cosmic Form by astounded Arjuna

ततः स विस्मयाविष्टो हृष्टरोमा धनञ्जयः ।
प्रणम्य शिरसा देवं कृताञ्जलिरभाषत ॥ १४ ॥
*अर्जुन उवाच ।*
पश्यामि देवांस्तव देव देहे सर्वांस्तथा भूतविशेषसङ्घान् ।
ब्रह्माणमीशं कमलासनस्थमृषींश्च सर्वानुरगांश्च दिव्यान् ॥ १५ ॥
अनेकबाहूदरवक्त्रनेत्रं पश्यामि त्वां सर्वतोऽनन्तरूपम् ।
नान्तं न मध्यं न पुनस्तवादिं पश्यामि विश्वेश्वर विश्वरूप ॥ १६ ॥

*Tataḥ sa vismayāviṣṭo hṛṣṭaromā dhanaṃjayaḥ* ।
*Praṇamya śirasā devaṃ kṛtāñjalir abhāṣata* ॥ *14* ॥
*Arjuna uvāca* ।
*Paśyāmi devāṃs tava deva dehe*
*Sarvāṃs tathā bhūtaviśeṣasaṃghān* ।
*Brahmāṇam īśaṃ kamalāsanasthaṃ*
*Ṛṣīṃś ca sarvān uragāṃś ca divyān* ॥ *15* ॥
*Anekabāhūdaravaktranetraṃ*
*Paśyāmi tvāṃ sarvato'nantarūpam* ।
*Nāntaṃ na madhyaṃ na punas tavādiṃ*
*Paśyāmi viśveśvara viśvarūpa* ॥ *16* ॥

**Meaning:** Then Arjuna, in an astounded state with his hair standing on end, bowed down to the Cosmic Form of God, folded his hands, and said, 'O Lord! I see all gods like Indra, Śaṅkara, all Ṛṣis, celestial serpents, Brahmadeva seated on a lotus, and all groups of moving and non-moving entities in Your body. You have numerous hands, stomachs, faces, and eyes. Your forms are infinite, endless from all sides. O Lord of the world! I am not even able to see Your beginning, middle, or end.

Arjuna was dumbfounded looking at the Cosmic Divine Form of the Lord. He was beholding the entire world in His vast, gigantic body.

**Arjuna's request to the Lord**

किरीटिनं गदिनं चक्रिणं च तेजोराशिं सर्वतो दीप्तिमन्तम् ।
पश्यामि त्वां दुर्निरीक्ष्यं समन्ताद् दीप्तानलार्कद्युतिमप्रमेयम् ॥ १७ ॥
त्वमक्षरं परमं वेदितव्यं त्वमस्य विश्वस्य परं निधानम् ।
त्वमव्ययः शाश्वतधर्मगोप्ता सनातनस्त्वं पुरुषो मतो मे ॥ १८ ॥
अनादिमध्यान्तमनन्तवीर्यमनन्तबाहुं शशिसूर्यनेत्रम् ।
पश्यामि त्वां दीप्तहुताशवक्त्रं स्वतेजसा विश्वमिदं तपन्तम् ॥ १९ ॥
द्यावापृथिव्योरिदमन्तरं हि व्याप्तं त्वयैकेन दिशश्च सर्वाः ।
दृष्ट्वाद्भुतं रूपमुग्रं तवेदं लोकत्रयं प्रव्यथितं महात्मन् ॥ २० ॥

*Kirīṭinaṃ gadinaṃ cakriṇaṃ ca*
*Tejorāśiṃ sarvato dīptimantam* ।
*Paśyāmi tvāṃ durnirīkṣyaṃ samantād*
*Dīptānalārkadyutim aprameyam* ॥ *17* ॥
*Tvam akṣaraṃ paramaṃ veditavyaṃ*
*Tvamasya viśvasya paraṃ nidhānam* ।
*Tvam avyayaḥ śāśvata dharma goptā*
*Sanātanas tvaṃ puruṣo mato me* ॥ *18* ॥
*Anādimadhyāntam anantavīryam*
*Anantabāhuṃ śaśisūryanetram* ।
*Paśyāmi tvāṃ dīptahutāśavaktraṃ*
*Svatejasā viśvam idaṃ tapantam* ॥ *19* ॥
*Dyāvāpṛthivyor idam antaraṃ hi*
*Vyāptaṃ tvayaikena diśaś ca sarvāḥ* ।
*Dṛṣṭvādbhūtaṃ rūpam ugraṃ tavedaṃ*
*Lokatrayaṃ pravyathitaṃ mahātman* ॥ *20* ॥

**Meaning:** I see You wearing a crown and bearing a club and a discus. You are like a mass of radiance blazing from all sides and the splendor of burning flares of the sun. It is difficult to contain you in the field of vision. You seem to have endlessly pervaded everywhere. You are superior to all and imperishable; therefore, You alone are worthy to be known. You are the ultimate resting place of this world, protector of the eternal Dharma, and indestructible, ancient Puruṣa – this is my genuine faith. You alone are without beginning, middle, end; the owner of infinite powers and infinite arms; the sun and the moon being your eyes, blazing fire being your mouth, and giving heat to the entire universe. You alone have pervaded the ten directions in between the earth and the sky. Beholding this astounding, extraordinary, and intimidating Cosmic Form, the three worlds are trembling with fear.

These verses describe a process of meditation on the Cosmic Form of Lord Kṛṣṇa. Just like meditating on a beautiful, small sculpture of a deity in a temple, this, too, is a way to meditate on His vast, all-inclusive Cosmic Form. There are countless knowable objects in the world; however, Lord Kṛṣṇa is the only ultimate knowable since knowing Him can lead the seeker to his lasting benefit. The world may seem to be supported by the gravitational force of the planets, but that force itself is supported by God. Creation, sustenance, and destruction verily occur on His substratum. He Himself is the protector of Dharma as mentioned by him in *Paritrāṇāya sādhūnāṃ* (*4.8*). All sentient beings need heat for their sustenance, which is supplied by Him alone. God is vast, expansive, all-pervasive irrespective of anything. Seeing His frightful Cosmic Form, the three worlds seem to be completely intimidated.

**More description**

अमी हि त्वां सुरसङ्घा विशन्ति केचिद्भीताः प्राञ्जलयो गृणन्ति ।
स्वस्तीत्युक्त्वा महर्षिसिद्धसङ्घाः स्तुवन्ति त्वां स्तुतिभिः पुष्कलाभिः ॥
रुद्रादित्या वसवो ये च साध्या विश्वेऽश्विनौ मरुतश्चोष्मपाश्च ।
गन्धर्वयक्षासुरसिद्धसङ्घा वीक्षन्ते त्वां विस्मिताश्चैव सर्वे ॥ २२ ॥
रूपं महत्ते बहुवक्त्रनेत्रं महाबाहो बहुबाहूरुपादम् ।
बहूदरं बहुदंष्ट्राकरालं दृष्ट्वा लोकाः प्रव्यथितास्तथाहम् ॥ २३ ॥
नभःस्पृशं दीप्तमनेकवर्णं व्यात्ताननं दीप्तविशालनेत्रम् ।
दृष्ट्वा हि त्वां प्रव्यथितान्तरात्मा धृतिं न विन्दामि शमं च विष्णो ॥ २४ ॥

*Amī hi tvāṃ surasaṃghā viśanti*
*Kecid bhītāḥ prāñjalayo gṛṇanti* ।

*Svastīty uktvā maharṣi siddha saṃghāḥ*
*Stuvantitvāṃ stutibhiḥ puṣkalābhiḥ* ॥ *21* ॥
*Rudrādityā vasavo ye ca sādhyā*
*Viśve'śvinau marutaś coṣmapāś ca* ।
*Gandharva yakṣā surasiddha saṃghā*
*Vīkṣante tvāṃ vismitāś caiva sarve* ॥ *22* ॥
*Rūpaṃ mahat te bahuvaktranetraṃ*
*Mahābāho bahubāhūrupādam* ।
*Bahūdaraṃ bahudañṣṭrākarālaṃ*
*Dṛṣṭvā lokāḥ pravyathitās tathāham* ॥ *23* ॥
*Nabhaḥspṛśaṃ dīptam anekavarṇaṃ*
*Vyāttānanaṃ dīptaviśālanetram* ।
*Dṛṣṭvā hi tvāṃ pravyathitāntarātmā*
*Dhṛtiṃ na vindāmi śamaṃ ca viṣṇo* ॥ *24* ॥

**Meaning:** These groups of gods are entering You. Some, who are intimidated, are praying to You with folded hands. Hosts of great Ṛṣis and enlightened people are praising You with sublime hymns while saying "May all be well." Rudra, Āditya, Vasu, Sādhyadeva, Viśvadeva, Aśvinikumāra, Marutgaṇa, dead ancestors, Gandharvas, hosts of demons, and enlightened people are beholding You with great astonishment. Seeing Your gigantic, fearsome form having many arms, mouths, eyes, thighs, stomachs, and many tusks, all people are struck with terror and so am I. Seeing You touch the sky, resplendent, colorful, having wide open mouths and large glowing eyes, I am absolutely terrified. I have lost my courage and peace.

All gods and Ṛṣis manifest from and dissolve in Him who is the Supreme Lord of the world. His Cosmic Divine Form is incomprehensible, astonishing, fierce, and frightful. An ordinary Jiva is but a minuscule part of the cycle of the birth and death shown in this Cosmic Form. One who is born as a human has an opportunity as well as the ability to liberate himself from the cycle of birth and death. Lord Kṛṣṇa's incarnation is the most pleasant, captivating, and compassionate form of the Cosmic Form. Today, He is available in the form of the Bhagavad-Gita to all of us. Despite being a part of the frightful Cosmic Form, every human who is graced by Lord Kṛṣṇa has the freedom to attain complete fearlessness in his life.

**The description of the fierce Cosmic Form of God**

दंष्ट्राकरालानि च ते मुखानि दृष्ट्वैव कालानलसन्निभानि ।
दिशो न जाने न लभे च शर्म प्रसीद देवेश जगन्निवास ॥ २५ ॥
अमी च त्वां धृतराष्ट्रस्य पुत्राः सर्वे सहैवावनिपालसङ्घैः ।
भीष्मो द्रोणः सूतपुत्रस्तथासौ सहास्मदीयैरपि योधमुख्यैः ॥ २६ ॥
वक्त्राणि ते त्वरमाणा विशन्ति दंष्ट्राकरालानि भयानकानि ।
केचिद्विलग्ना दशनान्तरेषु सन्दृश्यन्ते चूर्णितैरुत्तमाङ्गैः ॥ २७ ॥
यथा नदीनां बहवोऽम्बुवेगाः समुद्रमेवाभिमुखा द्रवन्ति ।
तथा तवामी नरलोकवीरा विशन्ति वक्त्राण्यभिविज्वलन्ति ॥ २८ ॥
यथा प्रदीप्तं ज्वलनं पतङ्गा विशन्ति नाशाय समृद्धवेगाः ।
तथैव नाशाय विशन्ति लोकास्तवापि वक्त्राणि समृद्धवेगाः ॥ २९ ॥
लेलिह्यसे ग्रसमानः समन्ताल्लोकान्समग्रान्वदनैर्ज्वलद्भिः ।
तेजोभिरापूर्य जगत्समग्रं भासस्तवोग्राः प्रतपन्ति विष्णो ॥ ३० ॥

*Daṃṣṭrākarālāni ca te mukhāni*
*Dṛṣṭvaiva kālānalasaṃnibhāni* ।
*Diśo na jāne na labhe ca śarma*
*Prasīda deveśa jagannivāsa* ॥ 25 ॥
*Amī ca tvāṃ dhṛtarāṣṭrasya putrāḥ*
*Sarve sahaivāvanipālasaṃghaiḥ* ।
*Bhīṣmo droṇaḥ sūtaputras tathāsau*
*Sahāsmadīyair api yodhamukhyaiḥ* ॥ 26 ॥
*Vaktrāṇi te tvaramāṇā viśanti*
*Daṃṣṭrākarālāni bhayānakāni* ।
*Kecid vilagnā daśanāntareṣu*
*Saṃdṛśyante cūrṇitair uttamāṅgaiḥ* ॥ 27 ॥
*Yathā nadīnāṃ bahavo'mbuvegāḥ*
*Samudrām evābhimukhā dravanti* ।
*Tathā tavāmī naralokavīrā*

*Viśanti vaktrāṇy abhivijvalanti* ॥ *28* ॥
*Yathā pradīptaṃ jvalanaṃ pataṅgā*
*Viśanti nāśāya samṛddhavegāḥ* ।
*Tathaiva nāśāya viśanti lokās*
*Tavāpi vaktrāṇi samṛddhavegāḥ* ॥ *29* ॥
*Lelihyase grasamānaḥ samantāl*
*Lokān samagrān vādanair jvaladbhiḥ* ।
*Tejobhir āpūrya jagat samagraṃ*
*Bhāsas tavogrāḥ pratapanti viṣṇo* ॥ *30* ॥

**Meaning:** Having seen Your gruesome form which has mammoth, fearsome tusks and mouths blazing like fire, I am losing my awareness of directions. I am unable to experience any joy at all. Therefore, O Lord of the world! Confer your grace upon me. Many groups of kings and all sons of Dhṛtarāṣṭra are entering You. Also, Bhīṣma, Droṇa, Karṇa, and leading warriors from our side are seen entering – rather hurriedly – your mouth which has terrible molars. Some are seen getting stuck in the teeth and having their heads crushed to powder. Just like many streams of speedy rivers rush towards the ocean, so do these brave men in the world are entering Your fiercely flaming mouths. Just as moths around the lamp jump into a burning flame for destruction, so too these men hurriedly go into your mouths for their own destruction. You are devouring all beings in the world by biting them with your fiercely blazing mouths, by licking them from all sides and later gulping them. O Viṣṇu! Your fierce light is pervading the whole world and burning it.

These verses remind us of the chapter named Mrutyūnirūpaṇa in the Marathi treatise Dāsabodha, which states – "Everyone from a king to an ordinary man must die someday." Brave warriors like Karṇa and Droṇa; staunch loyalists, Yogis, and wise men like Bhīṣma who are also valiant fighters; and courageous warriors like Abhimanyu and Drūpada on Pāṇḍava's side were all seen entering the mouth of the Cosmic Form. The implication of this visual for us is that nobody can escape death. A person may consider himself to be special, exclusive, or distinctive, but such right or wrong ideas cannot prevent his death. Only an enlightened person having Self-Knowledge learns that he is not the body, and he is Ātman. He knows the fact that Ātman – his true Self – will not die with the death of the body. Only by realizing this Self-Knowledge, man can be liberated from the otherwise inescapable cycle of birth and death.

**Arjuna's question and the Lord's answer**

**आख्याहि मे को भवानुग्ररूपो नमोऽस्तु ते देववर प्रसीद ।**
**विज्ञातुमिच्छामि भवन्तमाद्यं न हि प्रजानामि तव प्रवृत्तिम् ॥ ३१ ॥**
***श्रीभगवानुवाच ।***
**कालोऽस्मि लोकक्षयकृत्प्रवृद्धो लोकान्समाहर्तुमिह प्रवृत्तः ।**
**ऋतेऽपि त्वां न भविष्यन्ति सर्वे येऽवस्थिताः प्रत्यनीकेषु योधाः ॥ ३२ ॥**
**तस्मात्त्वमुत्तिष्ठ यशो लभस्व जित्वा शत्रून् भुङ्क्ष्व राज्यं समृद्धम् ।**
**मयैवैते निहताः पूर्वमेव निमित्तमात्रं भव सव्यसाचिन् ॥ ३३ ॥**
**द्रोणं च भीष्मं च जयद्रथं च कर्णं तथान्यानपि योधवीरान् ।**
**मया हतांस्त्वं जहि मा व्यथिष्ठा युध्यस्व जेतासि रणे सपत्नान् ॥ ३४ ॥**

*Ākhyāhi me ko bhavān ugrarūpo*
*Namo'stu te devavara prasīda* ।
*Vijñātum icchāmi bhavantam ādyaṃ*
*Na hi prajānāmi tava pravṛttim* ॥ *31* ॥
*Śrībhagavān uvāca* ।
*Kālo'smi lokakṣayakṛtpravṛddho*
*Lokānsamāhartumiha pravṛttaḥ* ।
*Ṛte'pi tvāṃ na bhaviṣyanti sarve*
*Ye'vasthitāḥ pratyanīkeṣu yodhāḥ* ॥ *32* ॥
*Tasmāt tvamuttiṣṭha yaśolabhasva*
*Jitvāśatrūn bhuṅkṣva rājyaṃ samṛddham* ।
*Māyāivaite nihatāḥ pūrvam eva*
*Nimittamātraṃ bhava savyasācin* ॥ *33* ॥

*Droṇaṃ ca bhīṣmaṃ ca jayadrathaṃ ca*
*Karṇaṃ tathānyān api yodhavīrān* ।
*Mayā hatāṃs tvaṃ jahi mā vyathiṣṭhā*
*Yudhyasva jetāsi raṇe sapatnān* ॥ *34* ॥

**Meaning:** (Arjuna said) O Supreme Lord! I bow down to you. Please confer Your grace upon me. You are the most primeval Puruṣa, and I desire to know Your real nature in entirety. Tell me! Who are You so fierce in form? I am indeed unable to understand anything about Your visible form.

(Śrībhagavān said) I am the time which constantly progresses and destroys the worlds. Here on this battleground, I shall be engaged in destroying these people. The people in your enemy camp shall not live in the future even if you are not there to slay them. [They will not exist even if you don't exist.] Therefore, arise and get ready for the war. Attain success in the battle. Conquer your enemies and enjoy the prosperous, unrivaled kingdom. I have already slain all of them. You need to act as a mere instrument for their death. Warriors like Droṇa, Bhīṣma, Jayadratha, Karṇa, and many others have already been slain by Me. You need to slay them only by acting as an instrument. Do not be struck with fear. You shall conquer these brave warriors. Therefore, fight the battle!

These are immensely important verses for a seeker. "I am the doer", "It happened because of my presence", "It will not happen in my absence," "I will not let it happen without me", "What would happen in my absence?" – These and similar thoughts cloud the minds of most ordinary people. Such thoughts are replete with the feelings of doership, grief, fear, worry, ego and disdain about others. Many people also wish to be given credit for the work accomplished. There are two key messages in these verses –

**निमित्तमात्रं भव ।** *Nimittamātraṃ bhava* ।

"Be a mere instrument or medium while executing actions."

**मया हतांस्त्वं जहि ।** *Mayā hatāṃs tvaṃ jahi* ।

"I have already slain them."

The seeker should abide by these messages by making them the chief navigators of his life. St. Tukārāma says, "Man is merely an instrument, but he thinks 'I am the doer' and thus lives a futile life." Īśvara has created a systematic plan for each person, his physical condition, and his relatives whom the person considers his own responsibility. The plan is merely executed through the medium of that person. Therefore, every seeker should perform all his duties – with utmost love and dedication – only by acting as an instrument. In fact, the seeker cannot even control how much he can really do for others. All he can do is act to the best of his abilities. This same fact is also mentioned in the verse that "Each person has a right only in action and not its results (*2.47*)." The five Pāṇḍavas, Sātyaki, Aśvatthāmā, Kṛpācārya and Kṛtavarmā were the only warriors who survived the war. All others like Bhīṣma, Droṇa were killed, and Arjuna got to see their death in the Cosmic Form before the war. Lord Kṛṣṇa showed those stunning visuals to Arjuna to enable him to fight fearlessly with absolute certainty and destroy the unjust side. Kṛṣṇa wanted Arjuna to aid Him in His duty of eradicating the evil forces from the earth (*4.8*). Even if a warrior meets death in fighting for a noble cause, it is indeed a befitting death for him. Kṛṣṇa has also said before, "Either you will be slain on the battlefield and attain heaven, or you will conquer and enjoy the kingdom of the earth (*2.37*)." A devotee should like what his beloved God likes, otherwise it does not beseem his devotion. "Fight the battle", i.e. "perform your duty," is the primal command of the Gita.

**<u>Sanjaya says to Dhṛtarāṣtra</u>**

*सञ्जय उवाच ।*

**एतच्छ्रुत्वा वचनं केशवस्य कृताञ्जलिर्वेपमानः किरीटी ।**
**नमस्कृत्वा भूय एवाह कृष्णं सगद्गदं भीतभीतः प्रणम्य ॥ ३५ ॥**

*Sañjaya uvāca* ।
*Etac chrutvā vacanaṃ keśavasya*
*Kṛtāñjalir vepamānaḥ kirīṭī* ।
*Namaskṛtvā bhūya evāha kṛṣṇaṃ*
*Sagadgadaṃ bhītabhītaḥ praṇamya* ॥ *35* ॥

**Meaning:** (Sañjaya said) Having heard Śrīkṛṣṇa's speech, Arjuna bowed down to him with trembling, folded hands. Overwhelmed with fear, prostrating himself, again and again, he said in a choked voice–

***अर्जुन उवाच।***
**स्थाने हृषीकेश तव प्रकीर्त्या जगत्प्रहृष्यत्यनुरज्यते च।**
**रक्षांसि भीतानि दिशो द्रवन्ति सर्वे नमस्यन्ति च सिद्धसङ्घाः ॥ ३६ ॥**
**कस्माच्च ते न नमेरन्महात्मन्गरीयसे ब्रह्मणोऽप्यादिकर्त्रे।**
**अनन्त देवेश जगन्निवास त्वमक्षरं सदसत्तत्परं यत् ॥ ३७ ॥**
**त्वमादिदेवः पुरुषः पुराणस्त्वमस्य विश्वस्य परं निधानम्।**
**वेत्तासि वेद्यं च परं च धाम त्वया ततं विश्वमनन्तरूप ॥ ३८ ॥**
**वायुर्यमोऽग्निर्वरुणः शशाङ्कः प्रजापतिस्त्वं प्रपितामहश्च।**
**नमो नमस्तेऽस्तु सहस्रकृत्वः पुनश्च भूयोऽपि नमो नमस्ते ॥ ३९ ॥**
**नमः पुरस्तादथ पृष्ठतस्ते नमोऽस्तु ते सर्वत एव सर्व।**
**अनन्तवीर्यामितविक्रमस्त्वं सर्वं समाप्नोषि ततोऽसि सर्वः ॥ ४० ॥**

*Arjuna uvāca* ।
*Sthāne hṛṣīkeśa tava prakīrtyā*
*Jagat prahṛṣyaty anurajyate ca* ।
*Rakṣāṃsi bhītāni diśodravanti*
*Sarve namasyanti ca siddhasaṃghāḥ* ॥ *36* ॥
*Kasmāc ca te na nameran mahātman*
*arīyase brahmaṇo'py ādikartre* ।
*Ananta deveśa jagannivāsa*
*tvam akṣaraṃ sad asat tatparaṃ yat* ॥ *37* ॥
*Tvam ādidevaḥ puruṣaḥ purāṇas*
*Tvam asya viśvasya paraṃ nidhānam* ।
*Vettāsi vedyaṃ ca paraṃ ca dhāma*
*Tvayā tataṃ viśvam anantarūpa* ॥ *38* ॥

*Vāyur yamo'gnir varuṇaḥ śaśāṅkaḥ*
*Prajāpatis tvaṃ prapitāmahaś ca* ।
*Namo namaste'stu sahastrakṛtvaḥ*
*Punaś ca bhūyo'pi namo namaste* ॥ *39* ॥
*Namaḥ purastād atha pṛṣṭhatas te*
*Namo'stu te sarvata eva sarva* ।
*Anantavīryāmitavikramas tvaṃ*
*Sarvaṃ samāpnoṣi tato'si sarvaḥ* ॥ *40* ॥

**Meaning:** (Arjuna said) The world takes pleasure in singing Your praises and rejoices in it. It is appropriate that scared demons run in all ten directions, and groups of enlightened people bow down to You. O Supreme God of gods! You are infinite; You are the abode of the world; You transcend *Sat* and *Asat*; You are imperishable; and You are the primal cause of even Brahmadeva; why then would all people not salute You? You are the most ancient Puruṣa and the primal God. You are the supporter and knower of the world. You alone are worth knowing and the supreme abode of all. You pervade this entire universe. You are wind (*Vāyu*), death (*Yama*), fire (*Agni*), rain (*Varuṇa*), and the moon. You are Prajāpati (not Prajāpitā) and also, as if, the great-grandfather of all people. I salute you a thousand times. I bow to you again and again. O Ātman of all beings! Salutations to You from the front, the back, and all sides. There is no end to Your brave deeds; Your prowess is infinite. Being all-pervasive and omnipresent, You are all beings.

There is a remarkable difference between scared demons who run in all directions and enlightened sages who bow down to God. It is only natural that evil people will fear God, and good people will respect Him. Having seen the incomparable ability and grandness of God, it is natural for anyone – irrespective of how prominent he is – to bow down to Him alone. To continue the game of creation and destruction of this vast world through just one conscientious wish is a massive task, which needs extraordinary and unimaginable power. Īśvara has that power named **Māyā** which operates through different forms like Ajñāna, Avidyā, Śakti, Prakṛti, etc. God governs all games of Māyā by His will alone and without Himself doing any action. This idea itself is incomprehensible for most people. The Jiva, who strives to learn about *Sat* and *Asat* (real and unreal), is himself neither real nor unreal hence indescribable (*Sat-Asat-Vilakṣaṇa-Anirvacaniya*). God transcends *Sat* and *Asat*, but there is no one else other than Him who may address Him in that manner.

## Arjuna seeks forgiveness

**सखेति मत्वा प्रसभं यदुक्तं हे कृष्ण हे यादव हे सखेति ।**
**अजानता महिमानं तवेदं मया प्रमादात्प्रणयेन वापि ॥ ४१ ॥**
**यच्चावहासार्थमसत्कृतोऽसि विहारशय्यासनभोजनेषु ।**
**एकोऽथवाप्यच्युत तत्समक्षं तत्क्षामये त्वामहमप्रमेयम् ॥ ४२ ॥**
**पितासि लोकस्य चराचरस्य त्वमस्य पूज्यश्च गुरुर्गरीयान् ।**
**न त्वत्समोऽस्त्यभ्यधिकः कुतोऽन्यो लोकत्रयेऽप्यप्रतिमप्रभाव ॥ ४३ ॥**
**तस्मात्प्रणम्य प्रणिधाय कायं प्रसादये त्वामहमीशमीड्यम् ।**
**पितेव पुत्रस्य सखेव सख्युः प्रियः प्रियायार्हसि देव सोढुम् ॥ ४४ ॥**

*Sakheti matvā prasabhaṃ yad uktaṃ*
*He kṛṣṇa he yādava he sakheti* ।
*Ajānatā mahimānaṃ tavedaṃ*
*Mayā pramādāt praṇayena vāpi* ॥ *41* ॥
*Yac cāvahāsārtham asatkṛto'si*
*Vihāraśayyāsanabhojaneṣu* ।
*Eko'thavāpy acyuta tatsamakṣaṃ*
*Tat kṣāmaye tvāmaham aprameyam* ॥ *42* ॥
*Pitāsi lokasya carācarasya*
*Tvam asya pūjyaś ca gurur garīyān* ।
*Na tvatsamo'styabhyadhikaḥ kuto'nyo*
*Lokatraye'pyapratimaprabhāva* ॥ *43* ॥
*Tasmāt praṇamya praṇidhāya kāyaṃ*
*Prasādaye tvām aham īśam īḍyam* ।

*Piteva putrasya sakheva sakhyuḥ*
*Priyaḥ priyāyārhasi deva soḍhum* ॥ *44* ॥

**Meaning:** Unable to recognize your grandness, I may have regarded You merely as a friend and addressed You casually or mistakenly as "O Kṛṣṇa, O Yadava, O friend, etc." I may have also crossed my line with You – just for fun – while playing, resting, sitting, or eating with you, either alone or in the company of others. O Acyuta with unimaginable influence! If so, I implore You to forgive me. You are the creator of the sentient and insentient universe, highly revered, and the Sadguru of all Gurus. There is no one more influential and prominent than You in the three worlds. Who can then be possibly superior to You? Therefore, I bow down to You. O Supreme Īśvara by prostrating my whole body and pray to You. Just as a father forgives his son, a friend forgives his friend, a wife forgives her husband, so too You are graceful enough to forgive my misdeeds.

Lord Kṛṣṇa was incarnated as a human being. Therefore, He had to take the Divine Cosmic Form in an extraordinary manner to show a miraculous vision to Arjuna so that Arjuna could really perceive His divinity and grandness. St. Tukārāma suggests that a spiritual person – even if young – should not be considered ordinary when we are in a casual, friendly setting. Arjuna had immense respect for Lord Kṛṣṇa in his mind; however, being in close relation, he occasionally interacted in a casual manner with the Lord. Arjuna's respect for Kṛṣṇa was such that he was ready to be Kṛṣṇa's disciple and surrender to Him (*2.8*), but there was no way he could have recognized Kṛṣṇa's true nature before. However, having recognized Kṛṣṇa's divinity here, Arjuna was Sāttvic and genuine enough to implore His forgiveness then. Without maintaining appropriate distance in a relationship, one cannot respect the other person; and without respect for the other person, one cannot obey his orders.

## Prayer to the Lord to come back to His previous form

अदृष्टपूर्वं हृषितोऽस्मि दृष्ट्वा भयेन च प्रव्यथितं मनो मे ।
तदेव मे दर्शय देवरूपं प्रसीद देवेश जगन्निवास ॥ ४५ ॥
किरीटिनं गदिनं चक्रहस्तं इच्छामि त्वां द्रष्टुमहं तथैव ।
तेनैव रूपेण चतुर्भुजेन सहस्रबाहो भव विश्वमूर्ते ॥ ४६ ॥

*Adṛṣṭapūrvaṃ hṛṣitosmi dṛṣṭvā*
*Bhayena ca pravyathitaṃ mano me* ।
*Tad eva me darśaya deva rūpaṃ*
*Prasīda deveśa jagannivāsa* ॥ *45* ॥
*Kirīṭinaṃ gadinaṃ cakrahastaṃ*
*Icchāmi tvāṃ draṣṭum ahaṃ tathaiva* ।
*Tenaiva rūpeṇa caturbhujena*
*Sahastrabāho bhava viśvamūrte* ॥ *46* ॥

**Meaning:** I felt great joy by beholding what was never seen before, but my mind is fearful and distressed at the same time. Therefore, be pleased with me and show me Your original form. I desire to see You, as you were before, having a crown on Your head and bearing a mace and a discus in Your hand. O Cosmic God with thousand arms! I request you to manifest Yourself in your original form which has four hands.

It is true that Arjuna was delighted since he felt blessed and fortunate to be able to see Kṛṣṇa's Divine Glories in person, and his desire was fulfilled. However, after seeing the fierce, gruesome transformation of Kṛṣṇa in His Cosmic Form, the brave, valiant Arjuna also started trembling with fear. It is indeed true that sometimes a person cannot bear even his good fortune!

The seeker may see thousands of different faces in his lifetime, yet he should know for certain that they all belong to one God alone. He may feel compelled to react differently to different people, but he should think of the same principle – Brahman – present uniformly everywhere, and thus keep his mind calm and steady. This practice enables the seeker to perceive God in all beings. Evidently, there are transactional boundaries to this line of thinking. St. Tukārāma has clearly said, "When one sees a serpent or a scorpion in real life, he should mentally bow down to them knowing them to be God, in principle, but not be foolish to actually touch them." He also teaches seekers to keep away from evil, malicious people in life, even though, in essence, they are forms of God. There is no place for gullibility in the worldly life or spiritual life of a seeker.

**Lord Krṣṇa narrates the eminence of His Cosmic Form**

**श्रीभगवानुवाच ।**
**मया प्रसन्नेन तवार्जुनेदं रूपं परं दर्शितमात्मयोगात् ।**
**तेजोमयं विश्वमनन्तमाद्यं यन्मे त्वदन्येन न दृष्टपूर्वम् ॥ ४७ ॥**
**न वेदयज्ञाध्ययनैर्न दानैर्न च क्रियाभिर्न तपोभिरुग्रैः ।**
**एवंरूपः शक्य अहं नृलोके द्रष्टुं त्वदन्येन कुरुप्रवीर ॥ ४८ ॥**

*Śrībhagavān uvāca* ।
*Mayā prasannena tavārjunedaṃ*
*Rūpaṃ paraṃ darśitam ātmayogāt* ।
*Tejomāyāṃ viśvamanantamādyaṃ*
*Yanme tvādanyena na dṛṣṭapūrvam* ॥ *47* ॥
*Na veda Yajñadhyayanair na dānaiḥ*
*Na ca kriyābhir na tapobhir ugraiḥ* ।
*Evaṃrūpaḥ śakya ahaṃ nṛloke*
*Draṣṭuṃ tvādanyena kurupravīra* ॥ *48* ॥

**Meaning:** (Śrībhagavān said) O Arjuna! Using the influence of My own Yoga-power, I have graciously shown you My supreme, Cosmic Form, which is resplendent, infinite, and magnificent. This Cosmic Form has never been seen before by anyone other than You. There are many practices such as studying the Vedas, performing Yajñas, engaging in self-study, donating wealth of different kinds, executing the duties prescribed by scriptures, or observing grueling austerities. I cannot be seen in My Divine Cosmic Form through any of these practices by anyone other than you in this world.

Lord Kṛṣṇa is the Lord of Yoga. His Yoga-power or Yogamāyā is unfathomable to the human mind. Science has discovered various forms of energy like speed, heat, magnetism, etc. and extensively used them in day-to-day life. Īśvara governs Māyā. The energy of Māyā's immense power is beyond the experimental understanding of human beings. Māyā's power needs to be accepted on faith and also by using logic. We have accepted the terms electron, proton, etc. based on scientific experiments. Akin to them, if we accept the word **Māyātron** based on spiritual findings of seers, only then the phenomenal world around us can be comprehended. The Cosmic Form of Kṛṣṇa cannot be seen by any human through the worldly practices of Yajña, Yāga, etc. This celebratory event took place only between the two divine beings: Lord Kṛṣṇa and Arjuna. Kṛṣṇa's mother Yaśodā was able to see only a glimpse of His all-pervasive form when He was a child.

**Lord Kṛṣṇa comes back to His original form**

**मा ते व्यथा मा च विमूढभावो दृष्ट्वा रूपं घोरमीदृङ्ममेदम् ।**
**व्यपेतभीः प्रीतमनाः पुनस्त्वं तदेव मे रूपमिदं प्रपश्य ॥ ४९ ॥**
***सञ्जय उवाच ।***
**इत्यर्जुनं वासुदेवस्तथोक्त्वा स्वकं रूपं दर्शयामास भूयः ।**
**आश्वासयामास च भीतमेनं भूत्वा पुनः सौम्यवपुर्महात्मा ॥ ५० ॥**

*Mā te vyathā mā ca vimūḍhabhāvo*
*Dṛṣṭvā rūpaṃ ghoram īdṛṅ mamedam* ।
*Vyapetabhīḥ prītamanāḥ punastvaṃ*
*Tadeva me rūpamidaṃ prapaśya* ॥ *49* ॥
*Sañjaya uvāca* ।
*Ity arjunaṃ vāsudevas tathoktvā*
*Svakaṃ rūpaṃ darśayām āsa bhūyaḥ* ।
*Āśvāsayāmāsa ca bhītamenaṃ*
*Bhūtvā punaḥ saumyavapurmahātmā* ॥ *50* ॥

**Meaning:** Do not be afraid or bewildered by My fierce, gruesome Cosmic Form. Dispel your fear and behold this form of Mine again lovingly like before.

(Sanjaya said to Dhṛtarāṣṭra) Having thus spoken to Arjuna, Lord Kṛṣṇa again showed His original form which was loved by Arjuna. He assumed his genial demeanor and consoled Arjuna who was struck by terror.

**Arjuna's response**

*अर्जुन उवाच ।*

**दृष्ट्वेदं मानुषं रूपं तव सौम्यं जनार्दन ।**
**इदानीमस्मि संवृत्तः सचेताः प्रकृतिं गतः ॥ ५१ ॥**

*Arjuna uvāca* ।

*Dṛṣṭvedaṃ mānuṣaṃ rūpaṃ tava saumyaṃ janārdana* ।
*Idānīm asmi saṃvṛttaḥ sacetāḥ prakṛtiṃ gataḥ* ॥ *51* ॥

**Meaning:** (Arjuna said) O Lord! Having seen Your gentle, amiable form, I now feel composed as I was before.

**The importance of the Cosmic Form narrated by God**

*श्रीभगवानुवाच ।*

**सुदुर्दर्शमिदं रूपं दृष्टवानसि यन्मम ।**
**देवा अप्यस्य रूपस्य नित्यं दर्शनकाङ्क्षिणः ॥ ५२ ॥**
**नाहं वेदैर्न तपसा न दानेन न चेज्यया ।**
**शक्य एवंविधो द्रष्टुं दृष्टवानसि मां यथा ॥ ५३ ॥**
**भक्त्या त्वनन्यया शक्य अहमेवंविधोऽर्जुन ।**
**ज्ञातुं द्रष्टुं च तत्त्वेन प्रवेष्टुं च परन्तप ॥ ५४ ॥**
**मत्कर्मकृन्मत्परमो मद्भक्तः सङ्गवर्जितः ।**
**निर्वैरः सर्वभूतेषु यः स मामेति पाण्डव ॥ ५५ ॥**

*Śrībhagavān uvāca* ।

*Sudurdarśam idaṃ rūpaṃ dṛṣṭvān asi yan mama* ।
*Devā apy asya rūpasya nityaṃ darśanakāṅkṣiṇaḥ* ॥ *52* ॥
*Nāhaṃ vedair na tapasā na dānena na cejyayā* ।
*Śakya evaṃvidho draṣṭuṃ dṛṣṭavān asi māṃ yathā* ॥ *53* ॥

*Bhaktyā tv ananyayā śakya aham evaṃvidho'rjuna* ।
*Jñātuṃ draṣṭuṃ ca tattvena praveṣṭuṃ ca paraṃtapa* ॥ *54* ॥
*Matkarmakṛn matparamo madbhaktaḥ saṅgavarjitaḥ* ।
*Nirvairaḥ sarvabhūteṣu yaḥ sa mām eti pāṇḍava* ॥ *55* ॥

**Meaning:** (Śrībhagavān said) It is very rare indeed to see this Cosmic Form of Mine which you have seen. Even other gods are constantly longing to see this Form. My Cosmic Form, as seen by you, cannot be seen by anyone else even by studying the Vedas or performing Yajñas or giving donations. It is possible to know Me, behold Me, and be One with Me in essence – only through unswerving, single-minded devotion. A person who engages in all actions only for Me, surrenders to Me, remains devoted to Me alone, removes all worldly attachments, and does not nurture enmity towards anyone – he verily comes to Me and unites with Me.

**ॐ तत्सदिति श्रीमद्भगवद्गीतासूपनिषत्सु ब्रह्मविद्यायां योगशास्त्रे श्रीकृष्णार्जुनसंवादे विश्वरूपदर्शनयोगो नामैकादशोऽध्यायः ॥**

*Om Tatsaditi Śrimadbhagvadgitāsūpaniṣatsu Brahmavidyāyāṃ Yogaśāstre Śrīkṛṣṇārjunasaṅvāde Viśvarūpadarśanayogo Nāma Ekādaśo'dhyāyaḥ*॥

The last three verses include the preface to the 12th chapter. Even chapter 10 has similar verses: "Those who contemplate on Me and take arduous efforts to attain Me (*10.9*)." "I give spiritual intelligence to those whose mind is centered in Me (*10.10*). " These verses, too, contain a prelude to the 12th chapter. Arjuna was the only one who got to see Kṛṣṇa's Divine Cosmic Form. Many other devotees who exclusively love and devotedly pray to Saguṇa God can see Him in His regular form with four arms. Mere rituals like studying the Vedas or engaging in austerities, donations, etc. do not help in seeing God. Such rituals help only to purify the mind. Only devotees having intense faith and feeling may get to see Saguṇa God. St. Tukārāma and St. Nāmadeva have written compositions which reflect the fact that they actually saw God in Saguṇa form, and they have expressed their pining to see Him again. Verse *9.14* describes various spiritual practices to nurture and intensify devotion. Comprehending the true nature of God as Brahman, seeing Saguṇa God, later being One with Him, and not remaining separate from Him – this evolution is possible only for a seeker who has ardent devotion. The Lord also says here that it is necessary for a devotee to not feel hostility towards anyone. Was it indeed possible for Arjuna, whose archrivals Kauravas were facing him in the war, to not feel hostile? The answer here is that eradication of injustice, destruction of evil, observation of warrior duties, and following the order of the Lord to fight the battle – all such actions can be executed without feeling hostility for others. War can be fought as one's duty with an equanimous mind by abiding firmly in the resolve that "I am Brahman and so is everybody else." Arjuna fought the battle in the end after he was free from delusion.

Chapter 12

# The Yoga of Devotion

## ॥ भक्तियोगः (Bhaktiyoga) ॥

This chapter is also known as **Saguṇa Bhaktiyoga** because Arjuna asks the question right at the outset about whether it is better to worship Saguṇa God with form and attributes or Nirguṇa God having no form and no attributes. Lord Kṛṣṇa has approved the importance of worshipping Nirguṇa God, but He has ultimately said that worshipping Saguṇa God is a better option. St. Tukārāma lovingly says to Viṭṭhala, "You got Yourself into trouble by manifesting as Saguṇa God. Now You cannot escape from us devotees by giving the excuse that you are formless and attributeless, and tell us that we cannot to see you." Worshipping attributeless, formless God is extremely difficult. Considering this, God manifested Himself in a visible form with attributes. Worshipping Saguṇa God is better and easier for almost all people. The debate whether the Saguṇa form of God pertains to Īśvara or Brahman is unnecessary; rather, it is necessary to recognize that the Saguṇa manifestation of Brahman is available only for the convenience of seekers. The followers of Vārakari Sampradāya (cult) firmly believe that the idol of Viṭṭhala is Brahman in reality. In the Sundarakāṇḍa chapter of Rāmāyaṇa, Lord Rāma has been addressed as **Vedāntaikavedya**, which means – the fact that "Lord Rāma is Brahman" can be known only through the studies of Vedāntic scriptures.

The prominent feature of this chapter is that it states four ways of devotion. These ways are described according to the readiness, eligibility, or inclination of each seeker. Lastly, there is a description of the characteristics of a devotee, which marks the end of this small chapter. Chapters 9 and 12 are considered the most significant in the Vārakari Sampradāya of Mahārāṣṭra.

## Arjuna's question

*अर्जुन उवाच ।*
एवं सततयुक्ता ये भक्तास्त्वां पर्युपासते ।
ये चाप्यक्षरमव्यक्तं तेषां के योगवित्तमाः ॥ १ ॥

*Arjuna uvāca* ।
*Evaṃ satatayuktā ye bhaktās tvāṃ paryupāsate* ।
*Ye cāpy akṣaram avyaktaṃ teṣāṃ ke yogavittamāḥ* ॥ *1* ॥

**Meaning:** (Arjuna said) Some devotees strive to unite with You by constantly worshiping You as Saguṇa God, and some worship You as formless Nirguṇa Brahman. Who is the better Yogi amongst them?

Most people worship Saguṇa God who has a name and a form by engaging in practices like chanting His Mantra, and singing His praises. There are a few who worship Nirguṇa God by meditating on the thought that "I am Brahman", which is called Ahangraha Dhyāna. Some worship Nirguṇa God by discriminating between real and unreal, Self and non-Self, core and peripheral, etc. Occasionally, there may also be a conflict between Saguṇa worship and Nirguṇa worship. Analysis of the Vedāntic Mahāvākya '**Thou art that**' (*Tat-Tvam-Asi*) is a spiritual practice recognized and approved by scriptures. Also, there is excellent support for lovingly adhering to Saguṇa God at all times. On one side, there are Upaniṣads which explain the true nature of God. On the other side, there are scriptures like Nārada Bhaktisūtras and other texts authored by the enlightened saints which illustrate the true nature of devotion. Which one of these is better for spiritual pursuit?

**Lord Kṛṣṇa's answer**

*श्रीभगवानुवाच ।*
मय्यावेश्य मनो ये मां नित्ययुक्ता उपासते ।
श्रद्धया परयोपेतास्ते मे युक्ततमा मताः ॥ २ ॥
ये त्वक्षरमनिर्देश्यमव्यक्तं पर्युपासते ।
सर्वत्रगमचिन्त्यं च कूटस्थमचलन्ध्रुवम् ॥ ३ ॥
सन्नियम्येन्द्रियग्रामं सर्वत्र समबुद्धयः ।
ते प्राप्नुवन्ति मामेव सर्वभूतहिते रताः ॥ ४ ॥
क्लेशोऽधिकतरस्तेषामव्यक्तासक्तचेतसाम् ।
अव्यक्ता हि गतिर्दुःखं देहवद्भिरवाप्यते ॥ ५ ॥

*Śrībhagavān uvāca* ।
*Mayy āveśya mano ye māṃ nityayuktā upāsate* ।
*Śraddhayā parayopetāste me yuktatamā matāḥ* ॥ 2 ॥
*Ye tv akṣaram anirdeśyaṃ avyaktaṃ paryupāsate* ।
*Sarvatragam acintyaṃ ca kūṭasthaṃ acalaṃ dhruvam* ॥ 3 ॥
*Saṃniyamyendriyagrāmaṃ sarvatra samabuddhayāḥ* ।
*Te prāpnuvanti mām eva sarvabhūtahite ratāḥ* ॥ 4 ॥
*Kleśo'dhikataras teṣāṃ avyaktāsaktacetasām* ।
*Avyaktā hi gatir duḥkhaṃ dehavadbhir avāpyate* ॥ 5 ॥

**Meaning:** (Śrībhagavān said) Those who constantly fix their mind on Me and worship Me with supreme, unswerving faith are perfected in the union with Me. But some devotees conquer their senses and appropriately worship that all-pervasive principle which is incomprehensible by the mind and intellect, beyond words, unfathomable, eternal, immovable, formless, and imperishable. These Yogis are engaged in the welfare of all beings; they see Me everywhere and ultimately attain Me alone. The only difference is that those who worship unmanifested Brahman find it very arduous. This is because people who identify themselves with the body find it extremely difficult and painful to attain the unmanifested.

The objective of Saguṇa and Nirguṇa worship is the same. They both lead the seeker towards the same goal. Lord Kṛṣṇa says in the 4th verse that both kinds of worshippers attain Him. However, those who constantly and firmly believe that "I am the body" find it easy to worship Saguṇa God who has a visible form. It is natural for an embodied person to feel close to some other embodied form. Every seeker gets a body in his present birth as a result of his past Karma. On the contrary, God manifests Himself in a body of his choice by using the power of His Māyā. This difference can be understood only through the teachings of God Himself. Enlightened saints can explain these teachings very well. First, it is necessary to know that Saguṇa God – having a name and form – is the same as Nirguṇa God who is originally formless, nameless, and attributeless. Knowing this, a devotee can worship Saguṇa God and realize that he himself is Nirguṇa Brahman.

After being enlightened with Self-Knowledge that "I am Brahman," the devotee continues being devoted to Saguṇa God as well. It is, however, difficult for any seeker to center his mind in Nirguṇa Brahman. The mind disappears in Nirguṇa for some time, but after coming back, it feels ungrounded as there is nothing to think about. But a devotee adheres to Saguṇa God after he comes out of Nirguṇa realization. His mind remains invariably centered in Saguṇa God. Therefore, he is the best amongst all Yogis. St. Tukārāma has expressed great belief in the worship of Saguṇa where he says, "Some enlightened people continually adhere to Nirguṇa Brahman. But there is so much sweetness and joy in the Saguṇa worship that I will make even such Nirguṇa seekers salivate over the joy of worshipping Saguṇa. Once they taste the sweet joy of Saguṇa worship, they will wish to step away from their adherence to Nirguṇa and rejoice in Saguṇa devotion." It is far easier to see Kṛṣṇa everywhere in all beings, rather than seeing Brahman pervading everywhere. All enlightened saints have nurtured their vision in the same way.

## The process of Saguṇa worship

ये तु सर्वाणि कर्माणि मयि संन्यस्य मत्पराः ।
अनन्येनैव योगेन मां ध्यायन्त उपासते ॥ ६ ॥
तेषामहं समुद्धर्ता मृत्युसंसारसागरात् ।
भवामि नचिरात्पार्थ मय्यावेशितचेतसाम् ॥ ७ ॥
मय्येव मन आधत्स्व मयि बुद्धिं निवेशय ।
निवसिष्यसि मय्येव अत ऊर्ध्वं न संशयः ॥ ८ ॥

*Ye tu sarvāṇi karmāṇi mayi saṃnyasya matparaḥ* ।
*Ananyenaiva yogena māṃ dhyāyanta upāsate* ॥ *6* ॥
*Teṣāṃ ahaṃ samuddhartā mṛtyusaṃsārasāgarāt* ।
*Bhavāmi na cirāt pārtha mayy āveśitacetasām* ॥ *7* ॥
*Mayy eva mana ādhatsva mayi buddhiṃ niveśaya* ।
*Nivasiṣyasi mayy eva ata ūrdhvaṃ na saṃśayaḥ* ॥ *8* ॥

**Meaning:** Those who remain continually connected with Me, offer all their actions to Me, worship My Saguṇa form with single-minded devotion, and constantly meditate on Me – I liberate and elevate them, without delay, from the ocean of mortal worldly life. Therefore, fix your mind on Me, and let the decisions of your intellect be about Me alone. Thereafter, you shall undoubtedly remain united with Me and live in Me alone.

The term ***Anusandhāna*** means mentally adhering to God or being constantly connected with Him. When desires in the mind, decisions of the intellect, and reflection in the memory are focused on God, the ego merges in God and the seeker becomes One with Him. [Note: mind = Manas, intellect = Buddhi, memory = Citta, ego = Ahaṅkāra i.e. awareness of oneself as a limited, individual being.] All of these are tools to remain connected with God. Every seeker has to engage in some or the other action. So, offering all actions to God, as per Karmayoga, is another way of connecting with Him. Chanting, Yoga, meditation, and contemplation on Ātman are some other ways of being connected with God. Beholding His beautiful form and smile, pining to see His Saguṇa form and meet Him, and longing to go to His holy places can be considered some other ways of adhering to Him. St. Tukārāma prays to the Lord, "May my mind be steadily focused on God." He does not pray for constant physical presence, company, or proximity of God. His poetry indicates that the mental state or attitude is much more inmportant that the state of the body in spiritual path. When the mind continually adheres to God and remains steady in Him, the Cidābhāsa in mind disappears in the real God (*Cit*). In other words, Reflected Consciousness in mind disappears in Pure Consciousness. God is *Cit*; He Himself is Pure Knowledge even in His Saguṇa form. There is no reason to differentiate between adhering to Saguṇa God vs. adhering to Nirguṇa Brahman. St. Tukārāma has said that while worshipping God, it is crucial to truly feel and believe that God is present in the insentient form like an image, sculpture, or a frame. The worship reaches real God even if an idol is worshiped. The outward appearance of the frame or sculpture is not important in this process. God is sentient, while His idol is insentient. The sentient Jiva strives to unite with sentient God by worshipping and meditating on an insentient symbol like an image or a sculpture of God.

**Alternative course**

अथ चित्तं समाधातुं न शक्नोषि मयि स्थिरम् ।
अभ्यासयोगेन ततो मामिच्छाप्तुं धनञ्जय ॥ ९ ॥

*Atha cittaṃ samādhātuṃ na śaknoṣi mayi sthiram* ।
*Abhyāsayogena tato mām ichāptuṃ dhanaṃjaya* ॥ *9* ॥

**Meaning:** If you are unable to fix your mind on Me, then seek to attain Me by the Yoga of constant practice (Abhyāsa).

The word **Abhyāsa** means doing the same thing over and over again. It is extremely difficult to fix the wavering mind on God. The failure to do so disheartens the seeker. Even the most evolved seekers falter in this effort. Therefore, the seeker should follow all dos and don'ts of spiritual pursuit and tirelessly strive to concentrate his mind. Some prescribed don'ts are – do not nurture unnecessary thoughts of the past and future, do not engage in superfluous reading and discussions, do not watch TV, do not read unnecessary sections of newspapers, and do not perform duties by desiring results or thinking that "I am the doer." Some prescribed dos are – perform daily worship of God, engage in some regular rituals, read scriptures and holy books, sing glories of God, attend spiritual discourses, go to pilgrimages when possible, chant a Mantra, memorize holy verses, etc. The seeker can repeatedly perform these practices to progess on the spiritual path. These actions together help the seeker fix his mind on God.

**Alternative course**

**अभ्यासेऽप्यसमर्थोऽसि मत्कर्मपरमो भव ।**
**मदर्थमपि कर्माणि कुर्वन्सिद्धिमवाप्स्यसि ॥ १० ॥**

*Abhyāse'pyasamartho'si matkarmaparamo bhava* ।
*Madartham api karmāṇi kurvan siddhim avāpsyasi* ॥ *10* ॥

**Meaning:** If you do not have the necessary potential to study (the aforementioned Abhyāsayoga), then be intent to perform all actions only for My sake. Even by doing actions for My sake, you will attain Me.

Some seekers do not possess the requisite Sattvaguṇa; they are unable to control the mind and senses i.e. practice Śama and Dama, and they lack other necessary qualities required for spiritual pursuit. They should perform each action while remembering Me, by offering it to Me, as prescribed by Me, as would be admired by Me, and for attaining Me. By constantly doing this, they would attain the perfection of being One with Me in due course of time.

**Alternative course**

**अथैतदप्यशक्तोऽसि कर्तुं मद्योगमाश्रितः ।**
**सर्वकर्मफलत्यागं ततः कुरु यतात्मवान् ॥ ११ ॥**

*Athaitadapyaśakto'si kartuṃ madyogamāśrītaḥ* ।
*Sarvakarmaphalatyāgaṃ tataḥ kuru yatātmavān* ॥ *11* ॥

**Meaning:** If you are unable to do even this, then take refuge in Me, conquer your mind, and renounce the fruits of all actions.

Every action is associated with fruits or consequences according to the governance of Īśvara. The fruit is not earned by the Jiva, but rather it is given to him by the Lord. If a seeker remembers this fact while performing actions, then actions do not bind him. The Prārabdha of such a seeker comes to an end by living through it in his current life, and his Sañcita is destroyed due to immense love for God. St. Tukārāma says, "All my actions and their fruits have now become Nārāyaṇa (God)." Engaging in duties without feeling that "I am the doer" is the same as performing duties by renouncing their fruits.

## The importance of renunciation of fruits of actions

**श्रेयो हि ज्ञानमभ्यासाज्ज्ञानाद्ध्यानं विशिष्यते ।**
**ध्यानात्कर्मफलत्यागस्त्यागाच्छान्तिरनन्तरम् ॥ १२ ॥**

*Śreyo hi jñānam abhyāsāj jñānād dhyānaṃ viśiṣyate* ।
*Dhyānāt karmaphalatyāgas tyāgāc chāntir anantaram* ॥ *12* ॥

**Meaning:** The theoretical knowledge is better than mere mechanical or perfunctory study, meditation on Saguṇa God is better than theoretical knowledge, renunciation of fruits of actions is better than meditation, and renunciation ultimately leads to supreme peace.

St. Ekanātha asks a question in his poetry Haripāṭha, "What is the use of reading a holy book without knowing its meaning?" Listening to profound spiritual discourses by paying specific attention to the gist of philosophy is better than mere emotional reading of holy books or mechanical memorization of verses. Listening provides more knowledge about Saguṇa and Nirguṇa God. Meditating on God is an even higher practice than only listening to the knowledge about God. A still higher practice is renouncing the fruits of actions, since it removes the feelings of doership and ownership from the seeker's mind, and thereafter he can find inner peace. On the contrary, when a seeker enjoys or experiences the fruits of actions instead of renouncing them, he invariably experiences the duality of joy and grief. By offering all fruits to God, the duality is removed from his mind, and he realizes that he himself is Pure Bliss.

**The characteristics of a wise devotee (Jñāni Bhakta)**

**अद्वेष्टा सर्वभूतानां मैत्रः करुण एव च ।**
**निर्ममो निरहङ्कारः समदुःखसुखः क्षमी ॥ १३ ॥**
**सन्तुष्टः सततं योगी यतात्मा दृढनिश्चयः ।**
**मय्यर्पितमनोबुद्धिर्यो मद्भक्तः स मे प्रियः ॥ १४ ॥**
**यस्मान्नोद्विजते लोको लोकान्नोद्विजते च यः ।**
**हर्षामर्षभयोद्वेगैर्मुक्तो यः स च मे प्रियः ॥ १५ ॥**
**अनपेक्षः शुचिर्दक्ष उदासीनो गतव्यथः ।**
**सर्वारम्भपरित्यागी यो मद्भक्तः स मे प्रियः ॥ १६ ॥**
**यो न हृष्यति न द्वेष्टि न शोचति न काङ्क्षति ।**
**शुभाशुभपरित्यागी भक्तिमान्यः स मे प्रियः ॥ १७ ॥**
**समः शत्रौ च मित्रे च तथा मानापमानयोः ।**
**शीतोष्णसुखदुःखेषु समः सङ्गविवर्जितः ॥ १८ ॥**
**तुल्यनिन्दास्तुतिर्मौनी सन्तुष्टो येन केनचित् ।**
**अनिकेतः स्थिरमतिर्भक्तिमान्मे प्रियो नरः ॥ १९ ॥**

*Adveṣṭā sarvabhūtānāṃ maitraḥ karuṇa eva ca* ।
*Nirmamo nirahaṃkāraḥ samaduḥkhasukhaḥ kṣamī* ॥ 13 ॥
*Saṃtuṣṭaḥ satataṃ yogī yatātmā dṛḍhaniścayaḥ* ।
*Mayy arpitamanobuddhir yo madbhaktaḥ sa me priyaḥ* ॥ 14 ॥
*Yasmān nodvijate loko lokān nodvijate ca yaḥ* ।
*Harṣāmarṣabhayodvegair mukto yaḥ sa ca me priyaḥ* ॥ 15 ॥
*Anapekṣaḥ śucir dakṣa udāsīno gatavyathaḥ* ।
*Sarvārambhaparityāgī yo madbhaktaḥ sa me priyaḥ* ॥ 16 ॥
*Yo na hṛṣyati na dveṣṭi na śocati na kāṅkṣati* ।
*Śubhāśubhaparityāgī bhaktimān yaḥ sa me priyaḥ* ॥ 17 ॥

*Samaḥ śatrau ca mitre ca tathā mānāpamānayoḥ* ।
*Śītoṣṇasukhaduḥkheṣu samaḥ saṅgavivarjitaḥ* ॥ *18* ॥
*Tulyanindāstutir maunī saṃtuṣṭo yena kenacit* ।
*Aniketaḥ sthiramatir bhaktimān me priyo naraḥ* ॥ *19* ॥

**Meaning:** He who has no hatred for anyone; who is friendly to all, selflessly compassionate, free from attachment and egoism, always content, Yogi, controlled, firm in conviction, forgiving, equanimous in joy and grief; and who has surrendered his mind and intellect to Me – such a devotee is dear to Me. He who is neither troubled by anyone nor troubles anyone and is free from elation, jealousy, fear, and anxiety – he is dear to Me. He who has no expectations from anyone, who is pious in all aspects, alert in duties, neutral, untroubled, and selfless in all actions – such a devotee is dear to Me. He who neither rejoices in favorable situations nor hates nor grieves, who is free from desires, and who renounces results of both good and bad actions – such a devotee is dear to Me. He who is the same to a friend and an enemy, honor and dishonor, heat and cold, joy and grief; free from attachment; equanimous in praise and criticism; and not attached to any place – such a devotee is dear to Me.

All these qualities are spiritual practices for a seeker, and they are natural characteristics of an enlightened devotee. E.g. it is natural to feel some jealousy and discontentment when a person is a practicing seeker and separate from God. As a seeker, he should strive to wipe out the negative traits from his mind through constant reflection and practice. The gist of devotion is unconditional surrender to God and being content with all results granted by Him after having done one's duty in the best possible manner. When the seeker becomes One with God, there is no one else for whom he may feel hatred or disdain as he can see God everywhere around him. He becomes ever-satiated in God, and there is no reason for any discontentment in his life. He becomes detached, untroubled, neutral, and serene in the same manner. Lord Kṛṣṇa has described these characteristics over and over again in many places.

## Conclusion and culmination

**ये तु धर्म्यामृतमिदं यथोक्तं पर्युपासते ।**
**श्रद्दधाना मत्परमा भक्तास्तेऽतीव मे प्रियाः ॥ २० ॥**

*Ye tu dharmyāmṛtam idaṃ yathoktaṃ paryupāsate ।*
*Śraddadhānā matparamā bhaktāste'tīva me priyāḥ ॥ 20 ॥*

**Meaning:** However, those faithful seekers who worship Me by firmly remaining connected with Me at all times and by following the teachings of Dharma as described above – they are exceedingly dear to Me.

**ॐ तत्सदिति श्रीमद्भगवद्गीतासूपनिषत्सु ब्रह्मविद्यायां योगशास्त्रे श्रीकृष्णार्जुनसंवादे भक्तियोगो नाम द्वादशोऽध्यायः ॥**

*Om Tatsaditi Śrimadbhagvadgitāsūpaniṣatsu Brahmavidyāyāṃ Yogaśāstre Śrīkṛṣṇārjunasaṁvāde Bhaktiyogo Nāma Dvādaśo'dhyāyaḥ ॥*

Utmost unwavering faith, steady awareness of God, and following His teachings are the three key aspects of spiritual success. The message of verse 9.2 is repeated here that these teachings are in accordance with Dharma, and the seeker should abide by them with unswerving faith. Later in verse 18.70, the Lord has imparted the same teaching again. **Mokṣadharma** means following the essential teachings of scriptures for attaining liberation. Lord Kṛṣṇa's teachings are consistent with those of Mokṣadharma. Being continually aware of the true Self and abiding in the thought that "I am Brahman" is the spiritual duty i.e. Mokṣadharma of each Jiva (18.73).

Chapter 13

# Distinguishing the Kṣetra from the Kṣetrajña

॥ क्षेत्रक्षेत्रज्ञविभागयोगः (Kṣetrakṣetrajñavibhāgayoga) ॥

It is believed that the 13th chapter marks the beginning of the section of spiritual knowledge (*Jñānakāṇḍa*) of the Bhagavad-Gita. In the 15th century India, there was an acclaimed distinguished scholar named 'Madhusūdana Sarasvati' in the Advaita Vedānta tradition. He classified 18 chapters of the Bhagavad-Gita in the three sections corresponding to ***Tat-Tvam-Asi***. [*Tat-Tvam-Asi* or *Thou Art That* is a Vedāntic Mahāvākya from Chāndogya Upaniṣad which states the Oneness of Jiva and Brahman]. Per his classification, the three sections of the Gita illustrate in detail the three words in the Mahāvākya, respectively:

- ***Tvam*** – You/Thou (Jiva) – Chapters 1 to 6
- ***Tat*** – That (Brahman) – Chapters 7 to 12
- ***Asi*** – Are/Art (Union of Jiva & Brahman) – Chapters 13 to 18

Madhusūdana Sarasvati states that the 13th chapter marks the commencement of study for the realization of the ***Asi*** word in Tat-Tvam-Asi. The Jiva (***Tvam***) must perform spiritual practice to realize Oneness with Brahman (***Tat***). Some aspects in the mental and intellectual makeup help this practice, while some hinder the practice. All such aspects are described from chapters 13 to 17. The seeker should remove the aspects which hinder his spiritual practice and embrace the aspects which assist and enhance his spiritual pursuit. E.g. the seeker is required to earn the divine qualities and remove the demoniac qualities which are described in Chapter 16. This is the primary goal of the last six chapters of the Bhagavad-Gita.

The term **Kṣetra** means a body. The term **Kṣetrajña** means Jivā who knows the body. At the outset of this chapter, it is necessary to understand the following terms clearly:

- Antaḥkaraṇa: Inner instrument or invisible inner organ of each Jiva comprising of mind, intellect, memory, and ego. It works in a fourfold manner; hence, it has four names according to each of its four functions. Antaḥkaraṇa is the real Upādhi of each Jiva.
- Upādhi: Limiting adjunct which helps to identify one object distinctly from the rest, but it itself remains separate from the object
- Pure Consciousness with no Upādhi: Ātman / Brahman / Kuṭastha
- Jiva / Jivātmā = Brahman + Upādhi of the body or Antaḥkaraṇa
- Īśvara / God = Brahman + Upādhi of the universe or Māyā

These concepts are explained in more detail in verse 13.2.

The meaning of the word **Kṣetrajña** in this chapter should be taken according to its context, and it depends on the Upādhi. To better understand the meaning of Kṣetrajña, it is necessary to learn the following two terms:

- *Vacyārtha* **(वाच्यार्थ)**: literal or explicit meaning.
- *Lakśyārtha* **(लक्ष्यार्थ)**: core or implied meaning.

E.g. consider the sentence "I flew from Mumbai to Delhi." In this sentence, the literal meaning is that "I myself flew from Mumbai to Delhi," while the implied meaning is that "I boarded an airplane which flew from Mumbai to Delhi." Thus, the literal meaning and implied meaning of some words change according to their context, and they need to be understood separately. Analogous to this, the meaning of the term Kṣetrajña changes when it is considered with or without Upādhi:

- The literal meaning of Kṣetrajña (with Upādhi): Jivātmā/Jiva/Cidābhāsa (sentient)
- The implied meaning of Kṣetrajña (without Upādhi): Ātman/Brahman/Kuṭastha/Pure Consciousness

Every Jivā is originally Brahman when the Upādhi of the body (Antaḥkaraṇa) is removed from him. Īśvara is originally Brahman when the Upādhi of the universe or Māyā is removed from Him. Jiva, Īśvara, Kuṭastha, and Brahman – these four kinds of Consciousness are considered separate from each other only due to the difference of Upādhi. In essence, they are all Brahman (Kṛṣṇa).

The Kṣetra (body) is insentient and illumined. It is the subject-matter of 'qualified knowledge' (*Vṛttijñāna*), which means that the Kṣetra is known by the mind, senses, and other epistemic sources of knowledge. Kṣetrajña Ātman is Self-effulgent and Pure Knowledge itself. It cannot be known by the mind, senses, and other Pramāṇas. By discriminating between Kṣetra and Kṣetrajña in this manner, the seeker can acquire true Self-Knowledge.

The Kṣetra has no autonomous existence. It is superimposed (*Adhyasta*); it is delusive like a snake on a rope. The rope has an autonomous existence, but the snake is an illusory appearance.

## Kṣetra and Kṣetrajña

*श्रीभगवानुवाच ।*
इदं शरीरं कौन्तेय क्षेत्रमित्यभिधीयते ।
एतद्यो वेत्ति तं प्राहुः क्षेत्रज्ञ इति तद्विदः ॥ १ ॥

*Śrībhagavān uvāca* ।
*Idaṃ śarīraṃ kaunteya kṣetram ity abhidhīyate* ।
*Etad yo vetti taṃ prāhuḥ kṣetrajña iti tadvidaḥ* ॥ *1* ॥

**Meaning:** (Śrībhagavān said) The wise philosophers know the difference between Kṣetra and Kṣetrajña – the body addressed by 'this' is Kṣetra, and the one who knows the body is Kṣetrajña.

"My body is aching", "I use my mind", "My intellect is sharp", "My memory is weak", "I am gasping for breath" – these are some of the ways in which 'I' address 'my' gross body and subtle body. My body or my mind is separate from me. The body which is seen separately is the Kṣetra, while the knower who knows it to be separate is the Kṣetrajña. In Vedāntic language – "The body is illumined by someone else." It is the Jiva (Jivātmā) who illumines the body i.e. he knows the body as 'this body.' The Jiva also knows activities of the mind, intellect, etc., and he uses them in his day-to-day transactions. The very nature of each Jiva is Self-effulgent Ātman, which means no one else can know Ātman, and it is not necessary to have anyone else. This is analogous to the example of a light where another light is not needed to see the first light. [The Jiva identifies himself with the body and thinks that he is a separate, individual being limited to his body. On the contrary, Īśvara is aware of his true nature as Brahman. He regulates the universe but does not identify Himself with the universe separately from Brahman. Brahman neither regulates the universe nor identifies itself separately. It is only one, non-dual principle.]

The word Kṣetra also means a field. A farmer harvests many different crops from a field. Similarly, one can reap the harvest of sins, merits, and pure merits (Pāpa, Puṇya, and Śuddha Puṇya) from the field of the body. The Jiva is free to decide what he wants to harvest from the field of his body. Lord Kṛṣṇa, scriptures like Upaniṣads, and enlightened saints guide all seekers in this regard.

**The spiritual characteristic of Knowledge**

क्षेत्रज्ञं चापि मां विद्धि सर्वक्षेत्रेषु भारत ।
क्षेत्रक्षेत्रज्ञयोर्ज्ञानं यत्तज्ज्ञानं मतं मम ॥ २ ॥

*Kṣetrajñaṃ cāpi māṃ viddhi sarvakṣetreṣu bhārata* ।
*Kṣetrakṣetrajñayor jñānaṃ yat taj jñānaṃ mataṃ mama* ॥ 2 ॥

**Meaning:** Know that the Kṣetrajña (Jiva) in all these Kṣetras is Me (Brahman). In My opinion, the comprehensive knowledge of the Kṣetra and the Kṣetrajña is the true Knowledge.

It is essential to understand the difference between information and knowledge from the spiritual perspective. All knowledge about the Kṣetra should be considered information, while all knowledge about the Kṣetrajña should be regarded as the true Knowledge.

The body is the Kṣetra (field) of the Jiva, while the universe is the Kṣetra of Īśvara. Brahman pervades them both, yet it is neither attached to them nor encaged by them. Both these Kṣetras are illusory, so in reality, there is no Kṣetra associated with Brahman. Brahman is separately seen as Īśvara due to the Upādhi of the universe, and it is seen separately as a Jiva due to the Upādhi of the body. Upādhi is imaginary, so both Īśvara and Jiva are imaginary as well. The Jiva is the Kṣetrajña of an individual being. Īśvara is the Kṣetrajña of the universe. The following diagram further explains this concept and the limitations of Jiva, Īśvara, and Brahman.

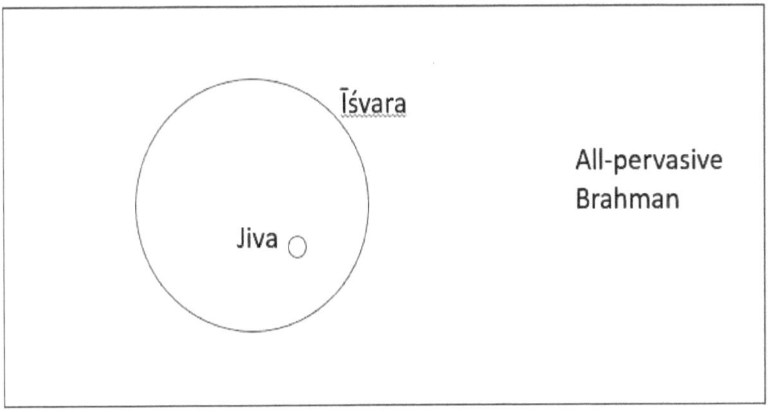


The white color in the outermost rectangle can be seen as Brahman. Brahman which is limited by the bigger circle can be seen as Īśvara. The white color limited by the inner tiny circle may be seen as a Jiva. White color pervades everywhere. The circles are called Upādhis i.e. limiting adjuncts. Upādhis are perishable; they are neither real nor unreal hence indescribable and illusory (*Sat-Asat-Vilakṣaṇa-Anirvacaniya-Mithyā*). Brahman exists constantly, eternally as it is, regardless of the presence or absence of Upādhis. Lord Kṛṣṇa says that He Himself is the Kṣetrajña.

An **Upādhi** is that which separates one object from others and which itself remains separate from the object. The existence of that object itself is not dependent on the Upādhi. E.g. consider a crow sitting on a tree. The crow shows that tree – on which it is seated – separately from other trees. Later, even if the crow flies away, the tree still exists as before. Therefore, the crow is the Upādhi of that tree, but the tree does not depend on the crow for its existence. Similarly, the body is the Upādhi of the Jiva, but the true nature of Jiva (Brahman) does not depend on the body in any way. Ignorant Jiva is deluded with the fact that "I am the Kṣetra (body)" and "objects in the Kṣetra (the world) are mine." St. Tukārāma has stated in simple words, "This Kṣetra i.e. my body may live or die, but I know that my true Self is the Kṣetrajña i.e. Pāṇḍuranga/Brahman, and I firmly adhere to my true Self."

**<u>Kṣetra and its modifications</u>**

तत्क्षेत्रं यच्च यादृक्च यद्विकारि यतश्च यत् ।
स च यो यत्प्रभावश्च तत्समासेन मे श्रृणु ॥ ३ ॥
ऋषिभिर्बहुधा गीतं छन्दोभिर्विविधैः पृथक् ।
ब्रह्मसूत्रपदैश्चैव हेतुमद्भिर्विनिश्चितैः ॥ ४ ॥
महाभूतान्यहङ्कारो बुद्धिरव्यक्तमेव च ।
इन्द्रियाणि दशैकं च पञ्च चेन्द्रियगोचराः ॥ ५ ॥
इच्छा द्वेषः सुखं दुःखं सङ्घातश्चेतना धृतिः ।
एतत्क्षेत्रं समासेन सविकारमुदाहृतम् ॥ ६ ॥

*Tat kṣetraṃ yac ca yādṛk ca yadvikāri yataś ca yat* ।
*Sa ca yo yatprabhāvaś ca tat samāsena me śṛṇu* ॥ 3 ॥

*Ṛṣibhir bahudhā gītaṃ chandobhir vividhaiḥ pṛthak* ।
*Brahmasūtrapadaiś caiva hetumadbhir viniścitaiḥ* ॥ *4* ॥
*Mahābhūtāny ahaṃkāro buddhir avyaktam eva ca* ।
*Indriyāṇi daśaikaṃ ca pañca cendriyagocarāḥ* ॥ *5* ॥
*Icchā dveṣaḥ sukhaṃ duḥkhaṃ saṃghātaś cetanā dhṛtiḥ* ।
*Etat kṣetraṃ samāsena savikāram udāhṛtam* ॥ *6* ॥

**Meaning:** I will briefly describe what that Kṣetra is, its exact nature, and its modifications (*Vikāras*). I will also explain the Kṣetrajña that is the cause of all Kṣetras and the power of Kṣetrajña. Listen to these explanations. The knowledge about the Kṣetra and Kṣetrajña has been sung by many Ṛṣis through various distinct Mantras in the Vedas and Upaniṣads which determine the cause and effect relationship. The Five Great Elements, ego, intellect, Avyakta (dormant state of the universe), eleven organs, 5 types of sensory objects, desire, hatred, joy, grief, the collection of organs in a body, sentience, and firm coexistence – these constituents (modifications) make up a Kṣetra which is briefly described here.

These verses discuss the details about the nature of Kṣetra, its modifications, the cause and effect regarding objects, and the power of Kṣetrajña. Change is the nature of a modification (**Vikāra**); The Kṣetra changes in 36 different ways and can be seen in that changed manner. These modifications are the elements of body composition. There are many different and strong arguments about what exactly the Kṣetra is, what its constituents are, and what its usefulness is, etc. The scholars are not able to resolve these complexities. Therefore, the Lord is giving His decisive opinion here. A seeker leading worldly life should embrace the decisive opinion given by the Lord and use it for his spiritual pursuit, without getting enmeshed into the intricacies of other opinions.

The Five Great Elements (Pañca-Mahābhūtas) are –

1 **Earth** (Pṛthvī)

2 **Water** (Āpa)
3 **Fire** (Teja)
4 **Wind** (Vāyū)
5 **Ether** or **Sky** (Ākāśa)

They were created in the reverse order: From Ātman, first Sky (Ether or Ākāśa) was created, and then the rest of the elements were created in the reverse order. In the beginning, they were in a subtle form and separated from each other. Such subtle elements are called **Tanmātrā**. These Tanmātrā were later mixed in a specific proportion through the process of Quintuplication (Pañcīkaraṇa); as a result of this process, the gross Five Elements were created. E.g. the gross Earth Element was created by mixing the Tanmātrā as follow:

- 50% of subtle earth
- 12.5% subtle water
- 12.5% subtle fire
- 12.5% subtle wind
- 12.5% subtle sky (ether)

The other four gross elements – water, fire, wind, and sky – were created by mixing the Tanmātrā in the same manner. Antaḥkaraṇa was created from the non-quintuplicated subtle elements (*Apañcīkṛta Tanmātra*), and the gross body was created from the quintuplicated gross elements (*Pañcīkṛta Mahābhūta*).

1. The gross body: The word 'gross' here does not indicate a physical form or color. The gross body means the visible body made up of muscles and bones, etc.
2. The ego: When the body is created, the ego manifests and remains attached to the body by thinking "I am the body." It flaunts itself by identifying with the body, the intellect, and the circumstances. The ego is defined as the continuous awareness of 'I,''I' that one feels within. (*Aham aham*

*kārayati iti Ahaṅkārah*). It is extremely difficult to transcend the ego since it is created from the earth element.

3. The intellect: It is created from the fire element and Sattvaguṇa. The Antaḥkaraṇa (mind) that makes decisions is defined as the intellect (*Niścayātmikā vṛttiḥ sā Buddhiḥ*). The Vāsanā that is responsible for the rebirth of a person resides in the intellect. The intellect is responsible for choosing between right and wrong.
4. The unmanifested (*Avyakta*): After the end of cosmos (Pralaya), the universe dissolves in Prakṛti and later manifests from it again. This Prakṛti, which stores the seeds of all beings in the universe, is known as Avyakta. When the Jiva rests in the deep-sleep, that state may also be known as the Avyakta.
5. The five sense organs (*Jñanendriya*): Eyes, ears, skin, nose, and tongue (taste buds) are the sensory organs. They can know form, sound, touch, smell, and taste, respectively. In Vedāntic language, it is often said that "A form is a subject-matter of eyes." (Tongue is both a sense organ and an action organ. For tasting, it is the sense organ; and it also contributes to the action of speaking.)
6. The five action organs (*Karmendriya*): Hands, feet, mouth, rectum, and genitals are the action organs. Holding, walking, speaking, excreting, and copulating are their actions, respectively.
7. The mind: This is essential for both worldly life and spiritual life. The mind is created from the wind element and Rajoguṇa, so it is wavering in nature. Kaṭha-Upaniṣad beautifully explains this concept using the metaphor of a chariot. The *mind* is equated to 'reins'. It is held by the *intellect* which is a 'charioteer' used to control the *organs* which are like the 'horses'. The mind is responsible for two ways of transmission. It transmits the decisions of the intellect – which itself is influenced by past Vāsanās – to the

action organs. The mind also takes in new imprints collected by the sense organs and transmits them back to the intellect. Therefore, all enlightened saints have imparted teachings to the mind to mold it properly for spiritual progress. The mind does the crucial job of taking in the new teachings of scriptures, saints, the Lord, and Sadguru through the sense organs. It then transmits back the new teachings to the intellect and gradually liberates the intellect from the clutches of old Vāsanās.

8. Desires: The nature of a desire is – "I wish to obtain something." Man desires to obtain five objects of senses, which are form, sound, smell, touch, taste, etc., and also other objects like power, wealth, success, fame, prestige, etc. for happiness. He is compelled to dance to the tunes of his desires for being happy; desires bring both joy and grief.
9. Hatred: Hatred is a strong reaction that rises while facing an adverse or undesired situation. When a desired or loved object cannot be obtained due to some obstacle, one starts hating the obstacle. Love and hatred constitute a duality.
10. Joy: Pure, unqualified joy – irrespective of the presence or absence of objects – is the very nature of sentient Kṣetrajña (Ātman). It is not necessary to seek it in the world outside. But a person experiences joy through worldly objects, favorable circumstances, good sleep, merits, and Sattvaguṇa – all of which are pertinent to the Kṣetra. Such joy derived through the Kṣetra is dependent on external aspects, so it is secondary or inconsequential as compared to the ever-available Pure Bliss of Kṣetrajña Ātman.
11. Grief: A person can never experience pure, unadulterated, lasting happiness due to his Prārabdha. Joy that comes by obtaining favorable objects is always coupled with suffering that comes by obtaining unfavorable objects or grief that comes by losing favorable objects. Only Ātman, Pure Bliss, is beyond the duality of this transient joy and grief.

12. Collection (*Sanghāta*): All bodily organs together are known as a collection or a Sanghāta. Organs are complementary to each other. Together, they constitute the day-to-day life of Kṣetra.
13. Sentience (*Cetanā*): Kṣetrajña is, in fact, sentient. Insentient objects are pervaded by sentient Kṣetrajña (Ātman). However, there is no mind (Antaḥkaraṇa) in insentient objects. Therefore, the sentience of Ātman cannot be manifested in insentient objects. The sentience of Ātman is also present in a dead body, but there is no Jiva in the dead body due to the absence of the mind.
14. Firm coexistence (*Dhṛti*): The properties of each of the Five Great Elements are contradictory to each other. Despite that, all the five elements coexist together amiably in the body and sustain the Kṣetra. E.g. water and fire are opposite to each other. Water can extinguish fire and fire can vaporize water. However, inside a body, they coexist together in harmony without any conflict, and only due to their collective co-existence, the body continues to function. Their firm power to remain together in this manner is called Dhṛti.

Thus, this Kṣetra (body) is made of thirty-six elements: the Great Elements – 5, intellect – 1, Avyakta – 1, ego – 1, organs – 10, the objects and actions of organs – 10, mind – 1, desire – 1, hatred – 1, joy – 1, grief – 1, collection – 1, sentience – 1, and firm coexistence – 1 = 36.

The Kṣetra (body) is insentient, while one who knows the Kṣetra is the sentient Kṣetrajña (Jiva). The real nature of a seeker is not the individual, limited consciousness (Jiva). Eternal, infinite, Pure Consciousness (Ātman) is his real nature. Ātman gives sentience to the Kṣetra. Cidābhāsa illumines the mind which pervades the gross body; hence the body and mind of a Jiva appear to be sentient. The main objective of any spiritual practice is that the Jiva should disregard his body (Kṣetra) through spiritual discrimination and realize Oneness with his true Self, Ātman (Kṛṣṇa).

As long as the Jiva identifies that "I am the body", he invariably gets caught in the life and death cycle after the death of his gross body. After death, the Jiva exists in the form of Vāsanās, and later, he is reborn as another body. He grows, changes, decays, and eventually dies. Thus, he is impermanent, transient, and the experiencer of joy and suffering.

As explained at the beginning of this chapter, the Jiva (***Tvam***) should unite with (***Asi***) Brahman (***Tat***). For this purpose, he needs to understand the impermanent nature of his body and also strive to acquire some other divine qualities. E.g. Humility or being indifferent to honor is a divine quality. A person may or may not receive honor from society for his work, but it is certainly not right for the person to seek honor himself or expect others to respect him. Humility does not mean tolerating dishonor due to meekness or fear. The overall appearance of the body and personality, intelligence of the mind, success or failure, affluence or poverty, self-regard or subservience, healthiness or unhealthiness – these traits can bring in honor or dishonor. All these traits are pertinent to the Kṣetra; therefore, the Jiva starts taking pride in his Kṣetra. Rather, the pride in the Kṣetra enhances these traits. The Kṣetra is impermanent. The pride in the Kṣetra, as well as honor or dishonor associated with it, are all impermanent. Consequently, one who expects honor for himself cannot realize that "I am Ātman." Therefore, it is necessary to consciously dissociate oneself from the dualities like honor and dishonor or see them in an impersonal, impassive manner.

The seeker who remains immersed in impermanent worldly life can never realize eternal Ātman as his true Self.

## The practices for attaining Self-Knowledge

अमानित्वमदम्भित्वमहिंसा क्षान्तिरार्जवम् ।
आचार्योपासनं शौचं स्थैर्यमात्मविनिग्रहः ॥ ७ ॥
इन्द्रियार्थेषु वैराग्यमनहङ्कार एव च ।
जन्ममृत्युजराव्याधिदुःखदोषानुदर्शनम् ॥ ८ ॥
असक्तिरनभिष्वङ्गः पुत्रदारगृहादिषु ।
नित्यं च समचित्तत्वमिष्टानिष्टोपपत्तिषु ॥ ९ ॥
मयि चानन्ययोगेन भक्तिरव्यभिचारिणी ।
विविक्तदेशसेवित्वमरतिर्जनसंसदि ॥ १० ॥
अध्यात्मज्ञाननित्यत्वं तत्त्वज्ञानार्थदर्शनम् ।
एतज्ज्ञानमिति प्रोक्तमज्ञानं यदतोऽन्यथा ॥ ११ ॥

*Amānitvam adambhitvam ahiṃsā kṣāntir ārjavam* ।
*Ācāryopāsanaṃ śaucaṃ sthairyam ātmavinigrahaḥ* ॥ 7 ॥
*Indriyārtheṣu vairāgyam anahaṃkāra eva ca* ।
*Janmamṛtyujarāvyādhiduḥkhadoṣānudarśanam* ॥ 8 ॥
*Asaktir anabhiṣvaṅgaḥ putradāragṛhādiṣu* ।
*Nityaṃ ca samacittatvam iṣṭāniṣṭopapattiṣu* ॥ 9 ॥
*Mayi cānanyayogena bhaktir avyabhicāriṇī* ।
*Viviktadeśasevitvam aratir janasaṃsadi* ॥ 10 ॥
*Adhyātmajñānanityatvaṃ tattvajñānārthadarśanam* ।
*Etaj jñānam iti proktam ajñānaṃ yadato'nyathā* ॥ 11 ॥

**Meaning:** Not expecting honor; humility; modesty; non-violence; forgiveness; straightforwardness; serving the Sadguru; purity; steadfastness; control of the mind; dispassion towards objects of the senses; absence of egoism; being aware of the faults associated with birth, death, aging, sickness, etc.; dispassion; not being excessively involved in wife, son, house, and the like; evenness towards desired and undesired; single-minded devotion to Lord Kṛṣṇa; liking for solitude; distaste for the company of people who are sinful, materialistic, and bound by worldly affairs; constant affinity to Self-Knowledge; and studying the scriptures of Vedānta – these are the practices to realize true Self-Knowledge, and these are also the characteristics of a person who has attained Self-realization. Anything opposed to it is ignorance.

The natural qualities of an enlightened person are the guidelines of spiritual practices for a seeker. The seeker must consciously and arduously strive to develop and attain those qualities. He is expected to continue his spiritual pursuit despite any intermediate success or setback he may face. Detachment and dispassion are immensely valuable traits for the seeker, and they can be evidently seen as undercurrents in all the aforementioned qualities. All elements of the Kṣetra pertain to the body, and they are the tools available to the Jiva for his functioning. The user of these tools (Jiva) is always separate from the tools themselves (body). The individual Kṣetra (body) and the cosmic Kṣetra (world) are both akin to each other and related to the Jiva, and both are illusory and impermanent.

Boasting or self-promotion is a manifestation of conceit. Even a small success in any field can be enough for boasting. Violence is targeted towards the Kṣetra, but it is the Kṣetrajña who has to bear its brunt. E.g. if one derides an ugly looking person, it is the Jiva in that body who gets hurt. Humiliating anyone is the same as humiliating God. It obstructs the unswerving faith in God (*7.7*).

If another person indulges in sinful behavior, the seeker should recognize that he is doing so under the influence of the three Guṇas, forgive him, and remain at peace himself. But forgiveness needs discretion. Lord Kṛṣṇa Himself condoned the first 100 sins of Śiśupāla but later immediately beheaded him. On a social or national level, forgiveness can be mistaken for weakness, and such unwarranted forgiveness helps political enemies. As a seeker, one should forgive those who mock him on a personal level. Real forgiveness is that quality where a man is capable of taking revenge but still forgives his enemy.

The seeker who is straightforward and upright in his actions can remain calm, and his credibility increases. His worldly life generally remains free from hassles, and there are fewer obstructions in his spiritual practice as well. The seeker should serve his Sadguru by being aware of the personal, familial, and social limits. The ancient tradition of students living in the Āśrama of the Sadguru and serving him is mostly over in today's age. Serving the Guru does not also mean adding to his financial assets and making him rich. It means assisting in his work wherever needed and in whichever manner. The seeker who maintains purity in all aspects of life can progress faster in spiritual pursuit. Impatience, anxiety, agitation, and wavering nature are the traits which do not enable the body or the mind to remain steady. Daydreaming, extreme ambitiousness, and comparing with others disturb the stability of the mind. The seeker cannot stick to any spiritual practice if his mind is not stable. It is necessary for the seeker first to control his mind in order to stabilize it. Traits like desires, anger, and greed make it difficult to control the mind. For that purpose, he can think about the negative effects of these traits. E.g. all objects of desire are impermanent in nature (*2.14*). They are subject to a beginning and an end; it is not wise to depend on them for lasting happiness. Through this thought-process, the seeker can avoid greediness regarding objects of pleasure and thus control his anger which usually arises when he does not acquire those objects. Detachment and dispassion towards worldly objects are necessary for this purpose.

The seeker who does not nurture any ego attains spiritual success very quickly. The ego is a manifestation of Antaḥkaraṇa (mind), so being egoistic is the same as being attached to the impermanent Kṣetra.

Events such as birth, aging, sickness, and death give rise to very little delight and enormous grief in life. There is no need to comment much upon them. Dāsabodha, the acclaimed treatise by St. Rāmadāsa, explains the events of birth and death in detail. The seeker can be detached from his body and the world through *Viveka* i.e. spiritual discrimination. He can think that the body and the world are peripheral aspects of life, while Ātman – the true Self – is the core, primal aspect. Peripheral will be eventually destroyed, while the core gist exists eternally.

Detachment and dispassion are essential, but the seeker should also gradually remove the sense of mineness which is falsely seen as love and is approved by society. He should renounce the feeling of mineness for his son, wife, husband, house, and other such relatives and acquaintances. This is the essence of spiritual practice. It has been presented many times in the Bhagavad-Gita.

The word ***Iṣṭa*** in Sanskrit means desirable, favorable, or good. The word ***Aniṣṭa*** means undesirable, unfavorable, or bad. Every person is faced with both favorable and unfavorable events in life as per his Prārabdha, but it is important to be equanimous in both situations. The seeker who is neither elated upon obtaining what is favorable nor distressed upon obtaining what is unfavorable finds it easy to progress further on the spiritual path. If he is able to remain steady with a single-minded focus in God, he will be able to attain devotion. Instead, if he remains immersed in matters regarding both Kṣetra and Kṣetrajña, he cannot surrender fully to God.

For most ordinary people, their minds are attracted wherever there is a big group of people due to the experience of sheer variety in such places. Being aware of this natural disposition of the mind, the seeker should prefer to remain in seclusion. He should attend public ceremonies like marriage, inauguration, etc. for as little time as possible. He does not need to mingle too much with people who do not have spiritual disposition and who revel mostly in worldly affairs pertinent to the body or objects of pleasure. Accompaniment exerts a great influence on the seeker's mind. Therefore, he should consciously avoid the company of bad people, nurture the company of good people, and calmly endure the company of familial members who are incompatible from the spiritual perspective. Sinful, evil, malicious people are bad company; they should be avoided at any cost. If immediate family members have no spiritual inclination, or they are against spiritual pursuit, then the seeker should quietly adjust with them knowing them to be incompatible. He needs to specifically nurture the company of good people having spiritual dispositions and strive to associate himself with enlightened saints. It is necessary to follow these guidelines for continuing the spiritual pursuit of Self-realization.

Just as a house is frequently soiled by dust, so too the mind is soiled by the influence of the delusive world. The house needs to be cleaned every day. Akin to this, the seeker needs to cleanse his mind and study the scriptures for Self-realization. The goal of the Vedāntic scriptures is Self-realization i.e. the direct realization that "I am Ātman." This is Pure Knowledge. Anything separate or contradictory to this is ignorance. In short, Ātman itself is Pure Knowledge, and all experiences other than the realization of Ātman are mere ignorance.

## Supreme Ātman

**ज्ञेयं यत्तत्प्रवक्ष्यामि यज्ज्ञात्वामृतमश्नुते ।**
**अनादिमत्परं ब्रह्म न सत्तन्नासदुच्यते ॥ १२ ॥**

*Jñeyaṃ yat tat pravakṣyāmi yaj jñātvāmṛtam aśnute* ।
*Anādimat paraṃ brahma na sat tan nāsad ucyate* ॥ *12* ॥

**Meaning:** I shall now describe that which is knowable, knowing which one attains Pure Bliss of Ātman. Brahman, the knowable, is beginningless; it can neither be known as real nor as unreal.

Even Māyā is said to be neither real (*Sat*) nor unreal (*Asat*), hence indescribable (*Sat-Asat-Vilakṣaṇa-Anirvacaniya-*

*Mithyā*). However, the indescribability of Brahman is of a different kind. ***Sat*** is Pure Existence and there is no one else who may address it as *Sat*. This is the reason why Brahman cannot be called *Sat*. Also, since Brahman transcends the three times, it cannot be called ***Asat***. The concepts of *Sat* and *Asat* are relative to each other, while Brahman is beyond them both. At least two entities are needed to compare them for relativity. This is not possible in non-dual One Brahman. St. Tukārāma says that Brahman can neither speak itself nor does it let anyone else speak about it. The actions of speaking and listening are both pertinent to Kṣetra while Ātman as Kṣetrajña is their Witness.

## The Cosmic form of Ātman

**सर्वतः पाणिपादं तत्सर्वतोऽक्षिशिरोमुखम् ।**
**सर्वतः श्रुतिमल्लोके सर्वमावृत्य तिष्ठति ॥ १३ ॥**

*Sarvataḥ pāṇipādaṃ tat sarvato'kṣiśiromukham* ।
*Sarvataḥ śrutimal loke sarvam āvṛtya tiṣṭhati* ॥ *13* ॥

**Meaning:** That Brahman has arms and feet on all sides; it has heads, eyes, and mouths on all sides, and it has ears everywhere. It exists in the world pervading and enveloping all.

Brahman pervades all beings in the world. Therefore, hands, feet of all beings are deemed as if they are Brahman's hands and feet. Organs belong to the Upādhi i.e. limiting adjunct, the body. Since Brahman pervades all bodies, the organs of those bodies are imagined to be of Brahman. In reality, Brahman is shapeless like sky or ether; it cannot possibly have any organs.

## The characteristics of Brahman

**सर्वेन्द्रियगुणाभासं सर्वेन्द्रियविवर्जितम् ।**
**असक्तं सर्वभृच्चैव निर्गुणं गुणभोक्तृ च ॥ १४ ॥**

*Sarvendriyaguṇābhāsaṃ sarvendriyavivarjitam* ।
*Asaktaṃ sarvabhṛc caiva nirguṇaṃ guṇabhoktṛ ca* ॥ *14* ॥

**Meaning:** The Jiva knows all sensory objects on the substratum of Ātman. However, Ātman itself has no organs. Ātman is omnipresent, yet it is not attached to anything; all organs are able to work due to the presence of Ātman. Ātman is an experiencer as a Jiva and non-experiencer as Ātman.

Objects of pleasure, mediums of pleasure, and feeling of pleasure do not belong to the true Self, Ātman. Ātman itself is Absolute, Pure Bliss, which is always present regardless of any object. A person should remember that the happiness felt by him while enjoying a worldly object is only a manifestation of Pure Bliss of his true Self manifested through that object. St. Tukārāma says that one should chant the Mantra of God while enjoying or renouncing a pleasure so that enjoyment or renunciation will not be binding for him.

## All-pervasive Ātman

**बहिरन्तश्च भूतानामचरं चरमेव च ।**
**सूक्ष्मत्वात्तदविज्ञेयं दूरस्थं चान्तिके च तत् ॥ १५ ॥**

*Bahir antaś ca bhūtānām acaraṃ caram eva ca* ।
*Sūkṣmatvāt tad avijñeyaṃ dūrasthaṃ cāntike ca tat* ॥ *15* ॥

**Meaning:** He pervades inside and outside of all sentient and insentient beings. Being highly subtle, He cannot be comprehended by the intellect. He is very far, yet very close.

The concepts of 'inside' and 'outside' are respective to the body. Human life is based on the concepts like 'inside the body,' 'outside the body,' 'inside the world,' 'outside the world,' etc. The space inside a pot (*Ghaṭākāśa*), the space inside a room (*Maṭhākāśa*), and open space (*Mahākāśa*) are present with reference to the Upādhi of the pot, the room, etc. The same is the case with a human body. The space in a pot and the space in a room are seen separately because the pot and the room are built inside wide-open sky. Analogous to this, the very concept of 'inside' and 'outside' is created with the creation of the body and the world.

Bodies of living beings are considered sentient because they have minds with Cidābhāsa (Reflected Consciousness) in them. Insentient objects do not have mind and Cidābhāsa; therefore, they are known as insentient. Space pervades inside the pot, in the body of the pot, and outside the pot. Analogous to this, Ātman pervades inside the body, in all parts of the body, and outside the body uniformly in the same proportion. There is no distinction of 'inside' or 'outside' in the realm of Ātman. It is the most subtle principle; it is Self-effulgent and illuminator of all. The existence of the intellect is known in the light of Ātman. The intellect itself is illumined by Ātman. An illumined object can never know its illuminator; so, the intellect can never know Ātman in the same way it can know other worldly objects. Ātman is the true Self; hence Ātman is extremely close to every Jiva. For those who do not realize "I am Ātman" due to ignorance, Ātman is very far – many births away. In other words, ignorant people do not know Ātman as their true Self despite going through many births.

**The creation, sustenance, destruction of the world**

**अविभक्तं च भूतेषु विभक्तमिव च स्थितम् ।**
**भूतभर्तृ च तज्ज्ञेयं ग्रसिष्णु प्रभविष्णु च ॥ १६ ॥**

*Avibhaktaṃ ca bhūteṣu vibhaktam iva ca sthitam* ।
*Bhūtabhartṛ ca taj jñeyaṃ grasiṣṇu prabhaviṣṇu ca* ॥ *16* ॥

**Meaning:** This Brahman equally pervades one and all, yet it is seen as divided in the bodies of beings. Brahman creates all beings, nourishes and sustains them, and destroys them.

Brahman appears to be multiple due to the sheer variety and multitude of Upādhis (bodies) it pervades. Upādhi is imaginary and impermanent; therefore, the perceived multiplicity in the world is imaginary and impermanent as well. For those who consider the world as real, Vedānta states that Brahman (Īśvara) creates the world by assuming the form of Brahmadeva, sustains it as Viṣṇu, and destroys it as Rudra. But when the seeker arrives at the conclusion that the world itself is a mere appearance, he can see that the three forms of Īśvara are imaginary as well. Brahman alone remains in the end. Brahman is one, homogeneous without divisions, subdivisions, or separations of any kind.

**Self-effulgent Brahman**

ज्योतिषामपि तज्ज्योतिस्तमसः परमुच्यते ।
ज्ञानं ज्ञेयं ज्ञानगम्यं हृदि सर्वस्य विष्ठितम् ॥ १७ ॥

*Jyotiṣām api taj jyotis tamasaḥ param ucyate* ।
*Jñānaṃ jñeyaṃ jñānagamyaṃ hṛdi sarvasya viṣṭhitam* ॥ *17* ॥

**Meaning:** Brahman is the illuminator of the light of the sun, the moon, and the mind, intellect, etc. It is beyond the darkness of 'ignorance' (*Avidyā*) and beyond insentient objects which are the 'effects of ignorance' (*Avidyākarya*). It is knowable, and it is Pure Knowledge itself. It can be attained through the knowledge of the philosophy, and it is established in the hearts of all in a special way.

There is more explanation of this verse in *15.6*. Kaṭha Upaniṣad has a Mantra with similar meaning (*2.2.15*). The sun, moon, and stars are the sources of light. They are physical, worldly lights. However, they can be 'seen and known' only in the light of Ātman. Ātman is Self-effulgent. The sun and the moon, etc. are illumined by Ātman; they are dependent on Ātman for their existence as well as for their knowledge. In day-to-day life, the sun is said to be self-radiant, but from the Vedāntic perspective, the sun can be 'known' only in the light of Ātman. Also, the material lights like the sun and the moon are created by Īśvara through His desire to create the universe. So, even from this perspective, Brahman is the illuminator of all lights.

Brahman also illumines the mind and the intellect. This simply means that functions of the mind and the intellect can be 'known' in the light of Ātman. Illumination of the mind is different from that of the sun. Illumination of the mind means knowing about functions of the mind in the light of Ātman, while illumination of the sun means seeing its physical light in the light of Ātman.

Brahman is the substratum of Māyā and far beyond the spread and reach of Māyā. In other words, it cannot be realized unless the seeker sublates the vast expanse of Māyā seen in the visible world. The very nature of Ātman is Absolute, Pure Knowledge, and it is the goal of every spiritual seeker. The highest welfare of human life is to realize that "I am that Pure Knowledge (*Sat-Cit-Ānanda*)." The worldly knowledge of millions of objects cannot make human life meaningful in a true sense. Pure Knowledge i.e. Ātman can be realized with the help of the Vedāntic scriptures, and it is ever available in the hearts of all beings.

Ātman is all-pervasive and commonly available as Pure Consciousness uniformly, everywhere, and at all times. This same Ātman is reflected in the intellect and thus available to every Jiva in a limited way as Cidābhāsa. Every seeker should make use of this limited Cidābhāsa through the medium of his mind to realize that "I am all-pervasive Ātman."

**Attainment of God through knowledge**

इति क्षेत्रं तथा ज्ञानं ज्ञेयं चोक्तं समासतः ।
मद्भक्त एतद्विज्ञाय मद्भावायोपपद्यते ॥ १८ ॥

*Iti kṣetraṃ tathā jñānaṃ jñeyaṃ coktaṃ sanāsataḥ* ।
*Madbhakta etad vijñāya madbhāvāyopapadyate* ॥ *18* ॥

**Meaning:** Thus, so far, we have seen the description of the Kṣetra, the knowledge, and the knowable Ātman. By learning about the underlying principle of them all, My devotee attains My real nature.

It is the responsibility of the seeker to learn about the insentient Kṣetra, the sentient Kṣetrajña, and the true nature of the Kṣetrajña. The Jiva (Kṣetrajña) should learn about the impermanence of his Kṣetra (body) and his own existence relative to the intellect. Ultimately, the Jiva should realize that "The true nature Kṣetrajña is Ātman, and I am Ātman."

**Prakṛti and Puruṣa are beginningless**

**प्रकृतिं पुरुषं चैव विद्ध्यनादी उभावपि ।**
**विकारांश्च गुणांश्चैव विद्धि प्रकृतिसम्भवान् ॥ १९ ॥**

*Prakṛtiṃ puruṣaṃ caiva viddhy anādi ubhāv api* ।
*Vikārāñś ca guṇāṃś caiva viddhi prakṛtisaṃbhavān* ॥ *19* ॥

**Meaning:** Know that both Prakṛti and Puruṣa are beginningless. Also, know that the three Guṇas and all qualities like attachment and aversion etc. are created from Prakṛti alone.

The very nature of Puruṣa or Ātman is that He is beginningless, transcendental, and the Eternal Truth. Prakṛti is said to be beginningless because no one can know for sure when it was created. Prakṛti is constant in the form of a stream, and it has a definite end. It can be ended by realizing the Knowledge of Ātman. The traits such as attachment or aversion belong to the realm of Prakṛti; therefore, they are not related to Puruṣa in any way.

**The different manifestations of Prakṛti**

**कार्यकारणकर्तृत्वे हेतुः प्रकृतिरुच्यते ।**
**पुरुषः सुखदुःखानां भोक्तृत्वे हेतुरुच्यते ॥ २० ॥**

*Kārya kāraṇa kartṛtve hetuḥ prakṛtir ucyate* ।
*Puruṣaḥ sukhaduḥkhānāṃ bhoktṛtve hetur ucyate* ॥ *20* ॥

**Meaning:** Prakṛti is the cause that creates the effect (the body) and the organs. Jivātmā – being the experiencer – is the cause of all experiences such as joy and grief, etc.

The Five Great Elements and the five objects of senses are known as the effect (*Kārya*) of Prakṛti. The five action organs, five senses, mind, intellect, and ego are together known as organs or instruments (*Kāraṇa*). Prakṛti is 'experienced' while Jivātmā is the 'experiencer.' A person feels joy when he gets what he desires and grief when he gets what is undesired. Grief is like an uncalled-for visitor, but Pure Bliss is the nature of each Jiva. Most people may not remember the innumerable pleasures experienced in life, but they brood on even the smallest of griefs experienced in the past. When the person is unable to center his mind in Ātman, and he gets attracted to Prakṛti, he is caught in the dual experiences of joy and suffering.

**The association of of Puruṣa with Prakṛti**

पुरुषः प्रकृतिस्थो हि भुङ्क्ते प्रकृतिजान्गुणान् ।
कारणं गुणसङ्गोऽस्य सदसद्योनिजन्मसु ॥ २१ ॥

*Puruṣaḥ prakṛti-stho hi bhuṅkte prakṛti-jān guṇān* ।
*Kāraṇaṁ guṇa-saṅgo 'sya sad-asad-yoni-janmasu* ॥ *21* ॥

**Meaning:** Puruṣa immersed in Prakṛti experiences the three Guṇas born of Prakṛti. Attachment to the Guṇas is the cause of his rebirth in higher and lower bodies.

Man has to live his life in the world which is the creation of Prakṛti. There is a difference between 'living life' and 'being immersed in life.' Recognizing this difference, one can also learn to differentiate between the accompaniment of a person and attachment to him. It is not possible to escape the company of family members or close acquaintances, but it is certainly possible to not remain attached to them. The seeker must also remember that the most intimate acquaintance of a person is his own body. The body, other related sentient people, and insentient objects are useful in life; however, the same entities can be detrimental if he gets excessively attached to them. When the seeker strongly identifies that "I am the body," only then is he reborn in the next life.

**Ātman and Brahman are the same**

उपद्रष्टानुमन्ता च भर्ता भोक्ता महेश्वरः ।
परमात्मेति चाप्युक्तो देहेऽस्मिन्पुरुषः परः ॥ २२ ॥

*Upadraṣṭānumantā ca bhartā bhoktā maheśvaraḥ* ।
*Paramātmeti cāpyukto dehe 'smin puruṣaḥ paraḥ* ॥ *22* ॥

**Meaning:** The Jivātmā in this body is, in fact, Supreme Ātman. Being Witness, he is also called spectator (*Upadraṣṭā*). There can be no actions without the substratum of Ātman, so he is called supporter (*Anumantā*). He nourishes and sustains all, so he is known as nourisher (*Bhartā*). Being the enjoyer or the experiencer as the Jiva, he is called enjoyer (*Bhoktā*). Being the Master of Brahmadeva and other gods, he is known as Maheśvara, the Supreme Lord. Being *Sat-Cit-Ānanda*, he is called Supreme Ātman.

In the word **Upadraṣṭā**, the prefix 'upa' means 'near' while the word 'draṣṭā' means 'the seer' or 'the perceiver'; therefore, Upadraṣṭā means the one who sees everything as a Witness by remaining very close to the body (effect). The word **Anumantā** means the one who remains very close to the body, organs, mind, intellect, etc. and when they are in action, He – even though actionless himself – inactively assists them in all activities without disrupting them. The word **Bhartā** means the one who sustains and nourishes the senses, mind, intellect, etc. by giving them existence and impelling them to action. The word **Bhoktā** means the experiencer of joy and grief in day-to-day life. Alternatively, Bhoktā also means the one that illumines the body and other insentient aspects through its own light, so that the Jiva can enjoy them. The word **Maheśvara** means the one who dwells in the hearts of all, who is autonomous, and who is the governor of all. The word **Paramātmā** means Supreme Ātman which is superior to the Jivātmā, whereas the Jivātmā is just a false appearance seen due to ignorance. This **Supreme Puruṣa**, described with different names so far, dwells as a Jiva in the body, which is the effect of Prakṛti, but Puruṣa remains unattached from everything. He, who is originally the Supreme Puruṣa, considers himself as a limited, finite Jiva due to ignorance. As a Jiva, he is constantly subject to the duality of joy and suffering, but as Brahman, He only revels in Pure Bliss.

**The result of this philosophy**

**य एवं वेत्ति पुरुषं प्रकृतिं च गुणैः सह ।**
**सर्वथा वर्तमानोऽपि न स भूयोऽभिजायते ॥ २३ ॥**

*Ya evaṃ vetti puruṣaṃ prakṛtiṃ ca guṇaiḥ saha*
*Sarvathā vartamāno'pi na sa bhūyo'bhijāyate* ॥ *24* ॥

**Meaning:** A person who thus knows the underlying principle of Puruṣa and Prakṛti is not born again despite being engaged in all kinds of actions.

Upaniṣad describes Ātman with this verse –

**असङ्गोह्ययं पुरुषः ।**

*Asañgohyayaṃ Puruṣḥ* । *(Bru. Up. 4.3.15)*

"This Puruṣa is unattached." Ātman is not attached to the body or imprisoned by the body, even if it dwells in the body and permeates it. When the Jiva knows and realizes his non-attachment as Ātman, he remains unattached like Ātman. Later, even if he performs actions as per Prārabdha, he knows them to be done by his body and not by himself. He does not think of himself as the doer of actions. Therefore, his *Kriyamāṇa Karma* does not yield fruits and his Sañcita is eradicated after the Knowledge of Ātman. As a result, he is liberated from the cycle of birth and death.

## The three practices for realizing the Knowledge of Ātman

**ध्यानेनात्मनि पश्यन्ति केचिदात्मानमात्मना ।**
**अन्ये साङ्ख्येन योगेन कर्मयोगेन चापरे ॥ २४ ॥**

*Dhyānenātmani paśyanti kecid ātmānam ātmanā* ।
*Anye sāṃkhyena yogena karmayogena cāpare* ॥ *24* ॥

**Meaning:** Having developed pure, sharp, and subtle intellect, some seekers behold Ātman in their hearts by meditation. Some attain Him by following Jñānayoga, the Path of Knowledge, and some attain Him by following Karmayoga, the Path of Action.

- The Path of Meditation: When the mind – firmly conquered by meditation (Yoga) – attains serenity, in that state, the practitioner unites with Supreme Ātman through his purified subtle intellect. Thereafter, he remains steadfast and content in *Sat-Cit-Ānanda*, his true Self (6.20).
- The Path of Knowledge: Wise people having equanimous intellect renounce the fruits arising from actions and thus liberate themselves from the bondage of the birth and death cycle. They attain the changeless, eternal, Supreme Ātman (2.51).
- The Path of Action: One who has put a leash on the impulses of his body, intellect, and senses, renounced all objects of pleasure even from his mind, and abandoned worldly hopes or expectations – even if such a Yogi performs actions with his body, he incurs no bondage or sin (4.21).

In this manner, the seeker should understand the three paths of Meditation (*Dhyānayoga*), Knowledge (*Jñānayoga*), and Action (*Karmayoga*).

## Attainment of God by listening to discourses

**अन्ये त्वेवमजानन्तः श्रुत्वान्येभ्य उपासते ।**
**तेऽपि चातितरन्त्येव मृत्युं श्रुतिपरायणाः ॥ २५ ॥**

*Anye tvevam ajānantaḥ śrutvānyebhya upāsate* ।
*Te'pi cātitarantyeva mṛtyuṃ śrutiparāyaṇāḥ* ॥ *25* ॥

**Meaning:** However, other seekers who do not have this knowledge of aforementioned three paths listen to the philosophy from other wise men and engage in worship accordingly. Those who believe what they have heard to be authentic and authoritative, they, too, certainly cross the ocean of worldly life and death.

All enlightened saints have given immense importance to listening discourses from the learned, wise Sadguru or other enlightened sages. For those seekers who do not have the required intelligence or who cannot study the scriptures on their own for some reason – listening to wise men is the only effective practice for spiritual pursuit. St. Rāmadāsa states that seekers should listen to the discourses on the Vedāntic texts, Purāṇas – ancient holy Indian scriptures, and the analysis of 'Thou art that' (*Tat-Tvam-Asi*) Mahāvākya. With the help of these discourses, they should learn the process of refuting or transcending the four bodies in meditation and realizing 'I am Brahman' (*Tanu-Catuṣṭaya-Nirasana*).

**<u>The synthesis of the Kṣetra and the Kṣetrajña</u>**

यावत्सञ्जायते किञ्चित्सत्त्वं स्थावरजङ्गमम् ।
क्षेत्रक्षेत्रज्ञसंयोगात्तद्विद्धि भरतर्षभ ॥ २६ ॥

*Yāvat saṃjāyate kiṃcit sattvaṃ sthāvarajaṅgamam ।*
*Kṣetrakṣetrajñasaṅyogāt tad viddhi bharatarṣabha ॥ 26 ॥*

**Meaning:** Whichever moving and stationary entities are created, know them to be created from the synthesis of Kṣetra and Kṣetrajña.

<u>Sentient, moving beings</u>: There is an imaginary relationship between the intellect (Kṣetra) and the Cidābhāsa (Kṣetrajña) in all the sentient beings. Cidābhāsa disappears in its origin Ātman in the deep-sleep, and it is not identified with the intellect while sleeping. There is only an imaginary relation (*Kalpita Sambandha*) between them. There can be no real relationship

between insentient intellect and reflection of Pure Sentience of Ātman in the intellect. Just as there is no relationship between a mirror and the reflection in it, but still it is said that the mirror contains the reflection. Similarly, intellect and Cidābhāsa are not united but they appear to be one. Their union is just an illusion, but due to this illusion, Jiva comes into being, which is why Jiva is also imaginary.

Insentient, stationary entities: All insentient objects have names and forms through which the Kṣetra is said to exist. Underlying this existence of Kṣetra is the substratum of Kṣetrajña ***Sat***. Insentient objects cannot exist without the sentient *Sat*. The relationship between Pure Existence (*Sat*) and the existence of insentient objects is imaginary as well (*Kalpita Sambandha*).

## The real knower of Ātman

**समं सर्वेषु भूतेषु तिष्ठन्तं परमेश्वरम् ।**
**विनश्यत्स्वविनश्यन्तं यः पश्यति स पश्यति ॥ २७ ॥**
**समं पश्यन्हि सर्वत्र समवस्थितमीश्वरम् ।**
**न हिनस्त्यात्मनात्मानं ततो याति परां गतिम् ॥ २८ ॥**

*Samaṃ sarveṣu bhūteṣu tiṣṭhantaṃ parameśvaram* ।
*Vinaśyatsv avinaśyantaṃ yaḥ paśyati sa paśyati* ॥ *27* ॥
*Samaṃ paśyan hi sarvatra samavasthitam īśvaram* ।
*Na hinasty ātmanātmānaṃ tato yāti parāṃ gatim* ॥ *28* ॥

**Meaning:** He is the real seer who sees that Supreme Īśvara equally pervades all beings, and He is the non-perishing ultimate Truth within all that is perishing. A person who sees that "All-pervading Supreme Lord is uniformly present everywhere" does not destroy his Self by himself. He attains the highest goal – Mokṣa.

Supreme Īśvara is present everywhere. But people who do not believe in His omnipresence engage in prohibited actions. Those who enjoy prohibited pleasures due to identification with the body, organs, and senses essentially destroy Ātman, their true Self. St. Jñāneśwara says, "Pure Consciousness pervades everywhere, uniformly, and at all times. Ignorant people see it divided in different sections like 'this is higher,' 'that is lower,' etc. (*4.70*)" Brahman is Pure Sentience. It is formless and the subtlest of all. It uniformly pervades all objects having names and forms as Pure Consciousness. It is not present in more or less proportion in bigger or smaller objects. All objects having names and forms are subject to creation, sustenance, and destruction. However, Pure Consciousness that pervades the objects is neither created nor destroyed with them. The seeker is supposed to recognize this fact mainly regarding his body. He should strive to see the uniform presence of Supreme Brahman in all bodies. This vision of sameness in all people helps in removing the duality of good and bad, desirable and undesirable, favorable and adverse, etc. from the mind. The seeker who has earned equanimous vision in this manner does not destroy himself due to the knowledge he has realized. In other words, by not identifying himself as the body and not seeing others as the body, he is not caught in the birth and death cycle.

**Ātman is the non-doer**

**प्रकृत्यैव च कर्माणि क्रियमाणानि सर्वशः ।**
**यः पश्यति तथात्मानमकर्तारं स पश्यति ॥ २९ ॥**
**यदा भूतपृथग्भावमेकस्थमनुपश्यति ।**
**तत एव च विस्तारं ब्रह्म सम्पद्यते तदा ॥ ३० ॥**
**अनादित्वान्निर्गुणत्वात्परमात्मायमव्ययः ।**
**शरीरस्थोऽपि कौन्तेय न करोति न लिप्यते ॥ ३१ ॥**
**यथा सर्वगतं सौक्ष्म्यादाकाशं नोपलिप्यते ।**
**सर्वत्रावस्थितो देहे तथात्मा नोपलिप्यते ॥ ३२ ॥**
**यथा प्रकाशयत्येकः कृत्स्नं लोकमिमं रविः ।**
**क्षेत्रं क्षेत्री तथा कृत्स्नं प्रकाशयति भारत ॥ ३३ ॥**

*Prakṛtyaiva ca karmāṇi kriyamāṇāni sarvaśaḥ* ।
*Yaḥ paśyati tathātmānam akartāraṃ sa paśyati* ॥ *29* ॥

*Yadā bhūtapṛthagbhāvam ekastham anupaśyati* ।
*Tata eva ca vistāraṃ brahma saṃpadyate tadā* ॥ *30* ॥
*Anāditvān nirguṇatvāt paramātmāyam avyayaḥ* ।
*Śarīrastho'pi kaunteya na karoti na lipyate* ॥ *31* ॥
*Yathā sarvagataṃ saukṣmyād ākāśaṃ nopalipyate* ।
*Sarvatrāvasthito dehe tathātmā nopalipyate* ॥ *32* ॥
*Yathā prakāśayaty ekaḥ kṛtsnaṃ lokam imaṃ raviḥ* ।
*Kṣetraṃ kṣetrī tathā kṛtsnaṃ prakāśayati bhārata* ॥ *33* ॥

**Meaning:** The wise person who sees that all actions are done by Prakṛti alone – and his true Self (Ātman) is actionless – is the real seer. When he realizes that all beings dwell in one Supreme Ātman and they evolve from Ātman alone, he becomes One with Ātman. The imperishable true Self, Ātman – being beginningless and attributeless – does not do anything despite dwelling in the body. Even though, such a person, who has realized Ātman, is engaged in actions from a transactional perspective, he is not tainted by actions or attached to actions. The space (Ākāśa) pervades everywhere as it is extremely subtle, but it is neither attached to nor tainted by nor imprisoned by anything. Likewise, Ātman that pervades all bodies is not attached to actions done by the body. Just as the sun alone illumines the whole world, so also the Kṣetrajña alone illumines all Kṣetras.

In Vedānta, it is necessary to clearly understand the terms 'non-doer despite being a doer,' 'non-experiencer despite being an experiencer,' etc. It is possible to misuse or misinterpret them due to ignorance. Muṇḍaka Upaniṣad (*2.2*) states that "Ātman is the Eternal Truth. It has no mind, no senses, and no life-forces (Prāṇas)." Therefore, Ātman cannot perform any action; hence Ātman is known as 'non-doer.' Every seeker needs to meditate on the resolve "I am Ātman" in Soham meditation practice. While meditating, he is expected to reflect on the thought, "If Ātman is non-doer, so I must be a non-doer as well." However, every seeker is conditioned to think that "I am the doer" and "I am the experiencer." So, it is necessary to find a smart way to resolve this apparent conflict. For that, the seeker must recognize that every Jiva is influenced by the three Guṇas, and he is impelled towards actions by the power of those Guṇas. He should recognize that he is the 'doer' as a Jiva, but he is 'non-doer' as Ātman. Vedāntic philosophy presents the concept of the three levels of existence –

- Empirical level (*Vyāvahārika Sattā*) – Entities having names and forms
- Divine level (*Īśvari Sattā*) – Existence, cognizance, likeability (Asti, Bhāti, Priya)
- Absolute level (*Pārmārthika Sattā*) – (Pure) Existence, Consciousness, Bliss (*Sat, Cit, Ānanda*)

The Jiva is considered a doer on the empirical level. From the spiritual perspective, every Jiva – being Ātman – is a non-doer. St. Tukārāma says, "I have realized that I am Ātman, so I am not engaged in worldly life in any way. Other people wrongly allege that I have a family and worldly life etc., but it is a false attribution from my perspective as Ātman."

To better understand this concept, consider two pots kept in space. One pot contains garlic, while the other contains saffron. The space in each pot appears to smell differently due to its contents, but space itself does not have any smell. Similarly, it may seem that the Ātman is engaged in actions due to its proximity with the Guṇas, but Ātman does not perform any action. It is ever-liberated from the bondage of actions.

The real rope illumines the illusory snake. Likewise, Ātman, the Truth, illumines the world through its eternal light. No characteristic of a snake can be seen in the rope. Just as a piece of magnet does not become iron when touched by iron, so too Brahman is not attached to nor tainted by nor imprisoned by any characteristic of the world.

## Ātman, the illuminator of all

क्षेत्रक्षेत्रज्ञयोरेवमन्तरं ज्ञानचक्षुषा ।
भूतप्रकृतिमोक्षं च ये विदुर्यान्ति ते परम् ॥ ३४ ॥

*Kṣetrakṣetrajñayor evam antaraṃ jñānacakṣuṣā* ।
*Bhūtaprakṛtimokṣaṃ ca ye vidur yānti te param* ॥ *34* ॥

**Meaning:** The apparent division between Kṣetra and Kṣetrajña does not exist in reality. In the same way, Māyā, which is the material cause of – the three Guṇas, all modifications of Prakṛti, and all beings – does not exist in reality. Seekers who know these facts realize "I am Ātman" and thereby attain the supreme goal of liberation (Mokṣa).

ॐ तत्सदिति श्रीमद्भगवद्गीतासूपनिषत्सु ब्रह्मविद्यायां योगशास्त्रे श्रीकृष्णार्जुनसंवादे क्षेत्रक्षेत्रज्ञविभागयोगो नाम त्रयोदशोऽध्यायः ॥

*Om Tatsaditi Śrimadbhagvadgitāsūpaniṣatsu Brahmavidyāyāṃ Yogaśāstre Śrīkṛṣṇārjunasaṅvāde Kṣetrakṣetrajñavibhāgayogo Nāma Trayodaśo'dhyāyaḥ* ॥

"Māyā as Kṣetra has no real existence" – this is the highest dictum of Ajātavāda – the theory of non-origination – in Vedānta. From this perspective, the three Guṇas, all beings, and their modifications have no existence at all. This is the highest spiritual knowledge. The seeker becomes One with Ātman by realizing this knowledge.

Māṇḍūkya Kārikā states the ultimate principle of Advaita –

न कश्चिद् जायते जीवो संभवस्य न विद्यते । (४.७१)

*Na kaścid jāyate jīvo sambhāvasaya na vidyāte* । *(4.71)*

"Jiva was never born, and it is not possible that he will ever exist." The seeker should remember this principle and continue his spiritual pursuit in that direction.

Chapter 14

# Division of the Three Guṇas

॥ गुणत्रयविभागयोगः (Guṇatrayavibhāgayogaḥ) ॥

This chapter describes the influence of Sattva, Rājas, and Tāmas Guṇas on human life. Disposition, behavior, thinking, speech, body-language, and mutual relations depend on the proportion of the three Guṇas present in human beings.

No Guṇa is completely absent in any person at any time. A Guṇa may be more dominant in a person, or it can be made dominant through practice. When we address a person as Sāttvic, it only means that his Sattvaguṇa is more dominant than the other two Guṇas, or he can adhere to Sattvaguṇa frequently and firmly. Every person has a unique nature or disposition which is a result of the composition of the three Guṇas in him. People behave in many different ways due to varying permutations and combinations of the three Guṇas present in them. If a seeker can recognize and calmly embrace this fact, he can react in a mild and composed manner to other people and their behavior. E.g. Anger is a result of his Rajoguṇa. When the seeker sees an angry person, he can recognize that such a person is under Rajoguṇa's influence, and thus react without anger while dealing with him. On the other hand, if the seeker is angry himself, he can recognize the rising Rajoguṇa in his own mind and reduce its impact by taking the necessary steps. If the seeker has a genuine wish to steady his mind for spiritual pursuit, he must invariably practice these two precautions of recognizing the Rajoguṇa or Tamoguṇa in another person as well as in himself.

## The supreme Knowledge of the Self

श्रीभगवानुवाच ।
परं भूयः प्रवक्ष्यामि ज्ञानानां ज्ञानमुत्तमम् ।
यज्ज्ञात्वा मुनयः सर्वे परां सिद्धिमितो गताः ॥ १ ॥
इदं ज्ञानमुपाश्रित्य मम साधर्म्यमागताः ।
सर्गेऽपि नोपजायन्ते प्रलये न व्यथन्ति च ॥ २ ॥
मम योनिर्महद्ब्रह्म तस्मिन्गर्भं दधाम्यहम् ।
सम्भवः सर्वभूतानां ततो भवति भारत ॥ ३ ॥
सर्वयोनिषु कौन्तेय मूर्तयः सम्भवन्ति याः ।
तासां ब्रह्म महद्योनिरहं बीजप्रदः पिता ॥ ४ ॥

*Śrībhagavān uvāca* ।
*Param bhūyaḥ pravakṣyāmi jñānānāṃ jñānam uttamam* ।
*Yaj jñātvā munayaḥ sarve parāṃ siddhim ito gatāḥ* ॥ *1* ॥
*Idaṃ jñānam upāŚrītya mama sādharmyam āgatāḥ* ।
*Sarge'pi nopajāyante pralaye na vyathanti ca* ॥ *2* ॥
*Mama yonir mahad brahma tasmin garbhaṃ dadhāmy aham* ।
*Saṃbhavaḥ sarvabhūtānāṃ tato bhavati bhārata* ॥ *3* ॥
*Sarvayoniṣu kaunteya mūrtayaḥ saṃbhavanti yāḥ* ।
*Tāsāṃ brahma mahad yonir ahaṃ bījapradaḥ pitā* ॥ *4* ॥

**Meaning:** (Śrībhagavān said) I shall again impart that Supreme Knowledge, the best of all kinds of knowledge, to you. Wise sages who have known it and contemplated on it have liberated themselves from worldly life and attained the highest goal of Mokṣa. Having known this Self-Knowledge and attained Oneness with Me, they are neither reborn at the time of the creation of the universe nor are they distressed at the time of the destruction of the universe. O Arjuna! My fundamental nature (*Mūla Prakṛti*) – in the form of Mahat – is the womb of all beings. I place the germs of all living beings in that womb. Thereafter, the birth of all beings takes place. Many beings having different forms are born in various kinds of wombs. My Prakṛti is the Mother of all these wombs, and I am the Father who plants seeds in those wombs.

Self-Knowledge is the highest of all kinds of knowledge (*10.32*). It is meant for the lasting welfare – which does not depend on worldly success or failure, prosperity or poverty – of human life. A seeker who realizes "I am Ātman" and constantly abides in it attains the supreme goal and enjoys lasting welfare and blessed life. Mere discussions and mechanical reading of the Vedāntic scriptures do not lead the seeker to this supreme goal.

We have seen before that chapters 13 to 17 in the Gita are meant to help the union of Jiva and Brahman i.e. realization of *Asi* in *Tav-Tvam-Asi*. The three Guṇas impede the path of Self-realization. In the initial stage of spiritual pursuit, the seeker should minimize the impact of Rājas and Tāmas Guṇas in him through Sattvaguṇa. Later, he should also get rid of the influence of Sattvaguṇa and attain Self-realization.

Lord Kṛṣṇa instructs Arjuna to transcend the three Guṇas (*2.45*). Ordinary people, who have not transcended the three Guṇas, live under the influence of some Guṇa. The seeker may often wonder when observing a person who behaves in a weird, wrong, evil, or malicious manner, "How can he behave like this?" After studying the 14$^{th}$ chapter in detail, the seeker can think, "How can he behave in any other way but this?" In other words, the seeker learns to see that every person is bound to behave as per the dominant Guṇa in him at any given time. This is an excellent thought process which can help the seeker tone down his reactions, and keep his mind at peace. Wise people liberated by this great knowledge are not born again nor do they become distressed with the idea of death. The body made up of the 36 basic elements and 3 Guṇas dissolves in Prakṛti; but, the true Self, Ātman, continues to exist eternally as ***Sat***. One who knows this Truth is neither scared nor distressed by death.

The seeds of all sentient or insentient objects remain in a dormant state in the principle named ***Mahat*** before the universe is created. At the time of the creation, all beings are created from their seeds by the will (*Saṅkalpa*) of Īśvara alone. There is a confluence of the sentient Jiva and insentient body in every sentient being. In day-to-day life, the sentience of Ātman is wrongly attributed to the body and the insentience of the body is attributed to Ātman. Therefore, a person may mistakenly feel, "I am born, and I am going to die."

**The Jiva is bounded by the three Guṇas**

**सत्त्वं रजस्तम इति गुणाः प्रकृतिसम्भवाः ।**
**निबध्नन्ति महाबाहो देहे देहिनमव्ययम् ॥ ५ ॥**
**तत्र सत्त्वं निर्मलत्वात्प्रकाशकमनामयम् ।**
**सुखसङ्गेन बध्नाति ज्ञानसङ्गेन चानघ ॥ ६ ॥**
**रजो रागात्मकं विद्धि तृष्णासङ्गसमुद्भवम् ।**
**तन्निबध्नाति कौन्तेय कर्मसङ्गेन देहिनम् ॥ ७ ॥**
**तमस्त्वज्ञानजं विद्धि मोहनं सर्वदेहिनाम् ।**
**प्रमादालस्यनिद्राभिस्तन्निबध्नाति भारत ॥ ८ ॥**
**सत्त्वं सुखे सञ्जयति रजः कर्मणि भारत ।**
**ज्ञानमावृत्य तु तमः प्रमादे सञ्जयत्युत ॥ ९ ॥**

*Sattvaṃ rajas tama iti guṇāḥ prakṛtisambhavāḥ* ।
*Nibadhnanti mahābāho dehe dehinam avyayam* ॥ *5* ॥
*Tatra sattvaṃ nirmalatvāt prakāśakam anāmāyām* ।
*Sukhasaṅgena badhnāti jñānasaṅgena cānagha* ॥ *6* ॥
*Rajo rāgātmakaṃ viddhi tṛṣṇāsaṅgasamudbhavam* ।
*Tan nibadhnāti kaunteya karmasaṅgena dehinam* ॥ *7* ॥
*Tāmas tvajñānajaṃ viddhi mohanaṃ sarvadehinām* ।
*Pramādālasyanidrābhis tan nibadhnāti bhārata* ॥ *8* ॥
*Sattvaṃ sukhe saṃjayati rajaḥ karmaṇi bhārata* ।
*Jñānam āvṛtya tu tamaḥ pramāde saṃjayaty uta* ॥ *9* ॥

**Meaning:** *Sattva*, *Rājas*, *Tāmas* – these three Guṇas created by Prakṛti – bind the Jiva to his body. Among these three, Sattvaguṇa is without any impurities. So, it helps to attain knowledge. Sattva is devoid of any faults, so it gives rise to the feeling of happiness in the mind. It binds the Jiva by increasing his affinity to knowledge and happiness. Rajoguṇa is of the nature of strong attachment. Know that it is created from craving and attachment. It binds the Jiva to fruits of actions. Tamoguṇa deludes all Jivas. Know that it is born of ignorance. It binds the Jiva by negligence, lethargy, and sleep. O Arjuna! Sattvaguṇa impels towards happiness, Rajoguṇa impels towards action, Tamoguṇa veils knowledge and impels towards negligence, carelessness, or laziness.

It is a part of Īśvara's system of governance that each Jiva is bound by the three Guṇas. No one can escape this system. Every seeker should be consciously aware of this fact when interacting with other people. If a seeker is indeed surrendered to Īśvara, he must embrace Īśvara's governance unconditionally, wholeheartedly, without any complaint. At the same time, he should be careful not to get duped or exploited by others in day-to-day transactions.

The intellect of a person remains pure and content when it is under Sattvaguṇa's influence. Even other people can see this purity; they respect and praise a Sāttvic person for his pure mind. The Sāttvic person may indulge in self-satisfaction by liking himself, being pleased with himself, or being happy due to the praise showered by others. As a result, he may become complacent and not reach the supreme goal of human life – Self-realization. This is the main binding of Sattvaguṇa on people. When influenced by Rajoguṇa, a person has irrepressible desires, ambitions, hopes, and greed; as a result, he remains incessantly busy in work. He gets increasingly attached to the fruits of actions, and this itself is Rajoguṇa's constraint on the Jiva. When influenced by Tamoguṇa, the intellect loses its power to comprehend anything. Consequently, it cannot grasp or delve in the Eternal Truth. A Tāmasic person cannot discriminate between action and inaction and hence engages in prohibited actions. Incorrect behavior, lethargy, sleep, etc. are the traits that bind the person who is influenced by Tamoguṇa.

## One Guṇa dominates the others

रजस्तमश्चाभिभूय सत्त्वं भवति भारत ।
रजः सत्त्वं तमश्चैव तमः सत्त्वं रजस्तथा ॥ १० ॥
सर्वद्वारेषु देहेऽस्मिन्प्रकाश उपजायते ।
ज्ञानं यदा तदा विद्याद्विवृद्धं सत्त्वमित्युत ॥ ११ ॥
लोभः प्रवृत्तिरारम्भः कर्मणामशमः स्पृहा ।
रजस्येतानि जायन्ते विवृद्धे भरतर्षभ ॥ १२ ॥
अप्रकाशोऽप्रवृत्तिश्च प्रमादो मोह एव च ।
तमस्येतानि जायन्ते विवृद्धे कुरुनन्दन ॥ १३ ॥

*Rājas tamaś cābhibhūya sattvaṃ bhavati bhārata* ।
*Rajaḥ sattvaṃ tamaś caiva tamaḥ sattvaṃ rajas tathā* ॥ *10* ॥
*Sarvadvāreṣu dehe'smin prakāśa upajāyate* ।
*Jñānaṃ yadā tadā vidyād vivṛddhaṃ sattvam ity uta* ॥ *11* ॥
*Lobhaḥ pravṛttir ārambhaḥ karmaṇām aśamaḥ spṛhā* ।
*Rajasy etāni jāyante vivṛddhe bharatarṣabha* ॥ *12* ॥
*Aprakāśo'pravṛttiś ca pramādo moha eva ca* ।
*Tamasy etāni jāyante vivṛddhe kurunandana* ॥ *13* ॥

**Meaning:** O Arjuna! Sattvaguṇa increases by defeating Rajoguṇa and Tamoguṇa. Rajoguṇa increases by defeating Sattvaguṇa and Tamoguṇa. And Tamoguṇa increases by defeating Sattvaguṇa and Rajoguṇa. When the light of knowledge shines in the body and organs, know that Sattvaguṇa is dominant at that time. O Arjuna! When Rajoguṇa is on the rise, one can clearly see indications like the undertaking of many actions, greed, restlessness, activity, hyperactivity, and desires. O son of the Kuru! When Tamoguṇa increases, the person cannot comprehend anything despite being guided by the scriptures or Sadguru. He has no desire to work; he neglects duties, feels sleepy, and his mind is deluded.

Each of the three Guṇas increases or decreases in a person according to the Prārabdha that needs to be experienced by him. When Sattvaguṇa rises by subjugating Rājas and Tāmas, it increases knowledge due to better comprehension capacity. A person can instantly learn and understand anything in this state. He can quickly gauge the circumstances and practice spiritual discrimination. He finds happiness since he attains success in worldly life and also gains more insight into spiritual knowledge in this state.

When Rajoguṇa is dominant, there is a proliferation of desires, anger, and greed in mind. Also, there is an inclination to perform actions with a selfish intent. Such a person works incessantly. He is restless, and he has endless desires for a variety of objects of pleasure. He feels happy if his desires are fulfilled and suffers otherwise. If the person gets his desired object in excess, he finds pleasure as his greed is fulfilled. If he does not get what he desires, he feels pain. Even here, the person is bound to get joy and grief as per his Prārabdha. St. Tukārāma has stated a rule of life in his poetry where he says, "Life is filled with little joy and enormous grief." Most people find more grief than true joy in life. Different people have different interests, so their actions involve competition, jealousy, selfishness, politics, and conflicts. The seeker may lose his inner peace while interacting with other such people. Lord Kṛṣṇa has asked a question:

**अशान्तस्य कुतः सुखं ।**

*Aśāntasya kutaḥ sukhaṃ* ।

"How can a person be happy when he is not at peace?" There is no joy where there is no peace. Peace and happiness are two sides of the same coin. If any one side is eroded, the coin has no value.

A person with dominant Tamoguṇa cannot learn any topic or gain any knowledge. He tends to neglect duties and exhibits carelessness in work, which gives rise to the possibility of him making mistakes at work. He is heavily impacted by lethargy and sleep. Therefore, his worldly life and spiritual practice are both impeded. He fails and feels distressed on both fronts.

## The resultant path due to the influence of each Guṇa

यदा सत्त्वे प्रवृद्धे तु प्रलयं याति देहभृत् ।
तदोत्तमविदां लोकानमलान्प्रतिपद्यते ॥ १४ ॥
रजसि प्रलयं गत्वा कर्मसङ्गिषु जायते ।
तथा प्रलीनस्तमसि मूढयोनिषु जायते ॥ १५ ॥
कर्मणः सुकृतस्याहुः सात्त्विकं निर्मलं फलम् ।
रजसस्तु फलं दुःखमज्ञानं तमसः फलम् ॥ १६ ॥
सत्त्वात्सञ्जायते ज्ञानं रजसो लोभ एव च ।
प्रमादमोहौ तमसो भवतोऽज्ञानमेव च ॥ १७ ॥
ऊर्ध्वं गच्छन्ति सत्त्वस्था मध्ये तिष्ठन्ति राजसाः ।
जघन्यगुणवृत्तिस्था अधो गच्छन्ति तामसाः ॥ १८ ॥

*Yadā sattve pravṛddhe tu pralayaṃ yāti dehabhṛt* ।
*Tadottamavidāṃ lokān amalān pratipadyate* ॥ *14* ॥
*Rajasi pralayaṃ gatvā karmasaṅgiṣu jāyate* ।
*Tathā pralīnas tamasi mūḍhayoniṣu jāyate* ॥ *15* ॥
*Karmaṇaḥ sukṛtasyāhuḥ sāttvikaṃ nirmalaṃ phalam* ।
*Rajasas tu phalaṃ duḥkham ajñānaṃ tamasaḥ phalam* ॥ *16* ॥
*Sattvāt saṃjāyate jñānaṃ rajaso lobha eva ca* ।
*Pramādamohau tamaso bhavato'jñānam eva ca* ॥ *17* ॥
*Ūrdhvaṃ gacchanti sattvasthā madhye tiṣṭhanti rājasāḥ* ।
*Jaghanyaguṇavṛttisthā adho gacchhanti tāmasāḥ* ॥ *18* ॥

**Meaning:** If an embodied Jiva dies when his Sattvaguṇa is dominant, he is reborn in a spiritual lineage of wise men (Knowers of Brahman), or he attains the pure worlds of Hiraṇyagarbha, etc. If the Jiva dies when Rajoguṇa is dominant, he is reborn in a family of people attached to actions. If he dies when Tamoguṇa is dominant, he is reborn in a Tāmasic species like a bird or animal, etc. The result of virtuous actions is pure and Sāttvic mind. Vedic and Holy scriptures state that the result of Rajoguṇa is suffering, and the result of Tamoguṇa is ignorance. Knowledge arises from Sattvaguṇa, and greed arises from Rajoguṇa. Negligence, delusion, and ignorance arise from Tamoguṇa. Those who are steady in Sattvaguṇa in their lifetime arise to heaven or Brahmaloka. Those who are steady in Rajoguṇa dwell in the middle (earth). Tāmasic people who are steady in inferior qualities go downwards to inferior planes.

If a person meets death when his Sattvaguṇa is dominant, he goes to the superior planes such as heaven or Gandharvaloka, which can be attained through good actions. When Sattvaguṇa and good actions evolve further, he is reborn in a spiritually advanced family conducive for his journey towards liberation. It is also important to remember that the pleasures in heaven or the other superior worlds are finite and impermanent, so they are inconsequential from the spiritual perspective. However, when the person is reborn in a spiritually advanced family, there is a favorable ecosystem available for his liberation. If the person dies under the influence of Rajoguṇa, he is reborn as a human who is attached to actions, and thus gets caught in the life and death cycle. However, he has a chance to redeem himself and attain Mokṣa as well. If the person dies when Tamoguṇa is dominant, he is reborn as a bird, a germ, a tree, or an animal, etc. and gets caught in the cycle of 84 lacs of species. Thus, Sattvaguṇa – which can be nurtured through virtuous actions – leads to pure fruits like joy, knowledge, detachment, etc. Rajoguṇa leads to greed, pain, jealousy, etc. Tamoguṇa, however, leads to complete destruction.

**A seer who transcends the three Guṇas attains liberation**

**नान्यं गुणेभ्यः कर्तारं यदा द्रष्टानुपश्यति ।**
**गुणेभ्यश्च परं वेत्ति मद्भावं सोऽधिगच्छति ॥ १९ ॥**
**गुणानेतानतीत्य त्रीन्देही देहसमुद्भवान् ।**
**जन्ममृत्युजरादुःखैर्विमुक्तोऽमृतमश्नुते ॥ २० ॥**

*Nānyaṃ guṇebhyaḥ kartāraṃ yadā draṣṭānupaśyati ।*
*Guṇebhyaś ca paraṃ vetti madbhāvaṃ so'dhigacchhati ॥ 19 ॥*
*Guṇān etān atīitya trīn dehī dehasamudbhavān ।*
*Janmamṛtyujarāduḥkhair vimukto'mṛtam aśnute ॥ 20 ॥*

**Meaning:** A seer, wise thinker knows that there is no separate doer other than the body, senses, and three Guṇas. He also knows that there is a separate Witness present in the body who is separate from the body, senses, and Guṇas. Such a person verily attains My true nature. The three Guṇas are the cause of rebirth. One who goes beyond them is liberated from the suffering associated with birth, aging, and death. He enjoys the eternal nectar of immortality.

It is necessary to explain "Who is the real doer" to let the seeker learn that "I am not the doer" (*18.14*). After recognizing the real doer, the seeker can see the actions of his body as a mere witness. Every action done by the Jiva is propelled by his three Guṇas. Actions take place involuntarily due to the force of the Guṇas. Only an extremely determined seeker can withhold the impulsive force of his three Guṇas to a great extent.

St. Ekanātha says, "A person engages in actions per the Guṇa dominant in him at any given time. The action-organs are subservient to the Guṇas, so actions are performed according to the influence exerted by the Guṇas." A person who knows this fact and sees all actions impassively as a witness is enlightened by realizing, "I am Ātman."

The universe is said to be created in the following order:

1. **Mūlamāyā** – The very first wish on Brahman
   "I am one and I shall manifest in many forms."
   *(Chān. Up. 6.2.3)*
2. **Guṇamāyā** – Mūlamāyā with the three Guṇas
3. **Jaḍamāyā** – Guṇamāyā with the Five Great Elements

Thereafter all beings were created from the confluence of the three Guṇas and the Five Great Elements. The body of every being was created in the same order. Thus, the seeker should invariably strive to be an impassive witness to the three Guṇas as well as their manifestations and liberate himself from the suffering associated with birth, decay, and death. Every seeker must remember that it is not possible to destroy any of the three Guṇas, rather it is only possible to witness or transcend the influence of the three Guṇas. Spiritual pursuit is not possible unless the seeker has a clear idea of what is and what isn't achievable by spiritual practice.

**Arjuna's three questions**

*अर्जुन उवाच ।*

**कैर्लिङ्गैस्त्रीन्गुणानेतानतीतो भवति प्रभो ।**
**किमाचारः कथं चैतांस्त्रीन्गुणानतिवर्तते ॥ २१ ॥**

*Arjuna uvāca* ।

*Kair liṅgais trīn guṇān etān atīto bhavati prabho* ।
*Kimācāraḥ Kaṭhaṃ caitāṃs trīn guṇān ativartate* ॥ *21* ॥

**Meaning:** (Arjuna said) O Lord! What are the characteristics of him who has transcended the three Guṇas? How does he behave? How does he transcend the three Guṇas?

**The Answer to the first two questions**

*श्रीभगवानुवाच ।*

**प्रकाशं च प्रवृत्तिं च मोहमेव च पाण्डव ।**
**न द्वेष्टि सम्प्रवृत्तानि न निवृत्तानि काङ्क्षति ॥ २२ ॥**
**उदासीनवदासीनो गुणैर्यो न विचाल्यते ।**
**गुणा वर्तन्त इत्येवं योऽवतिष्ठति नेङ्गते ॥ २३ ॥**
**समदुःखसुखः स्वस्थः समलोष्टाश्मकाञ्चनः ।**
**तुल्यप्रियाप्रियो धीरस्तुल्यनिन्दात्मसंस्तुतिः ॥ २४ ॥**
**मानापमानयोस्तुल्यस्तुल्यो मित्रारिपक्षयोः ।**
**सर्वारम्भपरित्यागी गुणातीतः स उच्यते ॥ २५ ॥**
**मां च योऽव्यभिचारेण भक्तियोगेन सेवते ।**
**स गुणान्समतीत्यैतान्ब्रह्मभूयाय कल्पते ॥ २६ ॥**

*Śrībhagavān uvāca* ।

*Prakāśaṃ ca pravṛttiṃ ca moham eva ca pāṇḍava* ।
*Ta dveṣṭi saṃpravṛttāni na nivṛttāni kāṅkṣati* ॥ *22* ॥
*Udāsīnavad āsīno guṇair yo na vicālyate* ।
*Guṇā vartanta ity eva yo'vatiṣṭhati neṅgate* ॥ *23* ॥

*Samaduḥkhasukhaḥ svasthaḥ samaloṣṭāśmakāñcanaḥ* ।
*Tulyapriyāpriyo dhīras tulyanindātmasaṃstutiḥ* ॥ *24* ॥
*Mānāpamānayos tulyas tulyo mitrāripakṣayoḥ* ।
*Sarvārambhaparityāgī guṇātītaḥ sa ucyate* ॥ *25* ॥
*Māṃ ca yo'vyabhicāreṇa bhaktiyogena sevate* ।
*Sa guṇān samatītyaitān brahmabhūyāya kalpate* ॥ *26* ॥

**Meaning:** (Śrībhagavān said) Light (knowledge), propensity towards action, and delusion are the three manifestations (effects) of Sattva, Rājas, and Tāmas, respectively. He neither hates these manifestations when they are present, nor does he desire them for his happiness when they are absent. He is not moved by the three Guṇas since he is neutral and nonchalant. He knows that Guṇas alone transact with the other Guṇas and remains absorbed in his true Self, Ātman. He views gold, a clod of earth, and stone as the same and sees beloved and unbeloved with evenness. He is forbearing. He remains the same in praise and criticism, honor and dishonor, and he sees a friend and an enemy evenly. He abandons undertaking of all gainful or fruitive actions (he performs all prescribed actions by not considering himself the doer and not desiring any fruits). Such a person having all these characteristics is said to have transcended the three Guṇas. One who serves Me through knowledge and unswerving devotion, and by being One with Me, is eligible for Self-realization of Brahman by transcending the three Guṇas.

The seeker may strive to keep his Sattvaguṇa in charge, but he will still see Rajoguṇa and Tamoguṇa rising intermittently within him. He is supposed to watch these Rājas, Tāmas influences in an impersonal, impassive manner, instead of being distressed by them. He should neither expect Sattvaguṇa's impact to last forever nor expect Rājas and Tāmas to vanish completely. The seeker who is thus not moved by desirable or undesirable effects of the Guṇas – while being a witness to their activities – knows that all activities are a mere play of the Guṇas amongst themselves. Guṇas themselves turn into Guṇi (Jiva) and execute their actions by becoming the Jiva. When such a seeker strives to abide in his true Self, he becomes eligible for the realization that "I am Brahman."

Māyā, action-organs, sense-organs, worldly objects, and Antaḥkaraṇa (inner instrument comprising of mind, intellect, memory, ego) are all made up of the three Guṇas. Vedānta states that the mind is made of Rajoguṇa, the intellect is of Sattvaguṇa, and the ego is of Tamoguṇa. Therefore, these three Guṇas impel functioning of Antaḥkaraṇa. When the Guṇas exert their influence through the organs, the seeker can recognize it to be a mere play of Guṇas within themselves and nothing else. The seeker is said to have transcended the three Guṇas if he revels in his true Self, Ātman, while being an impersonal witness to the three Guṇas. Such a seeker does not get swayed in the currents of joy and grief and remains steady in Pure Bliss of his true Self. He sees gold, clay, and stone as the same since all of them are made from the earth and thus impermanent. This 'vision of equanimity' is a description of his inner state from the spiritual perspective, but one should not confuse it with simple protocols of transactions in day-to-day life. E.g. St. Narahari Sonāra was an enlightened saint who was a goldsmith by profession. He used to create only golden ornaments while working; he did not create ornaments from clay just because gold and clay were the same to him. It takes immense patience and forbearance to nurture equanimous vision and even mind in day-to-day life in this manner. Such a person is neither attracted to favorable objects, nor is he repelled by unfavorable objects. He can neither be pleased due to praise nor be distressed due to criticism. One who remains centered in Ātman is not troubled by the duality of joy and suffering. He is not delighted by honor or friends, nor is he grieved by dishonor or enemies. He does not consider himself as the doer while undertaking any work. This doesn't mean he is inactive; rather, it means that he is not even remotely touched by the feeling that "I am the doer." Only the seeker of this stature is eligible to be known as the 'one who has transcended the three Guṇas.' To attain this ultimate stage of spiritual pursuit, the seeker who engages in single-minded devotion to Saguṇa God can remain witness to the three Guṇas. He becomes ready for the realization that "I am *Sat-Cit-Ānanda* Brahman." This is the path of praising and worshipping the Lord of the three Guṇas to transcend the Guṇas.

## The significance of Brahman

**ब्रह्मणो हि प्रतिष्ठाहममृतस्याव्ययस्य च ।**
**शाश्वतस्य च धर्मस्य सुखस्यैकान्तिकस्य च ॥ २७ ॥**

*Brahmaṇo hi pratiṣṭhāham amṛtasyāvyayasya ca* ।
*Śāśvatasya ca dharmasya sukhasyaikāntikasya ca* ॥ *27* ॥

**Meaning:** Brahman is imperishable, immutable, and the cause of all. As Supreme Ātman, I alone am the substratum (abode) of everlasting Dharma, and Absolute, Pure Bliss.

**ॐ तत्सदिति श्रीमद्भगवद्गीतासूपनिषत्सु ब्रह्मविद्यायां योगशास्त्रे श्रीकृष्णार्जुनसंवादे गुणत्रयविभागयोगो नाम चतुर्दशोऽध्यायः ॥**

*Om Tatsaditi Śrimadbhagvadgitāsūpaniṣatsu Brahmavidyāyāṃ Yogaśāstre Śrīkṛṣṇārjunasaṅvāde Guṇatrayavibhāgayogo Nāma Caturdaśo'dhyāyaḥ* ॥

Only for the understanding of ordinary people, Brahman is divided in two sections: pure and impure. 'Impure Brahman' indicates 'Causal Brahman' (Kāraṇa Brahma) since it is the cause of creation-sustenance-destruction of the universe. However, impure Brahman is based on the substratum of attributeless Nirguṇa Brahman. Nirguṇa is the real nature of Saguṇa. Nirguṇa Brahman is birthless, imperishable, immutable, eternal, non-decayable, omnipresent, all-pervading, and Absolute, Pure Bliss. Every seeker is always aware of Saguṇa i.e. entities having Guṇas; therefore, it is necessary to describe Nirguṇa Brahman with the help of Saguṇa. E.g. the body made up of the three Guṇas is perishable, but Nirguṇa Brahman is imperishable. The body is mutable, but Brahman is immutable.

Unless the Jiva is liberated from the clutches of the three Guṇas, he cannot realize "I am Brahman." All inclinations, traits, and preferences of the Jiva are present due to the influence of the three Guṇas in him. The root of all traits lies in Vāsanās, which are subtle imprints of pending desires from past births. The seeker should recognize this fact and see his own traits in an impersonal, impassive manner. E.g. the wavering mind is a mark of Rajoguṇa. The seeker should recognize wavering of his mind to be the influence of Rajoguṇa and disregard it. It is also necessary to always remember that the true Self, Ātman, is unattached from the impact of Rajoguṇa. The seeker is expected to apply this thought-process for all the three Guṇas and strive to go beyond them. By practicing in this manner, he will be able to realize "I am Brahman" as indicated by 'Asi' in the 'Tat-Tvam-Asi' Mahāvākya.

## Chapter 15

# The Supreme Self

॥ पुरुषोत्तमयोगः (Puruṣottamayogaḥ) ॥

This chapter describes the result of being One with the Supreme Puruṣa. Lord Kṛṣṇa says, "Having reached this goal, the person does not return to the birth and death cycle. (*15.4*)" So long as a seeker sees the tree of the world described in this chapter as real and remains attached to it, it is not possible for him to realize Oneness with Brahman, i.e. he cannot experience **Asi** in *Tat-Tvam-Asi* Mahāvākya. Most people are so immersed in worldly life that the thought of the world being unreal (Mithyā) does not even remotely touch their minds. This chapter illustrates in detail how the world is transient, unreal, and a mere illusory appearance.

**The allegory of Aśvattha tree**

*श्रीभगवानुवाच।*
ऊर्ध्वमूलमधःशाखमश्वत्थं प्राहुरव्ययम्।
छन्दांसि यस्य पर्णानि यस्तं वेद स वेदवित्॥ १ ॥
अधश्चोर्ध्वं प्रसृतास्तस्य शाखा गुणप्रवृद्धा विषयप्रवालाः।
अधश्च मूलान्यनुसन्ततानि कर्मानुबन्धीनि मनुष्यलोके॥ २ ॥
न रूपमस्येह तथोपलभ्यते नान्तो न चादिर्न च सम्प्रतिष्ठा।
अश्वत्थमेनं सुविरूढमूलं असङ्गशस्त्रेण दृढेन छित्त्वा॥ ३ ॥

*Śrībhagavān uvāca* ।
*Ūrdhvamūlam adhaḥśākham aśvattham prāhur avyam* ।
*Chandāṃsi yasya parṇāni yas taṃ veda sa vedavit* ॥ *1* ॥
*Adhaś cordhvaṃ prasṛtāstasya śākhā*
*Guṇapravṛddhā viṣayapravālāḥ* ।

*Adhaś ca mūlāny anusaṃtatāni*
*Karmānubandhīni manuṣyaloke* ॥ *2* ॥
*Na rūpamasyeha tathopalabhyate*
*Naānto na cādirna ca saṃpratiṣṭhā* ।
*Aśvatthām enaṃ suvirūḍhamūlaṃ*
*Asaṅgaśastreṇa dṛḍhena chittvā* ॥ *3* ॥

**Meaning:** (Śrībhagavān said) The scriptures – Śruti and Smṛti – speak of this changing world as 'the imperishable Aśvattha tree' whose roots are above, branches are below, and leaves are the Vedas. He alone is the knower of the gist of the Vedas who knows this Aśvattha tree. Objects of pleasure nourished by the three Guṇas are the leaves of this tree, and its branches are spread below and above. Bodies of men, who experience the fruits of good and bad actions, are the roots stretched below (w.r.t. Brahman). This tree is not what is described by people in the world. The origin, existence, or end of this tree cannot be perceived in any manner. Having cut asunder this deep-rooted tree of worldly-life with the ax of Knowledge of the true Self powered by non-attachment –

In general, every tree has its roots below the ground and branches as well as leaves above the ground. However, in this verse, the roots of the worldly Aśvattha tree are said to be 'above.' In this context, the word 'above' means 'superior' which is akin to the meaning in this statement "An order has come down from superior authorities." The substratum (*Adhiṣṭhāna*) of subtle Brahman is superior. On the contrary, the gross worldly tree, which is falsely superimposed (*Adhyasta*) on Brahman, is considered inferior. The superimposition (*Adhyāsa*) of the tree takes place on the substratum of Brahman, therefore Brahman is said to be 'up' or 'above,' and it is equated to the 'roots' of this worldly tree. Previously, Lord Kṛṣṇa has said that the Aśvattha tree is His Divine Glory (*10.26*). Traditionally it has been equated to the Peepal tree (Ficus religiosa or sacred fig).

The word **Aśvattha** in Sanskrit means dynamic and ever-changing. The nature of this worldly Aśvattha tree keeps changing constantly; it does not remain the same even for a second. The seeker, however, cannot see the world as changing since the changes are subtle. Brahman is the substratum of this ever-changing world, and Brahman is non-decaying and indestructible.

Leaves nourish, secure, and adorn a tree. Likewise, the Vedas are said to be the leaves of this worldly tree since they feed and secure it. This simply means, when the seeker acts by following the guidelines of the Vedas (leaves), those actions nourish and secure his life.

Śruti has stated that the world is expansion of Brahman.

**आराममस्य पश्यन्ति न तं पश्यति कश्चन ।**

*Ārāmamasya paśyanti na taṁ paśyati kaścan* । (*Bru. 4.3.14*)

"Everyone sees the expanse (Arāma) of Brahman in the form of the visible world, but no one sees Brahman." The seeker who knows the true nature of this Aśvattha tree along with its roots is said to be the real knower of the Vedas. Ādi Śaṅkarācārya has stated the gist of the Vedas in a succinct manner –

**ब्रह्मसत्यं जगन्मिथ्या ।**

*Brahma-Satyaṁ Jaganmithyā* ।

"Brahman alone is real; the world is unreal (*Mithyā*)." If this is indeed considered the gist of the Vedas, then it becomes necessary to know for sure that the worldly Aśvattha tree is unreal, while Brahman is the ultimate reality.

The creation, sustenance, and dissolution of the world continue in a cyclical manner, so here the worldly Aśvattha tree is said to be **Avyaya** i.e. constant (non-decaying). It is constant in the form of a cyclic flow, but permanency is not its nature. It is subject to a beginning and an end. This Aśvattha tree has grown enormously due to being watered with Sattva, Rājas, and Tāmas Guṇas; small new leaves of objects of pleasure have grown on this tree. Its branches of various species like humans, gods, animals, birds, Tiryaks etc. are spread above and below. [Note: All the species apart from humans move around by keeping their bodies in horizontal or oblique position. They are called Tiryak Yoni in Sanskrit. Only humans move in an upright position.] Among all the species, only humans are bound by their actions due to the roots of ego and mineness, and these roots have proliferated deep in the tree. The three Guṇas, objects of pleasure, the journey between various planes, doership, ego, mineness are the reasons due to which man remains constrained in the Aśvattha tree of this ever-changing world.

This tree is impermanent. One can recognize it as unreal by seeing it as such with the help of scriptures. The tree is real for ignorant people, and it is unreal for wise sages who have attained Self-Knowledge. Therefore, the tree is said to be neither real nor unreal, hence indescribable and illusory (*Sat-Asat-Vilakṣaṇa-Anirvacaniya-Mithyā*). It is not possible to comprehend when this tree was created, and it is not possible to imagine when it will end. Thus, it is not permanent. It is the sheer power of Māyā which does not let anyone remain permanently established in this world; hence, the Aśvattha tree of worldly-life has no permanent existence.

If one desires to know the real nature of this Aśvattha tree which is actually unreal but deemed as real due to the feelings of ego and mineness, then it is necessary to sever it with the weapons of detachment and dispassion towards worldly matters. Detachment and discrimination can together help sublate this falsely superimposed tree and know the substratum Brahman.

## Surrender to the Primeval Lord to know Brahman

ततः पदं तत्परिमार्गितव्यं यस्मिन्गता न निवर्तन्ति भूयः ।
तमेव चाद्यं पुरुषं प्रपद्ये यतः प्रवृत्तिः प्रसृता पुराणी ॥ ४ ॥

*Tataḥ padaṃ tatparimārgitāvyaṃ*
*Yasmin gatā na nivartanti bhūyaḥ* ।
*Tameva cādyaṃ puruṣaṃ prapadye*
*Yataḥ pravṛttiḥ prasṛtā purāṇī* ॥ *4* ॥

**Meaning:** Then that primal goal should be sought after. Having reached that goal, seekers do not return to the birth and death cycle. I have surrendered to that primeval Puruṣa – from whom this beginningless worldly tree has streamed forth – by being One with Him. (This is how that beginningless goal should be known or sought after).

Note: *Adhiṣṭhāna* = substratum (a rope)

*Adhyasta* = falsely superimposed entity (a snake)

*Adhyāsa* = false superimposition (seeing a snake on a rope)

One should try to infer the Adhiṣṭhāna when seeing the Adhyasta. Adhyasta is a delusive, superimposed appearance, and it is always based on an Adhiṣṭhāna. E.g. Adhyasta of mirage is falsely seen on the Adhiṣṭhāna of barren land in a desert. Knowing this, the seeker should surrender to Lord Nārāyaṇa who is the Adhiṣṭhāna of all, contemplate on His true nature Brahman, and sublate (Bādha) that which is Adhyasta on Brahman. Adhyasta is Māyic (illusory) in nature. Māyā can be inferred from its effects or actions. Brahman is the Adhiṣṭhāna of Māyā. The Adhyasta world has three aspects:

| **Mayic or Adhyasta world** | **Adhiṣṭhāna Brahman** |
|---|---|
| Asti – worldly existence | Sat – Pure Existence |
| Bhāti – worldly knowledge or cognizance | Cit – Pure Knowledge or Pure Consciousness |
| Priya – worldly likeability | Ānanda – Pure Bliss |

An entity 'exists,' it is 'cognized,' and it can be 'liked' or 'disliked.' Even though there is a huge variation in names and forms, the three factors of existence, cognizance, and likeability are common amongst all of them. ***Asti*, Bhati, *Priya*** belong to the visible world created by Īśvara; however, their origin is ***Sat, Cit, Ānanda*** Brahman. Brahman pervades everything in the world. Underlying every '*Asti*' of a name and form, there is the substratum of '*Sat*'. '*Asti*' is subject to beginning-state-end, but '*Sat*' is beginningless, stateless, and endless. '*Bhāti*' depends on the bodily organs, but '*Cit*' exists regardless of any organ. 'Priyatva' depends on a person, '*Ānanda*' is ever-available irrespective of any person.

**The practices for attainment of Ātman**

निर्मानमोहा जितसङ्गदोषा अध्यात्मनित्या विनिवृत्तकामाः ।
द्वन्द्वैर्विमुक्ताः सुखदुःखसञ्ज्ञैर्गच्छन्त्यमूढाः पदमव्ययं तत् ॥ ५ ॥

*Nirmānamohā jitasaṅgadoṣā*
*Adhyātmanityā vinivṛttakāmāḥ* ।
*Dvandvair vimuktāḥ sukhaduḥkhasaṃjñaiḥ*
*Gacchhantyamūḍhāḥ padamavyayaṃ tat* ॥ *5* ॥

**Meaning:** Those wise men whose ego and delusion are eradicated, who have conquered attachment to objects of pleasure, who are steady in Self-Knowledge, whose desires are wiped out, and who are freed from the dualities like joy and grief, attain the highest imperishable goal.

Attaining Self-realization is easy for those who do not seek honor or respect from society, who are not influenced by many kinds of lures, and who have renounced all attachments. Most people seek prestige which comes from intelligence, wealth, power, success, and fame. Their desires are based on the delusive notions that "I am the body" and "the world is real." E.g. intelligence is a part of the bodily existence; so, a person who strongly identifies himself with his body craves for recognition and appreciation from others about his intelligence. Śrīmad Bhāgavatam says that "Fame disappeared with Lord Kṛṣṇa when He ended His Saguṇa life. Now, the fame that ordinary people receive in their life is a mere reflection of the original fame that belonged to Lord Kṛṣṇa." People who crave for being famous will never find lasting fame in today's age. Their attraction for power, wealth, and fame is a result of not having faith in Īśvara. As per Īśvara's scheme of Prārabdha, everyone is bound to receive wealth, fame, etc. that he is supposed to receive in his lifetime. Nobody can receive more wealth or more power just by expecting it. The mind becomes restless for the seeker who has many expectations, and then he is unable to concentrate on his goal. The seeker must free himself from all attachments, such as "I am the body" and "The family and friends are mine." Unless he is free from these worldly attachments, he cannot be attached to his true Self, Ātman. Renouncing attachment simply means that he should not indulge in unnecessary thinking about people or objects. It does not mean physically abandoning family, house, or friends. The seeker who feels excessive and unnecessary love for his body and family cannot love God. He has to look after his body for spiritual pursuit and also tend to his family as his duty, but needless involvement in them is called attachment. Only the seeker who has consciously removed all worldly wishes and ambitions from his mind can continually contemplate on Self-Knowledge.

Every person is bound to get the prescribed fruits when he fulfills his duties meticulously, whether he aspires for the fruits or not. If the seeker expects specific fruits from his actions, he gets caught in the duality of hope and despair. He feels happy when he receives the desires fruits; otherwise, he feels gravely unhappy and dissatisfied. In a life invariably filled with such dualities, the seeker can never realize Absolute, Pure Bliss of his true Self. Constant experience of joy and grief is the central duality of human life. The seeker immersed in it cannot continue his spiritual pursuit and study the scriptures. Spiritual pursuit involves contemplation on Saguṇa Lord and Nirguṇa Brahman.

## The nature of the Supreme Ātman

न तद्भासयते सूर्यो न शशाङ्को न पावकः ।
यद्गत्वा न निवर्तन्ते तद्धाम परमं मम ॥ ६ ॥

*Na tad bhāsayate sūryo na śaśāṅko na pāvakaḥ* ।
*Yad gatvā na nivartante tad dhāma paramaṃ mama* ॥ 6 ॥

**Meaning:** Having reached that place (goal), enlightened people do not return to worldly life of birth and death. Neither the sun can illumine that place nor the moon nor fire. That is My supreme abode.

St. Tukārāma Mahārāja has said that worldly objects can be seen in the light of the sun or the moon. But Self-effulgent Ātman cannot be seen in the sunlight or the moonlight. Ātman can be realized only by following the teachings of enlightened saints. The eternal light of Ātman illumines the sun and the moon. In other words, the sun and the moon can be known only in the light of Ātman. In spiritual science, 'knowing' is 'illumination' (*Prakāśana*). How does one know the darkness? In which light does a person understand that "This is darkness?" This knowledge or illumination takes place in the light of Ātman, the true Self.

Ātman is extremely subtle, so it is formless; therefore, it cannot be seen with eyes. It is a well-known fact that only an object having a form or a shape can be seen with eyes. Ātman is formless, so it is untouchable; it cannot be known with skin. Ātman is non-dual; it is soundless since there is nothing else that can collide with it to create vibrations; therefore, one cannot know Ātman by listening with ears. There are no particles in Ātman, so it cannot be smelt and known with a nose. Ātman is not an object, so it cannot be tasted and known with a tongue. The knowledge gained through these 5 senses is known by a Jiva with the help of his intellect. Therefore, even the intellect cannot comprehend Ātman since Ātman is beyond the five senses. Thus, Ātman is Self-cognizant (*Swasaṃvedya*). It can only be known by being One with it. The seeker who realizes that "I am Ātman" is not caught in the cycle of birth and death. Ātman is the true Self of every Jiva; the realization that "I am Ātman" is the highest goal of human life.

## The relation between Ātman and Jiva

**ममैवांशो जीवलोके जीवभूतः सनातनः ।**
**मनःषष्ठानीन्द्रियाणि प्रकृतिस्थानि कर्षति ॥ ७ ॥**

*Mamaivāṃśo jīvaloke jīvabhūtaḥ sanātanaḥ* ।
*Manaḥṣaṣṭhānīndriyāṇi prakṛtisthāni karṣati* ॥ 7 ॥

**Meaning:** The Jivātmā in this body is an eternal part of Me alone. He impels the six elements (the five senses and mind) created from Prakṛti to seek objects of pleasure.

The Jiva resides in the body since the very origin of the universe, hence he is called 'eternal' in this verse. This Jiva is a part of Me i.e. Lord Kṛṣṇa, the incarnation of Brahman. The Jiva activates the senses and mind to work. The only difference between the Jiva and Ātman is Upādhi, imiting adjunct. There is no actual difference between them. E.g. only one moon gets reflected separately in the water filled in ten pots kept in the moonlight. They are not ten different parts of the moon. The fact that "Jiva is a part of Brahman" needs to be stated only till the Jiva realizes that he himself is Brahman. There is no concept of divisions or segments (part, whole, etc.) in Brahman. "Brahman is whole, and many Jivas are his many parts" – this is not a possible scenario. Brahman is only one, non-dual principle without divisions or subdivisions of any kind. The Jiva, who is perceived as a part of Brahman, impels the senses and the mind to their respective actions. Brahman, however, does not do anything. The 9th verse explains this in more detail.

## How does the Jiva leave his body?

**शरीरं यदवाप्नोति यच्चाप्युत्क्रामतीश्वरः ।**
**गृहीत्वैतानि संयाति वायुर्गन्धानिवाशयात् ॥ ८ ॥**

*Śarīraṃ yad avāpnoti yac cāpy utkrāmatīśvaraḥ* ।
*Gṛhitvaitāni saṅyāti vāyur gandhān ivāśayāt* ॥ *8* ॥

**Meaning:** When a Jiva, owner of the body and senses, leaves his prior body, he takes his mind and subtle organs with him to the next body, just as the wind carries sweet fragrances from one flower to the other.

Vedāntic scriptures state that the subtle body rides on Udāna Vāyu (a type of Prāṇa, energy) and enters the next body. This is a very subtle, delicate process like the example of particles of smell in flower. The Jiva takes his mind and all subtle organs with him when he goes to the next body. One should remember this while donating eyes or other organs.

## Various mediums to enjoy objects of pleasure

**श्रोत्रं चक्षुः स्पर्शनं च रसनं घ्राणमेव च ।**
**अधिष्ठाय मनश्चायं विषयानुपसेवते ॥ ९ ॥**

*Śrotraṃ cakṣuḥ sparśanaṃ ca rasanaṃ ghrāṇam eva ca* ।
*Adhiṣṭhāya manaś cāyaṃ viṣayān upasevate* ॥ *9* ॥

**Meaning:** This Jivātmā experiences the objects of pleasure by residing in nose, ears, eyes, skin, tongue, mind, and all action organs.

Sound, touch, form, taste, and smell are the five kinds of objects, and ears, skin, etc. are their respective senses. They are insentient in nature. E.g. sound is insentient; sound cannot know itself or anyone else. It does not know that "I am sound, and there is some other person who pronounces me." Insentient objects do not themselves have the power to make a person happy or sad. The Jiva feels happy after hearing praise or sad after hearing criticism. A person may feel unhappy seeing a lavish house of an unfriendly neighbor; however, the neighbor feels happy in the same house. If the house had the capacity to give pleasure, it would have made all people equally happy. The senses such as ears, nose, tongue, etc. are insentient like the house. They are considered sentient only due to the Jivātmā that pervades them. Therefore, a dead body cannot know anything despite having all senses and organs intact.

## Ignorant people do not know Jivātmā, wise people know him

उत्क्रामन्तं स्थितं वापि भुञ्जानं वा गुणान्वितम् ।
विमूढा नानुपश्यन्ति पश्यन्ति ज्ञानचक्षुषः ॥ १० ॥

*Utkrāmantaṃ sthitaṃ vāpi bhuñjānaṃ vā guṇānvitam ।*
*Vimūḍhā nānupaśyanti paśyanti jñānacakṣuṣaḥ ॥ 10 ॥*

**Meaning:** Ignorant people do not know about the Jiva while abiding in the body, leaving the body, being associated with the Guṇas, or while enjoying the objects of pleasure. However, enlightened people can see (know) the Jiva.

Whenever we discuss the actions done by the body, they are related to the Jiva in the body. As per the theory of Ābhāsavāda, the concept of 'Jiva' includes three constituents:

**Jiva** = Ātman (Pure Consciousness) + Intellect + Cidābhāsa (Reflected Consciousness in the intellect)

Ātman (*Kuṭastha* Caitanya), the true Self, is itself actionless, but it acts as a substratum for the Cidābhāsa in the intellect. Therefore, abiding in the body, leaving the body, enjoying objects – all these activities are performed by the Jiva or Cidābhāsa. The seeker can directly see or infer the presence of the Jiva in his body through his own actions. He can also indirectly infer the presence of a Jiva in another person's body by observing the person's movements. Wise people understand the presence of Pure Consciousness as the substratum for all actions performed by the Jiva. In contrast, ignorant people only remain immersed in actions.

## Pure mind is necessary for the Knowledge of Ātman

यतन्तो योगिनश्चैनं पश्यन्त्यात्मन्यवस्थितम् ।
यतन्तोऽप्यकृतात्मानो नैनं पश्यन्त्यचेतसः ॥ ११ ॥

*Yatanto yoginaś cainaṃ paśyanty ātmany avasthitam* ।
*Yatanto'pyakṛtātmāno nainaṃ paśyanty acetasaḥ* ॥ *11* ॥

**Meaning:** The seekers who are striving for Self-realization know Him (Ātman) dwelling in the Self or the heart. But ignorant people who have not purified their mind cannot know "I am Ātman" despite many efforts.

The word 'heart' (Hṛdaya) means Antaḥkaraṇa (mind-intellect-memory-ego) in spiritual studies. Ātman permeates the mind. Cidābhāsa, the reflection of Ātman, also permeates the mind. The mind permeates the whole body, so the Jiva occupies the whole body as well. If the mind is pure, then one can be aware of Cidābhāsa and Ātman in his mind. A person whose mind is impure dwells in the causes which pollute his mind (objects of desire, love-hate, etc.), instead of being aware of Cidābhāsa in it. In other words, the mind which is immersed in acquiring various kinds of 'qualified knowledge' (*Vṛttijñāna*) cannot know the substratum of Pure Knowledge which underlies all kinds of knowledge. The mind tainted by ego and mineness remains immersed in thinking about the body ("I am the body") and the world ("The world is mine"). It is unable to think about Pure Consciousness, which is the very substratum on which 'qualified knowledge' is known by the senses. A person whose mind is not tainted by ego and mineness can be aware of substratum Ātman illumining his mind. On the other hand, a person deluded with impurities can never know Ātman despite many efforts.

**The grandeur of the Lord**

**यदादित्यगतं तेजो जगद्भासयतेऽखिलम् ।**
**यच्चन्द्रमसि यच्चाग्नौ तत्तेजो विद्धि मामकम् ॥ १२ ॥**
**गामाविश्य च भूतानि धारयाम्यहमोजसा ।**
**पुष्णामि चौषधीः सर्वाः सोमो भूत्वा रसात्मकः ॥ १३ ॥**

अहं वैश्वानरो भूत्वा प्राणिनां देहमाश्रितः ।
प्राणापानसमायुक्तः पचाम्यन्नं चतुर्विधम् ॥ १४ ॥
सर्वस्य चाहं हृदि सन्निविष्टो मत्तः स्मृतिर्ज्ञानमपोहनं च ।
वेदैश्च सर्वैरहमेव वेद्यो वेदान्तकृद्वेदविदेव चाहम् ॥ १५ ॥

*Yad ādityagataṃ tejo jagad bhāsayate'khilam ।*
*Yac candramasi yac cāgnau tat tejo viddhi māmakam ॥ 12 ॥*
*Gām āviśya ca bhūtāni dhārayāmy aham ojasā ।*
*Puṣṇāmi cauṣadhīḥ sarvāḥ somo bhūtvā rasātmakaḥ ॥ 13 ॥*
*Ahaṃ vaiśvānaro bhūtvā prāṇināṃ deham āŚrītaḥ ।*
*Prāṇāpānasamāyuktaḥ pacāmy annaṃ caturvidham ॥ 14 ॥*
*Sarvasya cāhaṃ hṛdi saṃniviṣṭo*
*Mattaḥ smṛtir jñānam apohanaṃ ca ।*
*Vedaiś ca sarvair aham eva vedyo*
*Vedāntakṛdvedavid eva cāham ॥ 15 ॥*

**Meaning:** The splendor in the sun which illumines the whole world and that which is in the moon and in fire – know that light to be Mine. I permeate the earth and support all beings by using My power of retention. I nourish all herbs by becoming the fluid moon. I alone become the fire Vaiśvānara in the stomachs of all beings and digest four kinds of food by being ablaze with the help of Prāṇa and Apāna. I have entered the hearts of all beings. Hence, the 'knowledge' or the 'absence of knowledge' and 'memory' in all beings are from Me alone. I alone am worthy of being known through the study of all the Vedas. Also, I am indeed the author of the Vedānta Sampradāya as well as the knower of the gist of the Vedas.

The entire visible universe is a creation of Īśvara, so Īśvara's power can be experienced in many ways. Īśvara is omniscient and omnipotent. His power is coupled with His governance. The much-needed resources like energy and light are given to humans only as per His regulation. The seeker should remember Īśvara whenever he sees the manifestations of energy and light. The worship of the sun and the worship of fire have evolved from the same concept. The serene light of the moon gives pleasure. Knowing that Īśvara is present in the moon, there is a ritual of worshipping Him on specific festivities. Bṛhadāraṇyaka Upaniṣad says –

**यः पृथिव्यां तिष्ठन् पृथिव्या अन्तरो यं पृथिवी न वेद यस्य पृथिवी शरीरं यः पृथिवीमन्तरो यमयत्येष त आत्मान्तर्याम्यमृतः ॥**

*Yah Pṛthivyām tiṣṭhan Pṛthivyā antaro yaṁ Pṛthivi na veda yasya Pṛthivi śariraṁ yah Pṛthivimantaro yamāyātyesha ta Ātmāntaryāmyamṛtah ॥ (3.7.3)*

"He inhabits the earth and is also within it; however, the earth does not know Him. The earth is His body, and He regulates the earth from within. He is Ātman, the immortal Self, who controls each Jiva from within." The contradictory elements like fire and water, earth and water, etc. live together in harmony only due to the uninterrupted, continuous energy of Īśvara. It is verily His scheme that the seed of a fruit yields only the same fruit, not the other, and every Jiva lives as per his own Prārabdha. The moon, akin to nectar (Amruta), is His form. He nourishes herbs and plants through the moonlight. It is imperative for animals that the food they eat is properly digested. The job of digestion is done by fire, Vaiśvānara, with the help of Prāṇa and Apāna. This energy of fire belongs to the Lord alone. Food varieties that can be eaten, drunk, suck, chewed, or gulped are all digested due to the fire Vaiśvānara. The intellect in all humans is impelled only by Īśvara. One can gain knowledge by seeing, remembering, or using the other senses. Even the absence of memory or forgetfulness is a result of Īśvara's governance alone. The seeker should verily think of God every time he remembers or forgets something. Knowledge and ignorance are both His forms, so one should think of Him alone in both cases. Brahman is the core gist of all the Vedas; Brahman alone is worthy of knowing. Īśvara is the creator of the Vedas and Upaniṣads, and He alone is the authentic Knower of all the Vedas. Even the Jiva who strives to learn the Vedas is Brahman, in essence.

**The description of the three Puruṣas**

द्वाविमौ पुरुषौ लोके क्षरश्चाक्षर एव च ।
क्षरः सर्वाणि भूतानि कूटस्थोऽक्षर उच्यते ॥ १६ ॥
उत्तमः पुरुषस्त्वन्यः परमात्मेत्युदाहृतः ।
यो लोकत्रयमाविश्य बिभर्त्यव्यय ईश्वरः ॥ १७ ॥
यस्मात्क्षरमतीतोऽहमक्षरादपि चोत्तमः ।
अतोऽस्मि लोके वेदे च प्रथितः पुरुषोत्तमः ॥ १८ ॥
यो मामेवमसम्मूढो जानाति पुरुषोत्तमम् ।
स सर्वविद्भजति मां सर्वभावेन भारत ॥ १९ ॥

*Dvāv imau puruṣau loke kṣaraś cākṣara eva ca* ।
*Kṣaraḥ sarvāṇi bhūtāni kūṭastho'kṣara ucyate* ॥ 16 ॥
*Uttamaḥ puruṣas tv anyaḥ paramātmety udāhṛtaḥ* ।
*Yo lokatrayam āviśya bibharty avyaya īśvaraḥ* ॥ 17 ॥
*Yasmāt kṣaramatīto'ham akṣarād api cottamaḥ* ।
*Ato'smi loke vede ca prathitaḥ puruṣottamaḥ* ॥ 18 ॥
*Yo mām evam asaṃmūḍho jānāti puruṣottamam* ।
*Sa sarvavid bhajati māṃ sarvabhāvena bhārata* ॥ 19 ॥

**Meaning:** There are two Puruṣas in this world: Kṣara Puruṣa (perishable) and Akṣara Puruṣa (unperishable). Jiva having the Upādhi of Avidyā is the Kṣara Puruṣa, while Īśvara having the Upādhi of Māyā (the cause of the world) is Akṣara Puruṣa. Uttama Puruṣa is distinct from these two, and He is known as Supreme Ātman or Paramātman in Vedānta. One who pervades the three planes and nourishes them is the imperishable ultimate governor who is Uttama Puruṣa. I am known as Uttama Puruṣa since I am different from the Kṣara Puruṣa and Akṣara Puruṣa. For the same reason, I am known in the world and in the Vedas as Puruṣottama. O Arjuna! One who knows Me, the Puruṣottama, knows everything, and he worships Me with utmost devotion.

The word ***Kuṭastha*** does not mean Ātman in the 16th verse here. It means Īśvara (Witness) who does not consume the fruits of actions (Muṇḍak Up.). 'Jiva' having Upādhi of Avidyā (ignorance) is the **Kṣara Puruṣa**, while 'Īśvara' having Upādhi of Māyā is the **Akṣara Puruṣa**. Īśvara has a very long life compared to any Jiva. He is omniscient and omnipotent; therefore, He is addressed as Akṣara Puruṣa (imperishable). Both Kṣara and Akṣara Puruṣa are subject to birth, life, and death, so they are inferior. Uttama Puruṣa is beyond these two. The Upādhi of Māyā or Avidyā does not limit Him. In the 17th verse, the word **Īśvara** means 'Brahman', also known as Uttama Puruṣa there. Brahman upholds and maintains the three planes by being their substratum. Brahman pervades all entities in the sentient and insentient universe, yet it is not attached to those entities nor imprisoned by them. Therefore, it is called **Uttama Puruṣa**. The seeker should realize that his true Self is this Uttama Puruṣa. He should follow all commands of Īśvara, behold Īśvara in His Saguṇa form, worship Him, and realize that "I am Uttama Puruṣa" in this process. Īśvara is Saguṇa yet formless, so He cannot be seen in His unmanifested form. Only when Īśvara is incarnated as a Saguṇa Sākāra God like Kṛṣṇa or Rāma, He can be seen by a devotee who has deep faith and devotion. The seeker can realize Uttama Puruṣa by being One with Him. An enlightened seeker recognizes this and worships only Uttama Puruṣa through the Pure Knowledge of Brahman.

## Conclusion

**इति गुह्यतमं शास्त्रमिदमुक्तं मयानघ ।**
**एतद्बुद्ध्वा बुद्धिमान्स्यात्कृतकृत्यश्च भारत ॥ २० ॥**

*Iti guhyatamaṃ śāstram idam uktaṃ mayānagha* ।
*Etat buddhvā buddhimān syāt kṛtakṛtyaś ca bhārata* ॥ *20* ॥

**Meaning:** O sinless Arjuna! I have thus imparted the teaching of this highly profound and mysterious philosophy to you. Knowing this, the seeker becomes enlightened and accomplished in a true sense.

**ॐ तत्सदिति श्रीमद्भगवद्गीतासूपनिषत्सु ब्रह्मविद्यायां योगशास्त्रे श्रीकृष्णार्जुन संवादे पुरुषोत्तमयोगो नाम पञ्चदशोऽध्यायः ॥**

*Om Tatsaditi Śrimadbhagvadgitāsūpaniṣatsu Brahmavidyāyāṃ Yogaśāstre Śrīkṛṣṇārjunasaṅvāde Puruṣottamayogo Nāma Pañcadaśo'dhyāyaḥ* ॥

Just like the 9th chapter, Self-Knowledge is said to be mysterious even here. When we study the profound theory of Vedānta which leads to Self-Knowledge, we can see why it is called mysterious here. Therefore, the student of this Knowledge should be discerning, intelligent, and eligible for its study. "Brahman is that one principle knowing which everything as if becomes known (Muṇḍaka Upaniṣad)." The entire human life of a seeker who realizes "I am Brahman" becomes meaningful and glorious in a true sense.

## Chapter 16

# The Divine and Demoniac Traits

### ॥ दैवासुरसम्पद्विभागयोगः (Daivāsurasaṃpadvibhāgayogaḥ) ॥

St. Tukārāma has stated that bad qualities lead to utter failure on all fronts, both in worldly and spiritual life. The divine traits described in this chapter are good qualities, while the demoniac traits described here are bad qualities. A seeker who has divine traits finds it relatively easy to realize "I am Brahman" as stated with ***Asi*** in ***Tat-Tvam-Asi*** Mahāvākya. E.g. 'fearlessness' is a divine trait. One who is fearful by nature is attached to the body, and he considers the world to be real. He is scared for his body and fears the world. 'Attachment to the body' and 'perceiving the world as real' are both caused by ignorance. The ignorant seeker cannot realize "I am Brahman."

**Divine traits**

***श्रीभगवानुवाच ।***

**अभयं सत्त्वसंशुद्धिर्ज्ञानयोगव्यवस्थितिः ।**
**दानं दमश्च यज्ञश्च स्वाध्यायस्तप आर्जवम् ॥ १ ॥**
**अहिंसा सत्यमक्रोधस्त्यागः शान्तिरपैशुनम् ।**
**दया भूतेष्वलोलुप्त्वं मार्दवं ह्रीरचापलम् ॥ २ ॥**
**तेजः क्षमा धृतिः शौचमद्रोहो नातिमानिता ।**
**भवन्ति सम्पदं दैवीमभिजातस्य भारत ॥ ३ ॥**

*Śrībhagavān uvāca* ।

*Abhayaṃ sattvasaṃśuddhir jñānayogavyavasthitiḥ* ।
*Dānaṃ damaś ca yajñaś ca svādhyāyas tapa ārjavam* ॥ *1* ॥
*Ahiṃsā satyam akrodhas tyāgaḥ śāntir apaiśunam* ।
*Dayā bhūteṣv aloluptvaṃ mārdavaṃ hrīr acāpalam* ॥ *2* ॥

*Tejaḥ kṣamā dhṛtiḥ śaucam adroho nātimānitā* ।
*Bhavanti saṃpadaṃ daivīm abhijātasya bhārata* ॥ *3* ॥

**Meaning:** (Śrībhagavān said) O Arjuna! Fearlessness; purity of the mind; firm faith in the Yoga of Knowledge and the Yoga of Actions; donating wealth; conquering the senses; worshipping God; performing prescribed duties like Yajña; study of the scriptures and Vedas; chanting of Mantra; practicing austerities; forthrightness; non-violence; saying the truth; absence of anger; renouncing ego; steady mind; not criticizing others behind their back; compassion for all; non-attachment to objects of pleasure; gentleness; feeling ashamed of bad actions; absence of fickleness of the body; brilliant glow of intelligence or ability to influence others; forgiveness; fortitude; purity of the body; absence of enmity; lack of pride – these are the traits of a person born with divine disposition.

If the mind is pure, it becomes easy to be aware of Ātman i.e. Pure Consciousness in it. E.g. if the water is clear, calm, and steady, the moonlight reflects in it completely. However, more disturbed or polluted the water is, as in an ocean or a stream, more difficult it is to see the reflection of moon in it. Analogous to this, if the mind is disturbed or impure, the reflection of Ātman in it cannot be experienced clearly. But if the mind is pure, steady, and rested, one can naturally realize "I am Ātman" as a result. The seeker who leads his life by following the principles of Karmayoga (*Ch.3*) and Jñānayoga (*Ch.2*) can eventually realize "I am Ātman."

While donating wealth, the seeker should also think about the beneficiary who receives donations. Scriptures state that "One God resides in all beings." This knowledge makes it easy for the seeker to feel compassion for others and to help them in his capacity. Taittiriya Upaniṣad says – **(श्रद्धया देयं)** *Śraddhayā deyaṃ.* This means that the one should give donations with faith and self-reproach that "I am unable to give as much as I should be giving." The donor should genuinely care whether the donation is enough for the beneficiary's needs.

Every seeker should know that the senses are attracted to their objects as directed by the mind which itself is impelled by the past Vāsanās. If the seeker indulges in sensory attractions, he will have to spend his entire life in pursuing objects. No person can be motivated to restrain his organs as long as he finds illusory pleasure in worldly objects. All objects are transient, and they are subject to beginning and end. They give diminishing pleasure with time. Every person has to take many efforts and spend money to obtain these objects of pleasure. Therefore, the seeker should not be dependent on objects for pleasure. Instead, he is supposed to strive to seek Pure Bliss of Ātman. St. Kabira says, "An arrow cannot be thrown from the bow as long as the archer doesn't pull the string. Likewise, the organs cannot go out to the world when they are leashed by the person, even if his mind craves for objects." This is a great thought-process which can help every seeker since he can put a leash on his action-organs even when his mind craves for objects.

The seeker should engage in all day-to-day transactions while mentally offering them to God. This is just another form of doing a formal Yajña. He should study the scriptures of Vedānta, and texts written by enlightened saints. It is also important to sing the praises of Lord and chant His Mantra. All kinds of efforts needed to achieve one's goal in life are called *Tapas* (austerities). While being engaged in actions, the seeker should maintain the purity of the mind; stay away from treachery, insidiousness, and crookedness; and also help others to remain steady and at peace.

Non-violence is not hurting anyone physically, mentally, or verbally. St. Jñāneśwara says, "People who live their life for the very objective of making the entire world happy, theirs is the life of non-violence." If the seeker sticks to truth in day-to-day transactions, he can find the spiritual Supreme Truth relatively quickly. Being truthful is a great strength, and one who is truthful does not have to rethink or remember what he said to whom and at which time. As a result, his mind is neither unstable nor frightened. But when speaking what is true, one must express it in a way that will not hurt others, or else one must remain silent about it.

The seeker should abandon the feeling of being a doer and an experiencer. "I did this," "It happened because of me," "It will not occur without me," "I will not let it happen without me," "What would happen without me?" – All such thoughts indicate the sense of doership and they need to be consciously renounced. Anger is the very first enemy of human beings. An enraged person is defeated in worldly life as well as the spiritual life. Every event in life takes place under the governance of Īśvara. If the seeker or devotee believes in God but does not accept His governance, his worship has no value per se. Every person first thinks about his own happiness. By this rule, relatives, acquaintances of the seeker think about their own happiness as well. When the seeker does not accept this fact, he becomes angry. The absence of anger naturally results in peace. Peace and happiness are two sides of the same coin. Happiness or Pure Bliss is nothing but Ātman, the true Self. Upaniṣad describes Ātman as –

**निर्मलं निष्कलं शान्तं ।**

*Nirmalaṃ niṣkalaṃ śāntaṃ* ।

"Ātman is without impurities, parts of any kind; Ātman is peace itself."

It is a divine trait not to criticize anyone under any circumstances. In general, when two people meet, they discuss a third person. In most cases, they only talk about the bad or negative traits of the third person. St. Tukārāma has said, "The essence of worshipping the Supreme Lord lies in not feeling jealous of anyone in the world." Jealousy is one of the reasons for criticism. The seeker should nurture selfless compassion for all beings in the world. The compassion here means being conscientiously aware of the fact that "Other people feel happy or get hurt just like me."

Despite deriving pleasures from objects through senses, the seeker should not be attached to objects or dwell on them. The joy from objects is originally Pure Bliss of the true Self, Ātman. The mind becomes completely quiet as a result of the fulfillment of a desire. E.g. 'fame' is an object of pleasure which may give intermittent joy, but it does not give lasting happiness. When a person finds fame as he desires, his mind becomes quiet and retires or disappears for a while. As a result, the person becomes momentarily aware of his own Self Ātman, which was veiled by the activities of his mind, and thus experiences Pure Bliss of Ātman. But he mistakenly thinks that he felt happy due to external fame. The seeker should clearly know that the external pleasure is only a result of the fleeting union of the Jiva with Ātman which takes place when his desire is fulfilled. For lasting happiness, the seeker is expected to strive to center his mind in Pure Bliss of his Ātman, instead of chasing the external objects.

The seeker should also make an effort to be gentle, soft, and conscientious. This is foundational for building good society as well as for progressing in spiritual life. He is supposed to feel ashamed of indulging in unrighteous, unjust, or unholy behavior. The seeker, leading such a sublime life, should not engage in any meaningless, superfluous activity; rather, he is expected to purposefully and conscientiously execute all actions, so he can reach his ultimate goal.

The seeker whose life is pure and pious also has the ability to make impure beings pure. The seeker is supposed to forgive others for their petty mistakes and not ruminate over them in his mind. Forgiveness keeps the mind calm and steady, and such a mind can be used for spiritual practice. Fortitude is highly needed both in worldly life and spiritual pursuit. Lack of fortitude is a result of weak Sattvaguṇa. The seeker should take care of generic lifestyle aspects such as eating Sāttvic food, being in the company of Sāttvic people, and reading and watching only that which helps nourish Sattvaguṇa. If he keeps his own body, house, and surroundings clean, his mind naturally remains calm and cheerful. If there is enmity in his mind, it becomes agitated. It is not possible for any seeker to perform any spiritual practice with the agitated mind.

## Characteristics of people born with demoniac traits

**दम्भो दर्पोऽभिमानश्च क्रोधः पारुष्यमेव च ।**
**अज्ञानं चाभिजातस्य पार्थ सम्पदमासुरीम् ॥ ४ ॥**

*Dambho darpo 'bhimānaś ca krodhaḥ pāruṣyam eva ca* ।
*Ajñānaṃ cābhijātasya pārtha saṃpadam āsurīm* ॥ *4* ॥

**Meaning:** O Pārtha! Ostentatiousness, arrogance, conceit, anger, ruthlessness, and ignorance – these characteristics belong to the person born with demoniac disposition.

The pretentious show of one's own importance and flaunting one's own relatives everywhere is called ostentatiousness. There is no one superior to God in this world, so a person who strives to showcase his greatness to impress others forgets God. The same is the case with arrogance. If an arrogant person is taken down by others, he suffers a great deal. Every person gets his body, intelligence, and circumstances as per the governance of Īśvara, so there is no reason to take pride in them. By being proud, the person invariably remains immersed in his body and other related worldly aspects. The body, intellect, and circumstances are bound by well-known limitations, so there is no reason to feel proud of them. "Who am I?", "What is the nature of this world?" – Not even remotely thinking about these primal questions of human life is a mark of demoniac quality.

**The effect of divine and demoniac qualities**

दैवी सम्पद्विमोक्षाय निबन्धायासुरी मता ।
मा शुचः सम्पदं दैवीमभिजातोऽसि पाण्डव ॥ ५ ॥

*Daivī sampad vimokṣāya nibandhāyāsurī matā* ।
*Mā śucaḥ saṃpadaṃ daivīm abhijāto 'si pāṇḍava* ॥ *5* ॥

**Meaning:** It is believed that the divine qualities lead to liberation, and the demoniac qualities lead to bondage. Arjuna! Do not lament because you are born with divine qualities.

Divine qualities immensely help in Self-realization that "I am Brahman." Demoniac qualities strengthen the bondages of the Jiva: "I am the body," "I am the doer," "The world is real," and "I am born, and I will die." Lord Kṛṣṇa has assured Arjuna by saying that Arjuna is born with divine traits.

**Detailed description of demoniac qualities**

द्वौ भूतसर्गौ लोकेऽस्मिन्दैव आसुर एव च ।
दैवो विस्तरशः प्रोक्त आसुरं पार्थ मे श्रृणु ॥ ६ ॥
प्रवृत्तिं च निवृत्तिं च जना न विदुरासुराः ।
न शौचं नापि चाचारो न सत्यं तेषु विद्यते ॥ ७ ॥
असत्यमप्रतिष्ठं ते जगदाहुरनीश्वरम् ।
अपरस्परसम्भूतं किमन्यत्कामहैतुकम् ॥ ८ ॥
एतां दृष्टिमवष्टभ्य नष्टात्मानोऽल्पबुद्धयः ।
प्रभवन्त्युग्रकर्माणः क्षयाय जगतोऽहिताः ॥ ९ ॥

*Dvau bhūtasargau loke 'smin daiva āsura eva ca* ।
*Daivo vistaraśaḥ prokta āsuraṃ pārtha me śṛṇu* ॥ *6* ॥
*Pravṛttiṃ ca nivṛttiṃ ca janā na vidur āsurāḥ* ।
*Na śaucaṃ nāpi cācāro na satyaṃ teṣu vidyāte* ॥ *7* ॥
*Asatyam apratiṣṭhaṃ te jagad āhur anīśvaram* ।
*Aparasparasaṃbhūtaṃ kim anyat kāmahaitukam* ॥ *8* ॥
*Etāṃ dṛṣṭim avaṣṭabhya naṣṭātmāno 'lpabuddhayaḥ* ।
*Prabhavanty ugrakarmāṇaḥ kṣayāya jagato 'hitāḥ* ॥ *9* ॥

**Meaning:** O Arjuna! There are two types of men in this world: divine and demoniac. The divine qualities have been discussed in detail before. Now hear from me about demoniac qualities. Demoniac people do not do what should be done, and they do what should not be done. They are not pure inside out, nor do they have ethical conduct, nor do they stick to the truth. Those demoniac people say that "The world is unreal, it has no support, and there is no God. The world is born of mutual communion between man and woman, lust being its only reason. What else can be the reason for the creation of the world?" By accepting this fake knowledge, these people having dull intellect ruin the chance to reform themselves. These gruesome and destructive people are born only for destroying the world.

Green color has many shades, likewise, both divine and demoniac qualities have many shades due to the varying permutations and combinations of the three Guṇas in each person. Sometimes divine traits are on the rise, while sometimes demoniac traits are dominant. According to scriptures, Dharma is of two kinds: first, Pravṛttilakṣaṇa Dharma – the guidelines for worldly life, and second, Nivṛttilakṣaṇa Dharma – the guidelines for spiritual life or the life of renunciation. A demoniac person has no awareness of any Dharma whatsoever. The term **Pravṛtti** in Sanskrit means natural inclination to live worldly life. The term **Nivṛtti** means detaching oneself from worldly affairs at some stage of life. This stage paves the way for Mokṣa, and it contains the seeds for Blissful life. Dharma puts the boundaries of guidelines around human life mainly to aid in individual welfare and develop social harmony. Demoniac people dislike the boundaries established by Dharma. They cannot even remotely think of detaching from worldly life. On the contrary, they mock others who do so. Ātman, the true Self, is pure and untainted, so one cannot realize "I am Ātman" unless the mind, body, and all day-to-day activities are completely pure. Demoniac people feel no need for Self-realization, so they do not find it necessary to purify their minds or actions. For them, good action is akin to instant gratification. They do not bother about sticking to truth or resorting to lies. They completely reject the teachings of enlightened saints.

Demoniac people do not even believe that the world is created by God. They firmly believe that the world is neither real nor unreal nor is it supported by anything. [This opinion is from the spiritual perspective, not from a transactional perspective.] They believe, "The insentient entities in the world – the Five Great Elements and their creations – were automatically created, while the sentient beings are created by the communion between a man and a woman, so lust is the only reason behind the creation of this world. What else can be the cause for it?" These and similar thoughts are destructive in everyday life, and such a life is not even remotely spiritual. There is no provision for joyful, content, and peaceful life for people having such demoniac thoughts. These destructive thoughts pollute their mind. Their intellect cannot discriminate between good and bad, and they only end up living a bad and inferior life. People who engage in such gruesome actions lead the world to its destruction.

**More description of demoniac people**

**काममाश्रित्य दुष्पूरं दम्भमानमदान्विताः ।**
**मोहाद्गृहीत्वासद्ग्राहान्प्रवर्तन्तेऽशुचिव्रताः ॥ १० ॥**
**चिन्तामपरिमेयां च प्रलयान्तामुपाश्रिताः ।**
**कामोपभोगपरमा एतावदिति निश्चिताः ॥ ११ ॥**
**आशापाशशतैर्बद्धाः कामक्रोधपरायणाः ।**
**ईहन्ते कामभोगार्थमन्यायेनार्थसञ्चयान् ॥ १२ ॥**

*Kāmam āśrītya duṣpūraṃ dambhamānamadānvitāḥ* ।
*Mohād gṛhītvāsadgrāhān pravartante 'śucivratāḥ* ॥ *10* ॥
*Cintām aparimeyāṃ ca pralayāntām upāŚrītāḥ* ।
*Kāmopabhogaparamā etāvad iti niścitāḥ* ॥ *11* ॥

*Āśāpāśaśatair baddhāḥ kāmakrodhaparāyaṇāḥ* ।
*Īhante kāmabhogārtham anyāyenārthasaṃcayān* ॥ *12* ॥

**Meaning:** Demoniac people are filled with pretentiousness, excessive pride, and arrogance. They nurture insatiable desires, embrace wrong ideas out of ignorance, and lead their lives in a perverted manner. They also worry about many things until they die. Being immersed in objects of pleasure, they firmly believe that there is lasting happiness in materialistic life. Bound by many ties of hope, demoniac people remain subservient to their desires and anger. They strive to secure hordes of money by unlawful means for sensual enjoyment.

The minds of most ordinary people are filled with countless hopes and ambitions. Many of their desires are impractical, and there is no way of fulfilling them. Their minds are always restless, polluted, and wavering. Some people cover up wavering of their mind by calling it as a mark of 'ambitious mind.' Rajoguṇa is dominant in most people, so it is only natural that their minds are wavering. However, the seeker should discriminate between what is realistic and unrealistic and wipe out unrealistic ambitions from his mind. People who have unrealistic ambitions many a time cross the boundaries of righteousness and unrighteousness, right and wrong, and lawful and unlawful. E.g. some sport-players resort to taking drugs to surpass previous records, some students resort to copying in exams, and some people take enormous loans for their businesses. Demoniac characteristics include flaunting the wealth that is possessed and earned, expecting respect or honor from others, and being a snob due to arrogance. These traits invariably lead to restlessness, dejection, and outperformance of each other. Demoniac people having such traits cannot even enjoy simple pleasures of life, how may then they find eternal Pure Bliss?

This demoniac lifestyle includes umpteen worries which last till death. A wise person knows that life filled with worries cannot be called a happy life. A demoniac person craving enjoyment goes after any object of pleasure as soon as he sees it. He thinks only about momentary pleasures and cannot even remotely think about eternal Pure Bliss. The demoniac person pining for joy always remains restless, and he finds no peace in life. Caught in the intricate web of many hopes and desires, he gets angry when he encounters anything that obstructs the fulfillment of his desires. It is mentioned in the Gita (*2.63*) that "Anger leads to delusion, and delusion leads to loss of memory." Accordingly, the demoniac person forgets the difference between just and unjust, right and wrong, and develops unappeasable greed for collecting objects of pleasure.

**The mindset of demoniac people**

**इदमद्य मया लब्धमिमं प्राप्स्ये मनोरथम् ।**
**इदमस्तीदमपि मे भविष्यति पुनर्धनम् ॥ १३ ॥**
**असौ मया हतः शत्रुर्हनिष्ये चापरानपि ।**
**ईश्वरोऽहमहं भोगी सिद्धोऽहं बलवान्सुखी ॥ १४ ॥**
**आढ्योऽभिजनवानस्मि कोऽन्योऽस्ति सदृशो मया ।**
**यक्ष्ये दास्यामि मोदिष्य इत्यज्ञानविमोहिताः ॥ १५ ॥**
**अनेकचित्तविभ्रान्ता मोहजालसमावृताः ।**
**प्रसक्ताः कामभोगेषु पतन्ति नरकेऽशुचौ ॥ १६ ॥**

*Idam adya mayā labdham imaṃ prāpsye manoratham* ।
*Idam astīdam api me bhaviṣyati punar dhanam* ॥ *13* ॥
*Asau mayā hataḥ śatrur haniṣye cāparān api* ।
*Īśvaro'aham ahaṃ bhogī siddho'haṃ balavān sukhī* ॥ *14* ॥
*Āḍhyo'bhijanavān asmi ko'nyo'sti sadṛśo mayā* ।
*Yakṣye dāsyāmi modiṣya ity ajñānavimohitāḥ* ॥ *15* ॥
*Anekacittavibhrāntā mohajālasamāvṛtāḥ* ।
*Prasaktāḥ kāmabhogeṣu patanti narake'śucau* ॥ *16* ॥

**Meaning:** They think, "I have achieved this thing today, now I will fulfill the other desire as well. I already have this much wealth; I will get more wealth later. Today I have killed this enemy; now I will kill other enemies as well. I am the ruler; I am the enjoyer; I am the lord that ordains all. I am powerful; I am happy. I am rich and born in a good family. Who else is equal to me? I will perform fire sacrifices (*Yajña*), give donations (*Dāna*), and be happy by enjoying many objects of pleasure." Thus, deluded by ignorance, enmeshed in the web of delusion, strongly attached to desires and enjoyments, bewildered in many ways, these demoniac people fall into the impious, foul hell.

When a high-achiever – who takes pride in his work – remains discontent with his achievements and dreams of even bigger achievements, he leads a very anxious, restless, and unstable life. Greed is the main reason for instability, and greed is a result of Rajoguṇa. When a person performs his duties tirelessly, he gets the results even without desiring them. But if he fails to recognize this simple fact and harbors expectations for ensuing results, then he is bound to feel worried, jealous, and anxious. He may then have a strong feeling to somehow destroy those adversaries who obstruct the fulfillment of his desires or ambitions. In case he is able to eliminate some adversaries, he may feel the urge to destroy the rest. After that, the person starts feeling he has power to do anything and craves even more for objects that can be attained through power. His belief in the false power keeps increasing, and he starts feeling delusively happy due to the joy that comes from power. "I am rich; my family is highly reputed. Who else in the world is equal to me? I will undertake many new professional and religious activities, expand the business, give donations, and live a cheerful, festive life" – the person who is strongly attached to worldly pleasures indulges in such daydreams. He suffers the agonies of hell and forgets the fact that his real nature is eternal Pure Bliss.

**Characteristics of demoniac people**

आत्मसम्भाविताः स्तब्धा धनमानमदान्विताः ।
यजन्ते नामयज्ञैस्ते दम्भेनाविधिपूर्वकम् ॥ १७ ॥
अहङ्कारं बलं दर्पं कामं क्रोधं च संश्रिताः ।
मामात्मपरदेहेषु प्रद्विषन्तोऽभ्यसूयकाः ॥ १८ ॥

*Ātmasaṃbhāvitāḥ stabdhā dhanamānamadānvitāḥ* ।
*Yajante nāmāyājñais te dambhenāvidhipūrvakam* ॥ *17* ॥
*Ahaṃkāraṃ balaṃ darpaṃ kāmaṃ krodhaṃ ca saṃŚrītāḥ* ।
*Māṃ ātmaparadeheṣu pradviṣanto 'bhyasūyakāḥ* ॥ *18* ॥

**Meaning:** People who consider themselves venerable, who are bloated with pride and intoxicated by wealth, respect, etc., neglect the ritual of Yajña and perform it just for the namesake out of ostentation. Those demoniac people are filled with the arrogance of power, jealousy, ego, pompousness, cravings, and anger. They disdain and criticize Me who resides in their bodies and the bodies of others.

These demoniac people consider themselves superior in all aspects and live in a pompous manner. Intoxicated by wealth and respect from society, they engage in religious rituals merely for showcasing to others. In most cases, they sideline or disregard the traditional rituals. They only care about being called 'religious' by society. Their life revolves around the power of wealth, egoism, ostentatiousness, ambitions, and uncontrollable agitation arising due to non-fulfillment of ambitions. They criticize others due to ego and jealousy, which they feel when any other person is more successful than them. While criticizing others, they don't even faintly recognize that their criticism is directed towards God residing in other people. Arrogant people like Rāvaṇa, Hiraṇyakaśyapu considered themselves bigger than God residing in their bodies and criticized Him.

## Characteristics of demoniac traits and their effects

तानहं द्विषतः क्रूरान्संसारेषु नराधमान् ।
क्षिपाम्यजस्रमशुभानासुरीष्वेव योनिषु ॥ १९ ॥
आसुरीं योनिमापन्ना मूढा जन्मनि जन्मनि ।
मामप्राप्यैव कौन्तेय ततो यान्त्यधमां गतिम् ॥ २० ॥
त्रिविधं नरकस्येदं द्वारं नाशनमात्मनः ।
कामः क्रोधस्तथा लोभस्तस्मादेतत्त्रयं त्यजेत् ॥ २१ ॥

*Tān ahaṃ dviṣataḥ krurān saṃsāreṣu narādhamān* ।
*Kṣipāmy ajasram aśubhān āsurīṣv eva yoniṣu* ॥ *19* ॥
*Āsurīṃ yonim āpannā mūḍhā janmanijanmani* ।
*Māṃ aprāpyaiva kaunteya tato yānty adhamāṃ gatim* ॥ *20* ॥
*Trividhaṃ narakasyedaṃ dvāraṃ nāśanam ātmanaḥ* ।
*Kāmaḥ krodhas tathā lobhas tasmād etat trayaṃ tyajet* ॥ *21* ॥

**Meaning:** These beast-like cruel men unceasingly engage in evil actions. They disdain good people, sages, etc. I put these heinous people in the cycle of birth-death and in the wombs of demons over and over again. O son of Kunti! These foolish people do not attain Me. They fall into far more inferior births from demoniacal wombs and into hell. There are three gates to hell: lust, anger, and greed. They lead the Jiva to deterioration and destruction. Therefore, one should abandon these three.

These sinful people engaged in heinous actions and the lowest men who disdain Me out of ignorance have to be born again and again as demons. In other words, they are born with demoniacal traits in every life, and they keep revolving endlessly in the birth and death cycle. They cannot attain Self-Knowledge due to their bad traits. At times, these people are even born as animals, birds, etc. Lust, anger, and greed are the three wide gates for all kinds of suffering. One can never find complete happiness in life until these three gates are destroyed. St. Tukārāma says that one can find eternal, Absolute, Pure Bliss in life when these three traits are wiped out from the mind. Therefore, the seeker should gradually abandon these qualities.

**Conclusion**

एतैर्विमुक्तः कौन्तेय तमोद्वारैस्त्रिभिर्नरः ।
आचरत्यात्मनः श्रेयस्ततो याति परां गतिम् ॥ २२ ॥
यः शास्त्रविधिमुत्सृज्य वर्तते कामकारतः ।
न स सिद्धिमवाप्नोति न सुखं न परां गतिम् ॥ २३ ॥
तस्माच्छास्त्रं प्रमाणं ते कार्याकार्यव्यवस्थितौ ।
ज्ञात्वा शास्त्रविधानोक्तं कर्म कर्तुमिहार्हसि ॥ २४ ॥

*Etair vimuktaḥ kaunteya tamodvārais tribhir naraḥ* ।
*Ācaraty ātmanaḥ śreyas tato yāti parāṃ gatim* ॥ *22* ॥
*Yaḥ śāstravidhim utsṛjya vartate kāmakārataḥ* ।
*Na sa siddhim avāpnoti na sukhaṃ na parāṃ gatim* ॥ *23* ॥
*Tasmāc chāstraṃ pramāṇaṃ te kāryākāryavyavasthitau* ।
*Jñātvā śāstravidhānoktaṃ karma kartum ihārhasi* ॥ *24* ॥

**Meaning:** O Arjuna! The person who is liberated from these three gates of hell practices what is beneficial for him and thereby attains the highest goal. When he does not perform the actions ordained by scriptures and instead performs prohibited actions, he neither gets worldly happiness nor attains heaven nor attains the highest goal of Mokṣa. Therefore, know that the spiritual scriptures are the final authorities that decide which action should be performed and which should not be performed. It is right for you to act according to the commands of the scriptures.

ॐ तत्सदिति श्रीमद्भगवद्गीतासूपनिषत्सु ब्रह्मविद्यायां योगशास्त्रे श्रीकृष्णार्जुनसंवादे दैवासुरसम्पद्विभागयोगो नाम षोडशोऽध्यायः ॥

*Om Tatsaditi Śrimadbhagvadgitāsūpaniṣatsu Brahmavidyāyāṃ Yogaśāstre Śrīkṛṣṇārjunasaṅvāde Daivāsurasaṃpadvibhāgayogo Nāma Ṣoḍaśo'dhyāyaḥ* ॥

Unless one gradually frees himself from lust, anger, and greed, he cannot even try to attain his highest welfare. For every human, his highest welfare lies in realizing Self-Knowledge that "I am Ātman." Man can achieve this highest goal by following the commands of scriptures. Indiscriminate actions do not lead to happiness both in worldly life and spiritual life. The seeker who performs actions prescribed by scriptures does not face any conflict in his life. As a result, his mind remains pure, calm, and steady. He can thus engage in spiritual practices without any obstructions. Therefore, the seeker should stay alert and follow guidelines of good and bad actions given in scriptures. Here, the good (prescribed) and bad (prohibited) actions are not pertinent to religious rituals, rather they are related to one's behavior. Religious ritual is a part of worship. In today's age, there are alternatives like chanting a Mantra instead of the formal worship of God. Lord Kṛṣṇa has said in this regard that amongst all Yajñas, He Himself is the Yajña of chanting a Mantra (10.25).

## ☙ Chapter 17 ❧

# The Threefold Faith

### ॥ श्रद्धात्रयविभागयोगः (Śraddhātrayavibhāgayogaḥ) ॥

The three *Guṇas* described earlier in the 14th chapter are illustrated in more detail in this chapter. This chapter explains that the seeker should aim for Sattvic food and company so that he can continue his spiritual practice smoothly and efficiently. Sattvaguṇa assists in uniting ***Tvam*** (Jiva) with ***Tat*** (Brahman). On the contrary, Rājas and Tāmas Guṇas impede this union. In the last stage of spiritual pursuit, even Sattvaguṇa becomes an obstacle for Self-realization. Every seeker is required to perform spiritual practices only until he regards Ātman as a goal. In fact, Ātman is ever-attained and ever-available; therefore, it cannot be explicitly achieved like a goal. Spiritual practices are needed to remove the obstacles which veil and prevent the realization that "I am Ātman."

**Arjuna's question**

अर्जुन उवाच ।
ये शास्त्रविधिमुत्सृज्य यजन्ते श्रद्धयान्विताः ।
तेषां निष्ठा तु का कृष्ण सत्त्वमाहो रजस्तमः ॥ १ ॥

*Arjuna uvāca* ।
*Ye śāstravidhim utsṛjya yajante śraddhayānvitāḥ* ।
*Teṣāṃ niṣṭhā tu kā kṛṣṇa sattvam āho rajas tamaḥ* ॥ *1* ॥

**Meaning:** (Arjuna said) O Kṛṣṇa! Some people disregard the commands of scriptures out of ignorance and engage in actions like Yajña, donation, worship, etc. with faithful mind. What is the condition of their mind? Is it Sāttvic, Rājas, or Tāmas?

St. Rāmadāsa has said in his treatise Dāsabodha that every seeker should engage in spiritual practices by following the teachings of scriptures, and he is supposed to do so consciously by understanding the context, meaning, and objective of those practices. Faith (Śraddhā), donation (*Dāna*), austerities (*Tapas*) are spiritual practices, and they should be *Sāttvic* as explained in this chapter.

**The three kinds of faiths according to Guṇas**

*श्रीभगवानुवाच ।*
**त्रिविधा भवति श्रद्धा देहिनां सा स्वभावजा ।**
**सात्त्विकी राजसी चैव तामसी चेति तां श्रृणु ॥ २ ॥**
**सत्त्वानुरूपा सर्वस्य श्रद्धा भवति भारत ।**
**श्रद्धामयोऽयं पुरुषो यो यच्छ्रद्धः स एव सः ॥ ३ ॥**
**यजन्ते सात्त्विका देवान्यक्षरक्षांसि राजसाः ।**
**प्रेतान्भूतगणांश्चान्ये यजन्ते तामसा जनाः ॥ ४ ॥**
**अशास्त्रविहितं घोरं तप्यन्ते ये तपो जनाः ।**
**दम्भाहङ्कारसंयुक्ताः कामरागबलान्विताः ॥ ५ ॥**
**कर्षयन्तः शरीरस्थं भूतग्राममचेतसः ।**
**मां चैवान्तःशरीरस्थं तान्विद्ध्यासुरनिश्चयान् ॥ ६ ॥**

*Śrībhagavān uvāca ।*
*Trividhā bhavati śraddhā dehinām sā svabhāvajā ।*
*Sāttvikī rājasī caiva tāmasī ceti tāṃ śṛṇu ॥ 2 ॥*
*Sattvānurūpā sarvasya śraddhā bhavati bhārata ।*
*Śraddhāmayo'yaṃ puruṣo yo yacchraddhaḥ sa eva saḥ ॥ 3 ॥*
*Yajante sāttvikā devān yakṣarakṣāṃsi rājasāḥ ।*
*Pretān bhūtagaṇāñś cānye yajante tāmasā janāḥ ॥ 4 ॥*
*Aśāstravihitaṃ ghoraṃ tapyante ye tapo janāḥ ।*
*Dambhāhaṃkārasaṅyuktāḥ kāmarāgabalānvitāḥ ॥ 5 ॥*
*Karṣayantaḥ śarīrasthaṃ bhūtagrāmam acetasaḥ ।*
*Māṃ caivāntaḥśarīrasthaṃ tān viddhy āsuraniścayān ॥ 6 ॥*

**Meaning:** (Śrībhagavān said) The faith of embodied people is of three kinds according to their dispositions: Sāttvic, Rājas, and Tāmas. You should hear about it now. O Arjuna! The faith of each is in accordance with his mind (disposition). Man is full of faith by nature. He is Sāttvic, Rājas, or Tāmas according to his faith which is a result of the mix of his Guṇas. Sāttvic men worship gods; Rājas men worship Yakṣas and Rakṣasas (demons), and Tāmas men worship dead bodies and a host of ghosts. Men who are filled with conceit, ego, lust, desire, and the pride of power engage in gruesome austerities which are not approved by scriptures. Indiscriminate people torture and frail the Five Great Elements in the body and also torture Me who dwells in their body as the doer and enjoyer. Know that they are of demoniacal resolve.

The human mind is imprinted with Sattva, Rājas, and Tāmas Guṇas in more or less proportion. The disposition or nature of a person is borne of these imprints. Every seeker should recognize his natural disposition and make a conscious effort to mold it in such a way that it will be conducive for his spiritual practice. This molding can be brought about through the study of scriptures. Every person has innate faith in some person or object. Belief in scriptures is 'faith', and disbelief in scriptures is a kind of 'faith' as well. Therefore, there is no man without faith. Hopes and ambitions are integral parts of every person's nature. A person's faith is generally evolved in that direction which will help him fulfill his ambitions.

If the person is of Sāttvic disposition, he is inclined to worship God and consequently worship knowledge. The term 'God' is represented by the Sanskrit term 'Deva' (**देव**); its root word is 'Div' (**दिव्**) which means 'light' or 'the light of knowledge.' Thus, Deva (God) means knowledge; those who worship God in-turn worship knowledge. A predominantly Rajoguṇi person expects wealth and prosperity, so he worships Yakṣas and Rakṣasas to please them. A predominantly Tamoguṇi person is destructive and distorted by nature, so he worships dead-bodies, ghosts, etc. Amongst these three, the

Sāttvic person naturally makes quick progression on the spiritual path.

People who are influenced by psychological disorders discard the teachings of scriptures and engage in gruesome austerities by their own imagination. They feel proud of the traits like pretentiousness, ego, lust, attachments, and power. These traits are obstacles for spiritual pursuit. Practices such as animal or human oblations, sorcery, witchcraft, etc. are in no way related to the real spiritual pursuit. Same is the case with certain powers that can be gained through austerities. If the seeker attains any such supernatural power, it inflates his ego and eventually destroys him. Those people who torture their body – under the name of austerities – damage their bodies and torture the Supreme God residing in their body. Inflicting the body with torture or pampering it with excessive care has nothing to do with spiritual practice. Towards the end of the sixth chapter, there has already been a discussion about having balanced food, balanced thoughts, etc.

## Food and Yajña should be Sāttvic

आहारस्त्वपि सर्वस्य त्रिविधो भवति प्रियः ।
यज्ञस्तपस्तथा दानं तेषां भेदमिमं शृणु ॥ ७ ॥
आयुःसत्त्वबलारोग्यसुखप्रीतिविवर्धनाः ।
रस्याः स्निग्धाः स्थिरा हृद्या आहाराः सात्त्विकप्रियाः ॥ ८ ॥
कट्वम्ललवणात्युष्णतीक्ष्णरूक्षविदाहिनः ।
आहारा राजसस्येष्टा दुःखशोकामयप्रदाः ॥ ९ ॥
यातयामं गतरसं पूति पर्युषितं च यत् ।
उच्छिष्टमपि चामेध्यं भोजनं तामसप्रियम् ॥ १० ॥
अफलाकाङ्क्षिभिर्यज्ञो विधिदृष्टो य इज्यते ।
यष्टव्यमेवेति मनः समाधाय स सात्त्विकः ॥ ११ ॥
अभिसन्धाय तु फलं दम्भार्थमपि चैव यत् ।
इज्यते भरतश्रेष्ठ तं यज्ञं विद्धि राजसम् ॥ १२ ॥
विधिहीनमसृष्टान्नं मन्त्रहीनमदक्षिणम् ।
श्रद्धाविरहितं यज्ञं तामसं परिचक्षते ॥ १३ ॥

*Āhāras tv api sarvasya trividho bhavati priyaḥ* ।
Yajñas *Tapas tathā dānaṃ teṣāṃ bhedam imaṃ śṛṇu* ॥ *7* ॥
*Āyuḥsattvabalārogyasukhaprītivivardhanāḥ* ।
*Rasyāḥ snigdhāḥ sthirā hṛdyā āhārāḥ sāttvikapriyāḥ* ॥ *8* ॥
*Kaṭvamlalavaṇātyuṣṇatīkṣṇarūkṣavidāhinaḥ* ।
*Āhārā rājasasyeṣṭā duḥkhaśokāmāyāpradāḥ* ॥ *9* ॥
*Yātayāmaṃ gatarasaṃ pūti paryuṣitaṃ ca yat* ।
*Ucchiṣṭam api cāmedhyaṃ bhojanaṃ tāmasapriyam* ॥ *10* ॥
*Aphalāṅkṣibhir yajño vidhidṛṣṭo ya ijyate* ।
*Yaṣṭavyam eveti manaḥ samādhāya sa sāttvikaḥ* ॥ *11* ॥
*Abhisaṃdhāya tu phalaṃ dambhārtham api caiva yat* ।
*Ijyate bharataśreṣṭha taṃ yajñaṃ viddhi rājasam* ॥ *12* ॥
*Vidhihīnam asṛṣṭānnaṃ mantrahīnam adakṣiṇam* ।
*Śraddhāvirahitaṃ yajñaṃ tāmasaṃ paricakṣate* ॥ *13* ॥

**Meaning:** Three kinds of food are dear to all. Yajñas, austerities, and donations are also of three types. Now hear the distinctions in them. The food which is appetizing, oleaginous, bland, sumptuous and pleasing, and which increases life, intelligence, fortitude in the mind, strength, health, joy, and love, such food is dear to a Sāttvic person. The food which is bitter, sour, salty, excessively hot, spicy, dry, and tongue-burning is dear to a Rājasic person; such food verily creates pain, worries, and diseases. The food, which is stale, tasteless, unwholesome, stinking, cooked on a previous day, left-over by others, impure, and impious is dear to a Tāmasic person. When a selfless seeker performs Yajña as per the teachings of scriptures with composure and a firm belief that 'performance of Yajña is a duty,' it is called the Sāttvic Yajña. O best of Bharatas! When a Yajña is performed seeking pleasures in the other world like heaven or for self-glorification in this world, it is called the Rājas Yajña. And, a Yajña which is contrary to the scriptural teachings, in which no food is distributed, no Mantras are recited, no money is given to priests, and which is performed without faith, is called the Tāmas Yajña.

Just like food, Yajña, austerities, and donations are of three kinds. The seeker should eat simple, fresh, and hot food. It should be proportionate in all tastes like bitter, sour, etc. The seeker is supposed to be careful not to overeat or eat in a way that leads to indigestion. The setting for eating food should be clean and pleasant. The food should not be eaten while being engaged in mind-disturbing activities such as watching TV or reading novels, etc. There should be no arguments while eating food. The seeker is supposed to eat with a focused mind in a pleasant atmosphere. This is verily the Sāttvic way of eating food. The seeker should not eat Rājas or Tāmas food.

The Yajñas described in these verses are not prevalent in the current times. They are replaced by other worships, rituals, pious observances, etc. Even these practices have become infrequent in today's age. These actions should be performed without expectations of any kind, only then can they be considered Sāttvic Karma. When actions are done for mere prestige, show-off, or fulfillment of desires, they are Rājas in nature. When actions are performed reluctantly and merely because they are imposed, they are called Tāmas Karma.

**<u>Austerities of the three Guṇas</u>**

देवद्विजगुरुप्राज्ञपूजनं शौचमार्जवम् ।
ब्रह्मचर्यमहिंसा च शारीरं तप उच्यते ॥ १४ ॥
अनुद्वेगकरं वाक्यं सत्यं प्रियहितं च यत् ।
स्वाध्यायाभ्यसनं चैव वाङ्मयं तप उच्यते ॥ १५ ॥
मनःप्रसादः सौम्यत्वं मौनमात्मविनिग्रहः ।
भावसंशुद्धिरित्येतत्तपो मानसमुच्यते ॥ १६ ॥
श्रद्धया परया तप्तं तपस्तत्त्रिविधं नरैः ।
अफलाकाङ्क्षिभिर्युक्तैः सात्त्विकं परिचक्षते ॥ १७ ॥

सत्कारमानपूजार्थं तपो दम्भेन चैव यत् ।
क्रियते तदिह प्रोक्तं राजसं चलमध्रुवम् ॥ १८ ॥
मूढग्राहेणात्मनो यत्पीडया क्रियते तपः ।
परस्योत्सादनार्थं वा तत्तामसमुदाहृतम् ॥ १९ ॥

*Devadvijaguruprājñapūjanaṃ śaucam ārjavam ।*
*Brahmacaryam ahiṃsā ca śārīraṃ tapa ucyate ॥ 14 ॥*
*Anudvegakaraṃ vākyaṃ satyaṃ priyahitaṃ ca yat ।*
*Svādhyāyābhyasanaṃ caiva vāṅmāyāṃ tapa ucyate ॥ 15 ॥*
*Manaḥprasādaḥ saumyatvaṃ maunam ātmavinigrahaḥ ।*
*Bhāvasaṃśuddhir ity etat tapo mānasam ucyate ॥ 16 ॥*
*Śraddhayā parayā taptaṃ Tapas tat trividhaṃ naraiḥ ।*
*Aphalākāṅkṣibhir yuktaiḥ sāttvikaṃ paricakṣate ॥ 17 ॥*
*Satkāramānapūjārthaṃ tapo dambhena caiva yat ।*
*Kriyate tad iha proktaṃ rājasaṃ calam adhruvam ॥ 18 ॥*
*Mūḍhagrāheṇātmano yat pīḍayā kriyate tapaḥ ।*
*Parasyotsādanārthaṃ vā tat tāmasam udāhṛtam ॥ 19 ॥*

**Meaning:** Worship of Brāhmins, Guru, gods, and scholars; forthrightness; celibacy; and non-violence – these constitute the 'physical austerity' (Śārira Tapa). The speech which causes no distress and is meaningful, pleasant, effective, and beneficial; recitation of Vedic scriptures; and chanting of divine Mantras – these constitute the 'verbal austerity' (Vāṅgamaya Tapa). Contemplating on the Mantra, form, and the real nature of God; silence; control of the mind and purity of the mind are called the 'mental austerity' (Mānasa Tapa). When these three austerities are practiced with utmost faith and without any desire for results, they constitute 'Sāttvic austerity' (Sāttvic Tapa). When any austerity – which is impermanent and momentary by nature – is practiced with the objective of gaining respect, honor, and worship from masses; or for flaunting oneself as religious, it is said to be 'Rājas austerity' (Rājas Tapa). Austerity practiced out of foolishness and obstinacy with an objective to inflict torture upon one's own body, speech, and mind, and also that which is performed for destroying others is known as 'Tāmas austerity' (Tāmas Tapa).

The 'physical austerity' involves disciplining both the gross and subtle body. Worshipping God is a way to inculcate such a discipline in the gross body. The seeker is expected to respect and honor his parents, teachers, older adults, along with gods, Brāhmins, and Guru. An egoistic person cannot think about honoring any other person. So, the 'physical austerity' helps the seeker in taming his ego. Purity, piousness, and forthrightness of the mind are the practices to develop the 'mental austerity.' They help the seeker in keeping his mind quiet and conscientious. Celibacy indicates restraint; the seeker who lives his life with restraint can attain Self-realization of Brahman. The word **Brahmacāri** in Sanskrit traditionally means a religious person leading a life of celibacy. In spiritual pursuit of Mokṣa, the word Brahmacāri is understood as:

**ब्रह्मणि चरति इति ब्रह्मचारी ।**

*Brahamaṇi carati iti Brahmacāri* ।

"One who remains steadily absorbed in Brahman is Brahmacāri." So, the seeker should practice this true Brahmacarya with the help of celibacy in day-to-day life.

St. Rāmadāsa says, "Lord Nārāyaṇa pervades the entire world, and the seeker should worship Him who is omnipresent and all-pervasive. For that reason, he should try to please any one person every day. (*Dāsabodha 15.9.25*)." This simply means that pleasing any one person is a form of worship of the omnipresent Lord. In line with this teaching, we should not purposefully hurt any other person, his body, or mind. If there is a reason to say disagreeable things, it is essential to remember this rule:

**सत्यं ब्रूयात् प्रियं ब्रूयात् न ब्रूयात् सत्यमप्रियम् ।**

*Satyaṃ Bruyāt, priyaṃ bruyāt, na bruyāt satyaṃ apriyaṃ* ।

"One should tell the truth, say what is pleasant to all, and not tell the truth if it is hurtful or agonizing for others. If it is required to tell the truth, then one may say it in a way that is acceptable by others." This restraint on the tongue is the 'verbal austerity.' Studying the epic scriptures like the Bhagavad-Gita, Brahmasūtras, and Upaniṣads (*Prasthānatrayi*), contemplating on texts composed by enlightened saints, and chanting the Mantra of God – these are all various forms of the 'verbal austerity.' This practice also involves restraining the speech on all four levels:

1 **Vaikhari Vāṇi**: The gross level of speech where words are loudly spoken and heard by others
2 **Madhymā Vāṇi**: The inner and subtler level of speech where one thinks or speaks in mind to himself
3 **Paśyanti Vāṇi**: Even more subtle level of thoughts where one is just aware of thoughts within himself
4 **Parā Vāṇi**: The subtlest level of speech, Pure Awareness, beyond the comprehension of an ordinary person

Discussions on Ātman, describing the glories of the Lord, conversations about the greatness of Sadguru and enlightened saints – these are all forms of the 'verbal austerity' as well. One should also remember St. Jñāneśwara's guidance in Haripāṭha, "God can never be pleased with those who chit-chat continuously in day-to-day life."

The 'mental austerity' mainly involves keeping one's own mind happy and cheerful. St. Tukārāma has said that the cheerful mind alone brings success of all kinds. When the seeker makes an effort and does not allow petite issues to disturb his mind, he can remain calm and undisturbed in all circumstances. Most seekers do not pay enough attention to this practice. The mind is invariably disturbed when the seeker does not recognize the distribution of Guṇas, the inescapable Law of Karma

(Prārabdha), and the imaginary appearance of the world. The mind is also disturbed when the seeker does not understand the following rule of life –

**आत्मनस्तु कामाय सर्वं प्रियं भवति ।**

*Ātmanastu kāmāy sarvam priyam bhavati* ।

"The feeling of love for others is ultimately for one's own happiness, not for the pleasure of others." If actions and reactions of the seeker are soft and controlled, it becomes easy for him to practice silence, control his mind, and thereby contemplate on Ātman or God. Ātman or the real God is absolutely pure with no taints of any kind; therefore, by contemplating on Him, one can maintain the purity of one's own mind.

When all practices described so far are performed with utmost faith desiring no results, they are qualified to be known as 'Sāttvic austerities.'

'Rājas austerities' involve the practices done for getting respect and honor from others or for self-glorification. They are highly superficial, so they are not even qualified to be known as austerities.

The austerities practiced by demons like Rāvaṇa, Sunda, Upasunda, etc. are 'Tāmas austerities.' They involve the desire for one's own progress as well as the desire for someone else's destruction. Tāmas austerity also includes obstinacy and self-torture of all kinds.

## The donations according to the three Guṇas

**दातव्यमिति यद्दानं दीयतेऽनुपकारिणे ।**
**देशे काले च पात्रे च तद्दानं सात्त्विकं स्मृतम् ॥ २० ॥**
**यत्तु प्रत्युपकारार्थं फलमुद्दिश्य वा पुनः ।**
**दीयते च परिक्लिष्टं तद्दानं राजसं स्मृतम् ॥ २१ ॥**
**अदेशकाले यद्दानमपात्रेभ्यश्च दीयते ।**
**असत्कृतमवज्ञातं तत्तामसमुदाहृतम् ॥ २२ ॥**

*Dātavyam iti yad dānaṃ dīyate 'nupakāriṇe* ।
*Deśe kāle ca pātre ca tad dānaṃ sāttvikaṃ smṛtam* ॥ 20 ॥
*Yat tu prattyupakārārthaṃ phalam uddiśya vā punaḥ* ।
*Dīyate ca parikliṣṭaṃ tad dānaṃ rājasaṃ smṛtam* ॥ 21 ॥
*Adeśakāle yad dānam apātrebhyaś ca dīyate* ।
*Asatkṛtam avajñātaṃ tat tāmasam udāhṛtam* ॥ 22 ॥

**Meaning:** The Sattvic donation is that which is given at the right place and right time – considering it to be a duty – to a worthy person who has not done any favor to the donor. The donation which is given with a desire to attain something or receive a favor in return, and with a heavy heart or grudge, is called the 'Rājas donation.' That which is given at a wrong place and wrong time to an unworthy person, or given to a worthy person with disdain, it is called the 'Tāmas donation.'

Yajña, donation, and austerity are prescribed as spiritual practices for one and all. These rituals should be done because they ought to be done. Donation should be given to a worthy person. It needs a holy place and an auspicious time. Enlightened saints, sages, virtuous people, teachers imparting knowledge – these are the people worthy of donations. Holy places and holy times are considered right for this ritual. One should not give donations to a place where they will be misused. Giving alms to a beggar, contributing to social festivals, or helping an institution are not considered donations. These are parts of social responsibility. There may be expectations to gain fame or prestige behind such worldly donations.

Sāttvic donation is that where there is no expectation or possibility of any return in mind.

On the contrary, that which is given by desiring fame, reputation, etc. is the Rājas donation. One that is given unwillingly and under compulsion is also the Rājas donation.

Apart from these, that which is given by denouncing the beneficiary or given to an unworthy person is the Tāmas donation. One that is given at a wrong place or wrong time is also the Tāmas donation.

**Om Tat Sat**

ॐतत्सदिति निर्देशो ब्रह्मणस्त्रिविधः स्मृतः ।
ब्राह्मणास्तेन वेदाश्च यज्ञाश्च विहिताः पुरा ॥ २३ ॥
तस्मादोमित्युदाहृत्य यज्ञदानतपःक्रियाः ।
प्रवर्तन्ते विधानोक्ताः सततं ब्रह्मवादिनाम् ॥ २४ ॥
तदित्यनभिसन्धाय फलं यज्ञतपःक्रियाः ।
दानक्रियाश्च विविधाः क्रियन्ते मोक्षकाङ्क्षिभिः ॥ २५ ॥
सद्भावे साधुभावे च सदित्येतत्प्रयुज्यते ।
प्रशस्ते कर्मणि तथा सच्छब्दः पार्थ युज्यते ॥ २६ ॥
यज्ञे तपसि दाने च स्थितिः सदिति चोच्यते ।
कर्म चैव तदर्थीयं सदित्येवाभिधीयते ॥ २७ ॥
अश्रद्धया हुतं दत्तं तपस्तप्तं कृतं च यत् ।
असदित्युच्यते पार्थ न च तत्प्रेत्य नो इह ॥ २८ ॥

*Oṃ tat sad iti nirdeśo brahmaṇas trividhaḥ smṛtaḥ* ।
*Brāhmaṇās tena vedāś ca Yajñaś ca vihitāḥ purā* ॥ 23 ॥
*Tasmād om ity udāhṛtya yajñadānatapaḥkriyāḥ* ।
*Pravartante vidhānoktāḥ satataṃ brahmavādinām* ॥ 24 ॥
*Tad ity anabhisaṃdhāya phalaṃ yajñatapaḥkriyāḥ* ।
*Dānakriyāś ca vividhāḥ kriyante mokṣakāṅkṣibhiḥ* ॥ 25 ॥
*Sadbhāve sādhubhāve ca sad ity etat prayujyate* ।
*Praśaste karmaṇi tathā sacchabdaḥ pārtha yujyate* ॥ 26 ॥
*Yajñe tapasi dāne ca sthitiḥ sad iti cocyate* ।
*Karma caiva tadarthīyaṃ sad ity evābhidhīyate* ॥ 27 ॥
*Aśraddhayā hutaṃ dattaṃ Tapas taptaṃ kṛtaṃ ca yat* ।
*Asad ity ucyate pārtha na ca tat prepya no iha* ॥ 28 ॥

**Meaning:** At the beginning of the universe, Brahmadeva evoked Brahman with the three names **Om**, **Tat**, and **Sat**, and thereafter created the Vedas, Brāhmins, and Yajñas, etc. Therefore, the knowers of the Vedas begin all actions like Yajñas, donations, austerities, which are prescribed by the Vedas, by always invoking Supreme Ātman through the utterance of 'Om.' The seeker of Mokṣa should perform Yajñas, give donations, and practice austerities by uttering the word 'Tat' and not desiring any worldly gain in return. The term '*Sat*' is used to mean transcendence of the three times, or to indicate a virtuous action, which is Brahman itself. Unwavering faith in Yajña, donation, austerity, or Sāttvic belief in these rituals, is also known as '*Sat*.' The actions performed for Self-realization of Brahman, or actions performed while chanting a divine Mantra, are '*Sat*' as well. O Pārtha! Yajña, fire rituals, donations, or austerities which are performed without Sāttvic faith are considered '*Asat*'. They are of no use and do not give any result in this world or the other worlds hereafter.

**ॐ तत्सदिति श्रीमद्भगवद्गीतासूपनिषत्सु ब्रह्मविद्यायां योगशास्त्रे श्रीकृष्णार्जुनसंवादे श्रद्धात्रयविभागयोगो नाम सप्तदशोऽध्यायः ॥**

*Om Tatsaditi Śrimadbhagvadgitāsūpaniṣatsu Brahmavidyāyāṃ Yogaśāstre Śrīkṛṣṇārjunasaṅvāde Śraddhātrayavibhāgayogo Nāma Saptadaśo'dhyāyaḥ* ॥

There is a custom to evoke the words **Om Tat Sat** to purify Yajña, donations, austerities, and to eradicate possible defects in these rituals. Human beings are prone to making errors (deterioration); they may knowingly or unknowingly make mistakes. By evoking 'Om Tat *Sat*,' the mistakes in these rituals are wiped out.

Brahman is indicated by the following three words: **Om**, **Tat**, and **Sat**. 'Om' is a symbol of Brahman. Kaṭha Upaniṣad states that, "Om is a symbol to meditate on Brahman."

**एतद्ध्येवाक्षरं ब्रह्म एतद्ध्येवाक्षरं परम् ।**
**एतद्ध्येवाक्षरं ज्ञात्वा यो यदिच्छति तस्य तत् ॥**

*Etaddhyevākṣaraṃ brahma etaddhyevākṣaraṃ param* ।
*Etaddhyevākṣaraṃ jñātvā yo yadicchati tasya tat* ॥ *(1.2.16)*

**एतदालम्बनं श्रेष्ठमेतदालम्बनं परम् ।**
**एतदालम्बनं ज्ञात्वा ब्रह्मलोके महीयते ॥**

*Etadālambanaṃ śreṣṭhametadālambanaṃ param* ।
*Etadālambanaṃ jñātvā brahmaloke mahīyate* ॥ *(1.2.17)*

Karma is said to be complete and successful if 'Om' is uttered while doing it. Even if that Karma is faulty, it is purified and said to be complete if 'Om' is attached to it. The worthwhileness of Karma lies in the utterance of 'Om'. Upaniṣad has also said that 'Om' is an alternate name of Brahman. Brahman is formless and organless, so it cannot possibly have a name. Brahman is not the name of the principle i.e. Pure Consciousness. Ātman is also not the name of Ātman/Pure Consciousness. One can only discuss Brahman with the help of symbols.

The word 'Tat' means 'Brahman' in the ***Tat-Tvam-Asi*** Mahāvākya stated in Chāndogya Upaniṣad. Therefore, the seeker can think of Brahman while pronouncing 'Tat'. The word **Tat** is used to recognize and remember that everything in the world belongs to Supreme God, Brahman. The seeker is expected to perform actions like Yajña, donations, etc. without desiring anything that belongs to God. Only then those actions are considered helpful for attaining Mokṣa.

There is another Śruti mentioned in Chāndogya Upaniṣad –

**सत् एव सोम्य इदमग्र आसीत् ।**

*Sat eva somya idamagra Āsit* । *(6.2.1)*

"Only ***Sat*** (Brahman) existed before the beginning of this universe." Here the word '*Sat*' means transcendental, Absolute Truth. Brahman is the Absolute Truth, so the seeker evokes Brahman while uttering '*Sat*' even in this sense. The word '*Sat*' helps in the awareness that Ātman is permanent, and worldly objects (Anātman) are impermanent. The word '*Sat*' also means excellent and supreme. This indicates that actions which are performed by uttering '*Sat*' should also be excellent and superior. It is necessary to recognize that actions approved by scriptures are superior, while those prohibited by scriptures are considered unrighteous (Adharma). Also, one should know that all possible flaws and defects, which may arise while executing actions, are eradicated by uttering the word '*Sat.*' Firm, unwavering faith in Yajña, donation, and austerity is called '*Sat*'. Sāttvic belief in these rituals and the resultant flawless perfection (purity) is called '*Sat*' as well.

Brahmadeva received the power to create the universe by contemplating on Omkara. He learnt that there are three syllables 'A', 'U', and 'M' in Omkara. From A – the gross material world, from U – the subtle world, and from M – the causal world gets created. Brahmadeva created the three kinds of worlds – Ādhidaivika, Ādhibhautika, and Ādhyātmika – with the help of Omkara alone. He created Brāhmins (holy priests) to carry out actions, do worship, and accomplish knowledge which are necessary for the sustenance of humans. He created the Vedas and taught different kinds of Yajñas through the Vedas to ensure that Brāhmins remain virtuous and pious in their actions. Therefore, while reciting the Mantras in the Vedas, or following the teachings of scriptures about Yajñas, donations, austerities, etc., there is a convention to initiate them by pronouncing '**Om Tat *Sat*.**'

Pronouncing the words 'Om Tat *Sat*' while executing actions is known as the 'appropriation' (Viniyoga) of the Mantra. In the path of devotion, one may utter the Mantra of Viṭṭhala, Rāma, Kṛṣṇa, or any other God for the same purpose. When rituals like Yajña, donation, and austerities are performed without Sāttvic faith, they become meaningless and useless.

Lord Kṛṣṇa has said in the third chapter, "A human being cannot remain without actions even for a moment." In this chapter, He has given a definite direction to actions by teaching the nuances of sacrifice (*Yajña*), donation (*Dāna*), and austerities (*Tapas*). These are explained in detail in the Vedas created by Brahmadeva, so one should engage in these actions in a selfless manner and follow the orders of God. In essence, the chapter states that actions can be made rewarding by first appropriating the Mantra 'Om Tat Sat.'

Chapter 18

# Liberation through Renunciation

॥ मोक्षसंन्यासयोगः (MokṣaSaṅnyāsayogaḥ) ॥

The 18th chapter marks the conclusion of the Bhagavad-Gita, and it includes the revision of the teachings of Lord Kṛṣṇa. Some topics like the three Guṇas are described here again in detail. This chapter is considered the pinnacle of the Gita. St. Jñāneśwara has addressed it as the 'one-chapter Gita.' The concepts of renunciation (Saṅnyāsa) and abandonment (Tyāga/non-attachment) were explained before in chapters 4 and 5. But Arjuna asks a question regarding the same concepts again in this chapter.

**The principle of renunciation and abandonment**

*अर्जुन उवाच ।*
संन्यासस्य महाबाहो तत्त्वमिच्छामि वेदितुम् ।
त्यागस्य च हृषीकेश पृथक्केशिनिषूदन ॥ १ ॥

*Arjuna uvāca* ।
*Saṃnyāsasya mahābāho tattvam icchāmi veditum* ।
*Tyāgasya ca hṛṣīkeśa pṛthak keśiniṣūdana* ॥ *1* ॥

**Meaning:** (Arjuna said) O controller of the senses! O slayer of Keshi, valiant Lord Kṛṣṇa! I desire to distinctly understand the principles of Saṅnyāsa (formal renunciation) and Tyāga (abandonment).

*श्रीभगवानुवाच ।*
काम्यानां कर्मणां न्यासं संन्यासं कवयो विदुः ।
सर्वकर्मफलत्यागं प्राहुस्त्यागं विचक्षणाः ॥ २ ॥

त्याज्यं दोषवदित्येके कर्म प्राहुर्मनीषिणः ।
यज्ञदानतपःकर्म न त्याज्यमिति चापरे ॥ ३ ॥
निश्चयं शृणु मे तत्र त्यागे भरतसत्तम ।
त्यागो हि पुरुषव्याघ्र त्रिविधः सम्प्रकीर्तितः ॥ ४ ॥
यज्ञदानतपःकर्म न त्याज्यं कार्यमेव तत् ।
यज्ञो दानं तपश्चैव पावनानि मनीषिणाम् ॥ ५ ॥
एतान्यपि तु कर्माणि सङ्गं त्यक्त्वा फलानि च ।
कर्तव्यानीति मे पार्थ निश्चितं मतमुत्तमम् ॥ ६ ॥

*Śrībhagavān uvāca* ।
*Kāmyānāṃ karmaṇāṃ nyāsaṃ Saṅnyāsaṃ kavayo viduḥ* ।
*Sarvakarmaphalatyāgaṃ prāhus tyāgaṃ vicakṣaṇāḥ* ॥ 2 ॥
*Tyājyaṃ doṣavad ity eke karma prāhur manīṣiṇaḥ* ।
*Yajñadānatapaḥkarma na tyājyam iti cāpare* ॥ 3 ॥
*Niścayaṃ śṛṇu me tatra tyāge bharatasattama* ।
*Tyāgo hi puruṣavyāghra trividhaḥ saṃprakīrtitaḥ* ॥ 4 ॥
*Yajñadānatapaḥkarma na tyājyaṃ kāryam eva tat* ।
*Yajño dānaṃ tapaś caiva pāvanāni manīṣiṇām* ॥ 5 ॥
*Etāny api tu karmāṇi saṅgaṃ tyaktvā phalāni ca* ।
*Kartavyānīti me pārtha niścitaṃ matam uttamam* ॥ 6 ॥

**Meaning:** (Śrībhagavān said) Men of knowledge call renunciation of actions done for some gain as 'Saṅnyāsa,' other thoughtful men call abandonment of results of all actions as 'Tyāga.' Some intelligent people say that all actions should be abandoned since they are full of defects. In contrast, some people recommend that Yajña, donation, and austerity should not be abandoned. O best of the Bharatas, Arjuna! Hear from me the final word on Tyāga. O Arjuna, the bravest of men! Tyāga is of three kinds. The actions of Yajña, donation, austerity should never be abandoned. They must be performed because they purify selfless intelligent people. These actions should also be performed desiring no results and without the feeling of doership – this is My firm opinion.

The subject of Karma is profound and mysterious. Even the best scholars and distinguished men cannot concur on one final word on this topic. Every man who is bound by actions should know the final authoritative word on actions. In this regard, Lord Kṛṣṇa's teaching is the final word.

Actions are divided as follows:

- **Nitya Karma**: Daily obligatory duties
- **Naimittika Karma**: Occasional obligatory duties
- **Prāyaścitta Karma**: Actions performed for the expiation of sins
- **Kāmya Karma**: Rites performed for fulfilling worldly desires or removing worldly difficulties
- **Iṣṭa Karma**: Austerities and following the commands of the Vedas, etc.
- **Pūrta Karma**: Altruistic actions pertaining to social responsibilities

Out of these, Kāmya Karma should always be abandoned. Actions (rituals) which are performed for removing crises, eradicating diseases, obtaining wealth, etc. are known as Kāmya Karma. The seeker who is surrendered to Īśvara should have faith in Īśvara's governance as well as his own Prārabdha and not engage in any Kāmya Karma at any time. This is certainly ideal, but many seekers leading worldly life find it challenging to ignore crises and pursue the spiritual path during difficult times. When faced with conflict, struggle, challenges, emergencies, or crises, an ordinary seeker cannot be at peace, so he cannot conduct spiritual practices. Such a seeker can pray to the Lord to resolve or remove the crisis from his life. But he is supposed to pray for help only if there is a huge problem in his life or a massive crisis. It is not right to plead for God's help to resolve small, day-to-day petite issues. The seekers who are renunciates or detached do not engage in gainful prayers under any circumstances, and this is certainly an ideal state.

Nitya Karma (daily action) includes the five major Yajñas. These Yajñas were an integral part of Indian way of life in ancient times. Today, they can be conducted in newer ways which are synchronous with the newer times. The five major Yajñas are –

1. *Brahmayajña* (ब्रह्मयज्ञ) – Studying for attaining the Knowledge of Brahman (स्वाध्याय)
2. *Devayajña* (देवयज्ञ) – Traditional rituals which involve fire, oblation, etc. (होम)
3. *Pitryajña* (पितृयज्ञ) – Offering food and water to dead ancestors (पिंडक्रिया)
4. *Bhūtayajña* (भूतयज्ञ) – Serving other beings in some way
5. *Atithiyajña* (अतिथियज्ञ) – Serving visitors and guests at home who come without prior notice

'Nitya Karma' also include a daily bath and worship, etc. 'Naimittika Karma' include good hospitality, welcoming invited or uninvited guests (*Abhyāgata*), etc. In the old days, it was common to have visitors who would arrive without invitation or without any regard for convenient day and time since there were no means of quick communication in that era. It was considered a duty of a householder to invite any chance-met traveler or a student and serve him. These actions are supposed to be performed in a completely selfless manner.

Chanting a Mantra is a great 'Prāyaścitta (expiating) Karma,' mainly meant for worldly seekers. 'Pūrta Karma' include building hospitals, educational institutes, and the like. 'Iṣṭa Karma' include austerities and rituals like Vaiśvadeva. 'Pūrta Karma' are meant for fulfilling social responsibility, and 'Iṣṭa Karma' are meant for fulfilling one's own desires or earning benefit oneself.

When these actions are performed without desiring any fruit, they purify the seeker's mind. The purification of mind is the fruit of these actions. An action-prone seeker may think that such actions are akin to spiritual practices and remain immersed in doing them. Lord Kṛṣṇa has considered all aspects of Karma and given the final word that "Actions of Yajña, donation, austerity purify the mind, so they must be performed. However, they should be performed selflessly by abandoning the desire for fruits and attachment." Selflessness and detachment and are the two main pillars of Karmayoga which are explained in the Gita time and again. A seeker leading worldly life may not be able to take the vows of the monastic life, but he can certainly follow these aforementioned guidelines while performing actions.

**Characteristics of abandonment according to the 3 Guṇas**

**नियतस्य तु संन्यासः कर्मणो नोपपद्यते ।**
**मोहात्तस्य परित्यागस्तामसः परिकीर्तितः ॥ ७ ॥**
**दुःखमित्येव यत्कर्म कायक्लेशभयात्त्यजेत् ।**
**स कृत्वा राजसं त्यागं नैव त्यागफलं लभेत् ॥ ८ ॥**
**कार्यमित्येव यत्कर्म नियतं क्रियतेऽर्जुन ।**
**सङ्गं त्यक्त्वा फलं चैव स त्यागः सात्त्विको मतः ॥ ९ ॥**
**न द्वेष्ट्यकुशलं कर्म कुशले नानुषज्जते ।**
**त्यागी सत्त्वसमाविष्टो मेधावी छिन्नसंशयः ॥ १० ॥**
**न हि देहभृता शक्यं त्यक्तुं कर्माण्यशेषतः ।**
**यस्तु कर्मफलत्यागी स त्यागीत्यभिधीयते ॥ ११ ॥**
**अनिष्टमिष्टं मिश्रं च त्रिविधं कर्मणः फलम् ।**
**भवत्यत्यागिनां प्रेत्य न तु संन्यासिनां क्वचित् ॥ १२ ॥**

*Niyatasya tu Saṅnyāsaḥ karmaṇo nopapadyate ।*
*Mohāt tasya parityāgas tāmasaḥ parikīrtitaḥ ॥ 7 ॥*
*Duḥkham ity eva yat karma kāyakleśabhayāt tyajet ।*
*Sa kṛtvā rājasaṃ tyāgaṃ naiva tyāgaphalaṃ labhet ॥ 8 ॥*
*Kāryam ity eva yat karma niyataṃ kriyate'rjuna ।*
*Saṅgaṃ tyaktvā phalaṃ caiva sa tyāgaḥ sāttviko mataḥ ॥ 9 ॥*
*Na dveṣṭy akuśalaṃ karma kuśale nānuṣajjate ।*
*Tyāgī sattvasamāviṣṭo medhāvī chinnasaṃśayaḥ ॥ 10 ॥*
*Na hi dehabhṛtā śakyaṃ tyaktuṃ karmāṇy aśeṣataḥ ।*
*Yas tu karmaphalatyāgī sa tyāgīty abhidhīyate ॥ 11 ॥*

*Aniṣṭam iṣṭaṃ miśraṃ ca trividhaṃ karmaṇaḥ phalam* ।
*Bhavaty atyāgināṃ pretya na tu Saṅnyāsināṃ kvacit* ॥ *12* ॥

**Meaning:** It is not right to abandon 'Nitya Karma' (daily obligatory duties). Abandoning Nitya Karma due to ignorance is known as 'Tāmas Tyāga.' In some cases, seekers assume that all actions cause suffering and abandon actions due to the fear of physical pain. This is called 'Rājas Tyāga,' and it does not give the desired fruit of Tyāga. O Arjuna! When Nitya Karma are performed merely as duties by abandoning the doership and the desire for fruits – it is known as 'Sāttvic Tyāga.' A Sāttvic person does not disdain bad or ominous actions and does not take pleasure in good actions. Such a person performs 'Sāttvic Tyāga.' He is a wise man of Self-Knowledge, and he is a true Saṇnyāsi. It is indeed impossible for an embodied person to entirely abandon actions. But one who abandons fruits of actions is declared as a 'Tyāgi.' Those who do not abandon fruits of actions certainly get three kinds of results after death – 1. Undesired (*Aniṣṭa*) – birth in animal, bird species, etc. 2. Desired (*Iṣṭa*) – the attainment of Godhood 3. Mixed (*Miśra*) – birth as a human being. However, those Saṅnyāsins who abandon fruits of actions do not ever get these results.

One should indeed abandon Kāmya and Niśiddha Karma. It is equally true that one should not abandon Nitya and Naimmittika Karma. However, the intellect of some people becomes depraved due delusion. They develop a disdain for scriptures. They do not think about their welfare and abandon Nitya, Naimmittika Karma; this is called 'Tāmas Tyāga.' Execution of Nitya and Naimmittika Karma involve worship, duties, etc. which purify the mind. The seeker may experience certain discomfort while doing actions and think that all actions are painful. Hence, if he abandons actions like fasting, cold-water bath, etc. to avoid physical afflictions, it is called 'Rājas Tyāga.' There is no use of this kind of abandonment.

When actions prescribed in scriptures are executed as duties – renouncing attachment and desires for fruits – it is known as 'Sāttvic Tyāga'. 'Detachment' and 'not desiring fruits' – these are the two pillars that hold the key to spiritual pursuit. For detachment, the seeker needs to give up the feeling of mineness. For not desiring fruits, he needs to wipe out all hopes and ambitions from his mind. St. Tukārāma says, "One should not get attached to worldly matters, stay firmly rooted in Brahman, and refrain from mineness or affinity in worldly objects." The seeker who performs Sāttvic Tyāga does not consider some actions to be more prestigious than the others. The idea of avoiding inferior actions is deeply rooted in the Indian psyche. In comparison, western countries consider all jobs the same. The seeker who performs Sāttvic Tyāga is clear about the concepts of Karma, Akarma, and Vikarma. Such a wise seeker is a true seeker. Humans can never abandon Karma completely. Being born is a Karma and dying is a Karma as well. In between these two ends, Karma is invariably associated with every being. Hence, instead of making futile efforts to abandon actions, he is expected to perform all actions by abandoning attachment and the fruits of actions. If an elderly person is staying with his son or daughter, he can contribute to all necessary household activities in any possible way.

All actions are associated with good, bad, or mixed fruits. However, a person who engages in actions without genuinely desiring fruits will not gain worldly results for his actions, but his mind will be cleansed and purified as a result. Īśvara unmistakably gives worldly fruits to the one who desires them, and He does not give fruits to the one who does not desire them. There is a rule –

**यो यम इच्छसि तस्य तत् ।**

*Yo yaṃ icchasi tasya tat* ।

"One will get what he desires." But a person who abandons fruits is benefited from the spiritual perspective since such abandonment cleanses and purifies his mind and makes him ready for Self-Knowledge. The person who can mentally relinquish good fruits can also relinquish bad fruits.

**Five objectives of action**

पञ्चैतानि महाबाहो कारणानि निबोध मे ।
साङ्ख्ये कृतान्ते प्रोक्तानि सिद्धये सर्वकर्मणाम् ॥ १३॥
अधिष्ठानं तथा कर्ता करणं च पृथग्विधम् ।
विविधाश्च पृथक्चेष्टा दैवं चैवात्र पञ्चमम् ॥ १४ ॥
शरीरवाङ्मनोभिर्यत्कर्म प्रारभते नरः ।
न्याय्यं वा विपरीतं वा पञ्चैते तस्य हेतवः ॥ १५ ॥

*Pañcaitāni mahābāho kāraṇāni nibodha me* ।
*Sāṃkhye kṛtānte proktāni siddhaye sarvakarmaṇām* ॥ 13 ॥
*Adhiṣṭhānaṃ tathā kartā karaṇaṃ ca pṛthagvidham* ।
*Vividhāś ca pṛthakceṣṭā daivaṃ caivātra pañcamam* ॥ 14 ॥
*Śarīravāṅmanobhir yat karma prārabhate naraḥ* ।
*Nyāyyaṃ vā viparītaṃ vā pañcaite tasya hetavaḥ* ॥ 15 ॥

**Meaning:** The Sāṅkhya Darśana has explained the five causes for the accomplishment of all actions. O valiant Arjuna! Learn from Me these causes. Substratum – body, doer – Jivātmā, various organs, various actions, and Prārabdha – all of these are necessary for the accomplishment of actions. When a person engages in any prescribed or prohibited action – with his body, speech, mind – the aforementioned five are the very causes of that action.

The Sāṅkhya theory states that five causes are necessary for the accomplishment of any action. The body is the support, while the Jiva is the doer of every action. The doer (agent) needs the help of his organs when he performs actions. Prārabdha is one reason behind all of this. 'Ātman' – the true substratum – is actionless and non-doer; the Jiva who is impelled by his

Prārabdha is the doer. The Jiva executes many actions by making use of his sense and action organs with the help of his Prāṇas. The Jiva who overcomes the impulses generated by Prārabdha and follows the new direction given by scriptures is considered a real achiever from the spiritual perspective. The attainment of Mokṣa depends on this very skill. Any action, right or wrong, is impelled by the impulses of old Vāsanās or the impulses of new scriptural learnings. The seeker is supposed to remain vigilant and recognize his impulses. He should strive to transform his old impulses and channelize them appropriately for his spiritual pursuit. If this were impossible to practice, all scriptural commands would have been of no use.

**Ātman is non-doer**

**तत्रैवं सति कर्तारमात्मानं केवलं तु यः ।**
**पश्यत्यकृतबुद्धित्वान्न स पश्यति दुर्मतिः ॥ १६ ॥**
**यस्य नाहङ्कृतो भावो बुद्धिर्यस्य न लिप्यते ।**
**हत्वाऽपि स इमाँल्लोकान्न हन्ति न निबध्यते ॥ १७ ॥**

*Tatraivaṃ sati kartāram ātmānaṃ kevalaṃ tu yaḥ* ।
*Paśyaty akṛtabuddhitvān na sa paśyati durmatiḥ* ॥ *16* ॥
*Yasya nāhaṃkṛto bhāvo buddhir yasya na lipyate* ।
*Hatvā.api sa imāṃl lokān na hanti na nibadhyate* ॥ *17* ॥

**Meaning:** Despite this, a person who is wicked from the spiritual perspective considers his true Self, pure Ātman, as the doer due to his impure intellect and the lack of spiritual or religious conditioning. One who does not think – "I am the doer" – and whose intellect is not tainted by the thought – "I will enjoy the results of my actions" – does not slay anyone despite slaying all, and he is not bound (tainted) by sins of actions.

Ātman is not directly related to actions in any manner. Whether actions are accomplished or not, whether they are performed in accordance with scriptures or not – everything occurs on the substratum of Ātman, yet Ātman is neither attached to actions nor encaged by them. The intellect is considered spiritually impure when it is not influenced by this teaching of scriptures. The intellect that does not recognize "I am Ātman" is tainted. The intellect which forgets the spiritual conditioning done by scriptures cannot know or remember that "Ātman is not attached to anything." The thought that "I am the doer" is imprinted in the mind of every seeker from many past births. When the seeker eradicates it and replaces it with the thought that "I am Ātman, and I am the non-doer in reality," he is not bound by the world, his body, or actions. In Arjuna's case, his true Self does not slay anyone despite slaying all enemies. The topic that was previously explained in verse 2.19 is described here again. Lord Kṛṣṇa previously said to Arjuna, "I have already slain all according to their Prārabdha. Now, you should merely act as an instrument and be a medium to slay them (*11.33* and *11.34*)." Arjuna's delusion that "I am the slayer" has been expressed in *1.35* before.

**The motivation for action and its tools**

**ज्ञानं ज्ञेयं परिज्ञाता त्रिविधा कर्मचोदना ।**
**करणं कर्म कर्तेति त्रिविधः कर्मसङ्ग्रहः ॥ १८ ॥**

*Jñānaṃ jñeyaṃ parijñātā trividhā karmacodanā* ।
*Karaṇaṃ karma karteti trividhaḥ karmasaṃgrahaḥ* ॥ *18* ॥

**Meaning:** Knowledge, the object of knowledge, and the knower are the three activators of action. Action that needs to be performed, instruments (tools), and the agent (doer) are the three constituents needed to complete the action.

For engaging in any action, the knower of that action is needed. He must have enough knowledge of that action. The subject-matter of the action is the knowable. E.g. a warrior needs to possess the knowledge of war, and the enemy is knowable for him. Here, the knower is the Jiva. Ātman cannot be the knower. Also, for every action, the doer is needed, who, in-turn, needs the help of his organs to execute that action. Jiva is the doer, Ātman is not the doer.

## The distinction of knowledge, action, and doer as per Guṇas

ज्ञानं कर्म च कर्ता च त्रिधैव गुणभेदतः ।
प्रोच्यते गुणसङ्ख्याने यथावच्छृणु तान्यपि ॥ १९ ॥

*Jñānaṃ karma ca kartā ca tridhaiva guṇabhedataḥ* ।
*Procyate guṇasaṃkhyāne yathāvac chṛṇu tāny api* ॥ *19* ॥

**Meaning:** Knowledge, action, and doer are described to be of three kinds each according to the distinction of the Guṇas – Sattva, Rājas, and Tāmas in the Sāṅkhya philosophy. Hear about them carefully.

The three Guṇas influence individual human dispositions. Therefore, everyone behaves, speaks, and thinks under the impact of amalgamation of the three Guṇas.

## Characteristics of knowledge according to the three Guṇas

सर्वभूतेषु येनैकं भावमव्ययमीक्षते ।
अविभक्तं विभक्तेषु तज्ज्ञानं विद्धि सात्त्विकम् ॥ २० ॥
पृथक्त्वेन तु यज्ज्ञानं नानाभावान्पृथग्विधान् ।
वेत्ति सर्वेषु भूतेषु तज्ज्ञानं विद्धि राजसम् ॥ २१ ॥
यत्तु कृत्स्नवदेकस्मिन्कार्ये सक्तमहैतुकम् ।
अतत्त्वार्थवदल्पं च तत्तामसमुदाहृतम् ॥ २२ ॥

*Sarvabhūteṣu yenaikaṃ bhāvam avyayam īkṣate* ।
*Avibhaktaṃ vibhakteṣu taj jñānaṃ viddhi sāttvikam* ॥ *20* ॥
*Pṛthaktvena tu yaj jñānaṃ nānābhāvān pṛthagvidhān* ।
*Vetti sarveṣu bhūteṣu taj jñānaṃ viddhi rājasam* ॥ *21* ॥
*Yat tu kṛtsnavad ekasmin kārye saktam ahetukam* ।
*Atattvārthavad alpaṃ ca tat tāmasam udāhṛtam* ॥ *22* ॥

**Meaning:** That knowledge by which the wise person sees only one, indestructible, undivided Supreme Ātman in all different beings – know that as 'Sāttvic knowledge.' That knowledge by which a man sees distinctiveness in doing, experiencing, enjoying, etc. in all different beings – know that as 'Rājas knowledge.' But the knowledge by which one identifies strongly with his body and clings to the body out of ignorance – that trivial knowledge faraway from Mokṣa is said to be 'Tāmas knowledge.'

Here the word 'knowledge' means 'the vision evolved from the intellect which firmly abides in Ātman.' Sattvaguṇa has a close affinity to the Knowledge of Ātman. Ātman is one, non-dual, and undivided. The Sattvic intellect strives to see one Ātman in all beings rather than seeing many divisions or distinctions in the world. The world is full of many names and forms. Yet, this seeker is aware of one nameless, formless principle which is the reality underlying all variations. Sattvaguṇa is the main reason for joy, so this wise seeker naturally experiences joy when he sees Oneness everywhere. He does not experience the grief or fear that invariably comes with plurality.

When the seeker is influenced by Rajoguṇa, he sees many differentiations everywhere. He perceives names and forms as real and spends a lot of time in thinking about various objects. As a result, he experiences joy and grief from dealing with favorable and unfavorable objects. He tends to think about other people only for self-gratification and selfish interests. At the same time, he engages in rituals like Yajña and donations only to accumulate merits and enjoy his life.

When a person is influenced by Tamoguṇa, his intellect thinks solely about his own body and clings firmly to his body. It has no inkling of philosophy or logic. His intellect is completely blank or ignorant from the spiritual perspective. Such a person is disdainful about God, religion, rituals, and faith.

## Three kinds of actions according to the three Guṇas

नियतं सङ्गरहितमरागद्वेषतः कृतम् ।
अफलप्रेप्सुना कर्म यत्तत्सात्त्विकमुच्यते ॥ २३ ॥
यत्तु कामेप्सुना कर्म साहङ्कारेण वा पुनः ।
क्रियते बहुलायासं तद्राजसमुदाहृतम् ॥ २४ ॥
अनुबन्धं क्षयं हिंसामनवेक्ष्य च पौरुषम् ।
मोहादारभ्यते कर्म यत्तत्तामसमुच्यते ॥ २५ ॥

*Niyataṃ saṅgarahitam arāgadveṣataḥ kṛtam* ।
*Aphalaprepsunā karma yat tat sāttvikam ucyate* ॥ *23* ॥
*Yat tu kāmepsunā karma sāhaṃkāreṇa vā punaḥ* ।
*Kriyate bahulāyāsaṃ tad rājasam udāhṛtam* ॥ *24* ॥
*Anubandhaṃ kṣayaṃ hiṃsām anapekṣya ca pauruṣam* ।
*Mohād ārabhyate karma yat tat tāmasam ucyate* ॥ *25* ॥

**Meaning:** When a person executes a prescribed action without desiring any gain, keeping aside the pride of doership, and being free from attachment and aversion – it is called a 'Sāttvic action'. When an egoistic person desiring fruits performs an action with great effort – it is called a 'Rājas action'. When a person executes action without any regard for its consequences, physical or financial losses, violence, or his capability – merely due to ignorance and thoughtlessness – it is called a 'Tāmas action'.

Man is superior amongst all sentient beings, and he alone is eligible for Mokṣa. At the same time, he has the freedom to choose the kind of actions he wants to perform in human life, which is called 'Kriyamāṇa karma swātantrya'. Other species like animals, birds, etc. are meant for the enjoyment of pleasures or griefs that are ascribed to them by their Prārabdha. They do not have the freedom to choose or decide on actions, so they are not bound by good or bad actions. On the contrary, man is bound by the teachings of scriptures. The intellect that follows scriptural teachings is said to be Sāttvic. The journey to Mokṣa must be made on the path of constraints imposed by scriptures.

The Sāttvic intellect has the ability to tread on this path. Unwarranted thoughts like – "I am the doer, this work is done by me alone, what would happen after me? etc.," do not even remotely touch the Sāttvic intellect. All actions done by the Sattvic seeker are without any affinity or grudge towards any action, and he performs them without any desire for fruit, merely as his duty. When actions are performed as ordained by scriptures, the onus of those actions is on scriptures. So, the doer does not get distressed or affected by the fruits of actions.

The actions of Rajoguṇa are executed by people enmeshed in pleasures. They take arduous efforts to accumulate more objects of pleasure. These people justify their affinity to action by glorifying the statement, "Work is worship." St. Jñāneśwara has stated that "A person can worship God through his work," however, actions need to be Sāttvic for that purpose. Being proud of one's actions, being greedy about results, and the desire to flaunt the results are the characteristics of Rajoguṇa. "I am always busy, I do not have time for trivial activities, my work is unparalleled and unlike anyone else" – these thoughts are the manifestations of Rājas actions. The Rājas person desires that his actions should be recognized and appreciated by others. The feeling of dejection when no one notices or appreciates one's work is a result of Rajoguṇa as well.

Indiscrimination or thoughtlessness is the foundation of Tamoguṇa. Tāmas actions are born of delusion; therefore, there is no regard for consequences of actions, losses incurred, injuries, violence, or limitations of one's own capabilities. Such a person does not even think about gain or loss in day-to-day life. He has no regard for merits or sins from the religious perspective or for Mokṣa from the spiritual perspective. A person influenced by Tamoguṇa undertakes enormous work beyond his capacity, aborts or leaves the work in between, gets angry when there are adverse effects of the work, and occasionally even commits suicide.

**The characteristics of the three kinds of doer**

मुक्तसङ्गोऽनहंवादी धृत्युत्साहसमन्वितः।
सिद्ध्यसिद्ध्योर्निर्विकारः कर्ता सात्त्विक उच्यते ॥ २६ ॥
रागी कर्मफलप्रेप्सुर्लुब्धो हिंसात्मकोऽशुचिः।
हर्षशोकान्वितः कर्ता राजसः परिकीर्तितः ॥ २७ ॥
अयुक्तः प्राकृतः स्तब्धः शठो नैष्कृतिकोऽलसः।
विषादी दीर्घसूत्री च कर्ता तामस उच्यते ॥ २८ ॥

*Muktasaṅgo'nahaṃvādī dhṛtyutsāhasamanvitaḥ* ।
*Siddhyasiddhyor nirvikāraḥ kartā sāttvika ucyate* ॥ *26* ॥
*Rāgī karmaphalaprepsur lubdho hiṃsātmako'śuciḥ* ।
*Harṣaśokānvitaḥ kartā rājasaḥ parikīrtitaḥ* ॥ *27* ॥
*Ayuktaḥ prākṛtaḥ stabdhaḥ śaṭho naiṣkṛtiko'lasaḥ* ।
*Viṣādī dīrghasūtrī ca kartā tāmasa ucyate* ॥ *28* ॥

**Meaning:** A person who is free from attachment to fruits, non-egoistic about work, endued with fortitude and enthusiasm, unfazed by success or failure in actions, and free from excitement and distress is the Sāttvic doer. One who is attached to worldly pleasures, who desires fruits of actions, who is greedy and harmful, who causes pain to others, who is impure in mind and body, who is excited by success and distressed by failure – he is said to be the Rajas doer. One who has an unsteady mind, who is foolish, unbending in front of his teachers, malicious, lethargic, dejected, who destroys others for selfish gains, and procrastinating – he is the Tāmas doer.

The Sāttvic doer (actor or agent) executes his undertakings with utmost enthusiasm, thorough knowledge, and great fortitude, yet he is completely detached from those actions. He is neither excited by success nor dejected by failure. He is neither disturbed when the work is accomplished nor when it is aborted. He is aware that the work can remain unfulfilled due to bad health, or participation of many people, or other unforeseen circumstances.

The Rājas doer is excessively attached to actions and their fruits. His action is mainly impelled by greed. He holds many people accountable for accomplishing his work and inflicts torture upon them to get the work done. His behavior is unjust, unrighteous, and impure from the perspective of righteousness, justice, and Dharma. He indulges in these bad traits and uses them per his own convenience for his gain. People who support religious undertakings for securing votes come under this category. The Rājas doer is exuberant with joy when he succeeds, and he is despondent when he meets failure.

The Tāmas doer does not engage wholeheartedly in any action. He is uncultured, pretentious, and treacherous. At times, he does not even blink while destroying others for his selfish gains. Ancient moneylenders were of this kind. The Tāmas doer laments histrionically or throws tantrums when things go against his wishes. At the same time, he is lethargic, and he continually procrastinates.

**<u>The intellect according to the three Guṇas</u>**

**बुद्धेर्भेदं धृतेश्चैव गुणतस्त्रिविधं शृणु ।**
**प्रोच्यमानमशेषेण पृथक्त्वेन धनञ्जय ॥ २९ ॥**
**प्रवृत्तिं च निवृत्तिं च कार्याकार्ये भयाभये ।**
**बन्धं मोक्षं च या वेत्ति बुद्धिः सा पार्थ सात्त्विकी ॥ ३० ॥**
**यया धर्ममधर्मं च कार्यं चाकार्यमेव च ।**
**अयथावत्प्रजानाति बुद्धिः सा पार्थ राजसी ॥ ३१ ॥**
**अधर्मं धर्ममिति या मन्यते तमसावृता ।**
**सर्वार्थान्विपरीतांश्च बुद्धिः सा पार्थ तामसी ॥ ३२ ॥**

*Buddher bhedaṃ dhṛteś caiva guṇatas trividhaṃ śṛṇu* ।
*Procyamānam aśeṣeṇa pṛthaktvena dhanaṃjaya* ॥ *29* ॥
*Pravṛttiṃ ca nivṛttiṃ ca kāryākārye bhayābhaye* ।
*Bandhaṃ mokṣaṃ ca yā vetti buddhiḥ sā pārtha sāttvikī* ॥ *30* ॥

*Yayā dharmam adharmaṃ ca kāryaṃ cākāryam eva ca* ।
*Ayathāvat prajānāti buddhiḥ sā pārtha rājasī* ॥ *31* ॥
*Adharmaṃ dharmam iti yā manyate tamasāvṛtā* ।
*Sarvārthān viparītāñś ca buddhiḥ sā pārtha tāmasi* ॥ *32* ॥

**Meaning:** O Arjuna! Hear from Me the complete explanation of the three kinds of intellect and fortitude according to the three Guṇas. The intellect that can comprehend – duty and nonduty, the 'Path of Action' and the 'Path of Mokṣa,' the fear of birth-death and fearlessness, the bondage of being doer-enjoyer and liberation from that bondage – is the Sāttvic intellect. The intellect that cannot decisively think about Dharma, Adharma, duty, non-duty, etc. is the Rājas intellect. The Tamas intellect is veiled by ignorance, and hence it mistakenly takes Adharma as Dharma and misinterprets everything.

A person having the Sāttvic intellect knows how to progress on the spiritual path while being engaged in worldly life. St. Rāmadāsa has said, "One should be happily engaged in his worldly life, but also progress on the spiritual path at the same time." A person having the Sāttvic intellect is able to remember such teachings. He meticulously performs his duties and leaves the onus of results in worldly life on Īśvara while immersing himself in contemplating on Īśvara and practicing *Viveka*. He has a firm resolve to live life with detachment, and he is aware of his resolve even without taking the vows of formal Saṅnyāsa. He has no ambiguity about what is or isn't his duty. "I am my body" and "The world is real" – these two illusions create fear in mind. The Sāttvic intellect knows that liberation from these two illusions leads to fearlessness. The Sāttvic intellect is aware of the bondage of identification with the body, the bondage of doership, and the bondage of ego and attachment, and it also knows the ways to liberate from them.

The Rājas intellect has no understanding of any of the aforementioned aspects. It can only remain engrossed in eating, sleeping, and other activities of pleasure. It is devoid of knowledge and thus always subject to joy and suffering.

The Tāmas intellect considers injustice as justice, unrighteousness as righteousness, and Adharma as Dharma. Therefore, its decisions in all walks of life are perverted in nature.

**Dhṛti (intellectual power) according to the three Guṇas**

**धृत्या यया धारयते मनःप्राणेन्द्रियक्रियाः ।**
**योगेनाव्यभिचारिण्या धृतिः सा पार्थ सात्त्विकी ॥ ३३ ॥**
**यया तु धर्मकामार्थान्धृत्या धारयतेऽर्जुन ।**
**प्रसङ्गेन फलाकाङ्क्षी धृतिः सा पार्थ राजसी ॥ ३४ ॥**
**यया स्वप्नं भयं शोकं विषादं मदमेव च ।**
**न विमुञ्चति दुर्मेधा धृतिः सा पार्थ तामसी ॥ ३५ ॥**

*Dhṛtyā yayā dhārayate manaḥprāṇendriyakriyāḥ* ।
*Yogenāvyabhicāriṇyā dhṛtiḥ sā pārtha sāttvikī* ॥ *33* ॥
*Yayā tu dharmakāmārthān dhṛtyā dhārayate'rjuna* ।
*Prasaṅgena phalākāṅkṣī dhṛtiḥ sā pārtha rājasī* ॥ *34* ॥
*Yayā svapnaṃ bhayaṃ śokaṃ viṣādaṃ madam eva ca* ।
*Na vimuñcati durmedhā dhṛtiḥ sā pārtha tāmasī* ॥ *35* ॥

**Meaning:** [Note: The word Dhṛti in Sanskrit means the intellectual power or the ability to ingrain knowledge in the mind]. Sāttvic Dhṛti is that power which steadily contemplates on Ātman and with which one regulates the functions of his mind, organs, and Prāṇas. O Arjuna! Rājas Dhṛti is that unswerving power by which the man desirous of rewards holds firmly to Dharma, Artha, and Kāma, and considers the attainment of these three as his sole duty. And O Pārtha! That firm power by which a man – incapable of good thinking – does not abandon excessive sleep, fear, lamentation, depression, and arrogance is called Tāmas Dhṛti.

The word Dhāraṇā (Dhṛti) in Sanskrit means consistent and resolute adherence to a thought or an action. Sāttvic Dhāraṇā has no place for uncertainties or indecisiveness. For spiritual practice, the seeker has to regulate the functioning of his mind, Prāṇas, and organs. If his efforts are in accordance with scriptures, he can successfully regulate his mind. One of the Sutras of Aṣṭāngayoga states:

**योगश्चित्तवृत्तिनिरोधः ।**

*Yogashcittavruttinirodhah* ।

"Yoga is the complete cessation of activities of the mind." According to this Sutra, Sāttvic Dhṛti has the ability to quieten the mind. It does not ever make any compromise about following the teachings of scriptures. And it persistently engages in chanting, Prāṇāyāma, and Soham meditation.

Rājas Dhṛti gives immense importance to the body and materialistic life associated with it, so it invariably dwells on worldly thoughts. The characteristics of Rājas Dhāraṇā are excessive attachment and an intense craving for fruits of actions. Rājas Dhṛti strives for the attainment of only three aspects (Puruṣartha) – Dharma, Artha, and Kāma, as a Rājas person considers them to be highly important. [Dharma = righteous way of living, Artha = earning and growing wealth, Kāma = desiring worldly pleasures.]

A person with Tāmas Dhṛti firmly clings to his evil intellect, sleepiness, fears, worries, and arrogance. He is not affected by any teaching or any grief in life. He is always engulfed by fear for the present as well as future adversities.

**Happiness according to the three Guṇas**

**सुखं त्विदानीं त्रिविधं शृणु मे भरतर्षभ ।**
**अभ्यासाद्रमते यत्र दुःखान्तं च निगच्छति ॥ ३६ ॥**
**यत्तदग्रे विषमिव परिणामेऽमृतोपमम् ।**
**तत्सुखं सात्त्विकं प्रोक्तमात्मबुद्धिप्रसादजम् ॥ ३७ ॥**
**विषयेन्द्रियसंयोगाद्यत्तदग्रेऽमृतोपमम् ।**
**परिणामे विषमिव तत्सुखं राजसं स्मृतम् ॥ ३८ ॥**

**यदग्रे चानुबन्धे च सुखं मोहनमात्मनः ।**
**निद्रालस्यप्रमादोत्थं तत्तामसमुदाहृतम् ॥ ३९ ॥**

*Sukhaṃ tv idānīṃ trividhaṃ śṛṇu me bharatarṣabha* ।
*Abhyāsād ramate yatra duḥkhāntaṃ ca nigacchhati* ॥ *36* ॥
*Yat tadagre viṣam iva pariṇāme 'mṛtopamam* ।
*Tat sukhaṃ sāttvikaṃ proktam ātmabuddhiprasādajam* ॥ *37* ॥
*Viṣayendriyasañyogād yat tadagre 'mṛtopamam* ।
*Pariṇāme viṣam iva tat sukhaṃ rājasaṃ smṛtam* ॥ *38* ॥
*Yad agre cānubandhe ca sukhaṃ mohanam ātmanaḥ* ।
*Nidrālasyapramādotthaṃ tat tāmasam udāhṛtam* ॥ *39* ॥

**Meaning:** O best of Bharatas! Now hear about the three kinds of happiness from me. That pleasure, which is not tainted by pain or sorrow, in which a person remains immersed as it does not become stale despite repeatedly experiencing it, which is like poison at first since the mind is forced to detach from worldly pleasures, but in the end, gives the effect of nectar, and which is born of calmness earned by continually contemplating on the true Self, is called Sāttvic happiness. The pleasure, which arises from the contact of the organs with objects and which is like nectar in the beginning, but in the end, works like poison, is called Rājas happiness. And, the pleasure, which deludes the mind both in the beginning and at the end, which is born of laziness, lethargy, and carelessness, is called Tāmas happiness.

When a seeker is engrossed in singing praises of God, chanting, serving to God, worshipping, studying scriptures, meditating, and serving to every needy person by seeing God in that person, his day-to-day suffering is removed (forgotten), and he feels happy. This is known as Sāttvic happiness. The seeker may dislike spiritual activities in the beginning since engaging in them contradicts his natural inclination towards worldly enjoyments. However, the seeker who has Sāttvic Dhṛti recognizes the lasting benefit of spiritual path and resolutely continues his practice. Thus, he attains Sāttvic happiness. The student of classical music needs to take many arduous efforts at the outset only to get excellent results later. Spiritual pursuit is of the same kind. The initial joy felt while doing spiritual practice gradually evolves into Absolute, Pure Bliss of Self-realization. Thereafter, the seeker remains joyful at all times. This Bliss transcends even his Sattvaguṇa. Enlightened people always revel in a festive time, and saints attest to this fact.

The worldly pleasure derived from objects may be highly gratifying in the beginning; however, its results are adverse from the spiritual perspective. This is known as Rājas happiness. When a person uses all of his wealth only for worldly pleasures, he does not even think about the eternal, supreme, Pure Bliss of the true Self. St. Rāmadāsa has said in his poetry that "One can never find lasting happiness in material objects." The happiness born of indulgence in worldly pleasures is always subject to a beginning, state, and end; it is not perpetual. Profound thinkers of human life disregard what is transient and seek what is perpetual in life

Happiness born of sleep, boredom, lassitude, or objects like wine, etc. is Tāmas happiness. A person gets completely deluded in this state. He destroys himself and his relatives. Tāmas happiness is filled with delusion from start to end; therefore, it is pervaded with ignorance alone.

**The inevitability of the three Guṇas**

**न तदस्ति पृथिव्यां वा दिवि देवेषु वा पुनः ।**
**सत्त्वं प्रकृतिजैर्मुक्तं यदेभिः स्यात्त्रिभिर्गुणैः ॥ ४० ॥**

*Na tad asti pṛthivyāṃ vā divi deveṣu vā punaḥ ।*
*Sattvaṃ prakṛtijair muktaṃ yad ebhiḥ syāt tribhir guṇaiḥ ॥ 40 ॥*

**Meaning:** There is no being or object on earth, or in heaven amongst gods, that is free from the Three Guṇas born of Prakṛti.

The entire universe is made of the three Guṇas. There is no object anywhere on this earth without the three Guṇas. There was a detailed discussion of this topic in the 14th chapter.

**The discussion of the four social orders**

ब्राह्मणक्षत्रियविशां शूद्राणां च परन्तप ।
कर्माणि प्रविभक्तानि स्वभावप्रभवैर्गुणैः ॥ ४१ ॥
शमो दमस्तपः शौचं क्षान्तिरार्जवमेव च ।
ज्ञानं विज्ञानमास्तिक्यं ब्रह्मकर्म स्वभावजम् ॥ ४२ ॥
शौर्यं तेजो धृतिर्दाक्ष्यं युद्धे चाप्यपलायनम् ।
दानमीश्वरभावश्च क्षात्रं कर्म स्वभावजम् ॥ ४३ ॥
कृषिगौरक्ष्यवाणिज्यं वैश्यकर्म स्वभावजम् ।
परिचर्यात्मकं कर्म शूद्रस्यापि स्वभावजम् ॥ ४४ ॥

*Brāhmaṇakṣatriyaviśāṃ śūdrāṇāṃ ca paraṃtapa* ।
*Karmāṇi pravibhaktāni svabhāvaprabhavair guṇaiḥ* ॥ *41* ॥
*Śamo damas tapaḥ śaucaṃ kṣāntir ārjavam eva ca* ।
*Jñānaṃ vijñānam āstikyaṃ brahmakarma svabhāvajam* ॥ *42* ॥
*Śauryaṃ tejo dhṛtir dākṣyaṃ yuddhe cāpy apalāyanam* ।
*Dānam īśvarabhāvaś ca kṣātraṃ karma svabhāvajam* ॥ *43* ॥
*Kṛṣigaurakṣyavāṇijyaṃ vaiśyakarma svabhāvajam* ।
*Paricaryātmakaṃ karma śūdrasyāpi svabhāvajam* ॥ *44* ॥

**Meaning:** O Arjuna, the scorcher of enemies! The actions of the four Varṇas – scholars (Brāhmins), warriors (Kṣatriya), traders (Vaiśya), and workers (Śūdra) – are classified according to the Guṇas which are the cause of the specific disposition of each Varṇa. Serenity, control of the mind and the organs, austerity, purity, forgiveness, forthrightness, unswerving faith in Īśvara, Self-knowledge, and Self-realization are the natural duties of Brāhmins. Valiance, splendor, fortitude, alertness, not fleeing from battle, generosity, leadership are the natural duties of Kṣatriyas. Farming, cattle-rearing, and trading are the natural duties of Vaiśyas. Service and assistance to all the aforementioned Varṇas is the natural duty of Śūdras.

Over a period, human beings have led their lives by mutually depending on each other. This interdependence gave rise to human society. It is imperative that actions must be distributed amongst people to hold together the social structure and maintain the progress of society. The social fabric has been dramatically changing today due to globalization and the blending of cultures and religions. It will continue to evolve further. Till about 300 years ago, this social structure and distribution of work were largely determined by birth. Today these are determined by the aptitude and capability of each person. There are four kinds of actions necessary to sustain a society:

1. Knowledge – To maintain the teachings of Dharma, uphold the cultural heritage and continue the righteous and religious activities; to acquire knowledge in various fields, teach others, and work for intellectual upliftment of society.
2. Governance and Protection – To govern people with law, rules, and regulations; protect society from evil forces and crooks; protect the nation from foreign invaders.
3. Business and Agriculture – To cultivate the land, run various industries and professions for commercial advancement and materialistic progress of society.
4. Service – To assist people from all three aforementioned categories in their respective jobs and fields.

The kind of qualities needed for a person to work in each of these categories are discussed here in this section. If a person does not have the necessary skills and qualities to execute the given task, he cannot accomplish the work. The progress of society is hampered as a result. If actions in each category are appropriately executed and passed down to next generations, their knowledge is naturally preserved, and the execution of those actions can become better with time. On the contrary, even if a person is born in a particular tradition, e.g. a lineage of ironsmiths, but does not possess adequate knowledge of that trade, then his actions are impaired.

In today's financial, political, social atmosphere, it is nearly impossible that the ancient system of Varṇas is adhered to. In this case, people should make the utmost efforts to earn the skills and nurture the qualities required to do their chosen work to ensure that society continues to progress.

Following the teachings of Dharma, preserving culture, and doing the duties prescribed by Dharma are the actions of **Brāhmins** (priest class, scholars). They need control of the mind and senses, patience, fortitude, and painstaking efforts to nurture these qualities. The purity of the mind, thoughts, behavior, speech, and food are of the utmost importance for acquiring these qualities. Brāhmins need the ability to forgive wrongdoings and offenses done by many people, and they are required to be straightforward themselves. It is imperative for them to keep unswerving faith in the Vedas, scriptures of Dharma, Īśvara, and strive to learn the knowledge of Upaniṣads. Apart from theoretical knowledge, Brāhmins also need to aspire for Self-realization. These are the actions prescribed for them. Any person who has these traits and qualities can be successful (as a Brāhmin) and earn the respect of other people in society. As the role and necessity for Dharma declines in society, it will become difficult to execute these actions. The livelihood of this class is solely dependent on the good-will of society; therefore, it is difficult for Brāhmins to be wealthy like others. In ancient days, people in this category were known to perform the following six kinds of actions –

- Yajana – performing Yajña
- Yājana – instructing others to do Yajña
- Adhyayana – learning
- Adhyāpana – teaching
- Dāna – donating, charity

- Pratigraha – receiving donations

In the old days, Brāhmins were fully dependent on the king or the chief of town for their livelihood. Today, their livelihood is mainly dependent on society. Consequently, people in the Brāhmin class have now entered other professions such as the army, business, etc. to earn their living. Even in the era of Mahābhārata, Droṇāchārya, the teacher of Kauravas and Pāṇḍavas, fought the battle despite being a Brāhmin.

Valiance, fortitude, attentiveness, ability to impress others, and never turning back on duty – these qualities are highly necessary for the protection of society which is the main duty of **Kṣatriyas**. It is evident that these traits are needed for anyone who aspires to be in today's army, navy, or airforce. In ancient days, warriors were known invade other states, fight bravely, conquer wealth, and bring it back home. E.g. in Rājasuya Yajña, the four Pāṇḍavas invaded the states in four directions and amassed loads of wealth for their kingdom. (This was an indispensable part of the Rājasuya Yajña. Kings used to do it with the sole objective of becoming the sovereign king of kings.) Therefore, it was essential for Kṣatriyas in ancient days to be generous and donate their wealth. In the sovereign kingdom (राजसत्ताक), warriors were kings; so, they were expected to own wealth, glory, and control of the kingdom. In today's world, it can be clearly seen that people from all social orders (Varṇas) enter the army. They are provided with the required training for their jobs. After completing the training, a person born in any class or social order becomes a warrior (Kṣatriya). Today, people who are warriors by birth have entered many other professions like agriculture, business, trading, education, etc. Unless they have the necessary qualities to succeed in those other professions, they will not be successful.

The traditional **Vaiśya** (business) profession consisted of only agriculture, taking care of cattle, and trading. Today, there is an addition of industrialism. These actions need planning, regulation, and physical efforts. Water supply, roads, electricity are the new needs of this profession. This is considered the most critical and lucrative profession in today's world. It has maximum chances of earning wealth; consequently, people engaged in these activities also have the onus to donate wealth. Some professionals in this category recognize the need for donation and contribute to building temples, hospitals, or food distribution centers, and the like.

These three kinds of professions or actions require people who can assist/serve them in their endeavors. People who serve these professionals need to be known as **Śūdra** irrespective of their birth or lineage. None of the work above can be accomplished without their assistance. Unless there is a barber, laundryman, cook, and driver in the army; a worker in farming; a driver in business; and a coolie in travel, the work in these professions will not be accomplished.

**Attainment of the worldly prosperity and spiritual welfare**

**स्वे स्वे कर्मण्यभिरतः संसिद्धिं लभते नरः ।**
**स्वकर्मनिरतः सिद्धिं यथा विन्दति तच्छृणु ॥ ४५ ॥**
**यतः प्रवृत्तिर्भूतानां येन सर्वमिदं ततम् ।**
**स्वकर्मणा तमभ्यर्च्य सिद्धिं विन्दति मानवः ॥ ४६ ॥**
**श्रेयान्स्वधर्मो विगुणः परधर्मात्स्वनुष्ठितात् ।**
**स्वभावनियतं कर्म कुर्वन्नाप्नोति किल्बिषम् ॥ ४७ ॥**
**सहजं कर्म कौन्तेय सदोषमपि न त्यजेत् ।**
**सर्वारम्भा हि दोषेण धूमेनाग्निरिवावृताः ॥ ४८ ॥**

*Sve sve karmaṇy abhirataḥ saṃsiddhiṃ labhate naraḥ* ।
*Svakarmanirataḥ siddhiṃ yathā vindati tac chṛṇu* ॥ *45* ॥
*Yataḥ pravṛttir bhūtānāṃ yena sarvam idaṃ tatam* ।
*Svakarmaṇā tam abhyarcya siddhiṃ vindati mānavaḥ* ॥ *46* ॥
*Śreyān svadharmo viguṇaḥ paradharmot svanuṣṭhitāt* ।
*Svabhāvaniyataṃ karma kurvan nāpnoti kilbiṣam* ॥ *47* ॥

*Sahajaṃ karma kaunteya sadoṣam api na tyajet* ।
*Sarvārambhā hi doṣeṇa dhūmenāgnir ivāvṛtāḥ* ॥ *48* ॥

**Meaning:** A person who is alert and devoted to his own duty attains Mokṣa. Now listen to how anyone engaged in his own duty can accomplish detachment from this world. All beings arise from Supreme Īśvara, and He is all-pervasive. A person who worships Īśvara by performing his prescribed duty – to the best of his ability – attains the perfection of detachment. Better is one's own Dharma (duty) – though imperfect and inferior – than the Dharma of another that is more pleasant. A person who performs the duty which is considered appropriate for his nature incurs no sin. O Arjuna! One should not abandon the innate duty to which he is born, though he may find it to be faulty. All actions are enveloped by faults (evil) just as fire is covered by smoke.

Progress, welfare, and benefit in worldly life are called ***Preya*** (agreeable, dear), while the spiritual welfare is called ***Śreya*** (superior, beneficial). When a seeker resolutely fulfills the duties ascribed to him by his qualities, he attains both Śreya and Preya. By being loyal and honest to his duties, the seeker can attain these results. When actions are done consistently, accurately, promptly, and offered to Īśvara, they cleanse and purify the seeker's mind, and thereby he attains Mokṣa. The entire world is created from Supreme Īśvara. There is a law that states –

**जीवो जीवस्य जीवनम् ।**

*Jivo jivasya jivanam* ।

"One Jiva is the life of another Jiva." As per this law, all sentient beings depend on each other. Human beings have the onus to nurture and maintain other people. When man engages in his duties using the qualities given by Īśvara and accomplishes the work needed by society, the work itself qualifies as the worship of Īśvara. This is a natural form of His worship, and Īśvara loves it very dearly.

If a profession like medicine is practiced with the help of qualities or disposition of a Brāhmin, it is beneficial for society. If it is run like a business, it can exploit people. Therefore, one who works in the medical field should strive to acquire the traits of a true Brāhmin. For professions like the army, navy, etc., the disposition of a Brāhmin is of no use; rather, one needs the qualities of a Kṣatriya to protect the nation. In some cases, the person may feel that some other duty is better than the one ascribed to himself by virtue of his qualities. E.g. a person who is working as a Brāhmin may feel envious of the one working in the trading field because of his wealth. A businessman may feel jealous of a warrior because of his valiancy. However, only actions accomplished by using one's natural qualities meet success, and they are beneficial for the person as well as society. All four kinds of actions have their own merits and demerits; the seeker should engage in actions prescribed to him or chosen by him without paying heed to the demerits associated with actions and treating those actions as his duty.

## The perfection of non-action

**असक्तबुद्धिः सर्वत्र जितात्मा विगतस्पृहः ।**
**नैष्कर्म्यसिद्धिं परमां संन्यासेनाधिगच्छति ॥ ४९ ॥**

*Asaktabuddhiḥ sarvatra jitātmā vigataspṛhaḥ* ।
*Naiṣkarmyasiddhiṃ paramāṃ Saṅnyāsenādhigacchati* ॥ *49* ॥

**Meaning:** A dispassionate person who is not attached anywhere, whose mind is conquered, and who has no desire for any object of pleasure, goes beyond the 'Law of Actions' (governed by Īśvara) and thus attains Self-realization of Brahman.

Having transcended the three Guṇas, when a seeker performs actions by renouncing the feeling of doership and offering the actions to Īśvara, he attains the state where he is not bound by or attached to action. This is known as ***Naiṣkarmyasiddhi***. As a result, he does not need to endure the fruits of actions despite performing them. Actions are ascribed to a person on account of his Prārabdha. When he performs them in a detached manner without aiming for fruits, they do not yield fruits – virtues or sins – and thereby become moot. When such a seeker attains Mokṣa, all actions in his Sañcita are burnt to ashes i.e. they are eradicated. His Prārabdha comes to an end by living through it in a detached manner. This is the greatest accomplishment and epitome of human life. To get to this stage, the seeker needs to wipe out the desires of fruits from his mind, resolutely control the mind, and study the Yoga of Knowledge (Jñānayoga). [Note: Sañcita is the accumulation of actions from past human births which are still to be endured in a suitable future birth. Prārabdha is the set of actions whose fruits must be endured in the present birth.]

## Jñānayoga (Path of Knowledge)

**सिद्धिं प्राप्तो यथा ब्रह्म तथाप्नोति निबोध मे ।**
**समासेनैव कौन्तेय निष्ठा ज्ञानस्य या परा ॥ ५० ॥**
**बुद्ध्या विशुद्धया युक्तो धृत्यात्मानं नियम्य च ।**
**शब्दादीन्विषयांस्त्यक्त्वा रागद्वेषौ व्युदस्य च ॥ ५१ ॥**
**विविक्तसेवी लघ्वाशी यतवाक्कायमानसः ।**
**ध्यानयोगपरो नित्यं वैराग्यं समुपाश्रितः ॥ ५२ ॥**
**अहङ्कारं बलं दर्पं कामं क्रोधं परिग्रहम् ।**
**विमुच्य निर्ममः शान्तो ब्रह्मभूयाय कल्पते ॥ ५३ ॥**

*Siddhiṃ prāpto yathā brahma tathāpnoti nibodha me* ।
*Samāsenaiva kaunteya niṣṭhā jñānasya yā parā* ॥ 50 ॥
*Buddhyā viśuddhayā yukto dhṛtyātmānaṃ niyamya ca* ।
*Śabdādīn viṣayāṃs tyaktvā rāgadveṣau vyudasya ca* ॥ 51 ॥
*Viviktasevī laghvāśī yatavākkāyamānasaḥ* ।
*Dhyānayogaparo nityaṃ vairāgyaṃ samupāŚrītaḥ* ॥ 52 ॥
*Ahaṃkāraṃ balaṃ darpaṃ kāmaṃ krodhaṃ parigraham* ।
*Vimucya nirmamaḥ śānto brahmabhūyāya kalpate* ॥ 53 ॥

**Meaning:** Learn from Me in brief how he attains the Knowledge of Brahman and Self-realization. Listen to that supreme devotion to Self-Knowledge and the highest state of the Knowledge of Ātman. Purifying the intellect; resolutely controlling the body, senses, and mind; abandoning objects of pleasure; renouncing attraction and aversion; dwelling in solitude; eating limited quantity of food; subduing speech, mind, and body; practicing meditation; being always detached; abandoning the ego, power, arrogance, all kinds of desire, anger, and unnecessary collection of objects; getting rid of 'mineness' for family, close acquaintances and worldly possessions – the seeker who has thus attained serenity becomes eligible for realizing "I am Brahman."

Self-realization that "I am Brahman" and consequent freedom from the bondage of action i.e. ***Naiṣkarmyasiddhi*** is an arduous spiritual observance (Vrata). 'Desireless action' (Niṣkāma Karma) and 'unconditional worship' (Niṣkāma Upasana) are part of that process. Apart from these two, the seeker needs to abide by other grueling practices to attain *Naiṣkarmyasiddhi*. He is able to bring his spiritual practice to fruition only by fighting against his natural inclinations or temptations. The seeker purifies his mind by desireless actions and quietens the mind by unconditional worship. He eats limited, light, and Sāttvic food. He recognizes that pleasures arising from worldly objects are impermanent; so, he consciously gives up the efforts to attain material pleasures. He prefers being in solitude to avoid actions and reactions that surface in the company of people influenced by the three Guṇas. He avoids crowded places. He develops the power of Sāttvic Dhāraṇā (ability to ingrain knowledge in the mind and keep the mind steady) and conquers his mind as well as senses to tread the path of the supreme goal of Mokṣa. He completely controls his mind and speech and liberates himself from the duality of attachment and aversion. When a seeker is caught in a duality of any kind, his path to non-duality is completely closed. The seeker culminates his dispassion (*Vairāgya*) by practicing it with discrimination (*Viveka*). The aforementioned spiritual practices cannot be perfected without dispassion for worldly life. Such a seeker consciously keeps away from wealth, power, attachment to the body, and loftiness that comes with them. He abandons anger that arises from unfulfilled desires and ambitions and gives up his greediness to accumulate objects of pleasure. He liberates himself from the delusion of 'I, me and mine' and strives to meditate on Soham ("I am that – Brahman"). He unites himself with his true Self Brahman and thereby attains non-duality.

**Attining supreme devotion through Knowledge of Brahman**

**ब्रह्मभूतः प्रसन्नात्मा न शोचति न काङ्क्षति ।**
**समः सर्वेषु भूतेषु मद्भक्तिं लभते पराम् ॥ ५४ ॥**
**भक्त्या मामभिजानाति यावान्यश्चास्मि तत्त्वतः ।**
**ततो मां तत्त्वतो ज्ञात्वा विशते तदनन्तरम् ॥ ५५ ॥**
**सर्वकर्माण्यपि सदा कुर्वाणो मद्व्यपाश्रयः ।**
**मत्प्रसादादवाप्नोति शाश्वतं पदमव्ययम् ॥ ५६ ॥**
**चेतसा सर्वकर्माणि मयि संन्यस्य मत्परः ।**
**बुद्धियोगमुपाश्रित्य मच्चित्तः सततं भव ॥ ५७ ॥**

*Brahmabhūtaḥ prasannātmā na śocati na kāṅkṣati* ।
*Samaḥ sarveṣu bhūteṣu madbhaktiṃ labhate parām* ॥ *54* ॥
*Bhaktyā mām abhijānāti yāvān yaś cāsmi tattvataḥ* ।
*Tato māṃ tattvato jñātvā viśate tadanantaram* ॥ *55* ॥
*Sarvakarmāṇy api sadā kurvāṇo madvyapāśrayaḥ* ।
*Matprasādād avāpnoti śāśvataṃ padam avyayam* ॥ *56* ॥
*Cetasā sarvakarmāṇi mayi saṃnyasya matparaḥ* ।
*Buddhiyogam upāśrītya maccittaḥ satataṃ bhava* ॥ *57* ॥

**Meaning:** A person who is eligible to be One with Brahman and who has acquired serenity through Self-Knowledge neither desires anything nor laments for any loss. He sees all beings equanimously as his own Self, Ātman, and thus attains supreme devotion towards Me. Through this devotion attained by Self-Knowledge (*Jñānalakṣaṇa Bhakti*), he knows Me in truth, what I am, how big I am, and as I am. Then having known Me in essence, he unites with My real nature. Performing all actions for Me alone and taking refuge in Me, he attains My indestructible, eternal nature due to My grace. Therefore, O Arjuna! offer all your actions to Me while discriminating between Ātman and Anātman, seek Me as the highest goal, let you your intellect remain centered in Me, and always fix your mind on Me alone.

Brahman is Absolute, Pure Bliss which is undivided. When the Jiva realizes his Oneness with Brahman, he becomes Pure Bliss himself. That Pure Bliss manifests as serene joy in him. He sees Brahman everywhere; as a result, all dualities like birth and death, profit and loss, honor and dishonor, victory and loss, and anguish associated with these dualities are destroyed for him.

All beings seek and pursue happiness alone. An enlightened person who becomes Brahman realizes Absolute, Pure Bliss as his true Self; he does not expect or seek any separate happiness from outside. Brahman pervades uniformly everywhere; as a result, the enlightened person sees everything with the same vision. This is the very nature of supreme devotion (*Parā Bhakti*). St. Rāmadāsa has stated, "A devotee is the one who is not separate from God." In this way, after uniting with Lord Kṛṣṇa through devotion, the devotee remains absorbed in the true nature of God (Brahman). He is only seen as separate from God on account of the Upādhi of his body and pending Prārabdha. All devotees who are One with God may seem outwardly different from each other due to the difference in their Prārabdha, but they are all the same Brahman. The term *Naiṣkarmyasiddhi* – the perfection of non-action – does not mean 'not performing any action at all.' It is imperative for a devotee, a seeker, and an enlightened person to perform their own actions. Lord Kṛṣṇa says that a person attains the perpetual, indestructible, highest goal by My grace when he performs his ascribed or self-accepted duties while remaining centered in Me. Many enlightened saints were engaged in different professions. E.g. St. Gorā Kumbhāra was a potter, St. Cokhāmela was a worker, St. Sāvata Māli was a farmer, St. Tukārāma and St. Nāmadeva propounded the path of devotion, and King Janaka was looking after a kingdom. The devotee who remains centered in God is not affected or bonded by any action. Therefore, Lord Kṛṣṇa has ordered here that one should offer all actions to God, abandon the sense of doership and fruits of actions, and constantly remain centered in God or remain centered in Brahman.

**The tendency to perform action is inescapable**

मच्चित्तः सर्वदुर्गाणि मत्प्रसादात्तरिष्यसि ।
अथ चेत्त्वमहङ्कारान्न श्रोष्यसि विनङ्क्ष्यसि ॥ ५८ ॥
यदहङ्कारमाश्रित्य न योत्स्य इति मन्यसे ।
मिथ्यैष व्यवसायस्ते प्रकृतिस्त्वां नियोक्ष्यति ॥ ५९ ॥
स्वभावजेन कौन्तेय निबद्धः स्वेन कर्मणा ।
कर्तुं नेच्छसि यन्मोहात्करिष्यस्यवशोऽपि तत् ॥ ६० ॥
ईश्वरः सर्वभूतानां हृद्देशेऽर्जुन तिष्ठति ।
भ्रामयन्सर्वभूतानि यन्त्रारूढानि मायया ॥ ६१ ॥
तमेव शरणं गच्छ सर्वभावेन भारत ।
तत्प्रसादात्परां शान्तिं स्थानं प्राप्स्यसि शाश्वतम् ॥ ६२ ॥

*Maccittaḥ sarvadurgāṇi matprasādat tariṣyasi* ।
*Atha cet tvam ahaṃkārān na śroṣyasi vinaṅkṣyasi* ॥ 58 ॥
*Yad ahaṃkāram āśrītya na yotsya iti manyase* ।
*Mithyaiṣa vyavasāyas te prakṛtis tvāṃ niyokṣyati* ॥ 59 ॥
*Svabhāvajena kaunteya nibaddhaḥ svena karmaṇā* ।
*Kartuṃ necchasi yan mohāt kariṣyasyavaśo'pi tat* ॥ 60 ॥

*Īśvaraḥ sarvabhūtānāṃ hṛddeśe'rjuna tiṣṭhati* ।
*Bhrāmāyān sarvabhūtāni yantrārūḍhāni māyayā* ॥ *61* ॥
*Tam eva śaraṇaṃ gaccha sarvabhāvena bhārata* ।
*Tatprasādāt parāṃ śāntiṃ sthānaṃ prāpsyasi śāśvatam* ॥ *62* ॥

**Meaning:** By continually fixing your mind on Me, you will earn My grace and overcome all suffering. However, if you do not listen to Me due to your ego, you will perish and fail to attain the highest goal of Mokṣa. If you egoistically resolve not to fight war, it will be in vain, since your warrior inclination will compel you to fight. O son of Kunti,! You are bound by your trait created from your own blend of Guṇas and past actions. Therefore, that which you desire not to do due to delusion, you will helplessly do the same by being subservient to your trait. O Arjuna! Īśvara dwells in the hearts of all beings. He causes all beings mounted by their ego on the machine of His scheme of things to revolve through the power of His Yogamāyā. Surrender to that Īśvara with all your being. O descendant of Bharata! By His cordial grace, you will attain supreme peace and the eternal abode.

The human mind is filled with good and bad Vāsanās. Bad Vāsanās lead to destruction, yet people do not pay heed to them. A seeker may get temporary pleasure while pursuing bad Vāsanās, but the pleasure leads to suffering in the end. On the contrary, if the seeker follows good Vāsanās, listens to the commands of God, organizes his life accordingly, and continues to live in this manner – he attains the supreme welfare. The Sanskrit word ***Maccitta*** (मच्चित्त) means remaining in constant connection with the true nature of God. Alternatively, it also means living life according to the commands of God. When the seeker lives in this manner, his life becomes free of problems. Whichiver event takes place, he does not perceive it as a problem.

The events that are faced by the seeker on account of his Prārabdha can be favorable or unfavorable, and he perceives them to be good or bad accordingly. Ignorant Arjuna considered the destruction of his lineage and slaying his Guru in the war as calamities. When the seeker executes actions in any event as per the Lord's commands, the onus of actions is on the Lord. So, there is no reason to label any event as a problem or calamity. On the contrary, the seeker may mistakenly consider his ignorance to be knowledge and executes actions under the influence of his ego. As a result, he can invariably suffer in many ways, and that may lead to his destruction from the spiritual perspective. Even if Arjuna had resolved not to fight the battle due to his ego, he would have been compelled to fight on account of his natural trait as a warrior. However, the battle fought out of compulsion would have given him disgrace for not fighting in a timely manner. Even if deluded Arjuna had felt strongly, "I should not fight the war," he would have been impelled to fight due to the strong influence of his warrior instincts. His reputation as a strong warrior would have been permanently tainted as people would have thought that Arjuna fled the battlefield due to fear. He would not even have found the joy of fulfilling his duty had he fought with a dejected mind. Īśvara, who governs the world, impels every Jiva as per His system of governance. Lord Kṛṣṇa was resolved to eradicate evil forces and to reduce the excess load of humans from the earth. As a result of His wish, Duryodhana did not settle on mediation and did not turn away from the battle, and Arjuna was impelled to fight the battle. Īśvara residing in hearts of all beings impels each Jiva appropriately through the power of His Māyā. Every Jiva receives the impulses to act from his Vāsanās on account of his ignorance. But the lasting benefit of each Jiva lies in following the teachings of scriptures. Lord Kṛṣṇa has stated the following rule:

**ये यथा मां प्रपद्यन्ते तांस्तथैव भजाम्यहम् ।**

*Ye yatha mam prapadyante tan tathiava bhajamyaham (4.11)*

"With whatever intent men approach me, I grant them their results accordingly." Thus, Īśvara ascribes a particular trait or disposition to each person which helps him fulfill his Vāsanās from many past births. The seeker who desires lasting benefit in human life should nurture unswerving faith in Īśvara, surrender to Him, and follow all His commands. By doing so, He realizes "I am Ātman" and thereby attains supreme peace.

**Conclusion of the doctrine of the Gita**

इति ते ज्ञानमाख्यातं गुह्याद्गुह्यतरं मया ।
विमृश्यैतदशेषेण यथेच्छसि तथा कुरु ॥ ६३ ॥
सर्वगुह्यतमं भूयः श्रृणु मे परमं वचः ।
इष्टोऽसि मे दृढमिति ततो वक्ष्यामि ते हितम् ॥ ६४ ॥
मन्मना भव मद्भक्तो मद्याजी मां नमस्कुरु ।
मामेवैष्यसि सत्यं ते प्रतिजाने प्रियोऽसि मे ॥ ६५ ॥
सर्वधर्मान्परित्यज्य मामेकं शरणं व्रज ।
अहं त्वा सर्वपापेभ्यो मोक्षयिष्यामि मा शुचः ॥ ६६ ॥

*Iti te jñānam ākhyātaṃ guhyād guhyataraṃ mayā* ।
*Vimṛśyaitad aśeṣeṇa yathecchasi tathā kuru* ॥ *63* ॥
*Sarvaguhyatamaṃ bhūyaḥ śṛṇu me paramaṃ vacaḥ* ।
*Iṣṭo'si me dṛḍham iti tato vakṣyāmi te hitam* ॥ *64* ॥
*Manmanā bhava madbhakto madyājī māṃ namaskuru* ।
*Māṃ evaiṣyasi satyaṃ te pratijāne priyo'si me* ॥ *65* ॥
*Sarvadharmān parityajya mām ekaṃ śaraṇaṃ vraja* ।
*Ahaṃ tvā sarvapāpebhyo mokṣyayiṣyāmi mā śucaḥ* ॥ *66* ॥

**Meaning:** Thus, I have imparted the knowledge more profound than all secrets to you. Carefully reflect on it, and act as you choose. O Arjuna, the descendant of Bharata! Listen to My most profound, mysterious knowledge again. You are very dear to Me. Therefore, I am instructing what is right for you. Fix your mind on Me, be My devotee, worship Me, sing My praises, and bow down to Me. Then, you shall assuredly unite with Me alone. I promise this to you as you are exceedingly dear to Me.

Abandon all other Dharmas and surrender to Me alone. I shall liberate you from all sins. Do not lament.

The Knowledge of Brahman is highly subtle, therefore profound and mysterious. Brahman is the true nature of each Jiva. Every Jiva performs all transactions on the substratum of Brahman. Therefore, Brahman cannot be known by any seeker through the epistemic sources of acquiring knowledge. The science of spirituality (*Adhyātmaśāstra*) describes the way to learn about Brahman and realize it as the true Self. Therefore, it is the highest knowledge for people who seek higher and sublime life. There may be disagreements on the definition of a superior life; however, most people agree that the life filled with joy, peace, contentment, and fearlessness can be called superior. The Bhagavad-Gita describes the philosophy of living a superior, sublime life. After explaining this philosophy in detail, even Lord Kṛṣṇa did not insist that Arjuna must follow His teachings. He left it to Arjuna's discretion and discrimination. Having said so, Lord explained to Arjuna the very gist of spiritual life since Arjuna was exceedingly dear to him.

The first takeaway here is that one should remain continually connected with God in his mind. The word ***Anusandhāna*** is of immense importance in spiritual pursuit. The generic meaning of Anusandhāna is being constantly connected with God in one or the other way. It simply means that after having finished the important transactions and chores of day-to-day-life, the seeker should spend his spare time by being immersed in Ātman or Lord Kṛṣṇa. Such immersion or connection does not need to be monotonous. Lord Kṛṣṇa has described many ways to connect with Him in His teachings. The 10th and 11th chapters of the Gita describe those examples. Even Upaniṣads outline many ways in which the seeker can connect with the Lord. E.g. Anupraveśa Śruti of Taittiriya Upaniṣad states, "He created the sky, and He entered the sky." Therefore, beholding the sky is the same as beholding the Lord. By being constantly connected with God, the seeker naturally becomes One with Him. This can be seen even in day-to-day life. E.g. a person who passionately narrates an incidence forgets himself and becomes a part of it while narrating it. When Lord Kṛṣṇa Himself imparts teachings of philosophy on oath, the seeker should very carefully reflect upon them. He should not disregard them or take them lightly as mere casual dialogues. Only then the seeker can wholeheartedly embrace them and make them a living reality. The seeker can worship God, sing His glories, and thereby attain Him. The reason why Kṛṣṇa loved Arjuna was discussed in the introduction of this commentary. Any seeker can strive to become dear to Kṛṣṇa in the same manner.

The word ***Dharma*** has been always related to actions. Actions mainly involve duties. While performing these duties, the seeker should abandon the feeling – born of ignorance – that "I am the doer," and he should ultimately surrender to Lord Kṛṣṇa. If the seeker also abandons the fruits of actions by offering them to Kṛṣṇa, his delusive feeling that "I am the experiencer" is eradicated as well. The word 'surrender' has a profound meaning. Internal surrender of the mind is much more important than external surrender done by the body. "O Lord! I surrender myself to you" – merely saying these words is a 'verbal surrender.' Bowing down to the Lord is an external 'physical surrender.' However, the true 'mental surrender' involves quietly accepting whatever results come one's way and whichever is the state of the body while doing one's duties and worship God in the best possible manner. The Jiva, who is incomplete and feeble by nature, may find it challenging to surrender in this manner, but it is certainly not impossible for him. St. Gondavalekar Mahārāja says, "A person who complains cannot be a devotee." Īśvara has a track record of all actions of all Jivas from all past lives, and everyone gets fruits according to his past actions as per Īśvara's scheme of governance. The seeker who believes and embraces Īśvara's system, follows His commands, and offers the fruits to Him does not incur merits or sins of those actions. He has no reason to lament that he will be bound by merits or sins. Lord Kṛṣṇa promises here, "I will liberate you from all sins. Do not grieve." The discussion that started in 2.11 has been concluded here in this verse. Lord Kṛṣṇa has ordered that one should not lament on that which is not worth lamenting.

**Rules for spreading the teachings of the Gita**

इदं ते नातपस्काय नाभक्ताय कदाचन ।
न चाशुश्रूषवे वाच्यं न च मां योऽभ्यसूयति ॥ ६७ ॥

*Idaṃ te nātapaskāya nābhaktāya kadācana* ।
*Na cāśuśrūṣave vācyaṃ na ca māṃ yo'bhyasūyati* ॥ *67* ॥

**Meaning:** I have imparted this most profound knowledge to you for your benefit. Do not ever speak of this to him who is devoid of austerities, nor to him who is not devoted, nor to him who has no desire to listen to this philosophy, and nor to him who is envious of Me.

A seeker should be austere (*Tapasvi*) to realize the spiritual philosophy explained in the Gita or Vedānta. This means he should be able to perform spiritual practices without paying heed to physical or mental resistance. The seeker should patiently endure the physical strain while fasting or the mental distress felt while selflessly doing duties without any expectations. Such endurance is against his natural conditioning due to the past Vāsanās. Austerities also include putting a leash on the meaningless wandering of thoughts in mind and regulating one's diet, company, etc. The word 'devotion' in this verse also means faith. The philosophy of the Gita should not be instructed to a man who lacks faith in the enlightened saints, Vedas, Īśvara, Sadguru, and incarnations of God like Śrīkṛṣṇa. The Gita should not be taught to him who does not wish to listen to it due to his Rajoguṇa and past Prārabdha. The teachings of the Gita should not be undermined by enforcing them upon a reluctant person. Also, if one considers Lord Kṛṣṇa as a human being and finds humanistic faults in His biography or teachings, he, too, should not be taught the Gita. Lord Kṛṣṇa's teachings do not contain even a single fault that naturally pertains to the human intellect. His lessons are timeless and universal. His intellect is devoid of errors like delusion, blunder, and excessive greed. Dhṛtarāṣṭra was deluded by love for his son, so he was completely unaffected by Lord Kṛṣṇa's teachings. He was only seeing Lord Kṛṣṇa as a supporter of his enemies.

**The importance of spreading the Gita's teachings**

**य इदं परमं गुह्यं मद्भक्तेष्वभिधास्यति ।**
**भक्तिं मयि परां कृत्वा मामेवैष्यत्यसंशयः ॥ ६८ ॥**
**न च तस्मान्मनुष्येषु कश्चिन्मे प्रियकृत्तमः ।**
**भविता न च मे तस्मादन्यः प्रियतरो भुवि ॥ ६९ ॥**
**अध्येष्यते च य इमं धर्म्यं संवादमावयोः ।**
**ज्ञानयज्ञेन तेनाहमिष्टः स्यामिति मे मतिः ॥ ७० ॥**
**श्रद्धावाननसूयश्च शृणुयादपि यो नरः ।**
**सोऽपि मुक्तः शुभाँल्लोकान्प्राप्नुयात्पुण्यकर्मणाम् ॥ ७१ ॥**

*Ya idaṃ paramaṃ guhyaṃ madbhakteṣv abhidhāsyati* ।
*Bhaktiṃ mayi parāṃ kṛtvā mām evaiṣyaty asaṃśayaḥ* ॥ *68* ॥
*Na ca tasmān manuṣyeṣu kaścin me priyakṛttamaḥ* ।
*Bhavitā na ca me tasmād anyaḥ priyataro bhuvi* ॥ *69* ॥
*Adhyeṣyate ca ya imaṃ dharmyaṃ saṃvādam āvayoḥ* ।
*Jñānayajñena tenāham iṣṭaḥ syām iti me matiḥ* ॥ *70* ॥
*Śraddhāvān anasūyaś ca śṛṇuyād api yo naraḥ* ।
*So'pi muktaḥ śubhāṃllokān prāpnuyāt puṇyakarmaṇām* ॥ *71* ॥

**Meaning:** He who will teach this immensely profound philosophy in the form of verses or their meanings to My devotees, he will worship Me with supreme devotion and doubtlessly come to Me alone. There was none dearer to Me in the past, nor is there anyone dearer to Me at present, nor shall there be anyone dearer to Me in future than the one who skillfully imparts teachings of the Gita to devotees and establishes the teachings in their hearts. In My opinion, a person who will study this sacred dialogue of ours, he will worship Me alone through this Yajña of Knowledge. Also, when a person who is full of faith and free from enviousness listens to the Gita without finding defects in the philosophy, he will be liberated from the bondage of sins. He will attain the good world that can be attained through virtuous actions.

The sole purpose of Lord Kṛṣṇa's incarnation is to reestablish Dharma on the earth. If the word Dharma is understood as a duty, then it is easy to notice that both worldly and spiritual duties are included in Dharma. Such is the importance of the establishment of Dharma that formless Saguṇa Īśvara manifests Himself as Saguṇa God for that purpose. Lord Kṛṣṇa admires the tradition of spreading the teachings of the Bhagavad-Gita even after his incarnation has ended. He dearly loves his devotee who continues this tradition. We have already seen the immense benefit, blessing or grace that Arjuna received since he was loved by Lord Kṛṣṇa. The message for us here, in today's age, is that the seeker should realize the core philosophy of the Gita, understand the inclination and preference of Lord Kṛṣṇa, and continue the tradition handed down by the enlightened saints like Jñāneśwara, Adi Śaṅkara, and the like. The Gita should not be interpreted as per one's own wishes.

**Arjuna's condition after listening to the Bhagavad-Gita**

**कच्चिदेतच्छ्रुतं पार्थ त्वयैकाग्रेण चेतसा ।**
**कच्चिदज्ञानसम्मोहः प्रनष्टस्ते धनञ्जय ॥ ७२ ॥**

*Kaccid etac chrutaṃ pārtha tvayaikāgreṇa cetasā* ।
*Kaccid ajñānasaṃmohaḥ pranaṣṭas te dhanaṃjaya* ॥ 72 ॥

अर्जुन उवाच ।
नष्टो मोहः स्मृतिर्लब्धा त्वत्प्रसादान्मयाच्युत ।
स्थितोऽस्मि गतसन्देहः करिष्ये वचनं तव ॥ ७३ ॥

*Arjuna uvāca* ।
*Naṣṭo mohaḥ smṛtir labdhā tvatprasādān mayācyuta* ।
*Sthito 'smi gatasaṃdehaḥ kariṣye vacanaṃ tava* ॥ *73* ॥

**Meaning:** (Śrībhagavān said) O Arjuna! Have you listened carefully to My teachings with the single-pointed mind? Has this teaching eradicated your delusion?

(Arjuna said) O Acyuta! O Śrīkṛṣṇa! My delusion has been destroyed by Your pleasant grace! I have regained the memory of my true Self (Ātman) and my duties. My doubts are resolved. Now I shall act according to Your word.

Lord Kṛṣṇa is omniscient, and He knew it very well that Arjuna's delusion was eradicated. Here, He gives a subtle suggestion through His question that the delusion of seekers and the readers of the Gita should also be eradicated.

Lord Kṛṣṇa's question indicates that the seeker should listen to the philosophy of the Gita with unwavering attentiveness. The fact that ignorance is the root-cause of delusion is reiterated in these verses. Also, there is an insistence that the seeker should resolve all his doubts and wipe out the delusion from his mind. Arjuna is a seeker of high regard and eligibility. By surrendering his mind to Kṛṣṇa, he listened to the Gita with single-pointed, unswerving attentiveness. Therefore, he regained the memory of his true Self, Ātman. He was deluded earlier as he was oblivious of his true Self. Consequently, he was uncertain about his duty. In the end, his doubts were resolved, and he recollected the warrior duty prescribed for him. He was firmly established in his role as a warrior and ready to follow the orders of Lord Kṛṣṇa.

## The importance of the divine dialog of Gita

सञ्जय उवाच ।
इत्यहं वासुदेवस्य पार्थस्य च महात्मनः ।
संवादमिममश्रौषमद्भुतं रोमहर्षणम् ॥ ७४ ॥
व्यासप्रसादाच्छ्रुतवानेतद्गुह्यमहं परम् ।
योगं योगेश्वरात्कृष्णात्साक्षात्कथयतः स्वयम् ॥ ७५ ॥
राजन्संस्मृत्य संस्मृत्य संवादमिममद्भुतम् ।
केशवार्जुनयोः पुण्यं हृष्यामि च मुहुर्मुहुः ॥ ७६ ॥
तच्च संस्मृत्य संस्मृत्य रूपमत्यद्भुतं हरेः ।
विस्मयो मे महान् राजन्हृष्यामि च पुनः पुनः ॥ ७७ ॥

*Sañjaya uvāca* ।
*Ity ahaṃ vāsudevasya pārthasya ca mahātmanaḥ* ।
*Saṃvādam imam aśrauṣam adbhūtaṃ romaharṣaṇam* ॥ 74 ॥
*Vyāsaprasādāc chrutavān etad guhyam ahaṃ param* ।
*Yogaṃ yogeśvarāt kṛṣṇāt sākṣāt Kaṭhayataḥ svayam* ॥ 75 ॥
*Rājan saṃsmṛtya saṃsmṛtya saṃvādam imam adbhūtam* ।
*Keśavārjunayoḥ puṇyaṃ hṛṣyāmi ca muhur muhuḥ* ॥ 76 ॥
*Tac ca saṃsmṛtya saṃsmṛtya rūpam atyadbhūtaṃ hareḥ* ।
*Vismayo me mahān rājan hṛṣyāmi ca punaḥ punaḥ* ॥ 77 ॥

**Meaning:** (Sanjaya said) Thus, I have heard this brilliant dialogue between Lord Vāsudeva and the great noble soul Arjuna causing my hair to stand on end. By the grace of Sage Vyāsa, I have directly heard this most profound knowledge of Yoga being imparted by Śrīkṛṣṇa, the Lord of Yoga, to Arjuna. O King! Repeatedly recollecting this extraordinary and valuable dialogue between Lord Kṛṣṇa and Arjuna, I rejoice again and again. I am much astonished by frequently remembering the magnificent Cosmic Form of the Lord; I rejoice in it again and again.

The Bhagavad-Gita is an incredible dialogue between Lord Kṛṣṇa, the direct incarnation of omniscient Īśvara, and Arjuna, the Divine Glory of the Lord. Arjuna was a qualified but deluded listener. The reason this dialogue is called 'incredible' is that it is related to the highly subtle Knowledge of Brahman, and it has the power to remove even the most deep-rooted delusion from mind. If the student of the Bhagavad-Gita is indeed Sāttvic by nature, his Sāttvic emotions will surely be awakened, and his hair will stand on end. Sanjaya was endowed with the divine sight and divine hearing by sage Vyāsa so that he could narrate the proceedings of the war to Dhṛtarāṣṭra. Hence, Sanjaya was able to see the event of teaching the Bhagavad-Gita. Therefore, Sanjaya felt grateful and fortunate about himself.

If indeed any person does not consider himself fortunate despite hearing the imparting of this teaching of Kṛṣṇa, who is the Lord of Yoga, to Arjuna, who is the desirer of Yoga – such a person is indeed contemptible. Sanjaya was rejoicing again and again by remembering this dialogue. Even Sanjaya understood the profundity and great mystery of this dialogue, and the way it can lead to the highest and lasting benefit in life. But Dhṛtarāṣṭra was not even slightly affected by it. He was engrossed in the potential future result of the war. Sanjaya was ecstatic by recollecting Lord Kṛṣṇa's Cosmic Form again and again, but Dhṛtarāṣṭra remained immersed in the thoughts about his sons.

**<u>The conclusion of the philosophy of the Bhagavad-Gita</u>**

**यत्र योगेश्वरः कृष्णो यत्र पार्थो धनुर्धरः ।**
**तत्र श्रीर्विजयो भूतिर्ध्रुवा नीतिर्मतिर्मम ॥ ७८ ॥**

*Yatra yogeśvaraḥ kṛṣṇo yatra pārtho dhanurdharaḥ* ।
*Tatra Śrīr vijayo bhūtir dhruvā nītir matir mama* ॥ *78* ॥

**Meaning:** Wherever is Kṛṣṇa, the Lord of Yoga, and Arjuna, the prompt archer, there is prosperity, victory, wealth, and firm ethical policy. This is my conviction.

**ॐ तत्सदिति श्रीमद्भगवद्गीतासूपनिषत्सु ब्रह्मविद्यायां योगशास्त्रे श्रीकृष्णार्जुनसंवादे मोक्षसंन्यासयोगो नाम अष्टादशोऽध्यायः ॥**

*Om Tatsaditi Śrimadbhagvadgitāsūpaniṣatsu Brahmavidyāyāṃ Yogaśāstre Śrīkṛṣṇārjunasaṁvāde Mokṣasaṁnyāsayogo Nāma Aṣṭādaśo'dhyāyaḥ* ||

Lord Kṛṣṇa is Yogeśvara, the Master of Yoga. He is the originator and owner of Karmayoga, Jñānayoga, etc. The power of Yogamāyā, which is described in Bhāgavatam Purāṇa, is controlled by Lord Kṛṣṇa; hence, He was able to reveal His Cosmic Form to Arjuna. Thus, the word Yogeśvara also means "He is the owner of Yogamāyā." Being the incarnation of Īśvara, He is omniscient, omnipotent, and witness to all. Arjuna, the incarnation of Nara and a great qualified seeker, was deluded. So, he put down his bow and arrow before the war. In other words, Arjuna relinquished his duty. His delusion was not eradicated even though he was in a close company of Lord Kṛṣṇa. Arjuna heard Śrīkṛṣṇa's comprehensive teachings and remembered his true nature. Thereafter, he recognized his duties and lifted his bow and arrow again. Sanjaya believes that on whichever side there is the presence of Lord Kṛṣṇa and Arjuna, who is promptly ready for his duty, immensely faithful, and ardent devotee of the Lord, there will be prosperity, victory, wealth, and firm ethical policy on that side for certain. Lord Kṛṣṇa resides in the hearts of all beings as Ātman. If the seeker remains attentive to his duties, he, too, can overcome ignorance and attain the highest glory and spiritual prosperity. Mahābhārata is replete with examples of many teachings of Lord Kṛṣṇa in the areas of war-strategy, political strategy, etc. The core axiom behind those strategies is that the Supreme Truth should always be victorious in the end.

Let us pray to Lord Kṛṣṇa, "May we attain the same glorious victory in our lives!"

More information about the author –

**Dr. Shrikrishna Deshmukh**

http://vedantbhaskar.org

http://www.shrikrupaprakashan.com/

Select Hindi and English Translations at –

http://vedantbhaskar.blogspot.in